Where the Heart Was

Where the Heart Was

A NOVEL BY

Glenn G. Boyer

LEGENDARY PUBLISHING

Legendary Publishing, L.L.C.
3501 French Park Drive, Suite C
Edmond, Oklahoma 73034
www.LegendaryPublishing.com

First edition, first printing 2009
Manufactured in the United States of America

Library of Congress Control Number 2009923172
ISBN 978-1-887747-40-0

Original book design and typesetting by BW&A Books, Inc.
Cover photograph by Glenn G. Boyer
Cover design by Travis Clancy
Edited by Maura High

Publisher's Disclaimer:

The opinions and statements in this book are those of the author. Legendary Publishing has not verified and does not confirm or deny any of the information contained in this book. The reader should keep an open mind when reading this book and should independently judge the information contained herein. Legendary Publishing shall have no liability or responsibility to any person or entity with respect to any loss or damages arising from the information contained in herein or from the use or reliance of such information.

Environmental Statement:

Legendary Publishing is a proud member of the Green Press Initiative. This book and all books published by Legendary Publishing are printed on paper not harvested from endangered old growth forests, forests of exceptional conservation value or from the Amazon Basin.

To

ABRAHAM LINCOLN

Sixteenth President of the United States

Why?

This story reinvokes the *Soul of the Republic.*

A voice spoke in the night and said:

Write the biography of the Republic—
carve it in autobiographical vignettes, deeply etched cameos
that picture the lives of one pioneer American family;
cameos warm to the touch,
strange and fascinating,
like heirlooms discovered in a forgotten trunk.

Recall the lives of sacred ancestors,
recall our debts owed to them.
Owed to the Republic of Mankind, too,
the Human Race.

Listen by the Waters

CONTENTS

Where the Heart Was

PROLOGUE

The Drums of the Republic

— 1938

I remember . . .

I, Edwin Newton Cheek, rode off to war that spring I was eleven, in the warm fly-buzzing days—in the spring of the lush lilacs. 1861. I rode on my little Indian pony, Cannonball, beside my father, Lieutenant Colonel Robert Cheek. I wasn't exactly a drummer boy, though I was enlisted as one. I had more freedom. I never beat a drum. I was more a mascot. I rode down the main street at the head of the regiment with Pa and Colonel Smith, the regimental commander, passing between bunting-draped business houses, all closed in our honor.

You always ask me what it was like. You want to know about war because there hasn't been one that amounted to anything for almost a generation—or so you think. Let me tell you that you are just recovering from a worse, a sadder, war, where the guns fired every second, the guns of poverty, hunger, despair—"eyes looking for the light"—not "to see the dawn of peace," but a loaf of bread, a sack of beans.

You look back on my war as a noble war to free a chained race, and you glorify those few of us who survive . . . want to relive our adventure in words and pictures, but you don't want to relive your struggle against want. You wouldn't glorify my war either, if you really knew how it was.

I'll tell you then, goddammit, if you're sure you want to know! For one thing we weren't worrying about a dark, suffering army of slaves driven around like worker ants down south, "totin' the weary load." Not at first! Not till *freedom fighting* was good propaganda to stand off the goddam British. We were thinking about those arrogant bastards that fired on the flag at Fort Sumter, how we were going to go south and wring their necks, grind their noses in horseshit, drain out their noble blood with bullets and bayonets, not to make them atone for the blood drawn by the "bondsman's lash," not because the Lord's decrees were "altogether just," but because we thought the bastards needed a damned lesson. So we were marching south. (Christ, were most of us surprised to find just a bunch of good old boys down there with guns who hadn't any more idea what the hell we were fighting each other for than we did. As one said, "Because y'all 'r' down chere.")

Only we weren't marching south.

My war was pretty much always west—with a little jog east as far as Shiloh, then back west.

West, west . . . west toward the setting sun and adventures—the way the tide of empire flowed—though sometimes that ebbed east for a while too, but not often or very much.

The Americans who first went west weren't quitters, for the most part. Quitters came later.

The "busted by gosh" crowd who came back from the Pike's Peak Gold Rush of '59;

the "goin' home to the wife's folks" bunch of homesteaders. Skedaddlers.

Whipped.

The Americans I came down from built their cabins—if you could call such pigsties that—before the Revolution, settled in openings in the forests, where the English King said they couldn't go, squatted along streams, cut down trees, shook like rabid dogs from malaria—"fever and ague" they called it—and desperately put in a crop, even if they were almost too weak to stand up—had to have vittles for a fighting chance to survive the coming winter; delivered babies, sometimes in deepest, black night by firelight, or by no light at all if the Injuns were on the warpath, the expectant mother made even more desperate trying not to cry out a-birthing, so's not to attract the relentless red-death always creeping through the forests like blood-thirsty wild animals.

West they went. West and west and further west, starting out as one kind of people, and ending up another. Stolid peasants at first, English, Welsh, Scotch, Irish, Swedish, German, Dutch, farmers who'd never been allowed to own a gun, not even a knife decent enough to stab with. The first of them came west to the mountains and over them, not yet weaned, crying for a distant King's help—royal armies—to keep France's Indians from murdering them; the Shawnees, the Delawares, the Mingos up north, and down south the Creeks and Cherokees. Down there the Spanish bastards egged them on along with the French. You could count on both of those calculating countries to fight anything English anywhere in the world. It made life damned uncertain on the frontier.

Braddock's army came like waddling ducks, with young George Washington who knew better, loyally traipsing along, and was slaughtered in the Pennsylvania woods by the French and Indians. Braddock's regulars didn't know beans about fighting red wraiths that were like smoke drifting through brush, from tree to tree, as hard to hit with a bullet as winging birds, as hard to bring to bay for gutting with a bayonet as slithering snakes. Doltish Braddock bravely died there; his army staggered away, mortally wounded as far as armies went.

Armies came and went on the pre-Revolutionary frontier, and one day didn't even come anymore. Yet the settlers stayed, bit by a great yearning: *Westering*. Maybe most of 'em figured they had to stay because there was nothing east for them but poverty and they already had that aplenty, and they didn't need subservience to shopkeepers who knew how to get up in the world by licking the asses of their betters, the rich bastards who always ran things.

I can hear them a-sayin',
"Well, by Christ, we don't have any betters out here.
We'll take poverty and liberty."

And one day, across the whole frontier, north and south, ignoring government, they awakened. All they asked for after that was gunpowder and lead, gunflints; they said, "Bedamned to your dandy armies in leggin's and pipe-clayed belts, parade ground soldiers standin' in a row like sittin' ducks, shootin' by the numbers, with shit-faced, sherry-swilling officers having them flogged for penny-whistle offences.

"An' speakin' of swillin', give us whiskey. Good corn to fire a body up. Make you forget a rock-hard life for a while. And a smoke. Some 'baccy for your pipe and maybe venison spitted on the hearth, with the old woman having a snort along with you, and smoking her own corncob. Later we'll wallow together on a corn-shuck bed and plant a 'new nation, conceived in liberty'— to say nothing of good corn squeezin's, no pun meant."

And what about the red varmints then? Is that owl hoot on the hillside just before moonrise really a bird, or skulking death? Does the wind scrape a branch on the roof? Or was that moccasin feet carrying the murdering red bastards to the chimney to plug it up and smoke you out? You hope and pray it's nothing amiss, that they've finally decided to leave you be. But you know better. Buzzing rattlers and slithering copper snakes don't change. Neither do copper men. Still you'd leave them be, if they'd do the same.

And what if they didn't? Well, that got to be a different matter. You learned their sneaky ways of killing in the forests and fields, you followed them without letup if they raided, killing and carrying off your women and children. (Once they even carried off Daniel Boone, and like fools allowed him to live.) You learned to hate, to go after red varmints before they went for you. In any case, you finally struck back without pity, ambushed them as they did you, cut them to pieces, mercilessly killed them, their women and children, even their dogs, and savored it all, burned their villages and crops, brought home their scalps.

> *You, my ancestor, became a warrior,*
> *A killer without scruple.*
> *Times make the man.*

Descendants of that tough race—no different than us—were there when we went south, or as I said, more like west in my war—Missouri and Nebraska, and out on the plains after the Sioux. Always west after Shiloh. I was there. Anyhow we who went away to war stayed, in one sense . . . never came back, just like our forebears. And sons and daughters and grandchildren of pioneers just like the bunch I sprung from were out there waitin' for us with loaded guns. And *those* southern men were a different breed than their eastern brothers who eventually were whipped by New England shoe clerks with paper collars. These fellows were from Texas and Arkansas, famous for the Bowie knife and Arkansas toothpick, were hung down with Colts and Remingtons.

Colonel Smith's regiment marched down the main street of LaSalle with "measured tread," ladies and slackers lining the curbs, waving little flags, calling to friends, many—especially wives and mothers, sentimental sisters, sweethearts—eyes brimming with tears.

Teddy Smith, the barber, no relation to the colonel, was no longer a barber but a high private, whaling away at the bass drum, setting the tempo for the whole shebang, a center of attention for the first time in his life, bursting with importance in his baggy soldier suit with sleeves too long and pants too short, trying to look determined and heroic as he set the pace:

> Boom!
> Boom!
> Boom! Boom! Boom!

Left, right, left, right. Hayfoot, strawfoot. Even Nicodemus Cochrane in step this time—by now they'd drilled together enough so everyone knew he wasn't famous for it.

Going to war. We were all going to war. On a great crusade to kick ass down south. Only it was out west. We got as far south as Shiloh the next spring, but after that it was west. And I sat high and straight as I could in my saddle, age eleven, on my spotted Indian pony, Cannonball, riding beside Pa.

I can see and hear it yet, smell it too, mostly the smell of horse manure and sweat and dust.

I remember how I waved at Ma when I spotted her in the crowd. She waved back and waved and waved, calling, "Goodbye, Newt." But I knew that inside, so's not to embarrass me, she was sayin', "*Goodbye my little soldier, God bless you. And please God let him come home. Let them all come home.*"

But not a one ever did. Not those "moldering in graves," like poor old John Brown in the song, not those who trudged back (some still alive—old men now) who ever after had a special, haunted look sometimes capture their eyes, just like me, Edwin Newton Cheek, who saw it through the smoke that long time ago.

Our feet came home carrying us, some came on stretchers, like Pa, but a part of each of us always stayed out there where we fought—*or at least not where we seemed to be, but in some other place*—there and not there at the same time ever after, eyes darting into far distances, ears cocked, as though something startling suddenly moved out there, putting us on guard.

For what? For something. Beyond self. Beyond race. The great mystery we'd almost seen, touched, heard. *The Republic*. It was out there, calling. Asking something. *Beyond the Hills of History*. Recalling the drums:

Boom!
Boom!
Boom! Boom! Boom!

"Oh, mine eyes have seen the glory . . ."
See it yet . . .
Will see it till they see no more.
Till I come home at last,
To earth,
To the *Republic.*
To *God.*

CHAPTER ONE

Gettysburg, Pennsylvania

— November 19, 1863

A president of the U.S. always draws a pretty good crowd.

The crowd spreads all the way to the autumn-naked woods. The more influential members are seated near the speakers' platform or standing around it jostling each other. It is a dismal day. Most are thinking of the fried chicken and goodies they'll gorge on after the affair is over. Circus events were always hard on chickens in the U.S.

Abraham Lincoln sits on a too-small chair among the dignitaries on the platform, trying to stay awake while Edward Everett, "the foremost orator of his day," blasts the captive audience waiting to hear the resident, with rhetorical blank cartridges for two hours.

Honest Abe, the rail-splitter, sixteenth President of the U.S., looks at his big knobby hands, wishes he could scratch where he itches . . .

He thinks, "*These people will eat up all the fried chicken in Gettysburg while I get my hand wrung off after my little spiel by plow jockeys with grips like gorillas. I wonder what Mary's layin' on for supper at the White House tonight? Well, they're introducing me at last—where did I put my specs?*"

The tall, gaunt man, sallow and worn, rises to his full six feet four, takes a piece of paper from his pocket, fumbles out a pair of granny glasses and fits them on, then looks over them at the crowd, turning his head to take them all in. The crowd-murmur subsides into an expectant hush, as he knows it will in response to his silent appraisal.

When he starts his voice is high-pitched, but not squeaky, every word is heard distinctly to the farthest edges of the crowd. He has learned this trade well making stump speeches. The fact is he can yell louder than hell without getting goat bleat.

"*Four score and seven years ago our forefathers brought forth on this continent a new nation, conceived in liberty and dedicated to the proposition that all men are created equal!*"

Immortal words carry across the drizzly battlefield, echo from the melancholy, bare hills, will echo for centuries in men's minds.

The sad, gray eyes alight on a pretty woman in a green gown near the platform. They move on again, like a good speaker's, to include the whole crowd, but keep coming back to her. She soon realizes it, but doesn't appear flustered —rather, flattered and pleased.

He thinks, "*I'll bet she smells good. I'd rather speak at her than these fat-faced slackers.*"

(And the rest of the magisterial thoughts, if any, are nobody's damned business—history has to ride on an elevated plane if we're going to stay *dedicated* enough to survive.)

LASALLE, ILLINOIS

— May 1861

It had been a hard choice deciding whether Smith's Regiment of Illinois Volunteers should be a captive audience for the patriotic speeches or be strung out in companies four abreast, to parade without delay past the dignitaries and crowd as soon as the speeches were over. The latter option won out.

The South had fired on Fort Sumter at Charleston, South Carolina, the month before and started what was clearly an armed rebellion. Smith's was one of the first regiments in the Republic to rush to the colors upon Lincoln's call for seventy-five thousand volunteer soldiers.

Now the regiment is forming up awkwardly after waiting for hours in the hot spring sun. It has been drilled thus far only in the hay foot–straw foot of simple maneuvers by veterans of the Mexican War, which is already thirteen years past.

The front of the first company is a block from the town square, but out of sight around a corner, and happily for them, out of hearing of every word of the long, windy, patriotic speeches. Each company comes from a different locale in the hinterlands around the river town and there are community rivalries that soon will manifest themselves with entertaining results.

The tail of the last company is waiting almost half a mile out of the small town. A band will precede the whole shooting match. Colonel Steven Elephalet Smith, self-conscious in a new uniform with silver eagles in the epaulets on his shoulders, will ride with his staff in front of the band. The colonel is now approaching the leading company, riding well at a high lope on a big black horse, finally having been liberated from the speakers' platform, from which he gained many friends by making the shortest address of anyone:

"I'll be back in a few minutes with something for you to look at instead of listen to."

He was glad to escape the vicinity of the bomb-proof windbags who had just given their "first [and in many cases, only] *full measure of devotion.*"

Some of the troops have fallen out of ranks and straggled, sitting on curbs or looking in shop windows.

Colonel Smith gives the command: "Form up, men! Look smart now!"

So they form up *the best they know how.*

Riding to the colonel's left and slightly behind is his executive officer, Lieutenant Colonel Robert Edwin Cheek, who tried his last law case the afternoon before, and so far as he knows may never try another. In this command group is Regimental Chaplain Isaac Eaton Todd, Minister of the Church of God from the small village of Troy Grove up north, riding awkwardly on a small sorrel.

Beside Colonel Cheek rides his son, Newt, Todd's nephew, eleven years of age, and enlisted as a drummer boy, but looking more like a wild Indian on a spotted Indian pony.

The colonel gives the command, "Foor'd—Harch!"

The band strikes up, startling the horses; Todd, not much of a rider, almost loses his seat, does lose his hat. "Leave it there," Colonel Smith says. He is thinking, "*Thank Christ for small favors; at least no one fell off on his ass.*"

The bass drum starts them off with its solo:

> Boom!
> Boom!
> Boom—boom—boom!
> Fifes shrill.
> Bugles blare:
> Ta-da-ta-da . . . Da-da-da-dee-da
> Ta-dee-dee-da-dee-dee-da-da!
> Boom! Boom! Boom!

Everyone is feeling *dedicated* as hell, except maybe the horses. (As has been aptly observed about fighting, "No matter who won, the horses always lost!")

And that's the way wars start out.

High Private Nicodemus Cochrane, recently of Ireland, marches in the front rank of the first company, the tallest man in the regiment. The music (and several nips from the bottles that military planning stowed in various knapsacks) have elevated his spirits to the "busting" point as he strides out. He is usually the only man in the company out of step, but not this time. In any case, he is inclined by nature to think the whole company should keep in step with him.

Colonel Smith, developing military prescience early, senses something amiss behind him and turns to view the troops he assumes are following in martial splendor. The last eight of his ten companies, idle for two hours, have taken the occasion to visit the Last Chance and a couple of other neighborhood saloons at the edge of town. This inner reinforcement has emphasized various community rivalries that have been nourished for years by small-town editors, and the eight companies are now engaged in a huge, profane, scuffling fistfight and wrestling match from the town limits out into the surrounding cornfields, raising a respectable dust cloud.

Colonel Smith sighs, smiles bleakly.

To Cheek he says, "Well, Bob, at least we know the bastards will fight!"

ST. LOUIS, MISSOURI

(Slightly later that year)

A lot has been happening in border-state Missouri, which President Lincoln is anxious to have remain in the Union. The fly in that ointment is the red-hot secessionist Governor, Claiborne Jackson. Fumbling General Harney, representing the federal government, hasn't done a "damned thing about the bastard." At least in the eyes of the equally red-hot unionist Blairs, who are big sticks in Missouri politics and friends of President Lincoln. The Blairs intrigue Harney out of the state, and in cahoots with fanatical Captain Nathaniel Lyon, capture the arsenal (the contents of which Lyon has already spirited away safely to Illinois) and then, with Lyon promoted to Brigadier General by Lincoln, capture the Home Guard. A period of fruitless negotiation with Governor Jackson follows and relations disintegrate. Lyon runs Governor Jackson and his cronies up the pike.

"If I catch the sonofabitch," Lyon growls, "I'll stretch his goddam traitorous neck long enough to do a year's bookkeeping on with a blunt pencil."

Jackson, safely out of the way, places a fifty-thousand-dollar reward on Lyon, "dead or alive" and pronounces: "If I get my hands on that nigger-lovin' sonofabitchen abolitionist, Lyon, he'll be dead before I count out the reward. I'll drill him personally."

Things were getting decidedly more *dedicated* on both sides. Wars get that way pretty quick.

(And if it didn't happen exactly that way, it should have.)

It was already beginning to be apparent to Colonel Smith, whose regiment was now bivouacked on the outskirts of St. Louis, that Regimental Surgeon Colophon Bedel was going to be a great asset for the organization. Smith's exec., Colonel Cheek, was bound to agree. Just now Cheek was approaching Bedel's bailiwick, a large hospital tent, accompanied by his son, Newt. They heard a yelp inside and the clearly recognizable brogue of Nicodemus Cochrane complaining, "Jazus Kroist, Doc. Phwawt did ye roon awp me wand?"

Young Newt's mouth fell open when they entered and he saw the soldier, his pants and drawers down around his ankles, with a rubber tube shoved up his pecker. His father made no effort to shelter him from the scene—his attitude was that his son would see a lot worse than that if the war lasted.

Bedel removed the tube and dregs of a dark brown liquid dribbled from the end of it.

"Jazus!" Nicodemus yelped again, trying to get up his drawers and pants and dance at the same time. "When the hell will it stop stinging?"

"Taking a piss'll help. At least you'll be able to take one now."

Cochrane jumped, danced, and ran from the tent, headed for the latrines.

"Poor sap!" Bedel growled. "If he'd o' kept it in his pants he wouldn't be in that kind of trouble." He shook his head.

"What was that brown stuff?" Colonel Cheek asked.

"Silver nitrate. He's got the clap."

"Poor bastard."

ATHENS, MISSOURI

(Later that year)

Private Nicodemus Cochrane takes the opportunity during a lull in the fighting to relieve himself behind a tree. An almost spent minie ball removes what he's holding and two fingers on the hand that's holding it.

A week later in a field hospital Doctor Bedel examines the healing wounds and assures him, "You're going home. It could have been worse. At least you won't have any more trouble pissing—it took your chancre with it."

"I'd as soon be dead. I can piss. So what? What the hell else will I be able to do?"

He knows the answer. "Damn little!"

He will never feel *dedicated* again. Few are sufficiently informed to reflect on such sad aspects of wars.

CHAPTER TWO

Listen by the Waters

I remember you, Waubonsee, river town,
Indian-named,
place of summer waters flowing,
place of rustling green leaves.

I remember your stark winters—
bare branches etched against snow-deep hills—
time of coughing and runny noses,
of swift, reluctant sallies outside,
where even nuthatches hide from biting winds.

Waubonsee, Indian-named, river town.
Listen by the waters for rippling, alien tongue of dispossessed race,
rising like faint scent of cold trail.
Lift your head and don't breathe.
Hear the musical words?

Softly . . .
Wahbun—lost one.
Remember me! I am earth!
Listen! I give wisdom!

Wau-bon-see...!

1932
Was I coming down to Pearl Harbor all that time? "I remember Pearl Harbor."

— DECEMBER 1932

Bennie Todd was sick in bed often during those years. He'd been trapped for the past week in the dismal, smelly bedroom where he slept with Ma in a double bed. As usual he hurt all over, especially his head with his nose stopped up.

Tonight was one of his worst. A light had been left on so he could find his way to the toilet. It was a gas jet, survivor of an earlier era, set to burn low, but still consuming oxygen from the already stuffy atmosphere and creating an almost nauseating stink.

He had awakened in its dim light, confused by delirium. He stared at the pinpoint of flame that receded, winking like an orange star—beckoning. Where? He sensed where it beckoned. An awful destiny. Nine years old—he well knew about dying and was terrified. In panic he thought, "I don't want to die!" He frantically sought a god to propitiate, a colossal sacrifice to promise.

He wanted to yell, "Ma!" But he knew he didn't dare. She would ridicule him. Might beat him. Pa, far more understanding and kindly than Ma, slept in the next bedroom, but there was no way to go to him for help. Ma always kept the interconnecting door padlocked on her side. The other way over to Pa was a freezing trek in bare feet, through an unheated hall. In time Bennie would learn that all of Ma's entrances were locked on the inside.

How many times these unnerving incidents took place in those years he never tried to remember. When they were over, he only wanted to forget them. Eventually, as always, his mind escaped into sleep.

A sickly early light filtered through the narrow window. Ma was up. He could hear her storming around the kitchen, banging pans, dishes, and utensils. The unappetizing odor of cheap cornmeal mush scorching as it fried, coupled with his other discomforts, annoyed him. He hated cornmeal mush—and the necessity to eat it often because frequently it was all they had. He even disliked it freshly cooked and served as hot cereal with milk and sugar, which Ma sometimes did on the rare occasions when they had milk and sugar. But he especially detested it fried and swimming in cheap syrup, which didn't quite kill the taste.

Now he heard his older brother, Roy, suddenly yelp, "Aw, Ma!" He pictured the scene. He'd heard the whop of Ma's blow landing just before Roy yelled. He could see in his mind the sad picture of the food that had flown from Roy's mouth, see Roy's hurt expression, and almost feel his own ear stinging with the inescapable, unpleasant after-ringing. Ma always struck from behind without warning. With mean calculation she would catch him or Roy with their mouths full, or when they had their precious, rationed, single cup of coffee on the way to their mouths, so they'd spill it.

Roy's aggrieved voice came again. "Criminy! Why'd you have to do that?"

Ma snapped, "Next time leave some syrup for someone else! You're nothing but a hog!"

Sympathetic tears overcame Bennie. He was certain how Roy felt—he knew that his brother liked fried mush, especially with syrup, and could imagine that it had tasted so good and he was so hungry that he hadn't thought—now he would feel outraged and helpless, and half-sick. Often Bennie had to bear the same hurt himself for the same reason. Only Roy wouldn't cry anymore; that infuriated Ma.

Bennie imagined her look, the hard, hateful black eyes flashing, the unforgiving clenched jaw, heavily muscled, grown that way from almost constantly grinding her teeth in angry frustration. He often was awakened at night when she ground her teeth in her sleep. Without those boxer's jaws her features were regular and handsome, crowned by long, jet-black hair, which she wound in a bun. In his mind Bennie could see her out there now, globules of sweat gathered on her upper lip, glowering at Roy. She sweated easily. He guessed she could work one up standing still on a cold day. She always did while cooking.

Bennie heard Roy getting up now and gathering his school things—books, a pencil, a short, worn, too-thin and too-small jacket.

"Where do you think you're going, young man?" Ma asked.

"School," Roy said.

"You've got time to sit down and finish that breakfast. You dished it up."

"I ain't hungry anymore."

Bennie sympathized with that, knew it was actually so. He'd begun to get sick to his stomach just listening. It was easy to understand why Roy didn't want to eat anymore, even though he was undernourished, just like Bennie.

"You took all that syrup. You'll clean up that plate or get a good beating."

He heard Roy flop back down, knew he was picking, chewing sullenly without tasting, stomach rebelling.

Maybe that realization, more likely the apprehension that his turn was next—that Ma would take it out on him after Roy left—set off a coughing fit that seemed to drive fiery rods down his bronchial tubes. He almost choked on a rope of phlegm and finally got it up and spit it into the rag Ma had given him to avoid using one of their scarce handkerchiefs.

The sound of his gasping struggle brought Roy running in to help him. Ma followed and pushed Roy out of the way. She looked at Bennie and appeared unruffled, perhaps with an effort. She ignored Roy. Finally she said, "It sounds like your cold is breaking up." She put her hand on his forehead—they didn't own a thermometer—and added, "Your fever's broke."

He had fallen back on his pillow, gasping, exhausted, and couldn't talk. She gazed at him for a long time. He wondered if she was deciding whether or not to hit him for not saying something right away to confirm her opinion. While she was preoccupied, Roy grabbed his things and sneaked out.

Bennie was relieved when Ma returned to the kitchen, probably to see if Roy was trying to escape. He heard her wrenching a window open, even though it was the dead of winter, to yell threats after Roy for defying her. She was obviously too late. He prayed she wouldn't storm back into their bedroom fuming.

She had been right about him though. He was breathing easier and didn't feel so much like he was burning up.

He lay silent, staring at the dirty, gray ceiling and wishing he were completely well and playing outside. Since the bed faced away from the single narrow window, he couldn't even see outdoors. With nothing else to do, he looked up at the ceiling and made little shapes crawl around on it by staring intently for a long while.

He tried to think of some new way to amuse himself. Wishing for an Indian pony or a new sled was fun until he realized, as he always had to, that wishing wasn't getting. Kids whose fathers had jobs sometimes got new sleds. He didn't know anyone who had a pony or any prospect of getting one. Phillip's Park rented Shetland ponies in the summer for a nickel a ride, but that wasn't like having your own pony. Besides, he never had a nickel. Nonetheless, he loved every one of the little animals like they were his, and hung around where they were tethered. He even loved their smell. Ma called them stinky.

A familiar but always arresting sound attracted his attention. Ma said that recurring sound was probably mice chewing on something in the wall between the bedrooms. She liked to talk about such things, not only how mice infested walls of old houses such as theirs, but about Lord only knew what else might be crawling around in there.

"Snakes, maybe?" Bennie had asked once.

She had looked at him disgustedly. "Of course not! Maybe spiders though. Even lizards. We used to have them in the cabin *up north*."

He knew that Ma was one of the few women that were not the least bit afraid of spiders, or mice, or even snakes.

He wondered how or why a mouse would make a noise such as this one—a measured clicking sound, always exactly six clicks in a row. He considered the significance of that sometimes when Ma was out at night and he lay in bed alone, unable to get to sleep. He worried that the house might be haunted.

He was briefly shaken by a fear that the reason he heard the sound this time was because he was getting delirious again. He might be going to have one of his relapses. When he did, the second bout was usually worse than the first. He didn't see how he could survive another one the way he felt.

His older sister breezing into the room took his mind off that dreadful prospect.

"Hi. How's my sweetie this morning?"

"Hi, Sister," he said. He and Roy called her Sister; Pa had several pet names for her, and Ma always called her by her given name, Lillian, or sometimes Lil. She'd been named more or less for Pa's mother, Lillie.

"You look better," she said. She always said that—a great believer in the power of positive thinking. (Also at kidding herself; even Bennie recognized that.)

"I'm feeling better . . . a little . . . I guess," he said.

She felt his forehead just like Ma had, then nodded as though she'd divined his future. "You'll be up and playing before you know it. I'll bring you a surprise home from work tonight."

"Don't forget," he said and managed a grin.

Then something else seemed to capture her attention. He wondered if it was the clicking sound, which he'd just heard again. She did seem to be listening and frowned, then left quickly, saying at the door, "I'll be back before I leave for work."

Shortly he could hear her rap on Pa's door, but you could never make out voices too well from over there, at least not from where Bennie was; sometimes Ma would put her ear to Pa's door, but she never said what she heard, if anything.

CHAPTER THREE

Economic Winter

This was the GREAT DEPRESSION, a worldwide affliction. Economic Winter.

The clicks were thin, sharp sounds with a faintly metallic resonance—click—click—click—click—click—click! Pa frequently sat on the edge of the sagging, shabby bed in the cold, sparsely furnished back bedroom, staring at the floor and idly sighting his empty revolver, almost ritually snapping it once for each chamber, the six .45 caliber cartridges lying nearby on the dresser.

Sister hesitated and collected herself before she knocked on Pa's door, unnerved by the sounds coming from inside that Bennie had been told might be mice. She knew what made them.

Behind the door on which she was about to rap was the sad room to which Pa had been banished by economics—and Ma, who hated all men. Maybe once, long ago, she'd loved him.

Roy, thirteen, shared the bed with him. It always stunk of kerosene, with which the springs had been drenched to kill the bedbugs that swarmed in warm weather. The room was unheated. In winter their upstairs flat depended for warmth on a German heater in the kitchen. The only time the house wasn't cold was in the summer. Pa shivered silently in his icebox, even when wearing a heavy sweater and sometimes his overcoat. He seldom joined the family; often not even for meals.

The house, an 1870s cracker box over half a century old, was totally uninsulated; typical of most houses built then, too cold in the winter, too hot in the summer.

Pa and Roy suffered through the winter nights in that room with the hall door closed and their bedroom door also closed, so there'd be more heat for the other three small rooms. They didn't have enough blankets to be warm. Bennie, who was sick a lot, was given all the blankets that could be spared. Luckily they'd kept two horse blankets from the farm *up north* and these, augmented by Pa's shabby brown overcoat spread across the foot of the bed, helped in winter. Pa also had owned a once-fashionable blue overcoat, but had pawned it for seventy-five cents when they had nothing to eat. He'd never again had seventy-five cents to redeem it.

Sister, twenty-three, worked for the Bell Telephone Company and brought in the family's only money. It wasn't enough, but without it they might have starved. A lot of people were pretty close to it. Thousands would give up before President Franklin Delano Roosevelt's new government would take office in March and restore hope through government relief programs. Sister aimed to see that Pa didn't give up, no matter how remote relief might be.

She took a deep breath and knocked on his bedroom door with authority.

"Come on in," Pa invited. He knew who it had to be—Ma never came over there when he was home.

Sister breezed in just as she had into Bennie's room. She tried not to look at the revolver, and pretended not to see it. She stood touching Pa and put her arm across his shoulders and squeezed him. "Hi, you old sweetie," she said. "I came to get you for breakfast."

He leaned forward, not looking at her, and put the gun on his dresser. "I don't feel too hungry just yet. Maybe later."

"You ought to eat," she said. She knew he often didn't, sparing food so Ma and the boys could have more. She thought that was desperately unfair, since Ma saw that she herself ate enough to be putting on weight. Sister had been asleep during Ma's earlier hassle with Roy over the syrup, otherwise she would have correctly surmised for whom Ma wanted some syrup left.

Sister asked Pa, "You know what I dreamed about last night? I dreamed about Riverview—and how we used to go down to Jabby Dawson's on Sundays when I was little and get the paper, and you'd always buy something for me to eat while we walked home."

Pa smiled. "I wish we could go back and do it all over again," he said. Then after a long pause, added, "I'd do a lot of things different."

"Like not leave the farm," Sister suggested.

"Maybe not even go *up north* in the first place. If I'd stayed with Wolfel, I'd own the tannery now."

"It's not even running anymore," Sister said.

"Because Ed couldn't find anyone he trusted to turn it over to. He used to treat me like a son since he didn't have kids of his own. Even if it closed, we'd have made our pile during the war. We could be living down south like him, where it's warm even if you can't afford coal."

Sister nodded. "Maybe you should have. But that's past and done. Things can't stay bad forever."

Pa snorted. "Maybe not, but I've worn out my shoes looking for work. There isn't any."

"You'll find something. And promise me you won't sit around here getting morbid." It was an oblique reference to the gun, and he knew it.

"No place else to go. Guys like me are sitting around all over town, wherever it's warm, just to get out of the house—down at the terminal, the depot, even standing around in stores, or walking the aisles, with no money to buy anything. The floorwalkers look us over like we're going to steal something. I guess some do."

"You could at least sit out in the kitchen where it's warm and maybe read," she suggested. Pa wondered if she was so blind that she didn't know why he didn't.

"At least come out to breakfast and get warm now," she said.

It was a familiar scene in millions of places all over the world. The language, cast of characters, and surroundings might vary, but the underlying cause was universal.

It never occurred to Bennie that Pa was thinking of killing himself. Even if he'd known what was causing those clicking sounds, he wouldn't have suspected. Years later he would conclude that he must have been the only one in the family so comfortably ignorant.

CHAPTER FOUR

His Mother's Lovely Face

— Circa 1882–1886

Pa's first memories were of summer. He was in the yard under a tree in his cradle, discovering things. He'd already discovered the most important thing in his world. His mother. He learned that when he was hungry, she fed him. Papa sometimes picked him up and bounced him or swung him in the air, or hugged him and gave him a kiss—but his mother fed him. When he was cranky or afraid, she comforted him. She changed his diapers. She was now rocking his cradle occasionally with her foot while she sat beside him crocheting.

This place was suffused with golden light. Musical sounds came from the fluttering creatures overhead in the tree. Sometimes he would thrash his arms trying to point at them and make delighted noises or laugh. There was another sound that he heard and it too was charming, though he didn't know what made it; water flowed nearby, a brook gently purling over clean stones and through reeds where redwing blackbirds whistled.

He was always lulled to sleep by it all. His last recollection before his eyelids drooped would be of his mother's lovely face smiling at him. This scene was repeated often during his first summer. He would be one year old in November.

By the time he was three he'd learned a lot. He knew for sure that his name was Russell. When you had your own name it made you a lot more important.

He walked early and was allowed to play by himself in the yard, since it was entirely surrounded by a picket fence. When he was four, he was even allowed to play in the creek, since it wasn't deep enough for him to drown in. When he first learned to wade in the water and pick up smooth, clean rocks from its bottom, his whole world changed in a day. He couldn't wait to go back. Soon he was throwing rocks and watching them splash, squealing each time, or throwing his head back and laughing.

Pa was almost sure sometimes that he could actually remember details from that first summer. He had one of those spells now, as though he had jumped off onto a spiral slide and was whirling dizzily down into the past. He stopped the whirling by looking hard through the clear center of the ice-encrusted window into the wide yard now deep in snow. Across it was the long, two-story Hilger house. Sometimes Pa watched regretfully as the Hilger men went by to work carrying their metal lunch buckets. They had stayed in one place and still had jobs.

He crossed to the bed and flopped down on his back, pulling the two horse blankets over him. "What a hell of a way to end up," he thought.

Here was the fellow who had contemptuously rejected an industrializing world in exchange for a rustic retreat on a subsistence farm, now harried back into a factory town without even a job. He had his trunk shoved under the bed; in it was all he'd salvaged from almost half a century of struggling. He also had this smelly bed, an old dresser with chipped ivory paint and a wavy mirror, one rickety straight chair, and the big, hinged wooden storage box full of junk, mostly Ma's. The floor was bare. There was no closet, just a wire strung across the room to hang clothes on, and pitifully few clothes to hang on it. The walls were undecorated, except for ancient, faded-brown, floral-design wallpaper. The ceiling was gray, water-stained where the roof had leaked. There were two curtainless windows with ripped green shades that dated from the turn of the century. One shade, the one on the side where the landlord's house was located, he always kept down ever since he'd been unable to pay the rent, as though to protect himself from a disapproving eye from over there.

Pa usually had no trouble getting to sleep, since it was the one sure way to blot out his troubles for a while. He also did a lot of daydreaming about his childhood. Actually, it had been his happiest time.

— 1886–1892

A vision of the old place scrolled behind his eyes; he saw the neat white picket fence around the whole block—inside Gertrude, their cow, was grazing, also Papa's horse, Ned, which meant Papa was home. As superintendent of schools, his job took him to the county seat during the week. Gertrude and Ned both had their own stalls in a shed. Across from them inside was the area for storing hay and grain, where Pa (now young Russell again) sometimes napped with his big collie, Fritz.

During the summer or on weekends, Papa often took Mama and the kids picnicking or fishing, and sometimes gathering nuts or berries in season. He'd fill the back of the wagon with hay for the kids to ride on. Fritz would run around in the fields, generally following them, then jump right up into the back of the moving wagon when he needed a rest. He could remember Papa saying, "Fritz goes three miles to our one." One year they got a big, white tomcat named Man (short for Travelin' Man) and he would ride along too, never leaving the wagon except to share the family picnic lunch.

The lunches were mostly homegrown: fried chicken, Mama's delicious cake, homemade pickles, hard-boiled eggs from their own flock, home-canned fruit grown in their orchard, sandwiches with home-cured ham, and a big graniteware pot with the coffee already made, to be heated over a fire.

Their house in Spring Brook had originally been a cabin, but that was covered with board siding, and added onto so no part of it showed anymore, except the fireplace. The cabin had belonged to the first settler, a half-French Indian trapper name Bouyer, who'd settled there before the Revolutionary War.

Pa learned a lot about the outdoors when he was a boy, and even picked up a little "book learning" in school, though he hated school, a healthy boyish trait well described in Mark Twain's two classics, *Tom Sawyer* and *Huckleberry Finn*.

Sometimes he was allowed to ride Papa's horse, Ned, in the summer, with the understanding that he could explore *nearby* country lanes and fields. Fritz always came along. Even Ned seemed to get into the adventurous spirit of it. That was how they discovered the cave.

That day they'd been exploring over along the Illinois River, where Russell loved to watch the stern-wheelers passing up and down, chuffing, pouring out black smoke and making a rhythmic churning racket with their paddle wheels that echoed off the bluffs. There they stumbled onto a lane they'd never been down, beckoning from the edge of cool deep woods. A dilapidated stake and rider fence partly buried in raspberry bushes bordered it. This overgrown lane, now little more than two dim paths, promised some delightful surprise, although the overhanging trees that densely shaded it in spots made it spooky even in mid-afternoon. A snake slithered out of their path, causing Ned to shy and snort. Russell's heart pounded for a while against his rib cage. His palms were suddenly sweaty.

"Easy, Ned," he soothed the big black horse. But he didn't blame him for shying. Rattlesnakes and copperheads were not unknown over in this area toward Starved Rock. Horses could smell the difference between poisonous snakes and others. Most likely that had been a poisonous one. Anyhow, you couldn't be too careful. A rattler had bitten the blacksmith at Spring Brook, causing his leg to swell up big as a nail keg and he'd almost died. Papa had said to Mama, "Well, at least we know he didn't get *that* snake out of a bottle." They'd both laughed, but Russell hadn't understood why. However, he did think it was funny that the druggist in town kept a rattler pickled in a big jar of whiskey on his counter and had a standing offer of a dollar to anyone who would take a drink from the jar. Few did.

Heavy growth shaded the road, crowding them in. It reminded Russell of reading about the terrible Harp and Murrell gangs who had pulled riders from their horses right on the road, robbing and murdering them. But that had been way down south on the Natchez Trace, wherever that was. Nonetheless, he warily eyed each clump of bushes as they approached and urged Ned into a lope through each of them. He was too curious to back out now. In a while a set of weathered farm buildings came in view. He stopped and looked them over, then guided Ned to them across a final clearing covered with tall grass. He carefully surveyed the place for signs of danger. It looked like the sort of abandoned farm that hobos or robbers like Jesse James might have used. Both he and Ned started when an owl flitted out of a hole under the eaves of the decaying house with a noisy flapping of wings. Owls hated to fly in the daytime, but here was proof of what he'd been told—that they'd do it if they were startled.

The front door hung crookedly on a single hinge. Russell dismounted, cautiously, ready to spring back onto Ned and take flight if need be. His hair was standing up slightly on the back of his neck. He looked all around him on the ground, mindful of the snake they'd just seen. Snakes loved to lurk around old buildings such as this, staying cool beneath the rubble in the heat of the day. Finally, after listening a long while, he tied Ned to a porch post and started toward the door. The porch boards were rotting, but held him all right. He thought, "I sure hope my foot doesn't break through—no telling what's under the porch." Of course, his worst fear was of crashing through right onto a rattler. Finally he poked his head in the door and peered around quickly, trying to see every direction at once. He saw nothing threatening. Shards of plaster with tatters of faded wallpaper still clinging on them decorated the interior. It smelled of decayed wood and moldy plaster. Mustering his courage, he edged inside.

Gradually he gained confidence, since the place was absolutely quiet and seemed to be empty. A stairway led to the second floor, but he didn't feel brave enough to go up there. Instead he made a hurried inspection of the four downstairs rooms. The one he'd first entered had obviously been the kitchen; the remains of a cookstove were still standing, with a stovepipe precariously hanging in the crumbled chimney. Three bricks served in the place of a missing leg. A calendar on the wall showed the year 1879. He guessed that the place must have been deserted all the years since then—thirteen years.

Cautiously he returned to Ned, mindful still of where he walked, untied him, and rode to the barn. It was in better shape than the house. A wide alley led all the way through its center, doors open at both ends so you could see through with no trouble.

A few sparrows darted out the back way as he dismounted and tied Ned at the entrance. He walked inside, feeling a little more secure. He thought, "No one's been here for years, I expect." Then he spied the moth-eaten blankets spread on an ancient pile of hay. He looked around more carefully, noting imprints of large shoes in the dirt floor. "Uh-oh!" He told himself. "I'd best get out of here quick." He turned to leave and almost ran into a tall, bearded man who had approached quietly and was barring his way. This sight startled a yelp out of Russell. His heart was in his mouth for sure this time. He tried to dart around the giant and was caught by one huge, grimy hand and held firmly by his shirtsleeve.

"Hold on, sonny," the man said in a bass voice. "I won't hurcha."

Russell looked up into a fierce, bearded face with coal black eyes gleaming in it. Huck Finn's Pap flashed through his mind. He sure wished Papa was with him. Papa was never afraid of anyone as far as he'd been able to see. Just then Fritz came back from one of his excursions into the woods and instead of attacking the man, as he would have if someone threatened one of his people, sniffed him, then wagged his tail. Papa had always told the kids, "Dogs can spot the mean ones." It was some reassurance; a lot better than nothing to hang his hopes on.

The man leaned down and let Fritz sniff the back of his hand, releasing Russell as he did. Russell debated making a run for it, then decided not to try. The man was carefully scratching Fritz's ears, the big collie wagging his tail all the while. By then his heart had slowed down a little.

The man said, "I just come back for a look at the old place. I was born here, lived here till we went bust."

From that Russell knew the man was a tramp. Mama had cautioned the kids to be wary of tramps. "You can never tell what one of them might do to you," she had said over and over.

"What're you aimin' to do to me?" he asked.

The man threw back his head, laughing. "I ain't gonna do anything to ya, except maybe show ya where the best durned apples in the country are ripe just now." He pulled one from a deep back pocket and offered it to Russell. "The orchard's almost all still alive," he said.

Russell took the large, yellow apple mechanically, but didn't feel the least bit like tasting it. "Go ahead and bite into it," the man urged.

Russell was afraid not to obey. He took a small bite and chewed, which reminded him he hadn't eaten since breakfast. He took another bigger bite.

"How d'ya like it?"

He shook his head affirmatively. "Good."

"That ain't all," the man said. "How old're you?"

"Ten."

"You read?"

Russell nodded yes again. He didn't like school, but he read most of Papa's books that weren't too "old" for him. Besides, Mama and Papa often read something to the kids after supper.

"You ever read *Tom Sawyer*?"

Russell was getting interested now and had almost forgotten his fear.

"I sure did." Actually Papa had read that one to the whole family a little stretch at a time.

"Well, the man said, "I'll show you a cave just like Injun Joe's right down the slope."

Russell was torn between his natural fascination with seeing a cave like Injun Joe's and a chilling recollection of Joe's knife. Suppose this fellow was trying to lure him into the cave to do away with him? Then he remembered that Fritz trusted him. Besides he had a kindly voice and didn't look nearly so threatening anymore. Russell's curiosity won out. The other led the way, deliberately not looking back so Russell would see he trusted him not to run away like a ninny.

"C'm'on," he said. Still looking ahead he added, "By the way, my name's Mike Mullins. I farmed here till the bank took it. Doesn't look like they did as much with it as I could have if they let me keep it." He forged ahead, half talking to himself. "Gonna have to hang a few bankers one of these days. Maybe the Populists'll get 'em." Russell wasn't sure what a Populist was, except that Papa called them "plaguey Populists out to ruin the country."

With the fellow walking rapidly ahead talking to himself, Russell knew he could dart back to Ned and make a successful escape. He wasn't sure why, but he decided he didn't want to.

The thought of Ned prompted him to ask, "Should I bring my horse?"

Mike looked over his shoulder and said, "Naw, he'll be O.K. there." He continued down a dim path between sumac and ferns. "Sure has grown up since we left," he said.

Russell wondered who "we" had been, but was afraid to ask. They skirted a limestone outcrop where a broad sweep of river came into view, framed by an arch of elm trees. The man turned sharply left and in a few yards there was the mouth of the cave, a big one. The roof was at least twenty feet high at the front, then sloped back down, but Russell couldn't tell how far. A sort of porch formed by limestone lay across the front. From it he could see miles of winding river. The porch was overhung completely by a rock roof.

Cool, dank air swept out, hinting of the deep, secret recesses from which it came. Mike led the way inside.

He said, "They told my folks when they first come here that the Injuns used to camp here. Could still see their old, charred campfire spots, Pa said."

Russell followed slowly, watching where he was walking and not anxious to get in where it was too dark.

"The cave goes way back," Mike said. "We never did explore the whole thing though. Got too narrow and there wasn't any handy way to carry enough light along. Besides we was always too busy scratchin' fer a livin'."

When they were inside, the slapping paddlewheel of a passing stern-wheeler bounced loud echoes off the walls.

"This is far enough," Mike announced. "Need a torch or lantern to go further. Cain't tell when you might kick up a varmint in the summer. Rattlers like these cool rocky places on hot days."

They stood side by side, looking back. Mike put his big hand gently on Russell's shoulder, and Russell didn't even notice. They stood together and gazed at the shining river.

"Git yore paw to bring you up here picnicking sometime. There's lots of walnuts here in the fall. And you can pick them apples. Best jelly apples in the world. I notice you put that one away pretty neat too, come to think of it."

Russell hadn't realized he'd been eating the apple. Only the core remained in his hand. Mike went on talking, "Loaded with berries here too. And lots o' deer. There ain't no farms anymore for two 'r three mile up or down. All went busted like us. Less farmin' here than before the war, thanks to the hard-money cranks."

Russell had no more idea what a hard-money crank was than a Populist, and didn't care.

When they returned to the old barn, the man held out his hand. "Well, kid," he said, "I didn't knife you down there like Injun Joe, after all, did I? Don't look so surprised—I was a kid once. I know how kids yore age imagine stuff. Took some grit to foller me down there, I'd say. Out West where I bin livin' they'd say, 'I like yore style, pard!'"

Russell didn't know what to say. He was mightily pleased, but could only grin. Mike gave his hand another firm shake. "Good luck, kid. Tommorer I'll be hoppin' a freight fer the Wild West, as Buffler Bill calls it, provided the railroad dicks don't throw me off."

On the spur of the moment Russell blurted, "Take me with you."

"Cain't do 'er. Think how tore up yore maw'd be when you didn't come home."

"I could send her a letter when we get there."

Mike shook his head. "They'd have me in jail sure fer kidnappin', provided yer Paw didn't fetch me with a shotgun first. Nope. You come out West when yer bigger. It's a almighty rough place even yet. But when ya git there just ask fer Mike Mullins; there ain't nobody west o' the Missouri don't know me." He guffawed, and Russell wondered what the joke was.

He hadn't really expected that his new friend would take him with him; nonetheless he felt disappointed. Mike was grinning at him. "Tell ya what I will do, though," he said. "You can go a ways with me, provided I can hitch a ride on that horse o' yers. He's easy big enough to carry double."

"O.K." At least that way he'd be with Mike a little longer. He watched while his new friend rolled his blankets and slung them over one shoulder like the pictures he had seen of soldiers. Mike's only other equipment was a big tin can with a wire handle.

Russell rode behind Mike on Ned and noticed that his new friend smelled like he needed a bath pretty bad, also that Mike's long hair had gray streaks in it. He wondered how old he was. When they reached the road that led down toward the river and Peru on the other side, Mike pulled in Ned and nimbly swung a leg over in front and slid off so Russell didn't have to get down to let him dismount.

He promptly started down the road, turned briefly and said, "Don't take any wooden nickels, kid," a grin showing beneath his mustache as he said it. He turned again and resumed his way, looking back once and waving. Fritz followed him a short way, tail wagging, then trotted back.

Russell wondered if he'd ever see Mike again and guessed probably not. In any case he was already cheered by another thought—what a hero he'd be to the other boys he knew. Some of them could occasionally get a horse. He'd casually lead them up here and say, "Ya, wanna see something that'll knock yer eyes out?" Then they'd ask him how he knew the cave was there, and he'd spit and say, "Oh, me'n Ned do a lot of explorin'."

He knew better than to mention a hobo to anyone though, even to his brother, Ern, who'd be sure to let the cat out of the bag. If the folks ever found out he'd associated with a tramp, he could forget about riding Ned off by himself again. Besides, he'd learned long ago that you had to be sneaky sometimes and get scared pretty good to really have fun.

The sun was low in the west. He began working on a whopper to explain why he'd been too late to help with chores and get to supper on time. Mama would swallow almost any story he cooked up. He hoped Papa was in a good mood, though. When Papa swallowed a whopper it wasn't because he'd been fooled.

CHAPTER FIVE

A Small, Happy Boy Long Ago

— 1932

Bennie had a notion to ask Pa if he had any idea what was wrong with Ma.

Ma got out of the house as often as she could in those days. *Up north*, as they all referred to the farm in northern Wisconsin, they'd lived thirteen miles from town on a rutted, country road that was often deep in mud or snow. Beyond them another thirteen miles were unbroken marsh and cranberry bogs.

"The end of the world," Ma called it.

Her feeling of isolation deepened when she'd had to deliver both Roy and Bennie, with only Pa's mother to help. There was a doctor on the way both times, but he got there late; in Bennie's case, not till the next day, since it was January with a blinding blizzard howling through the bare, forbidding woods. So Ma now intended to make the most of being in a small city and made no bones about it.

Ma's oldest sister, Mary, was married to a Greek who owned a restaurant in the busiest spot in Waubonsee, with an entrance directly on the Chicago electric railway terminal. Mary's husband, Gus, had once owned the several-story office building in which the restaurant was located. He had exchanged it a little at a time for tickets on slow racehorses, but he hung onto the restaurant. It was a gold mine even during the Depression.

Mary had no hobbies, not even reading, except gossip columns, so she hung around the restaurant for something to do and acted as a waitress when it suited her—and as the Queen of Sheba at other times, as one of her sisters acidly commented. The observation smacked of envy, since Mary had no children and practically no domestic responsibilities. The court of the Queen of Sheba was usually where Ma went when she "got out of the house"; either there or to see friends from her youth who lived in town, all of whom, strangely, were named Helen—Helen Johnson, Helen Shannon, and Helen Hoyt. (When Ma said she was going out to visit "Helen," no one was sure where she was going, least of all Bennie; moreover, he didn't care. He was glad to be out of range of her abuse, regardless of where she went, and the longer the better.)

Two days had passed since his bad night. Ma said he'd soon be "feeling good enough to go back to school." This time, at least, he agreed. He felt good enough to go now. It was Thursday. He'd been sick almost two weeks. Missing school never hurt his grades though. He picked up in minutes what it took most of the kids all week to get.

After breakfast that morning Ma had drafted Pa as nurse, stomping out to his door loud enough so he could hear her coming to yell her "orders for the day" through the door at him.

"You stay with Bennie today. I'm going down to see Mary for a while." If he had other plans, that was too bad. Actually he didn't care. It was an opportunity to sit in the warm kitchen reading or writing letters without her hostile glare on him.

"Bennie's asleep," she told Pa, who'd come out into the kitchen just before she left. "Let him sleep. It'll do him good. And bring up a bucket of coal and take the ashes out."

He grunted. He knew he had to do all that, didn't look at her, didn't say goodbye, didn't ask when she'd be home. Knew if he had, she'd have said, "None of your business."

At first he'd wondered about her personality change. Now he tried not to think about it. The past few days he'd thought about Spring Brook a lot. It took his mind off his troubles.

He waited till she was gone before he went out for coal. She left wearing a hat, as all right-thinking women her age did when going out (to be "proper"), but she had sense enough to tie a scarf around it, both to protect her ears and keep it from blowing off. In addition she wore a shabby pair of once-fashionable women's galoshes. Under them were frequently resoled and patched shoes. She wore white cotton stockings (because they were cheap, not for warmth, though they beat rayon or silk) and an old, black cloth coat, which was decorated with a pretty well used-up imitation fox fur collar. She had frequently darned the fingers of her cotton gloves. Her purse was black imitation-leather. In it were a handkerchief, a small compact holding a mirror, rouge, and powder, and in the coin purse, four pennies and one streetcar token to be used in case it got bitterly cold. Tokens were three for a dime. She intended to use one of the pennies for gum, which was sold at the newsstand in the Terminal two sticks for a penny, since many people couldn't afford a whole pack. Beeman's Pepsin was her favorite. She'd break each stick in two so they'd go further.

To get coal Pa had to carry the bucket downstairs and outside around the corner to the cellar. On the way he glanced after Ma. She was already almost a block away, walking rapidly as she always did, leaning forward, chin out, "like she was going to save Napoleon from his Waterloo," as one of her sisters described it. Pa shook his head.

The routine for fetching coal included carrying out ashes in the empty bucket on the same trip (after they'd cooled off in the ash pan under the stove). Their cellar was reached by outside stairs over which a now almost extinct American architectural device was located: outside cellar doors. They were just like regular doors, only they were built against the house at about a twenty-degree angle from the ground, two doors hinged to join in the middle. These doors covered a stairway, in this case limestone—just like the foundation of the house. They shielded the stairwell below from rainwater, snow, and blowing paper, and warded off deposits by passing dogs.

The poor got a half-ton of coal from the county every once in a while. It was strictly rationed, first by the county, then by the user if the latter had good sense. (You could never be sure if or when you'd get another one.) It was the cheapest bituminous available, and came in chunks, some as large as a bushel basket. These had to be broken to stove size with a sledgehammer, which was one of Bennie's jobs when he was well.

Pa checked the thermometer at the side of the front door when he hurried back in with the coal. It was fifteen above. He thought, "It'll be below zero again tonight." He'd always dreaded December and January, except when he was down south.

Bennie's stomach woke him up. It was empty and growling. Aside from that, he felt great. He stretched, and that didn't hurt anymore. His head didn't hurt either. He got up to go to the toilet and was surprised to find Pa at the kitchen table.

"Where's Ma?" he asked.

"Down at the Terminal."

That translated to, "Visiting Aunt Mary," as Bennie knew.

When he came out of the toilet, he said, "I think I'll get dressed." It was actually a question. With Ma he wouldn't have dared to say that, but would have waited till she said, "It's time you got up. Get dressed." He knew when Ma got home she might get mad if she found him up and dressed, but hoped he'd get by with it on Pa's say-so.

"Go ahead," Pa said. "Are you hungry?"

"Uh-huh, real hungry."

They shared a concoction Pa made called "thickened milk," which he prepared by diluting condensed milk with water, adding a little flour and thickening the mess in a frying pan till it got like a sort of white gravy. They each had a slice of bread with this poured over it. Pa added a little of their scarce sugar to make it more palatable. Afterward they both had a cup of coffee. Bennie was still hungry and took another slice of bread, dipping it in his coffee as he ate it.

"When's Ma coming home?" he asked, not that he cared, but he wondered how much time they had to share some fun before she came home and spoiled it.

"I don't know."

Bennie decided to risk getting caught out of bed without Ma's permission. He went in and got dressed. Maybe he'd read. Or draw. He was already a pretty good artist. Maybe he could get Pa to let him play with the Winchester rifle.

He came back to the kitchen and stood at one of the two windows, both frosted at the edges, and looked out. It was a bleak prospect, mostly deep, dirty snow and bare trees. "It sure looks cold," he said.

"It is," Pa said. "Fifteen above when I got the coal. But it used to get a lot colder *up north*. In the old days it was a lot colder all over."

"I don't care," Bennie said. "I'd rather be back *up north* anyhow."

Pa thought, "Who wouldn't? Or down south." He'd been down there on construction work with his brother Ern, who was still a big shot with D & H Contracting (but not a big enough shot to keep his brother on the payroll when both owners had relatives to feed during these bad times).

Pa had just written to Ern again reminding him to send for him if anything turned up—anything at all. He'd also written everyone he could think of about a job, even his sisters who had farms, about coming to work free as a hired man, so there'd be one less mouth to feed here. But he was too proud to tell them that his family was almost starving. Up till now they'd stalled him, perhaps because of their husbands who were tight as wallpaper and didn't want another mouth to feed. Even Mary's husband down at the Terminal Restaurant turned him down for a dishwashing job. Gus had fellow Greeks doing that who were as hard up as Pa (and who'd work for almost nothing—as would Pa, but Mary's husband probably didn't think an American would).

Thinking of Pa's remark about how it had been colder long ago, Bennie asked, "How long ago was it a lot colder all over?"

"When I was a kid."

"How long ago was that?"

"Maybe forty years."

"At Spring Brook?"

Bennie'd heard a lot about the place, but he was never tired of hearing more, even the same old stories; it seemed like a magic time to him, closer to Indians for one thing. He also liked to hear about out west, and Alaska, and *up north*, but Spring Brook was right down the river and the country around there looked a lot like it did around Waubonsee.

"Yeah," Pa said. "At Spring Brook and at Riverview later."

"How cold was Spring Brook? Colder than here?"

"I remember it was thirty-five below one Christmas—I've never seen it lower than twenty below here. That time the water pump in our yard froze solid. We had to boil water in the teakettle and pour it down the pump to thaw it. One teakettle usually did it, but not that time. It was nip and tuck whether we'd run out of water in the cookstove reservoir inside before we got the pump thawed out to pump some more."

"Suppose you had run out?"

"We'd have melted snow, I guess. Wouldn't have done any good to chop a hole in the creek. When it got that cold, it froze solid to the bottom."

That made sense to Bennie. The two small creeks he knew about right here in Waubonsee did the same thing sometimes.

"Was it always that cold in the winter?" He was wondering how you dressed warm enough. He'd never had really good warm clothes, but he didn't realize that. His were all Roy's hand-me-downs that hadn't been adequate for a cold climate to begin with, and were frayed and patched when he got them.

"It wasn't always thirty-five below, but it was plenty cold, and the winter lasted longer, it seems to me. I can remember lots of snow as late as March, and sometimes we'd get our first snow already in October. I sure hated to get out of a warm bed on those cold mornings. I was the oldest boy and had to do most of the chores till Ern got big enough to help." He might have added, "and afterward too most of the time" Ern was a first-class gold brick if ever there was one.

"Where was Grandpa?"

"Gone away to work all week."

Bennie said, "I wish we could all go back to Spring Brook and have the big house with the fireplace."

He'd never seen a fireplace except in pictures or maybe in a movie. He imagined them all gathered around the fireplace in Spring Brook—even Ma, and they were all having such a good time that she didn't even hit anybody.

Pa had told him and Roy many times about Spring Brook.

Pa was thinking about it now and what else to tell Bennie.

Bennie couldn't remember earlier, better times very well. He only knew about good food because Ma took him *out home*, as she called her mother's farm. He never complained at home when they came back because he knew they were dirt poor like a lot of other people, and that was why they never had enough to eat. But it didn't keep him from remembering Country Grandma's farm. (Country Grandma was what Pa always called her, and everyone else did too after a while—except Ma.) Ma used to go *out home* for a few days about once a year. Grandma favored Ma because, although Aunt Mary had been the oldest child, Mary couldn't even manage to boil water. Ma had been the practical one, who'd helped her mother almost from the time she could walk—had kept her mother from going crazy with overwork. In later years Bennie would notice that Ma and Country Grandma talked to each other more like sisters than mother and daughter. Anyhow he was glad Ma took him down there with her, even if she always made him squirm, saying, "If I left you behind you'd only get into trouble."

He savored the memory of those visits long after he came home, particularly the meals. For breakfast there was always plenty of ham and bacon or sausages, and as many eggs fried sunny-side up as anyone wanted; fried potatoes too, and lots of homemade bread sliced thick, real butter, jelly, coffee with rich cream and plenty of sugar, pancakes, syrup, oatmeal with cream and sugar if you wanted some, and even homemade pie, provided you weren't too full yet. The other meals were on a par with that; for dinner (which was what noon meals were called then) chicken, fried or stewed, and sometimes both, with all the trimmings; and for supper usually a roast of some kind.

He always stayed on his extra good behavior so he wouldn't be sent away from the table and have to go hide somewhere so no one would see him cry over what he knew he was missing. Those visits were the high spots of the first years he remembered.

He always imagined that meals down at Pa's boyhood home in Spring Brook had been like those. He liked to have Pa tell about how they grew most of what they ate on the place and what a good cook his mother had been. But just now he wanted to hear about wolves. He knew he could get a good story out of Pa about that now that they were alone. When Ma was around and Pa was telling him and Roy stories, maybe after supper, she'd always horn in and say, "Don't you kids ever get tired of his wind jamming?" As though Pa wasn't even there. He often wondered why Pa didn't just crack Ma one side the head and get it over with.

This was a chance to hear a good story without Ma spoiling it, so now he begged, "Tell me about the wolves down at Spring Brook and how you used to go sledding on their hill."

Pa knew he was being prospected for the same old story. Well, if Bennie didn't think that the gold had been worked out of that old mine, he'd go along with him.

"You want me to fix us another cup of coffee before we start?"

Bennie suspected that would be sort of like stealing, the way Ma guarded the coffee, but he was game; "Sure," he said.

While fixing the coffee Pa had a minute to review in his mind what he'd tell Bennie this time—maybe some new wrinkle to make the old story more interesting. Lately those long-gone days were bright in his mind.

When Pa sat down, Bennie thought he looked happier than he'd seen him in a long while.

Pa started: "Well, you know we still had a few wolves around that country then. Mostly we only heard them howl in winter—maybe they came down from Canada to where winters were warmer, at least that's what people used to think."

"Do you think they really did?"

"Naw. I think they came closer to town in the winter to eat garbage, or chickens if they could catch one out. Anyhow, they'd sit up on top of the hill out where we used to go sledding and howl. The wildest sound you ever heard. Enough to make the hair stand up on the back of your neck. All the dogs in town would pitch in and make enough racket to wake the dead."

"How did the howl sound?"

He knew Pa could give an imitation of it, and he was egging him on, particularly since Ma always said a racket like that would probably peeve the red-headed woman who lived downstairs. That suited him fine. That dumb red-headed woman had hit him alongside the head once for no reason. He'd tipped her ugly daughter Lorraine out of her wagon while he was pulling her, because she'd leaned too far out and overbalanced it. Then, like a dumb girl she'd screamed like she was half-killed. She probably wasn't even hurt. Anyhow, her mother ran out and cracked him, but she wasn't his ma so he kicked her in the shins a good one. Then her shrimp husband had tried to catch him and tripped like a clumsy ninny and broke his thumb. After that they always glared at him, but never bothered him again. He ignored them all, except once, when he dodged out from behind the corner of the house and pasted Lorraine good with a snowball, then dodged back in quick and ran, without her ever knowing who did it. So whatever Pa did to get their nanny pleased him just fine.

Pa threw back his head and gave a real good, loud imitation of a wolf. Years later, when Bennie himself heard wolves, he knew Pa's imitation had been almost perfect.

Then he asked, "Why didn't someone shoot the wolves if they stole chickens?"

"Wolves are too darn slick. Some people tried, but the wolf was always gone when they got there, or if the hunter tried to hide out on the hill the wolf never showed up."

"How did the wolf know someone was coming or was laying for him?"

"They've got sharp eyes and ears and a good nose. They always move upwind so they can smell anything before they get to it, or if they have to go downwind they try to do it only where they can see a long ways—if they can't see they listen for a long while, unless something really has 'em on the jump."

"Did you ever see the wolf?"

"Not that one. Later I saw plenty of 'em *up north* and out west and in Alaska."

"What do they look like?"

"Like a real big police dog. Most are shaggy and a dirty yellowish-brown; some are almost black."

"Did you ever kill any in Alaska or anywhere?"

"Uncle Newt did. We skinned it for the fur—it's like wolverine and good for parka hoods because it doesn't frost up when you breathe on it."

Bennie knew from pictures of Eskimos in books what a parka was. It was the long fur coat they wore with a hood on it.

Pa suddenly laughed. "That was funny. I wanted to run right up and start skinning the wolf. Uncle Newt grabbed me. I wondered what the heck for—I said, 'The wolf'll freeze and we never will get his skin off.' Newt said, 'Wait'll tomorrow. We'll thaw him out in the cabin and skin him.' Well, I wanted to know what the devil for, you can guess."

"Well, what for?" Bennie wanted to know. He'd never heard this story before.

"Because if you came right up to him all the wolf's fleas would jump off the dead carcass onto you to keep warm and stay alive—they knew somehow as soon as the wolf died and that he'd soon be frozen stiff. Newt told me, 'Let the fleas freeze to death overnight. There won't be a one left.' And, sure enough, there wasn't."

Bennie thought that was mighty smart and figured to remember it if he ever killed a wolf. Then his mind turned to Pa sledding out there on the hill where there might be a wolf. "With that wolf around weren't you afraid to go sledding without a gun?"

"Naw. Wolves don't bother people, not even kids—unless maybe there's a pack of 'em and they're starving. That stuff you hear about wolves getting people is all hot air by writers like Jack London who claimed they were in Alaska. If Jack London was there, it was later. In any case, he sure stretched the truth, if he even found it out. Hell, even Robert Service showed up in the Klondike years after its heyday, but Dangerous Dan McGrew comes pretty close."

"Were there woods where that wolf, or maybe a whole pack of 'em, might hide on top of the hill where you went sledding?"

"I don't think there was a pack there, but there were woods up on the hill."

Bennie's eyes were drooping from the warmth of the kitchen and because he still was pretty weak. He could hardly keep them open. He thought, "Maybe it wouldn't be a good idea to go back to school just yet." Ma had a sort of natural feeling about that sort of thing, regardless of what else you said about her.

Pa tucked him back into bed. Before Pa left the bedroom, Bennie had a notion to ask him if he had any idea what was wrong with Ma, but decided against it. He suspected Pa might stand up for her anyhow; he usually did, bad as she treated him.

When Ma did come home she was in an extra good mood and even kissed him. Her sister had put a good, big hot meal into her and given her pie and ice cream for dessert, all free. (Mary had also given Ma fifty cents.) Then she'd given her a couple of pounds of not-quite-spoiled hamburger, and said, "You can still eat it, kid, if you cook it right away. It's just on the turn—hardly smells bad yet."

They *had* to cook it right away. It was a cinch it wasn't going into a refrigerator; they didn't have one, not even an icebox, though in the winter they kept a cold box perched outside the toilet window on a shelf as everyone did. Whatever you put in one of those froze, which wouldn't do with meat on the turn because when you thawed it you'd really have a poisonous mess, or at least that's what everyone said.

Ma fixed that hamburger for them, tainted or not, hard fried it so you couldn't smell or taste it, and with it she served boiled potatoes with brown flour gravy. She didn't even get mad when Roy parked his elbows on the table, although she said, "Get your elbows off the table and don't be a lout."

And no one got sick from the hamburger. Aunt Mary knew about such things, being in the restaurant business. She wouldn't have hurt anyone on purpose for the world. They served their customers meat not much better than that and got away with it.

Bennie lay awake a long time that night living in an imaginary Spring Brook, as he often did. Years later he would go there and find it little different from the way he'd imagined it, except he couldn't pick out that *high* hill Pa had sledded down. He found only knolls, the highest with some scattered trees on its crest.

The valley was filled with redwing blackbirds, whistling all through the summer days among the rushes where Pa had once hidden so he didn't have to play house with his pesky sisters. But the old homestead was gone; all that remained was the big, vacant lot that had been surrounded by a neat, white picket fence. No trace remained of the fence. Some rocks that may have been the foundation of the cowshed lay in an irregular rectangle. The big house with the fireplace had been carried off completely, even the foundation stones.

The enduring wind whispered messages from the past—a wolf's lonely diphthong, Fritz barking in reply, Travelin' Man scratching on the door to be let in on a cold night, the splash of a rock thrown into the brook by a small, happy boy . . . long ago.

CHAPTER SIX

Sacred Relics

Hear the drums, the drums,
The drums of the Republic marching.
Where are the drums of the Republic?
Beyond the hills of history . . .

Pa wasn't really old yet, but he had savored the adventurous times on the frontier during the Republic's late adolescence. Some said the frontier was dead. Every time that came up, Pa would snort and say; "If she's dead, the body is keeping pretty well."

Uncle Newt was even more of a pioneer than Pa. He'd been a drummer boy in the Civil War. As Newt himself put it, more or less tongue-in-cheek, "Mine eyes have seen the glory!" Uncle Newt was a *sacred* relic. Bennie didn't get to meet him till a few years later—when Newt came to live near them.

[FLASHBACK—SPRING 1930]

Waubonsee had other sacred relics that Bennie couldn't help but be interested in from the first time he noticed them. What attracted him was the way they looked, all dressed in blue uniforms like firemen or policemen. They sat around in front of a cut-stone building that had a bell tower with quaint cannons on wheels parked out front under the trees. The cannons weren't the main attraction though; the whole scene always had a mysterious air, as though it was a painting, or an exhibit of wax figures.

Bennie noticed these men first when he was about six, before Pa lost his job with Ern and came home. In those days Ma still had money and even laughed and whistled a lot. She used to take him downtown shopping with her. Most of the good stores were on the *Island*, as they called that part of town (since it really was an island). That day Ma was buying herself an overstuffed chair—the first she ever owned—in a furniture store right across the street from those blue-uniformed old men who, it seemed, just sat around and talked, and occasionally took off their tall, broad-brimmed hats, then readjusted them back on their heads. The hats looked like those worn by the Pilgrim fathers in a picture he'd seen.

"Who are all those men sitting around over there?" he asked Ma as they left the store.

"The G.A.R.," she said.

She must not have known that wouldn't mean a thing to him. They walked half a block before he concluded Ma might not know she hadn't cleared up the question.

"What does G.A.R. mean?" He asked.

"Grand Army of the Republic," she said.

That didn't mean anything to him either, but he decided to give up before he made Ma mad.

She would have told him, "Never go over there," if it had occurred to her that he someday would get out of her control. Ma thought of the G.A.R. as dirty old men who swore and drank and spit, and sat out there mainly to look at women's legs.

Ma's evasive attitude about them was what first gave Bennie the notion that he must get a closer look someday. Escaping Ma as often as possible was his prime aim in life even then, although he wasn't yet conscious of it. His first victory in that campaign was still a few months off, when she had to turn him loose to go to school.

The Island split the Fox River, and had bridges on both sides. At the Island's upper end both sides were dammed, but the mills they served were long out of business, one gone entirely. The other stood, boarded up, just across an alley from the Terminal Restaurant, perched on the river wall. The Main Street Bridge began just in front of that old mill and crossed to the Island. On the other side of the bridge, across the street, was the Fox Theater. Ma took him to movies there, and usually Aunt Mary went with them.

That's where Bennie saw the first movie he remembered. A railroad locomotive appeared to rush right at the audience. There were screams. "Probably dumb girls," Bennie thought, ignoring the fact that he himself almost wet his pants.

The big movie attractions for him were Westerns, already half-contemptuously called "horse operas," often pronounced "hoss oprees." By whatever name, he loved them. A huge audience loved them, probably the majority of Americans. *People were still close to the land and to their pioneer past.* Pa's stories and Western movies had the same appeal to Bennie's imagination. A city kid could escape to adventure in Western movies.

After he'd been somewhat liberated from Ma's smothering supervision,

Bennie got to go to a Western every Saturday, with Roy and other neighborhood kids.

Although movies cost only a dime, after the Depression set in Bennie didn't have a dime. It was a lot of money. But it didn't take a dime to go to the city library, which was on the *Island*, nor to the museum upstairs. It was a large, quiet hall filled with the delicious, musty essence of ancient happenings, and crowded with paraphernalia of the pioneers. Civil War relics especially fascinated Bennie—guns, uniforms, a bass drum with flags and a regimental insignia painted on it, a homemade drumstick. To make it, someone had whittled a handle from a small branch and attached to the end a leather pouch filled with sand. Who? Where? Bennie convinced himself that to make that drumstick the drummer had used one of the ancient willows that grew right along the edge of the Island a few yards away.

In addition to the guns and uniforms in the display cases were buckskin Indian leggings, bows and arrows, stone tomahawks, and arrowheads. (You could still find arrowheads anywhere in that part of the country though there had been no Indians roving free there for over a hundred years.)

Bennie had read about the Civil War, the War of 1812, with its Fort Dearborn Massacre over at Chicago, and Chief Tecumseh's and Pontiac's earlier wars. History books claimed that Tecumseh had been a barbarian. Bennie had studied Tecumseh's picture for a long time. He concluded the chief's face was actually kind, intelligent, and a little sad too. Maybe he'd already divined the Indians' fate—to be beaten and banished, leaving only names behind. The river at Waubonsee was named for the Fox tribe, and Waubonsee itself for the Pottawatomie chief who had fought with the whites against Blackhawk of the Sauk tribe, a historic ally of the Foxes, in the Blackhawk War only a century before. Sometimes, when he went to the edge of town and walked the fields, he would feel that maybe Waubonsee was still there, or at least had walked where he was now walking. It caused a strange chill to travel up and down his spine.

It all seemed long ago, but it wasn't that long. Country Grandma's stories made that clear. She was an Indian too, from out west, and she told exciting tales about her people fighting each other and the white soldiers, and how her father, Four Ponies, had been killed by the soldiers in a land named for her tribe: *Dakota*. (He didn't know yet that the Dakota of her girlhood was a vast Indian domain, not simply the two states in his geography book.)

The battles and chiefs sounded intriguing, even with the names given them by white men: Four Horns, Sitting Bull, Crazy Horse, Lame Deer, Two Moons; and the battles—Fort Phil Kearney, the Fetterman Massacre, Wagon Box, the Hayfield, Little Bighorn. His grandmother slid the names of the two greatest Dakota chiefs from her tongue with musical fluency: *Tatanka Iyo Taka, Tashunka Witko.*

Better even than Indians, almost next door to the library, was that big limestone building—the G.A.R. Hall. He still didn't know what "G.A.R." truly signified, but he knew that those old men who sat out front, dappled by sunlight and shadow into an enchanted natural painting, had actually fought in the Civil War over sixty years ago. They had done a noble thing—freed the slaves. He'd read about slaves in *Uncle Tom's Cabin*, and his school had shown a movie based on the book. Since he'd only been in first grade then, the main thing that had impressed him was that the Fox River was full of ice floes every spring, like the ones across which the hounds chased Eliza.

Movies were thrilling, but they were only make-believe; the Civil War vets were real. So were the new black cannons mounted out front, which were shaped like elongated tears. They replaced those on wheels and had been donated to the G.A.R. just that year. Volunteers from several local contracting firms had mortared them into stone, and they now were planted for posterity on either side of the front walk, hollow veterans pointing aimlessly, but not without memory. On their stone pedestals were brass plaques that told what they were and what they'd done. They were Dahlgren guns, naval cannons, from the gunboats of General Grant's river flotilla. The word "Dahlgren" itself was magical and alluring, even though Bennie wasn't sure he could pronounce it right. Added to the drama of it, General Grant had been from Illinois, just like Abraham Lincoln. The two of them had won the Civil War at last. (He knew that because he'd been told in school—but he didn't yet know that the history of wars was always written by the winners.) When he found out that Grant's river flotilla was actually from the U.S. Navy, that didn't dim the glory of it for Illinois either.

— Summer 1933

The G.A.R. veterans paid no attention to him when he started coming there, shyly watching and listening, trying to look as though his mother had told him to wait there while she shopped.

Sometimes, when he thought one of them was eyeing him a little sharply, he'd go throw rocks in the river to keep his cover. Huge willows grew along the bank there. Nothing could convince him that the drumstick in the museum hadn't been whittled from one of those venerable giants when it was a sapling, perhaps by one of the men sitting here under the trees. Or maybe by some comrade they'd volleyed muskets over in a parting salute, with tears of memory blurring the gunsights. Those ancient, spreading trees and the deep, swift river sweeping past, gave Bennie an eerie sense of time as a relentless torrent flowing all around him, a torrent that would engulf and obliterate everyone some day. Later he would realize that some of those men there were older than the willows, leaving him to plumb the significance of that. These speculations defied resolution; they slipped away as soon as he began to make them mean something and left him feeling sad. He realized that these fascinating old soldiers had only a few years left, that they would soon die and carry their memories away. He wanted to know everything they knew, learn what they thought, and preserve it because it might be more important than anything else—a terrible task for a small boy.

Because of that need, Bennie forced himself to risk slipping onto the end of a bench, close enough to hear the men talking. They looked at the sky a lot and talked about the weather. Some had been farmers or worked on farms during their lives. In the days when they'd grown up everyone had big gardens, even if they lived in towns and villages. It paid in those days to know about the weather.

He'd hear one of them say, "About time to put in corn."

The rest would think about that, spit—usually tobacco juice—then probably nod in agreement. Another might say, "Yep," or, "I reckon." This cryptic response would be followed by a general spitting. Most of them chewed tobacco or smoked pipes or, rarely, a cigar. Bennie never saw a one of them smoke a cigarette.

Every once in a while the talk would turn to "their" war, when they'd marched away, thrilled by the cadence of drums, the squealing of fifes and blare of bugles. It was their greatest adventure, not only of their youth, but also in most cases, of their whole life, the only time most had been very far from home. There'd been wars since, but they knew those hadn't been truly chivalrous wars fought in a noble cause as theirs had been.

When they talked about the Civil War, Bennie sharpened his hearing. By then they all knew why he was there. Many of them had listened to old soldiers of their day. In their youth, a few of them had seen and heard soldiers from the American Revolution, where America had won its independence from Britain. That too, was not so long ago then. Those earlier relics had told how they fought under General Washington; and had actually seen and heard Washington himself and described him and "what he done" to some of these very men sitting here.

The past lived only dimly in books, compared to how true and bright it was in the hearts of humans, and Bennie understood that without knowing that he did. This was how people could prevent the torrent of time from overwhelming them. By not forgetting.

What can history books tell? About Washington, they said:

"First in war, first in peace, first in the hearts of his countrymen."

That was the kind of stuff in history books. What do such high-flying pronouncements truly tell about George Washington?

Listen, goddammit!
Ancient voices live!
Hear the words—the reverent tone of remembering:

I can remember it clear—
We heard the commotion, men cheering,
Here come Gin'r'l Washington
On the biggest horse I ever seen.

Not like in them engravings.
Big as life, no wig
And musta lost his hat,
All hot and red in the face—sweating.

When he seen us fallin' back,
He started yellin' like a maniac.
You coulda heard him two miles away.
"What sonofabitch gave an order to retreat?
Form here! Charge, goddammit!
Goddammit, I say charge! Follow me!"

We couldn't help it. Nobody could.
We felt nine foot tall, and
Yelled like crazy,
Him yellin' loudest of all.
And we follered him—an' whopped 'em good,
Them damn lobsterback British bastards!

"Father of his country" like they say, I guess—
But let me tell you . . .
He come outa there with his sword all bloody . . .

That big sonofabitch was all fight!"

One afternoon an old-timer *spat*, turned and spoke to Bennie. "Sonny, you hang around here a lot, it seems to me," he said and waited, eyeing him severely.

Bennie figured this for his walking papers and didn't know what to say—he never thought any of them would say something to him except what he knew was coming next; an order to "git." Finally he managed to say, "Yes, sir."

"You got a home?"

"Yes, sir."

By then the others were alert, knowing the man was trying to get a rise out of the kid.

"How come you ain't home?"

Bennie squirmed, then blushed. "I'd rather be here," he said.

"What for?"

"To listen," he blurted. He figured they'd make him leave for sure then for being nosey. Instead they all laughed.

"Well," one of them said, glancing around at the others, "at least somebody's still around that wants to listen to us old coots."

That got a general laugh and a couple of words of agreement.

"You're O.K., kid," the first man said. "We figured that was your game. You can hang around as much as you like. C'm'on over here and sit down." He made a place for Bennie next to him. He smelled of tobacco and soap, and like old people.

He pointed his finger for Bennie to follow and said, "See them two big guns out there? Well, them big boys is what saved our bacon the first day at Shiloh."

Bennie was afraid to ask what Shiloh was, or to say anything for that matter, for fear of sounding dumb and being shagged off after all.

"The gunboats lobbed them shells as big as stovepipes down into the woods on our left."

Bennie's imagination leaped on the word "gunboats." That sounded powerful and deadly.

Some of the others nodded; one said, "That's a fact; them gunboats really pulled the fat outa the fire fer us."

"About half of Grant's army had run down under the bluff and hid by then, officers and all. Prentiss's whole division got captured. We was in a real mess. It rained that night with the clouds down low, an' whenever they shot off them big babies the whole sky lit up. Then we'd hear 'em hit down in the woods. Kabloom! Kabloom! Ran them Rebs plumb outa there."

There were more nods. Another white-haired relic chipped in, "Lordy, I was never so scared in my life with them big cannons a-boomin' an' lightin' up the sky. They sounded like thunder, only louder, cause they was shootin' right over where I was. Blew hell outa them Rebs though." He had a faraway look, his head held to one side, as though he was listening for the next salvo of big guns, and Bennie felt the old man wasn't really there with them but back at

Shiloh in the night woods and the rain. He shivered a little. For a minute he felt like he had been there, himself.

Bennie wasn't sure what Rebs were, but figured they must have been the other army. When the man said "blew *hell* outa them Rebs" he'd been a little surprised because not many adults cussed around kids then, not even that mildly. Yet none of them seemed to notice. The one who'd cussed, he learned, was Sergeant Ryan and in time, young as he was, Bennie sensed that the others deferred to Ryan. None of them ever told him it was because Sergeant Ryan had got a Congressional Medal of Honor for "outstanding valor at great risk to his own life."

Bennie was even more surprised when the first man brought out a bottle and they all took a big pull from it. Prohibition hadn't been repealed yet. Some of those old boys knew how to make their own corn likker, and bootleg whiskey wasn't hard to get either, if you had the money. In fact Bennie later discovered that a couple of his uncles were in the business—one cooked it down on the farm from his own corn—saying, "I might as well, you can't give corn away on the market." Another uncle sold that booze in the back room of his drugstore. That one, to Bennie's delight, had his own airplane, but Bennie didn't know then that he used it to fly the bootleg stuff up from the farm, landing in the pasture to pick it up.

These old soldiers knew they were now sacred relics of the glory days of the Republic, knew they could thumb their noses at the law. The police station was right next door, but the cops would as soon jump in the river as run them in for taking a pull on a bottle, unless they did it in the middle of Main and Broadway, or in church.

About two weeks later Bennie finally got up his nerve to ask something that had been on his mind ever since he'd come there. "Did any of you ever get shot?"

Sergeant Ryan opened his vest, shirt, and long-handle BVDs, revealing a long scar. "Like to cut my belly open," he said. "They flanked us at Chickamauga. A minie ball done that. They was as big around as a man's finger." He held out his index finger and marked off with his thumb how big a minie ball was. "A couple of inches further back and I'd 'o been a goner."

None of them seemed to think anything of Ryan undressing to show off an old wound to a kid. This was a golden opportunity for them to relive in retrospect a time they loved, regardless of what they'd thought of it back then. They'd seen it through the smoke long ago, in the springtime of their lives. God had granted them a part in a glorious saga. Bennie felt like one of them for a little while and wondered what it felt like to be shot, especially that bad. He didn't even like to cut his finger. But now he knew he wanted to be a sergeant even if he might get shot someday, or maybe even a general like Grant.

And he'd learned a wonderful new name—*Chickamauga*. It sounded like Indians, and deep, green woods—and long ago, when his new friends had been young, about the age of the men who'd been his heroes up till then, those who played baseball on the playground ball diamond. He wondered if these G.A.R. vets had ever played ball, but he didn't care to ask. Baseball didn't hold a candle to war.

Now he had a new feeling about the colored engravings of Civil War battles that were run every year on the weekend before Memorial Day and Fourth of July in the Chicago *Tribune* rotograph section. Sometimes they also featured General Washington on a white horse, waving his sword in a Revolutionary War battle. They didn't interest him as much anymore since he'd met Sergeant Ryan and his buddies.

Bennie suspected that if he knew the secret password he might be able to step right into the busy, glowing, colored lithographs of Civil War battles. He examined them all closely to see if he could recognize the youthful face of one of his G.A.R. friends—or perhaps his own face in an earlier life. (He'd heard that maybe people lived over and over again.) What if he'd been killed in the Civil War, at *Shiloh*, or *Chickamauga*? He could almost smell the smoke and blood, and hear the thunderous Dahlgren guns at Shiloh—feel it all turn his legs to jelly with paralyzing fear that he had to overcome and go on.

He often went to sleep thinking about that. One summer night a thunderstorm woke him up. He couldn't remember who he was, or where. He mistook the thunder for Dahlgren guns.

"It's *Shiloh*," he thought, "and I've just been killed."

Then he remembered who he was. He shivered and broke into a cold sweat. Ma was snoring beside him.

GETTYSBURG, PENNSYLVANIA

— November 1863

"We here highly resolve that government of the people, by the people, for the people, shall not perish from the earth."

When Bennie had to memorize Lincoln's Gettysburg Address in school, he wondered if Sergeant Ryan and the others had actually "*highly resolved*," in the words of Lincoln.

He would never believe that it was not so.

CHAPTER SEVEN

Buck Doaks versus Ma

Buck Doaks
Laughs and jokes,
But he don't talk
To other folks.

Bennie knew fairly young that losing the farm *up north* was a family tragedy and that, of them all, it was the greatest loss for Pa. It had been Pa's chance to return to a life next to the land, the life he loved. In time Bennie learned that the main reason they'd left *up north* had been Ma's constant bellyaching about living in "primitive isolation."

He was lying in the swing on their porch in Waubonsee, thinking about that sad affair. It was an upstairs rear porch facing the landlord's house, shaded all around in summer by mature box elder and ash trees that towered above the roof. Sometimes, if he lay real still, a robin would land on the railing, or a squirrel jump from a nearby tree and busily explore, hoping to find a tidbit. Without Ma finding out, Bennie managed to stash small pieces of bread, usually behind the mop bucket that was kept in a corner of the porch next to the door.

This porch had been his main window on the world until he started school.

Bennie was never sure what year Buck Doaks started talking to him. They were having one of their little talks now, Bennie lying on his back in the swing with his head on a pillow, a comforter folded several times under him for a mattress. He didn't fit on the swing anymore, so either had to lie with his legs drawn up or sticking over the end. Usually, before he got to know him really well, he could expect Buck to show up only when he squinted his eyes almost shut, sometimes with his eyes closed, but he didn't think he ever talked to Buck during the naps he took here, though he couldn't be absolutely sure. On the other hand . . . anyhow, he was sure Buck was real. He looked a lot like the picture of Huck Finn on the copy of the book that he drew out of the Brady School library and read every summer. This was the fourth time. He was eleven years old now, could read fast, and understand and remember almost everything.

He was getting sleepy from straining his eyes reading and from the warm weather; his eyelids had started to droop. Summer noises also lulled him—a robin chirped down on the lawn, another answered from a tree, a dove cooed far away, kids were calling to one another, somewhere carpenters were sawing and hammering, an occasional car drove past (out of sight since the high porch rail was solid), and lawn mower noise aroused his sympathy for whoever had to push it on this hot day (probably some kid—there were no power mowers yet), a radio was audible through an open window or door, a distant train whistled, and always flies droned.

He was almost asleep when Buck showed up and sat on the porch rail, chewing on a long stem of grass with seeds dangling from it.

"I've been thinking we ought to build that raft this summer and float down to the cave that your old man told you about," Buck said.

It never occurred to Bennie that there was anything unusual about his being able to converse with Buck without either of them making a sound—as though they were simply thinking to each other. What the heck, Ma would have him carted away if she heard him talking to someone she couldn't see, and he was satisfied that no one but he saw or heard Buck so far as he knew . . . except *Pro Bono Publico*. The latter had shown up for the first time during spring vacation from school just that year. Much to Bennie's and Buck's disgust she was a she, and obviously knew a lot more than either of them. They both had to admit, however, that she never tried to lord it over them on that account. She did make solemn pronouncements from time to time but they weren't able to argue about them. Hard as he tried to make her look a little more in style, she always looked like the figure of Justice on a coin. Because of that he and Buck sometimes called her *E Pluribus Unum* when she wasn't around, and sniggered over it. The trouble was, they were never sure she wasn't around because, like Buck, she could be invisible whenever she wanted to, even to Buck.

About the raft, the idea of which had intrigued Bennie ever since he'd first heard of the cave, he asked Buck, "What do you think we should build the raft out of?" He'd speculated with Buck over that, dozens of times but it was still fun to toss around.

They could have sort of borrowed a rowboat almost anywhere and it would have been a lot more practical, but Huck Finn and Jim had a raft. Nothing else gave quite the "high tone" of a raft under the circumstances.

"I think maybe some of those old railroad ties down by the river back of the ice plant," Buck said. "Or we could cut down cottonwoods along the river."

"I like the cottonwood idea O.K. except somebody'd be sure to notice and lay for us to come back and make us quit. Maybe even take us to jail." He could imagine what *Pro Bono Publico* would have to say if he landed in jail, not to mention what Ma would say—and do. She'd wear him out with Pa's hairbrush and call him a little degenerate like she sometimes did. He'd looked up "degenerate" and thought it didn't reflect much credit on Ma either, if he was one.

"All the same," Buck said, "we ought to be able to find some place to cut down trees for the job just in case. Someone might steal those ties for firewood or something before we get around to stealing them ourselves. Do you know where we can get an axe?"

"My old man brought one with us from *up north*. It's in the basement, but Ma won't let me touch it because it's sharp as a razor."

Buck snorted. "Ma won't let me touch it! Ma won't let me touch it! You're running away from Ma, right? That's one reason to build the raft, right? Forget Ma! You get the axe and carry it down there to the river tomorrow and I'll meet you there early."

"How do you expect me to carry out an axe, even if Ma doesn't see me, and then lug it down the street to the river without someone stopping me—maybe even the cops?"

"Put it in a gunny sack. I know you've got lots of them—I've seen them. I've got to go now. You be sure to be there. Early!"

Bennie had never dodged what Buck wanted him to do. He didn't really want to kipe the old man's axe, but didn't see how he could avoid it. He wished they'd move back *up north* where he wouldn't want to go looking for the cave in the first place because he'd be too satisfied right where he was, back on the farm. Besides it would be too far away. Here you could simply float downstream to it, down the Fox River to the Illinois and float down that past Starved Rock a short ways.

Bennie drowsily turned his thoughts to *up north*. He remembered a surprising amount about it even though he'd been little more than a baby. Or maybe he'd been told a lot of things and thought he was remembering them. In any case the images he got when he tried to remember that time were vivid. When he'd told Buck about his past Buck had said, "Yeah, I know. I was there. Remember?"

The devil of it was he really couldn't remember Buck there, but he took him at his word. Since he always assumed Buck was a lot older than he was and probably smarter too, he asked, "Am I imagining all this stuff about *up north*?"

"Naw," Buck said. "It really happened."

Right after Buck left, Bennie got another of his total recalls of the farm *up north*. It was fall; he was sure of that because the leaves were changing from green to startling yellows, reds so bright they hurt your eyes, subtle and rosy hues only duplicated in the transient colors of burning wood or sunsets. The leaf mat on the ground, coupled with partially decayed fruit, lent the brisk air a winey tang which, mingled with wood smoke, was such a heavenly smell you could hardly stand it.

His earliest recollection of the farm, one he was sure no one could have planted in his mind, was of being bundled up in a warm blanket, propped up in a chair at Grandma's cabin. It was night with the lamps lit, but dark in his corner. Firelight flickering through the isinglass on the door of Grandma's German heater fascinated him. He knew the night was frosty outside. They'd come over from their cabin beneath bright, winking stars with their breath like steam from a tea kettle in the air, the stars looking close enough to touch, though he wasn't yet sure what they were. Ma, Pa, Grandma, Aunt Nellie, and crazy Uncle Bob were in the room, talking like they always did, but paid no attention to him since he was being good and quiet. He felt snug and secure. It was harder and harder to keep watching the fire and finally he couldn't keep his eyes open and was soon asleep.

The only recollection he had of Grandpa Todd was from that time. They were sitting together on the old blue bench where Ma did the washing in galvanized tubs. The same bench was in the kitchen here in Waubonsee. It had been beside the stove in their cabin then. Grandpa had his arm around him, but he couldn't recall if the old man said anything to him, or hugged him. He remembered what Grandpa wore—a white shirt and black pants held up by suspenders.

Later he learned that Grandpa didn't live with Grandma anymore, but in Chicago and only came up on the train for visits in the summer. There was a lot of mystery about Grandpa Todd and how he made all the money he did, since he was supposed to be only a schoolteacher. The farm *up north* wasn't quite a paying proposition, so Grandpa bankrolled it to the extent of the shortage.

Bennie never forgot his best friend, Poochie White Cat. He was an orange-and-white kitty and smart as they came. Lord knew what prompted Bennie to dub the cat Poochie, maybe because he'd heard Ma address dogs as Poochie, and saw little difference yet between one four-legged furry animal and another.

One day Poochie White Cat figured out how to crawl up the screen door and unhook it, to let himself out. He then jumped down and pushed the door open as he'd already learned to do when it wasn't hooked. Inspired by the example, Bennie figured out how to use the broom handle to reach up and unlatch the same hook, which he knew was located so high just to lock him in.

One afternoon he was supposed to be taking a nap on the big bed with Ma, but got restless, slipped into the kitchen, unlatched the screen, and went outside. Escape gave him a great sense of satisfaction and exhilaration. He set off to explore, followed by Poochie White Cat, who shadowed him everywhere. They wandered down toward the creek, a fascinating place of mysterious movement, musical and strange sounds made by water wandering over and around rocks and through overhanging brush. Birds congregated in the trees and bushes and sang all day long.

The "creek" was actually the East Fork River, near its source, which was why it was narrow as a creek in most places, but behind the Todd cabins it ran over a rock bed and was wide and shallow. The rocky bottom could be seen through clear water that stayed cold even on the hottest summer day. Ma always warned Bennie to stay away from the creek so he wouldn't drown. If he'd known what "drown" meant he'd have been puzzled to figure out how he could manage that in such shallow water. Of course, in the spring when the ice thundered out, it rose out of its banks and anyone might have drowned in it.

When Ma woke up that day and found him gone, she went straight as an arrow to the creek. She had no idea that he had better sense than to go in the water. She spotted him easily in his white dress—she kept him in dresses for years—and recognized she needn't hurry since he was in no immediate danger. It was just like her to sneak up and give him a good scare. The first thing he knew, she had grabbed his arm and cracked him a good one on his bottom. He cried, more scared than hurt. Then she half-dragged him all the way back to their cabin, which hurt his arm so he really bawled.

As she marched him along she kept saying such things as: "You might have drowned" (which drew a blank). "Jerry the bull might have got you!" (Got me how? Although no one knew it Jerry let Bennie—and absolutely no one else—pet him, even on the nose.) "You might have got lost!" (Lost? What did that mean, and what happened if you did?) "Don't you ever run away again!"

If he'd known what "run away" meant he'd have wondered how you could do it in your own yard. Ma's idea of running away, he would learn, was getting out of her sight.

Such early incidents may have been what first implanted in him an obsession with escaping from her. *He would, in time, resolve to "run away" every chance he got.*

One day he managed to wheedle Pa into taking him along to cut wood. Then Ma put the kibosh on that. She harangued Pa, "You never watch him good enough. You'll let him get hurt—maybe killed—that half-wit Bob will probably hit him with an axe, or let the horses step on him. Besides you won't make him keep his coat buttoned up so he won't catch cold."

Finally Pa said, as she knew he would, "All right! You keep him here then."

Ma delighted in being a killjoy, especially if she could feel virtuous about it, as in this case where she appeared to be looking out for someone's welfare. It was years later that he finally figured out that Ma took pleasure in seeing that no one enjoyed anything since she hardly ever did herself.

Tearfully Bennie watched Pa and Uncle Bob drive away with the big wagon behind the bay mares, Nancy and Queen. He hated Ma so hard that it hurt his chest. It was the first time he positively recalled hating someone. It made him feel funny and half-sick because most of the time he still loved Ma. When he was older, he would try to explain to her that her over-possessiveness made him hate her and was a tragedy she could avert by giving him a little slack. It only got him a dirty look in response and the ungracious comment, "Someone has to order you around for your own good."

After crops were harvested *up north*, cutting and bringing in wood was the next big job. Wood was their only fuel and was used for cooking too. Pa and Uncle Bob cut down trees and trimmed them, then cut them into manageable logs that were loaded on the bobsled and dragged in after first snow. They always had a crop of dry logs cut and lying out since the year before. This day they had been going to chop down a new crop for the next year. They still had a large stack of wood, cut to stove lengths, and some split into smaller billets for the cook stove, stacked outside of both cabins. Bennie loved to go woodcutting because at that time of the year the woods were quiet and beautiful and smelled so good. On the few occasions when he *was* allowed to go with Pa and Bob, he never wandered off far from the sound of the axes and saws. Before a tree was felled Pa always made him get in the bobsled or wagon and stay there, far away from where they were going to drop the tree. So there actually was no danger.

Carrying wood into the house was one of his first triumphs as a kid. He stuck his arms out just like Roy did to be loaded up by Pa or Ma. "You're too young," Ma told him the first time. Pa loaded him up anyhow, a real load too. Bennie lugged it into the house and, far from discouraged by the effort, came back for more. Pa loaded him up again. "Look how much my little man can carry," Pa bragged. It was all Bennie needed. No matter how much they put on him he managed to get it in somehow, and Roy frequently overloaded him just to test him. In fact, when Pa bragged on Bennie's wood-carrying ability, Roy had overloaded himself, tripped on the edge of the porch and fell, scattering wood all over. Everyone laughed, even Roy.

Being a kid Bennie never noticed how stifling the cooking fire made the kitchen in the summer, and for that matter the whole cabin. Ma, hot and tired from other work, couldn't be blamed for not liking it. It was another score she held against living out there, even though the farm she'd been raised on was equally inconvenient. The possibility that she was doomed never to have city conveniences may have contributed to her dissatisfaction.

Another vivid recollection of Bennie's was the pitchfork that Pa had whittled for him out of a forked branch. With it he made a pretty good stab at helping Pa and Uncle Bob make hay. Pa kept him on top of the hayrack with him, while Bob pitched up the cured haycocks for them to stack evenly so the hay wouldn't fall off the wagon going to the barn. Their horses, Nancy and Queen, had learned just when to move to the next haycock without being told, wait while it was loaded, then move just the right distance for loading the next one. He loved both of the warm, shiny, brown-eyed horses that were never impatient over his constant attempts to stroke their silky noses. Whenever the hayrack was loaded and ready to head for the barn, Pa would put Bennie on one or the other of the horses. He sat astride just behind the collar where he held onto the hames for dear life, a long way off the ground but loving it even though he was scared.

Bennie sensed early that they were going to leave *Paradise*. He was too young to understand the endless arguments that preceded the decision, but he got the drift. The prospect was dreadful. Grandma must have thought so too. She cried a lot during those days when she held him on her lap. He would cry too, though he wasn't always too sure why, except he was sure he didn't want Grandma to feel bad. He couldn't bear the thought of leaving Poochie White Cat, Nancy and Queen, Grandma's two collies, Waggers and Laddie—the dogs weren't exactly his, but they might as well have been. They followed him around and licked him with big warm tongues and made him giggle, and if he'd pretend to be dead and lie on the ground real still they'd both try to revive him by poking him with their muzzles. In fact, once he refused to move or make a sound for so long that they both went for help and brought Grandma back.

If they left the farm, where could they go? What in the world could anyone do away from a farm in the woods along a creek? He knew they were all foolishly going to their doom and he wasn't prepared for it to happen. As it turned out he was dead right, and they weren't prepared for it either.

The final day came. It wasn't going to be like riding to town in the wagon behind the horses. Someone who had a car came to take them on the first leg of their exodus—to the little nearby town. As long as he lived he would hate towns—villages less than cities, but they were all confining, noisy, depressing places. Such furniture and household things as they meant to keep had already been moved to the village where they planned to spend the winter, just Bennie, Roy, and Ma, because Pa had got a job somewhere far away to make some money. They always were short of money. Sister already was living with Pa's brother Uncle John in a nearby city so she could go to high school.

This would be his first auto ride, but the prospect held no joy. He regarded the goodbye saying with mournful eyes, trying not to cry too soon.

Buck Doaks urged, "Save it up. Throw a real tantrum. This is your big chance to pay them off for pulling you out of Paradise." This was the first time he recalled Buck saying something to him. He had no idea what the word "Paradise" meant, but he knew what a paradise was.

When they came to put him in the car he threw himself down, screaming, clung to everything he could grab, and when Ma snatched him up he kicked, punched, clawed, and raved. Pa looked as though he'd have liked to throw a tantrum too. Later Pa would be plenty sorry he hadn't called the whole thing off right then. He could have. Grandma wanted him to. After all he was her first son. But Ma had Pa buffaloed. Bennie figured that out by the time he was twelve and never came to terms with it. He would have cracked her in the mouth for things that Pa meekly swallowed.

A big part of the problem was Pa's half-assed brother-in-law Bart, who'd married Pa's sister Nellie. He'd done that right quick when he learned she was going to go *up north* with her mother in 1914. He'd tried to make a go of this or that *up north*, but ended up living with Grandma. It made for too many mouths to feed on too small a subsistence farm. That, coupled with Ma's chronic griping, had been too much for Pa.

To shut up Bennie, Ma finally bashed him a good one alongside the head. Still he blubbered and sobbed bitterly, frantically squirmed loose and raced to Grandma, burying his head in her long skirt. "I'll stay up here with Grandma!" He pleaded.

Ma grabbed him again and hit him harder than the first time. Grandma gave Ma a look that should have turned her into a block of ice.

And that was how Bennie finally remembered his first meeting with Buck Doaks.

During the best part of his tantrum he recalled Buck yelling, "Go it, kid! Show 'em!"

Well, he'd shown 'em—and lost Paradise anyhow.

CHAPTER EIGHT

An Owl in the Full Moon

The only thing Indian left at Winnebago was the name—and perhaps the nearby forests and river.

Tell us, forest, do you miss your Indians?
Tell us, river . . .

"Listen by the waters!"

[FLASHBACK—1927]

Winnebago had been a logging town, a supply point for the *mercenary destroyers* who'd clear-cut the virgin pinewoods after the Civil War. The town was located on the Yellow River where, in 1856, a sawmill had been established.

Pa's sister Felice lived there with her new husband, Bertram, who looked like a cretin, but belied the appearance with a scheming, money-grubbing mind. He suited Felice exactly. Each thought they'd shrewdly entrapped a prize.

Ma and the boys stayed with them a couple of days then gratefully moved into their own cottage, even though it was dinky, cold, and bare. They had some potatoes they'd brought from the farm to eat and little money to buy anything else till Pa earned some.

They bundled up in winter clothes, even inside, since the only heat came from the cookstove in the kitchen and there wasn't much wood for that. Uncle Bart was going to haul in a load but hadn't got around to it and never did. A neighbor finally gave them half a cord on tick. After supper they'd sit around the kitchen table while Ma read to them or drew pictures, for which she had a fine talent. Usually they went to bed early to save kerosene for the lamp and to try to keep warm, which Bennie had no trouble doing since he slept with Ma and could cuddle up to her. Roy had to tough it out alone on a cot.

Bennie's main memory of that place was of one moonlit night so cold the trees popped. Powdery snow blew across the fields. They were sitting around the kitchen table after dinner when an owl hooted. "Hoo . . . hoo . . . hoo, hoo!"

Ma said, "Be real quiet and stay at the table till I tell you to come."

She blew out the lamp and slipped over to the window. At first Bennie couldn't see a thing and felt a shiver along his spine. Then he made out the rectangle of the moonlit window and Ma in front of it.

She called in a low voice, "Roy, bring Bennie over here and both of you be real quiet."

He looked out and saw a big owl framed by the full moon, perched on a branch of the bare oak just beyond the porch. The owl again sounded his "Hoo . . . hoo . . . hoo, hoo!" and danced down the branch, fluffing its feathers, seeming to keep time to its own mournful song. Then his big, feathered head swiveled, great, round, luminous eyes spearing them through the night. Bennie shivered again.

Ma was fun to be with when she did things like that. Often as not she'd say, "Ma used to do the same thing with us kids," and he wasn't surprised to hear her say it this time. He'd rather have stayed right there with Ma in the little cottage than go to yet another strange, new place that had no deep woods or a river, or even owls, to say nothing of wolves that sometimes howled close to town on winter nights and made his hair stand on end. They'd even seen deer walking right down their street early in the morning, just like back on the farm.

In time they left Winnebago, and Bennie felt as though he'd like to go to sleep and never wake up. His first train ride thrilled him, but his stomach and heart ached. It was late winter when their train finally pulled into Waubonsee. Pa was waiting for them. He hugged Ma, pulled Roy against his leg and hugged him briefly, then swung Bennie up in his arms and gave him a squeeze. He carried him into the cathedral-like depot in one arm and lugged Ma's cheap, battered suitcase with the other. Inside, it was overly warm and smelled of varnished wood, cleaning compounds and urine, the classic essence of American railroad depots.

A taxi was a luxury they couldn't afford, so they walked the ten blocks to Aunt Mary's Terminal Restaurant in biting cold, Pa slipping occasionally on the rough, melted-and-refrozen snow on the sidewalks, gripping Bennie harder when he did. Evening lights were just going on under a lonesome overcast sky. Electric lights were still new to Bennie. He didn't like them. Too bright. Candles or kerosene lamps beat them all hollow because they were friendly.

Aunt Mary knew they were coming and met them as they came in out of the cold. She pinched Bennie's half-frozen cheek, which hurt, and warbled, "How's my little squirrel?" He'd never seen her before, and her bright brown eyes and great toothy smile, showing one gold tooth in front, scared him—but for the gold tooth she looked like a piano keyboard. Heavily rouged cheeks simply added to her grotesqueness. He hid behind Ma.

Mary hugged Ma, saying, "Hi, kid." She was apt to call almost anyone but God and the Pope kid; she said nothing to Pa because he'd been there keeping warm, drinking coffee till it was time to go to the depot.

During two weeks of house hunting they all stayed at Aunt Mary's one-bedroom apartment—sleeping on the living-room couch and on the floor. Uncle Gus was seldom in evidence; he left early for the restaurant and came home late, grunted on the way through—his notion of spontaneous conversation—and vanished into the bedroom. If he didn't go to sleep right away, he sat up in bed and read pulp Western magazines (all of which Bennie would some day fall heir to) and smoked good-quality black cigars of alarming dimensions. Occasionally Aunt Mary prodded him out to join them, which he'd do for the minimum time he felt he could get away with. At such times he'd give Pa a big cigar, knowing Pa couldn't afford them, or at least not a good one. He regarded Pa impassively from unreadable, Greek eyes, almost Oriental in their inscrutability. What he thought was a different matter; probably, "So you married a sexless dud just like mine, *you poor sonofabitch*!"

Aunt Mary's meals were unforgettable; she always bought the best ingredients or brought them from the restaurant, then burned everything with fine impartiality, which was undoubtedly why Gus had eaten only one meal at home in the nine years of their marriage. Pa and Ma were in no position to complain and choked it all down.

Finally, before Aunt Mary's hospitality proved fatal, they found a place to live, a rental flat at twenty dollars a month, a week's pay for Pa, who had a job with a landscaper. He got that much only because he was good with a team of horses and could handle it working a block and tackle on the big tree-topping and removal jobs. His boss was Hugo Mundt, who drove a black Ford truck himself. (All Fords were black then.) Mundt drove the men to the job in the back of the truck, and on those jobs where horses were needed, Pa left early in order to get there at the same time as the others. Mundt's other two men were Pete Jensen and Ralph Esselborn. Pa was the oldest of the three at forty-five. Ralph had been in the World War, had been wounded and gassed and had medals for heroism. He was pretty much recovered *on the outside* by then.

Bennie took about a minute inspecting their new flat then started downstairs to look over the yard.

"Where do you think you're going, young man?" Ma yelled at him. "Get back up here. You'll get run over by a car or wander off and get lost. You stay right here with me. And stay out of the way of the men."

It didn't take long for the men to get things unloaded from the wagon Pa had borrowed from Mundt to bring their belongings up from the Burlington Freight Depot. The big pieces were few: a kitchen cupboard, beds, an oak kitchen table and four chairs, a couple of old rocking chairs and an end table, Pa's and Ma's battered dressers, Ma's blue wash bench and a big packing box full of odds and ends, her trunk, Pa's trunk, Ma's foot-treadle Brunswick sewing machine (which had kept the family in clothes *up north* and would here), several cardboard boxes of clothes, bedding, and kitchen utensils tied with binder twine. Last, the German heater in several sections, base, stove proper, fancy top, and pipes. They put the latter together and fitted them into the chimney flue in the kitchen. It was the only stovepipe outlet in the flat. Pa's tools they stored in the basement.

Bennie had got used to such marvels as a bathroom and running water and electric lights at Aunt Mary's. Here they had plumbing only after a fashion. The toilet was tucked in a small room above the entry hall, which was at the bottom of the stairs that were the only means of entry or exit to the place. Just outside the toilet door was a kitchen sink, cobbled to the wall somehow, jutting into the room like a big shelf. It had only a cold-water tap. Obviously the plumbing was something installed in an ancient house as an afterthought, but it beat an outside pump, or getting water from a creek in a pail, and the toilet they had here was better than an outside "two-holer."

For cooking they bought a two-burner gas plate and connected it up on a packing box next to the sink. Pa built a shelf in the packing box so it would hold all of Ma's pots and pans, and she hemmed a curtain of blue-checked gingham and hung it on a string across the front of the packing box. It was a house that any Revolutionary War vet could have marveled over. Ma's relatives all did too, eventually, but not for the same reason. Her sisters had all done pretty well at getting husbands who provided for them.

From the moment Ma issued her edict "You stay right here with me!" Bennie started to hate the city. After he finally left it, the place never entered his mind again, except in the bad dreams he had for years after.

They came to the city early in March 1927. Bennie had been four in January. He noticed and felt a lot for his age. For example, the sound of melting snow and icicles dripping off the eaves into puddles on the ground didn't pick up his spirits as it had *up north*; even birds chirping a greeting to long-awaited spring sounded less cheerful than he remembered.

He harbored a premonition of bad times ahead.

CHAPTER NINE

Bennie Wasn't the Playground Type

— 1927

Waubonsee, you were all America then.
Still between the land and man's contriving.
Nearer Plymouth Rock than an affluent society,
Close to the Founding Fathers.

Bennie remembered all too well how they came to Waubonsee, to the smelly, cavernous Burlington passenger depot, went to the Terminal Restaurant for a good (free) meal, which, God knew, they all needed, both nourishment and charity, like the Argonauts of '49 who had just crossed the Sierra Nevadas and arrived starved and numb. *Only in this case there had been no enticing report of a fabulous Golconda . . . only Ma's discontent, driving rather than beckoning.*

That summer he paced his new home, that small flat, ever remembered as more cage than shelter, looking out windows and off the back porch, never trusted alone down the long, steep stairs, across the small stoop, and into an enticing grassy yard full of dandelions and butterflies to a place called . . . *outside.*

Theirs was a corner house. Across Union Street to the west was Wolsfeldt's butcher shop, above which the noisy, red-faced Wolsfeldt boys lived in apartments. Beyond Grove Street to the south was Reder's sprawling house. Reder's owned the small I.G.A. grocery store two doors further down Union.

In those times many independent little stores, not really far apart, jointly served an equal population and the same needs that supermarkets would later. There were others within a few blocks. Clemens and Gangler's grocery in the second block west on Grove; Boudreau's bakery across the street a little beyond Wolsfeldt's; a candy and novelty store across from Brady School two blocks south of them; Gehring's candy store within a couple of blocks; and a store east of them on Grove at the end of their long block. Somehow these businesses all made a living—each had its regular customers, treated them right or they'd take their business to one of those other stores. Bennie didn't realize how nice it was in those days when the "customer was always right" (especially when he was wrong) until years later, when the opposite came closer to the truth.

He had yet to discover where most of those places were, but knew a wider world was waiting, and hungered to be away, like a chained hunting dog scenting the chase and whining.

— 1935 — Summer

It was too hot. No leaf stirred, and everything was still. Cumulus clouds, just forming, would create a different world by mid-afternoon. Bennie was in his swing almost asleep, his book open on his chest. He would remember that as "the summer in the swing," a time of reading and learning. He hungered to know everything. He was allowed to go places now, but didn't want to in this weather. When he did go, Ma expected him to tell her when he left, where he was going, and when he expected to be back. No matter where he was bound, even if he was going to the playground or library, she said the same thing: "You'll only get in trouble there." He doubted in time that she knew what she was saying since she said it so often and inanely.

She was right about the playground though. He wasn't the playground type. Too many regulations. He didn't think there was anything unusual about the fact that he simply couldn't conform. Even the playground swimming pool, where he could have gone to cool off, didn't hold the attraction it might have: you mustn't splash water, yell too loud, jump off the edge (because it would splash water and besides you might hurt yourself), duck anyone, especially girls; he didn't think girls belonged in a swimming pool in the first place. It was simply too much work to be good there, and besides he'd just barely healed the blisters from the sunburn he got the last time he stayed there too long. (He hadn't known you could get blisters; why didn't the smart-aleck lifeguard tell somebody that?) The lifeguard was a freckle-faced older girl they said was in college, and some of the older boys said they'd sure like to "do it" to her; he knew that was something dirty from the way they said it, but whatever it was didn't interest him even slightly.

Buck Doaks woke him up, rocking fast and noisily in the reed rocker. Bennie was startled and jumped, knocking his copy of Sabin's *On the Plains with Custer* onto the floor. Buck was fanning himself with a folded newspaper. "Man, it's a scorcher," he said, rocking faster, trying to create a little breeze for himself.

The Custer book was a re-read; Bennie had met Pro Bono Publico the first time he read it. Custer had gone to a place called West Point and *Pro Bono Publico* was one of their mottoes. He had been puzzling over the meaning of that when Pro Bono Publico materialized beside him for the first time. At first he'd thought she was some danged girl, then he could tell by her clothes that she wasn't.

She said, "Literally translated" (she never made anything easy), "*Pro Bono Publico* means, 'For the good of the public.' It's Latin, but it's in every dictionary; why didn't you look it up?" He had a notion to tell her where to go, but something about her looks suggested that wouldn't be a good idea. She looked sort of like she might wave a magic wand or something and send him where he'd just as soon not be.

He hadn't changed his mind about being a soldier and decided after he learned that Custer had materially assisted Sergeant Ryan, Lincoln, and Grant to win the Civil War, that he'd go to West Point someday himself, since Custer had. The trouble was, it was some kind of school. Custer had always been in trouble at West Point. Bennie suspected he'd meet the same fate there. His record was terrible enough in Brady School.

Buck, who could always read his mind, laughed and asked, "Remember how we got an 'F' in Milk Wagon in first grade?"

"I sure as hell do. What do you mean 'we'? I got the hair brush from Ma, not you."

"Yeah, but it was my idea to stiff-arm those dummies in the mush and take over the tools."

Bennie recalled all the nice little first-graders filing over to the big kindergarten room, which was handy for doing projects. Other grades frequently used the room in the afternoon since kindergarten only lasted till noon.

Miss Eichabraud had said, "Now I want you kids to be good because we have a special treat for you. They've paid a lot for a lady to teach you about building things." (*If she'd said what she was thinking it would have been more interesting, which was, "I've watched simpleton administrations throw away money on half-baked schemes for half a century and I'm about ready to hit the beach in Florida."*)

Miss Eichabraud had a good idea what was up—in a few years it would be fitted with a handle: progressive education, (cum life adjustment, cum situation ethics, cum bedlam). She thought a squint at Gibbon's *Decline and Fall of the Roman Empire* would suggest it was nothing new. First-grade teachers weren't supposed to think on that elevated plane, so she kept it to herself. One more generation would improve the strain of first-grade teachers so they not only didn't think on that plane anymore—or any other plane either, as far as the favorable evidence for a lot of them went.

Bennie's inchoate mind was untroubled by any such suspicions. Passage of a few years of serious reading gave him a better insight and he concluded that so-called educators with nothing better to do had decided to "pave the road to hell with a few good intentions" and introduce Utopia, perhaps over-influenced by Thomas Jefferson's inalienable right of man to "the pursuit of happiness." They cooked up an Alice in Wonderland "drink-me" phial filled with life adjustment. After the game played into overtime, the final "sudden death" verdict regarding their experiment would be that it was "a bunch of drivel" and that the only ideally adjusted individual in their terms (i.e., unre-sentful of anything) was found in a coffin.

"I can see us that day now," Buck recalled. "In knee britches like the founding fathers. I thought your Ma would never let you wear long pants. Anyhow, there was that lady 'rassler' or whatever she was . . ."

"Miss Morlach," Bennie put in. "She was a lion trainer or something during summer vacation."

"Pity the lions."

"Anyhow, they hired her as regular gym teacher the next year. You should have seen her shinny up a rope to the rafters."

"I'm not surprised. You should see a gorilla shinny up a rope. I can see her plain as day standing up there picking up tools and waving them around and warbling:

'This is a saw, children.' (The dumbest girl there knew it was a cotton-pickin' saw.)

'This is a hammer.'

'This is a stapler.'

'This is beaver board.'

'These are nails.'

'This is glue.'

"I went to sleep.

"I went to the can. When I got back everyone had been handed a tool to work with. Morlach didn't know what to give me, so she handed me the blue-prints. Everyone had to hold something. That was really neat. I started all the arguments. After an hour we hadn't sawed a lath, or even drawn a line."

"Yeah," Buck said. "It was the next afternoon when we really got started, and then nobody could saw on the line."

"Sad case. Pa put a saw in my mitts when I was two—*up north*. I watched as much as I could stand."

"I knew you were getting steamed."

"You gotta admit I was polite as pie when I asked Tommy Davin to give me the saw and let me show him how to use it."

"And he wouldn't give it to you."

"That's when I really got steamed. I could see we'd never build a milk wagon out of all that crap, the way that crowd was going at it."

"And that's why I said, 'Punch the sonofabitch out!' and you did and took the saw."

"Then old Morlach grabbed me and picked me up by the shirt collar and looked me in the eye. She said, 'You're supposed to be nice and learn to work together in harmony.' Her exact words. I didn't know what the hell harmony was, but I was ready to work in it—at least just then—provided she didn't bust me one."

"We got expelled for three days."

"A week."

"Three days. The week was when you pasted Hansel Mervyn in the mush for pushing you off first base and tagging you out."

"Yeah." Bennie laughed. "He had to have three stitches."

"Anyhow, Ma nearly laid a brick. When Pa heard about it he thought it was funny."

Bennie had obviously benefited a great deal from school in a short time. It took hold in first grade.

Only the previous fall his self-confidence had still been atrophied by Ma's smothering. He'd never been allowed to cross a street alone. On the first day of school Ma went with him.

"Give me your hand," she said at each street corner, and led him across.

"Have you got your handkerchief?" It was the third time she'd asked that. "Have you got your pencil? Don't lose it in school, and don't lose that tablet. They cost a nickel." All of this caused him a terrible experience that first day.

Miss Eichabraud, who'd been teaching school since Custer's Last Stand, shifted kids to other desks for singing, according to the pitch of their voices. He wasn't prepared for this and left his pencil and tablet behind in the drawer under the seat of his regular desk. He knew Ma would flay him for losing them. He nearly cried. He couldn't even remember for sure which desk was his regular one.

But he survived, and in a few days got a remarkable degree of self-confidence. Bennie learned to read and write far beyond the first-grade level in that year. Other wonderful educational experiences lay ahead of him, but very few were to be in schools.

He would recognize fairly early that school wasn't living up to its billing for him.

> *"A common aberration is to mistake schooling for education. HENRY ADAMS KNEW THIS PRETTY EARLY IN HIS LIFE."*
>
> —*Pro Bono Publico*

CHAPTER TEN

Hear the Musical Words

[FLASHBACK—AUGUST 1900]

Ma had been eight in May.

No one made a fuss over birthdays in her family, but they'd made a big fuss the winter before at Johnny Run School over the birth of a new century. She didn't see why. Nothing looked a bit different. A few sticklers commented that the new century actually wouldn't start till the next year, but no one paid any attention to them.

Pretty soon kids would be going back to school. She'd be glad to escape her Pa even if it was only during the day. So far only she and Mary went to school. Rob would be old enough the next year. Lizzie was only three, so she had a while to go before she went.

Ma was going to be in third grade, a matter of wonder to her. Third-graders had seemed like big kids when she started school the year before the war with Spain over Cuba.

Wars didn't make much sense to her, but big people got all excited over them. If people got hurt bad or died in them she thought they should stop having them. She'd seen George Spiller's arm that was all sunken-in below the elbow and had puckered up, and turned purple and red; she understood it got that way because he'd been shot by a Spaniard and might have been killed. He couldn't use the arm as good as he used to, but said the Army doctors had told him it would get all right again in time. She hoped so because George was nice. If he was out working in the field when Mary and she went by going to or from school, he always stopped his team of horses to talk to them when he was close enough to the fence.

Ma's name was Emma, but she hadn't been named for anyone special. Mary was named for their mother, and Rob was named for her Pa. She didn't care. You'd amount to just as much no matter what your name was if you were good like Abraham Lincoln or God. Abraham Lincoln was a martyr and was dead now. She wasn't too clear about what a martyr was or who God was either, but Pa was always reading in a book called the Bible and talking about God, and about being good because if you weren't you'd suffer hellfire.

She was old enough to know that Pa wasn't any too good himself. In fact she'd heard one of their neighbors, Old Jim Tynan, say to George Spiller, "Feltman is a mean little son of a bitch." She knew that was cussing and wasn't sure what it meant, but her guess came pretty close.

Pa used to beat up Ma, and the kids would all run, hide, and cry because they were afraid. Emma cried mostly because she wanted to help Ma and didn't know how. Then once Pa kicked Ma in the belly and chased her around and around the outside of the house, yelling and flourishing their butcher knife. Ma finally managed to get into the stone pumphouse and lock the door on the inside. Emma ran in panic the half-mile down to Tynan's to get help. Old Jim Tynan was hitching a team of horses in the yard. She ran up to him gasping and blubbering.

"For God's sake, what's the matter?" Jim asked, startled.

She couldn't get out a word yet.

Finally she blurted, "Pa's chasin' Ma with the butcher knife."

Old Jim was all of sixty then, but still big and strong. He jerked the harness off the team and jumped on one horse bareback. He yelled to his son, Young Jim, loud enough to scare the chickens. "Hey Jim, get the hell out here!" Jim Jr. rushed out of the barn. His father yelled, "Take the kid in to Ma and follow me. That son of a bitch Feltman is killin' his missus." Then he kicked the surprised work plug into a gallop across the fields. He'd been one of the few outsized cavalrymen in the Civil War.

By the time young Jim got there, his father had Pa Feltman down in the chicken droppings, straddling him and pounding his head up and down on the ground. Ma Feltman was tearfully begging him not to kill her husband. (The brotherly-love brainwashing they'd given her at "paleface" school had really taken in her case.)

Young Jim had yelled to George Spiller across the fence on his way down the road, "Come on! Feltman's killing his old lady." George got there at breakneck speed in a light wagon, bringing his Pa and two of the Bunton boys and their dad who'd been hunting rabbits in Spiller's field, all packing guns.

Before it was all over they had jerked Pa Feltman up on the big box elder with a hay rope around his neck so his toes just barely touched the ground. Emma didn't see it, but Mary told her. "Pa was blue in the face and his eyes were popping out something fierce. He was yellin', "I promise! I promise! Let me down!" They finally did let him down.

"What did he promise?" Emma asked.

"Not to hurt Ma ever again."

Emma hoped he'd keep his promise, but had her doubts. She wasn't the only one. Old Jim Tynan wanted to swing Pa off anyhow. The others talked him out of it. Then Old Jim shook his ham-like fist under Pa's nose and said, "You get this through your thick Dutch head good, you goddam little son of a bitch. This ain't Germany. We treat our women good. If I ever hear so much as a whisper that you lay a finger on this woman again . . ." He pointed at Ma Feltman who was crying, her belly awkwardly sticking out with Lizzie inside, "I'll come down here and blow your goddam head off with a shotgun!"

"The mean little son of a bitch's" face was no longer blue, but white as a sheet by then and he was shaking like a rabid skunk. The men took Ma Feltman and the kids down to Tynan's where Lizzie was born that night, about a month early.

Pa hadn't laid a hand on Ma since, though he still cussed her out. Emma thought it was a pity Old Jim hadn't mentioned not doing that too.

In any case it was not your usual naturalization hearing, but it had a sterling Americanizing effect. Pa was lucky Ma had been civilized at a good Christian school or, being Sioux, she would have fixed him so he'd only have been good to sing soprano in the church choir.

Emma was out in the cornfield now, being real quiet, trying not to move. She didn't know what she expected to happen but she felt like something might. She hoped no one would disturb her. A fresh northeast breeze was swaying the stalks, stirring the long corn leaves into a pleasant sibilance. Graceful tassels, already yellow, danced against a dazzling blue sky. The stalks were dense with fat ears. Emma knew that meant a heavy crop. Pa would be as happy as he ever allowed himself to be. The ears were a sign she might have a new pair of shoes to wear to school. Pa never spent money without having a pretty good idea where the money to replace it was coming from, plus a little over.

That wasn't on Emma's mind just then, however. *She was feeling good, knowing things without really thinking.* She imagined herself a stalk of corn, bare toes rooted in earth, feeling part earth, part corn, part flowing air that would join the passing wind as it eddied southwest. A spasm of pleasure rippled from the top of her head down into the ground.

Emma's mother had told all the kids to go play for a change. Pa was in town. When he was home everyone worked and, to his credit, he worked hardest of all. Except sometimes when he came home drunk and fell into the hay in the cowshed to sleep it off. Likely he'd be home drunk tonight. He'd left early with a rack of hay to sell in Coal City. After selling it he'd go to Peter Sabilio's saloon, wet his whistle, then go to his sister's place to eat, back to the saloon to really tank up, then home, often falling asleep on the empty hay rack while the horses found their way home. Once he'd fallen off and broken his wrist. He blamed everyone but himself; after he got home from seeing the doctor he even kicked both horses.

That had thrown the milking all onto Ma and the kids. Emma's older sister, Mary, never seemed to get the knack of milking, or any other work, so it really boiled down to Emma and her mother. Rob was too young yet. Emma was already convinced her older sister was pretty much a hopeless case.

"You're simple," Pa would tell Mary. To Ma Feltman he'd sometimes admit his frustration. "I'd beat her more if I thought it would help. If I hit her she just falls in a heap and blubbers."

Everybody in the family agreed that if Pa couldn't get Mary to work, then very likely no one on earth could. So Mary didn't milk. Pa once told Mary at supper, in German—they all talked German at home, "Mary, girl, your hands ain't built to work. They don't fit teats and they don't fit tools, but I notice they fit a knife and fork real good. Maybe we ought to take that knife and fork away till you learn to take hold of something that's work around here."

But Pa never did reform her. Deep inside he believed that everyone should eat as much as they needed to stay healthy and strong so they could work. Maybe someday Mary would meet a rich man—she was already a budding woman at ten, and very pretty. If Mary did catch a rich one, Pa thought he might get his hands on some of the money in time. Emma wished he really would try cutting off Mary's rations for a while to see if she'd start helping her and their Ma.

When Mary got chewed out by her father, she just ducked her dark-haired little head and grinned, as though she actually were a trifle simple-minded. She would grow up that way, but it was purely functional. As folks liked to say of people like Mary in those days, "She's dumb like a fox."

Now Emma was alone in the cornfield. She was hiding from Mary. Mary's idea of play was to dress herself, Emma, Rob, and Lizzie in the musty, frilly old clothes that their German grandmother had worn in the old country. They were kept in an ancient trunk in the attic of a lean-to attached to the barn. The two younger kids hated it as much as Emma did. Emma preferred to take walks, admiring flowers and inhaling the sweet smells of growing things, watching and listening to birds and animals. She felt really free then.

Maybe a train would come along rumbling on the Santa Fe tracks and she could watch that. She liked trains going west best. That was out where Ma had come from, far away, where Ma's Indian family still lived. There buffalo had run free by the millions; the Indians' food, clothing, and shelter all wrapped in one bundle. They were gone now. The Indians weren't gone, but they might as well be, cooped up as they were on reservations. The only thing free out there anymore was Cowboys.

Emma had never seen a buffalo except in a picture, but thought she'd like to. The pictures she'd seen of Cowboys also interested her because they were always on big, galloping horses. Sometimes men on horses drove cattle down the wide road past their farm, but she didn't know whether they were regular Cowboys. They didn't carry pistols or lassos, but swung long, leather whips to keep the cattle moving. Once, one of these men had ridden his horse up to the fence and stopped. The Feltman kids all stared, wide-eyed, looking awkward in their rough farm clothes, and were a little scared. The man offered them some candy but they weren't sure what it was.

"Don't be afraid—it's candy," he told them.

They backed away and shook their heads. Ma had told them never, never to talk to strange men; they might be tramps and no telling what tramps might do to a person. Emma was the only one who found her tongue, and in their bastardized, phonetic home-German she said, "Aber nix." ("Oh, but no.") The man probably didn't understand, but he laughed good-humoredly. "O.K. kids," he said. "Yer Ma probably warned you about strangers." He pulled his horse away and rode on at a graceful trot. The kids watched him and the cattle out of sight and felt a little sad.

Ma Feltman spoke English when Pa wasn't around. But she never tried to teach the kids Sioux. "It's no use. All my people will soon be dead and no one will speak Sioux anymore." Emma thought that was sad and terrible.

Emma had to go deep into the cornfield to hide or Mary would look in and see her. Mary would never come into the field though. She thought there might be snakes in there. Emma had never seen a single snake but was careful never to tell her sister that. Sometimes she took Lizzie and Rob into the corn with her.

"Now be real quiet," she'd tell them, "or Mary will find us, and we'll have to play 'dress up' and who wants to play that?"

"Not me," Lizzie would chime. Rob seldom said anything. He'd been three before he talked at all, and didn't talk much after that. Lizzie had a fat, round, cheerful face, pink as a primrose, and popping blue eyes, like Pa. Rob's eyes were hazel, but his face was pink too. Emma's was olive, more like her mother's. No one would have taken them for siblings.

Although Rob didn't talk much, he grinned a lot. Pa almost never found fault with him; after all, he was a male, and the first one at that. If he wanted something his older sisters had, Pa would order them, "Give it to the boy." Emma and Mary naturally resented that, and when Pa wasn't around ridiculed Rob by calling him "Gipsen boy," derived from "give-it-to-the-boy." Then he'd cry, especially when they shunned him and ran away to play somewhere.

Rob soon figured out why he was ridiculed and shunned and stopped whining for their things. After that he was allowed back into their good graces.

Rob idolized Emma and tagged around in her footsteps. She could do things, such as wash dishes, sweep floors, empty chamber pots into the back-house, shell corn, even cook some things like boiled potatoes, scrambled eggs, and fried cornmeal mush. More importantly, she fed him when Ma was too busy or when she was sick, even if it was only bread and milk.

Emma also washed clothes on the washboard in one big tub and rinsed them in another tub, then hung them on the clothes line to dry, and never let them trail in the dirt when she did it. Without being told, she'd pitched in before she was three and tried to help Ma. Now, at eight, she was really a big help, strong and hard-muscled. Even Pa recognized that and grudgingly gave her credit. Once he forgot his old-country male superiority and patted her head, saying, "You're a good girl, Emma." His voice was even warm when he said it. Then he was instantly embarrassed and puffed his pipe fast, pretending it was going out. Emma wasn't sure what to think about that. She wondered if maybe it meant that now she wouldn't get whipped quite as often. She judged that was probably expecting too much.

Now, out in the cornfield she was trying not to think about any of that sadness, in fact *she wasn't really thinking, but feeling, knowing certain things*, and also wondering what she might become someday. The kids at school had read about Florence Nightingale and Emma figured she'd like to be a nurse.

Then her mind turned to Indians as it often did, when she was all alone. She knew they were the original, romantic dwellers here. Even though her own mother was a real Indian and had once roamed wild as a hawk with her people, she was now just like anyone else.

It was the *old* Indians Emma thought of, the mysterious ones now gone who had once trod the ground on which she stood.

> *("Lift your head and don't breath; hear the*
> *musical words?")*

Were their spirits yet in this place?

> *("Listen by the waters . . .")*

Might she hear the legendary Shabonna, as he was called now, a typical pioneer mispronunciation? Shabonna, friend of the whites, buried not far away, in Riverview, the big market town where they traded—buried in what was now an alley behind a saloon. The whites were grateful that he had saved many lives by warning them of the coming of Blackhawk's warriors. Grateful for a while anyhow.

Once though, he had been *Chaubenee*, feared friend of *Tecumseh*, and almost a brother of the great chief. Their wars had killed a lot of whites in futile attempts to drive away the invaders of their home.

Emma didn't know that, but she thought she could sometimes hear Indian voices in the rustling corn, feel presences. She tried to make out what they were saying.

> *("Listen by the waters for rippling, alien tongue*
> *of dispossessed race,*
> *rising like faint scent of cold trail.")*

The deep mystery of it caused chills to run up her spine and her hair to stand up too. She knew these voices carried an important message from the ancients, passed down through the generations, *a message she couldn't miss or it would change her whole life and she would be nothing*, rather than the heroine she might be.

If it was Chaubenee trying to speak to her, she knew he could speak English pretty well, and that she'd understand what he said. This should be the place for him to come, here along the Mazon Creek where he'd camped so often. Not so far away he'd seen Tecumseh for the first time, just a few miles to the east where the Kankakee and Des Plaines rivers joined to form the broad Illinois. There had sprawled the camp of Chief *Spotka*. There as a youth of sixteen summers, Chaubenee came to learn the ways of a warrior and was entranced by the charismatic Shawnee, Tecumseh, and his older brother *Chiksika*.

Emma was now asleep. Her head was pillowed on black earth among corn roots.

> *("I am earth! Listen! I give wisdom!")*

This was the enchanted place, the place to commune with Indian spirits. No more than a shout away, the aging wife of Chaubenee pressing on to come home to him before dark, drowned in the rain-swollen waters of the Mazon.

Emma heard a voice calling her. "Emma. Emma. Emmmm—a."

It was not Mary this time. She fluttered open her eyes and was confused for a moment, then she realized that it was close to sunset.

"Emmmm—a."

It was her mother's voice. She experienced a sense of letdown. She had hoped it was the voice of Chaubenee's wife.

That voice had called out in the now-shattered dream, which she couldn't remember except that she had been about to make some colossal discovery about herself.

She felt like crying.

Her mother came closer among the cornrows. "Emma!"

She yelled back, "I'm coming, Ma!"

Her mother came to her and held her. "Where were you?"

"I fell asleep."

Her mother stroked her little-girl head. She knew Emma was often too tired—overworked. Well, so were they all. Even Pa.

CHAPTER ELEVEN

Who Was Johnny Todd?

America, you were rivers and streams,
Pioneer highways,
Ever flowing wells.
Your settlements were on waters.
Your people grew crops along waters,
First, for themselves,
Then, a little extra,
Floated to market on streams.

You heard the names of rivers—
Ohio, Mississippi, Missouri, Illinois,
Kentucky, Tennessee, Arkansas, Red—
And names of market towns—
Pittsburgh, New Orleans, Louisville,
Cincinnati, St. Louis, Chicago;
You grew like a rank weed, America,
Spread unrestrained.

In 1812, England, lusting for revenge,
Tried vainly to chop you down;
In 1846 Mexico suffered your sting;
In 1861 you fought one another
As though you'd run out of worthy opponents.
And the Mississippi, "Father of Waters"
Again flowed, "unvexed, to the sea."

The waters that flowed past Riverview joined the *Father of Waters* just above its junction with the Missouri—the Big Muddy. A little downstream was St. Louis; once Spanish town, then French town, and finally American town after President Jefferson, in 1803, doubled the size of the new nation with the Louisiana Purchase. It was St. Louis's fate to be the first Gateway to the Far West, supplier of fur traders, of the agents who rationed the Indians, of the army itself, an army sent to the frontier for the unusual purpose of protecting the Indian from the white man. *(Or so it was said; it was soon enough the other way around, and for good reason.)*

— 1893

Russell (Bennie's Pa) got back to the cave that Mike Mullins had shown him only once again because his family moved away from that country to Riverview. His father had obtained a better-paying job as superintendent of schools in a more populous county. Salary wasn't the reason he moved, however, but income was. (Grandpa had an *avocation* he could practice in a larger community, and they needed the money.) None except Bennie ever learned that story. When Uncle Newt came to live with them he told Bennie a lot of things. Newt never called Grandpa anything except Johnny Todd. Even Grandma had always called him Mr. Todd because he was a man of overpowering dignity and severity. Or was he?

There was a lot of mystery about Grandpa—or Johnny Todd, if one pleased. Bennie pleased. After Uncle Newt told him about free-wheeling Johnny Todd, Bennie never could think of Grandpa as anyone else, not as the "Papa" of Pa's stories about his youth, and certainly not as Grandpa. It was a shame that Bennie was sworn never to tell anyone what he knew because a lot of them would have loved to know—especially Pa. Bennie wasn't too old before he recognized the role reversal in some cases between himself and his father. When he *forgot* to confide in Pa with Uncle Newt's stories, it was more like keeping from a kid knowledge that *might* injure him.

- *RIVERVIEW—August 1893* -

Gardner Eichelberger was president of the Riverview Farmers' Trust Company. However, it was a fair bet that there wasn't a farmer in the county that trusted Gardy, as he was called. Gardy encouraged the diminutive of his name because he thought it lent him the common touch. An archangel couldn't have lent him the common touch. He had skin like the belly of a catfish and an eye like a stuffed lynx.

"Well, Professor Todd," Gardy was saying, "the school board has unanimously selected you as the superintendent of schools for the county. Congratulations." He rose magisterially from behind his desk; Grandpa Todd got up and shook his outstretched hand. Gardy had the knack of grabbing just fingertips so that no one actually shook his hand. Grandpa had gauged Gardy's skimmed-milk personality (masking a swordfish) and wasn't surprised at the half-assed, egg-sucking way he shook hands.

"Thank you, Mr. Eichelberger."

"Call me Gardy."

Grandpa put on his most sincere look. "That's mighty democratic of you, Gardy. Thanks again."

Gardy obviously didn't feel the need to have any other member of the board present. Grandpa would have bet Gardy *was* the board of education. The rest of them were probably hocked up to their eyeballs to his bank and wouldn't dare fart without coming to Gardy for permission.

"We may as well get right down to business, Todd. We brought you in because of Riverview's need for new schools. What you do about the rest of the county is your concern . . . *as long as it doesn't cost anything*. Do I make myself clear?" He gave out what passed for a laugh, a noise that sounded like a rusty nail being pulled in several installments out of a weathered board.

Grandpa Todd joined him with a genuine laugh. He thought, "This is a real gold-plated son of a bitch."

"No objections?" Gardy asked.

"Not a one. Where I came from we didn't even have money for schools in the county seat, much less out in the sticks—this will be a welcome relief."

"I'm not surprised. They're a bunch of rubes down there—no offense; you're not down there anymore, and for good reason. You'll find us progressive. Mighty progressive."

Grandpa thought, "I'll bet."

Gardy said, "I'll give you a few weeks to get acquainted," then caught himself and added, "myself and the board, of course—then you can make your report to *me* about what your plans are." This time he didn't catch himself. It was clear whom Grandpa would have to get along with.

"Good enough," Grandpa said. "I'll just need a few days to move the family up here, then you'll be hearing from me."

"Fine. I think we're going to get along just fine. Take the whole two weeks till school starts if you want to, then I'll take you around and get you acquainted with your staff." (He didn't mention that would also give him time to can the incumbent, who hadn't yet heard he was leaving.)

Grandpa stayed that night in Riverview to conduct a little business with some old friends . . . down the river a mile out of town at Dutch Liz's Parlor House. She'd run a similar place in Deadwood and later another in Tombstone. Her partner and husband, Red Kalbo, was also on hand. Red was a professional gambler. They were semiretired in Riverview, though it had enough action at night. It was Red's hometown. Sheriff Hank Kalbo was Red's brother, stone blind, but regularly reelected.

"Hell," Hank often said, "people won't admit it, but being blind is the finest qualification for a sheriff."

Brownlowe Kalbo, the boys' father, had been mayor of Riverview a long while, since the last mayor got drunk and fell in the Illinois and Michigan Canal and drowned; by coincidence the same day that Custer was wiped out at the Little Big Horn. Seventeen years and two months to the day to be exact.

The evening he was hired by Gardy, Grandpa played poker with Red, Liz, and a couple of safe people, in a private room down at Liz's where she and Red carefully screened who got in. Grandpa got a perfecto lit to his satisfaction, then sipped his bourbon, studying his first poker hand. Red grinned at him speculatively, a question obviously about to come out.

"How did our estimable banker strike you, Johnny?"

"A horse's ass." He was never to have any reason to change his estimate.

The next morning Grandpa took the downriver packet and was home to Spring Brook by suppertime.

"What kind of a man is Mr. Eichelberger?" Grandma asked.

"A pillar of the community."

"What kind of a pillar of the community?"

"A solid one. Does that suit you?"

She was well acquainted with her husband's independent streak. This really didn't sound encouraging. "We can always stay here."

"I'll manage to get along with him."

The fact was, Grandma really didn't know too much about her husband, even after fifteen years of marriage. All her folks had cared about his background was that he was a minister's son. All she cared about was that she loved him very much. She'd have willingly followed him to the jungles of Borneo or to the North Pole. She'd never met his earlier edition, Johnny Todd, and never would. If she had, she might have been happier in the end.

She'd have swooned if she learned that he and Newt had once joined a notorious character from their hometown of Troy Grove, on a little toot into LaSalle, and cleaned out a pool hall with swinging pool cues. Their bail was twenty-five dollars apiece, which Grandpa's father, the Reverend Isaac E. Todd, had paid after lecturing all three on the evils of drinking, which he correctly assumed they'd been doing, and on rowdyism. If he was aware that their companion, who took the lecture as contritely as they did, was the one and only Wild Bill Hickok, he never showed it.

When their benefactor was out of earshot, Wild Bill grinned as he said to the other two, "That sermon was a pretty steep price tag for a durned twenty-five-dollar fine, but the old boy's heart is in the right place."

– 1929 — Johnny Todd Is Laid Out in His Coffin –

"How natural he looks!"

The speaker was, of course, some idiot woman. One of his own daughters.

Bennie had never seen anyone dead before and was afraid to go near the coffin alone. Pa took him up to look. Bennie didn't think Grandpa looked natural at all, not like the big, robust fellow that sat on the blue bench behind the stove with his arm around him, out in their cabin. He looked instead like a withered ghost. (He'd been hit by a car in Chicago, and it had all been downhill from there.)

It was a pity Uncle Newt wasn't there. No one knew where Uncle Newt was, or even if he was alive. If he'd been there he'd have said, "Natural, my ass! I'll be goddammed if that's so."

But then, those others hadn't known Johnny Todd. He and Newt had seen far places together, seen big men—fighters—had fought plenty themselves. One day they rode out of Fort Abraham Lincoln with the Seventh Cavalry, Custer's Seventh, the band playing "The Girl I Left behind Me."

America, you were forts
Because of the Indians,
Because you were taking their land.
Empire building is a dirty business.
Ask England.
Now even England bleeds for poor Lo,
Confined to reservations.

Tell us, English bleeding hearts,
What happened to your aboriginal Britons?
Where are their reservations?
Where are they?

America was forts because of the French.
Fort Necessity, Fort Duquesne, Fort Ticonderoga.

And because of the English
(After the Revolution)
Fort Wayne, Fort Dearborn, Fort Mackinac.

Most of all America was forts
Because of Manifest Destiny.
We were destined

To people a continent.
So we built Fort Smith, Fort Leavenworth, Fort Dodge,
Fort Atkinson, Fort Howard, Fort Winnebago,
Fort Crawford, Fort Croghan, Fort Snelling,
Fort Gibson, Fort Riley, Fort Pierre, Fort Randall,
And Fort Abraham Lincoln,
Where Custer rode away to Glory
(To Garryowen in Glory.)
To Valhalla. A lion felled.
Custer's luck ran out.

"Of course he disobeyed his orders, you know."
("It's easy to kick a dead lion.")
Whose orders? That little pansy, General Terry's orders?
Custer acknowledged orders only from God.

Johnny Todd knew Custer,
Knew him well,
Saw him the day he died.
So did Uncle Newt,
But that's another story—perhaps later.

America, you were forts,
Waterways,
Manifest Destiny,
Bloody Manifest Destiny,
Peopling a continent,
Not wisely, but well.

Listen goddammit,
Don't moan about wisely!
Great things are seldom done wisely,
Wisely comes later, if ever.
Wise men rot safely at home
With their thumbs up their asses.
FUCK WISE MEN!
God will tell you you've made a good bargain
If you trade one hundred wise men
For one fighter.
"BID THE GUNS TO SHOOT!"

Well, Grandpa Todd built Riverview a model school system with shining Center School as its showpiece. Pa (young Russell) went there his last few years in school, then Grandpa went to Chicago alone, so Pa ran away with Uncle Newt. It bothered his conscience a lot, but didn't seem to rattle Newt's a bit. They were in Seattle when news arrived of the gold find in the Klondike; it was where Newt had been just before he'd come home for a visit; it was where he was taking Russell.

Grandpa went to Chicago because he got fed up with Gardy Eichelberger's sanctimonious crowd, the solid citizens. Several factors were involved, including Grandma's decision to have no more kids, but the main one that triggered his decision just then was the weekend poker club.

Quite gleefully, he'd been invited to join shortly after he took his new job. "Fresh meat," the others thought. After all, who ever knew a schoolteacher who could play poker (and mere teachers was what all superintendents of schools had been once, hadn't they)? And sure enough Grandpa had never even learned to shuffle and deal without fumbling the cards. But he took his losses in good humor, *such as they were.*

Gardy Eichelberger's chief ass-licker was Myron Troughtman, who managed Troughtman's Boot and Shoe Emporium: Wholesale and Retail. Myron featured weekly ads in the *Herald* that read:

> "Troughtman shoes everything
> Except chickens and horses."

He thought it was wonderfully clever. He used to show people the ad, nudge them with his elbow and say, "Get it? Get it? *Shoo* chickens! S.H.O.O., not S.H.O.E., get it? Haw!" He probably never heard the community paraphrase that went:

> "Troughtman screws everyone,
> Even chickens and horses."

A common suspicion was that Gardy Eichelberger owned a controlling interest in the store and in Myron. The latter was closeted in Gardy's office, as he often was on Friday afternoon, having a sly belt of Kentucky sour mash with the banker, from the bottle that Gardy carefully kept hidden in his private safe.

"I've been thinking . . . ," Gardy paused.

Myron's stomach knotted. When Gardy had been thinking Myron often had to pull off something extra shitty that would bother even *his* conscience. Gardy read his expression and experienced his usual distaste for the weakling.

Yet Myron was useful, perhaps indispensable, the closest thing to a friend Gardy ever had, loyal as a dog.

Gardy continued, "I've been thinking that son of a bitch Todd cheats at poker. Have you ever won any money since he's been sitting in our games?"

Myron thought a minute and confessed, "I never won anything before either." He went to the games because Gardy couldn't drive his own buggy horse.

"Well, I won something," Gardy said. "Pretty damned regular."

Myron might have said, "Because all us dumb bastards that you practically own had to let you if we didn't want to get put out of business."

"Anyhow," Gardy went on, "I've been talking to the other boys about this too."

Myron was silent, waiting for the rest.

"They've all been big losers over the long haul. Not a goddam one of 'em has won anything. I've dropped at least a thousand bucks in the last two years. How much have you lost?"

Myron squirmed. He was afraid to tell the truth because Gardy might suspect he had to be cooking the books on the store to have the kind of money he really lost. Finally he said, "Not much. I can't afford to stick in those big pots."

Gardy knew better, knew that a few belts of red eye turned this little pipsqueak into a tiger. "Bull!" He said. "You dropped at least as much as I have!"

Myron tried to get off that subject. "What makes you think Todd cheats? Maybe he's just lucky. Fact is I always thought he lost most of the time. He's always yelling poor by Sunday morning when we quit. Hell, he hasn't learned to hardly shuffle a deck of cards yet, or deal without dropping one or two."

The poker club got together one Saturday night a month and caroused and played cards all night, ostensibly fishing so far as the town knew. They all went to the rendezvous at separate times by different routes. Appearances were important in a town like Riverview.

"Looking clumsy is part of his game. He's a pro if you ask me. He just makes out he's clumsy."

Myron's mouth fell open at that. "You mean it's all an act?"

"Damn right I mean it's all an act."

"Why the hell don't you fire him and run him out of town then?"

"All in good time. All in good time. I want to get some of that sugar back." His eyes weren't smiling.

"How?"

"You'll see."

Gardy knew of a friend of a friend in Chicago who could make cards talk.

He was so good at it that he'd been shot once by a skeptic in Wichita who'd considered him unnaturally lucky. Gardy didn't know that. All he was sure of was that the fellow's name was Gerald O'Malley and he'd be up the next day, posing as Gardy's visiting cousin.

Seven players were on hand, none in on the secret except Gardy and O'Malley. Gramp, Myron Troughtman, and three substantial businessmen made up the balance of the group. Grandpa read O'Malley at first sight. The "profesh" had certain marks—a too-careful face, expressionless eyes, a handshake like a piano player protecting his dexterity. He'd have been careful about any new player, but this fellow was an obvious plant. He thought, "So Gardy is finally onto my game, the dumbshit."

O'Malley took his time about making a move. Then he dealt Gramp four sevens pat, never looking up. That was when "Johnny Todd" knew he'd read this guy right. The idea behind that kind of sucker hand was that Gardy, or someone else, would get a higher hand and knock Gramp's head off in high-stakes betting. So Johnny Todd tossed in his cards with the casual remark, "Boy, if they're all gonna look this bad, I'm in for a helluva night."

O'Malley looked at him sharply, almost forgot himself and started to reach for the "deadwood" Gramp had thrown away to see if he'd lost his touch.

"Uh-uh," Grandpa warned him, making as though to slap his hand. The look that went with the warning would have chipped diamonds.

O'Malley grinned, then sighed. He correctly figured he was in for a bad night. After a few hours of uphill work, he thought, "Todd has worked on the circuit somewhere. I wonder what moniker he used?"

Johnny Todd could read O'Malley's "readers," feel shaved cards, mark a fresh deck to suit himself with his fingernail or ring, restack a cut so fast it couldn't be seen, while appearing to be clumsy. And he played it smart and didn't win a thing himself, but managed to lose a little. However, he felt justice demanded that O'Malley be paid for his time and dealt him winners, alternating by setting up Myron Troughtman, who had never before won a dime and could use the money. He sweetened Gardy's hands just enough to play on his greed, so he'd bet like a damn fool. The rest didn't know what was going on, but secretly appreciated seeing Gardy get his.

Once Gardy forgot himself and, turning, snarled at O'Malley, "What the hell is going on?"

The best the hapless cardsharp could do for Gardy was manage for him to win from his own toadies, who, sensing something they didn't understand had turned into pikers.

When the bloodletting was obviously over, Gramp took over from Johnny Todd, shoved back his chair and said, "Excuse me, gentlemen."

He went out and walked over to the nearby Illinois River and arched a stream into its mighty waters, farting with great satisfaction while he did so. O'Malley had stepped out shortly after him and joined him in the ritual. He was grinning. He glanced around to see if any of the others were near before he said, "Boy, what a sweet deal you had here. Sorry to be involved in breaking it up. I didn't know what I was walking into."

"Eichelberger hire you?"

"Uh-huh. Boy is he steamed. Serves the bastard right."

Gardy was back inside filling in the others on what had been going on. "Something backfired," he said, "but I'm going to get that bastard Todd if it's the last thing I do."

Outside Gramp shrugged back into his Johnny Todd cloak. He said, "I was beginning to really earn my money associating with an asshole like Gardy Eichelberger."

"I can see what you mean. One night's enough for me. By the way, thanks for those good hands."

"Want to win a little sweetener?" Johnny Todd asked.

O'Malley looked puzzled. "How?"

"See that duck?" He pointed to a duck, its wake just visible in the dim early light, swimming near the far side of the river. "I'll bet you a hundred bucks I can drop a round within six inches of his ass." He had shucked a .45 from his back pocket as he talked, so smoothly O'Malley hadn't seen the motion till he had it in his hand, and hefted it once into an easier shooting position.

"Why six inches? Why not dead center?"

"I don't shoot anything anymore. Only people are ornery enough to shoot—that duck probably has enough trouble. Besides it might be a mother."

"Jesus Christ," O'Malley said, but it set him thinking. "O.K. You're on, a hundred bucks."

The pistol rose smoothly, paused a half-second, following the target's path as steady as a rock, then exploded. A splash almost took out the duck's tail feathers. It thrashed aloft, squawking indignantly.

"Teach it to be more cautious," Johnny Todd said.

O'Malley reached into his pocket for the hundred and was handing it over when Gardy and company poured out the door to see what had happened.

"I heard a shot," Gardy said.

"Firecracker," Johnny Todd corrected him. He'd slipped the .45 back into his pocket almost as fast and smoothly as he got it out.

But the straight story naturally got out. Almost. Like all good shooting stories it grew appropriately.

Someone would tell someone else: "That fellow, O'Malley, told Gardy that sonofabitch Todd whipped out a cannon so quick he couldn't tell where the hell it came from and dropped a slug right behind that duck at two hundred yards, just like he said he would. Jesus. Wild Bill couldn't have done any better." (In those days whenever good pistol shooting was the subject, the name of Wild Bill came up.) "And him our goddam school super for all these years." (It had only been three years.) "He's not only a gunman but a cardsharp."

"Yeah, and that ain't all from what I hear," an innuendo that would be followed, of course, by a lewd wink.

Well, Gramp was a lusty man—and good-looking.

School was out, but even at that the summons to meet the school board took longer than Gramp expected. (Gardy was working up his nerve.) The messenger found Gramp shooting pool in the back room down at Jabby Dawson's.

Gardy had the whole board in his office this time—he figured he was less apt to be shot in front of witnesses. As added insurance Marshal Shannon was on hand. Shannon had kept the lid on LaCrosse when it was the meanest town on the Mississippi. Gardy was unaware that the marshal wouldn't have lifted a finger to keep Gramp from perforating him, in fact would have considered it a public service, but Shannon was also sure that Gramp wasn't that big a damn fool.

When Gramp walked into the room he knew why Gardy had Shannon there and grinned, then winked at the marshal. They were good friends. He marched up to Gardy's desk, tossed his resignation on it, turned and left. Not a word was spoken.

— 1929

Sons and daughters who hadn't seen one another in years showed up for Grandpa's funeral. Their children included cousins who'd never seen each other before and, in some cases would never see each other again. Everyone brought their younger children; in those days babysitters who would stay for several days' duration were scarce, more like nonexistent. Bennie, Roy, Sister, and Bennie's parents had traveled several hundred miles; others further than that. Kids caused a problem, especially at bedtime, when they had to be parked wherever there was room. Bennie slept next to Ma on the living-room floor at Aunt Felice's.

Something woke him up the night after the burial. The light of a full moon flooded the room. Ma was snoring beside him. Others were snoring lightly. He wondered what had awakened him. It wasn't Ma's snoring; he was used to that. Then he heard Buck Doak's voice. "Hey, Ben, I wanna show you something. C'm'on. Hurry up."

He couldn't very well hurry without waking someone, though Ma was a heavy sleeper and went right on snoring. Cautiously he tiptoed between and over bodies.

Outside Buck set out up the bank of the Yellow River along a path made by livestock. Grazing horses looked up and watched them, then went back to grazing. Buck turned and climbed a steep hill, worked through a barbed-wire fence, headed across a field and through another fence into a hemlock grove. Bennie recognized that they'd come the back way into the cemetery where they'd buried Gramp that afternoon. A shiver ran up his spine. Graveyards at midnight weren't his favorite place to be. In fact he couldn't recall ever being out at midnight, much less on his own.

"Shh," Buck cautioned. "We're just in time." Bennie trusted him; he knew that Buck was a fey creature, like a good fairy. Buck pointed. Ahead was the lonely white stone with the carving plainly visible in the bright moonlight:

JOHN MEREDITH TODD
1853–1929

Something moved behind it just as his eyes followed Buck's pointing finger. He almost jumped out of his skin. He'd never been sure whether he believed in ghosts or not, but he was absolutely sure he didn't want to see one, even if it was a member of the family. He wanted to run.

"Hold still," Buck whispered. "He can't hurcha. Wouldn't want to if he could. You were his favorite grandson—the only one he figured had his wild streak."

A man's figure rose and turned toward them dusting himself off. He paused a moment, then his coattails flared out like wings and he silently rose into the air. Bennie could see his face clearly just as he took off. *He never forgot that face*. When the figure was high in the air he thought it waved at them, but he couldn't be sure.

He knew he must be having a nightmare, but as often happened he couldn't wake himself. He even dreamed he and Buck went back the way they'd come and he'd slipped down next to Ma again. That dream haunted him for many years, until finally the memory faded. When he did remember it, the face was always just as he'd seen it—not an old face, pinched and white like Gramp's had been in the coffin, but a young man's face, unlined, happy, smiling.

CHAPTER TWELVE

Our Boy Lindy!

— 1927

Before Bennie got pneumonia he got the first real thrill of his young life that he could remember in detail afterward. Shouting voices in the night had startled him awake, and he was afraid. He was not yet accustomed to city noises and encountered a lot of fears in his new surroundings. A farm in the woods had been comforting. His new environment was nerve-racking, especially to a little kid who understood little of what adults accepted as normal. He was not reassured when Ma quickly got up from the bed beside him. Dimly he made out her form moving out the door into the kitchen. He heard her cross that room to the windows.

He followed as far as the door and asked, "What is it?" He always thought something awful was coming to get them.

For once Ma answered a question she'd normally have brushed aside with, "None of your business—be still."

She said, "Something important must have happened. Maybe Lindy got killed like the others." You could always count on Ma to expect the worst, and not blame her either, since her life had taught her that was usually the way most things went.

Bennie risked following her with bare feet on the rough board floor of the kitchen from which he'd once got a big sliver in his foot. He could see her shadowy figure at the window opening it wide, which allowed the excited shouting that had awakened them to enter clearly:

He could make it out now:

"EXTRA! EXTRA! READ ALL ABOUT IT!"

In those days before radio was common or TV even heard of, newspapers capitalized on every least bit of unusual news by putting out an "extra" at a premium price. This time the voice was yelling:

"EXTRA! EXTRA! READ ALL ABOUT IT!
LINDBERG REACHES PARIS!"

So someone had finally flown the Atlantic Ocean alone. It had been done before by teams of pilots, but never solo. A big prize was offered for the first to do that, and others had died trying before "Lindy" made it. It had required sleepless hours of vigilant flying, partly by reference to the rudimentary flight instruments of the time. The whole world had been breathlessly awaiting news of this latest daring one-man assault on space. Bennie, only a little past four, had sensed his family's excitement and suspense regarding the outcome. Would another foolhardy, brave man sacrifice his life?

On May 31, 1927, Charles Augustus Lindberg (1902–1974), a young former airmail pilot became America's and the world's darling. He was a hero overnight, was dubbed "Our Boy, Lindy!" Shortly afterward he wrote a book about himself and his airplane, the *Spirit of St. Louis*, and titled the book "*WE*." No one cared that it might have been ghost-written or that the diffident, shy-appearing young man may not have had enough imagination to think up a catchy title like *WE*. He was a poor boy suddenly rich and famous and unaware that this eventually would bring unprecedented tragedy to his life. One day his tiny single-engine airplane would hang high overhead on wires in the Smithsonian Institute in the nation's capital.

– *Interesting Sidelight* –

The morning after Lindy reached Paris's Le Bourget airport and was nearly crushed to death by admirers: in Chicago, less than forty miles from where Bennie was startled awake in the night by the cry of "EXTRA! LINDBERG REACHES PARIS!," a self-made "rugged individualist" (the type America worshipped as the backbone of the country so long as it didn't have to rub elbows with them) sat in the rather plain cubicle from which he controlled a multimillion-dollar industrial business. His secretary rushed in, and knowing he was often there before sunup, assumed he may not have heard of the world shattering latest news. "*Did you hear that Lindy reached Paris?*" she asked, putting down some papers she was delivering to him.

A little tableau followed of more significance to mankind than the shrinkage of distances. Self-made man doesn't look up, doesn't stop writing the letter he's turning out in longhand, doesn't say a word.

She repeats, "*Did you hear me? Lindy got to Paris!*"

Without looking up, he grunts, says impatiently, "*Of course I heard you. One man can do almost anything alone. Tell me when a committee flies the Atlantic!*"

COSMIC MESSAGE FOR MANKIND

"Although organization man, the new molecule, is under development, his master—a lone person—is still alive and well."

A week or two after Lindberg's flight Bennie was again awakened from a deep sleep by a noise in the kitchen. He had heard Ma talk about robbers breaking in over and over and was instantly afraid. Suppose it was a robber and he killed them, as Ma said they often did? She also said they wouldn't get her if she got her hand on the stove poker first. Even in the summer it was stowed beneath the heater in the kitchen beside the ash tray. (Some people took their heaters down in the summer to have more room, but their four-room cold-water flat had no place to store it out of the way if they did take it down.) Bennie heard Ma get up, saw her shape at the kitchen door against the light, and was sure she was going for the poker. Young as he was, he thought that was foolish—a good way to ask for it. And if robbers got her, they'd surely get him.

His fear subsided when he heard Sister's voice high and excited, almost a squeal, "Look what I won at BANK NIGHT, Ma! A radio! It's an Atwater Kent!"

Anyone who knew a thing about radios knew that an Atwater Kent was the top of the line. Bank Night was a "giveaway" night, when theaters, to attract people, raffled off prizes to the holder of a winning number on their ticket stub. They must have made money at it, because it went on for years.

Bennie risked sneaking to the kitchen door and poking his head out to get a look at the radio. It was in a funny wood cabinet, standing high on spindly legs trying to look like an antique Chippendale sideboard or something (although he didn't realize that). Somehow Lillian's current flame, Howie Berkel, who'd taken her to the movie in his car, had hustled it up the steep stairs and into the flat.

Ma noticed Bennie, but was too excited over Lillian's luck to shoo him back to bed.

"See," Lillian said, "the controls are behind this little door." She let down a door with a click and it hung on a set of suspending metal braces that hinged down when the door was opened and held the door like a shelf. Inside were some gadgets to control the thing.

Lillian pushed up a toggle switch and said, "This is what turns it on."

Bennie half-expected it to come on and make some noise, not realizing that it had to be plugged into an electrical outlet.

Lillian went on, "These two dials are to tune in stations and control how loud it is," and she turned them to demonstrate, twisting them back and forth.

Bennie came closer and looked, but it didn't occur to him that he could learn to do that and might someday turn it on and listen all by himself.

Lillian said, "Tomorrow Howie is going to put up an aerial outside so we can receive programs on it." She hadn't known what an aerial was till Howie had told her on their way to the house.

Bennie could hardly wait till the radio made some noise—he didn't especially care what kind. Aunt Mary and Gus had had one in their apartment and although it spewed out only squawky voices and tinny-sounding music, it was enough to know that the people making that noise were miles away. He would soon learn that the top-quality Atwater Kent reproduced voices and musical sounds almost perfectly.

He didn't have many days to marvel over the radio when he woke up after a restless night feeling strange. He ate his meager breakfast but without his usual zest. There wasn't much in the house to eat anyhow because the money Pa usually sent from wherever he was "out working" hadn't got there on time. Besides, it was usually not quite enough to last all month. Lillian hadn't been paid yet either that week, and her money, which she generously chipped in to help out, went as fast as it came—not for foolishness either. Companies paid starvation wages before they gradually learned that it was bad economics. Strong unions helped them see the light.

Ma had caught Bennie eating ashes from the pan in front of the stove a few days before he got sick, and had really whipped him. Nutritionists, a later phenomenon, might have suspected he had a potash deficiency. The fact was, he had almost every kind of vitamin deficiency. Most people did in "the good old days," unless they lived on prosperous farms or were wealthy.

The day they discovered he was alarmingly sick, he had felt a compulsion to run wildly through the four-room flat. Ma told him to stop, and he did for a little while since experience had taught him he'd better follow her orders or get his. But he was driven by an irresistible compulsion. His body may have been having a last fling, sensing he was going to die, barring a miracle. Ma finally grabbed him in mid-flight, turned him over her knees, and inflicted one of her lunatic whippings, such as she had gotten from her father. Bennie vomited on the floor while she whaled away, sobbing and puking, which almost choked him. Only then did Ma realize that something serious might be wrong.

She pounded his back to get him breathing again, while dragging him to the toilet to get the rest of his breakfast out.

When he had regained his breath, pale and shaken, she asked, "How do you feel?"

He didn't know. He felt desperately alone in a hostile world and as scared as he'd ever been; absolutely terrified. Finally he got out through chattering teeth, "Funny! I never felt this way. I'm scared."

That shook her. He sounded like an adult. "Funny how?" she pressed him.

"Terrible," he said. Then he started to tremble with a chill.

She said, "I'm putting you in bed. You'll feel better after you lie down. Maybe you can nap."

He didn't think so. And he didn't care. All he wanted was to stop feeling terrified, stop feeling an unprecedented sense of unease and dread. His teeth chattered uncontrollably and soon chills overcame his whole body. He knew then that something dreadful was coming to get him. He knew that Ma couldn't help, and that if Pa were here, neither could he.

Ma felt his forehead and said to herself, "He's burning up with fever." She went out and returned with a cloth wrung out in cold water and put it on his forehead. It was the only home remedy anyone knew for a high fever.

Bennie's eyes on her, pleading her to help him, reminded her she'd just whipped him. Much as it went against her grain, she had to admit she'd been terribly wrong—too hasty to hit, as her Pa had been. She felt deep remorse and pity for her youngest, whom she loved dearly *in her warped fashion*.

"What if I lose him?" she asked herself, then refused to think of it.

By the time Lillian (Sister) came home, Ma was frightened.

She met Lillian at the top of the stairs and quickly said, "Come in here, Lil. Bennie is really sick and acting funny." Lillian sensed Ma's fear and it was so unusual that she herself was instantly afraid, not knowing what to expect as she rushed to the bedroom behind Ma.

By then Bennie was seeing grotesque things dancing in the air around him. He even saw the angels Ma had shown him in the big Bible she'd kept from when she was a girl out working, the book sent with her by her own Ma and Pa to ward off evil. When Ma had shown him pictures of angels in the Bible she also told him they were in Heaven, where good people went when they died, and he understood already that dying meant leaving his own familiar world, and Ma and Roy and Sister, and never seeing Pa again, either. The idea didn't suit him. He'd rather stay where he was. In fact, the idea of inevitable death scared him out of his wits when his mind could actually come to grips with the idea. The sight of the angels spinning around him convinced him they'd come for him and he would soon be leaving. He wanted to cry out to Ma or anybody to save him, but was too weak.

Sister put her hand on Bennie's forehead to judge if he had a fever and how high it might be, as everyone did in those days since fever thermometers were expensive and seldom needed. She thought the same thing Ma had, "Burning up!," but had sense enough not to say it because she knew it would further frighten an already terrified kid. Her fear increased at the sight of Bennie's eyes on her that didn't look like any eyes she'd ever seen before—as though an animal was inside a cave staring out wildly.

She drew Ma into the parlor out of Bennie's hearing and said, "I'm calling a doctor."

"We can't pay one," Ma objected.

Lillian, who seldom crossed Ma, came right back, "I don't care. He's got the highest fever I ever felt. Without a doctor he's going to die." And she tried not to think the next thought that crossed her mind, "And maybe he's going to die no matter what we do."

"We don't know a doctor," Ma said.

"I do," Lillian said, sitting down in the straight chair next to the phone, which was a luxury they had only because Lillian worked for the phone company and got one almost free.

Ma heard her describing to the doctor Bennie's symptoms, including those she'd passed along that Bennie had told her of chest pains and breathing difficulty. Those told the doctor all he needed to know to realize he might have a life-or-death case here.

Lillian hung up the phone and gave Ma a scared look. "He thinks it's pneumonia," she said.

"Did he tell you what to do?" Ma asked.

"He said he'd be right over as soon as he could."

In those days there wasn't a thing to be done for pneumonia even in a hospital that couldn't be done by a skillful doctor in a home, including the radical treatment known as "tapping" the lungs.

Dr. Richardson was a young, vigorous, tough-looking redhead. Ma thought he looked more like a gunshot surgeon than a general practitioner. He had the jutting chin of a warrior, but the tender look he gave Bennie revealed what he'd dedicated his life to war on—human afflictions.

The doctor placed a gentle hand on Bennie's forehead, and Bennie immediately felt better, felt the doctor's strength enter his own body. He knew he was in the hands of a healer and had hope for the first time since he'd puked while he'd been dangling terrified and helpless across Ma's knees.

The doctor said, "We're going to fix you right up." He'd have said the same inspiring thing if he thought the boy had only a few moments to live.

"I'm going to sit you up and take your temperature with a thermometer I have to put under your tongue. Don't bite down on it," he said,

He realized that Bennie probably didn't know what either big word meant, or have need to. To Ma he nodded his head and ordered, "Hold him up with your hands under his arms. I need room to check him all the way around with my stethoscope."

Lillian stood by feeling helpless, but more hopeful. There was something about Dr. Richardson that radiated strength and optimism to others. He was simply the old breed of fine healer.

As he listened to his instrument his face revealed absolutely nothing to Ma and Lillian, who were watching him intently. Ma thought, "He's got a poker face like Grandpa Todd." (When he'd come *up north* during summers, Grandpa had often got a poker get-together going.)

Dr. Richardson took out the thermometer and looked at it equally impassively, but thought, "106! Christ, I've got to move fast!"

In less than a half-hour he'd carefully sucked an enormous amount of sickening-looking pussy fluid from both of Bennie's lungs. It had been gradually suffocating him. It was a tricky, last-resort operation that could collapse the lung being sucked out and sometimes did. Unlike later years, when instruments had been invented to reinflate lungs, a collapsed lung then meant almost sure death.

Bennie could feel his breath coming easier almost as soon as the doctor went to work. When Richardson was through, he helped Ma ease the frightened kid back down and personally arranged his pillow for him.

He looked into his eyes for a long while, smiling a little, and finally asked, "How do you feel now that you're going to get well for sure, Bennie?" he asked. He had learned Bennie's name from Ma even before he'd come into the room the first time. It was an important part of the treatment that the doctor knew helped—everyone wants to feel their doctors knows them as a special person.

"Better," Bennie managed to say.

"You're going to be all well before you know it, Bennie. You're sweating. That fever you had broke."

He watched Bennie's eyes droop as he slipped into an exhausted sleep. He again felt the now-wet forehead, cooler with drops of sweat on it.

He replaced his equipment in his bag, and told Ma, "I'm going to leave the thermometer with you. Do you know how to use it?"

Ma nodded, "I studied to be a nurse years ago."

The doctor regarded her with greater interest, but didn't ask her why she'd given it up. He was glad she had had some training, since he knew Bennie wasn't out of the woods yet.

All he said was "Good. One of you stay with him all the time for at least a day. We don't want him to wake up alone and feel scared. And keep him covered up and warm. If he gets worse again, call me right away."

He left some aspirin to be pulverized and given with sugar if Bennie couldn't swallow one with water.

In the kitchen as the doctor was leaving, Ma asked, "What do we owe you"

Richardson had sized up their bare surroundings and said, "Two dollars. You needn't pay me right now if you can't spare it."

Lillian scraped up two dollars, a crumpled one-dollar bill in her purse and some change, and gave it to him. She had a dime left that she knew would buy her three streetcar tokens to use getting to work and back. They wouldn't last till payday, but it wasn't much of a walk down to the telephone office any-how—maybe two miles.

She asked herself, "What's Bennie worth?" He was her pet. She'd have walked thousands of miles to pay any doctor that could save her little brother's life. Ma felt the same, but probably would never have admitted it.

In a week Bennie could walk around on his own pretty well. At first he was wobbly and weak and could see stars when he got out of bed, especially when he'd had to go to the toilet while he was still sick. Ma had helped him because he fell down once trying to do it on his own. She was a different person when she had someone really sick on her hands, until she was sure they were going to live, at least. In two weeks Bennie was able to run around again, but Ma didn't whip him for it this time, or for a long while after that.

CHAPTER THIRTEEN

Brother, Can You Spare a Dime?

After Bennie was over his pneumonia Ma would often tell someone, "It permanently weakened him. He catches colds easy now."

Bennie liked to stand at the west windows and watch the men load ice into the high outside door on Wolsfeldt's Butcher Shop. Refrigeration for stores was far from common then. The ice, he later learned, was stacked in a loft above the downstairs cool room where they kept their bulk meat. The ice man or his assistant would back up the horse-drawn wagon to get under the door where the ice was unloaded. There was a steep cement drive, and it was a tricky business. The ice man would get one of the Wolsfeldts to block the wheels with bricks so the horses didn't have to keep it there, which would have been almost impossible for more than a few seconds. All in all it was a demanding task.

One day one of the horses slipped and fell as they were backing the heavy wagon. It started screaming in pain and fear, and Bennie was panicked. His heart went out to the thrashing horse, which had broken one front leg, yet was trying to regain its feet, hurting itself all the more. Bennie ran into the kitchen yelling, "Ma! Ma! Come quick!"

She thought he'd hurt himself doing something he shouldn't and snapped, "Now what have you done to yourself?"

He pointed to the window. "It's a horsy. Hurt."

Ma could hear the horse's cries by then. They watched it struggle to rise, biting the ground in desperation, as though it knew its fate. Its struggle reminded Bennie of his fight to remain *up north*. Hysteria foredoomed to failure.

Ma didn't let him watch the policeman who came on a motorcycle and shot the horse. She couldn't blot out the sound of the shot though. Bennie cringed as though he himself had been killed. He woke up sobbing during the night and thought of the poor faithful dead horse that had wanted to live so hard and couldn't. In the morning the horse was gone. (One day he'd wonder if the thrifty Wolsfeldts had agreed to dispose of the carcass free and had run a "beef" special.) But there was nothing funny about it even those many years later.

It was the first time he figured out that everything died one day, that he had to die and even Ma and Pa couldn't save him if his time came. He'd heard that if you were good, God took you into Heaven. He didn't want to go there. He wanted to live and go back *up north* where their horses were. He wondered if God let that ice horse into heaven. He sure hoped so. He wondered what happened to their horses. (Uncle Bart had already carelessly let one die.) He wondered where Poochie White Cat was. (Killed and eaten by wolves, which Bennie, mercifully, would never learn.) Baffled and helpless before this tragic riddle, which he now tried to solve, he often cried himself to sleep, stifling his sobs for fear Ma would hear.

About that time Pa and Ralph Esselborn quit working for Hugo Mundt and started their own landscaping business. Ralph got an old chain-drive truck. Sometimes he'd take Bennie and Roy for a "spin" in it, the chain howling, tooting the horn, which was one of those old "ah-ooga" kinds. Ralph knew what kids liked, since he had a bunch of his own. When he came over he'd get down on all fours on the floor and play "horsy" for Bennie.

"C'm'on, kid," Ralph said. "Climb on." Bennie got aboard and Ralph sailed around the floor.

Then Ma would say, "Oh, for heaven's sake, Ralph," but she didn't sound mad.

Ralph got up when Bennie had his fill and reached in his pocket and said. "What have I got in my hand?"

"A dime," Roy, who had been watching them, guessed.

"A nickel," Bennie guessed. They were bigger than a dime so he figured they were worth more.

"Right," Ralph said, and brought it out and gave it to Bennie.

"You'll spoil him," Ma said.

"Naw. It's good for him." He got another out for Roy. "No partiality," he said.

That was Ralph's way. He was always smiling and laughing. Pa and Ralph were both too easy-going and could never collect what was owed them. Most of the deadbeats were *big-bugs* with lots of money over on the West side, which was the ritzy part of town. After a few months Pa and Ralph went broke.

Pa finally found a job with his brother Ern, who was superintendent for a big Omaha contractor. Pa had to leave home and didn't get back for years except for visits between jobs. That was when he got his first car—a 1922 blue Buick four-door sedan. It was a noisy, four-cylinder thing, but smelled good inside and got him where he had to go.

Pa was gone most of the time from 1928 through 1931, when the Depression really settled in hard and dried up construction money. Pa had made good money but hadn't saved much of it. He'd have had to save more than he made to pull them through the Depression. Few had saved that much. People's lifetime savings eventually got wiped out. Many sold their possessions, but had to practically give them away, since money had dried up. People lost their homes and farms through foreclosure of mortgages.

While Pa had been gone was the first time that Bennie lived alone with Ma; Sister and Roy were home at night, but he was with her all day every day. Ma took him with her everywhere; of course she wouldn't have thought of anything else, even if she could have left him with someone. *He was hers.*

On Election Day in 1928 she took him with her to the polling place. She wasn't about to miss out on voting, because it was a right that had been denied to women since the founding of the Republic, and up till just a few years before with ratification of the Nineteenth Amendment to the Constitution in 1920. Ma was strong on asserting all the rights coming to her and any others she could rustle, too.

There was no doubt that she voted for Republican Herbert Hoover (that *goooood* man who had administrated war relief in Europe after the World War). She could never be made to confess though, since you voted secretly in a curtained booth, which deepened her natural secretiveness. After Hoover became the scapegoat for the Depression in the U.S., she certainly would not have confessed to voting for him.

On their way home from voting they passed a squirrel perched on a tree trunk, looking them over with his bright shoe-button eyes as though he'd like to make friends. Undoubtedly someone had fed him before, so he was looking for a handout. They didn't have anything to feed him, but Ma tried to touch him anyhow. He kept just out of reach. Finally she managed to give his tail a little tweak as he turned to dodge away and got a cussing for her pains. Ma was sometimes fun to be with. It was during that period, on a trip downtown with Ma, that Bennie first saw the G.A.R. veterans.

If Pa had never come home and just sent money, Ma would have been contented. She had no use for men. But in time Pa had to come home. He brought a newer Buick, a 1924 two-door cabriolet, an awkward-looking thing in which a third of the back seat was taken up by a storage well.

Eventually, as the Depression deepened, the Buick, like millions of cars, was jacked up and perched on bricks to preserve the tires, and its radiator drained to prevent freezing in the winter. (Antifreeze wasn't common then; most people used alcohol, which tended to boil away easily.)

Nothing looked more forlorn than a car on blocks, especially buried under snow, as useless as its owner had become. Nothing was more symbolic of the *Great Depression*, unless it was President Hoover chanting, "Prosperity is just around the corner!" But he didn't really care whether it was or not. The sonofabitch was rich already. When Social Security later became law "Hoover" groused, "When I was a kid social security came out of the root cellar." Suppose you didn't have a root cellar? Did money for medical attention come out of a root cellar? Royalty changes its ways hard. There was the story of the Queen of France who, when told that the peasants had no bread, allegedly said, "Let them eat cake!" Shortly after, she was handed her head.

— 1932

Pa had lost his job on "construction" and had been home for months, out of work. He and Ralph Essleborn were sunning themselves on a bench in front of the pool hall across the street from an A. & P. Store, one of the early supermarkets. Clyde Dillon, another war vet like Ralph, was with them. The click of pool balls floated out through the door. As demoralized as they were they might have thrown away a dime on a game, just to take their minds off their troubles, if they had a dime. More likely they'd have spent it for a loaf of bread and divvied it up. There were lots of hungry mouths at home and no bread to put into them. ("Let them eat cake," or, better yet, go to the root cellar.) Ralph had six kids by then.

Ralph said, "Why the hell don't we all just get together and go over to the A. & P. and take the goddam food? There's plenty of it if you got the dough. I didn't get my ass shot off in France to come home to this ."

None of the others said anything. A stranger leaning against the wall nearby, wearing patched bib overalls and shabby clodhopper shoes, looked their way and said, "Count me in." Others who had heard the remark nodded agreement. Talk like that was common across the country in 1932. A Hitler could have become America's first "man on a white horse" and overthrown the system; become a dictator. The army couldn't have done much—they'd withered away to a shadow. President Hoover's idea of how the Army should be used was to toss tear gas at World War veterans like Ralph, desperate veterans who were even then camped in Washington, D.C., honestly lobbying for early payment of a war bonus that had been promised to them. Those vets were called the Bonus Army. Their dispersal by violence (July 28, 1932) could have been the spark that ignited revolution if an American Hitler had been in the wings.

That wasn't in the cards. FDR was. Franklin Delano Roosevelt, as the next president, was destined to lead America back to the path the Founding Fathers had set it upon. The thought of becoming King Franklin the First never occurred to him, though he was accused of it almost every day by the Republicans.

How about that bonus *Pro Bono Publico*?

"A bonus would have stimulated aggregate demand. So would the Townsend Plan."

What the hell was the Townsend Plan?

"An idea similar to Social Security that was so popular it undoubtedly made the latter easier to effect into law." It simply came before its time by a few years. It was no different than the old-age pensions common in some countries.

Clyde had a more personal solution. That night just at closing time a masked man walked into the A. & P. Office, heisted the day's receipts, walked the manager with him out the back door, cold-cocked him with his pistol barrel, and rapidly drove away in a stolen car.

The last time Bennie saw Ralph alive, he and Pa took Bennie with them on a ride into the country in Ralph's old chain-drive truck, which now howled louder than ever. (Who could afford grease?) The men had heard where there might be a few jobs husking corn. When they got there, all the openings were filled. Such a job could have made them a couple of bucks a day for a week or two, enough to feed even Ralph's crew of kids for a month, maybe longer on cheap, filling stuff. Pa and Ralph were glum and silent on the way back to town. They ran out of gas a mile or so out of town and hoofed it the rest of the way in. (Hoofed it? Depression nostalgia definition: *walked*, especially when no other transportation was available.)

Ralph wasn't too glum to punch Bennie affectionately in the ribs when they parted and say, "Well, Skeezix, we'll have better luck some other time. Be good." He was smiling the way he always did.

That night Ralph took his longest trip ever and did it all alone like everyone must. They heard about it first in the paper. Someone had spotted a shadowy figure in the closed and locked K. of C. Hall late that night and called the cops. A cop with a reputation as "trigger happy" responded. He throttled his motorcycle back and coasted quietly into the parking lot. As he put down the kickstand a figure emerged from the front door, spotted him, and started to run. The cop—the sole witness—*said* he yelled, "Halt!" Then, "Halt or I'll shoot!" Whoever it was kept running. The cop, a crack shot, fired just once, the .45 slug catching Ralph in the spine. Bennie always hoped he never felt a thing. Beside his body they found a crumpled sack containing six stolen Baby Ruth bars—one for each of his kids. Thirty cents worth of candy. (Better even than cake.)

Ralph's executioner had a regular motorcycle patrol on the ritzy West side. A few days later a big, open touring car sped past him, then accelerated. The cop figured he'd bag a bunch of wild, rich kids out joyriding. Siren screaming, he gave chase. His cycle could accelerate faster than the car and was soon in a position to swing out and pass to pull them over. He was traveling over sixty miles an hour by then. People turned, or came to doors and windows to watch the excitement. They got their money's worth. At that point, two men who had been crouched on the floor in the back of the touring car, rose and hurled a bale of hay they'd carried on the back seat directly in front of the motorcycle. The cop had no time to swerve. His motorcycle upended like a bucking horse, siren still wailing, throwing him into the air. He struck the pavement, moving at a mile a minute, skidded across the curbing, limbs flailing, and flattened his head against a tree.

The touring car gunned west out of town. It was found the next day in a state forest, wiped clean of fingerprints.

EXTRA! EXTRA! READ ALL ABOUT IT. COP KILLED BY GANGSTERS!

Years later Pa told Bennie, "If that bale of hay missed, both those boys in the back seat had shotguns loaded with buckshot and knew how to use them." A movie Bennie saw in those days, starring Franchot Tone, which featured him as a World War vet gone bad, was called *THEY GAVE HIM A GUN*. Of course veterans knew how to use guns. Was the news story a cover? Did the cops suspect the truth and try to dupe the killers into becoming loose-mouthed?

Bennie wondered how Pa knew about the shotguns of the "boys in the back seat," but he never asked. He wasn't sure why, but he had a strong feeling he'd better not ask. He also wondered who'd driven the car, but didn't ask that either.

EXTRA! EXTRA! MERCHANTS AND SAVINGS BANK ROBBED!

Bennie thought that was great because the Merchants and Savings Bank had robbed him and his friends. Brady School's "Bank Day" was every Tuesday. It was some community leader's idea of the way to teach kids thrift—a major virtue (especially in the eyes of bankers). Teachers took in pennies and nickels and made entries in bank books on Bank Day. The money was placed in the kids' own bank accounts at the Merchants and Savings Bank. A time came when many of the kids, Bennie included, didn't have even a penny to save. By then he had over a dollar in his savings account. He should have withdrawn it, because one day, the bank closed. All the banks closed. Many never reopened. Some that did never made good on their deposits even after they reopened. The Merchants and Savings bank was one of them. Maybe that was why it was "knocked off." The robbers escaped in another touring car, only this one was never seen again in Waubonsee.

In the summer of 1933 Pa and Clyde Dillon found jobs somewhere in Indiana. Exactly what Pa did wasn't clear, but he started sending home substantial sums of money. He kept the job until the W.P.A. (one of FDR's ridiculed giveaway programs) opened up jobs in town and Pa got one so he could live at home. Pa always tried to be a family man. The pay was twelve dollars a week, a lot less than he made in Indiana.

Colonel Robert R. McCormick (Mr. *Chicago Tribune*) never missed a chance to report what the W.P.A. did (or mostly what it "didn't"). Cartoons in the *Tribune* invariably showed lazy men leaning on shovels, with taxpayers' dollars flying away into the blue above them. Those shovels, whether McCormick realized it or not, also propped up National Self Confidence (or N.S.C., which was the alphabet program really needed). In either case, Colonel Bob wouldn't have got the drill through his head. After all, he and his friends weren't experiencing any demoralization, except over FDR. Occupying the high economic ground focuses one's view a little above empty stomachs. In this case, if it hadn't been for Roosevelt, Colonel Bob and his cronies would also have been handed their heads.

The Republic gained from the W.P.A. substantial, economically built public facilities, constructed to last a long time, thanks to shovel-leaning beggars. Better shovels in their hands than guns, Colonel Bob.

CHAPTER FOURTEEN

We Hunted for Buried Treasure

One boy's hope, and imagination, could make a Wild West anywhere in those days—even along the noisy, smelly Burlington Railroad tracks with their bordering "public dumps" in Waubonsee. Tom Mix and Buck Jones were really alive then, wearing pistols and riding fast horses on the silver screen.

Things were a lot happier for Bennie when Pa got the W.P.A. job in Waubonsee. His W.P.A. money was enough to live on, with what Sister contributed. Also with Pa home Ma didn't get away with whipping Bennie so hard. Once, even after Pa was home, she pounded him on the head with the heavy end of a table knife, holding him by the arm so he couldn't get away from her. He yelled so loud that everyone came running. Pa came as close to cracking Ma a good one as he ever did—he grabbed her arm, twisted the knife out of her hand, and gave her a hard shove. He said in a level, deadly voice Bennie had never heard him use, "Don't do anything like that again."

Ma looked half-crazy, eyes blazing, like she always did when anyone balked her but she didn't try to fight Pa.

Pa warned her, "You could go to jail for that." Maybe that scared her. Maybe she'd scared herself. She never beat Bennie like that again. It was doubtful, though, that the law would have taken a hand unless she killed him. The community tried to stay out of family affairs, no matter what. In those days even the teachers at school "looked the other way" when kids came in with bruises, though they knew how they got them.

Pa and Sister's opinionated boy friend, Milton, who was handy around cars, got the old Buick running. Pa didn't drive it much, but Milton used it to go joy-riding with Sister and drive her home from work. The next year she married him.

On hot nights Pa, Bennie, and Roy would desert the stifling house and sit out in the deep, soft grass in the yard between their place and Hilger's. Pa usually leaned back against a tree, fished out his cheap tobacco and got his pipe going. Roy and Bennie would lie on their backs, hands folded beneath their heads for pillows. Bennie liked to cock one leg over the other knee. Pa told them a story almost every night. These episodes were one of the few good memories Bennie would retain of the city.

Pa started his best story, "Well, I got back to the cave at Spring Brook just one more time." Bennie was ten, so he could remember what Pa said very well. It would set him on a two-year quest. Pa continued, "I was riding Ned again, and Puss Daterman had a little Indian pony named Chunk. We took some camping stuff with us and Pa let me take his twenty-two rifle, the first time he ever did."

"To shoot tramps?" Bennie asked.

Pa laughed. "If Pa and Mama thought there'd be tramps out there, I can tell you for sure they'd never have let me go in the first place. Tramps stuck close to the railroad towns like LaSalle."

"How about Mike Mullins? He was out there."

"That was different. Mike used to live there and came back to look over the old place. If Pa ever found out about him, he'd have whaled the daylights out of me for not telling him in the first place."

"What do you suppose he'd have done to you if you had told him in the first place?" Roy asked.

"Lord knows. For one thing I'd never have got out of the yard with Ned again."

"How long was it after the first time that you got back to the cave again?" Precise information seemed important to Bennie; maybe it was Ma's German side in him.

"I got back the next summer," Pa told him. "Just before we left Spring Brook for good to go to Riverview."

"What happened when you went that time?"

"We hunted for buried treasure."

"Treasure?" Bennie almost squealed the word. "You never told us about any treasure."

Pa was simply going to tell how they pretended they were after pirate treasure, but he saw his chance to do a good "*Bear Story*."

"Sure. I thought I told you the James gang hid out there once. Everyone, just about, knew they'd buried treasure there."

Pa was glad they couldn't see his face in the dark. He puffed extra hard on his pipe. Roy had a notion Pa was pulling their legs, but it was a good story anyhow.

"Did you find it?" Bennie asked.

"Nope. I guess it's probably still there."

"Why didn't you go back after you moved to Riverview?"

"Hard to say now. I don't remember. Too busy doing other stuff, I guess.

Besides, Pa wouldn't let me. By the time I was old enough to go on my own, Uncle Newt took me to Alaska with him."

Bennie couldn't imagine anyone too busy to go hunt for treasure. That gave him a real keen idea.

"Why don't we go to the cave and find the treasure?"

"Yeah," Roy piped in, "we could go down some weekend in the Buick." He was fifteen and knew how to drive—it was about all he thought about. That and girls, but he never mentioned the girls.

Bennie thought driving down was about the dumbest idea he'd ever heard. He was disgusted to hear Pa say, "We might do that."

"What'll we do if we find the James gang's treasure?" Roy asked.

"Buy back the farm *up north*," Pa said.

"I think that'd be keen," Bennie said, "but I think we should make up a list of stuff to take with us and float down to the cave on a raft."

Pa and Roy both laughed, but Bennie was dead serious. Skeezix and his pal Spud in *Gasoline Alley* in the Sunday "funnies" had recently floated somewhere on a raft.

"Where are you going to get your raft?" Roy inquired, slyly.

"Build it. We got lots of tools."

Pa said, "If I get out of a job again, we could do that." He was ready for some pipe dreams if it made Bennie happy.

"What'll we take with us?" Bennie asked.

Roy got in the spirit of the game just for the fun of it, and they started to plan what they'd take.

Roy said, "Lots of pork and beans, some bread, and a lot of canned sardines." He loved pork and beans and sardines.

"We'll have to have blankets," Pa said. "By morning it gets pretty chilly down there along the river even in summer."

"And the Winchester .40-60," Bennie put in. He had the Tom Sawyer touch. Let others handle the routine stuff. "And shovels to dig for the buried treasure."

That was the first of several planning sessions. It was fun just being out in the yard at night with Pa. You could see a zillion stars; there was no air pollution in those days. Looking back later it seemed to Bennie that no air had ever filled his lungs so well, or smelled so wonderful. Usually there was the aroma of freshly cut grass like new-mown hay, and there was always the honeyed fragrance of the Hilger's peony hedge that divided the two yards. Some nights hundreds of fireflies flashed their little tail lights, and they could see "heat lightning" (actually lightning reflected off the bottoms of clouds from distant thunderstorms or simply off the moist night air). Sometimes a thunderstorm drove them indoors. They never shut the windows against the storms until the last minute, letting the cool gusty breezes clear the hot air out of the house. Sleeping after a rain was fine.

Ma never came out with them, even though she'd have been cooler. Pa always asked her anyhow.

"Too many mosquitos," she'd grouse. There were almost none. And she never failed to say, "Bennie will catch a cold out there." He never did. Even from inside she could put a damper on their fun because Pa knew she'd be at the nearest upstairs window, the one in the hall, trying to hear what he was saying. (Some more "wind jamming.") And she wanted to know if Pa talked about her to the kids—"knocking her" as she described it.

He never did.

Bennie did get infected with something out there. A terrible obsession with rediscovery of the James boys' buried treasure.

Their neighborhood had the usual "gang" of kids, not a bunch of dangerous degenerates like big cities would all have someday, like some already did, but a group of nice kids who hung around together because they lived close by. Sister took a picture of them all, including one of their dogs, named Trixie, which Bennie was holding.

In a popular kid phrase of that day, they were an "ozzie" looking bunch. "Ozzie" meant sort of ridiculous. Among them, with his pisspot haircut and buck teeth, was Cees (pronounced like "cease", short for Cecil). Till he met Cees, Bennie had never had a close buddy. Most of the kids had been too passive and lacking in imagination or energy. Cees was his match in all but imagination, and Bennie had enough for both of them. They were a Tom-and-Huck match.

Ma hated any rival for Bennie's affections, and particularly detested Cees, a typical go-to-hell Irish kid. She knew he was no good from the first time she set eyes on him. Bennie brought him home to play in the yard. Something in Bennie's voice warned her he liked the wild Irishman too well. She never let Cees in the house, and not in the yard again either. Cees's only reaction was to ask Bennie, "What the hell's wrong with your ma?"

Again and again Ma warned Bennie, "That degenerate will only get you in trouble."

She was dead right, but it was a two-way street. It was also the aspect of Cees's nature that made him worth knowing. An ounce of trouble was always worth a pound of Sunday school when it came to teaching a boy what he *really* needed to know.

A bigger problem for Bennie with Cees was keeping Buck Doaks from getting too jealous. For example, when Bennie first brought Cees along to cut cottonwood logs for the raft, the day he stole Pa's axe, Buck eyed Cees with disfavor. He asked Bennie, "What the hell did you bring that lout for?"

Bennie was sure that Cees couldn't see or hear Buck, and was relieved on that account.

"He's strong as an ox," Bennie told Buck. "It's hot as hell. We can divide up the tree-chopping." Buck was only partly mollified, even though it made good sense.

The first eleven years of life had been lonesome ones for Bennie, even with Buck to talk turkey with. Cees was Heaven-sent. It had taken years for Bennie to progress to having a buddy.

When he had been allowed out in the yard at the age of four, Bennie had spent a lot of time looking longingly across the street at Bobby Reder and wishing he could go and play with him. Bobby did the same thing back. He wasn't allowed out of the yard either. Bobby was an orphan who lived with his grandparents. Neither boy even yelled across the road at the other, as though their imprisonment imposed silence on them.

Then starting school "sprung" them both. Bobby went to St. Nicholas parochial school.

When Bennie came home after school, and Ma tried to put him back in prison on evenings and weekends, she suffered a rude shock. He didn't re-imprison for shucks. He ran away, got whipped for it, ran away again, got whipped harder and harangued for hours, then ran away again anyhow, over and over. At some point Ma conceded defeat. She tried half-heartedly after that on special occasions, such as going to Aunt Mary's for Sunday dinner, but Bennie would run outside and stand down on the sidewalk and thumb his nose at her when she ordered him back in to clean up and get dressed up. He got so he'd about as soon take poison as eat Aunt Mary's preparations, even her fudge with nuts in it. It was always hard as cement.

He wasn't about to be dragged somewhere all dressed up, especially there, so he'd tell Ma to go to hell, then disappear for hours, wearing his comfortable overalls. She always whipped him when she finally got her hands on him, but he became inured to that—a pittance to pay for freedom. No wonder poor, frustrated, balmy Ma half-killed him at last with the heavy handle of a knife. After all, she recognized that he must be going out of his mind if he didn't want to be with *her* constantly.

When Bennie refused to go out with her, she locked him out of the house, even in freezing weather, and left. "You can't be trusted in there alone," she told him, and may have believed it. Maybe he couldn't. After he'd got that treatment a few times, just for spite he might have trashed her precious junk, collected in her trunk and boxes. Probably he wouldn't have. He'd have been more apt to read or listen to the Atwater Kent.

In the coldest winter weather when he was locked out at night, he usually found some kids to play with until the last one of them had to go in, even Cees, then, shivering in his threadbare clothes, walked the streets, or sledded alone on some hill, till he was exhausted. Then he'd go home and roost down on the limestone cellar steps with the doors closed above him and get what fitful sleep he could. It was a tough row to hoe, especially only half-clothed.

One winter he got a dog of his own. Till then he'd owned every dog he could entice home, but only for a short while. He had Queenie longest. She was a stray, a black-and-white crossbreed of some kind, and although Ma never let him bring her in, he stole food for her, and sat down at the bottom of the steps sometimes and held her. One day he heard her yelping frantically in pain and fright and got to where she lay in the gutter just in time to hold her in his arms and see the life go out of her eyes, her tongue pathetically hanging from her mouth. The car that ran over her hadn't even slowed down.

He finally got his own dog that Ma accepted. He got him indirectly because Roy had quit school and gone to work on the farm of Ma's sister Aunt Ina and her husband, Lester. One cold night, a freezing, nearly starved mongrel scratched on their door. They did feed it and let it get warm, but were too cheap to feed a dog on a regular basis. (They only kept Roy there since he worked like a slave for no pay and would wear, without complaint, whatever they could get for him from the Salvation Army. However, such clothes were as good or better than the ones he'd had at home and the food was a damn sight better.) Roy couldn't stand it when they put the dog back out in the cold. He trudged with it the couple of miles to town, roused Ma in the middle of the night, and talked her into keeping it, at least for a while, then walked back. For a wonder, Ma took a liking to the dog and decided to keep it. By then they could afford to feed it something. (But it never got fat.)

So Bennie got his first dog. Sister's new husband, Milton, named it Mutt. Bennie thought that suited it as well as anything. Mutt looked like Buster Brown's dog in the shoe advertisement, sort of a miniature boxer with the markings of a Boston terrier, and not much bigger than the latter. Mutt didn't know he was a shrimp, had a warrior's heart—he fought anything despite his featherweight class, sometimes to his and Bennie's sorrow—and he followed Bennie everywhere.

Bennie, Cees, and Mutt became a three-member-gang that needed no others. Cees didn't like or dislike dogs, he simply accepted them as a fact of life. Bennie never saw him pet one, but he never saw him kick one, either.

This biologically diverse gang of three trooped the streets of the town, day and night; even penetrated the huge Burlington railroad storage yard full of cars waiting their turn in the repair shops. They effected this invasion despite the railroad detectives (known as railroad "dicks"). They played in the huge canyon that housed the railroad mainline, the yards, and two creeks, the last being the principal attraction for them. (Most people in town didn't even know Waubonsee had one creek, much less two.)

Cees and Bennie threaded the aisles of the downtown dime stores and were eyed suspiciously by floorwalkers (with good reason) while Mutt waited patiently outside.

They hiked both sides of the Fox River for miles, in town and out; terrorized sissies; played football and baseball with the large neighborhood gang, which was about the only contact they had with them; stole ropes from flagpoles at night; went to ball games and panhandled befuddled drunks; chased a hot-air balloon to recover the marked hoop in its mouth to trade for ten dollars' worth of fireworks at the store that sent up the balloon as an advertising gimmick.

This was an annual affair. Kids congregated at the fireworks store and ran, eyes fixed on the sky, after the balloon—often for miles. Ten dollars' worth of fireworks was a lot of bang.

One year Bennie breathlessly ran up just as the balloon landed on a trellis at a house in his own neighborhood. The man who lived there retrieved it, gave him a nasty look, and even though he knew Bennie was entitled to the hoop since he got there first, handed it to another kid. A lot of people in the neighborhood had spotted Bennie as the single-handed inventor of juvenile delinquency, and that fellow was obviously one of them and had decided (as it would turn out, to his sorrow) to make him pay for it. After passage of a few months, during which Bennie brooded over that mean trick, he burned down the son of a bitch's carriage house.

He was afraid to tell even Cees about how he sneaked inside at night, led out the goat that was kept there and tied it securely to the rear fence, before returning to torch a pile of straw inside. He ran like hell before the fire blazed, jogged to the end of the long block, turned right, then heard the first siren blast from the fire engine leaving Fire Station number 4, across from Brady School. He slowed down to a walk, intending to round the block and return to watch the fire.

"Well," Buck Doaks said just then, "we did it. I was kinda hoping you didn't have it in you."

By then Bennie was beginning to wish he hadn't had it in him either. He thought, "What the hell, I'm in for it now if someone saw me. They send you to reform school for that sort of thing. Shave your head." Ma always told him they'd shave his head when he went to reform school, which she frequently intimated he would. To Buck he said, "You hoped I didn't have what in me?"

"The wild blood. After all your great-grandfather, Four Ponies, stole horses, burned out ranches, killed palefaces and even Indians from other tribes. Maybe I shouldn't remind you of this. On the other side you had some killers too. Mentioning no names, one of them who was out west had to kill a man; the bastard was asking for it and got it. Old What's-his-name shot him dead as a doornail without blinking. Happened in a saloon. The fellow said, 'All I need from you is six feet of ground outside.' Old Whatsis shot him in his tracks and said, 'That's my distance.' It kinda put the taste for killing into him from then on. Got quite a reputation for it, but he only killed sonsabitches that needed it."

They were walking rapidly to get to the fire. "Who was old Whatsis?" Bennie asked Buck.

"None of your business. You'll find out if the time comes. I'll say this for you, at least you had sense enough to wait a couple of months before you burned this bastard out. Probably no one will suspect you. Not even him. He's probably screwed a lot of others worse than he did you."

"Jesus, I hope so."

"Don't worry. No one saw you. Just keep your mouth shut. Got that? Keep your mouth shut. Now, let's go watch the fire."

It was a great fire. Burned the lousy place to the ground. Bennie felt sort of sorry for the goat, with winter coming on. He was relieved to learn that they kept the goat in the basement that winter. Besides, goatshit in the bastard's basement struck him as a fitting reward for his unfairness.

As they walked home he asked Buck, "How come you know all this stuff about my family?"

"Never mind. I just know. Let it go at that. I've been around a long while, lucky for you. Not everyone has somebody like me."

"Why not?"

"They don't have enough brains to deserve it."

Bennie thought, "By Christ, that's a fact."

That night he lay awake a long while. He wondered, "Am I going nuts? Did I really burn down a building or did I dream it? Did Buck tell me all that stuff about the family? I sure had some neat relatives I never heard of. . . . I hope to hell Buck was right about no one seeing me." He half-expected Buck to show up again, but he didn't.

By this time, Bennie had a bed of his own in the room that used to be Pa's bedroom. Pa was sleeping with Ma now that he was the provider again. (There was a sort of economic protocol about that in those days—sexless duds like Ma and Mary had been conditioned to tolerate what amounted to rape as long as it was by a gainfully employed, self-respecting provider. The goddam work ethic even got between America's sheets every night.)

It was nice to be able to lie awake and thrash around to get comfortable and mull things over without Ma snoring in his ear or farting. Lord, how some of her farts stunk. He didn't think women should be allowed to fart. Especially your mother. It didn't seem delicate somehow. A strange thought for an arsonist.

Another nice thing about your own bed was you could play with your dong. That felt good. The summer before at the playground, the older guys (the ones who said they'd like to make out with the lifeguard) pointed out to some of the younger kids that you could see girls' "things" sometimes when girls got in the pool like they always did by cautiously edging over the side, which pulled their bathing suits aside at the crotch. Some of them had hair down there, just like he was beginning to grow. That was the first time that he noticed he was beginning to feel funny about girls. Then a bunch of the guys went off into the bushes and let the younger boys tag along, filing down to the creek which was heavily screened by willows. No one could see them there. They laughed sort of embarrassed and pulled out their dongs and began to milk them, or at least that was what it reminded Bennie of. Their dongs began to swell up like his own did sometimes, but theirs got a lot bigger, some of them real big. One with the biggest said, "How does that strike you short-cocked bastards for a hard-on?" He began to get real excited and work himself fast, thrusting like Bennie'd seen Mutt do on a female dog and pretty soon he let out a moan and jets of some white stuff shot out of his dong and arched to the ground. The rest got real excited too and pretty soon they were all shooting the same kind of stuff. He and some of the younger boys tried, but they could only get hard and excited. The older boys called it "shooting" when that white stuff that they called jizzum or jazz spewed out.

After that he always thought of girls' accidentally exposed hair when he jacked off in bed, though he wasn't really jacking "*off*" yet, which was a big disappointment. Thinking about it made his dong bigger and harder but he still couldn't "shoot."

He felt a lot different about girls after that. He was afraid they might read his mind and know he'd like to do something to them. The hell of it was he still didn't know exactly what you did when you did it to a girl. Nonetheless he'd have liked to have just about any girl to find out with. He used to look at some of the girls and get a hard-on in school, then he'd pray he didn't get called on to go to the blackboard or to stand up and read or recite.

And almost every night he played with his dong and hoped he'd "shoot." He knew what Ma would think about that. She'd think he was dirty. She called men, especially Pa when he wasn't around, "Dirty, nasty, forceful things."

Somehow he didn't feel dirty and nasty. He just wanted to get his jollies like the big guys and kept trying. He wasn't the least bit ashamed.

He never suffered a smidgeon of remorse over burning down that carriage house either. Only an occasional uneasy thought that he might still be found out. But he told himself several times, "I'm not the least damn bit sorry I did it."

By the time the Fox River froze that year, they had the raft ready to launch the next spring. They'd tried to build it of cottonwood logs but had given that up.

"Too damn crooked to fasten together," Cees summed up the case for cottonwood logs.

They'd cut a lot of them and never been caught, but they just didn't work. They decided to use the railroad ties after all. They wrestled one off the pile with their combined strength, but couldn't carry it, even together; could hardly pick up one end.

"These things must weigh a ton," Cees complained.

They tried to drag one but it would have taken them forever to get enough to the river, so they stole a kid's wagon and trundled them on that though the wagon kept tipping.

"This really doesn't work worth a crap either," Cees allowed. They were sweating like horses. It took them a week to move twelve ties.

"I don't think this'll make a big enough raft," Bennie said.

"Move the rest yourself then," Cees said. "I'm not moving another one of those big sons of bitches."

That was that. They went swimming instead.

That's where preparations for the big rafting adventure stood when New Year 1936 blew in. Pa was gone again. He was back in Wisconsin with a better job, not exactly *up north*, but closer. He was in another industrial city called Blackhawk, boarding with his sister, Nellie, and her husband, Bart. Bart had helped him get a job at the General Motors plant where he worked.

After Bart had carelessly killed that horse, he'd also let Grandma's cabin burn down while he was snoozing. Besides, he couldn't make it farming, so simply left Grandma high and dry and moved away to the city. Grandma had to live with Aunt Felice and then died about a month after Grandpa had. So much for Uncle Bart. When Bennie got to know him he reminded him of the rhyme that kids thought was clever then:

Bart, Bart,
  Let a fart.
Blew the baby
  Out of the cart.

If his job lasted, Pa planned to find a house and move Ma and Bennie to Blackhawk.

Buck told Bennie, "It looks like this spring or never to get to the cave. After the ice goes out we'd better launch the raft and take off."

Cees agreed. They planned never to come back till they got rich.

CHAPTER FIFTEEN

Bennie Sometimes Had Fun with Ma

Bennie hated to admit to himself that he had fun with Ma.

For instance, when they lived alone. That was after Roy left to work on a farm, Sister got married, and Pa was in Blackhawk. He and Ma would ride together on the Interurban car from Waubonsee to Riverview, changing cars at Yorkville along the Fox River. At Riverview one of her brothers, usually Johnny, would meet them and drive them out to Country Grandma's.

As the Interurban car sped along, Ma would talk about how that country had been when she was young. She might say, "This was all woods along here for miles," and sweep her arm around the horizon. "You could see deer, and there were wolves. I don't know who cut it all down." Her voice told that she was sorry it happened, whoever had done it. (Mercenary sonsabitches had done it during the World War, when lumber prices soared. One day Bennie would learn they'd ruined the Big Bend of Texas by overgrazing it for the same motive. Dirty old money.)

The Interurban was just like a big streetcar and ran on electricity. It hummed past farms and villages, at each of which Bennie wondered when the place had been settled, who lived there now, the sort of people they were and what they did. He was aware always that what he passed had belonged to the Indians only a century before.

Uncle Johnny would usually meet them in Riverview in his Dort touring car. Bennie never thought of the town by name, but as "the place with the statue of Chaubenee."

He liked best crossing the broad Illinois River on the old iron bridge at Riverview. If a stern-wheeler was in sight he'd get Uncle Johnny to stop on the bridge to watch it pass. They didn't block traffic since only about one car would pass every half-hour on weekdays.

Ma might have her memory jogged by crossing the bridge and say, "It took us all day to come to town in the wagon. We'd bring in eggs, butter, and milk to sell at the creamery. We had to stay overnight with some of Ma's friends from the old days when she was little. God knows what they thought of Pa, but they tolerated him on her account and probably felt sorry for her."

One time Ma took Bennie to Chicago on the Burlington commuter train. She had a special mission in mind—to see where John Dillinger had been killed. Ma and Aunt Mary were both crazy about scandal sheets that printed sensational stories about people like Dillinger. She'd read about "the Lady in Red" who had betrayed him and had to see where the Lady in Red had walked with Dillinger out of the Biograph Theater, wearing her distinctive red dress so the F.B.I. would know the man with her was the one they wanted. She must have been nervous as a whore in church.

When called on to surrender, Dillinger tried to get away, so they said, reaching for his automatic pistol as he ran, so they riddled him.

Ma bought tickets to the movie playing at the Biograph, but before they went in she coursed the sidewalk in front like a hound searching for faded bloodstains soaked into the bricks. "This might be one," she said, pointing at the sidewalk. Bennie couldn't see a thing. The ticket girl watched them with knowing eyes. A lot of weirdos came there for the same reason. If Ma had lived in St. Joe, Missouri, when Jesse James was killed, she'd have been over to visit the house about once a week in hopes of being let in to look around.

Bennie's existence alone with Ma was, however, drawing to a permanent close. He didn't look forward to moving to another city; even though a smaller one, it still would be a city. He saw himself instead running away with Cees, *working first for the understanding farmers they'd undoubtedly find down near the cave; then after finding Jesse James's buried treasure going west, where they'd buy horses, guns, and traps and start a trap line in Wyoming or Montana—maybe even Canada or Alaska.*

Raft-launching day had arrived. ("By the way, boys, have you figured out how you're going to get the raft over the dams downstream?" The voice is Pro Bono Publico's, but she isn't talking loud enough to be heard—it would spoil the fun.)

They had planned well, as far as they had planned, and built the raft on a slope where they could lever it down to the water with two long two-by-fours they'd stolen for that purpose months before. At water's edge was the remains of a stone foundation from the old ice works. The raft would slide over that and perhaps have a four-foot drop into deep water. They'd tied a rope to it so it couldn't float off and get away from them.

Cees and Bennie applied their two-by-four levers under the raft, one at each end, and were able to move it without too much strain, a few inches at a time. Finally it poised, precariously balanced, just above the last drop into the water.

Bennie rested a few seconds to prolong the feeling of being at a great juncture, between his past dull life and a glowing future of adventure. He felt a thrill like rapidly descending in a swing, which caused him to breathe rapidly.

Then they gave it a "one—two—three" together and over it went. As it dropped Cees gasped, "Well, there it goes at last."

They crowded up to the edge of the wall to admire their handiwork as soon as it bobbed back to the surface. Only it wasn't bobbing. The ancient, gravel-impregnated, creosote-soaked hardwood was as heavy as cement.

"Where the hell did the son of a bitch go?" Cees asked.

Bennie couldn't force out the answer.

The *son of a bitch* had sunk.

It sure looked like a real Indian. Bennie remembered the warning he'd read in some Western book, where a scout said, "When yuh don't see Injuns that's when the varmints are around."

He had been saying his secret goodbyes for a couple of days. Not even Cees was with him. Only Mutt. He visited the creeks and railroad yards, looking and listening, smelling the moist spring air with its many messages—spring beauties cropping up here, early violets there, wild irises, pungent pitch on poplar bark, swampy water with tadpoles and crawdads, new cattails. He remembered the games of cowboys and Indians played here with the gang, after being inspired by the Saturday Western movie. Mostly he thought of how he stayed after everyone else went home, how he savored the secret places, imagined he was in a still-living West where he would go some day to have adventures like his ancestors—especially that unnamed killer—had had there.

Well, the raft had sunk and put the kibosh on going west this spring.

He visited the haunted Moodore house, climbing through the rubble to the second floor. He looked out across the cottonwood and oak thicket behind the house. He was framed by a large brick window socket, now shorn of its window by some thief. (One glancing up there might have taken Bennie for the Moodore Ghost.) He could see the playground buildings across the fields. They were civilization; swings, teeter-totters, old-maid cards, a swimming pool with girls to ogle.

This deserted house was something other—a place where one Moodore brother had killed another and been hung for it. Tradition had the two ghosts returning on bright moonlight nights. Sometimes Bennie thought he could feel them beside him, perhaps in him, as though he himself were a Moodore Ghost, a weird notion he never revealed, not even to Buck. He wondered if this was how it was for the dead—unable to return no matter how much they wanted to go back to what they'd loved, in a world they could only look at, trapped in an endless future. He experienced a terribly lonesome feeling thinking of such a possibility.

He didn't bother visiting the playground. He did go to the Brady School library where he walked around. He often dreamed of that library thereafter; in some enchanted metamorphosis it had expanded. Shelf on shelf was filled with exotic, large books with covers all in glowing colors. He always knew they were books that could be obtained absolutely nowhere else. In one of them he would find the secret of creation and life, if only he opened the right book in time.

Miss Fisher regarded him suspiciously on his last visit as she always did, but she regarded all kids with suspicion, and could never tell one from another no matter how many times she'd seen them. From the first day he'd suffered her she had staunchly served her principal function, and denied him half of the books he wanted to take out, trying valiantly to dampen his enthusiasm for reading. (After all, she knew no boy his age could read that many books before they were due to be returned.) Bennie stifled an urge to stick his tongue out at her on this last foray into the happy land that she tried to turn into a sad domain.

Now he was alone at his favorite place of them all. Devil's Cave, a neat rock cavern four miles up the Fox River above Waubonsee. He'd lied to Ma and said he was going to camp overnight with several others of the neighborhood gang, which he was sometimes allowed to do.

He came with only Mutt, bringing canned beans, sardines, and bread (all ready-to-eat items), a can opener, eating utensils, two pie pans for plates, and a canteen of drinking water. For cooking he brought matches, some newspaper to start the fire, a hatchet to chop kindling, his jackknife. He also had a blanket, since it got cold toward morning there along the river, even in the summertime.

It started to rain before dark, a steady late-spring drizzle. His firewood was already gathered and inside the cave, so he and Mutt were snug. After sharing his meal with Mutt, they lay back to enjoy the solitude, staring into the ebbing fire. The roiling water of the Fox was faintly audible, mingled with the hiss of raindrops falling through new leaves.

He wasn't sure whether he'd dozed off or not when Mutt's sharp bark startled him. Mutt stood, hackles raised, glaring into the dark outside and snarling. Something big was coming toward them. Bennie's gut crawled and his hair rose on his neck; he was too scared to move and realized he probably couldn't get away past whatever was out there anyhow. He gripped the hatchet and thought, "Why didn't I sneak the .40-60 out?" He knew how to shoot it.

Then he thought, "Maybe it's only a cow." It sort of looked like one. But it wasn't. It was a man. An Indian, and dressed like one ought to dress, war bonnet and all. Bennie stared at him pop-eyed, scarcely able to breathe.

"Who are you?" he finally quavered.

"Waubonsee."

Bennie knew he had to be dreaming and began to feel better. But it didn't feel like a dream exactly. The details were all too clear.

"What do you want?" he asked Waubonsee in a steadier voice.

"You called me. What do you want?"

"I don't remember calling you. How? When?"

"All your life. I have been watching and listening. One day you will be one of us."

"An Indian?"

"One of us. That's enough."

"How?"

"Listen by the waters."

Waubonsee turned to leave.

"Don't go yet. I've got a question to ask you."

The chief turned back.

"Ask it."

"Am I dreaming?"

"Maybe. *Listen by the waters.*"

Then he was gone.

Mutt's hackles were still standing high.

"I'll be go to hell!" Bennie said, borrowing one of Pa's favorite exclamations.

He was very tired and too sleepy to puzzle over the whole thing.

Morning came clear, cool and bright, raindrops glistened on all the new leaves.

Bennie fixed the last of their food, divvied it up exactly, fair and square, then washed his eating stuff in the river.

He listened carefully to water rolling over and around rocks and through the willow branches that draped into it.

"I'll be one of what?" he asked himself. Then he spotted a single moccasin track in the sand on the river bank.

CHAPTER SIXTEEN

A Ride through History

— SUMMER 1936

Bennie kissed Mutt on top of his head.

"Goodbye, Muttsie," he choked, tears streaming down his cheeks. He hugged the little dog hard.

They were out behind Sister's garage, where no one could see him. In Blackhawk the new landlady didn't allow pets. They'd found someone who loved Mutt, the man who owned the filling station across from Sister's, where Mutt hung around when Bennie was in school. Mutt, at least, seemed wholly unaware of what was happening.

So, during that June of 1936, Bennie kissed his best friend goodbye and started the long migration home—*up north.* Only he didn't know that eventually he was going back home to Paradise. If he had, he'd have been happier. He thought he was exchanging one "dumb" city for another.

He was traveling the same trail north that he had in 1929 to Grandpa's funeral. He'd visited Blackhawk then, had seen photographs of himself, Pa, and Roy there, but recalled little about the town.

He was riding in the same old Buick, but this time he had the narrow back seat to himself, except that bundles and cartons surrounded him. He was crowded by the storage-well, which rendered the back seat uncomfortable for more than one person. In that tightly packed storage well, among other stuff, was the .45 pistol that Pa had clicked in that cold and lonely back bedroom. The New Deal had saved Pa's life, regardless of what it did to Colonel McCormick's blood pressure. The pistol was secure in a small box of underwear that smelled of mothballs. Money in Pa's wallet had mothballed that deadly weapon. The Depression itself needed to be packed away eternally in mothballs, a bad, yet valuable, memory to warn against repetition of the wage of unrestrained capitalism.

"Those who cannot remember history . . ."

Bennie asked himself. "What am I doing here?"

He was riding through history. Riding from the *Land of Lincoln* to the *Land of Blackhawk.* History was names. He was leaving Waubonsee to go to Blackhawk.

> *(River towns, Indian named.*
> *"Listen by the waters.")*

Blackhawk was also in the Land of Lakes.

> *Wahbesa, Kegonsa, Mendota,*
> *Wingra, Monona, Koshkonong.*
> *Devils Lake, Manitowish Waters,*
> *Pelican, Oshkosh, Tomahawk,*
> *Shewano, Chippewa, Winnebago.*
> *Waters for birchbark canoes.*

Once, not so long before, survival's taproot here was not money in a wallet but arrows in a quiver.

> *Indian woman,*
> *Be sure to save the arrowhead from the killed deer,*
> *Arrowheads cost long hours of chipping.*
> *Be sure to tan the hide well.*
> *It will be clothing,*
> *Moccasin for foot of warrior—hunter,*
> *Warm winter robe.*
>
> *Save the tendons for sewing,*
> *Hoofs for gluing,*
> *Bone for tools,*
> *Soup,*
> *Food for dogs that carry packs;*
> *Dogs that warn of approaching enemies.*
>
> *But watchdogs could not warn*
> *Of the annihilating enemy—*
> *Progress,*
> *The tide of Empire.*
> *(Manifest Destiny.)*
>
> *Where are you, native American?*
> *Alien in your own land,*

Where the Heart Was

Shuffling to the white-man store
With annuity check.
Did you progress?
What do the names of history,
Of the "Tide of Empire"
Mean to you?
What did they ever mean?

You seldom knew the names
Of those you fought.
Did Tecumseh really know
Daniel Boone?
Simon Kenton?
Maybe in books.
And if he did, then what?
Did these antagonists spout storybook
Speeches at one another
In paleface "biblical" words
And rhymes?

Not likely.
They shot hot lead,
Not hot air.

What do history-book names mean to Poor Lo's grandchildren?

Edison? Brings illumination, washing machines, radios—to palefaces.
And to Poor Lo? His women still wash clothes by streams, pounding them on rocks, or scrub on washboards in cheap tubs bought at the white-man store.
Does the radio tell Lo of the Hitler threat in Europe?
Indian sounds plucked from the "air waves" are not H. V. Kaltenborn or some other radio commentator with "cultivated urgency" in his voice.
They are, as always, the voice of God.
Mitchee Manitou.
Wakan Tanka.
Lo has never heard of Marconi or Tesla.
Lo doesn't give a damn.

Lo has heard of Winchester.
Lo buys Winchester arrowheads
At the white-man store
With annuity check,
Before the rest goes for booze.

Lo may still hunt for deer
As Blackhawk did.
If he doesn't get too drunk
And trade cartridges back for more booze.

Why does Lo get drunk?
Because he hunts the deer
And sees barbed wire fences
In Blackhawk's woods.
By Manitowish
By Pelican
By Tomahawk
Where canoes still float.
Paleface canoes
By Thompson,
By Old Town.
Floating
On the Tide of Empire.

Bennie was passing into a new geology. From uninterrupted prairie to rolling hills and occasional steep bluffs. *There were the same billboards, however. Walk a mile for a Camel. Buy Luckies. Come in and call for Phillip Morris. Buy Buick—ask the man who owns one. Motorists wise, Simonize.*

Bennie was rushing forward, looking back in his mind.

"What will happen to Mutt?"

"He'll be O.K." (He wasn't. The dumb son of a bitch who "loved" him stood by like a ninny and watched him choke to death on a golf ball he'd been throwing for him to retrieve. A desperate kid would have fished the ball out with flying fingers, or worked it up from outside with inspired hands.)

"Will Mutt miss me?"

"Especially *in extremis.*"

"What will happen to Cees?"

"Cees can take care of himself."

"Will I ever go back and roam the Burlington railroad yards?"

"No." *("But I'll remember them—especially the creeks—I'll sure as hell do that.")*
"Why did I love Brady School—school really stinks sometimes."
"You always loved the books!"
"Will I ever see the Fox River again at ice breakup time?"
"I hope so."
"Are the G.A.R. vets still there?"
"Fewer and fewer."
"Will I ever talk to any of them again?"
"Only in memory."

> *"It is for us the living, rather, to be dedicated here to the unfinished work which they who fought here, have, thus far, so nobly advanced."*
> *—Abraham Lincoln*

CHAPTER SEVENTEEN

I Am the Buckskin Land

Bennie was growing weary. Their old Buick, the road, and Pa's careful pace conspired to make an all-day grind out of what a decade would shrink to two hours. Finally he dozed off, sprawled among the boxes, packages, and bags, but not before Ma cautioned him when she heard him squirming to get comfortable: "Don't break any of those things. Don't squash anything. Be careful. Put that up out of the way. Give me that, I'll carry it on my lap."

When he woke up, they were stopped at a cafe in the little town of Marengo. Pa shook him. He said, "Wake up if you want some eats."

Ma was already outside, smoothing out her dress, looking at her shoes, glancing around to see if anyone was staring at her.

"Tuck in your shirt," she ordered him as soon as he got out. "One of your shoe laces is untied, you'll trip over it. Go in to the toilet and wash your hands as soon as we get inside—and wet your hair and smooth it down so you won't look like a tramp."

He was almost sorry he hadn't stayed in the car. Aspirations for a hot dog and some ice cream were all that got him out. He retied his shoelace.

"Your knee is in the dust. Brush it off. You could have put your foot on the bumper to tie your shoe."

It was a tennis shoe. Almost brand new. The dusty knee was on a pair of bib overalls. Those two items were the staples of boys' dress.

Marengo was a nice-looking town, founded shortly after the Chief Blackhawk threat was removed, old by the standards of the place and time. Tall elms spread over the streets. Some of the men who had helped chase out the Sac and Fox Indians in the so-called Blackhawk War had liked this unsettled country, theirs for the taking, as all unsettled land was. Land laws were not always clear and seldom were enforceable. Squatters' rights, the right of a man to keep what he'd developed beyond the fringe of civilization, were recognized as a necessity. When civilization caught up to him, he could do what was known as "prove up" and be issued a title at a federal land office. Very often, uncomfortable with civilization, he moved on to a new frontier rather than "proving up." Bennie had read enough history to know that this "nice old town" had begun in that manner. It was smaller than Waubonsee, and he liked the feel of it. No factory chimney was in sight.

Seated in a booth in the cafe, Ma closely inspected her silverware to see it if had been washed clean.

"What do you want?" Pa asked Bennie.

"A hot dog and ice cream."

Ma snapped, "You ought to have something *regular* to eat."

Bennie would have paid five dollars for the right to say, without getting popped in the mouth, "What the hell is *regular*?" He knew what she meant, though. It was tasteless meat, lumpy mashed potatoes and cold gravy, served on a plate with some rabbit-food salad and a soggy vegetable side dish, such as string beans, which he hated.

"Let him have what he wants for a change," Pa said.

Ma gave Pa a dirty look then changed the subject. "What are you having?"

Pa said, "I'm just gonna have some apple pie a là mode and a cup of coffee. How about you?"

For once Ma passed up a chance to stuff herself and had the same thing. Bennie got his hot dog and ice cream.

Back outside afterward Pa said, "I'm going to gas up while we're here."

Their Buick was one of the earliest cars with a self-starter. Before then drivers set the spark-and-throttle levers on the steering column to positions they prayed were right, then got out front and turned a hand crank that had to be engaged to the front of the engine shaft through an access port under the radiator. Cars like the Buick were built so they could be hand-cranked if the starter didn't work. Starters were activated by a floor pedal like the gas, except it was raised on an actuating rod with a spring on it to disengage the starter after the engine fired.

The sequence was "turn on the key, step down on the starter, and" (one hoped) "the old buggy fires off." This time it didn't. Pa had to get out and crank. As usual Ma cautioned, "Don't run over yourself."

"The emergency brake is set," Pa assured her, "and it's out of gear. It can't run over me."

Ma was never too sure about that; she thought cars had minds of their own, and might run away at unpredictable times, like horses. Bennie had a sneaking suspicion she was more than half-right, such as right now, when the starter decided not to work on a hot day. Pa got it started anyhow.

When he got back in out of breath he said, "I'll get the damned thing fixed at the gas station."

"You shouldn't swear in front of Bennie," Ma said.

Pa grunted.

Filling stations were almost all run by mechanics, since, in the early days of cars they'd started as "garages," which was what repair shops were then called.

Most garages started selling gas later as a convenience. Their owners all made a good living, since cars were notoriously cranky and undependable. A "long" trip was something of a gamble, and "long" was any trip beyond walking distance of home.

Gas pumps fascinated Bennie. They were tall metal columns with very thick glass cylinders holding ten gallons of wine-red gas on top. On the side of the cylinder were one-gallon markings like those on a measuring cup. When one turned on the hose, the gas fed by gravity, and the amount dispensed was shown by the mark to which the gas level fell in the glass cylinder. Sometimes when there was a "special" on gas you could get ten gallons for a dollar. If you needed more than ten gallons, you had to refill the cylinder from an underground tank. The handle to do this was on the side of the cylinder, worked by moving it back and forth, which was what led to the name gas "pump."

The gas station man fixed their starter by tapping it sharply with an iron bar. "The gadget that engages it was stuck," he announced. "Happens a lot on this model. Just crack it next time with a hammer or something."

As they resumed their way north, Ma said, "I hate to travel."

"Enjoy the scenery," Pa said.

They were crossing the Kishwaukee River, and the scenery really was something to enjoy. Many farmers had kept substantial woods with shadowed interiors that seemed to beckon.

Come, I am still the buckskin land.
Wild creatures imprint my carpet
with unfamiliar designs.
Once, a long time ago
Men could read my hieroglyphs.
You can't?
Come! You may learn.

A lone crow flew above the woods. In the distance a farmer rode behind a horse-drawn cultivator in a cornfield.

Bennie noticed that Ma was looking around—and even whistling, which she only did when she was feeling good.

Kishwaukee. Another river with an Indian name. Soon they would be in the valley of the Rock, which flowed straight through Lake Koshkonong, where Blackhawk's main camp had been during the long-ago summer of his last fight. The untrained troops of fumbling, uncertain General Atkinson had sought the Sac and Fox at Koshkonong, but not too earnestly. The penultimate curtain fell at Wisconsin Heights, and the final one at Bad Axe later. Despite the general's dismal record, a Wisconsin town bore the fumbler's name: Fort Atkinson. Bennie would become familiar with that name and place and others in the land of Blackhawk. That day they passed through Harvard, Walworth, and Darien, toward places named Milton, Edgerton, Albion, Janesville, Whitewater, Afton (wonderful name), Stoughton, Brodhead, Jefferson—places that all had the same reasons for being named as they were: once someone proposed a name, others agreed to adopt it. Now the Republic was beyond the naming stage. The land was settled up. The official Frontier had passed away in 1890.

Oh?
I am the buckskin land!
Come.
("Listen by the waters.")
Kishwaukee
Rock
Walworth
Delevan
Koshkonong
Waubesa.
("Hear alien tongue
Of dispossessed race.")

Or is that the rustle of leaves
Stirred by night winds
in vestigial forests?
Listen!

The Buick snorted up the last rise and they were poised on the bluff high above Blackhawk. Directly below was the town with evening lights just coming on, the shining river painting a broad, curved path through it toward the sun setting beyond hills to the west. On both sides of the Rock River were continuous hills, crowned by woods, some thick and black, others scattered like the spears of an ancient army. In the twilight the trees seemed to beckon, demanding exploration.

Like Balboa above Darien, the explorer had arrived. Three idle months of summer vacation lay ahead.

"If the frontier is dead the body is keeping pretty well."
Especially when one has known Chief Waubonsee and may meet Blackhawk some day.

CHAPTER EIGHTEEN

The Magic Place at Last

Rivers nourish,
Have secrets and moods,
Talk and sing,
Possess souls.
("Listen by the waters . . .")

The Rock River at Blackhawk wound through a land apart. Except for floodwalls downtown, it was not contained and meandered through wide, empty fields within the city limits. If it flooded in spring it harmed nothing, since most of Blackhawk was built on bluffs. Along the river's edge, willows arched supple branches into the water, trailing leafy ends like playful fingers. The swirling currents whispered, "I have been to the sea and back a million times."

A few days later, from Blackhawk's bathing beach Bennie scrutinized the far bank, the wildest one, and knew he had to explore there. A train passed, visible only between breaks in the trees then disappeared, leaving a dissipating smoke cloud, and sending back clattering echoes.

"*I'll go over there and find that track and follow it somewhere,*" he thought.

He had no trouble finding the double tracks and was following them out of town the very next day, wishing Mutt were with him—and Cees.

Railroads had their charm, but couldn't match the call of waterways, even though each train suggested that it had been to far, romantic places and was going to others. Blackhawk was still served exclusively by steam-powered locomotives, since it was not on a main transcontinental line as Waubonsee had been. The Burlington line at Waubonsee boasted diesel streamliners and was among the first to have them. Its famous Zephyr zipped from Chicago to the Pacific Coast in record time. Bennie never imagined that such growling, oil-belching, overgrown buses would replace steam.

Diesels never could evoke a sexual response in him like the rocking, swaying, black, steam behemoths, obsessed monsters that beat their way through space like cannonballs, pistons churning with machine-gun rapidity, clattering as though they were trying to throw themselves into a million pieces. They were alive, and their tracks became Bennie's high road to adventure.

Two major railroads served Blackhawk: the Northwestern and the Chicago, Milwaukee, St. Paul and Pacific, called the Milwaukee Road. One ran on each bank of the Rock. Both lines had depots near Bennie's house: old-fashioned, Victorian brick buildings, smelling as depots should of spittoons, urinals, and cleaning compounds; of old varnished wood, steam radiators—echoing with a chattering, never-silent telegraph instrument. Bennie frequently visited them to watch trains arrive and depart. The sound of the traffic on the tracks reached to his house, but there was hardly a place in town where trains couldn't be heard. Frequently, switch engines made up trains, bumping, banging and chuffing, usually at night, coupling lines of cars together. The red wigwag crossing light at Five Points was close enough for Bennie to hear its accompanying bell when he lay awake in bed.

The Northwestern line led him to his Mecca. Its tracks wound along the more heavily wooded shore of the Rock, then diverged into the equally woodsy hills, after crossing Three-Mile Creek. He followed those tracks that far the first day, and found what he'd been seeking for a long time.

The creek valley was walled by densely timbered bluffs, cut by ravines, each forming its own miniature valley, each demanding exploration. The farmers who owned these woods seldom came into them. Some farmers pastured cattle there, some merely used them for firewood. Both beef and dairy cattle were there, the former caring for themselves, the latter finding their way home at night for a supplemental feed and to have full udders milked before they became uncomfortable.

Here was the magic place at last. Here his imagination didn't have to fend off industrial surroundings to capture a wilderness. Here was genuine space—woods, meadows, a clear creek, deep pools for swimming, pure springs to refill a canteen (if only he had one, and he made a note to get one as soon as possible, since the one he'd used in Waubonsee had been Milton's). All he needed other than that was a gun.

Bennie started a wheedling campaign to get a B.B. gun. He knew a .22 was out of the question.

Naturally Ma was against it.

"You'll shoot out the windows. Put someone's eye out. Kill birds. Get in trouble with the police."

Buck Doaks grumbled, "I thought that's what B.B. guns were for. Don't let up. Pa'll get you one. Incidentally, Ma must be slipping, she forgot to mention:

shoot the neighbors' milk bottles, cats, mailboxes, apples, tomatoes (nothing does it for teeth like an apple or tomato with a B.B. in it), the ice man's horses so they'll run away, insulators on telephone lines, squirrels; and, sooner or later, our sour-puss landlady, Skinny O'Brien. Be sure to do that from across the street in the neighbor's bushes some damn dark night after she parks her car in the barn, then run like hell. Ma didn't come close to covering it."

"How about a reason I can give Ma why I should have a B.B. gun?"

"Try: 'All the other kids have them,' or, 'I'll only shoot it down along the river,' or, 'I'll never shoot anything but tin cans.'"

All of which he tried, and netted from Ma, "Kids that have B.B. guns are all delinquents." And, "I know you too well to take your word on anything."

So Bennie had to settle for his cap pistol for defense against Indians out at Three-Mile Creek and with cutting a crooked stick shaped like a rifle for long-range stuff. It didn't really take a gun to appreciate limitless land where he never saw anyone, no matter how long or far he rambled. From the edge of the woods on top of the bluffs he could see the distant farms and men in fields, but generally the cultivated fields were empty too. He might have been an Indian spying on early settlers. He knew the first time he came to the woods that this pungent place of mystic silence was his ancient home from which he'd strayed long ago.

("You will be one of us.")

Tall elms and oaks blended overhead with shagbark hickories, almost obscuring the sky. Hard and soft maples grew in clumps, an occasional locust or black walnut could be found; sumac, crabapples, chokecherries, ash, box elder thrived here, and always willows and cottonwoods crowding the waterways. Beneath was the perfumed carpet of prior years' sheddings: leaves, ferns, bark, decaying fruit and nuts, dead branches, providing sustenance for trillions of small organisms, each with a hidden abode or community, concealed in a separate world from giants walking over them. Spreading across whole hillsides were patches of gooseberries, raspberries, blackberries, attracting bees and birds, chipmunks, rabbits, and even sly- hard-to-surprise foxes. Above, hawks wheeled. Silent, sable crows glided over to spy out where an interloper had disappeared from sight of their lookouts, cawing loudly once they learned what they wanted to know and after they were safely past.

Birds were always in sight and hearing: redwing blackbirds in the reeds by the waters, seldom-seen brown thrashers in the bushes, scarlet tanagers, orioles, bluebirds, robins, sparrows, occasional cardinals, blue jays in tribes, meadowlarks, catbirds mewing in the brush, killdeer walking gingerly along sandy spits bordering the creek, owls sleeping in dark hollows in the upper reaches of oaks and seen flying only after dusk, whippoorwills calling at dusk, kingfishers, snipe, wood ducks, even the occasional cranes, shrikes, swallows, nuthatches, and in the meadows and cornfields, Hungarian partridges and pheasants.

In time Bennie would come to recognize them, their lurking places and ways, their calls. That first summer it was all cause for wonder. He made no close friends and was glad.

> *Friends? Why do I need friends?*
> *I have known Chief Waubonsee!"*

A person with him would have been a nuisance, wanting to talk when he wanted to listen, to go home when he wanted to linger and watch. He missed only Mutt. Then he discovered Silver, the great, white horse. He had no idea that twenty-five-year-old Silver was not beautiful, that he was sway-backed, that he was an old plug put out to pasture (*but if someone hadn't loved him he'd have been sent to a fox farm for food instead of pastured out*). What mattered to Bennie was that he was a horse, and that he wasn't the least bit shy.

Silver lifted his head from nipping grass when he sensed someone approaching, looked Bennie over, but didn't move away. Bennie started talking to him softly, holding his hand out as he'd done to the ice wagon and vegetable wagon horses in Waubonsee. Pretty soon he was stroking Silver's nose. He stayed around for a couple of hours just watching him and talking to him, petting him occasionally, all in wonder. He'd never been around a horse so long before. Silver might just as well have been his horse, because here he was with him, could stay as long as he cared to, and no one was around to chase him away for being a pest. Silver traveled with a small herd of grazing shorthorn beef cattle. After first looking Bennie over, the cattle paid him no further attention and resumed grazing. They were interesting to watch too, but not like horses.

Here Bennie had his ranch: cattle, a horse, privacy, and imagination; that was a ranch, wasn't it? He had everything but a saddle with stirrups so he could get on Silver.

"Horses came before saddles." It was Buck Doaks voice.

"So?"

"So, the first guy that ever rode a horse got on him somehow."

"How about steering him after I get on?"

"Steering him where? Where is he going to go? Where do you want him to go?"

"Out west."

"Fat chance. Just shinny up on him somehow. I'll bet he won't even move while you're getting on."

Silver looked as though he was listening to the conversation.

"He's nearly as high as a camel," Bennie protested.

"No guts, no glory!"

"Here goes."

Bennie grabbed Silver's mane with his left hand and jumped up, throwing his right arm over him. He landed with his stomach in the middle of Silver's back, draped like a sack and looking down from the far side with his feet on the other.

"Any more bright ideas?" he grunted.

"Sure. Get your left arm back over his mane and wiggle till you got your left leg back over his rump."

Fortunately Buck was right about Silver's steadiness. He stood like a rock while all that was going on, seeming to know all about it.

Most kids with a rudimentary knowledge of horses would have said, "Giddyap!" Bennie yelled, "Hi ho, Silver!" And kicked the old horse's flanks. It netted him about ten paces at a trot, then a stroll around the top of the hill, after which Silver felt he'd done his part and went back to grazing.

"I guess the show's over for now," Buck said.

"Just as well. His backbone is like a saw."

Bennie slid off, waited till Silver brought his head up between munching forays and kissed him on his velvety nose.

Then he hiked back to town on the railroad tracks, under a rising moon, happy as he'd ever been. Ma raised hell about how late he was.

Pa got a letter from Uncle Newt that summer.

"I'm coming home before snow flies," he wrote. "Alaska's getting a little nippy for old bones."

"I'll buy that," Pa said.

Pa read the letter to Bennie and Ma at the dinner table the night he got it. "I wonder how he found our address. I suppose we'll have to put him up for a while."

"I don't want him around," Ma said. "I never did like him."

"You only met him that once."

"That was enough."

"Well," Pa said. "We'll see when the time comes." He said that a lot, usually to put off a decision in case the need went away, or to avoid an argument.

CHAPTER NINETEEN

Prosperity Is Just around the Corner

Voices were speaking across the world but Bennie was scarcely aware of them, even though they were reported on the "air waves" and in newspapers and news magazines—two most popular of the latter were *Time* and *Life*, both started and published by Henry Luce. They were American staples. *Life* was Pa's most outrageous extravagance, other than an occasional cigar. A weekly issue cost ten cents. Ma looked at the pictures of movie stars in *Life* but read none of it. Pa still had to have his Saturday and Sunday *Chicago Tribune*. He ranted at reactionary Colonel McCormick, but loved the paper. He followed sports in its pages, was an avid baseball fan, his favorite team the Chicago White Sox. On weekends he never missed one of their games on the radio.

Sports were a national craze that salved troubled minds. The Depression was alleviated but was far from whipped. The man on the street knew the names and records of Lou Gehrig and Babe Ruth, Mickey Cochrane, Gabby Hartnett, Dizzy Dean, Rogers Hornsby (who had batted .424 in 1924) and was still going strong. Football "*Greats*" became household names, foremost Red Grange, the Galloping Ghost. Sports "*Greats*," such as Grange, were named *All-Americans*, a nomination started in 1889 by Walter Camp and carried on by Grantland Rice. (A committee inevitably took over selecting *All-Americans* and made the whole process suspect as a result—"*Tell me when a committee flies the Atlantic*, or hits a home run.") The Four Horsemen of Notre Dame (1922–1925) would remain in the public eye and consciousness for years, since three became famous football coaches. But they were not the Four Horsemen that shaped the next decades—*The Four Horsemen of the Apocalypse*.

Of those four horsemen, the rider on the Red Horse was about to take the stage front and center. As a result, Bennie's life would take the apocalyptic path, along with tens of millions of others worldwide.

But the *Drums of the Republic* were still muffled by far hills, restrained by Neutrality Laws. The Black Horse was preoccupation enough for a Depression-battered land. The Republic chose to see no evil and hear no evil; seers, critical of that shortsighted course (the main one being Winston Churchill in England) were even cautioned to speak no evil lest they antagonize dogs already frothing at the mouth. Fantastic! Hitler's legions were marching in Europe. The Rising Sun of Japan was ravaging Asia and had even sunk an American gunboat, the *Panay*, while it was peacefully anchored in the Yangtze River. Their "crocodile tears" of regret were accepted as a suitable apology.

Where were the *Drums of the Republic*? A lustrum must pass before the "sleeping giant" would "awaken," roused by the sneak Japanese attack on Pearl Harbor. They were five years that would bring Bennie . . . what?

His first orgasm, among other things.
His first B.B. gun; his first rifle.
His first job.
Social consciousness.
(Not necessarily unrelated items.)
A woman.

Prosperity is (still) just around the corner.

The new flat in Blackhawk was a trifle better than the last one in Waubonsee. The bathroom had a wash bowl in addition to the toilet, but no tub. There was central heating, especially in the summer; in the winter they suspected the landlady, an old maid with chicken legs encased in baggy white stockings, fired the furnace with a candle. Pa called her Skinny O'Brien. She reminded Bennie of a starved edition of Miss Fisher, the librarian at Brady School—same great bugs' eyes, staring eerily through thick glasses. Skinny's first look at Bennie was a glare through those milk-bottle lenses that didn't hide her thought, "Boys are no damned good!" He never gave her any reason to change that opinion.

Their flat was on the second floor of another Victorian chicken-coop, this one more interesting, with a front porch and gingerbread around the eaves. Skinny lived downstairs in the main house and they above her, with another tenant in a wing next to the landlady. That side of the house was hidden in bushes and rank weeds and enclosed by a high board fence on the lot line. Bennie never once saw that tenant, never heard anyone in that apartment, never saw a light there; the shades were always closely drawn. The only evidence that there was a tenant was that Skinny told Pa there was when he rented the place. Perhaps it was a vampire, and Bennie wouldn't have been surprised if he learned it was. In any case he was convinced something sneaky was going on there.

Mature trees—elms, oaks, hickories, and a locust—surrounded the house.

Behind it was a barn in which Pa had garage space, in a cell almost hermetically sealed from the rest of the barn with tongue-and-groove board walls. Later Bennie often wondered why none of them had learned for sure that Skinny was harboring a vampire in that dark wing of the house and hiding bodies in her part of the barn. He, at least, should have bored his way into the barn and explored it. Moreover, he should have enlisted some help to set a twenty-four-hour watch on the other apartment. That would have entailed finding some new friends, which wasn't turning out to be easy. He was looking for someone of Cees's caliber, or at least a reasonable facsimile. Of course, he was also busy exploring the wide open spaces around Blackhawk and the public swimming beach on the river where there were girls to ogle.

Regarding the first neighborhood kids he met, Buck Doaks opined: "Virgin sucks!" Bennie had to agree, especially after one of them squealed on him for sort of borrowing a bicycle that wasn't his. "Suck" was a stunningly appropriate term then used to denote a goddam Little Lord Fauntleroy: a little fink who cleaned his fingernails, went to Sunday School, and sucked ass with anyone and everyone who could do him some good, especially parents and teachers. Of course a "virgin suck" was the premier grade of that sort of loser. Finding a Cees in Blackhawk was an uphill proposition.

During that summer Bennie slept on what was commonly called a "sleeping porch"; this one with a full row of windows on one wall, screened so they could be left open. His bed was an antique that, a half-century later, would sell for a price that would have bought the whole house then. It was a wonderful place to savor a cooling nocturnal thunderstorm with the windows open, which was possible due to a big overhanging roof that prevented rain from blowing in. He would lie wide-eyed and watch the flickering lightning illuminate thrashing trees and wait for the crash of thunder.

They had none of their own furniture yet, so got by with the usual 1930s' furnished-apartment kindling in the kitchen and horsehair-and-plush torture racks in the living room, which were battered survivors of the Gay Nineties. Bennie felt like a wax dummy in a museum in that living room, which he avoided as much as possible except to shoot a pistol that fired a round wood stick with a suction cup on it at the porcelain doorknob. If his aim was true, it stuck to the doorknob.

He liked Pa's sister Nellie, who was the direct cause of their residence in Blackhawk. Her husband, Bart, and Pa were opposites, with no love lost between them. Nellie had had to twist Bart's arm to make him help Pa get his job with G.M.

Nellie was a twin—but she and sister Felice were not identical in either appearance or personality, as Bennie would discover in a few years. He'd learn that Nellie laughed a lot; twin Felice was a sourpuss. They both had sharp tongues, but Felice needled, Nellie tickled. She thought hell-raising boys were normal.

Pa was Nellie's favorite brother. Once, as an old man, Pa confessed to Bennie, "I got Nellie and a neighbor boy diddling each other out behind our woodshed. They were probably about ten. I heard Ma coming and ran to hell out of there through the orchard before Ma saw me, but she caught Nellie and the boy in the act. Nellie wouldn't squeal on me even though the little bastard who screwed her said, 'Her big brother put us up to it.' Lucky he didn't know one of us boys from the other. Ma always thought I was an angel, so she figured it must have been Ern. When he got home she grabbed him and whaled him without telling him what for. I can almost hear her saying, 'You know what for!' Anyhow, he figured he must have got it for something I did, so when he saw me he asked me, 'What the hell was all that about?' But I played dumb. I never did tell him."

Uncle Bart was a scoutmaster who tried to recruit Bennie into his "loyal, cheerful, kind, clean, helpful, reverent, etc." local contingent, but had tough going. Cheerful was the best Bennie could manage. He and Buck were sandbagged into attending a couple of meetings. Buck kept muttering so that Bennie laughed when he shouldn't have. Uncle Bart was lecturing on first aid: "To control arterial bleeding in the upper leg, you press hard on the pressure point in the groin. One of you boys come up here and I'll demonstrate."

"He needs some strong pressure applied to his fat ass with a size fourteen boot if you ask me," Buck growled.

Bennie guffawed and got several mean looks from the "loyal and reverent" crew, and also his uncle.

A little later Buck mused, "Do you suppose Fatso is in this racket because he likes young boys?"

That went over Bennie's head. Pro Bono Publico showed up about then and chipped in, "Shut up, Buck! That won't be popular again for years yet. We aren't quite that far down the Appian Way."

Whenever he'd remember that remark years later, Bennie would grin to himself and think, "Do you suppose that, unbeknownst to the public, there are esoteric merit badges that make one an Eagle Scout without tying so many square knots and grannies?"

"Anyhow," Buck said to Pro Bono, "these are a real bunch of epods."

"What the hell is an epod?" Bennie asked.

"Dope spelled backward."

"Moreover," Pro Bono said, "this is a glorified committee. No committee will ever pioneer anything—neither will a troop of these epods. It's like that fellow in Chicago said about Lindberg flying the Atlantic alone."

"What fellow in Chicago?" Bennie asked.

She told them about the fellow who, when his secretary excitedly told him about Lindberg crossing the Atlantic, said, "One man can do anything by himself. Tell me when a committee does it."

None of them ever went to another scout meeting. On the way home *Pro Bono* said, addressing her remark mainly to Buck, "Fatso would do better staying home and putting out the fire there before it burns the house down instead of telling a bunch of kids about rubbing sticks together to start a fire."

"Yeah," Buck agreed. "Did you ever see a fire started that way?"

"I never did," Pro Bono said.

"Me either," Buck said.

Bennie didn't get the drift but let it slide—he really wasn't interested in Bart's problems, although he couldn't understand how Nellie put up with him.

What Nellie saw in Bart was a mystery to more folks than Bennie. Bart had a nose like a cartoon Indian and was built like a turnip, wide in the hips and narrow in the shoulders, which wasn't alleviated by the fact that he was tall; worse yet, he was awkward, clumsy, and knock-kneed. Because of his high butt, Pa always called him "sky balls." Although Bennie learned it much later, at the time they came to Blackhawk, Nellie was having an affair with her doctor, which explained what *Pro Bono* had been talking about. The doctor wasn't a beauty either, but he had fire. He spotted Nellie's vulnerability—she was home with hot pants while Bart was down in the church basement pushing the wrong pressure points and rubbing the wrong stick, instead of rubbing something at home that would have been a damn sight more fun.

Nonetheless, Bart was about to become famous, and Bennie would witness his most glorious moment.

Before then, Bennie fell deeply in love. This happened at a brick pile called Grant School. (He never learned if it was named for the dime store chain, or for General Grant.) He was forced to repeat the first half of seventh grade again there, since Blackhawk didn't have half-grades like Waubonsee. They'd have done better to skip him into eighth grade if they were planning to challenge him—or better yet, twelfth.

Grant School had two rooms of seventh-graders and two seventh-grade teachers. The two groups were divided based on the school's estimate of their brainpower. The smarter kids somehow got the dumber teacher of the two, but weren't able to teach her much.

Every day the two groups would switch rooms for some classes, and Bennie noticed a petite blond girl, named Betty Lou, with whom he fell in love at about second sight. He would have spent the whole year with a hard-on if he'd been in the dumb group. As it was, he only had a problem because the two classes switched rooms and teachers for various subjects. His hard-on started coming up at the thought of crossing to the other room and seeing her in the hall on the way, and stayed up till he got back to his own room and cooled off after passing her in the hall the second time. Worse, he always thought he was sitting at her desk since he was sure he felt warm pulsations in the seat under him. (That was why he flunked penmanship and never got a Palmer Diploma, he figured. Actually it was because the Palmer people were handwriting analysts and could recognize and detest a nonconformist every time.)

Because of Betty Lou, when he crossed the hall, he carried his notebook in front of him and walked knock-kneed. (There may have been several other boys doing the same thing for the same reason, but he never noticed.)

In his own room there was another Betty, well-developed for her age, whose mother allowed her to wear makeup, silk stockings, and high heels, all of which kept that group of boys, Bennie included, in various states of tumescence. "Don't knock it," Buck said. "I don't know about you, but I do my best thinking with about a half hard-on."

Bennie's night fantasies were divided between Betty Lou, Betty, and movie actresses. One night while he alternately did to them whatever the hell it was you did while doing the real thing, he felt an unusually poignant sensation rising as he jacked away (right-handed, as usual). He became feverishly excited as a most excruciating sensation gradually possessed his body, spreading and overwhelming him. He creamed all over himself for the first time ever. He'd done it! He'd actually learned to "shoot!" He'd not only jacked as usual but jacked "off"! As quickly as he could get it hard again he tried to do it all over, but couldn't. He was drained.

He could never remember whether he'd "come" with his own true love, Betty Lou, with that hussy Betty, or with movie beauty Jean Harlow (whom, by coincidence, since Ma wasn't putting out again, Pa often fantasized about while he jacked off in the can). In any case, Bennie promptly figured out that sensation was why doing the real thing was so popular and wondered if girls got such sensations too. He wondered, as well, how he could approach either one of the Betties and bring up the subject of their letting him do the inconceivable to them. He concluded that he would get nowhere because Ma said that all girls thought it was dirty, just like she did.

Buck Doaks put in his oar just then and said, "We're going to have to be a little quieter about this business or you'll wake Ma up."

"Dynamite wouldn't wake Ma up."

"You came close to dynamite."

"Do you think I can find a girl that doesn't think it's dirty?"

"Not a chance."

"Why not?"

"Girls aren't honest."

"Why not?"

"Their mothers screw up their minds young."

"How?"

"With malarkey."

"Why?"

"Why does Ma try to make a saint out of you?"

"Ya, I guess mothers all suck . . . Say—does that "shooting" business always make you feel like your butt just fainted?"

"It gets worse."

"Good."

The next day at school Bennie looked at the two local targets of his "dirty, nasty" male mind with different eyes. Betty Lou, at least, knew he was lusting at her, because she was lusting back and recognized the look. As for the other Betty, she was usually too preoccupied lusting at herself to notice much of anything.

Bennie didn't know how Betty Lou felt and was too bashful even to ask her if he could walk home with her. Seduction was beyond him as yet. He thought you simply had to ask them. What words to use, except "Let's go somewhere and do it?" was a real puzzler. He was certain he was too bashful to be that blunt; in fact he was sure of it since he was too bashful to even say hello to her. He didn't realize that Betty Lou would have liked to cooperate, regardless of how he asked her; and she knew how, unlike him, even though she was in the dumb room. Nonetheless, if he'd had the guts to ask her right out, the "code" would have required her to bash him in the mouth. It would not have required her to kick herself in her delicate behind afterward, but that's what she'd have done. For his part, after she bashed him, he'd have turned scarlet, slunk away, and never looked at her again. (We should worry about wars with this sort of torture going on all over?)

She did a lot for him anyhow. Fantasizing about her fuzzy little bottom while he industriously fidgeted his dong kept him exhausted and almost out of trouble for nearly a year. Of course he broke out in pimples. They claimed you got pimples from jacking off; also that you went crazy, blind, and got hair in your palms. Closer to the truth, they claimed it was bad for your back and it may have been. That's when Bennie started to have back trouble. But, Jesus, the crime was worth the punishment.

Meanwhile, cosmic events conspired to move Uncle Bart along the path to fame. It related to something President Roosevelt observed:

"Wall Street hates me and I welcome their hatred."

> "Wall Street never changes."
> —*Pro Bono Publico*

Pa wouldn't have known the dog of "aggregate *demand*," the death of which caused the Great Depression, if it bit him. He wasn't alone. Neither did FDR until John Maynard Keynes, and others of similar economic views, worked on his case. When FDR figured it out, he came out even stronger for the working man. It took him too long, but he eventually learned that the little guy had to spend his paycheck as soon as he got it in order to survive, rather than buy art objects or yachts—that's where "aggregate demand" came from. FDR (and also that little fellow who might find a gun if he wasn't given a shovel) couldn't wait for manna to magically "trickle down" from the yacht set.

FDR had said, "I see one-third of a nation, ill-housed, ill-clad and ill-nourished. What this nation needs is a *New Deal*."

All Bennie knew about it was that he had often been hungry. He was never again hungry after Pa went to work for the W.P.A. and later General Motors. Ill-clothed and ill-housed, but not hungry.

The guts of the *New Deal* were the programs Colonel McCormick and his friends hated and derided. (The programs that they were totally unaware were keeping their skins from being converted into lamp shades.)

The programs were known as FDR's "alphabet programs" for their initials.

The N.R.A.,
P.W.A.,
W.P.A.,
C.C.C.,
A.A.A.,
T.V.A.,
N.Y.A.,
N.L.R.A., etc.

Those were the famous "alphabet" doodads that actually saved the "last best hope of earth" from a revolution that would have destroyed something precious.

Like big business and Wall Street, FDR preferred to save the country through the existing system, although they didn't give him credit for that. Unfortunately the "old" system was dying of constipation. The country couldn't wait for a coy prosperity to peep from where it allegedly lurked, "just around the corner." FDR damn well dragged it around. In doing so he changed the "old" system, kept what was good, tossed out what was bad, introduced new things and tried them, kept them if they worked, canned them if they didn't. America would never be the same.

Wall Street especially hated Roosevelt because of the S.E.C. That stood for the Securities and Exchange Commission. It was designed to eliminate the old evils that had triggered the market crash and ensuing Depression. The S.E.C. and the law on which it was based *torqued* Wall Street's jaws. What "excesses" were there to curb? Well, for example, there was Samuel Insull, head of the largest trust, who'd left thousands of stockholders goosing a ghost while he skipped to Europe to avoid a striped suit and bars. (He was eventually exonerated, but God knows how.) Investigation of another trust, Associated Gas and Electric Company, showed that by pyramiding a series of interlocking trusts schemers had been able to invest only $300,000 and control a billion dollars, in their own interest.

[FLASHBACK—1934, AT A CONGRESSIONAL HEARING]

"*You gentlemen are making a great mistake. The [Stock] Exchange is a perfect institution.*"

—*Richard C. Whitney*
President of the New York Stock Exchange
(Later jailed for embezzling securities.)

"Perfect" the Exchange may have been, but Richard obviously missed that boat.

Much was going on in Washington, D.C., in those days, where the groundwork of Uncle Bart's glory was being laid, which Bennie would observe at its height and which he would fully savor. It wasn't in the field of stocks and bonds, although Bart unaccountably saw eye to eye with Richard Whitney without owning bonds and stocks himself. Bart's glory had its underpinning in another alphabet agency, the N.L.R.B. (National Labor Relations Board), the executive agency created to enforce the terms of the National Labor Relations Act (known as the Wagner Act after the liberal New York senator who sponsored it and much of the other New Deal legislation).

The Wagner Act was one of the principal New Deal programs designed to jerk prosperity back around the corner. It gave the "forgotten man" (the little guy) a fair shot at more purchasing power by working through the system. Industry didn't see it that way. The provision that truly horrified them, and ushered in the Affluent Society over their fainting forms read:

"Employees shall have the right to organize and bargain collectively through representatives of their own choosing, and shall be free from interference, restraint or *coercion* of employers."

Great Heavens—would free enterprises coerce?

[FLASHBACK—JULY 1892, HOMESTEAD, PENNSYLVANIA]

The Carnegie Steel Corporation's hired guns, assisted by militia (in an action approved by the White House) shoot down striking workers.

That action's stench in the electorates' nostrils helped put a new president in the White House, yet set back the cause of organized labor (unions) by four decades. The four decades had just passed when FDR assumed office.

Later—too late—Andrew Carnegie, a "malefactor of great wealth," as President Theodore Roosevelt dubbed his kind, donated thousands of libraries to his fellow countrymen, no doubt with the Judgment Day in mind.

(Un*conventional Wisdom—the sonofabitch went to hell anyhow.*)

So much for industrial coercion of labor. The curtain came down on it when, in April 1937, the Supreme Court of the U.S. decided the Wagner Act was constitutional.

(*Conventional Wisdom—that particular Court would have decided against the act if FDR hadn't scared their principal ingredient out of them just about then by attempting to "pack the court" with new blood to inspirit "tired old men."*)

Even before then, organized labor under the leadership of the C.I.O. (which could be spelled "John L. Lewis," its organizing genius), had cowed General Motors and U.S. Steel in the winter of 1936 and 1937. The Wagner Act had got John L's foot in the door; the "tired old men" had simply cast holy water on a fait accompli.

Uncle Bart's Act was about to go on.
A new one, that is, not:

Bart, Bart
Let a fart,
Blew the baby
Out of the cart.

Up to that time, Bart's claims to fame had been letting Grandma's big cabin *up north* burn to the ground while he snoozed through the preliminaries when a bucket of water would have averted disaster. He had also installed a harness hook so low a mare backed into it, got hung up on her vulva, and panicked. She died in agony because Bart was too chicken-hearted to shoot her.

Nonetheless, Bart was a great hunter—yes, indeed. Pa told the story of Bart's repeated boasting of what a fabulous wing shot he was. Pa didn't see Bart make his first and only fabulous wing shot. By the time Pa turned around after the report of the shotgun, Bart had a bloody nose, two fatter lips, and loose teeth. It was obvious he hadn't known that you fired a gun with the butt held firmly to your shoulder, not directly in front of your face. Wow! Fabulous wing shooter!

"Bart-Bart, fame is about to come into the wings after you and drag you onto the stage of history."

Meanwhile, Bennie was discovering the "woods." (And, of course, conducting a fabulous, love life *single-handedly*—right hand to be exact.)

CHAPTER TWENTY

Now We Got the Sons of Bitches!

1936–1937. Labor unions declare war on General Motors and U.S. Steel.

> *General Motors "stands as a monument to the most colossal super-system of spies yet devised in any American corporation."*
> *—The La Follette Committee on Civil Liberties*

What the hell was that all about? Spies? In peacetime?

Let's hear it from Pro Bono: "Big guys had stolen something precious from little guys who were trying to get it back. The big guys desperately wanted to keep it."

"What?" Bennie asked.

"The right to earn a decent living decently. That's what *good* unions are all about."

All Bennie knew about that was that a union, the United Automobile Workers (U.A.W.), was trying to organize the local G.M. plant. He had no idea what organize meant in that case and didn't care. Whatever it was, Pa and Bart argued about it whenever they were together and both got hot under the collar.

> QUESTION: *Was the Great Depression inevitable after unrestrained greed sent aggregate demand down the tube?*

> *"Becher Ass!"*
> *—Buck Doaks*

> QUESTION: *Now, what was that the La Follette Committee said about super-spies?*

Who were we at war with, who was the
ENEMY?

Of the utmost importance to Bennie's livelihood, though he didn't know it then, was the identity of that enemy. Pa worked for him, reluctantly withal, but one has to eat.

The enemy was, if the truth were faced, General Motors, who had hired the spies in the first place. And who the hell did General Motors think they were? For one thing, in 1936 they were the biggest industrial corporation in the world. G.M. had tripled its net assets between 1933 and 1936 (when Colonel McCormick—remember him?—was planning to leave the country because the New Deal was going to be bad for him and his *friends*, such as G.M.). In the same period G.M.'s annual net profits had risen 3,000 percent to two hundred million dollars. Its rate of return on investment was 37.9 percent at a time when an interest rate above 8 percent was considered usury (i.e., the equivalent of highway robbery) in most places. Between January 1, 1934, and July 1, 1936, G.M. had spent around $1,000,000 on private detectives to spy on union organizers and dissatisfied workers. (It must have been quite a job, since everyone with any guts—which boiled down to everyone but Uncle Bart and his purblind kind—was dissatisfied with working for G.M.) A raise in pay amounting to 10 percent of G.M.'s net profit would have paid for decent food for all of the company's workers and their families, and gone a long way toward making satisfied workers. Also correcting the imbalance in aggregate demand.

Alfred P. Sloan, president of poor, "financially distressed" G.M., refused to talk to the United Automobile Workers union until they gave him a swift kick where it would do the most good: in his avarice. They struck Fisher Body Plants numbers one and two in Flint, Michigan, on December 30, 1936.

Why *those two plants*? They held all the key dies that permitted production to continue in all the other G.M. plants. This time workers didn't simply strike and walk around outside waving signs, like ninnies, waiting for militia to take pot shots at them; they sat down right on the job, right next to their machines and tools. The famous "sit-down" strike was born. In 1892, the militia, with the blessing of the White House, would have moved in and shot down the strikers. In December 1936, FDR, reelected by a landslide vote (a true public mandate) to which the unions had provided the then-unprecedented sum of six hundred thousand dollars in campaign funds, was looking the other way.

Pa, now a staunch member of the United Automobile Workers, went on strike with the rest of the Blackhawk Local. He was out of a job for all practical purposes. Living as they did from hand to mouth, they couldn't pay the rent and had damn little to eat again. It was January 1937—not only winter, and an especially cold one to boot, but *Economic Winter* all over again. Skinny O'Brien, their mummified landlady, tossed them out. Alfred P. Sloan, not quite next to God yet, probably would have sent her a medal if he'd heard about it.

Pa was spending his last quarter in the grocery store for a ring of baloney. Their few possessions were stacked on Skinny O'Brien's curb. Their own furniture was still in Waubonsee, so they didn't even have a bed, or chair, just a bunch of cardboard boxes and an old pair of suitcases, plus Pa's trunk. Ma was holding the fort in front of the house sitting on the trunk, staring off into the distance, trying to ignore passersby who were looking curiously at their spectacle. For lack of something to do, Bennie was making snowballs and tossing them at Skinny's trees.

That's when the cops showed up. The one who got out of the patrol car approached Ma, looking embarrassed.

"Is your husband around?" he asked. Since he knew who she was, it was pretty obvious who'd called the cops and filled them in on what to look for.

Ma looked at him dumbly, convinced that he'd come to take them to jail. She had no idea why she thought that, except that was what cops did.

"He didn't do anything," she said.

"We got a call that he was creating a disturbance here."

A light went on in Ma's brain. She glanced toward the house and caught Skinny just ducking her head out of sight behind the lace curtain.

"Who called?" Ma said.

"We're not allowed to impart that information." He sounded like the line was memorized, as it was, having come from cards provided to policemen to coach them on how to handle various situations. He didn't have a card to prepare him for what came next.

Ma said, "I know who called you." She motioned toward the window with her thumb. "That skinny old son of a bitch that just dodged her head back out of sight."

"Swearing at a police officer is against the law. I could run you in for disturbing the peace."

"I wasn't swearing at you. I was describing that skinny old son of a bitch in the house."

Bennie could see the other cop who was still in the car with the window down, where he heard it all shaking with laughter.

"She threw us out here. Russ promised to pay the back rent when he got back to work, but she wouldn't listen."

The cop already had the picture and sympathized with Ma. There were lots of other cases like theirs around town.

Just then Pa arrived on the scene, driven in a car by a woman Bennie had never seen before.

Pa got out and joined Ma and the cop, whereupon the other cop got out, as though he expected trouble.

"What's the matter?" Pa asked.

Ma didn't give the cop a chance to say anything. She said, "That son of a bitch Skinny O'Brien called the cops, as though we don't have trouble enough already."

Pa turned to the cop. "What's the charge?"

"Disturbing the peace, we were told."

Pa laughed. "That's rich. How?"

"She didn't say—I mean the complainant didn't say."

"I'll bet," Pa said. "Well, we're going to get our stuff out of here pretty soon. Can we, or are you going to run us in?"

Pa had already sold the Buick for ten dollars to pay rent, or they'd have had that to sit in out of the wind and to pack their belongings in.

The cop thought Pa's language sounded like someone that might have been "run in" before. He had a notion to do it. Just then the woman who'd driven Pa up in the car entered the discussion. She'd walked up behind the cop without his hearing her.

"I'm giving them a place to stay, Irv," she said quietly to the cop.

He spun around, startled. "Oh, hi, Nell. I didn't recognize your voice." His own voice was respectful now.

She said, "I heard Russ's story down at the grocery store. There's nothing wrong with these people that a little respect and a few weeks time won't clear up." Then Bennie's jaw dropped as he heard her say, "Now why don't you two get the hell out of here so I can take them home with me and give them a hot meal for starters."

Bennie was even more surprised when the cops meekly obeyed her suggestion. "O.K., Nell," the cop who'd done the talking said, and grinned.

That night they were installed in their new apartment. Pa explained how he'd met Mrs. Guenther down at the grocery. He was telling his troubles to Larry LaSage, to whom they'd been good customers till their luck ran out, when she'd horned in. She'd said, "I've got an empty place where you can stay." As Pa told them later, "She said that right out of a clear blue sky, and then she said, 'I got no use for G.M., any more than you do.'" It turned out her husband and sons were all on strike too. The difference was she was a big stick in local do-good organizations and had political clout.

Ma said to Pa, "It's enough to make you believe in God."

A few months later, after the finger of suspicion wasn't so apt to point their way, Ma, out on one of her "peculiar" nocturnal walks, threw a brick through the window from which Skinny had peeked to savor Ma's misery. Rather than run, Ma hung around to put another brick in Skinny's face in case she poked her head outside. She didn't. By the time the cops got there, Ma was back home.

Meanwhile, that staunch Republican, Uncle Bart (who had refused to let Aunt Nellie take in her brother and his family out of the cold), was dancing the G.M. tune. Bart, beguiled by the siren song of G.M., who followed the accepted historical union-busting precedent of manipulating gullible marionettes like Bart, was organizing a company union to combat the United Automobile Workers (U.A.W.), while down in Virginia, Thomas Jefferson was turning over in his grave. Bart's union was called the Loyal General Motors Alliance and he was elected its president.

> *"Ain't that enough to gag a maggot?"*
>
> *—Buck Doaks*

Company unions were one of the oldest weapons of "economic royalists." If workers didn't join, when the dust settled after the "agitators" were shot down again, those that survived the hot lead, were out of a job anyhow.

A peculiar thing happened this time. God visited Alfred P. Sloan. As is customary, His hand appeared indirectly. G.M. production, due to lack of those key dies on which the sit-down strikers were keeping "eternal vigil," fell from a rate of fifty thousand cars a month when the strike started in December, to one hundred and twenty-five per month the first week of February. Sloan condescended to arbitrate with the U.A.W. (What the old A.F.L. union had failed to accomplish in a half century, the parent of the U.A.W., the Congress of Industrial Organizations, C.I.O., had done in five weeks.) Sloan hauled down the Jolly Roger. John L. Lewis, head of the C.I.O. became an insta-hero. In the same five weeks, without even striking, the C.I.O. knocked off U.S. Steel, corporate heir of the Carnegie Steel Company that had shot down the strikers at Homestead, Pennsylvania, in 1892. U.S. Steel was capable of drawing an inference, like a crow that sees the dead carcass of another hung on a fence.

It was a truly amazing "great-religious-revival," with all those "brand new" minions of God volunteering to arbitrate with the lowly laboring class. As a result of their philanthropies, wages rose, hours dropped, the right of unions to collectively bargain for "wage slaves" was recognized. The five-day week and eight-hour day adopted for civil service years before, became almost universal.

SOME WAGE SLAVES SPEAK:

John L. Lewis is sick in bed when G.M.'s Sloan gets next to God and arbitrates. Lewis is visited by a delegation of grateful workers. One says in broken English: "Mr. Lewis, my heart is glad, the hearts of one hundred thousand are glad for the Union. Now we got the sons of bitches!" (It's the kind of language Lewis understands and appreciates.)

A trifle later, a former anti-union man who has seen the light says: "We are now treated as human beings, and not as part of the machinery. United we stand, divided (or alone) we fall."

Uncle Bart did not see the light, though he benefited like everyone else from higher pay and shorter hours.

By the end of August 1937, the C.I.O. had 3,419,000 members, 32 member unions, and 510 local unions. The Loyal G.M. Alliance at Blackhawk, once one thousand strong, had one surviving "loyal" member: Uncle Bart. G.M. created a special position for him—since the union had also forced a "closed shop" agreement on them, which meant that no one could work unless they were a union member.

Management, of course, was excepted, but G.M. didn't see Bart as management timber, especially as a foreman over men who now hated his guts. G.M. made Bart a department of one—he was the sole employee and his own foreman. (Who says that companies aren't loyal—especially when they'll look like even bigger assholes if they don't go through the required motions.)

The U.A.W. made a special missionary drive just on Bart's behalf, trying to convert him to the new godly views of Alfred P. Sloan, but failed. The drive culminated on one of the downtown bridges over the Rock River, which Bart always drove across on his way home from work. Some would suggest that the confrontation with an irate mob was not spontaneous. In fact, signs that had taken some time and thought to make appeared at the scene, reading:

> *A vote for Hoover and Bart Hawverty,*
> *Is a vote for perpetual poverty.*

The Hoover, of course, was "*Hoobert Heever*" (as an embarrassed radio announcer had accidentally pronounced his name at his first inaugural). *Heever* was in disgrace these days as the ex-president whose policy it was to tear-gas poverty-stricken veterans of World War I—"the war to end all wars"—when they'd shown up in Washington, D.C., pleading for bonuses that had been promised to them.

On the occasion when Bart's fame was finally secured, Bennie was wandering around on his way home from school, as he often did, and was attracted by the crowd. A mob of perhaps five hundred had congregated around Bart's car. He was inside with the doors locked. That, obviously, had been anticipated, since someone produced a sledge hammer and broke the window behind which Bart cowered. He somehow squirmed his ample form into the back seat, but was soon hauled out, white-faced and speechless. Several men roughed him up.

Bart had just become "management," so the time was actually past for asking him to join the union, but the mob wasn't in a mood to niggle over that.

"How come you drive a Nash if you're loyal to G.M.?" someone yelled, as much for the sake of the crowd as for Bart.

Someone else yelled, "We don't want you lookin' like a hypocrite!"

By then a few cops had arrived but recognized a good time to keep their distance. Fifty-to-one odds didn't suit them. Bennie noticed a couple of them grinning.

"We're doing this for your own good, Hawverty!" A loud voice assured him. (It was beginning to sound as though someone had written a script for the preliminaries.)

About two dozen strong men grabbed hold of the Nash, edged it up on the bridge railing and pushed it over into the Rock River.

A burly fellow shook his fist in Bart's face. "You're lucky we're not dumping you in with your car, you goddam scab sonofabitch!"

He spun Bart around and kicked his ass, to a chorus of laughing and jeering. Then the crowd jostled him through its ranks and pushed him out on his way home. Once free, Bart started to run, tripped and fell, struggled up and rapidly walked toward home, his knock knees wobbling, looking back occasionally and rubbing his fat ass. Only God and maybe Aunt Nellie knew the condition of his underwear when he got home, but Bennie had seen a large wet spot down one of his pant's legs as Bart departed the scene.

By then Pa was back to work at much higher pay and shorter hours. No more half days of work on Saturday.

Their new home was bigger, on the ground floor of a large Victorian house set among tall oak trees. Behind it, the whole barn was theirs. So was the full basement. There were three rental apartments on the second floor, which was its only drawback.

Routine returned to their lives. Bennie resumed his campaign to get a B.B. gun and finally won.

"He'll end up in jail," Ma predicted to Pa, who ignored her.

One night at supper Bennie brought up another thing that had been on his mind. "What do you suppose ever happened to Uncle Newt?" he asked Pa.

He had been deeply disappointed that they hadn't heard or seen a thing of him after that first letter. Bennie was sure there would have been a lot of excitement in having a genuine pioneer and G.A.R. vet living with them.

"Maybe he died," Pa said.

Ma didn't say, "I hope so," but the satisfied expression on her face said it for her.

"I sure hope not," Bennie said.

"Don't talk with your mouth full," Ma snapped around a mouthful, almost spitting some out.

CHAPTER TWENTY-ONE

Echoes from the Past

— Thanksgiving 1937

Pa and Bennie were playing checkers in the living room. Ma was in the kitchen banging pots around, getting dinner ready. Pa sat in his overstuffed chair and Bennie on a kitchen chair, with a checkerboard on another kitchen chair between them. They often played checkers on Pa's days off, sometimes at the kitchen table, which just then would have been a risky business with Ma in full swing in her domain.

Pa's chair was their first real luxury, part of a living-room set from Sears, bought for a few bucks down and a few per month for a long while. The sofa was across the room beyond the bay window. Bennie loved that bay window. Framing it on both sides and the top was another window made of beveled glass pieces, some colored, all leaded together in intricate patterns. The bevels refracted sunlight and threw rainbow-hued beams into the room on sunny mornings. They were the first thing he saw when awakening, since he slept on Sister's old day bed at the other end of the long room. Across from his bed was a fireplace, which they never used, much to his regret. (Firewood cost too much.)

The first snow of the season was filtering down softly through bare oak branches. Scattered flakes lightly dusted the autumn-brown lawn and chased each other around the street in occasional swirling gusts of wind. Earlier Pa had checked the thermometer on the porch, and quickly shut the door to the unheated vestibule behind him as he came back in. "Boo! Woo!" He blew the words through his lips. "It's cold out there. Probably go down to zero tonight." It was plenty warm inside though. Pa tended the furnace for the whole house, and this landlady wasn't stingy about coal.

The rich smell of cooking turkey wafted in. Ma was in a good mood, as she usually was when a lot of delicious food was a prospect. She came to watch them occasionally, wiping her hands on her apron and once even asked, "Who's winning?" Not that she really cared. Now she said, "This is the first turkey I've cooked in twenty years. I hope I haven't forgot how."

Pa said, "We'll eat her anyhow. It can't be any worse than Mary's."

Ma made a face. She knew perfectly well that she could cook a turkey. Then she said, "You shouldn't have got such a big turkey. There's enough for two families. We'll be eating leftovers for a week."

"Good."

Pa made a careless move on the checkerboard because she distracted him. Bennie made him jump one piece and lose two and got himself a king in the bargain.

"Oh, shoot!" Pa said.

None of them heard the taxi pull up or someone come into the vestibule, and if they had, they'd have thought it was one of the people who lived upstairs, since the stairs went up to the three other apartments through a common front entrance. The sudden loud knock on their door startled them all. Ma went over and opened the door.

"We don't want any!" she snapped and slammed the door shut. To Pa she said, "Russ, there's a *morone* out there."

Ma pronounced "moron" as though it were spelled "more-roan", and to her a moron meant one thing: a sex offender, an idea she got since the sensational tabloid stories she and Aunt Mary devoured always stated that rapists were "morons" (or worse yet, "beetle-browed morons"). Anyone Ma viewed as the least bit peculiar or suspicious became a potential sex-offender and therefore a *morone*.

Pa got up. "Let me see about this," he said.

"Don't open that door!" Ma cautioned in a rising, quavering voice.

He ignored her and pulled the door open. He studied whoever was there a second, then pulled the door open wide.

Bennie couldn't see who was there, but whoever it was said, "Is that you, Ed?" Bennie thought someone must have the wrong place, since he'd never heard Pa called Ed before.

Pa boomed, "Well, I'll be go to hell! Uncle Newt, you old son of a gun! C'm'on in!"

Bennie caught the look on Ma's face, a half-surprised grimace of displeasure. Bennie wasn't ready for what he saw either. A man who towered over Pa's five-eleven, whiskers like Santa Claus, wearing a long white fur coat and a wide-brimmed, undented black hat like the photographs Bennie'd seen of Navajo Indians that made him look even taller than he was.

Newt pumped Pa's hand, then grabbed him and hugged him. "You're the first family I've seen since I was in Riverview in 1909," Newt said. He looked around, ignored Ma, and speared Bennie with his almost transparent blue eyes. "Who's this, Ed?" He asked Pa, pointing. "Yours?" Notably, he didn't say, "Yours and Emma's."

"Yep. C'm'ere, Bennie and shake hands with Uncle Newt."

Bennie's hand disappeared into Uncle Newt's grizzly-bear paw. He expected to get a bone-crusher like he always did from Uncle Bart, but Uncle Newt didn't have an ounce of bully in him.

"This is Bennie," Pa said.

"Howdy, Bennie." He didn't patronize him like most older folks, with: "How old are you? What grade are you in? You're sure big for your age." (Bennie was that.)

"Hi, Uncle Newt," he managed to say. He was feeling bashful with this strange-looking individual, but he couldn't stifle what he knew might be an impolite question. "What's that coat made of?"

"Polar bear. Shot it myself years ago when I was up at Nome. I got another skin like it in my things—we can have you a coat made just like it."

For once Ma didn't say anything.

Bennie said, "I think I'd like one." He could imagine himself coming to school in that—and the reaction of the other kids, especially Betty Lou.

Then Newt pretended to notice Ma for the first time. "Hello, Emma. That is you isn't it?" The implication may have been that he thought Pa was crazy for having stayed with her. For the first time he removed his hat.

Ma said, "Hello," but didn't smile or offer her hand and certainly not her cheek to be kissed, even though Newt was blood kin to Pa.

Pa looked a little irritated for a second, then said, "Peel off that coat and come sit down. How about some coffee?"

"Fine." Newt was too cautious to ask for what he'd really have liked till he felt out the ground. Besides he had a flat pint bottle in his overcoat for emergencies. He slipped out of the big, heavy coat as spry as a young man and carefully laid it on the couch, mindful of its precious contents. He sat down beside it and said, "I reckon we got a lot of jawin' to do to catch up."

Pa was beaming. Bennie had never seen him look so happy. He himself felt strange, as though he was on the brink of a great adventure, or had just found a fortune. Newt's presence dominated the room.

"I'll get the coffee," Pa volunteered, since Ma stood rooted in the middle of the room. "How do you take it?"

"Everything the law allows, when I'm around civilization." Bennie didn't miss that; the implication that a lot of the time he wasn't.

Ma left with Pa. In the kitchen she said, "We don't have enough to feed him too."

Pa said, "Don't give me that stuff. You just said we had enough for two families." It was as rough as he ever talked to her, and she recognized his "that's-the-end-of-it" tone, and sighed. It came out almost a groan.

"Are you going to ask the big lout to stay?"

Pa gave her a look that would have shut Bennie up for a week. "Just as long as he damn well pleases. I owe him plenty, and besides he's family. He might be on the down and out. He'll be good for Bennie."

"You keep him away from Bennie!"

"I'll do no such thing—and neither will you."

Ma gave him her dirtiest look. "If you think I'm forgetting what he tried to do, you got another think coming."

"I didn't imagine you would. Nonetheless, don't forget what I just said."

In the living room Bennie and Newt were eyeing each other. Newt grinned. "Ain't used to seein' freaks like me very much, eh?"

Bennie laughed. "I wasn't thinkin' that."

"Wouldn't blame you if you did. I ain't gonna ask you if you'd like a gold nugget." He was reaching in his vest pocket. "Any damn fool in his right mind would." He produced a yellow object as big as a marble and handed it over. Bennie was amazed at how heavy it was. Newt said, "Don't lose that son of a bitch. It must be worth fifty bucks."

Bennie hefted it and looked it over closely, then shoved it into his pocket. "I'll have to keep it hid or Ma'll take it away from me."

Bennie would have fainted if he knew what Newt was thinking, which was, "Up Ma's ass with a wire brush." What he said was, "O.K. Don't let her see it. You got someplace where you hide stuff from her, I expect."

Bennie nodded. "Out in the barn." He was still gripping the nugget in his pocket and checked with a finger to see that the pocket didn't have a hole in it.

"You got a gun?" Newt asked.

"A B.B. gun—I got my first one last summer."

Newt snorted. "A man needs something that'll kill somebody if need be. You'd do better with a bow and arrow."

"I got one of those too. Made it myself."

"Think it'll kill a man?"

"I doubt it."

"I'll show you how to make one that will."

Bennie thought, "Great! Having Uncle Newt around is going to be the neatest thing that's ever happened to me."

Pa came back with the coffee and put it on an end table.

"I'll have to use the crapper first," Newt said.

Pa showed him the way. In a little while it sounded like an artillery duel was going on in there. Bennie didn't know what the noise was at first because it was so loud. Then Pa laughed and Bennie joined him.

Ma bustled in wiping her hands on her apron. "Hear that?" she said, with indignation plain on her face.

Pa snorted. "I'd be *deef* if I didn't." (He always pronounced "deaf" that way.)

"I told you he was a lout."

"Matter of opinion. He's been away from civilization so long he doesn't think about manners probably."

"He's not staying here."

"He's staying as long as he wants. He was more a father to me when I needed one than Pa was. He can stay till he dies, as far as I'm concerned."

Ma thought of saying, "No wonder you're like you are if he raised you," but managed to hold her tongue. She stalked out.

Pa suspected Newt had turned up the volume in the toilet as much as he could just to irritate Ma. When the old boy came back, he showed no indication of embarrassment, but there was a half-smile buried under his beard that was mirrored in his eyes. He grabbed his coffee and swigged down about half of it in one swallow, took out his bottle and filled the cup back up, then before he put it away, asked Pa, "You want a snort?"

"I've sworn off," Pa said.

"Suit yourself."

At dinner Uncle Newt was a model of good manners because he knew Ma expected just the opposite; nonetheless, he didn't stifle a wolfish appetite that helped assure there wouldn't be "leftovers for a week," as Ma had feared. The old boy did put his elbows on the table occasionally. Bennie figured it might be something in the blood, since he looked just like his brother Roy always did with his elbows on the table, always forgetting that Ma would chew him out for it and maybe crack him one side the head.

After dinner Newt fished out a couple of expensive, fat cigars from an inside vest pocket. He and Pa got lit up and had a second cup of coffee. Ma bustled around cleaning off the other dishes and trying to get in their way as much as possible.

Since she was sure Bennie wanted to listen to the men talking, she said, "Young man, you get out of here, you're just in the way."

Before he could get out an "Aw, Ma," Newt said, "Let's all us men clear out so Emma can clean up."

That reversed the tables, since Ma didn't want to miss anything they might say, especially about the years before she met Pa.

"You two men don't have to leave," Ma protested. "Besides I like the smell of cigars." (Everyone did, or at least pretended to for decades after King Edward VII of England had made cigar smoking ultra-fashionable.)

"O.K.," Pa said. "I think I'll have another piece of that mince pie. I notice you baked two of 'em; and some for Bennie too."

Ma made a face but was turned to the sink where no one could see it. "Fix it yourself," she said. "I'm too busy."

"Why don't you have some too, Em?" He suggested. He knew she'd love that; she was well on her way to getting fat.

That mollified Ma. This way she wouldn't have to wait till later and sneak out and quickly wolf down a second piece of pie on the sly. She said, "All right. And I'll fix us all another cup of coffee, but I have to make a new pot first, so why don't you wait on pie till then?"

Pa looked at Newt. "Suits me," Newt said.

Pa said, "I'll make the coffee." He knew Ma would make it too weak in order to be saving.

While he was making the coffee, Pa said, "I think we'll put you up in Bennie's bed tonight—the couch is too short. He can sleep on the couch."

"No shorter'n the bunks on that tub we went to Skagway on in '97," Newt said, referring to their first trip to Alaska. "But you ain't gonna have to put me up. I wasn't sure how you'd be fixed, so I got a room at that little flophouse down across from the depot. Got my bags already in a room down there."

"How'd you find our new place?" Pa asked.

"Phoned your sister, Nellie. She wanted to put me up there. I'll have to go over and see them pretty soon for sure."

"I was sure wishin' you'd stay with us," Bennie put in.

That got him a shut-your-big-mouth look from Ma. Pa, who had no idea whether Newt was close to broke or not said, "We'll bring your things up here tomorrow."

Ma quickly turned away to the sink to get a glare out of her system.

"Oh, boy!" Bennie said.

Newt pretended not to notice any of Ma's shenanigans, but he'd taken her measure almost thirty years before.

"The kid here'll pump you for Alaska stories," Pa warned.

"Nothin' wrong with that. I got a bunch of 'em—some I ain't even made up yet, and I'm gettin' old and gabby, so it'll work out first rate."

"Tell us one now," Bennie urged.

"Wait'll I finish my pie and coffee."

Bennie could hardly finish his. He'd read all of Robert Service's Yukon poems like "Sam McGee" and "Dangerous Dan McGrew," novels by Rex Beach, and the short stories of Hendrix about that country, all in *Western Story Magazine*, which was the best of the bunch. Those writers had really been there too, like Pa and Newt. For some reason Pa didn't like to tell Alaska stories though. Bennie always wondered if something bad happened there that Pa didn't want to remember. Bennie hoped Pa and Newt would get each other talking about Alaska.

Newt fired up his cigar again, shoved back his chair and said, "Well, just before I left I had to get in to Anchorage and catch the boat. I was only out a hundred mile or so across the Susitna Flats, so I allowed myself a half-day, 'cause I ain't as fast as I used to be."

Pa kept a straight face, and Newt looked as sincere as a proselytizing minister saving the soul of a pretty girl.

"As it turned out I overslept and it was about 8 A.M. when I rolled out, so I hitched up my trusty team of mukluks as quick as I could and mushed in across the williwaw straight as an arrow. The last mile or so I could hear the boat whistlin' to pull out. I thought, 'Here I ain't even gonna have time to say goodbye to my friends, especially the three widows I aimed to kiss goodbye.'" He watched Ma's face when he said that and was surprised to see her grinning. She'd been a kid around Old Jim Tynan and knew the earmarks of a *Big Windy*.

"Wait a minute," Pa said. "How'd you know they were widows? No gal ever stayed single up there for over twenty-four hours or so."

"As it happened, a bush pilot buzzed me on my way in and dropped a note tied to a wrench to let me know about them widows, him bein' a noted philanthropist. He'd just come from the funeral."

"Funeral?" Bennie asked. "Did they bury all three guys at once?"

"Not exactly. The pilot overslept like I did and only made it to the last one, but he heard about the other two, of course."

"Did you finally get there in time to catch the boat?"

"I sure did. It froze in. Probably still there. I spent two weeks kissin' them widows goodbye and havin' the boys see me off. *Timbered* every waterin' hole in town—some three or four times."

Bennie had no idea what "timbered" meant and wasn't about to stop a good story to find out; later he learned it was the sourdough custom of coming into a "joint" and yelling "Timber!" to signify that he was buying drinks for the house. (It was just as well that Bennie didn't recall, although he'd read of it, that mukluks weren't sled dogs but Eskimo fur-lined leather boots, and a williwaw was an arctic wind, not a piece of geography. Newt had slipped in those lies up front since frontier protocol for "*Big Windies*" demanded that they contain a clue early on that they were a put on, at least for anyone savvy.)

"How'd you get here then, if you missed the boat?" Bennie asked.

"Took the train over to Whittier and caught another one."

"You're pulling my leg," Bennie said. "There's no railroad in Alaska."

"Naw, I ain't. They put one in for them tenderfoot farmers they brought up there." (Actually, it had been there since the 1920s, but Newt didn't like tenderfeet and didn't miss a chance to get a dig in about them.)

"What'd you do with your trusty team of mukluks?" Pa slyly asked.

"Oh—them. I give 'em to them widows."

"Weren't they scared of half-wolf dogs?" Bennie asked.

"What gave you the idea they was part wolf?"

"I guess I read somewhere that most sled dogs were."

"Well, mine wasn't. I had two poodles, a Pekinese, a Chihuahua, one that was a cross between a billy goat and a Saint Bernard and the rest was pure blood Pomeranians."

Bennie finally caught on and laughed. "You been pullin' my leg. A Chihuahua is a little Mexican dog that looks like a skinned rabbit. You been kiddin' me. Was any of the rest of that true about you gettin' to Anchorage and all?"

"Would I kid you, a blood relative?" Newt asked.

Quoting laconic Gary Cooper, his favorite Western movie actor just then, Bennie gave a perfect imitation of his spare dialogue and said, "Yup," which got a laugh out of everyone.

A little later Pa got Newt alone for a minute and asked, "You know what they run in that hotel you put up at?"

"I can spot one a mile away."

"You can really pick 'em. It's the only one in town as far as I know. They always keep three gals there, sometimes good lookers."

"How does it come you know so much about it, Ed?"

"The young bucks down at the plant talk a lot," Pa told him, managing to keep an absolutely straight face.

"Do tell? It looked downright interestin'. I may have to stay there from now on."

"Save your money. We got an apartment empty upstairs if you can afford your own place. How're you fixed?"

"I can coast awhile, I guess."

"You're welcome here."

"Naw. Emma'd have a fit, and I'd rather have my own digs anyhow. I can get by. I'll look at that place upstairs tomorrow."

"You'll like it," Pa said. "The other two places up there are rented by a couple of chickens."

"Young good-lookers, I hope."

"Not too bad and not old."

"Hookers?"

"I don't think so. Not pros anyhow. They both got jobs somewhere."

"You tried either one out yet?"

"One night I got both of 'em—in my dreams, that is."

Newt laughed.

Bennie came in on the tail end of the conversation and got a rough idea of the drift. "I sure hope you do move in upstairs," Bennie said, just as Ma came in after finishing the dishes.

"Who's movin' in upstairs?" she asked, afraid to hear the answer.

"Uncle Newt," Bennie said, and this time got a "big-mouth" look from Pa.

"I ain't decided anything yet," Newt said. "I ain't even looked the place over yet."

"They're a noisy crowd up there. You'd never get any sleep," Ma said.

Newt grinned. "I don't need much sleep at my age. It kinda struck me as a good idea to move somewhere close because the kid here can prob'ly use a good Christian example." Then he guffawed.

"My foot!" Ma said. But even she laughed.

She'd have died before admitting it, but the prospect of having a "*morone*" of her own was exciting. Besides, Newt reminded her a lot of Old Jim Tynan who'd wanted to hang her father.

CHAPTER TWENTY-TWO

Stay Away from that Reprobate!

— THANKSGIVING TO CHRISTMAS, 1937

Bennie and Uncle Newt had a surprise for Ma.

Uncle Newt shaved off his beard the day he moved in upstairs. Bennie sat on the edge of the bathtub and watched him trimming it with a scissors first.

Newt said, "Gotta mow it down first with shears so it's short enough to lather up and razor off."

Bennie'd never known anyone with a beard and wasn't sure he approved, uneasy about the possibility that the family might lose stature in some unforeseen way as a result.

"How come you're shaving it off?" he asked.

"There's gals livin' up here." Newt had looked them over and approved of what he saw. "Beards scare off young gals."

"How about those widows in Alaska?"

"That's not the same. Got a different breed of gal up there. Used to beards. Used to lots of stuff."

Up till then Bennie hadn't paid much attention to grown women, leaving out movie stars, except once when he'd sat next to one of his younger aunts in a crowded back seat of a car going to a picnic and got a hard-on from contact with her warm, resilient leg. He figured women didn't notice boys and sure wouldn't be apt to do anything with him like Betty Lou might if he just knew how to ask her. Newt's remark prompted Bennie to wonder what the "lots of stuff was" that women in Alaska were used to, but he was afraid to ask. It did start him seriously thinking about older women for the first time, though.

Newt shaved off everything but a sweeping mustache. He combed that out carefully and shaped it, then turned full face to Bennie.

"Waddaya think, kid?"

"You look like a pirate."

"The hell you say. Not like Ronald Coleman, huh?" Bennie noticed that the old man's voice sounded just like Pa's when he said, "The hell you say." It was a remark Pa often used.

Bennie wasn't sure whether Uncle Newt was serious or not about looking like the famous movie idol Ronald Coleman. But he was sure the old boy didn't look his age, which had to be well up into his eighties at least. Bennie figured Newt was what Ma would have called "well preserved." Then it came to him who Newt, with his brigandish nose and massive cleft chin, resembled.

He said, "You look like the picture of La Salle in one of my books."

"La Salle?"

"Yeah, the explorer."

Newt eyed him sharply. "La Salle, eh?"

"Except his hair was black."

Newt turned and examined himself in the mirror, twisting his head to several angles. Finally he said, "I guess La Salle'll have to do. He must have been a handsome son of a bitch. My hometown's named for him, by the way. He spent a winter near there with the Illinois Injuns."

The next day Ma instructed Bennie, "Don't go up there and bother Uncle Newt. He'll be busy unpacking."

What she really meant was, "Stay away from that old reprobate." She had a hunch Newt might corrupt an adolescent. She'd have been hard put to make a logical case for that since she so often called Bennie a "degenerate."

Bennie protested, "He asked me to come up and help him unpack, so why shouldn't I go?"

Ma instantly assumed her nasty look, eyes turning black, glaring.

"You won't go up there because I told you not to, and that's all there is to it!" She said in what Bennie thought of as her "shitty" voice.

He steamed inside, but merely shrugged, went and got into old clothes and headed out the back door.

"Where do you think you're going?" Ma demanded.

"Out to play." He paused a beat while she looked at him from the sink; if she started his way to grab him he planned to run for it.

She didn't say anything, and he continued out the door, feeling her gaze on him through the window as he went to the barn. He ran through it and out the back door over to the next street. He doubted Ma knew the barn had a back door; he'd never seen her enter the building, or even look inside.

He circled the block slowly, giving Ma time to forget about him. Ten minutes later he darted toward their front porch at an angle so Ma couldn't see him even from the bay window. Praying she wouldn't pop out about then to get the evening paper, he scrambled over the porch rail, crossed to the door, slipped into the entry, and took the stairs two at a time as quietly as he could.

"C'm'on in," Newt bellowed in response to his light tap, so loudly Bennie cringed for fear Ma would hear. He whipped through the door and quickly closed it behind him before she could rush out in the hall, look up the stairs and see him.

"What the hell's after you?" Newt asked.

"Ma told me I couldn't come up here. If she heard you yell, 'Come in,' she's apt to come up and see if it was me at the door."

"The hell with yer Ma. If she comes up, I won't answer the door. Bolt the damn thing."

A truck had delivered Newt's steamer trunks and lots of wood boxes and cardboard cartons tied up tightly with clothesline. All were stacked in the middle of the big parlor of his apartment, a room that had once been the master bedchamber of someone's mansion.

Newt said, "I been waitin' on you to really dig into this stuff. I did unpack one little thing." He pointed to a polar bear robe that completely covered the long couch by the front window. "Unpacked that and had a little snooze on it already. Nothin' like a bear robe to nap on in cold weather unless it's a buffalo robe, and there ain't many of them around anymore. I toted one of 'em around for years till some bastard stole it. Hair was beginnin' to fall out of it anyhow." He paused and looked around.

"First things first—we'll dig in here," he said, grabbing one of his steamer trunks and standing it on end. He unlocked it and hinged the two sides open like a clam. Bennie had never seen how a steamer trunk worked. It had drawers like a dresser on one side and a hanging rack for clothes on the other. Newt fished around behind the hanging clothes and drew out a long object wrapped in a pair of underwear.

"Guess what's in here," he said.

"A rifle."

"You win the gold watch."

It was a lever-action Winchester like Pa's .40-60, but without the usual dark bluing. The barrel was case-hardened, a mottled blue and gold with indescribable mixtures in between. The gleaming, oiled stock and forearm were Circassian walnut, with striated burls of rich, deep brown ranging to almost ivory yellow; the whole thing bespoke art as much as lethal power.

"I shot them polar bears with this baby—the one I had the coat made of and that one on the couch. Years ago up near Nome." He hefted the rifle once, threw it to his shoulder with surprising speed, aimed briefly then quickly dropped it to a military "port arms" position, presenting it to Bennie. "Try it."

It wasn't as heavy as Bennie expected and fit up to his shoulder naturally, perfectly balanced, where the .40-60 was barrel-heavy.

"Wow!" he said.

"One-of-a-Thousand, Winchester calls 'em. Teddy Roosevelt never used anything else."

Bennie gripped it, not wanting to turn loose, as though it had grown to him. He imagined himself with that out at Three-Mile Creek.

"A .45-90," Newt said. "Stop anything that walks."

"Wow!" Bennie said again.

"It's yours."

"Mine?" His voice broke.

Newt eyed him severely. "There's a string attached. You gotta promise first to use it the way I show you."

"I'll do whatever you say."

"*We'll sure as hell do that.*" The voice was Buck's.

Newt said, "*Hello, Buck, you dirty-mouthed little bastard.*"

Bennie's eyes widened and his mouth dropped open. "You can hear Buck?"

"Sure can. Can hear him, see him, and sometimes smell him. I grew up with the little son of a bitch."

"*Aw,*" Buck said, "*I ain't so little.*"

The three got their heads together to work out a little Christmas strategy for getting around Ma.

Ma pretended not to be "big" on Christmas, partly because her whole life had taught her that if she enjoyed something, it would be spoiled or taken away. She remembered all too well how Christmas was *out home* when she was little. Usually her father managed to catch everyone in a whipping offense, and if they were being unnaturally good, maneuver them into one, so he could beat them before they got their present, giving them an advance opportunity to atone for enjoying something. He was weird enough to consider suffering a bonus Christmas present. On top of that, presents always had to be practical; never a doll or ice skates, but shoes, stocking caps, and mittens and even underwear.

She remembered the year she went home for Christmas right after Sister was born. By then her wild brother, Johnny, was seven. About October he found out where his Christmas shoes were hidden in the hayloft and started wearing them whenever Country Grandpa went to town. By Christmas they were pretty well worn. Of course he was found out when they wrapped presents on Christmas Eve, after the kids were asleep. Country Grandpa put his razor strop in the shoebox. When Johnny opened the box the next morning and wonderingly pulled out the razor strop, his father grabbed them both and whaled Johnny with the strop. Every time he brought it down he yelled, "How do you like this Christmas present, boy? And this one? And this one?"

They all felt sorry for Johnny even though he deserved what he got.

Bennie once heard Johnny brag, "I was the first one to finally whip Pa. I was only fifteen but big for my age like you. I was really scared at first, but—hell—it was easy."

Rob, eight years older than Johnny, should have done it long before then, but he was too gentle; and maybe the only one of the bunch who genuinely loved Country Grandpa.

When Bennie told Ma what Johnny said about whipping their father, she added a little embellishment: "Every time Johnny cracked Pa in the mouth and knocked him down, he yelled, 'How do you like this Christmas present, old man?' And when he tried to get up, knocked him down again and asked, 'And this one?'"

Country Grandma had told Ma about it, since she saw the whole thing and never lifted a hand or yelled at Johnny to stop. Ma said, "You could tell she loved to see it happen to Pa at last, since she laughed even when she told me. We were all tickled to hear Pa finally got his from one of us kids. He let Ma alone after the neighbors almost hung him, but still beat up all the kids till Johnny thrashed him."

Memories about Christmases "out home" came back to haunt Ma every year, and, like Scrooge, she would resolve to reform and not be so much like her father but was never able to manage it.

She actually looked happy when they all gathered around the tree that Newt had bought and decorated—electric lights and all. It was in front of the bay window. Another turkey was already cooking, just beginning to waft its savory aroma through the house.

Bennie and Newt had a surprise for Ma. The night before, Newt had brought down a bunch of packages and put them under the tree. There were three for Ma, three for Bennie, and two for Pa. Before then, if they could afford anything, the family had simply traded one present apiece, and naturally not anything expensive.

Ma was strong for eyeballing packages, and, if she thought she could get away with it, also hefting, pushing, punching, poking, and rattling, just like a kid, though she would never have admitted that she loved Christmas. That would be sure to activate the evil genie that would spoil it all.

After Newt went upstairs to bed, Ma said to Pa, "That's a lot of packages. We didn't get Newt much. Do you suppose they're expensive?"

"I don't know. But he knows we can't afford to get a lot. Besides, he's the kind that really believes it's the spirit that counts."

Ma looked doubtful. If she'd let out what was on her mind, she'd have said, "He can't have much money. Suppose he blows it all like a spendthrift and ends up sponging off us for the rest of his days?" Instead, mindful of how Pa felt, she said, "Do you suppose he can afford it?"

"I dunno," Pa said. "But he doesn't look soft in the head to me. I expect he knows what he can afford."

"I hope so."

Bennie chimed in, "Maybe he's got a gold mine in Alaska."

Ma gave him a pained look. Gold mines were beyond her imagination. People you knew didn't own gold mines. She'd have been more ready to believe that Newt had robbed a bank. Pa would have believed either.

The next morning Newt insisted on ladies-first in package opening.

"You go ahead, Emma," he urged. "Then Bennie and Ed; I'll go last. That's the way we did it at home when I was little—that way we all 'ooh-ed and ah-ed' over what everyone else got and had twice as much fun."

Ma gingerly picked up her biggest package first, holding it as though it were hot, then put it on her lap and looked at it. Bennie thought she looked just like a little girl for a moment. Finally she carefully took off the ribbon so it could be reused, then removed the wrapping. She opened the box like she was afraid to look inside, lifting just one corner. Bennie could see that whatever was inside was pink. Ma finally took the lid off.

"Take it out," Pa urged.

As though in another world, she caressed the soft, satin robe. Finally she took it out, unfolded it and stood up, holding the quilted robe to her body and looking down, her eyes totally unwary. For an instant Bennie saw a different person and felt like he was window peeping.

In a soft voice Bennie had never heard before she said, "I always wanted one of these."

Newt was beaming. She went over and kissed his high forehead.

"How about that?" Buck whispered to Bennie. "That really softened her up. Now the dooey hits the fan."

Bennie selected a long, heavy package about which Ma already harbored grave suspicions. She had sneaked in and nudged that package the night before. Now she watched closely as Bennie unwrapped it still stroking her precious robe on her lap.

Actually Bennie had helped Newt wrap the .45-90 and knew what it was. He also knew it wasn't his real Christmas present just yet. Newt had said, "We'll wrap 'er in tissue paper and then newspaper, so your Ma'll get her money's worth watching you get it out and wonderin' if it's really what she's bound to expect it might be, since she knows I'm a crazy old coot and a bad influence."

"Gee!" Bennie said when he got it unwrapped, hoping he wasn't overplaying his part. "A rifle!"

Ma blurted, "He's too young for that!" She had to say it, even if Newt took both it and her robe back.

"How young is too young?" Newt countered.

"He's only fourteen."

"That's old enough to learn how to handle a rifle."

"He'll kill somebody," Ma said.

"Maybe," Newt conceded. "But not by accident after I get through showing him how to use one. He just might save your life with it." By then Newt had found out about Ma and her "*morones*" and stifled a notion to say, "Hell, the kid might even stand off a *morone* for you."

Ma was in a corner now, trying not to get mad. "All the same," she stuck to her guns, "he's too young."

Newt played his last card. "I was his age when I killed the coward that shot Pa in the back."

"That was in a war."

Pa spoke up then. "I don't think this part of the country's ready for a cannon like that, Newt, whether the kid is or not. It'd be different if it was a .22. Lots of kids have those. What do you think, Em?" He asked Ma.

She stepped into their net. "My brothers all hunted with Pa's .22 at Bennie's age," she conceded. "It would be better if it was only a .22."

"Well," Newt said, "I reckon I'll just have to keep this cannon for the kid a few years. But it's his. If I croak before he's old enough, remember it's his."

Ma let out a long sigh of relief.

"Aw," Bennie said. "Can I handle it empty and learn how it works?"

"Maybe after while, if Newt doesn't care," Pa said. "It works just like the .40-60 though and you know how to work that."

Ma said, "It's your turn to open a package, Russ."

Pa unwrapped his first package and found a box of cigars more expensive than he'd ever expected to smoke.

"Whew! I'll really have to make these last," he said.

"Don't make 'em last so long they get stale," Newt cautioned. He was already opening his package from Bennie, who was still holding the .45-90 across his lap.

Ma said, "Lean that rifle out of the way somewhere safe. I hope it's empty."

Bennie jacked it open to see.

"It's empty," he said.

"Be careful anyhow." Ma thought that guns, like cars and horses, had minds of their own.

Bennie hadn't had the foggiest notion what to buy Newt. Since the old boy still used a straight razor, Pa had helped Bennie select a shaving set—a cup, cake of scented lathering soap, and a soft-bristle shaving brush.

"Nifty," Newt said. He winked at Bennie. "With them two young chickens upstairs I gotta shave every mornin' regular."

Ma sniffed.

"Open another package," Newt urged her, eager as any kid.

Ma unwrapped a small box with a bottle of good perfume in it. She almost said, "What will I do with perfume?" But she was pleased. She opened it and sniffed. "Um," she said. She knew what she'd do with it. Treasure it, hide it with the delicious knowledge that it was hers to be kept in a drawer with the other precious perfume she never used, some of it twenty years old.

Then it was Bennie's turn again.

"*Here goes for the World Series*," Buck whispered.

From a second long package, Bennie unwrapped a beautifully blued .22 with highly polished walnut stock and forearm.

"A .22," he said, emphasizing that it was *only a .22* for Ma's sake and watching for her reaction.

She looked discomfited for just a second then said, without too much rancor, "You three men set me up for this, didn't you?" She looked over all three, one at a time, with genuine humor in her eyes, pleased that her veto power was potent enough to demand a plot to circumvent it. Bennie wondered if she'd actually meant to include him when she said "you three men."

"You're going to bail him out when he gets in trouble, Newt," she said.

"You got a deal." To Bennie Newt said, "That's a Stevens Crackshot. One of the finest little rifles made. Single shot. It'll teach you to make that first shot count."

Bennie jacked open the trim little weapon and squinted through the mirror-bright barrel. He hardly noticed the rest of the package-opening ceremony—what else anyone got—but his last package was a 500-round case of .22 long rifle ammunition—ten boxes, untold wealth.

In his mind he was already out at Three-Mile Creek, with Uncle Newt along teaching him how to "make that first shot count." He wondered if the old man could walk that far. He had a lot to learn about Uncle Newt.

CHAPTER TWENTY-THREE

An Old Injun Trick

— December 26, 1937

Bennie showed Uncle Newt the way to Three-Mile Creek along the Northwestern tracks. It was cold under a lowering sky. Bennie wore an extra pair of pants under his bib overalls, a pair of knit wool socks over his regular ones, work shoes under overshoes, two shirts, a sweater, a mackinaw jacket over it all, and a hunter's cap with ear flaps.

Newt eyed his bundled figure and said, "You're ready for anything, I see. Expecting a blizzard?"

"I wouldn't be too surprised."

Newt looked at the sky. "Neither would I."

He was wearing the first pair of L. L. Bean shoepacs that Bennie had ever seen—leather tops, rubber bottoms. Other than that, he was dressed comparatively lightly in wool twill pants, mackinaw over a checked wool shirt, and a lumberjack's stocking cap. Bennie figured he was used to a lot colder weather than people around Blackhawk. The old man also had both mittens attached to a cord that connected them through a loop behind his mackinaw collar.

"So you don't lose 'em if you slip 'em off on the run with a dog team," Newt explained when Bennie asked.

They bucked a head wind that stung their faces and caused teary eyes. Uncle Newt set the pace, walking with a long springy gait. Bennie found himself almost trotting to keep up. He thought, "I guess I won't have to worry whether the old boy can make it or not." He concentrated on not appearing strained himself. Carrying the Stevens Crackshot helped. He wondered if his sense of impending adventure was the way Daniel Boone had felt crossing the mountains into Kentucky the first time.

A few scattered snowflakes that foretold a storm were drifting down when they reached the railroad bridge across the creek. Spry as a chipmunk, Uncle Newt descended the outsized steps formed by the stone abutment, reaching the creek level without drawing a deep breath. He looked around at the woods and hills crowding down to the creek.

"Looks like around home when I was a kid."

"I wish I'd seen it."

Newt laughed. "This'll do. If you'd seen it you'd be an old coot like me with one foot in the grave"

"Some old coot I'd say. I brought Pa out here last fall and the walk almost killed him."

"He ain't in shape for walkin'. I musta run a million miles behind a dog team in my day. If we tried lifting all day like your Pa does on the dock down at the plant it'd just about kill us too. All depends on what you're used to." He sniffed the air and swung his gaze over the hills. "Any deer or wolves here?"

"Naw. A few fox is all."

"Gray or red?"

"Both. I never saw a gray one though. Lots of squirrels and rabbits."

"I guess they'll be safe around us today. We'll have to get ourselves hunting licenses down here in civilization I guess."

"Seasons are all over."

"Next year then. Now, let's set us up some targets. We'll go up one of these ravines and get a good backstop."

Bennie knew Newt had some regular paper targets and thumbtacks; otherwise he'd have brought a sack of tin cans. They found a good spot not far from the creek and Newt put up a target on a fat oak tree.

"We don't have to back off too far at first till you get the hang of that gun. I'll show you how to sight it. We may have to adjust the sights a little at first—they don't always do it just right at the factory.

"I'll draw you a picture of how the sights'll look to you when you aim if you're holding the gun on the target right." He took out one of the other targets, folded it and started to draw on the back. What he drew looked like a letter "U" with an "I" in the middle of it. "That's the back sight with the front sight in the notch. Notice the top of both of 'em are exactly level. Then the bullseye is like an 'O' sitting dead on top of the front sight."

"I always thought you held the front sight right in the middle of the bullseye."

"Some people do. They call that aiming dead center. It's O.K. for target shooting if you can see the front sight against a black background. But for hunting, especially in bad light, it's best to use this sight picture. They call it aiming at six o'clock, because the bullseye is round like a clock and you aim where the six would be. That's the way the Army shoots, and I always found it best for production shooting, the kind you do out hunting. I never did any target shooting except to sight in my guns or to teach somebody like we're gonna do today. Now, let's try your gun."

Bennie took out a box of shells and carefully extracted one, dropping the lever of the gun, inserting the shell, and closing the action.

"You been carrying that goddam thing empty?" Newt asked.

"Sure, I thought you'd want me to for safety's sake."

"Safe? From what?"

"Accidentally going off."

"Christ, if you carry the son of a bitch on half-cock like God intended, the bastard won't go off in a million years. If you need the goddam gun, it's not worth a shit empty. And dump the rest of that box of shells out loose in your pocket so you can get another one quick, instead of like taking a book out of the library. Hell's bells!"

This wasn't even close to the sort of careful instruction in the use of firearms that Bennie had expected.

"You end up with the gun cocked after you jack it open and put in a round. Do you know how to put your thumb over the hammer and pull the trigger without letting the gun go off by accident, to get the hammer down on half-cock?"

Bennie nodded, still in mild shock. "Sure," he said. "It works just like the .40-60 or .45-90. I tried it with this one too."

"Always be sure to aim it somewhere safe in case your thumb slips when you do it."

He managed that all right and looked at Newt for approval.

"Good. Now that's the way you always carry it—loaded and on half-cock. Nobody but an asshole shoots himself by accident, especially going through a fence like we always hear about. Push your gun through the fence ahead of you and follow it, or shove it through and lay it on the ground pointing away from you, even lean it against a post where there's a wire to prop it against so it stays put. Only simple-minded bastards drag a gun through after them cocked and catch the trigger on a barb. Always watch how anyone with you handles their gun. If they're loose about it, never go with them again. If you have to, take their damned gun away from them."

"Suppose they won't give it to you?"

"Suppose it's you or them?"

That was a proposition to think about too. Bennie thought, "Jesus, I haven't fired a shot yet and got the whole catalog shoved down my throat in five minutes. Suppose I miss the target after all that?"

But he didn't. They walked up and looked at the target. He'd nailed it dead center from fifty feet with his first shot.

Newt didn't say anything except, "Let's walk back and try it again."

When they walked up to check the next shot, Bennie's heart sunk—he couldn't see a hole anywhere, not even in the white part of the target. Then Newt pointed it out.

"Doubled out the first one," he said. "Notice how that one hole is a little elongated. I guess you inherited the family touch for shooting—it's in some people's blood, Jim Hickok used to say."

"Who was Jim Hickok?"

"Wild Bill, I suppose you heard him called."

"You knew Wild Bill?"

"Like a brother."

Bennie could hardly believe that. He eyed Newt to see if he was telling one of his stories.

Reading his look, Newt said, "Cross my heart, kid. Like a brother. Knew his whole blamed family. So did your grandpa, old Johnny Todd. They was neighbors down at Troy Grove."

"Will you tell me about him?" This was almost too good to be true; he'd read everything he could find about Wild Bill.

"When the time comes. Now let's shoot up that whole box from back here, then we'll put up another target and move back a ways."

Bennie never shot out of the black once at either fifty or one hundred feet—no great performance with a rifle, but pretty good for his first time.

When they were through Newt said, "Leave the targets up for the birds to admire. In fact here comes someone, maybe the farmer that owns this place—if he don't bite our ass for trespassin' he can admire 'em."

"It's the game warden," Bennie said.

"How do you know?"

"He took my B.B. gun away from me last fall."

"You didn't tell me that. What for?"

"Claimed I was most likely shooting birds."

"Were you?"

"Sure, but he couldn't prove it."

By then the game warden was within hearing. He didn't even say howdy, but "What are you two hunting?"

"Nothing," Newt said. "Tryin' out the kid's Christmas .22."

"Let me see your hunting licenses."

Newt's voice never rose as he repeated, "We aren't hunting. You can look at the target over there on the tree. Every shot we fired is in that tree."

The warden's eyes took on a mean, official look. Bennie knew he was detested by everyone who hunted in that part of the country. He'd arrested countless people for petty or trumped-up offenses and was famous for confiscating kids' guns. Lots of people had threatened to kill him, but it was all just blowing off. He wondered how Uncle Newt would handle this situation.

The warden looked at Bennie. "Oh, it's you again. What have you been hunting?"

Newt broke in. "I told you we've just been target shooting."

"And I asked to see your hunting licenses." His voice was as nasty as his eyes.

"We don't have hunting licenses. We aren't hunting."

"The state considers carrying a gun as prima facie evidence of hunting. I'll have to take the kid's gun."

Newt slipped out a big army .45 automatic from under his coattail and hefted it once. He said, "I'm carryin' a gun. Am I hunting?"

The warden looked at the .45, his jaw dropped a little, then he moved to throw up the shotgun he'd held till then in the crook of his arm. The crisp click of the .45 safety being slipped off suggested the wisdom of not trying to point the shotgun at anyone, although Newt didn't actually point the .45 directly at him.

The warden looked scared now. Bennie felt his heart pumping hard against his breastbone. This was the last thing he'd expected when he'd set out happily with his first .22. He didn't see how Newt could get out of this without going to jail.

The warden decided to bluff it out. "That's a concealed weapon. I'm a deputy sheriff too. I'll have to run you both in."

Newt pointed the .45 dead center on him for the first time. He said, "You'll shit too, if you eat regular, partner. Just set that shotgun down on the ground nice and easy. It looks like a nice gun and you probably wouldn't want to get it scratched."

There was a long period of silence while the warden's thoughts registered on his face: "Is this really happening? Should I make a break? Is this guy nuts, or really serious? I wish to hell I was safe out of this."

"You can't get away with this," he said.

"Just do what I say and you'll be all right," Newt said. There wasn't the faintest quaver in his voice. He sounded like just what he was—a killer who'd done it before and had no qualms about doing it again. Anyone but a fool could read his killer eyes. A light went on in Bennie's mind when he looked at Newt's eyes—here was the fellow Buck Doaks had told him about, the one who liked killing sonsabitches that needed it. He felt his heart beating painfully fast. He wondered if Newt was going to shoot this *sonofabitch* in his tracks.

The warden lowered the shotgun carefully to the ground.

Newt said, "Now step back and turn around."

The warden complied slowly.

"Now head up the gully here ahead of me. I want to go up and reason with you." When he was several feet away, Newt ordered, "Stop right there for a minute."

Newt stooped and whispered quickly to Bennie. "Get under those spruce trees over there and stay out of sight. I'll be back in no more'n a half-hour. Take this shotgun with you and don't touch it with your bare hands."

It was one of the longest half-hours he ever spent, wondering what Newt aimed to do. He half-expected to hear a shot. There was no doubt in Bennie's mind that Newt wouldn't hesitate to kill if he thought he had to.

Snow began to fall heavily, blanketing the ground. The wind died completely. A flock of juncos flew under the low-drooping branches and startled him as badly as his presence startled them. He didn't hear Newt's return till he said, "Hey, kid. Time to go home. Leave the bastard's shotgun leaning against the tree under there. You didn't touch it bare-handed, did you?"

"No."

That's when Bennie knew. He came out and gave Newt a scared look. "What'd you do to him?" he blurted.

"Reasoned with him. He agreed to leave the country and never come back."

"How'd you get him to do that?"

"An old Injun trick. I'll tell you how it works someday."

"Why not now?"

"Never mind. Just get this straight. *You never saw that son of a bitch. No matter who asks you or how much they threaten or promise, you never saw that son of a bitch. Understand?*"

"*What son of a bitch?*" Buck Doaks asked. "*Got that, Bennie?*"

"Got what?"

"About the damned game warden?"

"What game warden?"

Bennie thought, "Jesus. Just like the Hatfields and McCoys."

He knew there were a lot of places up the ravines out here where water had carved deep caverns that would easily conceal a horse, much less a man. And it was easy to cave down the overhanging banks into them. He'd tried it just for the hell of it to see the earth falling in. Usually there were down trees around them with roots sticking up.

CHAPTER TWENTY-FOUR

I'm Callin' You and Raisin'

Pa had been talking about getting back *up north* as long as Bennie could remember. When cigarette company slogan contests came into vogue, paying as much as ten thousand dollars for first prize, Pa entered every one. When, as usual, he'd hear nothing from his entry, he might complain, "Why, I put some stuff in there right out of their own ads." Maybe that was the problem. Anyhow, he never rang the bell as others did with such prize-winning slogans as "I'd walk a mile for a Camel," or, for Lucky Strikes, "They satisfy." If he had, maybe they'd have been back on the farm.

Newt soon heard of Pa's *up north* fund that he was saving to buy back the old place. Also of the fund's repeated setbacks. It never got much above twenty dollars before Ma would have a tooth filled or Bennie outgrew his shoes.

Shortly after the Three-Mile Creek episode, Newt developed an avid interest in going *up north* too. Bennie suspected why. Pa might *not* have gone on his own even if he had the money. He was a dreamer. Newt was a doer. Pa liked to say, "We'll see when the time comes." It seldom came. When Newt started to talk about going *up north*, Bennie figured something might actually come of it.

Pa and Bennie escaped to Newt's apartment whenever they could slip out from under Ma's alert eye. If she suspected they were going up there—and she had an almost infallible instinct for divining when they were thinking about it—she always had an errand to be run. Pa had to go get something for her at the store. Bennie had to carry out garbage, help her clean out the closet and take the trash out, or carry unneeded things to the basement in a carton. She never went up to Newt's place, though Newt invited her to come anytime.

Newt had a neat set of professional poker chips that he'd get out so he, Bennie, and Pa could sit around his kitchen table and idle time away at poker, eating the cookies or rolls he always had on hand and drinking coffee. Occasionally the two pretty young women who had apartments up there would drop in. Bennie was sure that if Ma knew about that she'd have a fit. She thought they looked like "whores." Any woman that might glance at Pa, even though Ma professed to hold him in contempt, looked like a "whore" out to steal her prize, or so it appeared. This probably didn't apply to nuns, but

Bennie never thought of that. The two women who lived next to Newt, Kate and Grace, went out of their way to please Newt and didn't seem to notice his age.

After Bennie got over being bashful around them, he always hoped they'd drop in. Kate was a blue-eyed redhead and Grace had dark brown hair and eyes. Bennie overheard Newt telling Pa one day, "They both been on the line." That meant nothing to him, and if he'd known what it meant he wouldn't have given a damn. He was coming to regard availability as a virtue in women and wished he could find some. Later he'd realize that these women must have been Blackhawk's only call girls (he was sure the town couldn't have afforded two sets). One or the other might be gone for a night or take a trip with someone. Ostensibly they ran a little dress shop. If he'd known what they were he might have pan-handled them, since he thought a lot about what it would be like to get with them in bed, since he now had a better idea of what it was all about with men and women.

One Saturday in early March, after Pa and Newt had returned from grocery shopping, Bennie joined them up at Newt's place. They were having coffee at the kitchen table.

"Hello, kid," Newt greeted him. "Not out shooting?"

"Naw. Too cold and windy." Actually he'd been avoiding his most convenient shooting field since the game warden had disappeared. He'd found some abandoned gravel pits on the other side of the river, but the country didn't please him nearly as well as Three-Mile Creek, even though the pits provided ideal shooting backstops.

The missing warden had been the subject of a news story and a couple of follow-ups in the *Gazette*, dwelling on his mysterious disappearance. Fortunately he'd walked out from town just as Newt and Bennie had, otherwise there would have been a telltale car parked out near where he disappeared that might have directed searchers to that area. His wife told the investigators, "He'd never tell me where he was going. He just took his gun as usual and walked out. I told him he might get in trouble and be sorry someday." From her bitchy tone and look the police speculated that she might know more about his disappearance than she let on, or that he might have walked out on her and good riddance. In any case, no one seemed to be grieving over him, and the case died out and was forgotten by the public.

Newt knew what was bothering Bennie and teased, "You ought to get out there to the creek more often. It's a pretty spot. I was surprised to find so much woods back here around civilization. A man that knew how could hide out there forever." There was a wicked twinkle in his eye when he said that. Bennie was sure he meant a man could hide out *dead or alive*.

Bennie said, "Maybe I'll go out there tomorrow. You want to come along?"

"Why not?"

Just then Grace dropped in without knocking, which didn't seem out of the ordinary to Bennie. Pa grinned.

"Which one of you men are going to help me move some trunks and boxes?" she asked.

"Not me," Newt said. "I'm too damn old. You go, Ed. I'm gonna tell the kid here about old Wild Bill. He's pestered me to death about it for a month of Sundays."

After the two had left, Newt said, "Let's go sprawl in the living room?"

He had his polar bear robe spread out over a huge overstuffed chair that he'd had Bennie help him select at Montgomery Ward's. He pointed to it. "You sit in that, kid. I'm gonna sprawl out on the couch . . . Now what the hell did you want to know about old Wild Bill?"

"Everything."

Newt laughed. "That's a pretty tall order. But whatever you heard, it's probably true."

"What's probably true?"

"All that bull you read about him. Like that article you showed me from the Chicago *Tribune*."

"How come you call it bull then?"

"It's sorta like Lincoln's story about the old slave who was a long ways from home and tryin' to impress the local boys. He pointed at a star and said, 'Why I saw *dat berry stah* up home!' Lincoln said, 'He thought he was lying, but he was telling the truth.' That's the shape those guys are in when they scribble about Wild Bill. The son of a bitch did so much nobody ever heard about, no matter what they write about him, it's most likely pretty close to the truth."

"Did he kill all those men?"

"He killed plenty. Probably more'n anyone ever heard about. And he had to have killed at least a couple of dozen in the Civil War to boot—maybe twice that many. Who the hell knows?"

"Why did he kill so many?"

"Well, everybody kills in a war because they have to. The others were ornery skunks that needed it, like Dave Tutt who was beggin' for it."

Bennie knew about Dave Tutt "begging for it" and almost said, "Like that game warden?" and just remembered in time he was supposed to have eternal amnesia about that. He thought, "If Uncle Newt wants to tell me what happened to the bastard, he will." He figured from the fact that he hadn't heard a shot that Newt had probably finished him with a rock like the Indians did, then buried the body.

"What sort of person was Wild Bill?" he asked.

Newt thought about that, wanting to give a precise answer in as few words as possible. He said, "For one thing he was as good-natured a fellow as you'd ever meet. Hell, he was just a farm boy at heart. Laughed a lot. If you were his friend, that was that. He'd kill for you if need be, lend you his last cent, give you the shirt off his back. Christ, he gave the sonofabitch that shot him in the back some eatin' money after he cleaned him in a poker game the night before."

He paused and looked as though he was suddenly far away. He finally said, "Me'n' Johnny Todd, was just back from Custer's Last Stand and on our way to hunt down that bastard—that little shit, Jack McCall—when they picked him up and tried him for killin' Hickok. Run him down in Yankton. We stayed for the trial and hangin'. If they hadn't jerked McCall to Jesus we'd have beefed him. We flipped a dollar to see which of us was goin' to gun him down if the judge didn't sentence him to hang. Had the fastest hoss we could steal waitin' to ride for it afterward."

"Who won the toss?" Bennie asked, making a note to pump Newt about Custer's Last Stand sometime.

"I did. Had my big Sharps in a hotel room with a good view of the route where they took McCall back and forth every day. I couldn't have missed. I'd have been out the back way and gone before anyone got organized, not that they'd give a damn. Might not even have chased me. Maybe give me a medal if they caught me. I almost shot McCall on general principles before they even found him guilty."

"Gee," Bennie said. He felt sort of funny lots of times around Uncle Newt. He was no different than Wild Bill himself. The difference was he'd survived.

"Was Wild Bill as good as they say with a pistol?"

"He was good enough when it come to shootin' men."

"How about that trick shooting?"

"Lots of us could do that. The acid test is getting a big pill into someone who's shootin' at you, or fixin' to, before they get you. At that he was aces. Nobody was any better. People get pantin' to shoot too quick, and they miss. He was cool as ice in a tight spot. If you hurry, unless the other fellow is a greenhorn, you're a dead duck."

"Did you ever have any gunfights?"

Newt laughed. "You mean like in Western movies?"

"Sure."

"Not really. I made sure the other fellow was dead before the fight started."

"You ain't kiddin' me?"

"Huh-uh."

"Where'd you ever do that?" he asked, since it sounded like Newt wouldn't mind telling.

"Tombstone, for one. A damn fool called me out. Said, 'Step outside, all I need from you is six feet of ground.' Sounded like a dime novel. I shot him in his tracks right where he was and it seemed like I ought to say something gaudy, so I said, 'That's my distance.' Some drunk guffawed at that and that didn't strike me like due respect for the dead so I knocked his teeth out with my six-shooter, forked my bronc, and sloped."

"What'd they do to you?"

"The first thing they had to do was catch me."

"Did they?"

"I'll tell you that story some other time, *maybe*."

Bennie didn't get time to wheedle him any more just then since Pa came back. Bennie didn't notice that Pa had been gone a long while just to move a few trunks and boxes. He flopped down in Newt's other chair and looked cheerful.

"You look tired out," Newt said. "Musta been pretty heavy trunks and boxes."

"They were," Pa said.

"By the way," Newt said, "I been thinkin . . ."

"Uh-oh!" Pa said. "Here it comes—we're in for it."

Newt ignored that. "I been thinkin' I'd like to go back to a little farm somewhere and end my days like I started 'em."

"Who wouldn't?" Pa said. "But it takes do-re-mi."

"Suppose you won one of those contests and had the dough?"

"Hell, I'd go any way I could get the money. I've thought of robbing a bank."

Newt said, "I always wondered why they say 'robbin' a bank.' Anything you do to a banker is a public service, almost. I sorta liked the James Boys on that count, even if Jesse was trigger-happy."

Bennie burst in, "Did you know them too?"

"I didn't say I knew 'em. I said I liked 'em. I liked their style." To Pa he said, "How much do-re-mi would it take to get a farm?"

"I've seen farms advertised in the *Trib* or the *Milwaukee Journal* for little or nothing. They're almost givin' 'em away and still can't can get any takers, especially *up north*. People can't make a go of it with prices for farm truck as low as they are, even with Roosevelt helpin' out."

"So? How much?"

"We could probably get the old place back for a thousand bucks. Maybe as little as eight hundred. It wasn't much of a farm to begin with. If Pa hadn't bankrolled us, we'd have gone bust every year."

Bennie's Pa had never learned that the state's social engineers were trying to depopulate the Cutover, as the area where they'd farmed was called, and turn it back to woods. That benevolent effort was another reason besides Ma why they couldn't make it *up north*. Those Ph.D.'s down at the state capital seemed stunned to learn that a lot of *ignorant mudsills* would rather starve on a farm in the Cutover than leave. It was beyond the comprehension of social engineers to grasp the reason why, that the ignoramuses simply liked the isolated back country.

Pa recalled, "That farm was Ma's and Pa's way of keepin' my nutty brother Bob out of the city so they wouldn't put him in the nuthouse."

Bennie had heard Ma call Bob simple-minded several times, but this was the first time he'd heard Pa admit it. Later he learned that the last straw had been when they'd caught Bob pissing on the streetcar track in Riverview at high noon and the city fathers told Grandma Todd to get him out of town or they'd put him away. Bob was twenty-six at the time.

Newt asked, "What would a *good* farm cost?"

"I'd guess a good '120' would run around twenty-five hundred bucks with most of the machinery thrown in; another few hundred would probably get you the livestock."

Pa liked to daydream about that kind of thing. He and Bennie had gone over it dozens of times. Pa would describe his ideal place. "No tractor. Too much like factories with stinking machines. Four horses are the ticket. A horse will do anything if it learns to trust you, as long as it knows what you're asking from it. A few cows. Some chickens. Maybe some pigs. How I loved that good home-cured ham with eggs and pancakes on those crisp fall mornings *up north*."

Sister once told Bennie, "The trouble was Pa had all the piglets named. They'd have died of old age before he killed them. Same with beef. We'd get too many calves, but Pa wouldn't want to butcher them. He wouldn't have killed his own beef if his life depended on it."

That might have been another reason why Grandpa Todd had to bankroll the place. That, and old "Bart-Bart-let-a-fart."

Newt broke out a new box of cigars and passed the box to Pa. They both got fired up and took a few luxuriant puffs to get their stogies going to suit them. Newt knew that Bennie was already smoking roll-your-own cigarettes and offered the box to him too, glancing at Pa to see how that sat with him.

Pa said in response to Bennie's questioning look at him, "Go ahead. A kid has to learn sometime. Don't inhale the damn thing though or you'll get sick as a dog. Just puff it in your mouth and blow it out. It tastes good anyhow."

Newt leaned back, drew in a big drag, inhaled, blew it back out at the ceiling and looked as contented as a man could get.

"Ed," he said. "I'm callin' you and raisin'. I got five thousand dollars for you to buy the old place and a good one somewhere right around there to boot. I want the old place myself for sentimental reasons. Johnny Todd used to write me about goin' up there in the summer; he loved the place as much as you did. It'll be a place for me to remember the good old days I had with him when we were young. I aim to batch and live out my last days there."

Newt's remark about "callin' and raisin'" was an apt one. Pa looked like he'd got caught betting into a full house with a pair of deuces.

Newt said, "I didn't heist a bank, but I really got the money. I didn't spend fifty years in Alaska because I liked the weather."

Pa said, "The last I remember, you lost your poke on a faro table in Nome and Pa had to send us both the fare to get home. Remember, we both bent a shovel for Big Alex McGlaughlin while we waited for Pa to send the dough?"

"I ain't forgot. But we got a new stake in Tonopah. When you went home, I went back to Alaska and been addin' to my pile ever since. The last time I went 'outside' after that was 1909, when I came back and tried to knock some sense in your head about gettin' married—or not gettin' married. I guess Emma never forgave me."

"She never did. In fact she mentioned it the day you showed up at the door."

"Don't surprise me."

"Anyhow, I made my pile in Alaska, but keep it under your hat. I got that five grand and plenty more where that came from."

"I'll have to quit my job if we go up and look around. They won't give me any time off," Pa stalled.

Newt snorted. "Boy, city life has got to you."

Pa looked hurt. Newt simply didn't understand how the Depression had broken men like Pa; how demoralizing it had been to live with years of hopelessness. Now Pa had a little security and didn't want to lose it. The undecided look on his face mirrored his thoughts.

"Let's do it," Bennie urged, hoping hard that Pa would come to his senses.

Newt was equally impatient. He said, "I'll give you till this cigar burns down."

Pa wondered if he was serious and searched his face for a clue. Newt managed to be blowing another cloud of smoke at the ceiling and avoided his look.

Bennie tensed up painfully as he often did when Pa dragged his feet about something Bennie thought he ought to do. He found himself hating Pa for the worst foot dragging he'd experienced yet. He wished Pa was more like Uncle Newt.

Pa tried another dodge. "I'll have to see what Emma thinks," he said.

"Jesus Christ!" Newt exploded. His face hardened. "You ask her a goddam thing and the deal is off. I'm goin' whether you do or not."

Bennie thought, "*And I'm runnin' away to join you as quick as you do.*"

"O.K." Pa said, abruptly. "I should have left her years ago. If it wasn't for the kid here I'd have done it."

Bennie thought, "*If I'd known that I'd have run away long before now.*" As it was he ran away almost every summer, at least in his mind and sometimes literally.

Newt said, "You shouldn't have married her in the first place. Bennie is the only good thing I've seen come out of it. You should have come back to Alaska like I wanted you to. Anybody might have knocked her up. Lillian doesn't even look like any of us, judging from the pictures I've seen. You were suckered in."

Ignoring the fact that Bennie was there, Pa asked, "Why did she pick me then?"

Newt thought, "*Why you? You're the dumb ass that just said, 'I'll have to see what Emma thinks.' She probably wanted someone she could boss around.*"

But, all that Newt said was, "God knows. Maybe she was in love with you once."

This all went over Bennie's head, though he understood the drift. He'd never heard any of it before and didn't give a damn. What he was interested in was going back *up north*. This was their chance and he hoped Pa wouldn't muff it.

Pa was still thinking about what Newt said. He said, "I can still hear Mama saying, 'If there's any chance it was you, you've got to do the right thing and marry the girl.' Well, there was a good chance it was me."

Newt said, "How about the slick medical student where she was workin'? She still talks about Don Juan right in front of you as though he was Prince Charming."

Bennie had heard all he could stand of that Prince Charming bull himself. He thought he sounded like a sissy and a virgin suck to boot.

Pa didn't answer. Instead he asked, "How do you aim to get *up north* and shop for a farm?"

"In the Lincoln I bought."

He went on as though he hadn't noticed Pa's and Bennie's surprised looks. "It's only two years old and in prime shape. It's even got bud vases and fancy woodwork in the back. I aim to get up there with you chauffeuring and me ridin' in style. Now let's go down and drive it up here, if you've still got strength enough."

Bennie didn't catch onto that remark either. Later he learned that Grace's timely arrival to ask for help with trunks had cost Newt ten dollars—not the first time either.

Newt added, "Monday you go down and tell G.M. to shove their job where the sun don't shine. If you're scared to, I'll put five grand in a checking account for you first."

Bennie thought, "*I'd have snapped up Uncle Newt's offer in the first place without all the bull; so fast it would have made his head swim.*"

He already knew he wasn't anything like Pa, or his brother Roy, who took after their father. Roy was still back in Illinois, happy plowing the same furrow for his board.

Bennie said, "How about me comin' along to shop for a farm with you?"

Without even looking at Pa, Newt said, "Sure. You can ride in style with me in the back and we'll smoke cigars."

After they got past Ma's amazement and clucking over extravagance, Newt invited her for a ride in the Lincoln. He held the door for her to get in the back with him. Bennie rode up front beside Pa.

They stopped at a little restaurant out on the highway that Ma had gone to once with Aunt Nellie and never stopped talking about. It was Newt's idea. "Soften her up," he said.

Now they were back in the car riding through a typical sloppy Wisconsin spring, fields partially bare with slushy snow lingering here and there. The lowering sun painted the hazy western sky solid red.

Pa thought, "It's now or never." He yelled back to Ma, "Newt is going to put up the money to buy us a farm back *up north*."

She looked at Newt to see if she'd heard right.

"That's right," Newt said. "A real good farm."

"I'm not going back up there!" Ma said, setting her jaw.

Newt said, "It won't be the same place in the woods. It'll be a regular farm with a good house, indoor plumbing, and the whole shooting match. I'll even get you one of those gas washing machines. You can get to town quick in the car."

Ma said, "Without electricity I'll be back to cleaning kerosene lamp chimneys again."

"Bennie can do that," Newt countered.

He thought, "*What the hell am I doing, wheedling her? I ought to pitch her in the drink at the first river we come to.*"

Ma said, "I think I'll go to Iowa to take that job with my cousin's husband. You men don't need me."

Her cousin Ella had burned to death when the kerosene can from which she was pouring kerosene into a coal cook range exploded. Her widower had asked Ma to come keep house for him, since he knew from her letters to Ella that she wasn't happy at home. He even told her to bring Bennie along, he'd be a father to him. Ma was too naive to grasp the full implication of the offer. Until the prospect of *up north* had materialized, Bennie had been all for Iowa, even though his conscience tweaked him a little over having to leave Pa behind. Notwithstanding, a farm was a farm. It would be away from town and there would be animals to work with, even if you owed it all to a farmer named Ezra.

Buck Doaks had said, "*Ezra? Jesus Christ!*"

Pa astonished everyone, including himself, by yelling back at Ma, "Go ahead. I'm taking Bennie with me."

Newt grinned.

They drove in strained silence for a few miles.

Ma was fiddling with her old white gloves, picking at the frayed ends of the fingers. Then she kicked the footrest on the floor a couple of times. Looking sulky, she finally blurted, "I guess I'll come along to pick out that farm. You men won't know enough to pick out the right place."

"That's probably true," Newt said.

CHAPTER TWENTY-FIVE

It Beats Miss Morlach's Hygiene Lectures

— 1797

George Washington, in his Farewell Address as he leaves the presidency, warns his countrymen against "foreign entanglements."

Perhaps good advice in an era when crossing the Atlantic Ocean barrier took six weeks or more. On the other hand, America gained its independence in a foreign entanglement.

In 1938 Howard Hughes rounded the globe by air in 3 days, 19 hours, and 14.28 minutes. The ocean of air recognizes no shorelines or boundaries.

— March 31, 1938

Former president *Hoobert Heever* (closer to 1797 than 1938) criticizes FDR's foreign policy thrust in a speech to the Council on Foreign Relations and recommends not allying ourselves with the European powers opposing the brutal madman Hitler, because that will lead to war.

> *"If you could expose the stupid to themselves, it wouldn't be necessary."*
> *—Pro Bono Publico*

> *Hoobert Heever was an all-around loser.*
> *—Buck Doaks*

That was what had been going on in the outside world, and Bennie, although vaguely aware of it, couldn't possibly have cared less.

— March 1938

Bennie's stomach periodically had been visited by butterflies ever since they'd finally decided they were going back *up north*.

They'd reached that decision a couple of weeks before. They were taking him out of school to go *up north* with them farm-hunting. Pa, Ma, and Newt were downstairs making plans. Bennie was in Newt's apartment trying to concentrate on reading an article in one of the four volumes of Newt's *Battles and Leaders of the Civil War*.

Kate came in and asked, "Where's your uncle?"

"Downstairs. They've got their heads together about movin'—we're planning to go back up where we used to live and buy a farm."

"I know." She sighed. "Newt told me. I'll miss you all."

She flopped down on the couch, pulled a pack of cigarettes and a kitchen match out of her blouse pocket, and lit up.

"Want one?" She extended the pack to him. He got up and took one, handing the pack back. She offered him a light off the end of hers. As he bent down he smelled her perfume and could see down her blouse, which caused a pleasant sensation in his groin.

"Cripes," he thought, "I hope I don't get a hard-on and have her notice it."

He resumed his seat and crossed his legs. He noticed that she was watching him closely and quickly averted his eyes.

"How old are you?" she asked.

"Fifteen last January."

"You're big for your age. I thought you were at least sixteen. Taller than most men already. How tall are you?"

"Six feet even."

"How much do you weigh?"

"A hundred and sixty the last time I weighed."

"You'll probably fill out and get a lot taller."

He looked at her directly then, curious about why she was saying such things. Since he wasn't getting a hard-on after all, he got up and flicked his cigarette ashes in her ashtray. Close up he noticed that she had really pretty eyes, surrounded by thick, dark-red lashes. He didn't realize that they were artfully accentuated by a subtle application of mascara and eye shadow. Her full, red lips fascinated him as she talked and smiled. He thought, "I never noticed how pretty she is. I wonder why?"

She was saying, "I've got a present for you before you leave. Might as well give it to you now."

"What is it?"

"It's a surprise. Something nice that will last you as long as you live."

"What?"

"I told you, it's a surprise—I'm not gonna tell. C'm'on with me. You'll have to come see it. I can't give it to you over here."

He'd been in both the girls' places on occasion for cocoa and cookies or some other treat, so had no hesitation about following her.

Her apartment was typically feminine, but furnished with better than average taste and an ample budget, with the sort of furniture that would become collectors' pieces in a few decades: select, well-finished walnut and mahogany and fine upholstery. Bennie didn't realize that all the paintings were originals and, if he had, was too naive to appreciate the significance of that.

"We don't want anyone to bother us for a while," Kate said, and bolted the door behind them.

Only then did he get an inkling of what she had in mind. The way Ma had raised him, he might have run for the door if it wasn't bolted. He felt weak and couldn't understand why—confused. She put her palms on his shoulders, looked up at him. Her hands were gentle and warm. He noticed that her pupils dilated slightly. Her perfume assailed him strongly. He was anchored as though turned to stone.

"Did you ever kiss a girl?" she asked.

"No."

"I'll show you how." She pressed hard against him. "Put your arms around me."

He held her awkwardly, his arms like limp reeds.

"Squeeze a little," she said.

He did, and she pressed tightly against him, one arm around his shoulders. He was getting a hard-on now; half-scared though he was, it was coming up and he didn't care.

She held her face close to his.

"Pucker up," she said, pressing his lips with the fingers of her free hand to get them into the shape she wanted.

"I'll kiss you first like you should learn to kiss a woman."

She wetted her lips with the tip of a small, red tongue while he watched like a rabbit hypnotized by a fox. Her lips were warm and soft. She pressed them to his and tickled them with the tip of her tongue. Then she drew back.

"Open your mouth," she said. "You don't want to grow up kissing like a dead mackerel like most men."

He did, and this time when she kissed him he felt her tongue enter his mouth and probe its depth. At first he was startled then delighted when he realized that it made his already poker-hard cock start throbbing.

"Now you try that on me."

He complied eagerly, no longer uncertain. They clung together and he felt her breathing as hard and as rapidly as he was.

When they broke apart, she gasped, "My! You're really cut out for this." She took his hand and led the way to her bedroom.

"Take your clothes off," she said. She was already out of her panties and pulling up her blouse.

"We're going to take a shower together," she said. "It's not only a good way to get real excited, but you've always got to be clean about this. That's important."

He was getting out of his clothes blindly, watching parts of a woman emerge that he'd never seen except in "dirty pictures." Her breasts, white and full, pink-tipped, came out of her brassiere. Pubic hair emerged fully exposed when she stepped out of her skirt. He thought it was beautiful, thought her whole body was beautiful and couldn't take his eyes off her.

"Go ahead and look," she said. "It's natural. All men do; they never get over it."

She pulled his naked body to hers, but kept her hand between them and stroked his penis with a hand more expert than his own. He wondered how she learned that and almost groaned.

"You're pretty big all over. It must run in the family."

He missed that at the time. Later he'd know what she meant and why she said she'd miss Uncle Newt. He would also wonder what special touch Newt had to intrigue young women even at his age.

In the shower she made sure he knew how and where they needed to wash especially clean. He expected to hear Buck Doak's snide voice say something like, "It beats Miss Morlach's hygiene lectures," but the little devil respected his privacy for once.

Kate washed him gently with slippery suds and he almost came. She felt his quiver and said, "Don't do that yet. You'll be like your father. I pity your poor mother."

He didn't miss that. She didn't intend that he should.

"You and Pa did this too?"

"Why not? Your mother never does anything for him that he really needs."

"I don't know. It just seemed funny for a minute."

The shock took his mind off coming, as she hoped it would.

"Your father is what experienced women call a 'rabbit.' Or he was till Grace and I got hold of him. He came the first time I did that with him. Couldn't stop like you just did."

He thought, "The hell with Pa."

She quickly got off the subject. "Feel this," she said, taking his hand and placing it between her legs. "Now give me your finger." She placed it where she wanted it. "Feel that little swelling? Move your finger around on it."

He tried it and she gave a little moan. "That's what they call 'the little man in the row boat,' the most sensitive part of a woman. In doctor books it's a clitoris. In either case learn how to work it."

Then she thrust strongly toward him and said, "There. That's the spot exactly." He tried to keep it under his finger and massage it just right. "Keep it up," she sighed. She was now thrusting her body at him spasmodically. He felt the swelling grow. "Don't stop now, whatever you do," she gasped. "I'm going to come." It was the first time he'd heard that women came too.

Her excitement, which he knew he'd caused, and her intensity, all aroused him to a peak he'd never imagined possible without creaming all over himself; but something new grew in his mind that held him off—a desire for this delightful woman, now in the throes of passion, to have as much or more pleasure than he. He sensed her need fully, knew that something, perhaps his innocence, had unexpectedly aroused her to a surprising peak.

"I'm coming," she gasped. "Oh, my God, how I'm coming! Kiss me hard!" She clung to him and surprised him with her strength, then almost collapsed in his arms, spent, totally out of breath. After a little while she recovered and giggled. "What a lover you're going to make," she said, breathlessly. "Let's get out of here, dry off and get into bed."

They snuggled close and started all over. He kissed her this time with a little more skill and confidence, no longer afraid she might laugh at him. The thrill, he discovered, was mental as well as physical. He thought, "So this is what it's like. No wonder everyone in their right mind wants it."

Kate whispered, "It's important to take your time with most women. As good a way to get them ready as any is kiss them a lot and learn to do what you did to me in the shower."

He kissed her again, slipping his tongue deeply into her mouth and caressing her, seeking "the little man in the row boat" with his finger.

"You don't need to do that again. If you do, I won't be able to get out of bed. Try kissing my nipples a little. Run your tongue around on them and suck them. I like that. Most women do."

So did he. He was especially aroused by the fragrance the soap had imparted to them, and to her whole body. For the first time he realized why perfume was so popular.

She laughed after a while. "Roll over on top of me." She parted her legs to receive him.

When he was above her, holding himself up on his elbows, she raised her legs in a scissors grip around his buttocks. She said, "Now, let me take your cock for a minute." She slid the head of his hard shaft expertly up and down her entrance. "Feel where to put it in? It's already slippery. That's because I'm hot and ready. If a woman isn't lubricated you'll hurt her if you try to force it into her, especially with a cock as big as yours. Now you take hold of yourself and slide the head around there on me, up and down and then start it in slow and gentle."

He did as she directed, feeling an overpowering urge to push it in fully as soon as he got it in a little ways. She gave a pleased moan and came to meet him.

"Now kiss me," she said, "and don't lose control too soon and start humping like a riveting machine."

He felt his orgasm starting as soon as he got inside her, regardless of what anyone might caution. He thought, "I'm going to come too soon and spoil it." It was so impossibly better than jacking off he could hardly believe it. He started to thrust more quickly. Instead of trying to restrain him, she came to meet him each time, pulling his body strongly to her with her hands on his buttocks.

She gasped, "Get it in as far as you can each time."

That was the last thing either of them could say. As though outside of himself, he heard their groaning and gasping as they thrust to each other, and had to remind himself he was contributing part of that animal sound. Then he exploded inside her; the longest, hardest orgasm he'd ever had, jetting off through his tube as he held it deeply into her. He knew his cock had never been as big as during the final swelling. He felt her contracting around it but didn't know enough to realize she was coming with him. He almost fainted, remaining up on his elbows only with an extreme effort, so he wouldn't crush her. Finally he rolled off.

They lay side by side, regaining their breath. She laughed, an elated, breathless little sound of pleasure, then wiggled over and put her head on his shoulder. He held her tenderly, kissed her hair lightly, and with newborn ferocity, wanted only to protect this source of tremendous pleasure and triumph.

He was in love for the first time.

CHAPTER TWENTY-SIX

Paradise Regained

Bennie was again about to ride through history, this time in a little more style. Uncle Newt had gone downtown with Pa to gas up the Lincoln for the trip to Winnebago. When they returned there was a red rose in each bud base in the back seat. God alone knew how Uncle Newt got them at that early hour. After supervising the loading of suitcases into the trunk, Ma got in and couldn't help but notice the roses immediately. Their fragrance dominated the whole interior.

She was silent, sitting erect and looking at the roses, then looking out the window, trying not to look happy. She knew they were there for her.

Buck whispered to Bennie, "It smells like a funeral in here."

Bennie grinned. He didn't care. He was headed back *up north*.

The only home where his heart had ever truly been.

And this time he was occupying the copilot's seat in place of Ma. The rising sun peeped over the houses and sent slanting light through the still-bare trees across the street as Pa backed the long Lincoln out of the driveway, swung its rear across the street, came to a halt to change gears from reverse to low, and headed north, accelerating slowly.

Bennie glanced at Pa's profile and wondered what he was thinking. There was no sign on his face of a twin to Bennie's own elation, only concentration on the road. Bennie would have been puzzled if he'd sensed Pa's trepidation over having just burned his bridges. Pa had stood siege alone too long before the cavalry charged to his rescue in the person of Uncle Newt. Now he came close to simply not giving a damn. He didn't know he would live decades longer and be part of a "silent majority" whose membership, like him, had had to confront and vanquish one dragon too many, and had all the fight kicked out of them in the process. They would abandon their responsibility to exert a moderating influence on society and see America come as close to being "the Land of the Spree" as "the Land of the Free." It would survive that too. Above all, the Republic was a survivor.

Like Waubonsee's schools, those in Blackhawk *hadn't* taught Bennie much history—in the latter case they had certainly not acquainted him with the historical sites he knew they'd pass through going north. The misapplied educational theories of John Dewey had taken care of that. And that misapplication had miscued further in that Bennie wasn't especially "well adjusted." Young as he was, he had become dimly aware that "well adjusted" in practice meant indifferent to injustice. It was an ideal cloak for those too ignorant to know injustice if it bit them. Bennie would never be fat, dumb, and happy.

"Of what possible use are facts about dead eras?"
"Those who cannot remember history . . ."

"History repeats itself."
"But, that can be an avoidable tragedy."
—Pro Bono Publico

"Yah! Like Hoobert Heever and Bluebeard.
Is he coming, Sister Ann?
Is Prosperity just around the corner,
Sister Ann?"
—Buck Doaks

Bennie had skipped school often in Blackhawk and gone to the library to read all day—mostly history and biography. He was, by then, in Junior High. The principal, R. E. Lowry, hadn't regarded Bennie's impending permanent departure from the local halls of learning as occasion for other than celebration. Bennie's only scholarly achievement had been an embarrassment to the school. Annually, the Daughters of the American Revolution (D.A.R.) offered a one-hundred-fifty-question American history test. The person correctly answering the most questions received a gold medal. As usual, so-called educators poisoned the well. They assured that only students upon whom they'd already conferred an A or B in history were allowed to take the test. Why? Because educators were constitutionally unprepared to recognize that others might do as well or better than A students, especially since As are more often a function of ass-kissing than knowledge. (Who is better adjusted than a born ass-kisser?) And if Lowry and his kind had recognized these things, they would have been indisposed to lose control over the rewards and punishments which grades actually were. Grades were *all too seldom* what lip service said they were: assessments of knowledge.

Miss Tandy generously had given Bennie a C+ for his A+ historical knowledge and had done it to rap his knuckles because he rarely attended class, hadn't turned in a single homework assignment, and frequently read a book in class or slept. In doing this she had rendered her fastest horse ineligible to race, ineligible to shed reflected glory upon Miss Tandy. (Horrors, girls!

What to do? Why cheat, of course!) She recognized that a little late, and obtained a waiver for him to take the D.A.R. test. He scored 142 on it, while the runners-up, two girls, scored 101 and 95 respectively, winning a silver medal and honorable mention.

Aside from the fact that the system was geared to exclude anyone who lacked conformity, winners or not, other priceless sociological lessons of the situation escaped Bennie; for example: that living on the wrong side of the tracks as he did, his picture was not in the *Gazette* alongside second prize and honorable mention, who lived in the country club district; that the text of the article accompanying the pictures almost forgot to mention him at all, then belatedly recognized that bobble and lamely reported what amounted to: "OOPS! We just remembered what this article was supposed to be about—the D.A.R. Medal, which *old whatsis* won." Actually, *old whatsis* couldn't have cared less.

Now he was leaving the arena of that great honor; worse yet, he was leaving Kate, whom he desperately wanted to bed as often as possible. He was the type to choose orgasms over gold medals—even C+ orgasms.

He couldn't manage kissing Silver goodbye, since the honorably retired old horse was kept close to his owner's barn during the cold months, where he could get out of the wind if he wished.

Going out Washington Street in the Lincoln, Bennie thought of asking Pa to detour through Riverside Park.

"What if I never see it again?" ran through his mind. "I've had some good times there."

He'd climbed its cliffs above the river, stolen the picnic lunch of a fat-assed cop who made a life work of harassing kids and did it right under Fatso's nose, drunk from the many ever-flowing artesian wells that filled pools with delicious, though slightly sulphurous, ice-cold water; had caught the greased pig at a G.M. Fourth of July picnic, climbed the greased pole and clung to the top the same day, achieving double glory; and that night when everyone watched the fireworks, pissed in Uncle Bart's lemonade jug, but only because he knew that only Bart drank lemonade.

He'd miss Riverside Park. It might even miss him . . . sometimes land does. (Walk beside the Little Big Horn.)

> *"Where are you, George Armstrong Custer?"*
> *"Where are you Sitting Bull—Crazy Horse?"*
> *"Where are you, Blackhawk?"*

"Where are you, Ben Edwin Todd?

"Where are you, Bennie, our own, he who pissed in Uncle Bart's lemonade jug? Rare are they with the guts to prescribe poison, or 'bid the guns to shoot!' (Or even piss in a jug of lemonade.)

"Where are they all?"

BEYOND THE HILLS OF HISTORY.

Some like Bennie, faceless—oops, old whatsisname!
(While insipid runners-up are pictured in Gazettes.)
Nameless—except as pro forma afterthoughts.
Some, gone forever.
Others waiting—like Bennie—
Until the DRUMS OF THE REPUBLIC
Sound the long roll—the call to fight injustice.
The call to Glory.

CHAPTER TWENTY-SEVEN

Ma Gets a History Lesson

— 1660

"The country was so pleasant, so beautiful and fruitful that it grieved me to see that the world could not discover such enticing country to live in."
—Pierre Radisson

Just wait, Pierre!

— 1848—Regarding the Blackhawk War

"If General Cass" (then running for president) "went in advance of me in picking whortleberries, I guess I surpassed him in Charges upon wild onions. If he saw any live, fighting Indians, it was more than I did; but I had a good many bloody struggles with the mosquitoes."
—Abraham Lincoln,
Congressman

— April 1938

The ice was gone from the Rock River. The last scattered pieces had disappeared downstream and were undoubtedly metamorphosed into water on its way to the sea. Pa drove the Lincoln slowly over the river at Four-Mile-Bridge so they could admire the vista. They went that way because Uncle Newt wanted to see Fort Atkinson.

He said, "My grandpa Cheek was there during the Blackhawk War. Come to think of it, so was that Rebel son of a bitch, Jefferson Davis. He was a lieutenant just out of West Point then. Pity old Blackhawk didn't cut his balls off."

Ma, used to her "*morone*" by now, ignored the language. In fact she had a hard time suppressing a guffaw.

Bennie was well aware that Jeff Davis had later been president of the Rebel Confederacy during the Civil War.

Whenever Newt thought about Jeff Davis, he remembered some company or other of Union troops marching while they sang at the top of their voices:

We'll hang Jeff Davis
To a sour apple tree!

Sung to the tune of John Brown's Body. Later the tune was appropriated for the inspirational favorite of the Union: *The Battle Hymn of the Republic.* That also lived in Newt's memory, and still caused a lump in his throat when he remembered how it sounded with a band accompanying a thousand homesick troops singing "by the watch-fires of a hundred circling camps":

Mine eyes have seen the glory of the coming of the Lord:
He is trampling out the vintage where the grapes of wrath are stored.
* * * * *
As He died to make men holy, let us die to make men free,
While God is marching on.
* * * * *
Glory, glory, hallelujah!
Glory, glory, hallelujah!
His truth is marching on.

Ma had Pa stop along Lake Koshkonong so she could look at the geese that harbored there awhile on their way north to nesting places in the Arctic. The first thing Bennie heard when he got out of the car was the inimitable piping of a long V of them, sparkling specks against a deep blue sky, following a leader as they had done for eons in almost unchanging pattern. Only shotguns had altered their habits—they learned of hunting seasons and in the fall flew high, landing in the middle of wide lakes, beyond the range of the ring of shotgun-studded blinds along the shores, slyly dropping into cornfields and raiding the plenty there only at night.

But environment altered only the grace notes. The instinct of survival, as always, scored the melody.

In the spring it was entirely different when there was no hunting season; the honkers were their ancient selves, flying low, heedlessly squawking and screaming.

"Hear them?" Ma said, cocking her head. "How wild they sound. They're right over there on the lake. Here's a path. I'm going down there to look at them."

She left the men to follow if they pleased or not. Bennie was right behind her, skirting puddles and muddy spots and noting how nimbly she did the same. Pa and Newt stayed at the car, lighting up cigars. Bennie heard Newt say before they were out of hearing, "Seen one goose, yuh seen 'em all."

Pa laughed. "Like elephants."

Unlike Pa, Bennie also went to see every elephant he heard might be near.

Ma stood beside the lake a long while, raptly observing the bobbing birds as they paddled slowly, like tall ships getting under way, ducking heads beneath the surface to pluck succulent bottom-growing tidbits, with pointy-tailed rumps sticking out of the water. Occasionally one of them decided to take a spin aloft, flailing mighty wings to work up takeoff speed, then climbing rapidly and circling, only to come right back after a turn or two, gliding down, feet extended like huge skis to break its speed as it hit the water, plopping in with a rocking motion, spraying white water and honking. As far as Bennie could see they flew for the pure joy of it, sometimes inducing others to join them for a formation flight. It didn't occur to him that this was a calisthenics program to stay in shape for the next lap of their journey.

Bennie wondered what it would be like to fly that freely. Up till then his flying had been in a Ford Tri-motor (aptly called a Tin Goose) and in J-3 Cubs, on the few occasions when he could hornswoggle a flight at the Blackhawk airport. Compared to geese, it seemed to him that both those aircraft were pretty unwieldy, though he felt free in the air like nowhere else.

When he and Ma came back, Newt said, "We thought maybe old Blackhawk come back and got you two."

Bennie grinned. Ma ignored them if she even heard, looking pensive and distant, quiet for a long while after they drove on. Bennie thought she looked like she'd have been glad if Blackhawk had come and spirited her away. Or maybe she wanted to sprout wings and fly off with the geese, seeing a different earth far below, inhabited by inferior, plodding beings.

They stopped for lunch in Madison, the state capital. He admired the view of the capitol building as they drove down State Street, thinking it looked just like the one in Washington, D.C. He'd seen pictures of the nation's capitol and others but had never actually been near one. It was a hallowed picture to one who thrived on history. Such signs as the Orpheum and Capitol Theaters, or the beer billboard proclaiming "Now Better Than Ever—Old Heidelberg!" seemed to desecrate this sacred scene. His patriotic fervor might have been watered down somewhat if his reading had introduced him to James Duane Doty, father of Madison.

Doty, a federal judge due to political sycophancy at age twenty-three, used his skill along those lines to "log-roll" Madison (then called Four Lakes) into the site for the new state capital before so much as a log cabin existed there. However, title to the land did exist in the pockets of Doty and his friends. Odd how the course of Empire sniffs down the path of the money.

Pa saw a handy restaurant right on State Street with a parking spot open out front. They got lunch there. Bennie rushed through his hamburger and French fries to go out and look at the capitol building some more—also to roll a cigarette from the Bull Durham hidden in his jacket pocket. He walked up the street, rolled his weed, then walked back inhaling with great satisfaction, but ready to toss it down if Ma came out of the restaurant.

Buck Doaks, eyeing the capitol building said, "Just like Washington, D.C., in those Civil War pictures. Maybe Old Abe will come down the street."

Bennie grinned. "I wish he would. I've got a question I'd like to ask him."

"Like what?"

"Like why someone as smart as him didn't hire a bodyguard that was worth a shit."

They headed west out of town, then north. A few fields still held snow beneath evergreen trees and in gullies, or on the north slopes of steep hills. Farmers were out with tractors or teams, preparing fields for planting. Most farms had a herd of familiar black-and-white Holstein dairy cows somewhere in sight, either on early pasture which wasn't much to brag about yet, or in farm lots near the barns and silos. New calves were eyeing the world curiously, staying close to their mamas.

Ma exclaimed several times, "Oh, look at that cute little calf!"

Bennie agreed. Nothing was more innocent-looking or prettier than a new calf with its melting brown eyes and big floppy ears. The only fault he found with most of them was they were too shy to let you walk up and pet them.

Crow lookouts criss-crossed the land, the only birds plainly in evidence, though Bennie knew the scattered woods were full of others kinds of birds that had just migrated north like the geese, or native birds that were getting active now that it was warming up. Ducks and geese were paddling in the shallows of the Wisconsin River when they crossed the bridge into Sauk City. Pa drove right through town, then through its twin, Prairie du Sac, and continued north on Highway 12 toward Baraboo.

"Baraboo," Ma said, reading the mileage sign. "Ringling Brothers winter there—maybe we can see some animals, especially elephants."

"They aren't there anymore," Bennie said. "They winter in Florida now."

Ma didn't look pleased. He didn't look back, but knew what she looked like from the familiar gravel in her voice when she said, "How do you know?"

"I read it somewhere."

"You're always reading something somewhere," she grumbled.

He thought, "You'd be better off if you read something somewhere besides those 'rape magazines' about *morones* that you and Aunt Mary gobble up."

Ma said, "They wouldn't have left there. They've been in business in Wisconsin since the Civil War."

"1881," Bennie corrected, and shouldn't have.

"You don't know what you're talking about!"

He thought, "Why don't I get my foot into it all the way?" Besides he sometimes liked to bait Ma. He said, "Yes I do. You're probably confusing Ringling Brothers with Barnum, since the shows later combined. Barnum started his Museum in New York before the Civil War in 1842. Ringling Brothers didn't join Barnum and Bailey till years later. Or maybe you were thinking of the tour Barnum arranged for Jenny Lind in 1850."

"Where did you hear of Jenny Lind? You don't even know who she was."

Bennie wished he could say, "The hell I don"t!" What he did say was bad enough, "She was a famous Swedish singer who toured the world."

"You think you're pretty smart now that you got that history medal, don't you."

Newt pitched in, "He is pretty smart—that's why he got the medal. By the way, I heard Jenny Lind sing once. Not too bad for a 'furriner' either."

That didn't mollify Ma or get her off Bennie's case. She was scowling as she said, "He'd do better to get a job delivering papers instead of sitting around with his nose in a book all the time."

Bennie shrugged. He thought, "*Not all the time. You should have seen me and Kate in the shower, old girl.*" He reckoned they didn't have paper routes up in the woods. To Buck he said, "I could really steam her ass if I told her that I know Barnum didn't start his circus till 1871, merged with Bailey in 1881, the year that Ringling Brothers gave their first performance right back there where we just passed a little while ago at Mazomanie, Wisconsin."

Buck said, "You wouldn't have the date, would you?"

"November '81; there were fifty-nine people at the first show."

"I shouldn't have asked."

Ability to remember that kind of stuff was what won the D.A.R. medal. On the other hand there was algebra—a complete mystery to Bennie, as well as a puzzle regarding what anyone normal could do with it during their life. Geometry was more his speed. You could see geometry.

He figured he'd bugged Ma enough and didn't throw in any of those details, or mention that Sauk Prairie, which they were then passing, had been the site of the Great Town of the Sauk Indians in the 1700s. The latter had been great farmers and supplied traders for miles around with corn, beans, and melons to get them through the winters. Ma most likely thought the first white men in Wisconsin had been the lumbermen in the 1800s. In fact, Jean Nicolet had set foot ashore at Green Bay in 1634. A French fur trading empire had thrived for a century before the British drove them out in the French and Indian War, which ended in 1763. Shortly after that, an American, Jonathan Carver, visited the Sauk village in October 1766. He reported that they had snug houses, regularly laid out streets, and even front porches on which to sit smoking and admiring the scene.

Blackhawk may have been born there. He was later a Sauk war chief, after the tribe migrated southwest around the mouth of the Rock River in Illinois. It had been the appropriation of their land there, particularly their main village Saukenuk, which was at the root of the Blackhawk War in 1832.

There was still plenty of light when they got to Devil's Lake, so Pa drove in and parked the Lincoln in the campground.

"We can get out and stretch our legs," he explained his decision to stop there.

Bennie got out and looked up at the purple-tinted cliffs surrounding the oval green lake. The area was dotted with coniferous trees. The cliffs towered four or five hundred feet above them. The air was heavy with the piney smell even though a wind was blowing.

"Let's walk up there," Uncle Newt suggested. "Here's a path goin' that direction. I really do need to stretch my legs."

"Go right ahead," Pa said. "I'm staying here. It looks to me like you'll get more leg stretching than you bargained for if you go all the way to the top."

Newt and Bennie set out on the path. "I'm coming too," Ma said."

Bennie thought, "*I'll bet you don't make it to the top, old girl.*"

He lost his bet. She was barely puffing when she got there right alongside him. A half-hour brisk climb had taken them to a lookout point where the whole lake spread out beneath them, so clear the bottom was visible. It suggested a colossal glittering emerald.

The pines stirred musically in the chill wind, reminding them that some years Wisconsin had only two seasons—winter and Fourth of July—and even in good springs, winter sometimes returned with a rush for an indefinite stay. The sun was flirting with the treetops to the west, settling into a deep blue sky, and little puffy clouds criss-crossed it, chilling them whenever the sun was blotted out.

Ma was taking it all in, standing on a projecting rock like the figurehead on a sailing ship, breathing deeply of the balsam-scented air, oblivious to the chill and the two males with her.

Bennie was about to remind her that they ought to get back down before dark, but Newt restrained him with a hand on his shoulder and a head shake.

Bennie understood. Perhaps for the first time since she was a farm kid, Ma was feeling just like he and Uncle Newt did about the outdoors and its wide, empty spaces. He could have played tour guide and told Ma how the glacier had formed the lake that enthralled her, but the thought fled his mind as soon as it entered.

When they reached Baraboo, the streetlights were just coming on. Ma had them stop and ask someone where Ringling Brothers' winter quarters were located. The local man they asked looked like they might be a little "tetched" and said, "If we was any closer to where *they used to be* they'd bite us. That's what all these old empty brick and stone barns are along here. The circus hasn't wintered here for years." The buildings were practically in the center of town. Bennie had thought they might be some old warehouses.

Ma didn't look happy. Bennie had sense enough not to say, "I-told-you-so." He didn't even look her way. Why embarrass her? For once he was sorry for her, knowing how disappointed she must be.

They found a tourist court, then went to the restaurant recommended by the owner. When Uncle Newt and Bennie returned to their cabin, full of chicken fried steak and home fries, the old man flopped in the wicker rocker and puffed contentedly on his cigar. Bennie pulled the other chair to the opposite side of the table and rolled a cigarette. He was looking forward to reading the latest issue of *Western Story Magazine*.

Before he got started, Newt said, "I was up in this country with Pa before the Civil War. I was just a kid, but he used to take me all over with him."

"How about school?"

"Pa always said school was for turning out imitations of great men. He took me out whenever he wanted to. One teacher fussed about it and pestered Pa until he told him he'd shoot out his lights and liver if he didn't shut up."

Bennie waited, knowing that there was a story coming.

"Pa owned some timber land and had money in a railroad up here. The railroad went busted in the Panic of 1857 like most of 'em did. Later he come out smellin' like a rose though. His interest got picked up as part of the Milwaukee Road. A big crooked sonofabitch of a banker from Milwaukee pulled it all out of the fire. Made Pa rich before he croaked."

"I thought he was killed in the Civil War."

"Not by a jug full, though he might have been better off if he was . . . I shouldn't say that, I guess. He did a power of good for a lot of folks before he went. Went to court to try cases in his wheelchair. They tried to make him a judge so he could sit down all the time, but he knew their game and told them to go to hell. In any case he damn well croaked way before his time."

Bennie was sorry he'd asked since he had merely wanted to know about the family. He looked at Uncle Newt cautiously to see if he'd hurt his feelings and concluded that the old man didn't look irritated, though it was obviously a sore subject.

Newt finally said, "In the end he killed himself."

"Why?" Bennie blurted.

"He was crippled. Hurt all the time. Never walked after that sonofabitch shot him in the back."

Newt was silent for a while—remembering—puffing on his cigar. Bennie waited. If Newt didn't want to tell him the details, he understood why, but he was eager to hear them.

When Newt finally opened up again, he said, "Pa waited till Ma was gone. He must have hung on all those years just to look after her. I don't think either of them ever looked at anyone else. People talk about love, but they were the only ones I could say for sure loved each other. They was kids in school together."

He was silent a while then laughed gustily. "I sure as hell didn't take after Pa that way. But I might have if I'd met the right gal."

"Were you ever married?"

"Almost." Newt grinned and looked at Bennie speculatively, debating whether this was the time to tell him more about that. He decided to change the subject.

He said, "Today we went right past where Pa's dad was in a battle with Blackhawk's Injuns—down by Sauk City."

"Yeah," Bennie said. "The battle of Wisconsin Heights."

"I ain't surprised you heard of it—read it, I reckon." There was pride in his voice, something Bennie wasn't used to hearing even from Pa.

Bennie said, "Yeah. I read it in a book somewhere, but I forgot which one. I sure as hell never heard about it in school though, I know that. Probably Wisconsin is ashamed of what happened to old Blackhawk."

Newt nodded. "They ought to be. Anyhow, I never had much use for schools myself. I went off adventuring too early. Which reminds me, we ought to have stopped at that battlefield. I had half a notion to mention it."

"You should have," Bennie said.

"Pa took me over there in 1860, less'n thirty years after the fight. I was only ten then, but I can remember it clear as yesterday, clearer in fact; at my age you sometimes forget what happened yesterday." He snorted. "Gettin' old is hell, kid, but it beats hell out of not gettin' old as long as you still have some piss and vinegar left in you.

"Anyhow the battlefield was in the middle of nowhere back then. Plenty of arrowheads and Injun truck, and lead balls—I even found a ramrod. I wouldn't be surprised if you could still find stuff like that today."

Bennie said, "Maybe the two of us can come down some day after we get settled *up north*. It ain't all that far away."

"Good idea. You'll have to start driving the Lincoln. We can go over to Bad Axe too—where they finally slaughtered old Blackhawk's outfit. I suppose you know about that too."

Bennie felt his heart leap at the thought of being allowed to drive the Lincoln and had to catch his breath.

Finally he said, "I read about the battle of Bad Axe too. Up on the Mississippi south of LaCrosse. The Sacs that escaped across the Mississippi were massacred by the Sioux under Wabasha."

Newt snorted. "That brings to mind an article I saw not long ago. We didn't look pretty in the affair, but like you say, the Sioux killed women and kids too, musta been a hundred or more of 'em at least. Injuns was always killin' each other. If we hadn't whipped the hell out of all of 'em they'd have killed each other off. Maybe been best if they had. Not many of the poor buggers have any self-respect left. Can't blame 'em for that either."

Like most whites, even Newt hadn't learned that the Indians didn't kill each other off until trading with whites set them against one another in competition for furs and trade goods, to say nothing of whiskey. Before then they had their own economy, trading with other tribes and bringing goods up to that country from as far away as Mexico.

Bennie thought about what Newt had said before he went to sleep. He remembered Waubonsee, who had fought with the whites against Blackhawk. He figured Blackhawk would never pay him a call, since he most likely would know he was a friend of his enemy, Waubonsee. That night he dreamed he was trying to stop the Sioux from killing the women and kids of Blackhawk's tribe. The Sioux laughed at him at first, then started chasing him, showering arrows his way, but miraculously none hit him and he finally dove into the Mississippi and swam a long ways downstream under water and got away.

In the morning Pa came over alone. Newt was already up, but Bennie was still drowsing in bed.

"Hear the fuss last night?" Pa asked. He was trying to keep from laughing.

"Nope," Newt said. "Slept like a log."

Pa finally couldn't hold himself in and guffawed. "A cop pinched Em."

That woke Bennie up all the way.

"What happened?" Newt asked.

"Ask her. It'll be more fun that way."

"For you, maybe. Something tells me I just ought to pass on that one. Why don't you tell us?"

"Well, you know Em is half-cracked about walking around at night. She musta sneaked out after I was asleep. Anyhow, a cop caught her trying to crawl through a window into one of the old Ringling Brothers' barns. She got the cop to bring her up here instead of booking her. Lucky he was a nice guy or we'd be down bailing her out."

"Did she say what the hell she thought she was doing?"

"I asked her that as soon as the cop brought her up here. If you live to be a million you'll never guess what she said . . ."

Bennie said, "I'll bet I can guess. She said she wanted to see an elephant."

Pa gave him a funny look. "How did you know?"

"I just guessed. But she said last night, sort of to herself, 'I still think there's elephants down there.' You two were talking about something else and didn't notice."

"Who knows," Newt said, "maybe she saw one? Or an elephant spook. She's half Injun ain't she? They're funny. Sometimes they see things we don't."

Bennie thought, "Like Chief Waubonsee." He had half a notion to tell them about that, but decided not to. They'd only laugh. He'd never told anyone.

"Anyhow, I think the cop figured she was a little dotty and he'd best let me handle her. He was laughing when he left. Good thing. After he left she said, 'Didn't he look like a morphadite to you?' You know, if they're not a *morone*, they're a morphadite according to Em. I told her she ought to be damned glad he was a good guy, whatever he was."

Ma was exceptionally quiet at breakfast and didn't eat much. The rest of the trip north she said very little, not even wanting to stop at the Dells.

Looking over the roadside clutter there, Newt said, "Just as well not to stop here. Looks like a tourist trap."

Not far north of there they were fairly in the sand country, with marshes and tamaracks along the road. The houses and barns were run down and needed paint. The land had a nice feel to it though. The government had tried to relocate these poor farmers and got very few takers. It was a deep mystery for the bureaucrats.

Bennie was really taken with the view, desolate though most people would have considered it. They were all quiet, taking it in. Pa stopped on a long straight stretch of road with marshes along both sides. They all got out, stretched and rubbernecked at the scenery. Bennie inhaled one deep breath after another of the wet fresh air. A rattletrap Ford pickup slowed to see if they needed help then speeded up when Pa waved; the two men in the front seat smiled and waved back.

"People always were friendly up here," Pa said. "Like the West. Everybody's game to help. I loved this country."

Ma gave him a black look. She was obviously thinking of saying, "I didn't!"

Pa hadn't given birth to two babies in it, both without a doctor. Pa also didn't care for good clothes or miss city conveniences. His prune of a sister, Felice, snidely had called him "Honorable Patches" in those days due to his shabby dress—at a time when he was still her main support, before she'd captured her prize cretin, Bertram.

They reached Felice's in the middle of the afternoon. Her farm lay just across the river bridge from Winnebago. She knew they were coming, but sure didn't welcome "Honorable Patches" with open arms.

Bennie couldn't remember her at all, hoped she'd be like her twin, Aunt Nellie, but read the opposite at first glance.

Buck Doaks summed it up: "*Skinny O'Brien and Miss Crane wrapped in one lousy package.*"

A girl Bennie guessed must be a year or two younger than he came out and stood behind Felice, peeking around her with wide, curious eyes that also held a shadow of fear. She was skinny and looked embarrassed, rubbing one bare foot on top of the other. Bennie wondered if he had a nutty cousin that the family was keeping a secret, like they had his Uncle Bob.

Buck said, "The kid there is rushing the barefoot season, isn't she?"

"I guess," Bennie said. "But take a gander at pruneface and her old man with the Orphan-Annie eyes and elephant ears. They're probably too cheap to buy her shoes."

"Or something to eat either, from the looks of her."

"Yeah. Pity."

He caught her looking at him speculatively, open interest in her innocent dark eyes for just an instant, then she realized he'd caught her and cast her eyes down at her bare feet and blushed. Bennie was sorry he'd caught her and told himself, "She's thinking that we think she's funny and outlandish. She looks to me like the only honest one in the bunch."

She whirled and ran off around the house. Felice yelled, "Stay here, Rose," but the girl kept going. He saw her dodge across the backyard toward the barn and disappear behind it. "Maybe they make her sleep out there," he thought.

"She's shy," Felice said.

Buck snorted, "If you ask me, 'a trifle tetched' would come closer."

Bennie wasn't too sure. He'd liked something in her eyes—also, she was so clean she sparkled, especially her long chestnut hair. He thought, "What the hell am I thinking about her for? She's just a skinny little kid."

He glanced around then—remembering. The scene came back clearly from the time when he and Buck had traipsed off from this yard to the cemetery on a moonlit night long ago—almost a decade—and he'd seen Grandpa Todd's ghost. Now he wondered if it had really happened, or if he'd been dreaming.

He wondered if he should ever tell Uncle Newt; if anyone would understand, it would be Newt.

In any case he knew they'd see Grandpa's grave again pretty soon because Newt had said to him, "You'll have to show me old Johnny Todd's grave because I want to put some posies on it first thing. I lived the best days of my life with him."

CHAPTER TWENTY-EIGHT

Up North Again

I am still the buckskin land.
Tarry beside the waters that divide me,
Sleep with me in starlight,
Winnebago and Chippewa silently slip through my aisles,
One with earth;
Kill their brother, the deer,
Speed bullet with prayer
For the soul whose earthly shrine they steal.

Bear, and wolf,
Lynx, coyote, fox,
Walk my fastnesses,
Drink my waters;
Hunt:
Rabbits and mice, deer,
Each other.
Survival rules—the need to eat.

Hear my trees?
Musical in breezes,
Threatening in storms
When birch and poplar roar.

Listen. It is timber wolf.
Only bear does not fear him.
Why do you hold your breath?
Both fear man.

Do not hate my violence,
Fear my shadowed places.
I am what you make of me,
Friend or foe.

The Indian knows,
But is silent.
I am an open book.

Read me if you can.

— 1938—April

I told you we'd get stuck in the mud if you came this way!" Ma told Pa.

Pa only grunted. He gunned the engine and rocked the Lincoln back and forth, trying to free it by alternately snapping it from low to reverse and letting the clutch out easy each way, but only spun the wheels and buried the Lincoln in the mire a little deeper.

"We can get out and push while you gun it," Bennie suggested.

"We're buried too damn deep," Pa said. He shut the engine off. "I'll go over to Old Nelson's place and see if I can get him to bring over his team to pull us out."

Newt was admiring the woods. He didn't give a damn if they ever got out. This country looked like what he liked—wilderness. He got out, stretched and looked around. Bennie followed him, eyed the dark woods, heard some strange, large bird squawk as it took wing from a tall rampike down the road. The high, dead growth on the road told him that nothing had passed that way in a long while. It had only two dim ruts to show where it had been.

Ma climbed out and said, "I'd think you'd have sense enough not to come down here the way it looked."

"Aw, dry up!" Pa said.

Bennie thought, "Oh, boy! It looks like this may be a new game." He'd never heard Pa tell Ma to dry up.

Pa then said, to no one in particular, "I'm going to cut through the woods over to Nelson's; it's a lot shorter. The creek'll be down enough—maybe the old crossing log is still there."

"I'll come along," Bennie volunteered.

"Hadn't better," Pa said. "Old Nelson's wife was always down on kids."

Newt wondered if Pa had noticed that this kid was an inch taller than he was and concluded he probably hadn't.

Bennie shrugged. He was happy just breathing deeply of the pungent, moist air and trying to see into the deep hazy woods as far as possible. These were real woods. He knew that dozens of beady, little eyes were covertly observing them. Pa had often told him that these woods ran unbroken for twenty miles to the west, except for marshes here and there. He could scarcely wait to explore them. In them, deer would be plentiful, there were still bears and wolves, as well as coyotes. Thinking of the future when he'd go rambling, he was hardly aware of Ma and Pa volleying words.

"You'll fall off the log and drown if the creek is high."

"It probably isn't high. Hell, I can most likely hop across on rocks at the ford this late—ice's been out for at least a couple of weeks."

"I'm going with you anyhow," Ma said.

It had always been a mystery to Bennie why Ma, who didn't seem to care much about Pa, always tried to protect him at times like this.

Pa said, "You'll probably slip off the log or a rock and fall in and get soaked."

"I'm going if you do," Ma persisted.

Pa suddenly guffawed. "Why not? Old Nelson was always a little sweet on you. It might help get the team."

"He was not!" Ma snapped. "He was nothing but a dirty old sot."

Newt thought, "*Dirty old sots get sweet on gals too.*" He'd been listening, grinning inwardly. He loved to hear Ma and Pa go at it, reminding him that he'd been wise never to buy a cow with milk so cheap. Ma would have poisoned him if she knew his motto about women: "*If they didn't put out, there'd be a bounty on 'em.*"

Bennie had wandered up the road a hundred yards or so to get away from the wrangling. He'd rather hear the woods talking. Besides, this place of his birth was laden with not-so-dim memories even though he'd left it so young. He was sure he remembered the road here that he'd traveled many times with Pa and Ma in a buggy or wagon, sometimes in a bobsled or cutter; first in Ma's arms, then able to sit up between Ma and Pa. When he was real little, they had to point out things to him. It came back to him clearly just then that Ma had once said, "Oh look at that eagle. You don't see many of them," and pointed. Sometimes Pa would stop when deer were in the road; the first time, Ma took Bennie's head in her hands and aimed his eyes at them. He had been very small then. Later he was often the first to see something and point it out.

"Home," Buck interrupted his thoughts. "Remember?"

"I guess I do. I remember Ma showing me an eagle along here somewhere."

"On this very spot," Buck said. "Smell this air. There's no goddam air better'n in the woods. You'll have to get a camping outfit and get way to hell back in them."

Bennie would later recall that Buck had said, "You'll," rather than, "We'll."

"Suits me," Bennie said.

"Here comes the debating society."

Ma and Pa were briskly walking their direction, Newt staying well behind. When they got closer Pa told Bennie, "We're going over to Nelson's. Why don't you and Newt go up to our old cabin? I'll point out the way."

"I know the way," Bennie said, and was sorry right away.

"How would you know the way?" Ma snapped. "You were too young to know anything when we left here."

Bennie thought, *"I wasn't too young to know that we shouldn't be leaving."*

He fell in behind them, dropping back to where Newt was. He wondered if Newt had his .45 in his back pocket, then thought, "Foolish question. Of course he does." Ma would have had a hissy if she'd known that.

Ma and Pa left them where the road to the old cabin took a sharp turn to the left. The old Todd farm was on a knoll above the East Fork, which everyone simply called "the creek."

"God knows when we'll make it back," Pa said. "But sometime for sure."

Bennie thought, "Who the hell cares?" And when they were out of hearing, said it.

"Amen," Buck said.

"Ditto," Newt added.

They walked in silence. The weathered shingles of their old cabin came into view through a break in the woods. It had survived the brush fire that started when Uncle Bart let Grandma Todd's big nearby cabin burn to the ground. Grandma had hung on there for another year, living in the little cabin, then she'd regretfully moved in with Aunt Felice. She'd tearfully sent Bob to an institution, since she could no longer cook and wash for him. Aunt Felice said, "I'm sure not going to wait on that lout." Grandma thought it was a hell of a way to talk about your brother. But she was getting helpless herself and needed them. Felice and the Cretin had been careful to have her sign over all her property to them before letting even her move in. They sold off the old farm as soon as she moved out.

As they approached, something darted away from the house down the hill toward the creek and disappeared in the underbrush.

"Lynx," Newt said. "Good sign no one's been around here lately. Probably hunting mice in the old cabin. There'll be lots of 'em in an old cabin like that."

"Or in the lynx by now," Buck said.

"Most likely a little of both. Sorry to spoil his breakfast." He stopped walking and sized up the abandoned cabin. "So this is where you let out your first squawk, eh kid?"

"I guess."

"What the hell do you mean, 'I guess'?"

"I might have been born over in Grandma's cabin."

"Why don't you ask your Ma?"

"I will."

"Well, I reckon there's worse places to be born. It looks homey to me."

Bennie felt peculiar here and tried to figure out why. He thought, "It's not only because I know I was born here, but something else." He had the weird notion for an instant that he'd always been here and the place had been born in him, as much as the other way around. "How could that be?" he asked himself. He was assailed by the conviction that some titanic revelation or adventure was in store for him here; maybe both. He knew the Indians thought everything was One, and he was more Indian than his blood suggested.

He ducked through the low door into the front room, which had been the kitchen. The heavy plank door sagged on one hinge. Still in fair condition was a plank floor he couldn't remember. It was littered with leaves, also twigs, perhaps blown in, perhaps dragged in by squirrels or birds. Small piles of mouse droppings proved the accuracy of Newt's surmise about what business a lynx had there.

The brick chimney to the left of the door was in good shape and had a brass plug in the stovepipe hole. Stairs to the loft ran behind the chimney from its right, a narrow pantry beneath them to the chimney's left. The place was permeated by an essence of dead leaves and bark, as well as the mustiness of a long-vacant log cabin. Years ago, someone in need had appropriated the windows. It was a wonder they hadn't torn up the plank floor and taken the brass chimney plug. He passed into Ma and Pa's former bedroom through a door in the far left corner at the base of the stairs.

This room was about the same size as the front room, taking up the full eighteen foot width of the cabin and about equally splitting the length, which Bennie estimated at around thirty feet. When he'd approached the building he'd thought, "How little it is." It seemed a trifle larger inside, but hadn't provided much room for a family of five.

The bedroom had no closet, only a shelf with a pipe for hanging clothes under it, hung to the wall immediately to the right of the door and running the full length of that wall. He thought, "As persnickety as Ma is about dust, this must have driven her nuts, she probably put a sheet or something over her clothes." It didn't occur to him how pitifully few clothes there had been after they wore out what they'd brought up there with them.

The interior walls had been plastered by Ma's brother Rob, who had visited them one summer. He was a plasterer by trade. He'd also put down their first "dug" well and cribbed it. Before that they'd got their water by dipping it from the creek in a bucket. That had made getting enough water in the winter a real problem. The creek froze a foot thick or more and sometimes almost to the bottom in a real cold winter. A hole had to be chopped in the ice with an axe and kept open every day without fail. The horses and cows would go down to the hole and take their turn at drinking, but if there was young stock born unseasonably, water had to be carried to them since they couldn't stand the weather unsheltered and, moreover would have been a meal for wolves or coyotes if they ran away. So water was laboriously packed up to the barn every day for little pigs or calves and to the hen house. A hell of a job, even after the well was put in. In the winter, baths were also an ordeal, the same tub of water was used by everyone, a little warm water added from the tea kettle each time.

All of that ran through Bennie's mind while he looked around. It dawned on him for the first time that Ma had a point in wanting to leave such a place, "dug" well or no "dug" well. It wasn't much to brag about.

Newt came in and surveyed the bedroom. He said, "Right fancy compared to some I've lived in. This could be fixed up first rate."

"Think it's for sale?"

"Huh-uh."

Bennie felt his heart sink. He'd been living here again in his mind; now he looked glum.

"The reason I know that for sure," Newt said, "is 'cause I bought it myself."

Bennie's face brightened again. "Bought it? How'd you do that? You've been with us all the time."

"The U.S. mail. Remember, I got all them books—yer old Unc can read and write, kid. I got it for only five hundred bucks, and the guy that owned it thought he'd robbed me."

"Wow! You plannin' on us livin' here too?"

"Why not, if your Pa can't find anything else better. Can build another house, or a fancy cabin like your Grandma had."

Bennie left the bedroom and mounted the stairs cautiously. He had to duck his head to keep from hitting the sloping roof at the landing, but the ridge pole had been set high to provide the steep roof necessary to shed snow, making for plenty of head room in the center of the loft. The windows had been stripped from their openings at each end, just like those downstairs. He was surprised someone hadn't stolen the flooring, since it was in good shape. Probably rough-sawed pine was too cheap to make stealing it worth while.

Newt followed him upstairs. "Roof's still good," he said. "Hardly a water mark down here. Musta done a good shingling job."

Bennie thought, "I'll bet this was a cold place to sleep in winter." He knew that Sister and Roy had slept in the loft while Ma had kept him downstairs with her and Pa, often in their bed in real cold weather. He wondered if they had enough covers, recalling their few, inadequate blankets in Waubonsee. When they had finally got a little money ahead, he recalled how Ma made comforters from big rolls of cotton and cheap muslin, which she stitched together with string in a checkerboard pattern, with a stitch about every four inches or so. Had she done that here—*up north*? Probably. Grandpa had plowed money into the place when they needed it.

He dimly remembered how Ma or Pa got up occasionally to put more wood in the stove. It took an iron will for either of them to do that, especially as dog-tired as they were sometimes. Neither of them could afford the luxury of staying in bed if they got sick either, especially Pa. Bob and Bart couldn't be depended on to do anything right, if at all. Left up to them the cows would go dry from not milking them or the chickens starve or do without water.

These realizations all crowded in on Bennie, but failed to dampen his enthusiasm. He did begin to see how Ma might have hated such a situation, though. Who could blame her? Even a place like Waubonsee had looked better to her till the Depression came along. That was when they remembered that here, despite all the inconveniences, they'd at least had enough to eat. Even when there was little or no money, which had been most of the time, there were eggs, potatoes, milk, home-canned fruit and vegetables, delicious homemade bread and butter, jelly from wild berries, limitless easy-keeping cranberries from the marshes to the west, and nuts gathered all over the woods. Both cabins had root cellars to keep this plenty in. The root cellars were warmer in winter than the cabins. With dirt and straw banked around the cabin foundations, nothing ever froze in the root cellars.

Newt led the way back downstairs and outside, then made a round outside the cabin.

"Yup," he said. "It kin be fixed up real snug. A little creosote and some mortar on the rotten spots, maybe a new shingle or two. It'll last longer'n I will."

He sat down on the kindling chopping stump outside the front door, took out a cigar, bit off the tip, fired up, and crossed his legs, blowing out a huge cloud of smoke and watching it drift away.

"Home," he pronounced.

"Do you inhale those things?" Bennie asked.

"Sure as hell do. That's why I'm in such good shape for my age. Hell, I just had my semi-annual hard-on when I woke up this morning. Pity Kate or Grace wasn't around."

Buck said. "More like your semi-hourly hard-on."

Bennie rolled a cigarette and savored that first drag while his gaze swept over the woods. Second growth had crept into the long-uncultivated fields. Birches were already becoming respectable trees. Through them he saw dark, hazy woods, principally oaks interspersed with pine and full-grown birches, though he didn't know that yet. Along the creek were willows and poplars as well as more birches and scattered pines.

The sun was burning off the haze and would soon shine through, drying the dewy undergrowth.

"Let's walk up the creek a ways," Bennie suggested.

"You walk up the creek," Newt said. "I'm gonna sit here and calculate about fixin' up this place."

CHAPTER TWENTY-NINE

You Will Be One of Us

Bennie walked off, wishing he had his Stevens Crackshot. Ma naturally had nixed bringing that with them, with him hating her for it every second while she laid in her arguments until Pa caved in. Newt hadn't been in on that discussion, or Benny would have had it with him. However he wasn't nervous without a gun.

At the creek bank he stopped to listen to the rushing water. A woodpecker hammered in the distance; the flutter of small birds was all around in the brush. Snow patches survived under deadfalls and in nooks beneath the caving creek banks. He breathed deeply, savoring the mingled sweet musty smell of decaying old growth and green, budding new.

A blue jay belled and was answered by another. "*Most people don't even know that jays can make such a musical sound*," he thought. Writers always referred to their raucous cries.

A crow "scout" drifted over. Well after it was safely past, it announced its mission with a sudden, noisy flapping of wings and furious cawing, telling its gang that the two-legged monster was tarrying by their creek, had no bang-stick in his hands, and was standing still so it was hard to predict if he'd head toward their nesting ground. Bennie watched it out of sight, then spotted a hawk circling, and watched till it drifted away beyond the tree rim, all the time inhaling the invigorating air, unable to get enough of it. He resumed his walk then, looking constantly about, anxious not to miss anything.

He climbed an odd-shaped knoll above the creek and wondered if it might be an Indian burial mound. At its top he sat down on a deadfall that overlooked a long, straight stretch of the creek. By now the sun had risen over the trees and burned off the fog, warming the woods. He leaned back on a broad limb that provided a comfortable back rest and pulled up his feet. The warmth made him drowsy, which reminded him he'd been up since long before dawn. Through squinted eyes he peered directly at the sun. Ma claimed that would ruin your eyes, but the Indians did it for hours during their sun dances and were noted for their acute vision. Bennie thought, "Like a lot of things that's a bunch of bull too, I guess."

Staring at the sun made him feel like he was soaring toward it at incredible speed. A similar experience sometime in the dim past tugged at his memory. Lazily he searched his mind for what it had been, with nothing to do right away, anticipating many days ahead of him like this one, knowing that almost anything might happen, and no matter what it was it would be all new. Then he remembered what the sun reminded him of. He recalled how he'd wake up sick and stare at the bright ball of the gaslight in his stuffy bedroom in Waubonsee, where he'd suffered through so many childhood illnesses. That orb had seemed to beckon to a frightening fate, being close and infinitely distant at the same time. The sun didn't suggest death, but life—a new exciting life, an explosion of wonderful days.

The memory of that foul room, of the sad days when *up north* had been only a grail, cast a shadow over him. During those unpromising years of childhood he'd often been sure he'd never live to find his grail, the place of his dreams. Ma had almost convinced him that he'd die because "pneumonia weakened him," and she surely had taught him that he was undeserving; a "degenerate" who would probably go to reform school and have his head shaved and eat bread and water. She'd tried to deny pleasure to everyone around her unless they first made some sacrifice, just as her father had made everyone suffer to have pleasure, especially in order to get their Christmas present, even if it was a lousy pair of socks.

Worse, life had shown him that what he loved would be taken from him. By now he had known for months that Mutt died a terrible death from which he could have saved him. Sister had written them one of her sentimental letters telling them how poor Mutsy died. It had reminded Bennie that Pa hadn't even thought of looking for a landlady in Blackhawk who would have let him keep Mutt. As a sort of ritual of protection, Bennie had learned to conceal love; he even tried to deny its existence to himself.

Well, he was at least back *up north*. But would that too be denied him? Maybe he would be made to wait for months, in suspense over whether they'd find the right place to live, months during which Pa might "chicken" about the whole thing, go back and beg G.M. for his old job back. He didn't know, but his mood switched from one of elation to one of apprehension. Maybe he'd get sick and die here before they even went back and got their things and brought them to a new home. This caused a lump of self-pity to rise in his throat and brought tears to his eyes.

Then he remembered the words of Waubonsee, "You will be one of us."

"I won't be 'one of them' unless I live, will I?" He asked himself. The thought didn't occur to him that he might have to die to be one of them. He answered his own question, "*Hell no! How about that, Buck*?"

He got no answer. It was the first time he'd ever addressed Buck without getting an answer. He was shook by that, then thought, "I'll bet the little son of a bitch is back having a nip off Newt's bottle and smoking his cigars."

Bennie didn't know whether he went to sleep or not, or if he was dreaming when the wolf-mother walked past between him and the creek with her cubs following her. He thought, "Isn't it a little early for cubs to be out?" He knew that Ernest Thompson Seton had probably written something about that, but couldn't remember what it was. He hardly breathed, watching them. There were two cubs close behind her and a third having trouble keeping up, stumbling over branches and brush and occasionally whining as though to say, "Hey, Ma, slow down." The little cavalcade disappeared into the woods, without detecting his presence.

It seemed as though they'd hardly gone when he heard a voice somewhere saying, "Well, Skeezix, we'll have better luck some other time. Be good." The voice was very familiar, perhaps even someone in the family. He looked around to see who'd sneaked up on him and could see no one. He was troubled because he'd heard the voice say the same words somewhere. "Who? Where?" Then he knew because its owner sat down on the log near him. It was Ralph Esselborn. Those words had been the last Ralph had ever spoken to him—the day he was killed. Bennie's hair stood on end.

"You're dead!" He gasped.

Ralph grinned his old grin. "Was. Dead depends on if you want to *really* die, or if you change your mind and don't want to stay dead."

"What're you doing here?"

"*It's a nice day so I thought I'd take a little flight around.*"

"I figured you'd be back in Waubonsee."

"*I never really liked the place. Besides I had something I wanted to tell you.*"

Bennie waited.

"*I was in the war. We're going to get into another one. You'll be in it.*"

Bennie was ready to believe they were headed for war, familiar with world news from Pa's dinner-table discussions with Newt.

"Will I get killed?"

"*I can't tell you that. I came to tell you in war, never run; no matter how scared you are, never run!*"

"Why?"

"*Because cowards suck.*"

"How come you say 'suck?' I thought only us kids knew about it."

"*I get around. Anyhow, don't forget. I'm going now.*"

"Will you be back?"

"*Listen by the waters.*"

The words and Ralph faded away together.

"How the hell did he know about '*listen by the waters*'?" Bennie wondered. "Waubonsee said that too. Well, here I am by the waters with nothing much to do but listen. Somebody say something."

A small bird landed on a branch above him and asked, "*What would you like me to say*?"

That's when he was sure he'd gone to sleep and was dreaming.

"Sing something. You're a bird."

It drew in a deep breath and sang in an operatic voice:

> "*Oh say can you see*
> By the *dawnzerly* light?

Pretty snappy, for a sparrow, eh?"

"On key, too," Benny said. "Do you sing anything else?"

To the tune of *The Girl I Left Behind Me*, it sang:

> "*Oh, she jumped in bed*
> *And covered up her head*
> *And thought I couldn't find her.*
> *But I knew damn well she lied like hell.*
> *So I jumped right in behind her!*
> *Which reminds me, what do you*
> *Think Kate is doing about now*?"

"I don't know, but I can think of something I'd like to be doing with her."

"*You and Uncle Newt. You're a horny family.*"

With that the sparrow flew off.

Bennie thought, "*Just when I was going to ask if it knew what I was going to be one of.*"

"*Ask me*," a deep, gruff voice said.

Bennie looked around to find the source of the voice and could see no one.

"Who are you?" he asked. "And, come to think of it, where are you?"

"*Up here.*"

Bennie looked up and saw a hawk like he'd watched earlier, perched high in the tree over him.

"So, what will I 'be one of?'"

"*A warrior, you dumbahit! Couldn't you figure that out for yourself?*"

"I kinda had that notion."

"*Very astute!*"

"Do you talk with people much?"

"*You're the first one. I really don't give a damn for people.*"

"I'm flattered."

"*Don't be. I don't particularly care for you either. I was sent.*"

"Who sent you?"

"*None of your damned business.*"

The hawk took a little hop, launched himself into a glide and silently drifted out of sight. Bennie thought, "If I had my rifle I'd take the wise ass's tail feathers out."

He couldn't remember waking up, but when he slid off the log his gloomy mood was gone. He wasn't blind from staring at the sun either. In fact it seemed like he could see more clearly. He stretched and yawned. "I guess I'd better be getting back in case they got Old Nelson's team and are wondering where I went."

Then something whined nearby in the brush. He turned and took a step, causing whatever it was to scuttle away ahead of him. He picked up a club in case it was a wounded animal with some fight left in it, then went to investigate.

The tall grass stirred a short ways ahead, then stopped. He edged cautiously forward and got his first good look at his quarry. "One of the wolf cubs," he said aloud. "I wonder why Mama left it?"

Then he knew. It was the runt. She'd left it to die. "A wonder she didn't kill it," he thought. "Probably couldn't bring herself to do it. I hope she doesn't change her mind and come back." He knew a she-wolf would be no picnic to handle when it was defending its young.

He approached the little thing slowly, all the while saying, "I won't hurt you, little guy. Stay there and I'll come get you and feed you something." He could imagine what Ma would say when he dragged back this flea-bitten little thing. It was too weak to get away and shook like a leaf when he put his hand on it. It tried to snap at him, but was too weak to do even that. He took out his gloves and put them on, then gently petted it, scratching it behind the ears just as he would a dog. It didn't try to snap again, simply closed its eyes and fell over.

"Poor little thing. I hope it didn't die," Bennie said to himself. He scooped up the bony, limp body and shoved it inside his jacket, then headed toward the cabin at a brisk pace. They had a lunch in the car from which he could feed it some meat from a sandwich.

"That ain't a wolf," Newt said when Bennie opened his coat and showed it to him. "It's a dog of some kind."

"How did it get with a wolf?"

"Are you damn sure you saw a wolf?"

"Like I said, I could have dreamed that. I dreamed a lot of other screwy stuff. Maybe somebody abandoned it."

Newt said, "It's sure as hell got a long ways in the woods for a pup that small if someone abandoned it on the road."

"I hope Ma lets me keep it."

"If she don't I'll keep it for you."

Bennie shoved it back inside his coat and could feel it wiggle.

"It's still alive," he said. "I'm gonna take it back to the car and give it something out of our lunch."

"I'll go with you. I saw what I came to see."

"How long was I gone?" Bennie asked.

"A half hour at the outside."

That surprised him. He thought he'd napped for an hour or more considering all he'd dreamed about—if it had been a dream.

CHAPTER THIRTY

Where Are You, Buck Doaks?

Bennie tenderly cradled the pup inside his jacket all the way back to the Lincoln.

"You think he'll live?" He asked Newt, thinking of how he'd lost Mutt.

"Dogs are tough. Sometimes the runts are toughest of all if they pull through. I was a runt. Ma said I must have caught everything that came down the pike before I was five. But I always knew I was gonna pull through—every time."

Bennie thought, "*Just like me. I hope the pup is like us, too.*"

Bennie gave the pup an extra squeeze. "You're gonna pull through," he assured it, wishing he was as confident as he tried to sound. "What do you think, Buck?"

Again he got no reply. Now he was alarmed. To Newt he said, "What the hell do you suppose happened to Buck?"

"Why?"

"Whenever I talked to him, as long as I can remember, he was right there. This is the second time he wasn't."

"*It was time for him to bow out, I reckon. He did it with me after we come home from the Civil War.*"

"Why now?"

"You're growin' up fast. Got your first piece of tail. What the hell! He stayed around when you really needed him. Just thank God you had him."

Bennie missed that about his first piece of tail, too concerned about Buck to realize that Newt knew about him and Kate.

"Will he ever come back?"

"I don't know."

Newt had a pretty good idea when Buck would come back to either of them, if he ever did.

Bennie carefully set the pup on the front seat and took off his jacket to cover him. He got the lunch basket and started to unwrap a sandwich.

"Before we do that," Newt said, "give me the coffee thermos."

He poured coffee into the lid and mixed it with whiskey. Then he improvised a funnel from a ten-dollar bill. "Get the critter out here on the ground for a minute and we'll give him an injection of something hot. Hold his head up to one side. We can't pour this stuff straight down him or he might choke."

Newt carefully trickled the hot mixture into the funnel.

"We're gettin' some out on the ground," Bennie said.

"And some in the pup," Newt grunted. "We're shootin' for the bunch; can't be finicky. He's startin' to work his jaws; that's a good sign."

After a few swallows the pup opened its eyes briefly, then closed them and took all the liquid Newt poured down, sucking greedily.

"That got the little fart's attention right smart," Newt said. "Now take the meat out of that sandwich and shove it in him a little piece at a time. He's old enough to eat solid stuff."

Bennie started to feed it, first having to shove it in, but shortly the dog tasted the meat and came to life, grabbing for the pieces.

"Ouch!" Bennie pulled back his hand. "He's got teeth like needles."

"More like razors," Newt said. "Gotta be careful. I had a wolf pup once. He finally learned the difference between my hand and a bone, but it was tough at first. Don't feed him too much—he'll only puke it up."

When the meat was gone, Bennie lifted the dog back onto the front seat and wrapped him in his jacket. The pup relaxed, let out a contented groan and went to sleep almost in a wink of an eye.

Newt watched how tenderly Bennie handled the little dog and smiled. "You're good with critters," he said. "I judge with your help that one's gonna pull through."

Bennie and Newt heard the trace chains jingling before Pa and Old Man Nelson came in sight, riding work plugs, the clattering trace chains tied across the hames with twine to keep them off the ground. Nelson was packing the evener and singletrees across his horse's withers. Bennie thought that Nelson, with the stuff across the horse's withers, looked like a picture of a mountain man with a rifle balanced across his saddle. Nelson tossed his load on the ground, then nimbly slid down. Pa didn't do half as well, tangling one foot in the harness and almost falling.

Nelson was a startling sight, with tobacco-stained walrus mustache, bristling gray whiskers, craggy pink face now dirt-smudged, and long iron-gray hair that he cut himself. He wore an oft-patched pair of dirty bib overalls, a ragged blue shirt with a red bandanna worn like a necktie and an ancient, cast-off suit coat out at the elbows. Grimy white socks showed between clodhopper shoes and the turned-up bottoms of his overalls. He topped it all with a greasy felt hat with an Alf Landon button pinned on it.

When Bennie made out what the button was, he thought, "I'll bet that

Landon button went over like a loud fart at a wedding with a strong FDR man like Pa."

Newt had seen a lot worse sights in his travels, but Bennie had his mouth open, staring.

"Newt, this is our old neighbor, Mr. Nelson," Pa said.

The two old men eyed each other like a couple of prima donnas, which Pa didn't seem to notice. Bennie did, though.

"You got a first handle?" Newt asked.

"Come again," Nelson said.

"What's yore first name?"

Nelson thought that over. "I had to stop and think," he said. "Mostly they called me Old Man since I was thirty or so. And after I got married, 'that old son of a bitch, Nelson!'"

He laughed a series of raspy "yuh, yuh, yuh's" half-gasped out.

"I bin called that a time'r two myself," Newt said, and to Pa, "What happened to your shotgun guard?"

"Em?"

"None other."

Nelson snorted. "Haw! She's sittin' over at my place lookin' mad as a wet hen, dryin' out in front of the oven—she fell in the goddam drink. Tell 'em, Russ." His eyes looked like shiny little berries as another series of yuh, yuh's came out of him.

"Em fell off the crossing log. She was so damn busy telling me how to do it, she slipped off. I heard the splash and looked around." Pa started laughing and he couldn't go on. Finally he said, "She was spraddled out on her butt in the water, yelling, 'Help, Russ! I'm drowning!' Hell, the water wasn't over a foot deep right there." He broke up again and had to stop a while to get his breath before he continued. "Jesus, it was funny. I said, 'Hell, Em, get up and wade out—it's shallow all the way,' so she got up and then she squawked, 'What if I fall in a hole?' I said, 'If you do, I'll come in and get you.' She wanted me to come in and help her out anyhow. I told her, 'I ain't gonna get my feet soaked in ice water just because you pulled a damn fool stunt, not paying attention because you were mouthing at me.' That made her so mad she stormed out of there like a bull. I figured she would. At least I didn't get my feet wet for nothing. Anyhow, like Nelson said, she's over at his place sittin' in front of the oven drying out."

"I'd've given a hundred bucks to see it," Newt said.

Pa, still chuckling, said, "Let's drag the car out. Oh, by the way, Em wasn't too mad to agree to fix some of Nelson's grub for us when we get done. Maybe she worked up an appetite in the creek."

"Hell, Emma was born with an appetite," Newt said.

"That's a fact," Pa agreed. "An outsize one at that."

The pup, probably having a bad dream let out a yowl. "What was that?" Pa asked and looked in the car where the sound came from.

Bennie said, "There's a new member of the family on the front seat."

Pa opened the car door. "What the heck have you got?"

"A pup. Found him in the woods, abandoned." He didn't go into a full explanation. "I want to keep him."

"We'll see," Pa said.

"No we won't," Newt said. "I already saw."

Pa grinned. "Like that, eh?"

Nelson, standing back out of hearing with the team, said, "What the hell you all looking at?"

"Bennie's got a dog he found in the woods," Pa said.

Nelson had to come get a look too. "Don't look like much right now, but he might pull through." He gave the dog's head a little pat.

Bennie was grateful to the old man for the encouraging words. He hadn't really thought too much of Nelson till then, but obviously he liked animals, a big plus in Bennie's estimation.

Pa and Nelson decided to pull the Lincoln out backward into the woods so Pa could turn it back the way they'd come. The horses barely strained dragging it out, although the car must have weighed three tons. When it hit dry ground, Pa started the engine and as soon as he was sure he had traction he signaled Nelson to cut loose from the horses. Then he gunned it and stopped well beyond the muddy spot to make sure he didn't get stuck again.

He reeled the window down and yelled back at Newt and Bennie, "O.K., you two galoots. Get in."

Before driving away, he waved out the window at Nelson who stood in the road and watched to see that they didn't get stuck again, then headed the team back the way they'd come.

Bennie looked back and said, "You suppose Nelson's gonna ride back or wade the creek?"

"No tellin'." Pa said. "Old Nelson is apt to do damn near anything. He used to be the nicest fellow around till he got married. Then he turned into a brass-riveted son of a bitch. His old lady died last year, and he's just like he used to be as near as I can see."

"He looks like a good man," Newt said. "And I'd bet he's almost as crusty as me if he wants to be."

He lit up a cigar and leaned back in the rear seat. Bennie rode with the pup cradled in his lap. All three were wrapped in their own thoughts, under the spell of the silent woods.

After he turned back onto the graded road, Pa said, "Nelson wants to sell his place and take life easy."

Newt said, "He doesn't look to me like he'd know how to take life easy any more'n I do." If Pa expected advice about buying Nelson's place, Newt wasn't putting out any.

"Good place," Pa went on. "As good as any around. A one-sixty with ninety cleared and the rest good wooded pasture. Said he'd throw in the tools and that team and harness."

Finally Newt said, "So, what're you gonna do?"

"I wanted you to look over the place before I do anything."

"I don't know doodley-squat about farming. I worked on our place for Pa when I was a kid. That's about the size of it."

"It'll eat up a big chunk of that five thousand."

"How much?"

"Thirty-five hundred bucks."

"You gotta learn to take a chance sometime, Ed. You played it careful" (he thought of saying scared) "all your life except that once when you ran away with me, and that would have worked if you'd come back to Alaska instead of letting Em talk you into making a damned nest. Money is to spend. Especially at my age. If you need more, I reckon I can scrape it up. I ain't gonna take it with me. Shoot the moon. Buy the son of a bitch before someone comes along and snaps up a good deal right under your nose. And don't haggle. Old Nelson needs a nest egg to learn to take it easy on."

"Hell, he's got the first dollar he ever made."

"Mebbe so, but he can use a windfall just like anyone else."

"Well, I thought I'd better ask, since it's your money."

"Was my money. I gave it to you. Use it. If the place looks good, buy it. You're my hoss and I'm bettin' on you."

Bennie would have been shocked had he realized that Pa was scared to death—so scared his bung hole puckered—scared he'd make a sorry go of it again and lose everything, older this time, tireder, maybe wiser but broke again and too old to start over. The *Depression* did that to a whole generation, and Bennie himself would always have some of it in him as well—not as scary, but always there ready to ask, "What if everything falls apart again?"

Bennie was worried over how he'd approach Ma about keeping the pup. He knew Newt would keep it, but he wanted Ma and Pa to agree he could have a dog of his own because he figured they owed it to him. That worry fled as he sighted Nelson's place and Pa said, "There she is."

Nelson's house stood on a knoll surrounded by pines and beeches, one of the few virgin groves of white pines that had survived when the loggers cut over the country. Entering the drive Bennie got a good look at the two-story white house trimmed with green. The lilac bushes and flowerbeds had obviously been well kept, already spaded up for spring. He wondered what the interior would be like, hoping he'd have a bedroom of his own, on the second floor. He imagined the wind sighing in the pines outside his bedroom window and thought, "This is the sort of place I always dreamed of living in. A real first-class farm place. I hope to hell Pa doesn't get cold feet, or do something dumb at the last minute."

Ma came out on the wide porch that surrounded the front and one side of the house. She was smiling even after her embarrassing little accident. Normally losing face would have kept her in a bad mood for days.

She said to Pa, "*This is a real nice place. Buy it.*"

"Just like that, eh?" Pa said. He looked stunned.

"*Yeah. Just like that,*" she said. "*Now hurry up and get in here. I've got dinner fixed keeping it warm.*"

"We'll have to wait on Nelson," Pa said.

"We'll save him something in the warmer. Go in and wash up."

Bennie, unable to restrain himself, butted in. "C'mere, Ma, I got something to show you."

He led her back to the car where he'd left the pup. "Somebody dumped him and I rescued him in the woods," he said when she looked at it. He didn't mention the wolf, knowing she might think he made that up and would get into a bad mood and deny him the dog to punish him for fibbing.

She looked at it a long time while Bennie held his breath. Then she silently patted it. "It's cold," she said in a soft voice. "Bring it in and we'll put it in a cardboard box or something near the stove."

Pa and Newt exchanged a "well-I'll-be-go-to-hell" look.

"You ought to call it Tam-o-Shanter," Ma said.

"How come?"

"Because it's just a rag, a bone, and a hank-o-hair."

"That's a good name," Bennie said, ready to agree to anything to keep Ma in a good mood. "Or maybe we could call it just Hank."

Ma found a box, put the pup into it on her own sweater, and set it on the floor in front of the open oven door. She patted its noggin and said softly, "Sleep tight, Hank."

Bennie knew Ma too well to believe she hadn't realized her sweater might get infested with fleas. He wished Buck were around to see it.

CHAPTER THIRTY-ONE

Those Who Cannot Remember History

HORSE TRADE: Definition: A transaction in which—traditionally—the third party (i.e., victim, not always a horse) is seldom consulted.

— 1812

Fort Dearborn (Northwest Territories—now Chicago, Illinois).

Leaders surrender arms, believing besieging Native Americans' craftily told lie that they will accept them and in return guarantee the gullible whites safe passage away from there; cowardly leaders obtain "peace in their time" for everyone, and wolves erect a suitable memorial for such leadership: the whitened bones of eternally peaceful slaughtered mothers and babes scattered on the prairie.

— 1938

Munich, Germany.

British and French leaders, Chamberlain and Daladier, trade German megalomaniac Hitler a big chunk of Czechoslovakia for "peace in our time." This appeasement directly invited six years of war in which fifty million or more people were granted eternal peace.

- HISTORICAL PERSPECTIVE -

Yellow bellies and white flags have sacrificed infinitely more lives than they've saved. The sonofabitch that said there was never a good war or a bad peace may have got it backward, so long as the war started early enough and for the right reasons.

- HISTORICAL LESSON? -

For a majority—absolutely none!

THOSE WHO CANNOT REMEMBER HISTORY ARE CONDEMNED TO REPEAT IT!

— April 1938

"Johnny Todd was a helluva man!"

Uncle Newt may have addressed that remark to Bennie, standing beside him by the tombstone inscribed "John Meredith Todd," perhaps was talking to himself or to the world at large—maybe to Johnny Todd.

"I wish I'd known him," Bennie said.

"So do I. Hell, he could be alive yet. He was a couple of years younger'n me, healthy as a bull moose. What a goddam shame some sonofabitch run him down with a car. Think of it. A goddam lousy car with a clumsy half-blind woman drivin' it."

They spent a week living with Aunt Felice and the Cretin while they got the papers worked out to buy the Nelson place. Now Ma and Pa were headed back to Blackhawk in the Lincoln, aiming to come back with all their stuff and Newt's in a moving van.

Bennie was allowed to stay *up north* with Newt practically over Ma's dead body. She had her reasons, of course:

"He should get a few more days of school while we're packing."

Bennie thought, "Jesus Christ, how much could I *teach* dumb teachers in just a couple of more days."

Ma added, "He'll only get in trouble." (He usually was.) Then she had her variation of that for Pa alone, "*They'll* only get in trouble." (They usually were, or at least working on it.)

Also, "Nelson doesn't like kids around, you said so yourself," and "Felice doesn't want to have one extra mouth to feed, much less two, you know her."

Finally Pa blew up. "Christ! Bennie's growing up. Of course I know Felice. Screw Felice! And I said Nelson's *wife* didn't like kids; the old bat is dead; Nelson likes Bennie. The kid can stay with Newt and that's all there is to it!"

Bennie was tickled to see Ma look stunned and shut up, faced with this change in Pa. He thought, "Pa should have cracked her in the mouth and made her knuckle under long ago. If he'd done it back in Waubonsee, we'd all have had it easier." He couldn't imagine the crushing, almost total demoralization of Pa's generation. He'd just thought Pa was soft. Well, he was a natural gentleman, but so was Wild Bill.

Bennie and Newt had watched the Lincoln pull out and head down the road, Rose silently standing beside them. She never said much as far as Bennie could see, but hung around him like a leech for some reason. He felt sorry for her. "Probably doesn't have many friends," he thought. "She's nice enough. I suppose old Prune Face and Elephant Ears won't let her have any friends."

They'd got her as a county ward, obviously not motivated by charitable impulses, but expecting to get her board out of her in spades. When Bennie first saw her tackling a pile of after-dinner dishes he thought about the old ditty:

> *Little Orphan Annie came to our house to stay,*
> *To wash and wipe the dishes and brush the crumbs away.*

He'd pitched in to help her with the sink full of dishes and got a funny look from Ma. He was relieved that for once Ma didn't say anything. He knew why she looked at him that way—he never helped with dishes at home. Of course, he wasn't expected to since she always thought he'd "just break them."

Bennie didn't see the wink Pa gave Newt, who grinned and nodded his head. If he had noticed, it would have puzzled him. After all, Rose was just a skinny, homely little kid that he pitied.

After the Lincoln was out of sight, Rose sighed and said, "I guess I've got to go to school now."

She sounded to Bennie as though she had about the same opinion of school that he did. He noticed that she was allowed to wear shoes for school. He thought, "Prune Face and Old Elephant Ears are probably afraid of what people would think if she came to school the way they make her run around here to save on shoes."

Rose paused, as though she might be waiting for them to invite her to skip school and join them doing whatever they were going to do. She glanced at them timidly, then averted her eyes and raised her arm and wiggled her fingers in a diffident goodbye wave. Just before she turned to go, her eyes met Bennie's. Blushing, she left at a trot, books beneath her arm.

Newt got out a cigar and performed his usual ceremony of getting it lit to suit him. He blew out a big cloud of smoke and watched it float away.

"Let's go uptown," he suggested.

They stopped on the middle of the bridge and watched the yellowish spring flood retreating beneath them. As always Bennie savored the illusion of speeding upstream when he stared down at the water. It was a mild day, one you could enjoy with your jacket open. Out of sight of Felice's place, Bennie rolled a cigarette and took a deep drag on it, savoring the taste and tang of the first deep puff.

"That's a nice girl," Newt said.

"Huh?" Bennie said.

"That Rose is a nice girl."

"Oh? Yeah. I feel sorry for her."

"Don't. She knows already what she wants, and if I'm any judge she'll get it."

"What does she want?"

"Hard to tell exactly," Newt parried the question. "I expect what most gals want. But that's a deep *young'un*."

Newt thought, "If I told you what I think she really wants, it might hurt her chances of getting it." And he thought what she wanted might be good for Bennie.

Through wiser eyes he'd watched the look she'd given Bennie just before leaving them, and it said, "*I'm a woman, no matter what you might think now*." He rightly suspected Bennie thought she was just a gawky kid, but he'd seen others just like that grow into tall, lush women, budding all of a sudden one day like a new blossom that opens and looks at itself with surprised satisfaction.

Side by side they strolled across the bridge into town. Bennie had been told about Winnebago but remembered nothing except that cold, bright night just before they'd left for Waubonsee, when Ma had shown him and Roy the owl in the tree, silhouetted by the moon.

"We need some kind of contraption to get around in and haul some stuff," Newt said as they walked uptown. "A little truck would fit the bill. I saw a Model A Ford the other day that ought to do. I hope it's still there. I'd have bought it at the time, but it would have set yore Ma to thinkin' about who was gonna drive the sonofabitch. You're it."

Bennie's heart took a bounce at that news. He was the age Roy had been when all he thought about was cars (and girls). Bennie hadn't thought much lately about girls, but a lot about Kate. He'd almost agreed to go home with Ma and Pa on account of Kate. A vivid picture of Kate's body frequently occupied his mind, her hot, blue eyes watching his, mirroring thoughts she wasn't ashamed of, a look that had aroused him as much as the sleek soft warmth of her body when they were tightly entwined, hotly thrusting to each other. This clear recall always brought up his cock. Now, only she was the object of his fantasies when he jacked off, which happened pretty often because of her.

"This here thingamajig ain't like a horse," Newt told the salesman who was showing them the Model A pickup. "I never even drove one. What if she busts down right after I buy it?"

The young man grinned, looking like what he was, an honest kid just off the farm on his first sales job. "I'll guarantee she's sound in wind and limb; bound to make it to the street at least."

Newt snorted. "Is that the best you can do?"

"The boss says we can't afford to guarantee the used ones. I can give you a driving lesson or two though if you never drove one."

"Give it to the kid here," Newt said. "If it snorts around the block a time or two, we'll take her and hope for the best. It don't look like it's been used up too bad."

The salesman gave Bennie a lesson while Newt watched the store. It only took about ten minutes for him to get the hang of it, since he'd driven Uncle Johnny's Dort, and Pa had let him handle the old Buick several times, though he didn't trust him with the Lincoln.

"You can pick up the rest on your own," the salesman said when they got back. "I learned mostly on my own. Started driving on the old man's tractor; was plowin' an hour after he first put me on 'er. I was eight."

In those days no one ever bothered about drivers' licenses and certainly never heard of a learner's permit or driver's school.

As Bennie carefully drove them away, Newt said, "The first thing we're gonna do with this contraption is get our duds the hell out of that sorry-ass place and move out to the farm. We'll help Nelson move too when he's ready."

"Where's he movin'?"

"Into your old cabin to help me fix it up. He's gonna sorta camp out there, then build himself a shebang of some kind over there."

"He'll freeze his ass at night," Bennie said.

"Not likely. He said he's got a couple of bear robes and a bunch of blankets. Plans to move over his regular bed."

"How's he plan to cook, and wash?"

Newt looked startled. "Wash? You saw him. He'll wash come summer unless he falls in the creek before then. As fer cookin', he'll manage."

"You figure you can live with him the way he smells?"

"He'll keep the damn mice out of the place and the mosquitos away after they come out. Hell, he smells like a rose compared to Eskimos. Besides he'll be in his own place pretty quick."

Bennie wondered how Nelson had kept his house clean enough not to turn Ma off on buying the place. Actually it had been pretty spic and span. He supposed it hadn't had time to run down since the old man's wife had died. He was soon to learn that Eben, Nelson's hired man, was also the housemaid. Eben had agreed to stay on and help Pa till he found another job.

As they were driving out of Aunt Felice's driveway, Rose turned in, coming home from school early. Bennie pulled up beside her and rolled down the window.

"School out early?" he asked.

"I thought you'd be leaving. I left school early to tell you goodbye. Your aunt will probably give me the devil, but I'm going to play sick. I wish I could go with you." All of this came out in a breath and she had to stop, looking fearfully toward the house.

Newt leaned over toward the window on Bennie's side and asked, "They don't mistreat you here, do they?"

Rose's face colored. "I just don't like it here."

Bennie thought, "Boy, I can't blame you for that." The atmosphere even shut off his normal horse-like appetite.

"Can I come out and see you?" She was looking at Bennie when she said it, then quickly shifted her eyes to Newt.

"You bet," Newt said. "I'll send Bennie in for you on weekends. If they won't let you come, I'll be in to see about that."

She smiled, the first time either of them had seen her smile, and it changed her wonderfully, lighting up her serious countenance in some remarkable way. Bennie thought of the pictures he'd seen of angels and got a strange feeling about her he couldn't define, like he'd like to hold her and comfort her like he would a little scared puppy or kitten. He should have been surprised, but wasn't.

As they drew away, she gave them the same little wave she'd given them that morning, a tentative gesture as though she wasn't worthy to be saluting people above her who might not accept her.

Eben heard the Model A coming when they pulled into Nelson's place with their stuff, and came out of the kitchen door to meet them. He looked over the truck briefly but wasn't surprised. Before either of them got out he grabbed the two suitcases from the truck like a bellboy.

Newt said, "Give me my damn bag. I ain't helpless yet."

Eben only grinned, then made a beeline for the house, saying over his shoulder, "Likely you ain't had much service in your day. Everybody deserves a little before they croak."

Newt grunted, "I ain't dead yet by a danged sight."

"Didn't mean to say you was."

He put down the bags and turned to give Newt an apologetic look. "I just like to be helpful."

"Suit yourself," Newt said. "Only in case you got the wrong idee, I ain't even decided *whether* I'm gonna die yet, much less *when*."

Bennie thought, "By Christ, I believe that." His main concern, however, was his new pup. "Where's Hank?" He asked Eben.

"In his box behind the stove, I'd guess."

Bennie went to look. Hank hadn't even heard them come in; he was sprawled on his back, snoring, all four feet in the air and his tongue hanging out just a trifle at the corner of his mouth. Bennie reached down and put his hand on him. That got one eye open, a faint tail wag, then Hank dropped off again with a happy sigh. Eben watching, said, "He's still a mite tuckered out, but gettin' stronger every day."

While that was going on Newt sneaked upstairs with both their bags. They each had a room, Newt occupying the bedroom that would be Pa and Ma's, Bennie in the corner room he'd asked for. Tall pines towered outside the windows on both sides of the room. There were two more bedrooms, one was Eben's and the last was Nelson's, a boar's nest full of all sorts of old junk, too valuable to toss out because Nelson knew that whatever you threw out you always needed the next day, if not sooner.

"Where's Nelson?" Newt asked.

Eben said, "Moved over to yer place already. Took one 'o the teams. He's puttin' up firewood for yuh."

"The hell you say? He shoulda waited fer me to help him."

"I been helpin' him. Come back to milk and clean up a little. I figured you'd be out today. I wanted to look after the pup, too. Keep him locked in a stall full o' straw in the barn when I ain't here; I brought him in to feed him and warm him up good. Fed m'self too. Are you two guys hungry? I kin fix breakfast or dinner, whatever you want."

"Not me," Newt said. "How about you, kid? I was always hungry at your age."

"I could use something," Bennie said, borrowing a frequently used phrase of Pa's.

"Breakfast or what?"

"Breakfast, I guess, if we can call it that in the P.M." He recalled the skimpy fare Felice had given them earlier: one hard-fried egg apiece, burned toast with oleomargarine, and coffee with canned milk, the margarine and lack of real cream despite the fact that they ran a creamery.

"We can call 'er anything we want to, I reckon, breakfast, lunch—I read in the paper they have something called brunch in the cities," Eben said. His idea of breakfast was ham and eggs, pancakes with all kinds of preserves, homemade maple syrup, fried spuds, coffee with rich, fresh cream, topped off with apple pie.

After Bennie downed a big meal, Eben brought out dessert. "Made that pie myself," he said as he served it in a bowl with cream poured over it. "Got a barrel of apples in the cellar."

Bennie hadn't known there was a cellar. He figured to go down and look it over after eating. Newt interrupted his thoughts and said, "I guess I could go get a piece of that pie and some coffee myself."

Bennie had been looking over the kitchen while Eben cooked and later while he ate. He watched Eben, busy at the stove, cramming wood in the firebox, and some extra small pieces through the four round, removable iron lids. Most wood-burning cookstoves had four round lids that could be removed with a lid-lifter. The lifter was a device common to all cookstoves, with a nickel-plated coil spring wrapped around the handle to keep if from getting too hot. People left it stuck up in the lifting slot of one of the lids when it wasn't in use, to avoid mislaying it. Like most cook ranges, this one had a warming oven across the back, with the stove pipe routed through it as the source of warmth, and a water reservoir at one end of the stove, right next to the firebox. The bottom part of the stove was an oven, which was a challenge to keep at any set temperature, especially for anyone not familiar with using one. When you finally got the hang of it, nothing baked quite so well. Country Grandma, Bennie reflected, had the hang of it, and this range was exactly like hers.

The room was a warm cozy one, even though it was plenty big as farm kitchens went. A low, beamed ceiling helped keep it warm; the beams were an architectural style that Nelson probably adopted from his native Sweden—there were certainly few of them in that part of the country outside of the Swedish and Norwegian communities. Another oddity for a farm kitchen was a window seat wide enough to sleep on, with a cushion from end to end. Bennie could see himself perched there for long hours, reading, or napping with Hank beside him (till the pup got too big, and if Ma let him) with the screened windows wide open in warm weather. The whole place sent a delightful chill through him when he thought of how it would be living there.

CHAPTER THIRTY-TWO

Two Bucks a Whack

"Best we get over and help Nelson," Newt said, shoving back from the table as soon as he finished his pie.

Eben said, "Nelson ain't easy to help. He figures the help most folks give is more like hornin' in."

Newt thought about that awhile. He said, "Sounds like me. But I made a study of helpin' crusty bastards like the two of us."

"Nelson says most folks can't find their own ass with both hands."

Bennie laughed. It was the first time he'd heard that expression.

Eben had the table cleared and the dishes in the sink in a jiffy. "Wash 'em later," he said; "they'll keep."

"What'll we do with Hank?" Bennie asked. "He's too pooped even to beg scraps at the table."

"Leave him where he is," Eben said. "If he craps or pees on the floor I'll clean it up. It's nice and warm for him in here."

Eben scouted up the tools Newt wanted to take over to the cabin, including another axe. Newt swung it around in one hand like a baton, tested its edge, and laid it in the pickup.

"I'll ride back here," he said.

"Like hell!" Eben snorted.

Newt eyed him for a second, trying to look offended, then grinned. "Hop right in, then."

Bennie bet Newt had figured to fake Eben out like that in the first place.

When Bennie got to the still-muddy spot where Pa had bogged down the Lincoln, he dropped the Model A in second and gunned right through. If he'd bothered to think of it, he might have recognized that Pa's getting stuck illustrated the difference between his and Pa's approach to life.

"Barney Oldfield," Newt commented, mentioning the name of a famous pioneer racecar driver. "You're really gettin' the hang of this contraption."

Bennie tried not to choke up over such high praise, but didn't succeed. He couldn't stifle a grin either.

Nelson was leaning on his axe waiting for them, though he didn't look like he needed a rest, even after half a day at wood cutting. He looked even less tired when Newt hopped out and produced his usual flat pint bottle of whiskey.

"Restore your youth," Newt said, offering it to Nelson first. After a big pull, Nelson let out a long, satisfied "Ahhhh!" He held the bottle up and squinted one eye, looking it over with approval, then took another big swig. He said, "Beats Lydia Pinkham's."

Bennie knew that *Lydia Pinkham's Vegetable Compound* for women was a standing joke, since it was about half alcohol.

"Where the hell did you drink *Lydia Pinkham's*?" Newt snorted.

"All during Prohibition. It was all us rubes up here in the sticks could get regular. Besides it was handy. My old lady always kept a case around for the vapors."

"My ass," Newt said. "I heard your old lady was about as delicate as a rhinoceros."

"At least, maybe twice as," Nelson said, then drained the bottle a trifle lower and handed it back to Newt, who passed it to Eben.

"Nope," Eben declined. "I done quit. Got tired of somebody steppin' on my hands every Satiddy night."

Newt bit. "How was that?"

"Over at Aunt Kay's tavern—crawlin' out on my hands and knees when they closed up."

They all laughed.

"No joke," Eben said. "I usually puked too. Finally decided it was dumb, so I up and quit. Been savin' money in the bank for the first time in my life."

"How long ago?" Newt asked.

"Five years, pret near."

"Jeezuz," Newt said. He turned to Bennie. "Hear that kid? Never start." He took a big pull, capped the bottle, and shoved it back in his mackinaw pocket.

To Eben Newt said, "How about a good cigar then?"

"Don't smoke anymore, either."

Newt eyed him severely. "Anything else you don't do anymore, either?"

"Huh-uh. Twice a month. Costs two bucks a whack."

Newt brightened. "You'll have to show me where."

"I'm due Satiddy night."

Nelson interrupted. "I'll take one o' them seegars, if you don't mind."

Newt fished one out and handed it over. Bennie knew that Newt bought the best cigars money could buy, mailed to him from New York City. He was tickled at the expression on Newt's face when he saw Nelson take his expensive Perfecto, crumble part of it off the end and shove it in his corncob pipe; the rest he stowed in his side pocket for use later. Nelson lit up, took a few puffs with satisfaction, and said, "Damn near as good as Union Workman," mentioning a well-known nickel pipe tobacco.

"How about Plowboy?" Newt asked, naming another.

"That too," Nelson said, keeping a poker face. Later Bennie would learn that Nelson was sly enough to have set up that whole thing to get Newt's goat, if he could.

"Well," Nelson said, "gotta get back to work," and he headed into the woods, not caring whether anyone was going to join him or not. Eben grabbed an axe and trotted to keep up with Nelson, who moved with a determined, long stride. Newt yelled after, "I'll be along in a while."

"Take your time," Nelson yelled back. "At your age you don't want to over-exert yourself."

By the time Newt thought up something to say, Nelson was too far away to hear it. Bennie heard Newt mutter, "In a pig's ass," under his breath.

Newt led the way into the cabin. It contained a jumble of Nelson's stuff. His bed was stacked high with two mattresses, his blankets, and the two bear robes on top. Altogether, it was about four feet off the floor.

"I hope the old bastard doesn't fall out of that hay stack and break his leg," Newt said.

The cabin was beginning to smell a little like a chicken coop.

"Ah," Newt said, inhaling deeply, "just like my place in Alaska."

Bennie thought, "Christ Almighty, he must be kidding!" He contrasted it with all the romantic movies he'd seen about cabins in the West and Alaska and figured it was a good thing you couldn't smell movies or they wouldn't make a cent.

Newt looked around. "I'm gonna be measurin' some things up in here. Tomorra we'll drive to town and start haulin' out some lumber and stuff. Why don't you take a ramble in the woods? When I'm through in here I aim to go help Nelson and Eben."

Bennie was glad to get away by himself again. It was still new, of course, but he'd never get over the delicious thrill of being alone in the woods. Whatever gripped him then was never definable. The best he ever did at explaining it to himself was that only then did he truly understand life—his kinship with everything around him, his reason for being, or even that there was a reason for being. It was too holy to be put into words—it could only be felt. Those who gained that insight became woods addicts, or "woods queer" as some said. In any case they returned again and again just to savor the essence of druid silence, of isolation, total privacy. He guessed that the vast western deserts and mountains imparted the same heady sense of escape into oneself or, perhaps, completely outside oneself. *Would that be the gift that dying granted everyone some day?*

He walked along the creek and wondered if he might be able to recall Ralph Esselborn to that place again. Ralph could tell him about dying. First, Bennie figured he'd ask, "Were you really here, Ralph?" On the other hand, wouldn't recalling him be an unforgivable violation of privacy? Besides he wasn't sure he wanted to know. That mystery might be as precious as its solution. It spoiled some things if you found out about them too soon.

He'd read about the Vision Quest of the Plains Indians and wondered if his experience here with the hawk, with Ralph, a few days before, had been akin to the Indians' visions, especially in view of his Sioux blood.

Even now he wondered, "Is the Hawk my brother? Are Ralph and I and the Hawk one? "A strange, poetic thought ran through his mind, as though he himself wasn't really thinking it, but receiving a message:

> *Will I escape the fetters of place?*
> *Of time?*
> *Fly far beyond earth,*
> *Unbound?*
> *Not in a dumpy Cub,*
> *Or a Tin Goose,*
> *But in mystifying visions?*

A pocket of wind provided wild music to accompany his wondering. It fluttered new leaves, flattened the tall, still-brown grass, spiraled upward, leaving a momentary hush.

> *Poor Lo,*
> *Hears God's voice*
> *In the wind.*

Bennie moved on toward his mound, planning to sit again on the log where Ralph had come to him.

"Maybe he'll come back," he thought. "I hope he does. I've got a few questions I'd like him to answer."

He leaned back on the log he would come to regard as his private perch. It was a place for dreaming. Soon Hank would grow big and strong, be his companion on treks into solitude. Nothing was a less intrusive outdoor companion than a dog, unless you were trying hard to listen to something while it was panting. Small thing, on balance, when you considered that a dog asked nothing more than to be with you. They were even faithful to cruel masters. He thought sadly of poor dead Mutt. How he'd have loved this. How he missed him—and Buck Doaks.

"*Are you really gone, Buck?*" he asked.

Bennie figured he must have dozed off. It was a good place for that. He rubbed his eyes and looked around. Something dark and bulky was edging toward him from the farthest visible reach of woods, pausing occasionally, like an animal stopping now and then to sniff. It walked upright like a human, but he knew that bears could do that too. And bears could be out of hibernation by then—also ravenous. He kept his eyes on the moving body, ready to take off; not run, mind you, just lope back to the cover of Newt's .45. Hell, even Custer had retreated to reinforcements when scouting alone and surprised by a large body of hostile Indians. Why commit suicide? Bennie squinted hard at the creature, not wanting to retreat before he was sure he had to, because he was anxious to know what it was. Closer, it lifted its head and he made out a man's face under a hunting cap. He thought, "Who the hell would be out here? It's not hunting season."

Then he recalled that for locals in isolated places, there was no closed season, especially not on overly officious game wardens, like one he recalled. Maybe this was another game warden. He thought, "If Uncle Newt has to fetch another one he may be over his bag limit." While these thoughts prowled through his mind, he didn't take his eyes off the approaching man.

As the man drew closer, Bennie saw that the other was swarthy, with coal-black hair just like his own. He was working his way directly toward Bennie, now close enough for him to make out the single-barrel shotgun carried in the crook of his right arm. He wore a threadbare black pea jacket that had made him resemble a bear, and patched overalls tucked into badly used-up shoe pacs like Newt's. About ten feet from Bennie he stopped and silently surveyed him.

Neither spoke. Bennie finally said, "I thought you might be a bear when I spotted your black jacket." He tried a smile. This was obviously an Indian. Could he possibly be one of those broncos that carried on a vendetta against whites even yet? Bennie didn't think that was likely, since those had been western Indians—Apaches and Yaquis. This fellow didn't look mean, or hostile, and was a lot younger than Bennie had thought; about his own age and not as tall, though he was broad. Bennie figured he could handle him, if need be, provided he could grab the shotgun away from him first.

The Indian finally smiled back. He said, "I am a bear. In the tribe my name is Stumbling Bear. They laugh at that at school—when I go. My white-man name is Sylvester Kinsolving. Ain't that a laugh? Some name for an Indian, huh?" He threw back his head and guffawed, showing white teeth, black eyes glistening.

Bennie said, "Well, I guess we can't pick our own name. Be better if we could. Mine's Bennie—Bennie Todd." He stepped up and put out his hand. Sylvester didn't hesitate to shake, transferring the shotgun to his left hand to do it.

"How," Sylvester said. "I go to a lot of movies so I know how us Injuns are expected to handle that ceremonial greeting." He laughed again.

Bennie joined him. "What should I call you?" he asked Sylvester.

"Try Kid. The guys at school called me Silly when I was little, till I found out what they meant and I kicked the shit out of a whole bunch of 'em."

"O.K., Kid. How come there's no school up here today?"

"There's school today, all right. Only I don't go much. School is a bunch of shit for guys like me. This out here is school. What're you doing here?"

"My folks used to own this place."

"*So did mine.*"

What could you say to that?

"You get in trouble skipping school up here?"

"Naw. At least *I* don't. The truant officer came to see my folks once. Ma said he looked like he was gonna faint when he saw the dump we live in. He told her he'd have Pa put in jail if I didn't come to school. That's a laugh. Pa's chief of the tribe, by the way. Circling Hawk. High muckity muck. Anyhow, Ma told this asshole he'd play hell puttin' Pa in jail. He wanted to know where she got that idea. *She told him, 'He's already doin' three to five in Waupun for knifin' a sonofabitch like you.'* He dug out like he had a lit cob up his ass and we never saw him again. Maybe he thought Ma might take the butcher knife to him. She might, too, come to think of it." Sylvester laughed.

"I hate to be nosey, but how come your Old Man knifed somebody?"

"Some big gorilla tried to beat the shit out of him when he was drunk, so he knifed the big bully."

"Kill him?"

"Naw. Just bled him a little. Said the big yellerbelly squealed like a pig and ran like a deer. Anyhow, Pa got three to five even though the other bastard was twice as big as him, almost, and asked for it in the first place. Of course, the other guy wasn't an Injun. Pa's due out pretty soon. Ma said she'll be glad to see him back; she's horny as hell and says she'll be damned if she's gonna screw any of those worthless bastards sniffing around the chief's wife." Kid didn't seem to think there was anything unusual about spilling all this family dirt, spitting occasionally as he talked.

"Served the bastard right, if you ask me," Bennie said.

"Damn right," Kid said, looking surprised. After a while he added, "You sure don't think like most money grubbin' palefaces."

"I'm quarter Sioux," Bennie said.

Kid looked him over closely. "I can see that. I'm full blood. We stayed here in Wisconsin. Ain't many Sioux here anymore. We don't have a regular reservation, just a village on the Winnebago Reservation. My great-granddad was Wabasha. Ever hear of him?"

"Sure. I read a lot." He had a sly notion to tell Kid that Wabasha's braves had chased him into the Mississippi after the battle of Bad Axe, recalling his recent dream about that. Kid probably would have appreciated it, but you could never tell.

"I read a lot, too," Kid said. "I may start going to school more if you're gonna be there. The two of us could kick the crap out of that whole bunch of sucks."

"I guess I'll have to finish up this year for sure, if Ma has her way, but I'd just like to quit and help Pa on the farm."

"I know what you mean. She sounds like my ma. She says, 'You gotta get an education if you're ever going to amount to anything.' But she never says what she thinks I ought to amount to or mentions how the hell she got the idea you can get an education in school."

Bennie laughed.

"Sounds like my ma, too. Mostly she says I'll end up in reform school. If you ask me, you'd probably learn more there than in regular school."

Kid laughed. "What grade you in?"

"Ninth."

"Me too. We could play football together next fall if I make it to tenth. You play football?"

"I went out last fall—made the Junior High team."

"What do you play?"

"End."

"You must be able to run some."

"Pretty good. What do you play?"

"Full back. I got a hard head. They need a couple of yards, they give me the ball. Football is the only reason I might stay in school a while yet."

"My ma is the reason I'll stay in school. Forever, if she has her way. I'd rather go out west and start a trap line."

Kid gave him a new sort of look. "Me too. I run one right around here. About all you can catch is muskrat and fox and a mink occasionally, but I make a little at it."

"Maybe you could show me how to do it," Bennie said.

"Sure." Kid looked around. "You out here with someone?"

"My uncle Newt. Why don't you come down and meet him. He's been out west and to Alaska. He's over at our old cabin."

"Why not? You got any tobacco on you?"

Bennie passed over his makings, and watched Kid roll about the fattest cigarette he'd ever seen. He wondered if he'd get any tobacco back. Kid noticed his look and said, "Us Injuns make the most of it when somebody gives us something."

Bennie rolled a cigarette himself from the skimpy remains of his makings and led the way back toward the cabin.

Kid said, "Your old place up there, huh?"

"Yeah," Bennie said. "I was born there."

"My tribe used to pow-wow with the Winnebagos right about where the barn used to be. In fact, our old burial ground is back there where you were when I came up. Down the creek a little ways. There's a big boulder there. I'll show you one of these days. Great swimming hole right below it."

"The hell you say? A burial ground. I felt kind of creepy there for a fact." He was afraid to tell Kid the whole story, at least yet, but he had a notion that Kid, being Sioux, would understand. "When did your tribe live out here and pow-wow with the Winnebagos?"

"I dunno. A hundred years ago. Maybe two hundred. Who knows? They still pow-wow together in town—every year. They did it out here till the loggers came and run us out. They're gone. So are the pines. We ain't."

Newt was outside the cabin and saw them coming. He said, "You wasn't gone very long."

"I met Kid down there. Kid Kinsolving. This is my Uncle Newt . . . Kid is an Indian."

"So I see. Howdy, Kid." He offered his hand and Kid didn't hesitate to shake, looking Newt over closely, almost insolently, grinning. He said, "You look like all the old Injun fighters I've seen in movies."

Newt laughed "You can really read 'em, Kid. I even knew Custer, but I swear I never killed more'n one Injun at a time . . . or less either, come to think of it."

After that remark Kid looked Newt over again, a little more carefully, obviously not sure if Newt was kidding. Bennie figured the old man had expected as much; Newt's offhand remarks usually weren't all that offhand.

Kid said, "You wouldn't woof a poor, ignorant redskin, would you?"

"I might." Newt left that hanging.

Kid decided to let it drop.

"Kid's folks have lived here a long time," Bennie said.

"I ain't surprised," Newt said. He nodded at Kid's shotgun. "What you huntin'?"

"Nuthin' really. Everybody carries some kind of gun. Apt to get picked up as a nut if you just walk around empty-handed."

Newt nodded. He'd spent most of his life in places just like that. He took out his bottle and took a short pull. Kid's eyes followed the bottle like a cat watching a mouse, which Newt didn't miss. He offered the bottle. "Have a slug."

Bennie watched about half of what was left disappear and thought, "He handles booze like he did my makin's. Well, he probably can't afford his own." He noticed Kid didn't choke on it like he was sure he would, so he knew it wasn't his first slug of it by a whole lot.

Kid said, "Bennie says you're movin' in here and fixin' the place up." He glanced around.

Newt said, "I aim to spend my last days here."

Kid said, "My folks and I lived here one year after the old woman and crazy guy moved away."

Bennie said, "That'd been my grandma and nutty Uncle Bob. They put him in the loony bin right after Grandma moved in with my Aunt Felice. She wouldn't have Bob, even though he was her own brother."

Kid laughed. "He busted out of the nut house. Come back here and lived with us. They come lookin' for him, but we always hid him. He was crazy like a fox."

That surprised Bennie. Till a few months before he hadn't even been told about Bob. They must have caught him eventually, though, since he remembered they had to let him out to come to Grandpa's funeral.

"They ever catch him?" He asked Kid.

"Once. He busted out again." He looked evasive, as though he could have told more, but wasn't sure he could trust them yet.

"Good," Newt said. "Hell, most nuts *do* have more sense than the average Joe. Even Custer was crazy as a bedbug. Most good cavalrymen were."

Kid eyed him closely. "You wasn't kiddin' about knowin' Custer then?"

"Not by a jug full."

Bennie vowed to pump Newt dry about Custer the first chance he got.

Newt took out a cigar, which Kid eyed like he had the bottle. Noticing, Newt offered him one. Kid leaned his shotgun against the cabin and made a ceremony of getting the cigar lit.

He said, "I'm sure as hell glad you're movin' in. You couldn't use a shiftless, thievin' redskin to help fix the place up, by any chance?"

Newt looked Kid over impassively for several seconds.

"Why not?"

CHAPTER THIRTY-THREE

No Milk, No Cream, No Butter, No Moola

– PRO BONO PUBLICO IS INTERVIEWED BY VOX POPULI –

"What endures?"
"Love."
"And . . . ?"
"The Land."

— Spring 1938

Eben shook Bennie awake at sunup. "Time to milk," he said. "Roll out."

It was the last thing Bennie felt like doing. Instead he felt like he'd rather sleep forever. The tangy fresh air that had drifted through his bedroom all night made for really good sleeping.

When they reached the barn, carrying milk buckets, Eben explained, "This time of year you don't have to run the cows up from the pasture first, 'cause there ain't no pasture yet. After you get 'em up here, which they already are, you jest let 'em in the barn. No problem there. You throw down hay first and they know it's waitin' for 'em. Or maybe feed some silage or bran."

He led the way up a ladder to the hay loft. It had a sweet, musty smell, one that Bennie always savored. Above the horse stalls on one side and cow stanchions on the other were rows of holes for throwing down hay into the mangers below.

"Not too much, not too little," Eben explained, showing Bennie how to use the pitchfork to pick it up from the tightly packed hay. "Don't want to waste any. It's gotta last till next haying season. On the other hand, pasture's no good yet so yuh gotta feed the critters enough or you won't get milk. No milk, no cream, no butter, no moola from sellin' at the Creamery, no store-bought stuff. Hosses need more to eat than cows, and a lot more when you're workin' 'em. You feed 'em hay and corn both, if you got it, or oats, or all three when you're workin' 'em hard. Otherwise you break 'em down and they won't be able to work worth a damn. Remember all this. Yore paw'll be countin' on you to know it. Prob'ly countin' on me to teach you while I'm still around."

He was working as he talked, tossing down hay. The team that Nelson left were in their stalls below, stamping impatiently, knowing they were about to be fed.

"Here, you try it," Eben said, handing the pitchfork to Bennie.

Bennie shoved it into the hay, too deeply the first time, and couldn't lift what he got hold of because the hay was intertwined and packed down. He looked at Eben.

"Slack off," Eben said. "Pull the fork out and next time just kinda skim it off the top. You'll get the hang of it. And you'll learn when it's just right from how heavy it feels."

Bennie tried again and got a forkful, looking at Eben for guidance. The hired man nodded and said, "That's about right, pitch 'er down."

Bennie did the same for the rest, Eben only grunting as Bennie looked at him each time for approval. When he was through, Eben said, "Not bad for a city kid."

They were milking eight cows, not many, but about what diversified farms around there usually kept. Two other cows waited in a lean-to attached to the barn. Bennie tossed down their hay through the ladder hole, as directed by Eben, then they went down and forked it into the lean-to that adjoined the barn's alley. "This here is the calving shed," Eben explained. "It's too damn cold yet to let 'em calve in the pasture."

The barn's planked center alley separated the four horse stalls plus a box stall on one side from the ten cow stalls on the other. In the alley were a hand-cranked corn sheller and a gas-engine operated hammer mill that made meal from shelled corn. If there was a particularly early frost, ear corn wouldn't ripen and these machines stood idle. In any case every farmer in that country made green corn silage every year, and it did wonders for milk output. In the case of silage, the corn had to be cut before it ripened and really eared out.

Eben led the way into the cow section of the barn and walked up the alley behind the stalls to a door, Bennie close behind him. "Open the door," Eben directed, "then stand back unless you wanta get stomped to death by hungry critters."

The cows were waiting eagerly outside, impatient to file in and get their bellies full. Bennie, unlike most city kids, wasn't the least bit afraid of cows since he'd spent a couple of years rambling the woods around Blackhawk where they grazed. He'd learned they were a lot more afraid of people than vice versa. Bennie suspected Eben was telling it scary, but he was about to learn plenty he hadn't known. Up till then he'd mostly watched from his distant woods when cows went into the barns where they were milked, except for his brief excursions at Country Grandma's.

Bennie opened the doors and stood aside while the cows filed in, paying no attention to either him or Eben, going directly to their own stanchions and sticking their heads in to attack the hay. Eben stepped in between the first pair and snapped the stanchions shut around their necks. "Watch how I do it," he told Bennie, "then you do the rest. We ain't got a kicker in the bunch so you don't have to be careful. Besides you can do almost anything to 'em while they're eatin'."

Bennie examined his first stanchion, a wood-lined metal clamp about three feet long, shaped like a big paper clip, hung by a chain from a sturdy overhead beam that ran the full length of the stalls and chained to the floor on the bottom. "Cows ain't as dumb as you think," Eben said. "Notice how they poke their heads in the stanchions with no argument. Even the two with horns." Bennie had noticed how cleverly those two had twisted their heads and slipped them through the stanchions with their horns aligned almost vertically so they didn't catch on the sides. All he had to do after that was clamp the hinged side of the stanchion shut on the cows' necks so they couldn't pull back out.

When they were secured, Eben said, "Now the fun begins. Watch what I do. Then you try 'er. Ever milk a cow before?"

"Nope," Bennie said. "I tried a time or two down at my grandma's in Illinois, but my uncles figured I was only in the way and holding up the parade, so they always finished."

As a matter of fact, he'd avoided milking, in favor of playing, and besides it seemed like a long time ago.

Eben took a bucket in his right hand and a stool in his left, then squatted down on the right side of the first big Holstein, just in front of its hind legs. Bennie already knew the black-and-white spotted cows were Holsteins. All Nelson's were. They gave more milk than Guernseys and Jerseys, the other two popular breeds, but Holstein milk wasn't as rich in butterfat.

Eben edged his stool closer to the cow's flank after he sat down, but not so close Bennie couldn't see what he was doing.

"Watch," Eben said. He grabbed a pair of big teats on the cow's bag. "See? Now watch me squeeze; you start with your pointing finger, then squeeze the next and so on, down to your little finger and then start all over. Folks that don't milk think you're pulling on the teat, but that ain't so, it just looks that way."

He had two steady streams of milk shooting into the bucket with a pinging metallic echo, which soon shifted to a rich sudsy sound as the bucket filled and began to foam. By then three farm cats had showed up waiting for their act to go on. "Git over a little," Eben said, "and watch this." He angled the teat just right and shot a stream of milk at one of the cats and it quickly sat up and caught it in its open mouth. He did it for each of the cats in turn. "That's enough for now," he announced, returning the stream to the bucket. The cats stayed around, meowing plaintively, and occasionally Eben gave them another squirt.

"Now you step in here and finish this one," Eben said. "She's the gentlest one we got—name's Gertrude."

Bennie took the stool, a homemade affair with a two-by-four seat about a foot long, nailed to a piece cut out of a small tree, about four inches across and a little over a foot long. He got settled on the stool, but the unfamiliar maneuver threw him off balance and he almost fell over and spilled the bucket. Eben steadied him. "You'll get the hang of it," he said. "Lean the stool a little toward the cow and brace back ag'in' it. Between the stool's leg and yore two you're makin' a three-legged stool."

Bennie did as he was told and managed to grip the bucket between his knees as Eben had.

"Good." Eben said. "Now grab the teats and go ahead."

After watching him for a minute Eben said, "You're a natural, just keep it up and pump away till you've stripped those two teats dry, then do the same on the other two. That's all there is to it."

Eben moved to the next cow and started milking her. Bennie managed to finish his cow and get about halfway through a second by the time Eben finished the rest. Eben came back and checked on Bennie's first cow and said, "You really are a natural. You milked old Gertrude dry."

Bennie felt a warm sense of accomplishment at that praise, and his aching hands and arms took on a new surge of strength. Even at that, he had to rest occasionally so the cow got restless and shifted her hind feet around.

"Stand still, dammit," he growled, not wanting to be stepped on or spill his bucket. He was surprised to discover that the cow responded.

"Cussin' helps," Eben said. "Cows 'r' like mules thataway. If they really get ornery, get up and crack their hind leg with your stool. That gets their attention right smart. Of course you better be ready to scramble in case the sonofabitch decides to kick you."

Bennie thought, "Big help." He looked at the huge leg on the monster he was trying to milk and imagined what a hell of a kick it could deliver.

He also learned about cows' tails, good training for the future, when the tails that only nervously swatted him a time or two now would be switching at flies constantly, and, moreover, were usually drenched with fresh manure and urine. He was to learn, come summer, what a true delight that experience was after a hard day in the field, sitting next to a hot cow's flank in a stifling barn, sweat running in his eyes, flies swarming around his face and neck and an empty stomach growling for food. That was calculated to give a farmer the inspiration to reflect on the poetic effusions of writers about idyllic rural existence. Those who'd "been there" knew it was best perceived from afar, despite the clean fresh air, peace and quiet, personal freedom, and association with humble, honest beasts and the nurturing land.

Later he would learn another poetic fact about humble, honest beasts: what they did most was eat and pass waste. About that, Eben said, "The quicker yuh run 'em back out after we finish milkin', the less you'll have ta shovel." Nelson's barn was one of the more modern. It boasted a cement walk and gutter behind the cows and an overhead tram bucket for running the offal outside on a cable arrangement to be dumped across the barnyard on a manure pile. But first someone had to shovel the waste into that bucket after each milking. As yet Bennie hadn't figured who that most often would be. In fact he hadn't yet given a thought to how the manure got out of there.

Bennie and Eben emptied their milk pails into ten-gallon cans to transport to the milk house. The cans were carried on a hand-drawn cart with large iron wheels.

They turned the cows out and Bennie pushed the milk cart out the door at the other end of the barn. He shortly discovered the cart might as well have weighed a ton in the soft ground. Eben gave him a hand. "Pull it, and it'll move easier. Hell, kid, wait'll yuh have to fight lots more cans on this contraption because the cows're all in fresh and maybe it's rainin' to boot with the ground soft and muddy."

"Fresh?" Bennie's tone implied the question.

"Yeah! Fresh. Cows put out a lot more milk then."

"How?" Bennie asked.

Eben looked startled. "By havin' a calf, facrissakes!" Then he softened his tone, "I fergot yer a city kid. You don't act like most of 'em do though."

High praise coming from that source and Bennie recognized it. Nonetheless, he felt really dumb. He'd felt superior to city kids he'd read about who didn't even know where milk came from, except a bottle at the store, or delivered to the back door, but it dawned on him he had a thing or two to learn about it himself.

By then they were at the milk house. Eben said, "Stop to think, when we milk, we're actually stealin' from the calf. You breed a cow, it gets a calf and has milk for a long while afterward, pretty much as long as the calf nurses, or we milk her—o' course she goes dry in time, so before then, when her milk drops off, we breed her again. She goes dry before she has the next calf. Then she drops the calf, and comes in fresh an' we start milkin' her again. We just divvy with the calf till its weaned and can eat regular stuff."

It was an unending cycle, Bennie learned, since you had to milk morning and night, or find someone to do it for you if you had to be away.

They trundled the cart into the milk house after Eben's little sermon and Bennie was thinking, "Thank God that's over. I'm hungry enough, as Newt says, to eat the asshole out of a skunk."

Eben jolted him again, saying, "When we finish separating the milk I'll show you how to slop the hogs and feed the chickens, then I'll go up and start breakfast."

"Holy shit," Bennie thought. "I'll collapse before then."

The separator was like the one at Country Grandma's, a contrivance that looked something like a hand-operated well pump, set on a cast iron frame, this one bolted into the cement floor. It had a crank that you turned to "rev" up the machinery inside to several thousand revolutions per minute, using gears, and the contraption actually separated cream from the whole milk by centrifugal action, in a manner he never understood till he took a physics course. He'd been allowed to turn the handle on the one at his grandmother's, but he'd always pooped out and couldn't keep it revved up, so that his uncles would take over. It wasn't going to be that way this time. Eben poured the milk in the big metal bowl on top and Bennie turned the handle, discovering a few more muscles, just as he had milking, but he wasn't about to flag this time. He'd lost about enough face. He was going to keep it revved up till he dropped, if need be.

He watched the skim milk come out one spout and the cream out another, skim milk into a milk can and the cream into the container Eben set beneath that spout. Bennie would always enjoy seeing the rich, yellow cream fill the container, thinking of all the good things that could be made from it, especially home-made ice cream, but also butter, and he never again liked coffee without real cream after he tasted fresh farm cream in it.

The cool, stone milk house had been built almost directly beneath the windmill, and above the well, which was right next to the milk house. The windmill could pump water only when enough wind blew to move the wheel; but when there wasn't enough wind the pump was worked with a long handle that moved the pump leathers up and down, simulating the action of the sucker rod on the windmill. That had to be disconnected in order to pump by hand. In either case, water was first pumped into a tank inside where they washed the milking stuff and stored cans of cream to keep them cool. From the inside tank the cool water ran out an overflow pipe into a galvanized metal trough outside where the farm animals drank. One of his jobs in freezing weather would be breaking ice off it so the animals could drink. That tank overflowed into a duck pond through a stone ditch. Bennie would come to love the cool, dark milk house in the hot, sultry summer days, and never complain then about separating, or churning butter, which were both done there.

By the time they'd finished separating, Bennie had forgotten about the hogs and chickens, and had a picture of one of Eben's breakfasts going on the table.

Eben had run the skimmed milk from the separator back into the cans in which they'd carried the milk down from the barn. "Toss these two cans back on the cart," he told Bennie. "I'll show you where to slop the hogs—they get it all when we ain't got any weaner calves."

Bennie groaned inwardly, but grabbed a can and discovered that it weighed a ton. The thick metal can alone probably weighed twenty pounds. He heaved and tugged and finally got a can on the cart by bracing it against his legs but found out he couldn't dead-lift one. Eben came to his rescue and one-handed the second can onto the cart like it was a feather. That caused Bennie to look him over carefully since he wasn't big and he wasn't broad either—just strong as an ox.

Eben said, "By tomorrow you'll have the hang of all this and can handle it alone, except for the milkin'. That'll take a little building up to."

Bennie thought, "Maybe I'll handle it alone. If I pull through."

Eben led the way to the plank-fenced farrowing yard. "These're all sows," he said of the huge pigs that crowded up to the fence, grunting and shoving, knowing the trough would soon be running full of skim milk. They even bit one another, in a definite pecking order, but after the trough was full they were all too busy to fight each other, inhaling the skim milk with greedy sucking noises. Bennie thought, "No wonder they call it slopping the hogs." No one with hogs ever needed a garbage can for waste food. Hogs could inhale everything but razor blades and tin cans.

"Jeezus, they stink!" Bennie said.

"Farms ain't no flower garden, kid. Wait'll some nice summer night so 'close' you can strike a match on it, when you got the window open, hopin' to get even one breath of air and that breath comes from over this way. I've been on farms all my life and never got used to it. By hot weather they'll all have litters too. Maybe a dozen piglets apiece. We sell most of 'em off, but there's always plenty left to perfume up the air. The only way I like those bastards is on the table as ham or bacon or sausage, or fresh pork."

Bennie thought, "I can hardly wait." He was as close to being starved as he'd ever been.

"I'll start breakfast while you shell some corn for the chickens. C'mon, I'll show you where everything is. You can gather eggs after we eat."

"Thank God for that," Bennie thought.

He followed Eben back to the barn where the corn sheller stood in the middle alley, stopping at the corncrib on the way to fill a big metal basket with ear corn. The crib formed one side of the granary, in the middle of which was an alley wide enough to drive a wagon through the building. An oat bin stood on the other side.

The corn sheller was operated by a hand crank and had a flywheel to help keep it turning. Ears of corn fed into the top came out a waste chute as cobs, while the kernels were shelled off and fell into a metal basket beneath the machine. It was an ornery contraption, hard to keep up to shelling speed, despite the flywheel. Eben left Bennie struggling with it, saying, "Come back here when you're done feedin' the chickens and get those cobs and bring 'em up to the house in that basket. We're running a little short."

Bennie was glad he at least knew what cobs were used for—starting fires in the cook stove, or making a fire a little hotter. (He recalled his Uncle Johnny used them in the back house for another purpose, as well.) Eben added over his shoulder, "Scatter that corn around the chicken pen good. By the time you're through and washed up, I'll have breakfast about ready to put on the table."

While Bennie was washing up in the kitchen he asked Eben, "Want me to go up and roll out Uncle Newt?"

Eben gave him a pitying look, which Bennie missed, since his back was turned. "You don't know old Newt very well, do you?" Eben said. "He was up and et before you rolled out. Said to let you sleep late, you probably needed it. He's prob'ly been over cuttin' wood since it was light enough to see what he was doin'."

"I might have known," Bennie said.

Bennie heroically destroyed a truly memorable breakfast of ham and eggs, hot rolls with butter, jelly, and jam, fresh-fried spuds, and a big piece of Eben's apple pie swimming in cream, with coffee to wash it down. Eben didn't stand short on eating his own cooking, Bennie noticed. The hired man was clearing off the dishes while Bennie rolled a cigarette, first putting the plates on the floor to let the pup, Hank, do the preliminary wiping with a big red tongue.

"The little feller is lookin' right pert, I'd say," Eben observed.

Bennie said, "I thought I'd walk over to Newt's through the woods. You think Hank's in good enough shape to make it?"

"You'll never know till ya give 'im a chance," Eben said. "You'll prob'ly have to pack him over the creek though. I wonder if you'd give me a hand with a couple of things before you go."

"Sure," Bennie said, unsuspectingly.

Eben thought, "I'm gonna really like this kid. He's a sticker. Never grumbled once about doin' a thing." On the other hand he recognized in Bennie another independent soul, just like himself. He wasn't about to do anything that looked like ordering Bennie around.

Eben said, "Yore Uncle Newt reckoned you'd like to know how to hitch up a team and maybe drive it around—get the hang of it before yore Paw comes back."

Bennie forgot about the woods for a while. "I'm game," he said. "Lead the way."

Eben had slyly omitted mentioning where and what they were going to "drive around," and mentioned the horses before he got Bennie out to help him "manure out" the cow barn. Next they manured out behind the horses.

"We'll toss the harness on the hosses in here," Eben said, "then lead 'em out."

He showed Bennie each piece of harness and named it as he used it, but first introduced the two big mares, "This here bay is Nancy, and the black is Queen."

Bennie watched the deft harnessing up, but the names of the pieces of harness simply created a confusing jumble in his mind. "I'll never be able to remember all this," he thought.

After the team was hitched up, Eben gave Bennie some rudimentary instructions on controlling the team, then turned him loose to drive while they dragged a bunch of tools and fence material on a stone boat down to the "back forty." There they reset a couple of posts and corner braces, restretched some barbed wire, and replaced a lot of staples that had weathered out over the years.

Back from that, Eben set Bennie to work with a hammer, helping him nail down siding on the outbuildings that had been worked loose during the winter by a combination of wind buffeting them and moisture warping them. They did this on the barn, granary, and machine shed, which was a lean-to attached to the barn. Bennie had hardly noticed he never got over to Newt's place yet, when they sat down to the noon meal.

He pushed back his chair and rolled a cigarette. The thought crossed his mind, "Cripes, it seems like I was just doin' this, right after breakfast no more than a half hour ago." It had been six hours.

He stubbed out his cigarette, took a last swig of coffee and said to Eben, "If you don't mind, I'm gonna stretch out on the couch over here for a minute. I ain't used to this much work."

He woke up with Eben shaking him.

"I figured you could use a leetle nap," Eben said, "so I didn't bother you. It's time to milk again."

Bennie looked out the window and was dismayed to see the sun just setting.

"I'll get the buckets and meet you out to the barn," Eben said.

It got dark quickly after sunset that time of year; before they could finish milking they had to light lanterns and hang them on the spikes, located along the barn wall for that purpose. Bennie ended up stumbling across the yard under the stars, dragging the milk carts. They lit another lantern in the milk house to "separate." Bennie dragged the skim milk over to the hogs by starlight.

Eben told him, "I already done fed the chickens before I woke you up. Gotta get them inside before dark."

Newt showed up just in time for supper, with Nelson along.

Newt looked at Bennie, grinned, and said, "I expected you'd be over to help out. I guess you been layin' around takin' country life easy, eh kid?"

Bennie had enough fizz left in him to give Newt his Gary Cooper act. "Yup." he said.

He was almost too tired to have his cigarette and coffee after supper and soon dragged himself up to bed. When he was part way up the stairs, he heard Nelson say, "Either of you galoots care for a game of cribbage?"

"I'm yore man," Eben said.

Newt said, "Good. I wanta read a little while before I turn in."

"Cripes," Bennie wondered, "will I ever get like them?"

As he was getting out of his clothes Bennie thought, "It ain't no picnic, but I'm really going to like it here when I get the hang of things."

He was sound asleep when his head hit the pillow. If someone had looked at him, they'd have seen a grin splitting his face from ear to ear.

It was 7 P.M. Later he'd realize that hadn't really been a long day by farm standards.

He was home. *Up north.*

CHAPTER THIRTY-FOUR

'Twas Not The Moon That This Did

[FLASHBACKS—1930 THROUGH 1938]

Bennie Todd had seen only the local effects of what was happening in the world in those years. A kid, even one of fifteen years who knew his history, could be excused for not realizing that the world was shrinking. *But he wasn't the only one who had to learn that the other fellow's hard luck soon could be yours.* In the years of the worldwide Depression, lunatic forces were released by the economic hardship suffered by little people who forgot everything but their stomachs. (It's the way animals are built—few deny that in the jungle hunger gives birth to daily mass murder.)

If he'd been told, Bennie wouldn't have realized the meaning of what would someday be termed "important indicators." For example—a 70 percent shrinkage of world trade. (It goddam well meant what Keynes, a British economist, called "aggregate demand," had dried up and stalled the machine of prosperity.) Governments, such as Britain's Labor Party, were forced from office. Germany plummeted into economic chaos that killed its first weak democratic government, and in time condemned fifty million people to death while Germany got even. France put in one government ministry after another at about one-month intervals. Ten Latin American countries suffered revolutions. All because of empty stomachs—and no roofs overhead. Those two conditions breed chaos.

Hoobert Heever, supposedly a smart man, didn't know that. If, figuratively speaking, Caesar didn't understand what the hell was going on under his nose, why should a kid of fifteen? Well, the kid was hungry, so was better prepared to learn it. His ears and eyes were opened by that gnawing pain in his gut.

He'd heard often that sad *Hooverism* "Prosperity is just around the corner."

Nonetheless he'd been hungry for years after. Bennie knew that what *Hoobert Heever* had stood for was a "bunch of shit." Free enterprise was a dodo as far as its unrestrained phase went. If the public learned its lesson permanently, there would be no more robber barons who were accountable only to themselves. Their final grade was F. The old ways were condemned by their own excesses, and their executioners were Franklin Delano Roosevelt and the New Deal.

But FDR couldn't have done it if the times weren't ripe. And he wasn't looking to get even with anyone. The winds of rampant greed had blown unchecked since the Civil War, and ushered in the inevitable whirlwind that blew away the last of the robber barons. (Was a new crop in the wings?)

> *"NATCH!"*
>
> —*Pro Bono Publico*

Bennie heard it all discussed around the dinner table almost every night. The Depression that stubbornly refused to die, the growing threat of world war, the new willingness of government to listen to the little man's voice, the question whether the common people were smart enough to hang onto what they'd gained. (When were they ever?)

THOSE WHO CANNOT REMEMBER HISTORY . . . !

The most significant historic change that Bennie noticed, however, was in Ma. It showed on her face when she and Pa returned from Blackhawk. She stepped out of the Lincoln smiling and quietly looking around. He didn't blame her for smiling. Every time he looked over the Nelson place, now theirs, he felt like jumping up and down and hollering. She'd have been more hopeless than he thought if she hadn't felt at least a little like he did.

When she stepped down from the Lincoln and surveyed her domain, Ma was thinking of how she'd come *up north* that first time. And why. The why was simple. She'd had no choice. It seemed as though she'd always been the slave of some man—of Pa *out home*, of Prince Charming in a different way, finally of a husband she'd never loved, and no longer even respected.

She wasn't given to retrospection, therefore her thoughts as she stepped out were both heartening and surprising:

"This is my last chance—*our* last chance. And I'm going to see that Russ doesn't fumble it. I'm going to run this show and I know how. In the first place Russ is a weakling, a quitter, a dreamer. Well, he's quit for the last time."

It conveniently escaped her that he'd just finished a couple of years of slavery for G.M. and hadn't quit, in fact hadn't wanted to. She was also totally unable to see, or at least admit to herself, that she was the reason he'd quit *up north* the first time, or admit that they'd have been a hundred times better off even on a poor, subsistence farm in the woods than on the dole in Waubonsee during their leanest years. The nearest she came to admitting that was in her plan of action now.

She'd looked over Nelson's big orchard and garden spot before she decided they should buy the place. Like *Hoobert Heever* she thought social security could come out of the root cellar—at least in this case, since they had both a root cellar and some *roots*. The first day she'd been there, she'd found the late Mrs. Nelson's canning equipment. While the men had been in the woods getting the Lincoln unstuck from the mud, she'd carried a kerosene lamp down into the dim cellar to snoop.

There she found at least a year's supply of food, mostly home-canned stuff in Ball fruit jars, neatly stacked on shelves from floor to ceiling, all labeled, though she could tell by sight what most of it was: jams and jellies, apple sauce, peaches, berries (either home-grown or wild, they grew like weeds in that country), carrots, beets, string beans, peas, and in ventilated bins, potatoes and onions, turnips and rutabagas. There were also bulk staples in sealed cans, undoubtedly bought or traded for in town: coffee beans, sugar, flour. Finally, a large stone crock was full of homemade maple syrup, and, carefully wrapped in cheese cloth and secured in mouse-proof screened cages, at least two dozen home-cured hams. Looking at all this food brought her as close to sexual arousal as she'd ever come. Little shivers of pleasure rippled through her body. She felt like she had as a kid, standing in the tall, ripe corn, listening to it whisper that some wonderful revelation was in store for her. This was security. She planned never to lose her grip on it again.

And she aimed to improve on their self-sufficiency this time around. An icehouse could be built and stocked from the East Fork, which frequently froze all the way to the bottom. With an icehouse available, they could butcher and keep meat from spoiling the year round. Unlike before, there would be plenty of help. Then Russ had complained that Nutty Bob and lazy Bart had been more a hindrance than a help, which Emma conceded. Bennie could help; she thought of him as a "big hulk," already bigger than most men. Both Newt and Nelson were spry as young colts, considering their ages, and she planned to levy on them whenever she needed help. She'd taken Eben's measure in one meeting, after he told her he was the maid who kept the house immaculate, and Nelson had snorted and added, "And he ain't only a heck of a wife, he's the best farmer I know, except me, of course." If Eben wanted to stay on, she planned to offer him just board and spending money, since jobs were hard to come by.

Realizing she was thinking like this surprised Ma. It would have stunned Pa and Bennie, but not Newt. All three would recognize her guiding hand, in time, and adjust the best way they could. Bennie would do a better job of it than Pa, and Newt would applaud what he saw. Bennie was heartily tired of

Pa's shilly-shallying. A home needed someone at the helm. Bennie needed a father, *even if it was Ma*. He would find his whole attitude toward her changing, especially since she never again was prone to slug him for little or nothing. (He didn't realize that was because he'd got so big she was afraid to.)

"*We own something decent at last*," Ma thought.

This profound change had started to come over Ma when she told herself, "*We can hold up our heads. Be somebody.*" As she looked around she smiled.

Their household things had come in a moving van paid for by Newt, and she had inspected each item as it was carried in, believing that the moving men would ruin half the furniture. After their work passed inspection, she even fixed them something to eat, still smiling that triumphant little smile.

Now two days had passed. Almost everything was settled in its place to her satisfaction. The men were gone. She'd seen Pa and Bennie head for a field with a four-horse, two-bottom riding plow. Bennie was going to get his first plowing lesson. She'd been so astounded to see how he willingly dived into doing the chores, and keeping her kitchen stocked with cobs and wood, that she hardly grumbled over the decision to keep him out of school for the rest of that year. Newt had been the deciding agent, arguing, "Hell, he knows more than most of the teachers I've ever met. Besides he can earn some money. When you don't need him, I'll pay him to help me. We can start a savings account for him."

That decided Ma. She knew that you had to save something if you weren't going to be miserable. Bennie wasn't so sure. He'd never forgotten that the Merchants and Savings Bank in Wahbonsee had cleaned out his accumulation of pennies and nickels without so much as an apology. But he didn't give a damn if it happened again, so long as he didn't have to go back to school right away. Learning about a farm was too much fun.

Ma was looking out the open window above the kitchen sink, the dishes she'd been washing forgotten. A warm, spring breeze carried in the happy noises of birds seeking nesting places and the vital smell of budding greenery.

"How long has it been since I've been this happy?" she thought, and rested her arms on the sill.

"A long while." She answered her own question. When she'd worked for Browns as a girl and a certain man had come along. It reminded her that you had to wait a long while for even a fleeting encounter with happiness. Then you were apt to see it wither and die.

"*How long will it last this time?*" she asked herself.

Then, she set her jaw. "*Till the day I die, if I have any say about it!*" she vowed. "*And I'm going to have a lot of say about it. I'm still young. Forty-six.*"

She repeated it to herself. "*Forty-six. Think of it. It seems like yesterday I was six and wondering what it would be like to start school.*" Forty years past. The school years had fled by, her happiest years as she looked back on them, despite all her father did to make life *out home* miserable.

[FLASHBACK—1905]

Emma knew she was going to have to go "out working" as soon as she finished eighth grade, just like her sister Mary had. Sometimes she looked forward to it. At other times she'd think that it would be nicer to stay home always and just help Ma. Lord knew, Ma needed help. Between keeping house for Pa and the five other kids, she had to be a man part of the time and help in the fields.

Electric power hadn't even been imagined for rural homes, and if it had been, most of the labor-saving appliances that would someday relieve housewives of drudgery hadn't been invented. Emma must have heard her mother say a hundred times, "I'm so busy I don't even have time to go out back." That was the common term for going to the outdoor toilet, or back house.

Mary came home to visit in the summer when the Stough family she worked for went on vacation to someplace cool. They always hired another girl wherever they went to save paying Mary's railroad fare. On top of that they sent her home without pay. The rest of the year when Mary was at the Stoughs', Pa would take in some vegetables or butter and eggs to sell once a month and pick up Mary's pay, which he was accumulating in a bank account to build a new barn. (All except the part he'd spend to get drunk, which wasn't much, as small as his capacity was and as cheap as whiskey was.) Mary got seven dollars a month, her clothes, room, and board. Emma supposed she'd get about the same.

If she went, the best part would be getting away from Pa. That and being around the wonderful things the people always had who could afford hired girls. On rare visits to Ma's well-to-do childhood friends, Emma had ogled everything. Dark, shiny furniture, deep carpets with colored designs, good mirrors in which you weren't all wavy and yellow-looking, real pictures in frames—even toilets in the house, and a furnace in the cellar that heated the whole place, one that you never had to polish with stove blackening like you had to with an old German heater.

There was some secret about her mother's past, in the time when she'd had rich friends. It wasn't just that Ma was a Sioux, although that was exciting enough, especially since she had belonged to Sitting Bull's tribe until she'd been captured and adopted by Major Brown. He hadn't even had to be in the Army, since his family was rich. The major had been on the campaign in which the Army was chasing Sitting Bull and Ma somehow was captured when they were all running away.

Emma knew that Chief Sitting Bull had been like an uncle to Ma and was a real kind man, even though he'd "massacred" General Custer and his men. Ma almost never talked about that, but Emma knew Ma had been a little girl and was right there when that battle took place. Ma did tell Emma once that she'd been swimming in the river with some other kids and not expecting any trouble at all when the shooting started and almost scared her to death. She told how little splashes dappled the water, and they thought at first that some mischievous boys were hiding in the bushes and throwing rocks into the water until one of the little girls was shot, the bullet almost taking her arm off. Then they thought evil spirits had attacked them, until they heard the soldiers' rifles and all ran screaming back toward their camp, even the little girl whose arm was dangling by a rope of flesh, spraying blood all over.

Once, after that, Country Grandma had said, "They killed Sitting Bull later to get even."

(It wasn't so, but might have been—actually a son of a bitch named McLaughlin arranged to kill the chief in a power struggle over whether he, as Indian agent at Standing Rock, was going to run things, or Sitting Bull, as hereditary chief of the Uncpapas was going to run them.)

The real mystery was how Ma had been cheated after Major Brown and his wife died from a fever, just a day apart. Ma was their adopted child and was supposed to get all the money and property. Instead, Major Brown's brother came out from Pennsylvania and ended up with the money and property, even the mansion where Emma was now going to work. He gave Ma the puny little farm they lived on now. Emma heard Jim Tynan say, "*Brown married the girl off to that little German son of a bitch, just to get rid of her. I suppose he figured he was doing a big thing giving her the farm that belonged to her anyhow.*" Emma knew Jim meant her mother. And Jim usually knew what he was talking about, so she believed it.

She wondered why Ma had anything to do with the Browns after that, and why in the world she wanted her to go to work for them and slave in the big house that was rightfully theirs. All her ma said was, "They were good to me and took care of me after Pa Brown died and I was all alone."

Emma thought, "If you ask me, they didn't take care of you very well," but she didn't say it. Maybe there was something she didn't understand. There had to be, and that was the mystery. Maybe she'd discover what it was when she worked at the Browns'. Emma had no way of realizing how lost an Indian girl was in the white culture, even after twelve years in white schools; or how confused and powerless such a one felt, unable to comprehend what "*rights*" really meant, or that she had any. She'd simply been grateful to the major's brother for explaining everything to her, making out the papers she had to sign, and keeping a roof over her head.

If her Ma had told Emma how scared she'd always been back then, maybe it would have been easier to understand. She was so terrified of soldiers in blue she couldn't watch a parade. They looked like the soldiers on the big horses who'd come shooting, and might have killed her like they did her father, *Four Ponies*.

At times she dreamed she was in a court and the judge would glare and point his finger at her and say in a grave voice, "You were there when the soldiers were killed. You're guilty! Guilty!"

Then a gang of big, rough men would drag her away, and she'd wake up trembling and wet, unable to go back to sleep for hours. She wondered where they had been going to take her, but always woke up before she found out.

(Fifty years after the Custer "massacre," she read that a commemorative ceremony was held on the battlefield, but few of her people had gone because they suspected it was a ruse to get them there and kill them at last, for revenge. She knew exactly how they felt. She read that Mrs. Custer declined to come as well. She could understand that too. Mrs. Custer had lost there the dearest thing in the whole world to her. She herself wouldn't have gone where they killed her father that terrifying day unless she'd been dragged.)

All Emma knew about her ma and those days was the little snatches Ma let out now and then, always ending up by saying, "It's all past. It was terrible. Terrible! I wish I could forget it." She'd always have a faraway look in her eyes, seeing it again, and Emma felt sorry for her.

Emma knew that Ma had loved Major Brown as a real father. His wife had been kind, but never loving, and Ma seldom spoke of her. Now Emma was going to work for Major Brown's nephew, who'd inherited Ma's stolen legacy, but she didn't feel he was a relative in any sense of the word. In fact she was apprehensive about the whole thing. At least it was a change, and a chance to get off the dull farm with its relentless routine. If she didn't like it "out working," she'd eventually grow up and could leave and be a nurse like Florence Nightingale. She knew she was going to be a nurse or die trying. Maybe there'd be another war and she'd be a famous nurse too, and get her name in history books. If you had to die someday, it seemed a lot better if your name was at least remembered.

When the day came for Emma to go out working at Riverview, Pa hitched Old Charlie to the Democrat wagon for the ten-mile trip. Pa called the wagon the *Lunatic* because it would never track just right, or at least he said it didn't—and he was sure right about that on the nights he came home drunk.

Ma said, "Why don't we take Emma in with the buggy and we won't look so poor?"

Pa gave her a disgusted look and it was a wonder he answered her, but he said, "Because this way we can take in butter and eggs at the same time."

Emma knew Ma wanted to look a little less "countrified," as people called it then, especially in front of her rich relatives and friends, but such an idea never entered Pa's head. He came from where peasants were peasants and couldn't get away with trying to look like anything else without being laughed at—maybe even being whipped on the orders of some nobleman.

So they were in the *Lunatic* when they drew up in front of the Brown mansion and Ma led Emma up the long walk. The Browns made sure Pa knew he was never welcome there, and he waited in the wagon. Emma carried her little bundle of possessions tied up in a clean apron. She was painfully self-conscious, her feet wanted to run away, as though she had no control over them. She even got a picture of herself breaking away, wildly diving through the neighbor's hedge, dashing blindly across lots and jumping in the river to drown, like Chaubenee's wife had. Emma didn't know how to swim.

In the back of her mind was the thought, "*Maybe dying isn't so bad if you have to live always afraid, or poor and embarrassed half to death.*"

Her knees felt wobbly and weak and her bowels and bladder too; she was trying not to dribble in her pants right then. She wasn't sure she might not throw up though. She hoped no one had been watching them come up the walk like a procession of beggars. Maybe if someone were watching they'd see how dumb and common she looked in her poor clothes and change their mind about wanting someone like her working for them. Fat chance. She knew from Mary what people like that wanted. A cheap slave. Appearances didn't matter.

Ma twisted the brass key that rang the doorbell. Eventually Mrs. Brown herself answered the door. Emma had seen her before, since they were relatives—almost. They invited Ma in to a duty tea about once a year, scheduled at one of the times when Ma and Pa brought garden truck in to sell. Pa always dropped Ma off, never coming in himself, though he and Ma sometimes stayed overnight with one or the other of Ma's well-to-do girlhood friends. It was as though the Browns didn't want to be reminded of what they'd done to Ma, stealing everything from her and marrying her off to a foreigner, and a damned mean one at that.

And that was how Emma went "out working."

Ma's final advice as she kissed Emma goodbye was, "Don't go out after dark." Before they'd left the farm, Pa had told her, "Keep your legs crossed, girl." Emma vaguely comprehended the meaning of both remarks. It was a simple era that didn't seem to realize that girls could be impregnated at high noon, as well as after dark—also that good advice was a damned poor contraceptive.

— 1909

Four years passed quickly for Emma. She'd learned a lot. Her photos from that time show a very good-looking girl. She was even dressed comparatively well in one picture, wearing a beribboned straw hat perched on top of raven-black hair, piled in a pompadour. She was seventeen. Also pregnant, regardless of good advice, or conscience either.

As Byron put it:

> You may think it was the moon that this did,
> But I cannot help but think, that puberty assisted.

A couple of thousand years of whining morality always made a poor showing against a million years of braying biology.

To paraphrase Byron, "What then, was it that this did?"

The newspapers of that day were always reporting on what they referred to as "the true inwardness of the situation," and in this case would have said, "The trouble started with a summer boarder who was a medical student from Chicago."

He was handsome and debonair (by local standards) and a good dresser. Emma, by then, was studying at night to be a nurse, while still drudging for the Browns. She sometimes assisted Dr. Barker with simple surgery. He was gratified to get a neophyte who didn't rush for the bathroom at the first sight of blood.

The medical student from Chicago spent his summer vacations working with Dr. Barker. That was bad enough, but this fellow, never mind his name, learned that his father and Mr. Brown were old school chums from back in Pennsylvania. A letter or two soon assured that he was living with the Browns. After all, the son of old friends shouldn't be exposed to the evil influences of a strange town—such as "going out after dark," and things of that nature.

Details? The usual. A smile. Flattery. Candy and flowers. The light touching of fingers. A brotherly arm around the shoulders. A buggy ride and picnic. A light kiss, another, even serenading with a ukelele. Emma was in love, whether she knew it or not. He knew what he was in—a familiar pattern. This was an experienced young seducer. The cause, of course, as someone said, was passion, or musically defined with a touch of wry punning: "*A duet from gland uproar.*"

As it happened, the back stairs from his large, airy second-floor bedroom to her smaller, equally airy, third-floor bedroom didn't even creak when walked on carefully. Emma knew positively she was in love after his first ascension. Like a ninny she wondered when he was going to ask her to marry him, since he told her he loved her too. After she told him she was pregnant, he wondered if she'd show in front before he could gracefully get out of town. He left, after a tearful parting, and she waited anxiously for the promised letter telling her of his plans for their future together.

The letter came from Paris (sounding brotherly in case someone else read it) and told how he intended to continue his studies in Europe. It was a carefully crafted little note, such as a casual acquaintance (who had never laid a finger on a girl) would write. A light came on in Emma's untutored mind. She was too damned mad to cry.

She told her sad story to Mary and their girl friend Flora, who was reputed to be a "fast" woman.

Flora asked, "Who was it?" Then quickly said, "Never mind. It was that oily rich kid that worked with Doc Barker, wasn't it?"

Emma mulishly refused to accuse anyone.

Flora gave her a disgusted look; also pitying.

"Have Doc Barker knock the kid for you," was Flora's suggestion. "Tell him it was his fair-haired boy who did the dirty deed."

Even Emma laughed at Flora's choice of words. "Dirty deed, indeed!" Normally it was called "getting a girl in the family way." Surprisingly, Emma knew what "knock the kid" meant. Only she didn't want to do that, not that she thought it was sinful. She'd been around Pa long enough to laugh at the idea that many earthly things were sinful—or God would have struck him dead long before then. Her heart simply told her it was wrong to kill a love child. And she had loved the cad. Still did. Perhaps always would.

Mary was her usual helpful self. "You could run away," she suggested. Her mind was overwhelmed by the thought of what a fit Pa would have when he found out. She didn't want to be around when he did. (Especially since the new barn wasn't quite paid for.)

Flora, who'd once got in the same pickle herself, had a better idea. "If you don't want to get rid of it, find some dummy and blame it on him. You'll never hang it on the slick son of a bitch that did it."

Mary and Emma sucked in their breath to hear such language coming out of a woman. Flora looked at them disgustedly.

She went on, "Find a local boy who can't run for it. A good-looking one with money would be best, if you can find one. How about Gardy Eichelberger's boy? He's the richest skirt-chaser in town and a real catch, even if he is a fink."

"I don't even know him," Emma said. "Besides he's never done it to me. No one else has."

"Holy cow!" Flora exploded. "You're really green. You get them to do it to you. They all want to."

Such an idea was beyond Emma, in fact stunned her. She thought most men would think it was wrong to "do it" before you were married, just as she'd been taught from the time she could understand anything. She had thought she might be the only girl in town "being bad" with a man, not that she was sorry she was doing it.

She finally let that advice soak in and asked Flora, "How do I get a man to do it to me?"

"Just look at them right."

"How?"

Flora showed her. "Like this," she said, batting her eyelids then letting them droop, her lips parted and head canted to one side. She then wet her lips, showing just the tip of her tongue, and smiled—only a brief hint of a smile. She said, "And then turn and walk away like this." She swayed her hips in an exaggerated fashion, causing her buttocks to bounce like a couple of puppies trying to fight their way out from under a blanket.

"I don't know if I can do that," Emma said. But, under the circumstances, the thought of not trying to get the hang of it never occurred to her. She knew she was in a hell of a jam. She naturally shared Mary's horrifying apprehension over Pa's probable reaction. It was a hell of an inspiration to learn acting, or anything else necessary.

"Practice in a mirror," Flora said.

"Yeah, kid," Mary put in. The performance had given her a couple of new ideas.

"I do know a nice man," Emma said. "He might have some money. He went to the Gold Rush in Alaska at a place called Nome. I met him at the roller rink. He always wants to skate with me, but I told him I was engaged."

"O.K. But now you need to get his attention again. Fall down in front of him and pretend you're hurt," Flora said, then brightened at another thought. "Maybe you'll really fall and have a miscarriage. What's his name?"

"Russell Todd."

"I know him," Flora said. "He's cute. And dumb. Just the kind you're looking for if he has some money. Or even a steady job, in a pinch."

"He works at the tannery."

"Well, that lets out money. Nobody with money would work in that crummy place. But it is steady work. That's something."

Emma's campaign worked like Flora predicted, and Russell was actually "doing it" to a girl for the first time in his life. Not only that, but to a pretty girl. He'd never done it to the whores in Nome or Tonopah and places like that because he was deathly afraid of catching something from them. Besides he was painfully bashful. But here he was in the bushes in Poole's Park, getting his first nookie with that good-looking girl Emma. He got his first thrilling feel of it and soon started thrusting—too soon—and panting, streaming off his big load of jizzum in her, practically right away. He almost fainted that first time, sagging on his elbows and rolling to one side to keep from crushing Emma, gasping for his breath like a dog that just lost a fight.

Emma thought he was pretty dumb about it compared to the medical student. But they did it every night for a week after that. He'd probably have been married inside of a month except that Uncle Newt dropped back from Alaska just then.

"I'm gonna get married," was almost the first thing Russell told Newt.

For once, Newt looked as shocked and disconcerted as he was.

"Hell, kid, you must be nuts. I just struck it rich and come back to cut you in on it."

Russell had seen (or heard) Newt strike-it-rich before. Sometimes he really did in a small way, and lost it all before the year was out at the gambling tables. Russell tried not to look mulish, but couldn't. He'd grown to hate Alaska for several good reasons other than having his balls frozen off in the winters, and just then thought he wouldn't go back if they gave him the place.

Newt saw he wasn't going to make any progress on that tack and switched to another. "Well, I guess I oughta get to see this gal, if it's that serious. Maybe I'd better give you away with a dowry." He guffawed.

Russell and Emma accepted Newt's invitation down to the ice cream parlor so Newt could meet her. Newt noticed right off that Emma showed a little in front and rightly figured Russell was too green to notice.

Alone again with Russell, Newt asked, "How long have you known this gal?"

"I guess maybe a year," Russell told him, not getting his drift.

"I mean how long you been jumpin' her?"

Russell actually blushed.

"Well?" Newt pressed the point.

"Maybe a month, I guess." Russell confessed.

Newt didn't spill his suspicions just then. Instead he managed to accost Emma when Russell wasn't around. Unfortunately, his first chance was when she was with Mary and Flora, just going into the ice cream parlor. Newt followed.

He sat down with the three without invitation and said, "I'll buy."

Flora could read the trouble signs all over him at one glance. She almost said, "Who the hell do you think you are, grandpa, hornin' in on a private party?"

Emma introduced him. After they downed their ice cream, Newt eyed Emma and said, "I guess you know I'm kind of a second pa to Russell. I'd like to have a word with you alone about your wedding plans."

Emma didn't suspect a thing. Flora did, and gave Emma a warning look that she missed completely. "You gals won't mind if I go over in a booth for a minute and have a private word with Emma."

He didn't wait to hear whether they did or not, rising and taking Emma's arm, almost dragging her with him. They sat down in the back booth, and he managed to have her facing the wall where Flora wasn't able to shoot her any signals. Newt had read Flora as well as she did him. (In fact he was planning to see her privately as soon as he could arrange it, but not about Emma's wedding plans. He knew that with her kind it was only a matter of price.)

Newt said only two words before Emma started to get scared.

"You're pregnant." He said. "At least three months by now, and Ed—Russell, that is—ain't the father. Right?"

She blushed and avoided his eyes.

"Don't try to get out of it," Newt growled. "I've been around this world a long while. I can read the truth in your eyes. Some bastard knocked you up and dumped you and you're tryin' to hang yourself and the kid around Ed's neck for the rest of his days, or until you can skip out and leave him stuck with the kid. Well, you ain't gonna get away with it, sister!"

"I never thought of running away," Emma protested.

"Do you love, Ed?" Newt asked.

Emma looked down and didn't answer. The truth was she thought he was a clumsy dolt compared to her lover, which was true. He not only didn't know how to screw, he didn't even know how to kiss. Most men were that way in those days; they had no chance to learn to be any other way.

Later, Newt laid it on the line to Russell. He had him out of town before sundown the following day. They headed west on the train, planning to spend the winter with Grandpa Isaac Eaton Todd who'd moved to western Iowa from Troy Grove. Newt thought the Reverend "Ike" Todd, as he called him, was a big hypocrite, but had a soft spot in his heart for him anyhow, ever since he'd bailed his son, Johnny, Newt, and Wild Bill out of the hoosegow in La-Salle, years before. Newt's evaluation of him was, "He's a Bible-spoutin' son of a bitch, but as Jim Hickok used to say, 'His heart's in the right place.'" He never forgot either that the Rev. had almost fallen off his horse going away to the Civil War.

Newt and Ed even went to church pretty regular that winter, in Newt's case to prospect for women with a roving eye. By the next May, not much improved morally but somewhat fatter, they were thinking of taking the train to Seattle and hopping a steamer to Alaska as soon as the ice went out.

Then Russell got a letter from his mother. It said: "*If there's the slightest chance you're the father of Emma's pretty little girl, you have to do the right thing.*"

He wasn't sure, not absolutely sure the baby wasn't his, and he also thought he might be in love with "pretty little Emma," regardless of the "pretty little girl" baby. He'd missed Emma. He'd never had another woman and wanted to "do it" again regularly.

Newt gave him up as a hopeless case, didn't even see him off on the train back to Riverview. Earlier he'd told him, "You're too damned soft for Alaska anyhow. But, good luck. You'll need it." He gave him five hundred dollars and shook hands with him.

Newt thought, "You're a gold-plated sucker. You're going to be stuck with the worst kind of woman, one that doesn't love you and never did."

Russell never saw him again till that day in Blackhawk twenty-eight years later, when Newt became Emma's "*morone* of her own."

Just in case Russell changed his mind, Emma's father had the sheriff meet the train. Russell spent the night before his wedding in the county jail—except when Sheriff Ed Hoyt took him with him down to Dutch Liz's Parlor House. "Let's get some nookie, kid?" Hoyt suggested. It made Russell feel like puking. He'd never been the whorehouse type. But he went along anyhow, and waited in the parlor, to humor the sheriff. It beat sitting in a desolate cell.

Emma liked the comfort of a home where someone loved her. She didn't love Russell, but she at least became fond of him and tolerated his demands, but she didn't understand what someone got out of sex so often, or at all. She'd never even had an orgasm with the great lover who'd got her pregnant, though she'd come close a couple of times before he had left her in the lurch. But mostly, she'd liked his cleanliness, the fact that he smelled of shaving lotion and had an engaging line of blarney. She never came close to an orgasm with Russell, because he knew nothing about taking his time, or even trying to.

Inevitably, as the years passed, sex became what the grannies and aunties had warned Emma it would be: "*A woman's painful duty*." She came to hate men, all men, except the glowing ghost of Prince Charming, but especially Russell, who demanded his "marital rights" all too often. In time, she even blamed him for the fact that she never became Florence Nightingale. And about making love she said, "*It's just like sawing wood*."

How goddam exciting can it get?

CHAPTER THIRTY-FIVE

Grandma Todd Was Walking History

— 1914

Ma remembered how the train brought them into Babcock siding long ago, before the World War. It backed their freight car of goods onto the siding and chuffed away a few minutes later, disappearing around a curve in the spring-green corridor that had been carved through the dense woods years before, probably by men now old, and horses long dead. Their presence could still be felt, if one had enough Indian in them.

It was not a very well-kept railroad, overgrown as it was in brush and weeds close to the track, with decaying ties and crooked rails. In dry years there was always the danger that the smoke-and-cinder-belching-locomotive would blast sparks into the dry weeds along the track and start a forest fire. Not then, however. A cheerless, lowering sky had dripped rain intermittently all that week.

Ma and Lillian, who was just past her fifth birthday, stood on the long, empty, plank platform like fledgling wood ducks that had leaped from their nest without really knowing why, creatures fallen to earth and confused, frightened by new, threatening surroundings. The difference was that Ma didn't scare worth a damn.

After their weathered freight car had been sided and the train steamed off, the scene was even more stark. They may as well have been stranded on Mars.

Grandma Todd had put on her shawl and tied a scarf around her head and trudged off down the tracks in the intermittent drizzle, out of sight around the curve, seeming to sniff her way like a hound. This place where they'd been stranded looked to Ma just like the sort of place to run across a hungry bear not long out of hibernation, which it was. She was sure Grandma Todd had never considered such a thing. Ma always thought of Grandma Todd as more Indian than her own mother, full of silent self-contained ways and receiver of secret messages that few seemed to sense. Pa was defensive of his mother when Ma mentioned this to him. Yet Grandma Todd might suddenly cock her head to one side and command: "*Listen*!" her voice too insistent to ignore.

"To what?" Ma might ask, hearing nothing even with her sensitive Indian ears.

Maybe Grandma would be silent a long while, perhaps not answer at all, or maybe she'd say in a low, pensive tone, "*I don't know*." But she would still have her head cocked, listening, her calm, gray eyes fixed on something far away. It was odd that Pa never noticed.

Grandma Todd was walking history. Her people had known Lincoln because they were his neighbors. As a girl she herself had heard his haunting farewell address to his lifelong friends at Springfield, Illinois, when he reluctantly left to take the lonesome job as President. She remembered for sure only his final, mournfully spoken words . . .

"*I bid you an affectionate farewell.*"

His mortal remains had returned four years later in a special car on a flag-draped train. His train had threaded the land, whistle wailing its melancholy diphthong at every wayside village, stopping at larger towns so the mourning people could solemnly pass the coffin, take one last loving look at Father Abraham, at rest in calm death. Grandma Todd had looked—and been strangled by a terrible, sob-wracked sense of loss. Everyone, even children, knew how Lincoln had shepherded them through four dreadful years of war . . . saved the Union, freed the slaves . . . not only for America then, but for man's vast future, "*the last best hope of earth*."

And now he "belonged to the ages." He'd been taken back, a strange, unique, beloved traveler here for a short, shadowed time, taken home by God who had sent him in the first place. And she had known the sun would never shine on another like him. She felt like she had experienced the wanton destruction of some irreplaceable personal possession, too dear even to try to define, had seen an indescribable treasure taken from her forever. It was an almost universal feeling that would grow with the passing years.

She asked herself, "*How can life go on without him?*"

It was then that she decided that there was a God and that He really did care about human affairs because when people needed him, God had sent them Abe. And that thought comforted her even though she still felt bereft. God had willed that it was Lincoln's time to go—perhaps return. He'd made the ultimate sacrifice for America, for all nations—all people forever—if one thought about it. There would be plenty of trouble finishing the work he had "so far nobly advanced," but it had to be done.

Grandma Todd could remember, too, seeing the drifting smoke from the great Chicago fire of 1871, over one hundred miles away across the Illinois prairie, dimming the sky, telling them in Farmer City of some enormous calamity even before the wires carried the news. As usual many were ready to assume the end of the world was coming. She suspected it would be a while yet, long after her time, in fact. She stubbornly knew by instinct that she hadn't been born to suffer an apocalyptic end before she'd lived a full life. She loved children and aimed to have a lot of her own.

The smell of wood smoke lingered for weeks, poignantly urging them to respond to appeals to chip in their pennies, nickels, and dimes at school for relief of the poor Chicago survivors who'd lost everything, including loved ones in many cases.

People said the fire had started when Mrs. O'Leary's cow kicked over a lantern. Maybe it had. Anyhow, most of Chicago was gone from the face of the earth for all practical purposes . . . then, almost instantly, started to rebuild—"bravely," as the newspapers said. In her opinion it would have been better if the place had gone back to the empty prairie it had been before Fort Dearborn was built. She thought that, especially, years later, after Grandpa Todd (Johnny Todd) moved to Chicago, leaving her on her own in Riverview with Crazy Bob and the younger kids, waiting for him to come back for occasional weekends or for summer vacations.

Everyone told her she ought to be thankful that he was such a good provider and sent home lots of money every month. She'd rather have had him home—every night! She knew why he was gone. He'd left when she decided not to risk having any more babies. Being a "respectable" woman of her era, she only knew one way to prevent that. She suspected, moreover, that he'd had his other women even before then.

"Well, let him!" she'd thought, "If that's what he wants." But it caused a stabbing pain near her heart whenever she thought about it. She had never looked at another man; never would. She would die a month after he did. "Heartbreak," Ma would say, and add, "I don't see what she saw in the arrogant bastard." But Ma didn't know about that warm, incomparable family life they'd lived at Spring Brook—Grandma Todd's happiest years.

Pa, and Crazy Bob, and Bart brought out from the freight car the horses that had been carried *up north* in their end of the car, along with their household goods in the other. One set of car doors had been left open so the animals could get plenty of air and light. A sturdy removable plank gate was fastened across it. The gate also served as a loading ramp when removed and set in place. Pa rode in the boxcar with the horses, feeding them from bales of hay stowed aboard, and watering them from a bucket dipped in the water barrels. There was plenty of room in the car, even with the three families' possessions in one end and the horses in makeshift stalls in the other.

The rest of the family rode in a passenger car on the same train. At longer stops Pa would come down and see how they were doing. He was eager and in good spirits, his eyes bright with the prospect of getting back to dirt farming, "away from a factory life." Ma had different notions. She'd got her belly full of dirt farming out home, as a kid. Town, even "out working," had been a lot better. Besides she might have been Florence Nightingale, except for one dumb mistake, a mistake a lot of girls had made, she discovered, and one that countless other "little simps" would make after her. She supposed there was no way to warn them. Sometimes she thought people were no more in control of their own lives than ants, condemned to run willy-nilly about their monotonous business.

She looked over the drab, wet woods, *up north* for the first time, and thought, "I don't even see a spring flower."

Lillian distracted her attention, saying, "I've got to wee."

Ma looked around for a privy, but the Soo Line didn't budget for such frills at remote points of deposit. She led Lillian into the woods.

"Go here," she said.

"Here?" Her little voice squeaked her incredulity.

Ma said, "Just squat down. You'll get used to it. *You'll have to get used to a lot of things.*"

The next week *they got used to* their first tornado of the season. They were renting the Favel place till Pa built a cabin on the farm. Grandma Todd and the others had moved into the big cabin that was already on their farm. Pa, who was destined to do most of the work and all of the thinking, drove the team a mile to and from the farm every day. They had a barn for the horses at the Favels' and were building one at Grandma's. Ma never thought of it as "their" place. Building a barn before a cabin for them to live in was a good example of why she thought that. She grumbled to Pa, "Why don't we find a place of our own? Favel says there are plenty of jobs over on the river in the mills."

"I can't do that. Besides I didn't come up here to go back to work in a damned factory," was all Pa volunteered. He couldn't bring himself to leave his mother at the mercy of Bart, with his dreamer's mind. But he thought about leaving a few times over the years, especially when even his patience wore thin over doing all the work with damn little credit, seeing the lion's share of the money his father sent them go to Bart and Nellie. He would mull the option over a time or two, even if checking out of there meant going into another factory. Playing second fiddle to a couple of dingleberries like Bart and Bob didn't please him anymore than it did Ma. And there was also his prune-faced sister, Felice, making fun of him behind his back. He knew she called him *Honorable Patches*.

Pa was over building the barn when the tornado hit. Ma heard it coming, recognized the sound—like a freight train traveling at high speed bearing down on them. Her first thought was of Lillian playing outside somewhere. She rushed into the yard, yelling, "Lillian! Lillian!" and almost stumbled over her, just around the corner of the house mounding up pyramids of dirt with an old teaspoon. She grabbed Lillian's hand, dragged her back inside and down into the shallow root cellar beneath the kitchen. It was dark and musty.

"What's the matter, Ma?" Lillian wailed. "Is it the end of the world?"

Ma almost laughed. Even kids had heard of such cataclysmic things, on which simple, superstitious minds had dwelt from the dawn of time, or at least for sure as long as she could remember.

"It's a tornado." Her voice was calm and even. She'd been through them before and expected she'd probably pull through this one. She was as fearless as any man (a fact that somehow had never penetrated into Pa's mind). Ma would have made a first-rate gunfighter—an unflinching frontier marshal.

Rain drove down in sheets as soon as the funnel passed. They were up to their knees in water before the roar died away. Lord knew how water got in around the stone foundation of the house. Ma thought maybe the wind had lifted the house a little without her noticing. Later she'd learn that the sandy soil was so porous that a deluge would turn it into a sponge. At least the house and their possessions hadn't blown away.

All that ancient history had scrolled past in Ma's mind as she stood, elbows on the window, at the Nelson place (their place), *up north* again. "I wonder when we're in for our first tornado this time?" She mused. She answered the question to suit her. "Never, I hope."

The possibility that they wouldn't be that lucky didn't dampen her spirits, however. You met what you had to, and hoped you'd survive somehow. Besides she had plenty else to think about; how to hang onto Eben, for instance, and break him in to her ways. She'd already figured out he'd be better than gold—a counterbalance to Pa's procrastination that had grown on him over his years of adversity. She also planned to siphon all the indispensable farming dope she could get out of Nelson. And there was always Newt as their banker. She suspected he had a lot more money than they'd seen, probably had a gold mine in

Alaska, just as Bennie had speculated. Like a good general, Ma knew how to build a good staff, and also knew that information was power. And so was the hand that held the frying pan, if you knew how to cook.

Bennie felt his senses growing keener. Everything challenged him. Yet he wholly missed the drift of Ma's strategy sessions at the supper table, deliberate staff meetings in every sense of the word. He was only eager to shovel in as much as he could handle of the delicious meals that had suddenly come his way. Ma could cook, had fed them pretty well, even when she had almost nothing to work with. Now she turned into a prodigy of the stove.

Maybe if she hadn't been so handy at that she'd have had more trouble persuading Eben to stay around at little more than half pay. Eben liked having a family. Nonetheless, being a topnotch cook himself, Eben wouldn't have tolerated some uppity *shemale* botching that job. He'd have gone and worked with Newt for his board till he found another paying job. Instead, Kid Kinsolving became Newt's hired man—sort of.

Bennie had been there at the interesting session when Newt formally hired Kid. Nelson had exploded, "He'll steal you blind!"

Kid grinned, "Naw, I won't. With your stuff around, I'll steal you blind instead."

Newt guffawed. So did Nelson. Actually Nelson kind of cottoned to Kid's easygoing ways, which Kid had learned to use to conceal his innate competence at almost everything. It was protective coloration. Injuns weren't supposed to know anything, and if they did and let it show, were considered uppity. Happily for Kid, he liked to go along with pretending that all Injuns were no-count, lazy, thieving, lying drones. It was hard for a crusty old fellow like Nelson to abandon a lifelong credo and a community standard in the same bargain and admit that Kid was a jewel. In any case, Newt had a hired man—sort of.

Eventually Kid came to Bennie's house for supper, invited by Ma after Newt told her about him. The first time, Kid felt his way like he was walking on eggs, having heard a lot about Ma from Bennie.

Newt introduced him to Ma, "This is my new sidekick, Kid."

"Kid is a Sioux, like Grandma," Bennie put in. Then added lamely, "Like us. Only he's a full-blood."

Ma shot Bennie a glance that clearly said, "How come you know so much about him and didn't mention it to me before now?"

He could hardly have explained to her why, even if she'd openly asked. Bennie hadn't forgotten Ma's frosty reaction to that happy-go-lucky hulk Cees, a few years before, and her insane jealousy at the thought Cees might be stealing Bennie's affection. So he'd managed to forget mentioning Kid to Ma.

Kid didn't look Ma directly in the eyes at first. His diffidence reminded her of the way she'd felt at Browns' her first night "out working" and a lot of days and nights at Browns' after that, for that matter.

Ma said to Bennie, "Get another chair and set him a place at the table."

Kid looked directly at Ma. "Thanks. I hope I'm not hornin' in," he said, then cast his eyes down again.

"There's plenty to eat. Wash up and it'll be on. Show him where, Bennie."

Kid had scrubbed himself almost raw in the cold creek before coming over, but dutifully went back to the bathroom with Bennie.

"I can tell your Ma is Sioux, all right," Kid said. "Too good-looking to be any scrub Injun."

Bennie laughed. "Handsome, like us, huh?"

"Yeah."

Over supper Ma said to Nelson, including Eben in her remark with a glance his way, "You'll have to help us for a while." She had thought of saying, "I hope you'll help us for a while," but decided to shoot the moon instead. Frontier marshals didn't ask, they commanded if they wanted to get and keep the upper hand.

Nelson looked up, but kept on chewing, and only nodded, his mouth full.

Ma shot a glance at Pa, who was pretty busy himself putting away meat, potatoes, and gravy. If he sensed anything coming, he didn't show it.

Nelson swallowed his mouthful and said, "Eben can tell you just about anything I could," and crammed in another mouthful, sensing that something was afoot, and wondering if he might be about to step into a cross fire. He put his head down, shooting a quick glance toward Pa.

Pa said, "We already talked it all over. I guess we ought to keep on about like Nelson's been doing."

Everyone went on eating. Newt found something to grin about but didn't look at anyone particular while he was doing it.

"Talked over? With who? I must have missed out on that," Ma said.

She didn't have to spell out a demand for a replay of the talking over. For all their differences, she and Pa, like many couples, could almost read one another's minds.

Pa tried to play burnout with Ma and lost. He avoided a direct answer, though and lamely recited, "I guess we'll put in some oats and corn, plenty of hay, buy maybe another cow or two, keep the garden, raise some pigs."

"Don't name all the little pigs this time," Ma said.

She was saving her plans to go into truck gardening until later, when she had Pa alone, also raising potatoes in a big way—maybe twenty acres of them as a money crop. She knew their sandy soil was good for hundreds of bushels an acre, just like Maine and Idaho.

Ma's remark about naming the pigs intrigued Newt. He hoped Ma would elaborate, sensing some snide joke, since Pa got extra busy with his plate when she mentioned that. Pa said, "How about passing the ham?" Which Eben did.

Ma needled some more, "If it's up to Russ, we won't be having much ham when this is gone."

"How's that?" Newt asked, and got a "why-don't-you-lay-off" look from Pa for his pains.

Ma said, "He's too soft-hearted to butcher 'em. We had the only pet pigs in Wisconsin before."

Pa managed a sheepish grin and shot back, "And you named all the calves and said how cute they were."

It reminded Nelson that the neighborhood used to talk about "those dumb city folks, the Todds, over there. Too soft-hearted to kill their own meat." He almost laughed.

Ma countered, "So did your mother."

Nelson thought, "So that's why they hired me in those days to do their butcherin'? Well, I can still do it."

It was a proposition that Pa had already considered. Either Nelson or Eben. He also wondered if Bennie had the stomach for butchering. Kids a lot younger than Bennie—and a lot smaller—managed to do it, and smoke the meat afterward too.

Kid kept out of the discussion and tried to appear he wasn't watching their faces, nonetheless didn't miss a word or facial expression. At the same time he managed to eat twice as much as anyone. Eben ran him a close second there.

Ma noticed Kid chucking it away and thought, "The poor kid must be half-starved." He reminded her of her mischievous brother Johnny. She thought, "He's probably just as full of beans as Johnny was at that age." She had no trouble getting a second piece of cherry pie down Kid at dessert time.

Bennie staved off a fainting spell when Kid pitched in to help Ma clean off the table, then volunteered to wash dishes. "Bennie'll wipe," Kid said.

Bennie thought, "Thanks a heap, podner. If it wasn't for your big mouth we'd be outside taking a big drag off a roll-your-own about now."

Ma came to the rescue and said, "You two kids'd probably break all the dishes," but she didn't really mean it. At least not where Kid was concerned.

She figured Kid was raised never to break anything because he knew if he did there wasn't anymore. Ma added, "It's still light out. Get some air—get Hank out of here too."

By then Hank had grown, got some strength, and learned to make the rounds of the table. That is, if he could get away with it, which was a snap—everyone there was "dog simple" as Eben put it. Hank, as a result, was putting on a puppy paunch.

Outside Bennie said, "I was dyin' for a weed when you mentioned doin' dishes."

"Me too," Kid said. "But I want an invite back. Your Ma can really cook."

"No lie. She likes you, too."

"How can you tell?"

"I just can. That second piece of pie for one thing."

Kid grinned. "Good."

By then they were far enough down the lane to roll weeds and light up without being seen.

"Ahhhh!" Bennie sighed, inhaling and letting out a huge cloud of Bull Durham smoke, watching the breeze carry it away.

Spring's caressing moistness clung in the air, which was perfumed delicately by blooming lilacs. The four horses, kept in the small pasture near the house during work season, looked up and watched them. Hank ventured through the fence to get acquainted, but lost his nerve in a sniffing match when a big set of flared nostrils snorted on his nose and he scampered back.

Kid laughed and reached down, patting him reassuringly, "They won't hurcha, Hank."

Hank looked like he understood him and might be saying, "I ain't too sure about that yet."

"This is Paradise," Bennie said. "What a life."

"Yeah," Kid agreed, "an' wait'll I show you where I camp—out in the marshes. There's a couple of little lakes out there nobody but me's been to in years." He paused a beat and said, "Well, almost nobody," but Bennie made nothing of it just then. "One's got an island in it, maybe a half acre, with birches all over it. I call it Bear's Island, for my Injun name."

Bennie chuckled. He was glad to see that his new buddy had learned to make fun of whites making fun of Indians. He thought, "It's probably easier for him since he knows he's as good or better'n any of 'em so he doesn't give a damn for anyone's opinion but his own—sorta like me 'n Uncle Newt."

The first stars were winking above them.

CHAPTER THIRTY-SIX

That Crazy Son of a Bitch Hitler!

It was dark when Bennie and Kid returned to the house, Bennie to hit the hay, Kid to drive Newt and Nelson back to their cabin in the Model A pickup.

Before they were inside Bennie could hear the after-supper rag chewing still in progress at the table over smokes and coffee. What he caught of it made him wish he'd never left. Newt was saying, "It looks to me like the world's gettin' into the same kind of mess the U.S. was in just before I traipsed off with Pa to the Civil War, and for just about the same egg-sucking reason."

"How's that?" Pa wanted to know.

"By tryin' to bury its head in the sand over a hell of a lot of bastards running around loose that'd be better hung."

The two boys slipped in quietly, Bennie signaling Kid to join him on the window seat. Ma was nowhere in sight. She wasn't strong on political discussions or world affairs either, although she thought Hitler was a mean son of a bitch who reminded her of her German father. For that reason he remembered she'd once contributed her two cents to the talk about a war coming. She'd said, "Pa had some Jewish blood, and I'll bet Hitler does for all of his raving about Jews stabbing Germany in the back after the war."

The rest were all up on current events from papers and magazines, and all read everything else they could get their hands on. Bennie'd been surprised to discover that Nelson and Eben had quite a library between them, and Newt had a lot of books. He thought, "I guess I come by my reading naturally." He knew also that Grandpa Todd had written a couple of textbooks on geography and history.

War news dominated the newspapers and such magazines as *Life* and *Time*. His schools had all had a weekly discussion called "current events," covering Germany's land grabbing, Italy's trying to steal Ethiopia, and Spain's revolution, as well as the Japanese rape of China. Everyone, even kids his age, had a sneaking suspicion that things were shaping up for another World War. If Europe got into it again, the U.S. would eventually have to come help, just like they did in the World War, despite what isolationists and America-firsters ranted about. Of course Ralph Esselborn's ghost or whatever it had been had told him, unless he'd been dreaming, that a war was coming and he'd be in it.

Bennie'd heard Pa say at least a hundred times, "That crazy son of a bitch Hitler is worse than the Kaiser ever was. If England and France get into it again with Germany, we'd better not wait like we did the last time, till it's almost too late."

Of course Pa's attitude about Germany may have been influenced some by the fact that Country Grandpa was a typical German, who'd had the sheriff goose him to a shotgun wedding even after he'd agreed to marry Ma of his own free will—more or less.

Newt said, "I don't want to sound like a know-it-all, but after spending four years in the Civil War pickin' cooties out of my clothes, when I grew up and looked back it sorta came to me to wonder what the hell wars are all about. I've been readin' on the subject ever since, especially on *my* war."

"So, what was your war all about?" Pa asked, not that he hadn't heard Newt's opinions before, but he wanted to draw him out for the sake of the others, especially the two boys.

"Slavery," Newt said.

Eben guffawed over the simplicity of the answer.

"Damned if it wasn't. None of that high fallutin' crap I've read in books about states' rights and national supremacy, though it came down to that in the end."

"Dead right," Newt said. "It happened because the blacks are human. Slavery was dead wrong. The South wouldn't admit that—at least the bastards running the show, like that son of a bitch Jeff Davis; they couldn't admit it, because slavery was their bread and butter. *The poor bastards were stuck with it.*"

Nelson said, "I was a school kid in the old country when the Civil War started here and I can remember my teachers talked about it. We even had to read a translation of *Uncle Tom's Cabin*. Everybody in Sweden thought slavery was dead wrong, maybe everybody in the whole world, except for France and England, who were blind on the subject because they needed the South's cotton. And come to think of it, that was one of the first times anyone ever pointed out something damned well wrong and got it corrected no matter what it cost. I recall I read somewhere that Lincoln, at one of those White House doin's, met that old battleaxe Harriet Beecher Stowe who wrote *Uncle Tom's Cabin* and said, 'So you're the little lady that started this war.'"

Bennie gave Nelson a close look when he finished his remarks. He hadn't thought he had that sort of ammunition in his magazine. What Nelson, and even Lincoln, said were oversimplifications. What that old battleaxe had written was only what a lot of others were already thinking, and thinking it because there were more compelling reasons than righting a human wrong. But it was damned well the truth about getting results from pointing out a wrong.

Pa said, "We still haven't got the job done. I worked a couple of years down south on construction in the twenties. If anyone thinks the Civil War freed the slaves, they got another think comin'."

"I know that," Newt said. "We got a long ways to go. It ain't gonna be easy for us—or them."

"You think we owe 'em?" Eben asked.

"You mean like Eleanor Roosevelt?" (Racists were already calling her "The Niggers' mama," for trying to make life a little easier for them, especially in Washington D.C.) "We don't owe this crop a damn thing except the respect we owe each other. We owed plenty to that other bunch that were slaves, and we tried to pay the debt the best we could and made a pretty fair fist of it. All we owe this bunch is a fair chance. But they won't get it till we get color-blind, if I'm any judge."

"They ain't gettin' a fair chance down south," Pa said.

Eben said, "They don't get much chance up here either, as far as I can tell. But would they do anything if they got one? Most of 'em I've seen are pretty damned shiftless."

"How many you seen?" Newt asked.

"About two outside the Army in the war." He laughed.

"Ah," Newt said, "you was in the war?"

"Two damned years. Got stuck in the occupation after it was over. West Point Regular Army bastards only used 'Niggers' to do work, or cook, mostly."

"Didn't the Army think they'd fight?" Newt asked.

"I dunno."

"Do you think they would've?"

"I dunno that either."

"I do."

"Would they?"

"As good as you or me. Maybe better if their heart was in it. Look what blacks did to the British in Africa."

Pa interjected, "They must be hard to kill. The marshal down in Flora, Mississippi, told me if I ever had to shoot one to drill him in the head—it was the only way to stop one."

That got a general laugh, but Bennie didn't think it should have. This was all part of the crap people heaped on good guys like Kid, or Kid's old man, who got sent up when he was in the right, just because he was an Indian.

"How come you know they fight so good?" Bennie risked asking.

The old man looked at him, but didn't answer. Instead he pulled his Turnip watch out and squinted at it.

"Time to be gittin' back," he said. He eyed Bennie. "You been pesterin' me to hear about the Civil War. C'mon over Sunday and I might answer yore question."

Bennie's heart speeded up. Maybe Newt would tell him how he killed the "son of a bitch" that shot his pa in the back. It was a matter that had intrigued Bennie since he first heard of it.

CHAPTER THIRTY-SEVEN

Young Newt

"*When lilacs 'first' in the dooryard bloomed, alack!*"

Whenever Newt remembered the spring he'd set out to war with his Pa, the redolence of lilacs recurred to him—lilacs drooping heavy with dew at dawn, or perfuming their yard and house after a spring rain. His father and mother both loved flowers, and especially lilacs. Their oak- and elm-shaded yard was dappled with lilac bushes, and they also partially hedged the porches, interspersed with bridal wreath, forsythia, and snowballs. On the south and west, honeysuckle and clematis climbed on trellises, shading the porches there.

Their house was considered a mansion in the time and place, solidly built of yellow brick brought in from New York State. It was two and one-half stories high, tall as any building in town, with its sloping mansard top half-story, which was pierced by dormer windows.

Up there was the attic he loved to browse in, experiencing a delicious queasiness, induced by anticipation of one day discovering some wonderful secret hidden in the accumulation of the past, a secret that would explain those baffling years before Newt.

How could there have been a time when he never was? Yet he'd been made to understand that was the case. Was it possible that he had been simply in storage waiting his time to be unwrapped as a Christmas present or something? But nowhere? You can't be nowhere! That was entirely too hard to swallow.

He and his best friend, Leland, were allowed to play up in the attic whenever they wanted to. Of course they were only there on rainy or snowy days because it was too much fun to be outside at other times.

Leland was the son of Magawn Washington, their man of all work, whom Newt knew could do anything. He was gardener, groom, carpenter, shoemaker and harness maker, farmer, doctor (with strange herbal remedies and incantations). Newt never made anything of the fact that Leland, Magawn, and his missus, Rebecca (Beckie) were black. Some folks were black and some weren't. Aside from eating in the kitchen they were just like regular members of the family. He never heard either his father or mother say a harsh word to any of them, except sometimes Leland when he and Newt were bad together, and even then it was generally Newt who caught it because Newt's parents knew he'd probably been the ringleader and instigator of any mischief.

It didn't occur to young Newt that Magawn was an unusual name. When he was older he realized he'd never again heard it. He wished he'd asked Magawn how he came to be named that, but by then the old darkie was dead. Newt conjectured he might have been a slave once, and that was a name taken from the last name of some master or overseer. Even at that, it would have been a pretty unusual last name as well. When Newt was young, maybe four, he assumed Magawn and his own parents, and all of his elders, had always been around, even though there was a time before he himself had joined them. Why such things should bother him he never asked himself. There was simply something fascinating about time. When he discovered that they would all die someday, that the fun of living would stop no matter how much they didn't want it to, that seemed the most unfair thing he'd ever heard of. He confided to Leland, "I don't think I'm going to die like other people do."

Leland laughed but didn't say anything, if he even thought seriously about it. Newt was a ringleader, and if he said he didn't aim to die, maybe he wouldn't. Maybe he could even fix it so Leland wouldn't die, since he didn't want to either.

They were up in the attic when Newt decided about that. Rain was drumming on the roof. An occasional swaying limb scraped the eaves in the wind. It seemed snug and safe inside, illuminated by the soft light of a candle to augment the gloomy outside light that filtered in through the dormer windows. By then Newt was seven and had been instructed how to keep from accidentally setting the house on fire with a candle or a Lucifer. His best instruction was his father's admonition "If you burn the house down, I'll wear you out with a tug strap."

Though his father seldom laid a hand on him, Newt wasn't sure he might not use a tug strap on him under those circumstances. The saying in LaSalle—and Newt had heard it often enough—was "If Cap'n Cheek says he's gonna do something, most likely he will."

Newt was aware his father was called Captain, locally pronounced "Cap'n," because he'd been a captain in the war with Mexico. Up in the attic was a big, wood-hooped, round-topped trunk secured with leather straps buckled stoutly around it. Inside was Pa's uniform from that war. It was blue, trimmed in gold on the sleeves, with gold tassels at the shoulders, pendant from the epaulets. With the blouse and pants was a yellow sash. But best of all was the black sword belt with shoulder strap, and gold-trimmed black leather scabbard with the sword still inside. Pa never said the boys couldn't delve in that fascinating trunk, if he even thought about it.

The sword was intricately engraved on the blade and had a filigreed gold-and-silver hand guard around the knurled ebony handle. Also on the sword belt was a pistol scabbard, but the gun was not in it. Pa kept it in his dresser drawer, and sometimes carried it to court in his belt, under his coat when, as he put it, he had, "a hot case." In those days men hadn't yet forgotten the last of the three pledges of the signers of the Declaration of Independence. A later time would be more concerned with the first two, but the whole concluding clause read "to which we pledge our lives, our property and our *sacred honor*."

Newt could recall his father saying, "You notice they didn't say anything about *sacred* lives and property, only *sacred honor*."

Since Cap'n Cheek agreed wholeheartedly with the founding fathers' feelings in the matter, he sometimes felt it was prudent to carry a huge Walker Colt .44. Newt had been shown how to use it by the time he was six, loading it, cleaning it, shooting it—and hitting something too, though it was a struggle to hold it up long enough to sight it even with both hands, since it weighed almost five pounds. But he managed. His father said, "You're good enough for your age. You could hit a man every time at twenty-five yards. And that's what pistols are made for when you come right down to it."

If his pa ever fought a duel over a matter of honor, Newt never heard about it. Most likely word of his marksmanship had circulated and no one felt like trying it out as bullseye. One look into Captain Bob Cheek's icy blue eyes suggested he wasn't apt to flinch when he drew a bead, even with someone shooting at him. If they called him out, it would more likely be with swords, except that at six-foot four, and two hundred ten pounds, all bone and muscle and quick as a cat, that didn't look like a good proposition either.

Once, when Newt's Pa and Abe Lincoln shared a room on the Illinois court circuit, Abe looked over that well-muscled body while they were getting into their nightshirts and said, "By God, Bob, I believe if they dropped you, you'd bounce." His Pa told that to his ma, and they both laughed. Newt couldn't imagine how they'd get anyone as big as his pa up high enough to drop him; maybe if he fell off a horse, but that wasn't too likely, since he rode like he was part of a horse, and taught Newt to do the same.

Newt knew his pa hadn't got hard by accident, and he knew why. He had plenty of muscles and calluses himself for the same reason: helping his pa and Magawn farm an "eighty" at the edge of town. They also owned a section up at Troy Grove and farmed it on shares with Ma's brother, Ike Todd. (The Todds were from Pennsylvania, but related to Mrs. Abe Lincoln's family of Todds, who lived in Kentucky.) The whole family would go up to Troy Grove sometimes for haying or harvesting. Newt thought it was fun, even if they had to tolerate Uncle Ike spouting scripture as they shocked oats or pitched hay, and suffer through his long, windy prayers before meals.

Pa once pretended he'd gone to sleep with his head bowed in prayer at the table and stayed that way so long no one was sure he hadn't, or maybe even died, and his wife finally shook him.

"What happened?" he asked, pretending to be startled awake.

He got a withering look from his wife who, after all, was Ike's younger sister.

He only smiled and said, in a trifle too-hearty voice, "I thought I'd died and God was haranguing me about my bad manners or something."

Uncle Ike didn't know for sure whether to be honored or insulted and for once held his tongue, in fact almost laughed.

Newt's ma was Amelia Todd, and her family moved from Pennsylvania to Illinois before she was old enough to remember much. Her first recollection was of being at the rail of a steamboat, somewhere on a wide, bright river during that trip west. Her mother, Grandma Todd, used to recall how, back in Pittsburgh, she'd helped care for young Stephen Foster, and never suspected he'd someday compose all those wonderful romantic songs like "Come Where My Love Lies Dreaming" and "Jeannie with the Light Brown Hair." The Fosters had been their neighbors, maybe even distant relatives. Newt never knew or cared. But he remembered his ma playing all of Foster's songs on the piano that stood in the big, high-ceilinged drawing room.

She always played the piano in the evening, before lamp-lighting time, when long sun rays slanted across the room and mellowed the outlines of everything. She sang along with the music in an untrained, but sweet and true voice. If he were home, Pa would come in and listen, tapping his foot, and looking at his wife with loving eyes, proud of her talent. Sometimes he'd try to sing too, in a strong baritone, but if there were high notes he'd botch it and they'd all end up laughing. Newt knew he couldn't sing for figs and was reconciled to it and didn't try. He liked to turn the music, though, when his mother used it, which was only for classical pieces. She knew by heart all of Foster, and a lot of others too.

Looking back Newt recognized his happiest days had been spent in that big house. Maybe childhood was the happiest time for everyone, and God had meant it to be that way. The house, with its high ceilings, was always cool in the summer, kept even cooler by the shutters hung inside all the windows, with adjustable slats to let in just as much light as you wanted, or almost none if you wanted it dark. Sometimes Newt would go into the library and draw the blinds shut and nap during the long afternoons. Whatever kitty was in charge of the house at the time would jump up on his lap and sleep with him, after kneading and licking as required to get properly settled. The big house was usually very quiet because noises drowned in its vast innards, except when he and Leland would chase each other around, up and down stairs, or when Beckie, Leland's mother, would sing loud in the kitchen while she worked.

Pretty often Newt's mother entertained her sewing or reading circle, and when she did the boys would be shooed outside, or if it was raining, banished to the attic or stable, where Magawn might be mending or oiling harness or shoeing the horses. Newt could never remember him idle.

The two boys often rode double on Newt's sturdy pony, Cannonball, and went down to the river to watch the stevedores loading or unloading the stern-wheelers. Or they'd ride into the woods, which was easy to do since they came right to the edge of town in places. Out there they stuffed themselves with berries and gathered nuts in season. It was a place to play pioneers and Indians too, and if you knew how to play it right, you could really scare yourself good, imagining Indians lurking in every dark spot. Cannonball wasn't a Shetland, but what they called an Indian pony then—a runt horse, tough as nails, coming by his name honestly. He could run. Even with two boys on him he could go some, and at his jog trot he was smooth and tireless.

— 1938

Newt had been telling Bennie, Eben, and Kid about those days back home as a boy. "I never had a better horse than little Cannonball," he said.

They were down on the creek bank, sitting in the shade in tall, soft grass. Nelson was up in the cabin, sleeping off a heavy dinner, which Eben had come down and cooked for them.

"Cannonball carried me all through the war, was never gun-shy even the first time, and the easiest keeper I ever owned. Lived to be thirty-two. Pa and Ma kept him for me and buried him, with honors, I guess," he chuckled, "buried him out by the stable. I put up a regular monument for him. Maybe we oughta go see sometime."

"Is the house still there?" Bennie asked.

"Oughta be. I gave it to the town for a library and museum when Pa and Ma were gone. Put it in the deed that they had to keep the place up."

"Did they?"

"They better. I have a lawyer check on 'em every year. I figure the place is a memorial to my folks, and to the 'good old days,' I suppose."

Bennie thought about that. What had Ma and Pa ever done that he'd want to leave a memorial to them?

"Not much," he told himself. If he'd been a little more mature, he'd have concluded they had both deserved medals for letting him grow up pretty much his own way.

To Newt he said, "You really loved 'em, didn't you?"

Newt was silent awhile. Finally he said, "They were two of the finest people that ever lived. A kid couldn't have had better parents."

Kid broke the silence that followed Newt's remark, and said the last thing Bennie would have expected to come out of him. He said, "So're mine. Even if Pa's up in the can at Waupun just now."

Newt said, "That don't cut any ice. I'd trust a lot of convicts a lot further than I would the types they hire to guard 'em."

That brought to Bennie's mind the fact that Newt had killed a man, or maybe several, out west in the wild old days, and probably the game warden back in Blackhawk. And he'd been pretty evasive about whether he'd ever been caught out west. Had Newt done time, maybe in the famous Yuma Hellhole prison he'd read about? He wasn't about to ask him.

"How come you got to go off to war, as young as you were? Didn't your ma raise a fuss?" Bennie asked.

"She sure did. Even Pa wasn't for it at first. I talked them into it. We had a black family lived with us as long as I could remember. They were actually just like part of our family. I told Pa I wanted to go do something to free all the others, so they could live decent too, and not be sold down the river and split up, with everyone cryin' and maybe never seein' one another again no matter how much they loved each other. We'd seen how that worked right in LaSalle. U.S. marshals rammed the Fugitive Slave Law down our throats.

"Like as not they'd have some slaveholder or two along with 'em to identify a runaway. They weren't choosy about who they identified either. One year they grabbed Magawn Washington, who lived with us. He'd practically grown up with Pa, at least from the time they were both maybe twelve, so we knew the man who claimed he'd run off from his plantation in Mississippi the year before was a damned liar. Fellow by the name of Yancey, as I recall. Maybe kissin' kin to that son of a bitch Jeff Davis, bein' from Mississippi too."

"What happened?" Bennie asked.

"Well," Newt said, "normally the U.S. commissioner that heard such cases woulda decided in favor of Yancey. The way the law worked, the commissioner was paid ten dollars for deciding against the fugitive and only five dollars for him. You can see how that'd work out most of the time. Only in this case the commissioner was Colonel Smith, a judge then; later he was the colonel of our regiment. He'd known Magawn almost as long as Pa had, so he threw Yancey out on his ear with a little talkin'-to, like he'd prob'ly never heard down south of the Smith and Wesson line."

Bennie grinned at the notion of calling the Mason and Dixon line the Smith and Wesson line. It was the first time he'd ever heard it called that, but it made sense. According to Bennie's Pa, six-shooters (and Smith and Wesson was famous for making good ones) still figured as the law in controlling blacks down there. He knew, of course, that Pa'd spent a couple of years right in Mississippi where this Yancey had come from.

Newt went on, "That wasn't the end of it either. Down where he come from, Yancey was some kind of big stick. Didn't cotton to not gettin' his own way a-tall. He hired some plug uglies and tried to kidnap Magawn—took him right out of our front yard the next mornin' while he was spadin' around some bushes. Ma heard the fuss and looked out and saw 'em through the window. They hustled him into a buggy, the rest ridin' horses, and whipped outa there right smart.

"I remember Ma yellin' for me. 'Newt! Newt!' I thought maybe a snake or skunk or something got in the house and come a-runnin'. She said, 'Ride down and tell your Pa they just kidnapped Magawn!' Well, I lit a shuck outa there on Cannonball, ridin' bareback and goin' like Paul Revere. I found Pa in court."

"'They kidnapped Magawn!' I yelled, as soon as I busted through the door. Everyone looked at me like I'd lost my mind. It's a wonder I didn't get fined for contempt. Instead, Judge Smith adjourned court and joined Pa and a bunch of others in a little posse to chase old Yancey. I raced back to the house and grabbed my old muzzle loader and followed along, hopin' nobody would make me go back if I caught up."

Newt stopped and doctored himself a cigar, got it going to suit him, then pretended he'd forgot he was in the middle of a story and was quiet for a long while.

Even though Bennie was onto his tricks, he couldn't stand waiting and asked, "Did you catch Yancey?"

"Damn well told. Pa told the bastard he had a notion to give him a hiding with a horsewhip. Yancey made a move for his Colt but was a trifle late and Pa shoved his old Walker in Yancey's face. I can remember clear as hell Pa sayin', 'Go ahead and jerk it, because after makin' that bad move you just did, if you don't, I'm gonna take you out here in the woods and stretch your neck.' Yancey turned white as a sheet, but didn't make another move except to turn loose of his iron."

"What happened then? Did they hang him?"

"Pa mighta done it, if there wasn't a lot along that he didn't entirely trust, although he woulda trusted Colonel Smith, even though he was a judge. With only a few close friends along he'd have 'hided' old Yancey for sure, at the least. If Yancey'd had guts enough to jerk his Colt, Pa'd 'a' killed him too and never blinked. It wouldn't 'a' been his first. He probably knocked over a couple of dozen men in the Mexican war."

Eben chipped in his first remark. "What happened to Yancey? Did they hold him for kidnapping?"

"Naw. It probably wouldn't have stuck even around there, because Magawn was black. Judge Smith gave old Yancey another dressing-down I'll bet he took to the grave with him, still making a face over it, and goosed him onboard a boat headed south and told him to light a shuck. It made a different man outa Pa. I remember him tellin' Ma, 'I got outa bed this A.M., still an old-line Whig, and I'm gonna get up tomorrow a fire-and-brimstone Abolitionist. Abe was right.'"

"Abe who?" Bennie asked, suspecting he already knew.

"Abe Lincoln. Pa took me up to Ottawa the year before that, to hear Lincoln's first debate with Douglas. I didn't understand all of it, but I figured out the chief difference between 'em was Abe thought slavery was wrong and Douglas didn't give a damn one way or the other. Douglas didn't win the debate by a country mile if you judged by the hollerin'. If you wanta know what I meant the other night about dodging the issue and gettin' into a mess, read what Lincoln said there that day."

"I don't remember a whole lot about the debates," Bennie confessed. "I never read any of 'em. Just pieces in history books."

"I got 'em all in a set of books," Newt said. "Read 'em. In a nutshell, the founding fathers, even the slaveholders amongst 'em, thought slavery was wrong, figured it'd go away by itself. Then the cotton gin was invented. With it they could clean three hundred pounds of cotton in the time it took to clean three before. It made slavery the South's main support, because Southern whites were too damned lazy to pick cotton, and I can't say I blame 'em. All the rest was in the works from then on—the Compromise of 1820, Nullification, the Wilmot Proviso, the repeal of the Compromise of 1820, the Compromise of 1850, the Kansas Nebraska Act, crazy old John Brown—the whole works. All leadin' up to the war. It finally came to a head when old Abe was elected president. The South was afraid he'd put the kibosh on slavery for good. He probably wouldn't have, but as it was they forced him to do it. The North wasn't all that clean either. They had a gun in the South's ribs for years with high protective tariffs, keepin' 'em from buying sometimes-better goods cheaper, that was made in England and France."

"And you got to go off to war."

Newt was silent remembering. Hearing the speeches and the bands.

The Drums of the Republic, marching . . .

And he remembered the soft lips of his ma, who kissed him every night of the world, as she tucked him in bed. He remembered how fervently she'd kissed and hugged him, the last time, the night before he rode away to war on Cannonball . . . and came back a man, too big to be tucked in and kissed goodnight by his ma anymore.

He remembered that he'd never really come back; realized that she'd known that was how it would be. He saw her as she was then, with a halo of blond hair, fine as silk, still young and lovely, limned in the warm candle glow, tears misting her deep blue eyes.

Tears misted his eyes . . . remembering.

I remember Ma
And the eternal smell of lilacs
On the night air
drifting in the window.

I remember, too, the smell of war in the air,
Hear the Drums of the Republic,
echoing still.

I can remember Uncle Ike almost falling off his horse.
Old Bible-spouting Uncle Ike.
All of them gone for years.
"Mine eyes have seen the glory
Of the falling off the horse . . .
Almost."

That's the way wars started out. Funny and tragic both.

Newt looked at Bennie and Kid, sure their war was coming.

"*Well,*" he thought, "*I hope they pull through and both live to be old coots, like me and Nelson.*"

He yawned and stretched. "I'm gonna go join Nelson. I'll tell you some more later."

CHAPTER THIRTY-EIGHT

Likker and Fast Women

Bennie was finally allowed to drive the Lincoln, the first time, even though it'd be dark before they got back. Ma had a fit, and Pa wasn't exactly approving since he'd fallen in love with the big limousine and didn't want it wrecked, but it was Newt's car, and Newt said Bennie could drive it, so that was that, short of forbidding Bennie to go out. Even Ma was afraid to try that, because Newt could take the car away from them. She loved it as much as Pa did. In fact, she was trying to figure out a way to go down to Country Grandma's in it—and be sure to visit her sisters who all lived close by. They'd have to be sure to have it washed and polished before they did.

Newt told Pa, "You can come along tonight and drive instead of Bennie if you want to."

Pa gave him a look. He knew that Newt, Eben, and Nelson were going out for a little "toot" and needed a driver who'd stay sober and get them home in one piece. It wasn't Pa's idea of a fun evening. And if they pulled in at two A.M., he knew he'd never hear the end of Ma's questions. "Did you have a drink?" She could have smelled on his breath if he did. "Were there fast women down there drinking? What did you do while all the rest were tanking up? I suppose you were looking over all the women."

"No thanks," Pa said. "I guess Bennie can manage, come to think of it."

Bennie, with Kid as copilot, drove them down to the most popular local gathering place, actually more of an institution, known as Aunt Kay's, and so proclaimed on a large, flashing neon sign outside that also advertised Old Heidelberg beer.

Immediately inside the front door was the barroom with a rustic, beamed ceiling. It boasted a fireplace that made it an especially popular rendezvous in the winter. Nonetheless, it was equally well patronized in this sweltering June weather for several good reasons. The place served anyone except Indians (and Kay made certain individual exceptions even for them, such as Chief Circling Hawk, Kid's pa). Moreover, a ten-year-old could get a beer there if he looked like he could handle it. This reflected the neighborhood German, Norwegian, and Swedish conviction that "likker" wasn't sinful and, in fact, might be beneficial. Prohibition candidates for public office had had a piss-poor time of it around there for at least a half-century. The second reason Kay's was popular was that sooner or later at least all the males in the neighborhood dropped in with the latest gossip and news, making the barroom better than a newspaper for keeping abreast of neighborhood happenings. But the main attraction, accounting for an all-male clientele, was the whorehouse Kay operated in the back rooms. After Newt's eyes got accustomed to the dim interior he stared across at the lady bartender.

"Who's she?" he asked Eben.

"That's Kay. Don't try to lay her unless you want a load of buckshot up yer ass."

Newt laughed. "I wasn't aimin' to—but come to think of it, she's a pretty spry lookin' heifer."

"Must be all of forty-five," Nelson objected. "Too old for the likes of us."

"Sheeit!" Kid said.

Nelson gave him a look. "What's ailin' you? You ain't even had a beer yet."

The waiter, who was also the bouncer, and looked it, came over to their table.

"Hi, Ace," Eben said. "I'll have my usual."

Ace made a face. "One root beer," he said. "Christ! You used to pay the electric bill." He gave Kid a hard look.

"He's O.K." Eben said.

"Yah," Nelson added his endorsement. "He lies and steals, but he's peaceful."

"Sheeit!" Kid said again and gave a short laugh.

"What'll it be?" Ace asked him.

"A tap beer."

Ace looked at Newt.

"Straight Old Granddad. Make it a double. And one for my father, too." He pointed at Nelson.

"My ass," Nelson said.

Ace grinned, breaking up his pug's face into a series of craters that made it look like a sack of marbles. He had a sprinkling of gold teeth in front.

Newt thought, "Probably lost his real ivories in the ring." Ace had a couple of cauliflower ears that fitted that picture too, but he wasn't just another punchy old pug; his body was obviously still hard and he was flat as a board in front.

"How about you?" Ace asked Bennie.

"An orange pop, or Squirt if you don't have orange."

"We got both," Ace said. He thought, "Good to see a kid with sense enough not to drink."

Bennie wasn't being either virtuous or sensible, he simply hated the taste of all booze, couldn't see why anyone drank the stuff. He got out the makin's and poured tobacco into a paper, then passed the Bull Durham to Kid after he rolled his. He knew Kid was always out of makin's, or maybe never in.

Newt fired up a cigar, the smoke permeating the air with the rich aroma that only a very expensive cigar imparts. He was careful not to offer Nelson one. He hadn't offered him another since he'd crumbled one up for pipe tobacco.

Ace brought over their drinks and left, saying, "I'll run a ticket."

Nelson said, "How about a cigar?" Looking innocent. "I forgot my pipe."

Newt eyed him appraisingly. He'd been waiting for Nelson to say that for a couple of months at least. He reached into an inside pocket and pulled out a cheap White Swan stogy and passed it over. Nelson looked it over and frowned, smelled it, wrinkled his nose and asked, "Where'd you get this dog turd?"

"Been savin' it. It's damned near as good as Union Workman," Newt said. "Or Plowboy either." Both were two of the cheapest pipe and "chewn" tobaccos around—some kidded that they were probably made from the sweepings on tobacco warehouse floors, but that didn't make them unpopular—they were probably the two most popular going.

Kid guffawed. Everyone laughed. Even Nelson, who said, "I meant one o' them good seegars."

Newt passed him one. He really didn't give a damn what he did with it. Then he tossed down about half his double shot, rose, and said, "I reckon I'll get acquainted with Kay."

"I'll introduce yuh," Eben said, quickly.

"No need."

"Watch yer step. I wasn't kiddin' about her."

Newt eased up on a barstool and puffed on his cigar, looking pleased with the world. Kay came over shortly and waited to find out what he wanted, hands on the edge of the bar. She knew he had a drink over at a table and thought he might be an old smart ass who'd bragged to his crowd that he was going to proposition the madam. She glanced at their table to see if anyone was watching, but they didn't seem to be.

"Hi, Klondy," Newt said.

Kay's expression hardened, then, after studying him for a minute, relaxed. She said, "Newt? Is that really you? You must be a hundred."

"It's really me. And thanks a heap. I'll be eighty-eight shortly."

"What're you doin' here? Dodgin' a paternity suit *up north*?"

Newt laughed. "Not as I know of. I got kin around here."

"I didn't recognize you when you come in. I hate to wear glasses." She had them cocked up in her hair. "Got bifocals, but I never learned to walk with 'em. Always stubbin' my toe. But I can't make change without the damn things."

Newt looked her up and down. "I might ask what the hell you're doin' out here in Rube-ville."

"It's home. I own a farm up the road. Was born there."

"Married?"

"Nope. I was, but he wasn't. Goosed him off with a scattergun years ago."

"Anyone I knew?"

"Kid Goldfine."

"That little sonofabitch! You shoulda had yer head examined."

"He was rich. I was broke."

"He *was* rich, you said?"

"Prob'ly still is. He was a moneymakin' little such-and-so."

"And you?"

"Would I be runnin' a joint like this if I was rich?"

"Maybe."

She gave him an inscrutable look. "You're too derned smart sometimes, Newt."

"That's how I lived so damn long."

Someone pounded his mug on the bar and yelled, "Hey, Kay. Dry down here."

"O.K. Comin'. Keep yer shirt on." To Newt she said, "I'll be over to your table in a while."

When Newt sat back down, Eben said, "You hit if off right smart with Kay. I wasn't kiddin' about her—she doesn't cotton to everybody, and for sure she don't take from nobody."

"I wasn't tryin' to hand her any. She looked like someone I used to know."

"Was she?"

Newt pretended not to hear, glancing around the room, watching the girls hustle the place. Three young women showing ripe bodies in tight slacks and halters, that revealed all but their nipples, were circulating among the customers when they weren't busy in back.

"Not a bad lookin' bunch of chippies if you ask me," Newt said.

"Kay don't keep any old hags," Eben said. "Never seen an old homely one in the place—or an old one at all, come to think of it."

"I ain't surprised," Newt said.

"How come?" Eben asked. "You know Kay from somewhere before?"

"What gave you that idea?"

"She ain't that chummy with strangers. In fact, I wonder if she didn't run off from somewhere after puttin' a hatchet in her old man's head, or something. She gets all fired nervous around strangers sometimes, like maybe she's expecting the Pinkertons to show up. Or the F.B.I."

"Just a hunch," Newt said. "She looks smart."

If Klondy hadn't told anyone she'd made the Gold Rush way back when, he wasn't about to blow her cover. It was forty years ago. She didn't look a day over forty-five, had to be at least ten years older though, and maybe was husband hunting, or at least man hunting.

Eben broke in, "I guess I'll go back and get my ashes hauled."

Kid said, "Someday you'll get a dose."

"Had clap four times," Eben said. "Cured it all but the first time."

"Bull," Kid said. "You'd o' drowned in yer own piss before now if you had four doses."

"Naw," Eben said. "Git my dong reamed out down at the garage every so often."

"What with?"

"A wrist pin fitter."

Bennie snorted. He knew what a wrist pin fitter was—something like a big articulating metal-link bull dick that was revved up with an electric drill to size holes for the pins that went into pistons when you overhauled an engine. But it wasn't all that funny. Eben could do whatever he wanted to, but Pa had scared Bennie half to death with stories about what you could catch from whores. Bennie would have died if he knew Kate, back in Blackhawk, whom he now loved, was actually just a high-class whore.

The youngest of the girls had rubbed her big boobs on his shoulders earlier and said, "How about you, big boy?"

It got a laugh from everyone at the table but him. He flushed, but even though he felt a pleasant tingling in his dong, he wasn't having any, thank you, no matter what. He said, "No thanks."

"O.K., honey," she said and drifted away.

He was grateful she hadn't stayed around and pestered him. He suspected she'd thought he was older than he was, as Kate had.

Eben got back in short order, looking a lot happier.

"Quick trip," Kid said.

"It don't take long to blow your brains out," Eben said. "First one always is quick."

"Waddaya mean first one?"

"I'm gonna get a waltz outa all three tonight."

"Quick trip" reminded Bennie of his first time with Kate and how he felt himself coming right away. He got horny as hell remembering. To make it worse, the young, willowy blond who rubbed her tits on him was now out on the dance floor with a big farm kid in bib overalls, swaying against him to the juke box music, getting him all hot and bothered. Bennie watched the sway of her hips and where her ass curved down between her legs. She pushed hard against her partner and Bennie knew how that felt and started getting hard himself, his dong throbbing against his pant leg. Pretty soon the girl and the kid left for the back, hand in hand. Bennie wondered if he should risk it, too. Newt was eighty some and hadn't died from patronizing whores.

Newt was watching the direction of Bennie's gaze and said, "You thinkin' of changing your mind?"

Bennie grinned. "Maybe."

Kid said, "Don't do it. She might have syph, too."

Bennie knew syphilis could kill a person. His hard on started back down. It had actually started to lubricate, and he felt the wet spot inside his trousers leg. He knew he'd probably have to jack off later to release the pressure so he could get to sleep. He'd think of those tights pants on the blond and imagine what was under them when he did.

Knowing that Indians had a reputation for being widely victimized by venereal disease, Bennie wondered where Kid had got his Puritan attitude. He hadn't yet met Kid's mother, or he'd have known.

Bennie's mind was taken off that by the arrival of Kay at their table. She'd turned the bar over to Ace for a while. Before she pulled up a chair she said, "How about another round on the house?" And didn't wait for an answer. She fetched that, then sat down with them.

"I know these two old rips," she said, indicating Nelson and Eben with a nod, "but who're these two?"

Newt pointed at Kid, "This one works for me. And Bennie here is my nephew."

"Nephew?" Kay said, raising her eyebrows.

"Grand," Newt said.

"Howdy boys," Kay said.

Kid, by now in his "Injun ceremonial" mode, said, "How," and raised his beer in a salute to Kay.

Bennie thought, "He sure don't run to that business about Injuns not holding their liquor." He'd had at least six and his voice wasn't even slurred. "Maybe a hollow leg."

Kay said to Bennie, "Your Unc and I are old friends," giving Newt his cue it was O.K. to bring up the past. She added, "From the Gold Rush."

"Which one?" Nelson asked, with a straight face.

Kay gave him a mock glare. "Watch your tongue, old man, or I'll cut you off."

"O.K." Nelson said. "I was just leavin' for a spell. I thought I'd take the gal with the most padding and go interview her in the back for a while."

Kay said, "That'd be Suzie." She looked around and found Suzie on a barstool, resting up from her labors, sipping a coke.

"Hey, Suze," Kay summoned her.

Suzie ambled over to the table, eyeing the group, not knowing what Kay might want her to do for what were obviously friends.

Kay pointed to Nelson. "This is Father Nelson, our retired parish priest. He's never been laid and would like to try it before he dies. How about taking him back and busting his cherry?"

Suzie looked flabbergasted.

"You ain't Catholic are you honey?" Kay asked.

"I was raised one."

Kay said, "Don't worry, this one is about as far from a priest as you can get. I was ribbing."

Suzie looked relieved. She'd had plenty of old fossils spoil her night, usually because she couldn't get them up, but she'd never had to worry about maybe pissing off God while she tried to raise the dead.

As she moved off with Nelson they could hear him say, "Don't worry, sweetheart, I felt my annual hard-on coming up for a week now, and this is the day. And I even took a bath in the crick."

He really had, much to Newt's amazement. Also put on clean overalls and blue work shirt. Underwear too. But he still wore the battered hat with the Alf Landon button.

Kay started back to tend bar. As she got up, Newt whispered in her ear, "You don't want to break a standing rule, do you?" He grinned. So did she and whispered in his ear, "That's not a standing rule, it's a laying rule—and it don't apply to old friends."

A little later they were gone quite a while in back together.

Eben got back from his third heat and said, "Where's Newt? Gittin' his ashes hauled?" He looked around. "Who'd he pick; I bet on the young blond."

"You ain't gonna believe this," Nelson said.

"Try me."

"Him and Kay have been back there for quite a while."

"Maybe Newt's dickerin' to buy the place."

"Ask him when he gits back."

"I will."

Kay got back first and put on her apron, going back behind the bar. Newt came out a little later, looking like the cat that ate the canary.

Eben didn't even ask. He simply looked at Newt and said, "I'll be go to hell. I never expected to see Kay go back there with anybody."

"We was in her office," Newt said.

"Talkin' business, right?"

"Correct."

"Is there a couch back there?"

"I didn't notice."

Bennie'd been yawning for the last couple of hours, had thought of going out to snooze in the back seat of the Lincoln, had mentally bedded the blond at least twice, and was ready to go home.

He was happy to hear Newt say, "Let's hit the road?" Then pretending he hadn't seen Eben's frequent business excursions to the back rooms, Newt said, "That is if you been laid yet."

"Tried 'em all."

"Yer a better man than I am, Gungha Din. I envy you."

"You oughta stop jackin' off in between—you'd have more stamina."

"Why? It's adjustable; that's more'n you can say for ass. And a damn sight cheaper too in most cases."

CHAPTER THIRTY-NINE

This Is Really the Life

Kid only mentioned his lake and its island when he and Bennie were alone. From the way Kid talked about it, Bennie realized that it was special to him and that it was secret and mysterious. Of course he realized it was hidden and that alone was mysterious enough. He thought it might be sacred Indian ground, as their old place had been before the loggers came and drove the original owners away. Kid would get a distant look in his eyes when he said "*my lake*," and Bennie concluded, even after they were pretty good friends, that the other was still sizing him up, trying to decide if he could really trust him to see his secret place.

Just to be ready for camping out, Bennie had been spending the money he earned from Pa and Newt to order supplies from an outfit in Richmond, Virginia, the Army and Navy Supply Company. He'd sent for their free catalogs even when he was in Blackhawk, but had never been able to afford anything. Now he could, and ordered a pup tent with a ground cloth and mosquito net, an army canteen and mess kit, a coffee pot, a wire grill with folding legs, a waterproof match holder with a compass on top, an army knapsack, and even some tins that were to keep bacon and butter in, and stuff that needed to kept away from bugs and hungry animals.

One late spring day they went swimming in the East Fork up by Bennie's log. The thing Bennie really liked about the place was the big rock that marked the Indian burial ground, just down the hill. The rock itself overlooked a deep pool, deep enough so you could safely dive in off of the rock. It was the best place for swimming anywhere near the farm. After tiring themselves out diving and water fighting, they got out and flopped in the sand over on the far bank. Bennie sighed and said, "This is really the life."

"Amen," Kid agreed, then casually added, "I guess we ought to go swimming in my lake one of these days. It's colder than here by a jug full, but there's lots you'll wanna see out there."

Bennie was almost afraid to ask and hesitated. Finally, since he sensed that Kid wanted to be prompted, he asked, "Like what?"

"A big heron rookery, for one thing. That should tell you how far off the beaten path it is. Nobody goes there except maybe a hunter or two, and they're all from the tribe. No palefaces get out that far—*except Nelson sometimes, and he's an Injun and doesn't know it.*"

Bennie thought about that a minute and laughed. "Damned if that ain't so," he agreed. He didn't add that Nelson even smelled like most of them did, except when he took a bath to go whoring, but thought better of it. Kid sure didn't smell bad, though. Bennie was sure that Kid's ma would wear him out if he didn't stay clean. Even his clothes, patched though they might be, were always freshly washed. Bennie hadn't met Kid's ma yet, but looked forward to it. He wondered if Kid wasn't ashamed to take Bennie to the place they lived in since he'd called it a dump.

Kid went on, "One reason no one goes out there to the lake is that it's in the middle of the marshes and you have to know your way through the swamps and bogs or you'll be up to your neck in muck. There's twenty miles straight west out there without a road in it and another dozen or so beyond the first road you come to. By then you're getting over toward Black River Falls."

"I'm set to go whenever you want to," Bennie said.

"One of these weekends. I don't want to miss old Newt tellin' us about the Civil War and he's got started on that. Let's give him a couple of Sundays to gab, then we can go. Maybe your old man will give you a Saturday off. Better to take a couple of days and stay overnight. It takes the better part of a day just gettin' in and out of there."

Going to the lake kept coming back into Bennie's mind pretty often after that, even while he was concentrating on getting the hang of farm work, learning to handle a team, even plowing without getting much complaint out of Pa about how he managed it. He'd learned to put down a straight starter furrow and come back and throw another against it to begin a land. The horses knew how to do the rest. He started with a sulky plow on a small field, but Pa graduated him to the big two-bottom job and four horses. It probably helped that he was "horse simple," had always loved them and every one of them knew it as soon as he got near them.

He'd even learned the name of every piece of harness and how to hitch it up right. He loved to go along at the slow pace of the horses, feeling like part of the woods that edged the field, hearing the squabbling birds following him, fighting over the worms and bugs that the plow turned up. The soft, damp soil had its own special smell, the sacred aroma of the annual rebirth of the earth. He felt that the land was awakening from hibernation, stretching and yawning after a long winter and happy to discover it was still alive.

Sometimes he'd almost dream with his eyes open when the horses took over on the long stretches and he'd feel then that he was part of the land. He didn't know his ma had felt that way as a kid when she used to hide in the cornfield from her sister Mary, but he would have understood in a second.

At times like that, he felt like the air went through rather than around him and the woods reached out and touched him gently. Sometimes he felt he could probably take off and fly around the clouds if he put his mind to it. He wondered what the birds would think—or the horses, if they looked around and saw him flying away. They'd probably spook. It called to his mind the night he and Buck Doaks had seen Johnny Todd, his grandpa, rise into the moonlit night and wave to them as he soared away to Valhalla, or somewhere. He'd never been absolutely sure it really happened though. If it had, he wondered if his gramp hadn't gone to join Custer and Wild Bill, whom he'd known before he came back home and got married and respectable.

At night, with the windows open on each side of his corner bedroom, he savored the spring breezes stirring through the room, laden with the almost unbearable fragrance of new plant life. The two new calves bawled occasionally, and their mamas answered them with reassuring moos, undoubtedly telling the little ones where Ma was, if the calf had wandered off in the dark pasture on its own. Gusts of wind sometimes stirred his white pines, to which they responded with what sounded like a grateful sigh as they scraped their branches against the eaves. Hank stirred occasionally on the floor beside the bed, sometimes groaning contentedly. Far off, another farm dog barked. The sound traveled at least a mile on the still night air, since nobody was any closer than that, except Newt and Nelson, and they didn't have a dog yet.

Bennie no longer got so tired that he almost went to sleep at the dinner table. In fact, he had more energy than he could burn up and often had trouble going to sleep right away. He didn't mind. It gave him time to think about things. For example, the Civil War, which had always interested him after he met the G.A.R. veterans. And about getting out to Kid's lake. He wondered what the big mystery was. "Well," he told himself, "I'll find out soon enough." In the meantime he resolved to wheedle Newt out of as much Civil War as he could get him to tell about. He hoped someday they'd go to LaSalle so he could see where Newt's pony Cannonball was honorably laid to rest, as much a veteran as any of those G.A.R. vets he'd known. He also wanted to look through the museum they'd made from Newt's boyhood home and maybe see the attic where he'd played as a kid with his little black buddy, Leland. He thought, "I'll have to ask Newt if Leland is still alive." He also wondered if Newt had a picture of Cannonball, maybe with him and Leland on him, or just Newt sitting on him during the war somewhere. He made a mental note to be sure and ask Newt that, too.

Newt and Nelson were over for dinner most Sundays. Ma would have hated to admit that she missed her favorite "*morone*," Newt, when he wasn't around regularly. And Nelson was also one of her favorites. Bennie could see that, but he was puzzled why. He sure was pretty crude to look at. Bennie wasn't yet old enough to appreciate that Ma liked honesty more than anything else, and Nelson was honest to the bone and as straightforward as they made 'em. Even though Pa still kidded Ma about Nelson being "sweet" on her, she invited the old Swede over with Newt whenever she wished. She even "forced" an extra piece of pie on him every time, which was something like making a cat lick an ice-cream dish.

Since the weather had turned warm, they usually sat outside after Sunday dinner. Ma, and Rose if she was out visiting them for Sunday, which she often did, would join them as soon as they cleared off the table and washed the dishes. Usually Ma had worked up a pretty good sweat and would sigh when she came out fanning herself with a folded newspaper. She would sit down in the swing and always say, "I had to get out of that hot kitchen," as though a person had to make an excuse every time they started to enjoy themselves or get comfortable.

Nelson was usually asleep in a matter of minutes, flat on his back in the grass, snoring, with a newspaper over his face to keep the light out and the flies away. About that, Newt said, "He's as good as having a bear around to keep the flies off us—most of 'em go for him."

Newt and the young ones would sit around in the grass under the ancient maple tree that shaded the porch, and Ma and Pa held down the swing or the old rockers that had been retired to the porch. Pa would sometimes get up and say, "I think I'll take a leaf out of Nelson's book and go in and snooze awhile where the flies won't bother me." He'd heard Newt's Civil War stories years before. Ma hadn't and had always been interested in the Civil War from the time she learned that old Jim Tynan had fought in it. She tried not to appear to be listening closely, but took in every word—Rose did too. The girl was interested in everything, eager to learn and painfully aware of how much there was to learn. It never occurred to her that she already was much better informed and a lot smarter than the average kid her age.

Newt enjoyed being on stage and was a helluva good storyteller.

CHAPTER FORTY

The Mystic Chords of Memory

Newt closed his eyes and leaned back against the veteran maple tree.

He wondered if the maple had been there the year he went to war. "Probably," he thought. He'd heard maples lived as much a six hundred years.

Tell me, tree, the reason's reason, behind the people of the bygone season.

Pictures played through his mind and he saw and heard the past and sometimes smelled it too. His hometown, LaSalle, floated into his vision and anchored itself there; he could see again the busy waterfront where traffic from Chicago came down the Illinois and Michigan canal.

Tell me, Time: "Was I really a boy once?
Was I destined to be a witness to history?"

I remember the arching elms over the dirt streets and how I loved to look west at the setting sun in the green tunnel they made. Did I see Manifest Destiny waiting out there? If I did, it was always beautiful and made me feel like a giant.

I remember how I could hear horses passing out in that road through my open bedroom windows on summer nights. I always imagined a faithful old nag, plodding by in the dark, hoofs plopping in the soft dirt, taking someone home or maybe pulling the wagon of a farmer headed out of town after he'd sold his load of produce. They always camped out to save money.

Did anyone know at the time when the railroads first invaded rivertown LaSalle, that the iron horse was going to save the Union—"the Last Best Hope of Earth"? The competing canalmen fought tooth and nail to keep out the competition, would have even if they'd known the railroads would keep the Union together when Lincoln's "mystic chords of memory" weren't glue enough.

Only dirty old trade routes that shifted to east and west with the iron horse instead of north and south on the Mississippi River got the job done. Trade was money, and money put supper on tables. Only that made "mystic chords" of the kind that, when it came down to it, swelled the "chorus of union." Bread and butter tied Illinois to Yankeeland, instead of the mint julep chivalry living south of the Smith and Wesson Line.

There was nothing left to tie the South to Yankeeland, either mystic or economic, or so the folks running things down there thought.

So I rode Cannonball to war with Pa and Colonel Smith, no more knowing about Manifest Destiny than about the Ark of the Covenant and not giving a damn. We were going off to a big circus—an adventure for sure. It was just fun to be riding, going somewhere beyond the horizon. Even Cannonball knew it, and I could feel it in him.

Newt learned about Manifest Destiny later—in a book. But that wasn't what he was thinking about as he tuned up to spin one of his Sunday yarns about his war. He was thinking of a song that told about the carefree feeling of going somewhere new on a horse better than he could. It wasn't even one that had been written yet when he and Cannonball went to war. He heard the song's lines again as plain as the first time he'd heard it.

Newt opened up to his Sunday audience on that theme, and said, "They used to have a song," . . . and Bennie knew the Sunday story was about to start. "The part of the song I remember best went:

and this is the way we'd go,
forty miles a day on beans and hay
in the regular Army-o.

The cavalry sang it after the Civil War, but it was pretty much true long before then. It was part of a song that a couple of minstrel show songwriters by the name of Harrigan and Hart wrote."

Bennie thought, "He remembers little stuff like that, just like I do. It must run in the blood."

Newt was quiet a while, and no one prompted him to go on because they knew he was remembering, so he could tell it right. Finally he said, "But that wasn't *the way we went* at first. We were still only walking infantry. Later we got to be mounted infantry and had to beg, borrow, or steal a thousand horses or so to do it. I didn't know we'd end up fightin' Injuns instead of Rebs. At first we left LaSalle on river steamers. Some of 'em had famous names during the war. Some of 'em got sunk. I don't know for sure anymore which ones they were, but such names as the *Die Vernon* and *Carondelet* come back to me because of the sound of 'em. I don't even remember how you spell those two for sure.

"Anyhow Pa and Colonel Smith supervised loading up, getting officers' horses on board and all our regimental gear. We were pretty well equipped since the Colonel and Pa both had a lot of political drag. Both knew old Abe real well, and Governor Yates, of course. In those days that had a lot to do with being able to get guns and ammunition. We even had a couple of cannons the Colonel bought out of his own pocket, though they weren't really authorized for infantry regiments. We had horses to pull those, too. Colonel Smith hung onto them babies through thick and thin. Even Grant couldn't get 'em when we left Shiloh to go west again. The Colonel went to the top with a telegram, and Grant got one back from Washington that got right to the point. I remember Colonel Smith showing around a copy of old Abe's wire that he sent to Grant and laughing. It said:

> *Grant.*
>
> *Leave Smith's cannons alone. He bought them out of his own pocket and he can keep them.*
>
> *A. Lincoln.*

He kept his cannons, but Grant could be petty, and Smith made an enemy who saw that he never wore a general's star like he should have.

"Abe knew how to play politics and he wasn't the softy people thought he was. He could come to the point right smart, and if need be he was 'loaded,' as the old saying went. No one ever blew in him to see if he really was 'loaded,' either, after the first time. The saying came from how we used to blow down the barrel of an old muzzle-loader—if it was, empty air came out the hole where you put the cap on the back. Stanton, who called Abe 'the great ape' behind his back at first, tried blowing in him just once and found out the boss was not only loaded but went off in his ugly puss. Stanton made the mistake of telling Abe he wasn't going to do something and got a note back just like Grant did about those cannons, and it said, '*My dear Stanton. I'm afraid you'll have to.*' Stanton knew it was an invitation to resign if he didn't feel like behaving and he never tried Abe out again. Stanton, like most who wrestled Abe back at New Salem when Abe was a young feller, 'got throwed.'"

Newt snorted, "Anyhow, the big gun Stanton picked to blow in damn near blew his head off."

This was what Bennie liked about Newt. It seemed like he was going around Robin Hood's barn with a story, but you figured out you were learning more than most of the history professors in creation could tell you, because the run of the mill didn't know how to tell a story. Maybe didn't even know the story or get it right. Newt did. And besides he'd been there.

"The Illinois was runnin' full when we set out. I can still see it, a mile wide some places, and water flooded into the low places along the banks, six or eight feet up on some of the trees. The kind of water that makes a truce between rabbits and rattlesnakes since they both crawl up on the same high spot to keep from drowning. Nature's like that. *Same thing that makes allies in wars.*

"The river was prettiest in the early morning with haze hanging over it. I got up early and followed the rail and walked all the way around the boat. It was foggy enough I could imagine the boat was the only thing in the whole world. I can still hear the paddlewheels hittin' the water—thwack, thwack, thwack—and the big walking beams creaking and squeaking, and the noise of escaping steam hissing while we left a trail of black smoke rising up and floating away. And way up above us was the pilot in his house, running the whole shebang so we didn't end up on a sand bar or sink ourselves on a snag."

Newt remembered thinking as they ghosted through the fog: "Suppose I'm dead and this is Heaven. Where are all the angels? Where is God? I guess the pilot will have to do up there in his private domain."

"The pilot was boss. Even the captain kept his mouth shut around him, especially in tight places, where it took a lot of know how to get through. The pilots even ran at night unless there was a storm, ran just so long as they had enough light to see the banks. Read Mark Twain's *Life on the Mississippi* to get the real hang of it. He was a pilot himself before the Civil War. We've got so harnessed up in the idea of schools today that people don't know old Mark was one of our best historians. They can't see that because he never went to college. Fact is he probably didn't go to much of any school but his own . . . like me."

Bennie thought, "*And me.*" Then added the thought, "*And Kid.*" He should have added Ma, but didn't think of it because she was *only a woman*. It was still a pretty tough world for women to get recognized as worth much in those days, especially as warriors, and it was worse the further back in history you went. Joan of Arc, a warrior by any measure, really must have had a hell of a time.

"It took us a day and a night to make it to St. Louis, even goin' downstream like we did. Fog held us down to a crawl for a while. When we got there it was a big hassle finding someplace to tie up. It always was busy, but there must have been two or three hundred steamboats there, and some anchored out in the river waiting their turn to get in and unload and load back up. It got even worse later. The war started it, of course, but at that time it was only getting going. Naturally they built a lot more docks, but that took time.

"It was a noisy place and stunk to high heaven too, and the air was full of smoke from the steamers. At least then it was wood smoke. I never have liked coal smoke."

Bennie thought Newt looked almost like a boy with his head back remembering, nodding forward every once in a while to emphasize a word or two. Obviously he was enjoying himself back in the past. He never opened his eyes, though. He seemed to be looking into himself, and in a way he was, since that's where memory is stored.

"Anyhow we finally got unloaded and marched through town to a campground they had reserved for us. Somebody's pasture up till then. Colonel Smith and Pa, of course, knew how to lay out a camp from bein' in the Mexican War. They both knew how to handle men, too. They were quiet men and never asked anybody to do anything dumb, and if it looked dumb at first and really wasn't, they explained why it had to be done. Some of the younger officers, and some not so young, didn't have the feel for that yet and Colonel Smith soon spotted them and had a little talk with them. A couple went home without their shoulder straps, too. Pa and Colonel Smith both knew that it didn't do to peeve a bunch of independent western men if you expected to get something out of 'em, and that applied particularly to those off farms. Especially if you expected them to stand up and shoot and get shot at. I didn't know that yet. It only takes one big shootin' affair, though, to figure that out, unless you're pretty damned dumb. Some of the officers were. They were the ones that Colonel Smith sent home. He didn't even give some of 'em one battle to cut it before that was it."

Newt nodded his head in rhythm with his voice, like a poet beating his foot to his meter. Even the pup, Hank, knew Newt was the center of attention and that something important was going on. He went over and lay beside him and put his head on his knees. Newt only opened his eyes then and looked fondly at him, scratched behind his ears, and left his hand on Hank's head. The pup sighed, closed his eyes, and looked like he was going to sleep, but his ears pricked up occasionally as though he understood Newt's words. Maybe he did.

"We had our share of pooches and cats that went along to war, too," Newt said. "Cats were handy to keep rats away around camp or in the hospitals. We had plenty of hospitals after the shootin' started, but not many were worth a damn."

Ma perked up at that, the natural born nurse in her rising. She said, "I'd have straightened out those doctors and improved those hospitals or knew the reason why."

Newt opened his eyes and nodded. "I'd bet on you, Em," he said.

Bennie wished she'd shut up for fear Newt would lose his train of thought, but he didn't. He went right on:

"Nobody knew what they aimed to do with us, but Colonel Smith knew it paid to discipline his troops. He started in pretty easy, since most were country boys used to having their own way. They didn't care much about saluting and spit and polish and he didn't push that at first, and didn't really get firm about anything except to keep the camp clean. He knew that disease killed more men than bullets. Our camps were always set out right and proper from the very first day and kept clean. The Army called the picking up 'policing the camp.' If you've read much about the Army you know they even call the duty when you're assigned to help out in the mess hall, doing duty as *kitchen police*, or K.P. as they called it. Everyone hated it. Especially if a sergeant came around and sucked them in for it when they were lounging around planning a free day.

"It was fun watching the boys learn to drill. Only a few like Nicodemus Cochrane had two left feet, though. Most got the hang of it in just a couple of hours. We had some sergeants that had been in the Mexican War just like Pa and the Colonel, and they took over the drill business and taught the men the manual of arms, which was mainly how to hold their guns and get them on their shoulder or shift from one shoulder to the other, or ground them and stand at parade rest, and like that. It was extra-important to get through their heads the fact that they might accidentally slice their buddy with that butcher knife bayonet on the end of a rifle if they didn't know the manual of arms.

"Of course we made a few new corporals and sergeants, and you could tell who was apt to be promoted after you watched a while and got a feel for men."

He saw it all again, spreading out in his mind as he talked, each old friend or place coming into view like the names and the shifting scenes at the start of a movie. He kept on with his story, but it drifted through his mind in pictures just like it had been. He told about it so well that Bennie could almost see it, and feel and smell it too.

Newt was no longer with them after a while:

Well, here I am again back in Missouri in the spring of '61.

Dammit! It keeps flapping by like a Keystone Cops movie. Slow down! Slow down, dammit, so I can get you in focus!

"Adventures never slow down."

It was Buck Doaks talking out of the past and Newt was a little surprised. "Is that really you, Buck?"

"Becher ass it's me. I was there, too, you know."

"Yeah, I know. Why don't you say hello to Bennie while you're here. He misses you."

Buck changed the subject. "Remember the day yore Paw got on Mike Mullins case about them swiped pullets?"

Newt laughed. "How could I forget."

Bennie had thought maybe Newt was asleep until he laughed. The old man opened his eyes and said, "I remember one day we was in camp on our way up north in Missouri. Pa was sittin' in one of those folding chairs that officers were issued, in front of a field desk that had folding legs, too. They were both designed so's not to take up much space in a wagon or packed on a mule. He was sittin' under the canvas awning in front of his tent, with Mike Mullins at attention in front of him, or what passed for attention for a farm boy in those early days of the war.

"Mike looked embarrassed and a little scared. Everyone knew Pa was no one to mess around with and Mike realized he was in trouble.

"I was off to one side and knew how Mike felt facing Pa's hard look. I also knew the other side of Pa and knew that he loved every one of his boys.

"Mike Mullins had got in Dutch because everybody's belly was just about sayin' howdy to their backbone. We were headed north to help a fire-eating colonel, Dave Moore, clean up the last patch of the Reb sympathizers out of northern Missouri or make good Indians out of 'em. We'd outrun our rations and everyone was hungry, especially me, who was hungry all the time anyhow.

"Colonel Smith had issued strict orders against unauthorized foraging or burning farmer's fences to cook coffee. He told the boys, 'We don't want to peeve these sonsabitches so there's one behind every hedge shooting at us like the Minutemen.'"

Newt snorted as he said, "Later in the war rules were relaxed to allow taking *only the top rail*. But as some typical Irish soldier observed, 'That makes the next rail the top rail, don't it bhoys?'"

Newt was back there again, seeing it plain as the day it happened:

"Pa tried his best to look severe when he asked, 'Did you steal those chickens, Mike?'"

"'Yes, sir,' Mike admitted.

"By then almost the whole regiment had learned to say 'sir' to officers, even the officers they didn't like.

"Pa asked him if he knew there was an order out against it.

"I can hear his voice yet when he said, 'Yes, sir, Colonel Bob.'"

Again Newt wasn't with them under the maple tree, but back in Iowa:

"Why did you do it then?"

"We wuz all hungry as bears, Colonel, and it was gettin' dark and it seemed like a shame to pass up such a big chicken coop. I figured a rich farmer could spare a few."

"Who helped you?"

"I don't remember, sir."

Colonel Bob loved him for the lie. Here was a man who'd take the knocks for his sidekicks and never squeal. This was the kind that made a soldier who'd died in his tracks before he'd desert his friends in a tight spot. That kind won battles. You had to win battles to win wars.

"You got anything else to say for yourself?"

"Well, Colonel Bob, I reckon not, unless maybe you ought to know I gave one of them pullets to your cook. Likely you and young Newt over there ate him."

Newt almost split and his Pa guffawed so loud everyone within a hundred yards turned to look his way. They hadn't expected that. Newt had seen the pullet arrive the night before but never squealed on the men, any more than they did on each other.

"O.K., Mike," Newt's Pa said. "I reckon I'm as guilty as you. Let's just forget all about it this time."

Mike saluted and managed an almost professional about-face and started off. He stopped and half-turned when Colonel Bob said, "Oh, Mike." He expected maybe the Colonel had changed his mind and was mighty relieved when he added, "That was a damned tasty bird. Now get the hell out of here—and don't get caught next time."

Newt sighed. "Well," he said, seeming to come back and see them all around waiting for him to say some more, "we saw it through the smoke the first time up at Athens, Missouri. It's right up on the Iowa line. How well I remember old Colonel Dave Moore. He was a dilly. He could cuss longer without repeating himself than anyone I ever heard. And Christ was he tough. He once had a—pardon my French, ladies—'no good sonofabitchen Secesh minister' that didn't shout for Uncle Abe, stood up on a cannon trail every morning for nine days running and made him yell out prayers for Old Abe in Washington. If it looked like the sky pilot was winding down, he had a sergeant poke him in the ass with a bayonet, and it wasn't a pinprick either.

"Anyhow, before we met Moore we heard his cannons working. He had a personal grudge fight going with a Reb named Martin Green—Mart Green as they called him. Mart had a pickup regiment just like Moore and said he was coming up to Athens to clean up on Moore and run him out of Missouri. It didn't work out that way. I'll bet Moore never said any prayers for old Mart when a sharpshooter got him a few years later at Vicksburg. By then the sonofabitch had made general in the Reb army.

"Some of Moore's troops didn't stick and we saw a bunch on horseback skedaddle past us over on a ridge to one side, on our way up there. We almost got there too late for the shootin'. Colonel Smith sorted out two companies and they double-timed—that means trot, in case you wondered—up there ahead of the rest of us, but old Mart Greene was already skedaddling. Still, a few were shootin' right smart and we could hear cannon. Mart Green had some old relics of cannons, and I heard one was a hollowed out log that busted the first time they shot it. That sort of thing was pretty typical during the first few months of the war—if you could call it a war yet.

"By the time I got there the shootin' was almost over. I heard it pretty loud, and then it just died out with a few final pops while Green's crowd hauled their freight. If I'd have been close enough, I'll bet I'd have heard feet pounding the ground and brush popping while those boys ground in their feet running for their lives.

"They had a sort of hospital in a dry goods store in town, and Doc Bedel helped out Moore's doctors and the local sawbones with the wounded. I heard a few noises coming out of there that I didn't care for much and didn't go in to look. Sounded a lot like a dog sounds when it gets run over by a car and not quite killed, if you'd like to know."

Oh, mine eyes have seen the gory (that's gory, not glory, no mistake).
War is blood above all, goddamit!
Glory comes half a century later
If you pull through.
Then the grandkids get the big windies.
About how you lost that leg
(But not how you shit your pants when you got shot.)
Tell 'em how you can still feel the rhematiz in the leg that's gone.
They won't believe that but it may be the only God's truth you tell 'em.
What the hell, it's your story and they're stuck with it.

"I wandered around on Cannonball and saw my first dead soldiers. They didn't look any different than any other dead men I'd ever seen except most of 'em was layin' on their backs with their legs pulled up, like their backs had been bothering them just before they croaked. Funny, but most of the dead on battlefields died like that. I don't recall that lookin' at a bunch of bloody bodies shocked me much if at all. I was sort of like Huck Finn. Not much shocked me after living in a town like LaSalle with the river workers around there all the time. They were always shooting or knifing each other or putting an axe in somebody's head. Like all boys, whenever we heard there was another fracas, we had to run see, so I'd seen enough blood before then. But not so much of it all in one place."

And how about you, Nick Cochrane, our only casualty. You had sense enough to get behind a tree to take a leak, but some skulking sonofabitch got left behind, hiding in the brush and took all the fun out of life for you from then on. The bastard sneaked in one last shot and ran like hell. But not far. I saw Pa swing up that fancy English breechloader he had and pick that bastard off like a runnin' rabbit. Got him right where the suspenders cross. The damned Secesh shot two fingers off Nick's hand that was holdin' his pride and joy, and ripped his tool off right down to the root.

Newt was trying to decide if he should tell them about that, especially with Rose there, and decided maybe it would be just as well to forget that. Besides Ma would probably look mean and say it served a dirty, nasty man right to have his "works" shot off.

Well, Nick, I remember running into you in Chicago in the '90s. You was a big stick in politics by then, running' the whole Southside. I remember how you told me, "I never run for office, just run the sonsabitches that do. Who the hell would vote for a guy that everybody calls Cockless Cochrane behind his back? But the nuns love me. I keep all their charities runnin'."

Where are you now, Cockless? Up strumming a harp with the vets, I guess.

"Jesus, Newt!" It was Buck Doaks snide voice again. "Can't you see Cockless in long flowing robes strumming a harp?"

"Not exactly," Newt allowed, "to tell the truth. Maybe Nick got his dong back and is making charitable contributions to needy angels."

Bennie wondered if he'd get sick to his stomach seeing a bunch of dead men and didn't think so.

"Well," Newt said, "we didn't do much but chase our tails for a couple of months around northern Missouri, but we learned a lot about marching. There was all sorts of Reb guerrilla outfits roaming around trying to tear up the Hannibal and St. Joe Railroad and raise hell generally. Every piece of woods might be full of 'em ready to shoot and run, and every creek and river we come to was apt to have a bunch trying to hold the bridge against us. We gave a few of them fits, lost a few men, and they lost more, and finally we run most of 'em south of the Missouri, where they joined up with Pap Price and his Rebs. Down there Price won the battle of Wilson's Creek about the time Moore was winning the skirmish up at Athens.

"One of the most important things we learned was how to keep from going hungry again like we did on the way up to Athens. After that first march Colonel Smith got us a herd of cows and pigs to run along behind the regiment. I drew the duty pretty often to help herd them back there in the dust. In a few days cows would follow a bell steer and pigs would follow the cows, so we didn't have so much trouble keeping them on the road and out of the woods and pastures. Cows are funny like that. They're born to do almost nothing but eat, but they forget that and think they're goin' to die if they stray out of a herd once they get used to it. That's why they stampede like they do. When the leader goes, the rest go. In this case they died for stickin' with the bunch. We'd butcher however many we needed every night. It didn't make for aged beef. In fact, sometimes we tossed it into the pan almost quivering. I remember one of the troops, Joe Black, held up a piece after it was cooked and said, 'I seen cows hurt worse'n this one get well.'"

Newt said, "That herd had its drawbacks because it's hard to sneak up on the enemy with a herd of bawling cows and a bunch of chicken coming along. Every wagon had a few crates of chickens hanging on it somewhere, and camp at night sounded like a farm. I guess that's not the way you expected to hear how a war was, but that was all part of it too. There weren't as many battles as you'd think, and bein' sick killed more men than bullets.

"We were due to see our first real fuss—I mean one that came anywhere near to a real battle—when we got on a couple of steamers at Hannibal and went south to join Grant down at Cairo, Illinois. He was spoilin' for a fight. He was one of the few generals in those early days—or ever for that matter—that knew what the hell an army was for. He could never figure out anything to do but pull one together if they'd let him and look up a scrap where he'd go for the enemy's jugular. That's what folks don't know about him. One of his staff recalled that the first time he saw old *Ulyss*, he struck him as a fellow that looked like he could butt his head through a stone wall and was just about to do it. When we joined him, he was just about to do it for the first time.

"I'm gonna save that and take a leaf outa old Nelson's book and get a snooze, if you don't mind. Youth has to have its rest."

Ma snorted. "Youth, my foot. Why not stretch out inside, out of the flies. And you and Nelson stay for supper."

Ma loved her *morone*. He had fire, and it wasn't ready to sputter out by a long shot. She thought, "I'll bet he'd ride off to war tomorrow on Cannonball, or any horse he could get, if they still rode horses."

Where are you Cannonball? I think I know.
In the great green pasture where horses go.

As he was dozing off, Newt could see the little horse plain again.

CHAPTER FORTY-ONE

Women Are Handy in Bed

Bennie noticed a big change in Pa right after he and Ma got back *up north* from Blackhawk. Pa still let Ma boss him around when it didn't make any difference, but he walked straighter and with a spring in his step.

Especially around horses, Pa was a man Bennie had only seen once before and that was a dim memory. He remembered how Pa had hurried across the snowy street in Wahbonsee, politely shoved aside a few perplexed men that obviously knew little about horses, and gently got the milkman's poor scared horse up before it hurt itself, after it had slipped and fallen on the ice.

The thing that made Pa's metamorphosis all the more singular in Bennie's eyes was that his father had never been demonstrative or inclined to outward displays of affection. And he sure wasn't the kind anyone would suspect of having much baby talk in him, but with horses he had a way of getting their whole attention with a soft voice and whispered words with which only lovers' ears were normally favored.

Newt and Bennie were watching Pa talk a team into pulling out a stump they'd have to dynamite otherwise. He got the two big mares to pull exactly evenly and the stump almost flew out of the ground.

Newt said to Bennie, "Yore Paw knows how to get the last ounce of pull out of hosses." To Pa he said, after he'd got the job done, "You been humpin' them mares on the sly?"

Pa just grinned.

"Speakin' of humpin'," Newt said, "I think we ought to go down and see Aunt Kay tonight. How about comin' along, Ed?" he asked Pa.

Bennie was surprised to hear Pa say, "Maybe. Depends."

"Depends on what?" Newt asked cautiously.

"Depends on if Ma will let me out."

Bennie examined his face to see if there was any trace of humor in the remark. He was perfectly poker-faced.

"Maybe I can give teacher a note," Newt said.

"Holy shit!" Nelson exploded disgustedly. "Crack da whip!"

"Easier said than done. I notice you talk mighty sweet to keep getting that second piece of pie from Em," Pa said.

Nelson grinned. "Yah, but I don't have to hang around her all the time on top of it."

Newt laughed. "Women'r handy in bed." He watched Pa for reaction, but it was Nelson who had something to say about that.

"Ha," the old Swede said. "My old vooman vas always getting' off *rich ones* in bed. Phew!"

Everyone guffawed at that. Bennie remembered how Ma's farts stunk up the bed when he was little and had slept with her.

"Anyhow we don't have to spend all night with the ones down at Kay's," Newt said.

Bennie said, "I got a better idea to get Pa out. I don't like it down there at *Aunt Kay's* smelling stale booze and sitting around swilling pop while I wait for you guys to get your ashes hauled. Somebody has to drive the Lincoln. It'll have to be Pa if I don't go. I can say I'm too sleepy and want to go to bed early. If Ma doesn't go for it, I'll say I don't feel good. She'll have me in bed with an onion poultice or something inside of five minutes."

His proposed sacrifice wasn't entirely inspired by charity. He knew that the new *Western Story Magazine* had come in the mail.

Newt grinned wickedly. "Good idea, but suppose Em wants to come along?"

"Let her," Pa said. "Do her good to watch how a whorehouse works. Besides, if she thinks Bennie's sick you couldn't pull her out of the house using the 'girls' there that I just got to jerk out that stump."

"Haw," Nelson burst out, ignoring the second part of the remark "Emma wouldn't even know she was *in* a whorehouse."

Bennie thought, "*Probably not even if she worked there*." Then he caught himself and thought, "*What a hell of a thing to think about your ma*." Then he justified himself with the thought, "*She deserves being ridiculed. She's damn good at it where Pa is concerned. She's really mean as hell, deep down*."

In any case Bennie's idea made sense to all of them.

"All the same," Newt said, "for your sake Ed, I sure hope she stays home. You need to have your hose drained."

Pa didn't say anything to that. He thought, "*That'll be the day*." He wasn't any more inclined to risk a dose or the syph than he had been in Alaska, or bumming around the West with Newt. But something he recalled from his Alaska days had aroused his interest in going down to Aunt Kay's.

Bennie had made an innocent remark to Pa after he'd chauffeured Newt and the boys down to Kay's the first time. They were out in the barn and he didn't see any reason not to spill the beans about what happened between Newt and Kay down at her place.

"You say Newt knew her from the Gold Rush?" Pa asked.

"Yup."

"What does this heifer look like?"

"Well, she ain't bad-lookin' actually, but she can't be very young. Blond, blue eyes, wears glasses, short like Ma but not plump."

That was enough to prompt Pa to pump Newt.

"Klondy," Newt explained. "You remember her?"

Pa thought, *"Who the hell wouldn't, especially if they saw her bare ass when she was in first bloom."*

Pa remembered her all right. He recalled with wry humor that Nelson said Ma wouldn't even know she was in a whorehouse. *"True,"* he thought, *"but I was that dumb once and maybe it's nothing to be ashamed of."*

[FLASHBACK—1900]

The name *Klondy* took Pa back to a dancehall in Nome—at the Palace Variety Hall. A very pretty blond who filled out a tight, low-cut dress in all the right places was on stage singing requests from an all-male audience. They applauded and cheered wildly after each piece and threw money on the stage too. Some even tossed a gold poke to her. Money meant nothing to lonesome men who were full of booze. They requested mostly tearjerkers like "After the Ball," but also liked the sprightly popular tunes like "There'll Be a Hot Time in the Old Town Tonight."

Pa had no idea in those days what the term "Variety" really meant. He was only there because Newt dragged him out. "Do you good to get out on the town," Newt had urged. Pa doubted it. He stayed at their table near the stage in the smoky room while Newt went to a crib out back with one of the house ladies of the night. He suspected what was going on when Newt left, but nothing could have dragged him back there with one of them. If he'd known where he was being taken before he came out with Newt, he'd have stayed in the cabin and read.

His ideal woman was a clean, wholesome girl like the one singing. He couldn't have brought himself to believe it if someone had told him that she was available at a high price to a few selected favorites. She'd been *Swiftwater Bill*'s girl at Dawson when she was only sixteen and just a couple of years off the farm. In his comfortable ignorance Pa was satisfied to daydream about her from a distance. He thought, "That's the kind of girl I want to marry someday."

He hadn't the slightest suspicion what was about to happen to him when she gracefully undulated down from the stage with swaying hips and continued to sing as she moved through the crowd, rumpling a few men's hair or playfully pulling down someone's hat brim as she went, and if he'd known, he'd have run for the door. He wondered why she picked him from the bunch that included a lot of mature men with plenty of money when she edged in and quickly sat on his lap before he realized what was happening.

That got some hooting and hollering from the crowd who had seen her do that before to some other clean young kid. He was hugely embarrassed and showed it with a deep blush. She put her arm around his neck and snuggled up to his chest, wiggling to get comfortable as she continued her song while soulfully looking into his eyes. The crowd loved it, and envied the kid's good luck. It was all the funnier since they all sensed his uneasiness. At nineteen he felt himself quickly getting a hard-on and blushed even more deeply. He didn't know that his innocent appearance and clean looks were why she sat on his lap—doing that might have got her in trouble with more mature men who would want something for nothing later. She laughed pleasantly when she finished her song, a little breathless sound that enchanted him, that and her perfume, but even more by how a woman felt rubbing a soft, warm ass on his lap.

"What's your name?" she asked in a little girl voice that he was too green to suspect she had practiced to perfection to render men's heads suitable for woodpeckers to work on. It worked on him for sure.

"Ed."

"How old are you?"

"Nineteen."

"You're sweet," she said. "Stay that way." She wiggled artfully some more on his lap and he knew she must feel his hard prick just as he felt the soft body that had caused it, and he was so overwhelmed by it for a little while that he didn't even think what his mother would say about that if she learned of it.

When she left his eyes followed her like a newborn calf keeping an eye on its ma. His face looked like a kid that just dropped his sucker. He was in love for the first time. His pecker throbbed for a long while before his hard-on folded up and his pants were wet from his dick drooling in them.

When Newt came back to the table, he stopped to chat with several of their acquaintances and learned of Pa's encounter with an angel. When Newt sat back down he said, "If I'd known you had the touch to get that one over here, I'd have stayed here. *Klondy* is famous from Dawson to Honolulu."

Pa didn't think that such a clean, young girl would care for old men like Newt, even if they were rich, which Newt was temporarily (the usual case with Newt and riches). He'd vaguely sensed what Newt was implying and doubted if she'd have anything to do with any man, especially an old rip like him. She looked like the girl next door.

That night in their small cabin Newt heard him jacking off, breathing hard, thrusting at his new love and trying not to make too much noise. He didn't manage to do that as he involuntarily groaned with pleasure when he rocketed off in his hand and on his belly while he imagined doing it to Klondy. He knew what men and women did, but had never done it, and didn't think he would until he got married. Right afterward he was ashamed of himself for thinking what he had about a sweet girl like Klondy, but he woke up just a few hours later and did it all over again. By then Newt was sawing wood.

The first time he'd heard Pa loping his mule across the room, Newt had thought, "The kid probably isn't the only one in Nome that Klondy made get it off with old mother-five-fingers tonight, and probably she gets a few dozen that way every night." He grinned at the added thought, "I might have to fist off myself thinking about that ripe young piece if I hadn't just had my ashes hauled. Pity she can't charge them at least a cut rate for the service. I'll have to try the lady out myself."

He had no doubt he could—maybe even free. He had a "gift for the shit," as he called it, and knew that was sometimes more valuable to women than money. They all loved to hear they were the most beautiful women a man had ever laid his eyes on.

Up till then, Pa usually hadn't wanted to come out to the Nome joints at night with Newt, but he did after that, hoping Klondy would notice him and sense his true heart and that he could love her like no other man. He'd bet he was older than she was and would know what to do, too. But she seemed not to notice him again after that first time. He didn't care. He was still in love with her. Then one night she came over to his table again when Newt was out back, and plopped into his lap.

"Hi, keed," she said. "Been bein' good?" He thought her smile was like a sunrise.

He was tongue-tied.

She came right to the point about why she was there this time.

"I need someone to shovel for me on the beach. I lost my shovel man. Some bastard shot him."

Pa couldn't believe his ears. His pure love had just used a word that only the coarsest men used. He tried not to think about it, and also tried not to get hard again and failed at both.

He knew what she meant by "shovel man." She wanted some one to work a footage claim with her and do the hard work.

"Want the job?"

He was breathing hard and staring at her like a bug-eyed rabbit stared at a snake.

"Well?"

"Sure."

He could only gasp out his agreement because he couldn't keep from shooting off his wad in his pants just then. He suspected that she knew because as he involuntarily thrust toward her. He wasn't experienced enough to wonder if she'd had the same sensation with him, since her lips were parted and she was breathing rapidly. Newt would have known that plenty of women used men that way to get it off, a gentle rape after a fashion. The experienced ones got extra-excited over bringing off some green kid without risking getting pregnant in the bargain.

In any case she was able to calmly say, as though nothing had happened between them, "Come by in the morning. I'll meet you in the Polar Restaurant next door at 8 A.M."

She lightly kissed his cheek, jumped up and in her sweet soprano swung into "I Don't Want to Play in Your Yard." The band quickly picked it up on her lead.

Newt had missed this performance for the same reason he'd missed the last one. When Pa told him what happened (with one singular omission—or emission, more accurately), Newt eyed him with respect. "I'll be go to hell!" he exclaimed. "I gotta take a closer look at you. I must have missed something."

"She wants someone that won't paw her," Pa said, with unusual insight. He couldn't have pawed anyone just then even if he wanted to.

Newt said, "Be damn hard to get away with pawin' in any case, out on the beach in this blessed Land of the Midnight Sun."

Pa laughed inwardly, and entertained an unusually bawdy thought for him: "It'd *be hard in my case for damn sure*."

When she met him that first morning at the Polar, he was surprised to find her in a fancy dress and wearing a bonnet. He wasn't sure what he'd expected her to wear, but it wasn't a spiffy rig like she had on. She had dabbed perfume on, which aroused him as she knew it would. He couldn't take his eyes off her. Finally he managed to say something.

"Aren't you afraid of getting that nice dress all mussed up?"

She laughed. "I don't have any other kind. I'd like to wear overalls, but I'm afraid it would shock a lot of the boys that come to hear me sing. Could be bad for business."

He thought she looked absolutely adorable, and his heart took a little leap when she looked him straight in the eyes. "*I'd come to hear you sing no matter what you wore*," he told himself. He was too shy to even think that he'd come in more ways than one if she wore nothing at all, as she always did in his daydreams, or when he thought of her when he tried to get to sleep. Thinking of that, he blushed, because he knew it was going to bring up a big hard. There was nothing he could do to stop it, and he hoped she wouldn't notice. If he had realized that women like her could tell by the look in a man's eyes without looking for a bulge in their pants, he would have been too innocent to suspect how she knew. This was a girl not yet twenty who'd had hundreds of men in bed with her. He didn't know she might want him, and perhaps already was beginning to, for a different reason than she'd wanted all except a very few of the others. Most had been for money, of course.

After a few weeks on the beach together, for which Klondy paid him well, Pa felt a lot more comfortable around her. But he never once came close to making a pass at her. He always apologized if he happened to touch her by accident. He had no idea that very pretty women like her who discovered that they couldn't get an obviously masculine fellow into bed by just snapping their fingers were challenged by that, attracted more than the cleverest seducer could have managed.

The fact was, she had started to get genuinely horny around him all the time and sometimes felt herself involuntarily lubricating. Only that didn't embarrass her like his erections did him. Of course her condition didn't show. If he'd known how vulnerable she was to him, he wouldn't have known how to take advantage of it. All he knew was that her perfume was tantalizing and she was beautiful, the most beautiful women he'd ever seen. Seeing small tendrils of her blond hair slipping from beneath her bonnet as she worked alongside him always made him want to hold her tenderly and hug her.

One day as they were taking a break from their work, Klondy stood beside him and leaned against him companionably. He didn't pull away for fear of hurting her feelings. Besides he liked it. "I'm pooped," she said. "This is hard work."

He startled himself by managing to say, "I don't care how hard the work is. I like being with you, Klondy. But you take a rest for a while. I'll do the shoveling and rocker work both." He never wondered why she kept coming out with him, since he could have done the whole job alone. Some others did though, and nudged one another and asked, "Do you suppose that kid is getting in there?"

Klondy said, "Eddie, you're such a darling. I like to be with you too. I really like you. Do you really like me?"

It was the last thing he expected her to ask. He loved her. He was at a loss for words for a while, and finally managed to say something, "Sure. Of course I like you." He was afraid to say how he really felt about her.

"I mean like men like women."

He blushed deeply, and somehow managed to blurt out, "I'd die for you, Klondy!"

"Would you marry me?"

He almost fainted at the thought. He wondered if perhaps she was losing her mind, and looked around to see who was nearby that might help him if she had a fit or something.

"Would you?"

"If I had the money. I love you."

"We can do the next best thing, if you want to."

He had no idea what she meant and was afraid to ask.

"Come around to my cabin behind the Palace tonight and we'll have a nice long talk without having other people around. Be there exactly at 2 A.M. so I know it's you, and I'll let you in. We can *really talk* there and *do whatever we want to*. It's number 8, the last one in the row along the boardwalk. Don't fall off in the mud."

Pa had no idea what she'd be doing until 2 A.M. and certainly didn't catch the meaning of "do whatever we want to." Something cautioned him not to tell Newt what he aimed to do. Newt surely would have told him what was up, and spoiled it for him. As it was, his upbringing (or lack of it as it turned out) spoiled it anyhow.

He was there exactly at two and knocked, looking around and hoping no one would look out and see him. The door opened promptly, and she met him wearing only a nightgown, which he didn't notice at first. He was hypnotized by her eyes looking directly into his as she said in a low voice, "C'mon in, Eddie." She caressed his name in a practiced stagy whisper that almost melted him.

When he did notice what she was wearing, it didn't register on him. His sisters had run around the house in night clothes and he'd thought nothing of it, and he aimed to treat her with the respect he'd shown to his sisters. In those days that sort of courtesy to women was considered a national character trait to brag about. Properly brought-up men were always "gentlemanly." Every *decent* man was raised to be that way. At least on the surface.

"Did you get rested up?" he foolishly asked. "It's pretty late. Maybe you want to get some sleep. I guess I shouldn't stay very long."

She almost laughed out loud.

"You're such a dear," she said, approaching him closely and putting her hands on his chest. She tilted her head back and even he read the genuine warmth in her eyes.

He was petrified. Finally she lifted his arms and put them around her. "Squeeze me," she invited. "I won't break."

"Are you sure I should?"

She giggled. "Sure I'm sure. If I wasn't I wouldn't have asked you."

He did as he was told and knew he was going to get a monstrous hard-on and that she might feel it. He tried to hold that part of his body away from her the best he could, but she slid her arms down onto his buttocks and pulled him against her hard and thrust at him. He was surprised how strong she was.

"Did you ever kiss a girl?" she asked.

His face was red as a beet and he could only shake his head no.

"Would you like to learn? Would you like to kiss me?"

"I don't know how!" he blurted.

"I'll show you."

By now he was too fascinated to want to do anything but follow her lead. He couldn't believe his luck and surprised himself by admitting that he intended to pursue it, even if he was embarrassed. She first kissed him, then said, "Now do that to me."

As he tried it, he was astonished to feel her tongue enter his mouth, warm and soft, yet demanding. She ran her hands down his back and then around to the front and stroked him. He wondered if she was horrified to discover his huge erection, but he couldn't get it to go down no matter how much he thought about it.

Lord only knew how Klondy managed to get him out of his clothes. She quickly disrobed, and he watched, fascinated as exciting parts he'd heard and thought about and seen in dirty pictures emerged. He was also scared half to death and pretty damned sick to recognize for the first time what sort of girl she had to be to do this. A girl that would do that simply had to be what Newt had implied and it was a real shock to him. He almost couldn't believe it. Nonetheless he was too horny to resist when she whispered, "C'mon over and let's get into bed." He still thought she was the most beautiful woman he'd ever seen.

Her warm, responsive body felt wonderful and his misgivings gradually left. He was too fully aroused by then to wonder what his mother might think of him for doing this. He asked himself, "Is this really happening?" He loved the way her breasts and hips felt pushed against him and the way she kissed him with her tongue in his mouth again. But he experienced a fairly common problem anyhow.

He was clumsy and nervous and she wasn't surprised. She'd expected it and the predictable result. Much as he then needed it, his erection had folded from nervous apprehension. She knew some men were that way—not too many—but a few, and they were the nice ones. And mostly the young ones doing it for the first time.

She had learned that green kids when they were with a naked woman for the first time acted like they were standing on a rattlesnake and wondering how to get off safely—they damn sure wouldn't be able to get a hard-on while they were in that mental shape.

"Relax," she urged him, knowing you couldn't scold spaghetti into shape to push it uphill. You had to coax. She took the lead in kissing, although he'd started to get the hang of how to kiss a girl. He wasn't especially good at it, and in fact like some men, simply wasn't cut out for it. She thought, "He'll learn." She had no idea it would take about forty years in his case.

Bennie picked up the knack of kissing expertly from another lady named Kate about the same age his father had started to learn from Klondy. He wasn't cut off the same ordinary bolt of cloth as Pa.

"Only laying here squeezing each other and kissing is going to be hopeless." Klondy concluded after a half-hour or so. "He likes it just like I do, but he's too nervous to get hard again."

By then she was hot as a firecracker. Under the circumstances she wasn't about to give up. She stroked him, gently at first, then skillfully harder and faster, and finally got him up and tried to help him get it in, but it folded up before he could enter her. She almost laughed. She wasn't the type to get mad over something like that.

Finally when she got him up again he was lubricating heavily, and she jacked him off. He thrust spasmodically like a passionate dog and too quickly streamed off in her hand. He realized he'd never had his dong get so big, or that he'd never come so hard before in his life, not even doing it with dirty pictures. He was too green to know that she came with him from grasping his leg in a scissors grip and thrusting her clitoris against him. She not only came, but as hard as he did, kissing him passionately and making it last a lot longer.

"You were just green and scared," she assured him as she let him out a little later. "Next time will be better."

As he left she asked herself, "I wonder if I'm falling in love with a nice young kid?" She lay awake a long while thinking about him, and smiling.

Regardless, there was no next time. He didn't show up for work again and avoided her like she had measles the few times he spotted her coming down the street. He hoped she didn't see him hasten across streets and duck up alleys whenever he spotted her coming.

Newt naturally asked him why he quit his job. Like an oaf he confessed, "I found out she's a whore."

With unaccustomed consideration Newt kept a straight face, and didn't ask, "What the hell did you think she was?" but let it go at that. All he said was: "Most are up here. She's a lot classier than the average."

Pa didn't jack off for a long while after that. Instead, he leaked a few unhappy tears into his pillow because he couldn't keep from being in love with Klondy. Even thinking over and over about what his mother would think about him being in love with a whore didn't drive the picture of her from his mind. As the years passed, and he finally had his first woman, then another, the bittersweet memory of Klondy became just another score he always held against Alaska.

But the sad recollection didn't keep him from a powerful curiosity now, even after almost forty years. He wanted to know how Klondy had turned out. He hoped she was still a looker for her age, but didn't question himself too closely about why he wished it. He knew most whores didn't age well, but both Newt and Bennie thought she was still a looker for her age.

He snorted at a surprising thought, "The hooker is still a looker."

The thought crossed his mind of taking her a bouquet from his newly blooming flowerbeds, but he didn't see how he could sneak one out past Ma.

As the three old rips, Nelson, Eben, and Newt, left for Aunt Kay's Place after supper, dragging Pa along behind, Ma called after them, "Keep Russ out of trouble."

Newt ducked his head back in and said, "I'll make him wait in the car." (And neglected to add, "In a pig's ass!")

Ma wondered if Newt was serious. She vowed to stay up even if they didn't get in until 3 A.M. and aimed to smell Pa's breath even if she had to kiss him. It would never have occurred to her to check his underwear to see if there was a damp spot in the crotch. If she'd done that she'd have been in for a hell of a shock. She thought of Pa as an old man—a nasty old man who was after "*just one thing*" still, like all of them, but an *old* man nonetheless. She made damn sure he never got "*just one thing*" anymore. She didn't need him to support her, and was sure it was the other way around, in fact. She pushed him away if he touched her, especially in bed and snapped, "*Act your age.*" After a while he never bothered and wished he had his own room so he didn't have to go down to the can and jack off when he got horny after he went to bed.

Pa wondered why she was so damned possessive about him if she didn't want him herself. He sometimes had a notion to ask her. He savored what he imagined would be her reaction if he said, "*Em, just what the hell do you think acting my age is? Hell, Newt is almost ninety and still gets it off.*" But he never said it. He was fifty-six and not dead on either end by a long shot. He considered Ma dead on at least one end, and sometimes wished she were on the other so she couldn't run her mouth. The fact was, he simply didn't give a damn anymore and was happy anyhow.

Newt had warned Klondy he was bringing Ed over to her place. He'd always suspected that more had gone on between them than he'd ever learned. He wouldn't have been especially surprised at the special preparations she planned to make for meeting "her Eddie" again.

Newt and Klondy had had quite a discussion about "her Eddie."

"Has he ever had a drink? He only drank sarsaparilla when I knew him. Or water." She made a face. You couldn't sell water, except maybe out in the desert and she was sure there were damn few customers out there, even if most of them were bound to be good ones, provided they had money.

"Yeah," Newt said. "I was just getting him almost raised when he went back home and met Emma." He made a face and said "Emma" with an unmistakable negative emphasis. "She'd got herself knocked up by some slick-talking bastard and when he skipped out she picked Ed as the victim. I almost rescued him from even that, but his ma got in the way."

"Christ!" Klondy said. "I pity the poor son of a bitch."

"Amen," Newt said. "And you don't know the half of it. He probably hasn't had any nookie for years. I almost walked in on him when he was jacking off in the barn, so he's still got plenty active in his jeans."

Klondy laughed, but didn't mention what that brought to mind. She remembered a stock Jewish response which her ex, Kid Goldfine, used to use when he learned of problems that needed to be worked on; he'd say: "*It can be fixed.*"

She added the very private thought, "*And I'm just the little girl for the job. No man is going to make a woman scorned out of me, even if it takes me thirty-eight years to fix it.*"

"Is Ed still cute?"

Newt looked baffled. "Never occurred to me he was before!"

"He was a sweet kid."

"Well, I reckon he's sweet enough if you want to take it that way, but he's got a lot of miles on him. Not wrinkled though. It don't run in our family. You probably noticed how blindingly handsome I still am and like you said, I'm pushing a hundred."

Klondy knew something else that *did* run in the family, however. Big dongs. She preferred them. Most women did after they got a sample of what one could do for them when they were really hot. And most claimed to the contrary—even the honest ones, until they found out they hadn't known what they were talking about.

CHAPTER FORTY-TWO

She's Remembering Just Like Me

Klondy pulled her specs down off her forehead when she saw Newt walk in the front door of Kay's Place, which was to say: her joint. Nelson and Eben were with him. But Ed wasn't.

She thought, "Am I doomed to be a woman scorned again?" But she didn't really give a damn. She'd been curious—and no more—about how that sweet boy, Eddie, whom she'd known and liked, maybe even loved, so long ago had turned out after all those years. She felt she'd live happily ever after if she never saw him again.

The three took a table, and she came over to wait on them personally.

Looking them over critically she said to Nelson, "I suppose you dunked yerself in the crick again."

"That iss koe-rect," Nelson assured her. "Gittin' to be a regular habit. Used to be once a year unless I fell in."

"It won't kill you," she assured him.

Taking in all of them with a glance she asked, "What'll it be, and I don't mean you Eben, I got your Squirt in my pocket." She handed it to him with the cap off.

"Don't I get a glass?"

"And ice cubes too. I'll bring 'em when I serve these two."

Newt said, "Kentucky straight, and I've civilized my pard here," he indicated Nelson with a thumb, "and got him off Canned Heat so you can bring him the same."

Nelson grunted, looking over the girls all the while.

"Where are the two kids?" Klondy asked, meaning Bennie and Kid.

"Home."

"Anybody else home?" she asked Newt, pointedly.

"Ed's out talking with some neighbors about crops and his flowers. He's aces at growing flowers."

Klondy said, "Maybe I can get him to come over and work on my beds."

"Which ones?" Newt asked. "I didn't know it took more'n one."

"Watch yer mouth, old man. I've gone back to being a virgin. It saves a lot of trouble."

"My ass!" Eben snorted. "Yer just particular."

"Boils down to about the same thing," Klondy said.

Eben thought about that. "Damned if that ain't so," he agreed. "I'm sure as hell glad I ain't particular."

Klondy left and they all watched her swaying hips and switching buns. From the back she looked like a voluptuous young girl.

"Ummm!" Eben made just that one expressive sound. "How is that stuff really, Newt?"

"Like I told you, we only talk business back there. She ain't my type. Too much business and not enough romance. I suspect she was at least half serious about goin' back to bein' a virgin."

He thought, "*Man, that's one of the best lies I've got off in a long while.*"

Eben snorted. "Bull makes the grass grow green."

Just then Pa came in the door, looked around for them, and came over to their table. He glanced around and spotted Klondy behind the bar. If he hadn't rehearsed ahead of time so he could control himself, his jaw would have dropped. At that distance in a dimly illuminated barroom, she looked exactly like the eighteen-year-old canary he'd first seen up on a stage in Nome when he fell in love with her. A pleasant nostalgia overcame him, but he didn't imagine she'd even remember what he'd looked like after all these years. He could recall how she looked as though it were yesterday. He wondered why Newt hadn't told him who it was that owned the favorite local watering spot before Bennie's remark brought the subject up. Newt, who was soft-hearted in a lot of surprising cases, hadn't wanted to risk hurting him in case his suspicions about Nome had been right. The way Pa was, he might never have gone down to Kay's Place if he lived around there the rest of his life.

Pa realized that and thought, "*He was probably sparing my feelings—he must have known what a hell of a time I had getting over her.*" Then another surprising thought occurred: "*Hell, I should have married her—I'd have been a lot better off. Could have made my pile in Alaska like Newt and kept a gal like her in style.*"

If he had been assured by a good fairy at that moment, regarding what raising flowers was going to get him with this old flame, he wouldn't have believed it. On the other hand he wouldn't have dodged his duty. He'd matured a lot since Nome in some respects. That was one of them. Duty was his middle name. If it hadn't been, he'd have tossed Ma out years before. He suspected he may have helped make Ma ornery, but was stumped to know how. He'd have been completely unable to realize that Ma would have had a happier life if he'd allowed Klondy to complete the education she'd started on him in Nome. Ma's problem, like that of a lot of women in the Victorian age, was that she'd simply never had an orgasm. (And the fault lay with the clumsy men she'd known—in her case only two, but the world was full of dodo men.) As Klondy started over with their tray of drinks, Pa watched her and appreciated the suggestively swaying hips that the boys had admired going away a short while before. He got a boob shot to boot since her blouse was cut pretty low and showed quite a lot of Klondy. That brought him an instant recall of how the whole set looked, young and pert, with pretty pink nipples hypnotizing him as their platforms swayed freely. He felt himself getting a hard-on and thought, "*At least I'll get something out of this show without paying for it. Maybe I'll even come in my pants again. At least it doesn't give you a dose.*"

Her eyes met and locked with his. He wondered what she was thinking. Then he came to his senses and asked himself, "*What the hell do I think she's thinking? She's remembering just like me.*" He wondered if she thought he was the world's biggest dummy. When she gave him a friendly million-dollar smile he didn't think so. Or realized if she once had, he'd been forgiven.

"Hi Klondy," he said. "Long time."

"A real long time, Eddie," she said, setting the tray down and still holding her eyes directly on his. "You were my favorite shovel slinger, and besides you didn't go and get yourself shot."

Pa guffawed, and the memory led him to think, "*I'm surprised she didn't shoot me for being a dumb shit.*"

"What's that all about?" Eben asked.

Kay sat down. "It's a long story, isn't it, Eddie?"

"Try us," Eben suggested.

She told about what footage rights were on the beach at Nome, and how they worked together out there. But that's all she told them. Pa didn't give a damn what she told them. He was enjoying himself more than he had in years. He almost felt like he was nineteen years old again, back in the Palace Variety Hall. Klondy looked damn good, too. Hardly a wrinkle yet. "*She's got to be my age almost*," Pa thought. "*Must have found the Fountain of Youth*." His hard-on reminded him that he'd like to finish that earlier episode now that he was smart enough to do it right. "*I wonder if she's got a steady. With a farm and a place like this, a chicken like her probably has every stud for fifty miles around panting after her—would even if she was homely with all that property, come to think of it*."

Pa said, "I should have stayed up there in Nome like you two did."

"Don't say I didn't tell you," Newt put in, irritated all over again, remembering how Pa had stayed in Riverview like a damn fool and for all practical purposes ruined his life by becoming a foster father to some philandering son of a bitch's bastard kid. And that said nothing of being tied to his Ma's apron strings, which was what hamstrung his good sense.

"I know," Pa said. "I know. I used to think about it every day when I was out of work down in Waubonsee. I thought about shooting myself."

Nobody had anything to say to that. It had happened too recently and so many had thought of killing themselves, and too many had actually done it.

Klondy was sizing up Pa and thought, "I'm sure glad he didn't shoot himself. I got plans for Eddie boy." She remembered what he'd done for her with only his leg for her to get a scissors grip on, and could still see the handsome nineteen-year-old boy in his unlined face.

"I understand you're a whiz at growing flowers," she said to Pa.

"I make out. Always loved 'em and that helps."

Eben chipped in, "He took over my beds and they look better'n they ever did already and it's early in the year."

Suzie drifted past and stopped a minute at the table, looking over at Pa, and wondered who the new meat was. She was still a little nervous around that bunch, remembering Klondy's practical joke on her when she'd told her Nelson was the retired parish priest, and looking at the boss, pointed a thumb at Pa, and all-too-pokerfaced, asked, "He ain't a retired bishop is he?"

"He's not retired yet."

Then Klondy laughed and came clean. "Actually he's a real old friend."

Suzie looked him over good, and thought, "He ain't bad lookin' for an older guy, and he sure looks cleaner than the average. *I wonder if he's got money and would like to run off with a young piece of ass.*"

Pa eyed her appreciatively and grinned. If he'd known what she was thinking he'd have told himself, "*If I had money, I'd think that proposition over real good.*"

She moved on and prospected the boys at the bar. Pretty soon one of them put a quarter in the jukebox and took her out on the dance floor, rubbing hard against her. She didn't know him and wondered, "Is this guy just getting primed to go back with me, or is he jacking off on my tummy for a quarter?"

Klondy said, "Don't you ducks laugh, but I want Eddie to come back to the office after a while and look over my flower seeds and catalogs and the beds out back . . ."

Newt guffawed. "Shut up," she said. "I'm talking about the *flower beds*." To Pa she said, "You can't love flowers any more than I do. I reckon I got it from Ma. She always had some growing, even when we lived in some pretty awful dumps, like in Chicago when I was a kid. It's probably what kept her alive. When we finally moved up here she spent so much time in the flowers that Pa threatened to shoot her."

Pa nursed his beer while the others were back sampling the girls. Klondy was glad to see that her "Eddie" hadn't changed in that respect.

When Newt got back, Pa wasn't in sight. Newt said to himself, "Not like the Palace at Nome anyhow. He had sense enough to get her alone."

The other two came in one after the other and sat down. Nelson had another whiskey, Eben still had part of a Squirt in his glass and sipped the now-flat stuff without pleasure.

"Where the hell is Ed?" Nelson wondered out loud. "Did he finally decide to get his ashes hauled?"

Newt said, "I suspect he's back in conference with Klondy over them seed beds *and like that*." He kept a straight face, but grinned inside.

Nelson gave Newt a look and snidely asked, "You sure he ain't back dickering to buy the place *like you was*?"

"I don't think he's got the money," Newt said.

"Maybe it won't take money," Nelson said. "She looked like she was sweet on him."

Newt thought that over. "They was damn good friends once. A gal like her didn't have many real men friends in Nome. That counts for a lot with a gal."

Back in Klondy's office where she'd taken Pa, and carefully locked the door, she was saying, "My farm is only about two miles from yours through the woods as the crow flies."

"I'll have to start taking long walks and going hunting like I used to," Pa said.

Later he lit a Twenty Grand and inhaled part of it by accident and coughed.

"That makes your dong jump up and down," she said. "You think we can get it up again?"

Pa grinned. "We can try."

After an hour or so, when Pa joined the boys, he knew he'd get a lot of kidding and didn't give a damn.

Eben said, "Something about back there attracts your family. Newt must have been back there for an hour just like you. He said he was talking business."

Pa looked over Newt. "Prob'ly he was. He's too damn old for much else."

It was the beer talking in him.

Newt eyed him amiably. "My ass, kid," he said.

"Anyhow," Pa said, "I don't give a damn whether you believe it or not, but we was going through seed catalogs. And if you weren't all degenerates you'd know Klondy is a real lady, even if she does run a whorehouse. If you'd have looked out the window back there you'd have seen us moseying around her flower beds."

"Sure," Newt thought. "Sure we would. In a hog's ass. The family blood is finally coming out in you. It took long enough."

Eben said, "It's dark as the bottom of a well out back."

"Not with the floodlights on. Go look."

Pa whistled all the way home, stopping first at Newt's. The latter had noticed that Pa was tooling the Lincoln casually, and more expertly with a few beers in him, and noticed him savoring the night air blowing in the window, occasionally sniffing at it like a dog. Newt was dead sure he read the signs right.

Pa dropped off Newt and Nelson and didn't let up whistling going home. Eben, too, was satisfied he knew why.

CHAPTER FORTY-THREE

Nutty Uncle Bob

Lights were on in both the kitchen and front room when Pa parked the Lincoln.

"What the hell time is it?" Pa asked.

"Early. Not much after midnight, I'd guess." Eben said.

Pa grunted. He suspected Ma would meet him and do her snoopy duty to find out if he'd been drinking. Sure enough she met him just inside the door and tried to kiss him. He turned his head away so that the best she could manage was his cheek. He laughed, and decided to dig her.

"You horny or something? Once every twenty years or so ought to satisfy an *old* lady. I recall you attacked me a few years back." That time in one of her more weird moods she'd worried that her bottom might be growing shut from lack of traffic, but hadn't told him her game. He'd even obliged like a dutiful dummy.

His remark got a look from her that said, "*Not with Eben here*."

Eben didn't even notice. He knew almost any snide remark could come out of either one of them when it came to digging each other. He pitied them both. They reminded him of his own parents and he pretty much understood the problem. Nonetheless, he liked them both, especially Ma, whom he helped with the work around the house and with her vegetable garden. He quickly headed upstairs to get away from them. He wasn't certain he wasn't getting a little sweet on her. She was younger than he was and since she'd lost some weight from working outside had turned into a pretty damn good-looking woman again. She didn't have a wrinkle in her face or any gray in her hair.

"I'll see you two in the morning," he said over his shoulder. "I'm pooped."

"*And half stewed, too*," Ma thought.

She'd smelled the beer on Pa and figured he had a lot more than one judging from his frisky attitude.

She went to bed right with him, and snuggled up to him, though she usually stayed up for hours after him, "*messing around with her junk*," as Pa thought of it.

"Not tonight," Pa said. "I'm pooped like Eben and we got a big day ahead of us tomorrow."

"Doing what?" Ma asked. "You're always wanting me to *do it* when I don't want to."

Pa just grunted. He thought, "*Hell, she doesn't want to do it now, either. Just wants to be bossy and act like she still owns me. Well, she's got a hell of a surprise in store for her from now on.*" Then another thought occurred to him and he had to stifle a laugh. "*Suppose Klondy has the clap. In her business she might. Wouldn't it be a laugh if I gave Ma a dose? Maybe I ought to oblige her, but I doubt if I'll be able to get it up for a week after tonight.*"

Ma sulkily pulled away and lay very still on her back, staring up in the darkness for a long while. Like people do after living together for years, she sensed a great change in Pa and it troubled her. Her confidence that she could control him was slipping. What caused his sudden change? She was almost sure that he wasn't the type to have taken up with some whore, but you never knew. Some men got old and turned strange about things. That possibility really disturbed her, especially since he had turned down a chance for sex.

At the breakfast table Pa said to Bennie, "You and Kid been wanting to take off and camp in the woods. If you put in a good week, you can have off next weekend—take Friday too and have three days."

The boys hadn't mentioned Kid's lake to anyone, only that they wanted to go camping in the woods, but Pa was all for kids having fun. People grew up all too soon.

Ma said, "I may need him here."

Pa didn't even glance her direction when he said. "Well, you'll be out of luck. He deserves some time off."

Ma sulked, but had nothing to say. She had a few days to think up something to spoil the fun for Bennie and it would be something so necessary that Pa couldn't let him off.

Bennie read her mind and glared at her when she wasn't looking. If looks would have killed Ma would have gone up the flue right there.

He couldn't wait to tell Kid the good news about getting a couple of days off and remind him to make sure Newt let him off work too. He suspected that a few days off for Kid wouldn't be a problem. Newt would have given a boy three months off if the kid had some real fun in store doing it. Bennie envied Kid. He didn't really have a job since neither Newt nor Nelson were doing much besides making themselves a couple of boar's nests to spend their last years in. They worked when it suited them, and made sure that berry picking and fishing had equal priority.

Bennie went over through the woods right after supper that night and gave Kid the news.

"Great," Kid said.

"Should I bring my tent?" Bennie asked.

Kid thought about that. He knew they probably wouldn't need it since they could get over there in a half-day's good walk and there was shelter on the island. And that wasn't all. He was aces at keeping a secret and he thought he had one that would make Bennie's eyes pop out.

"Bring it so nobody will suspect we might be going where there's a shack to camp in. Bring all your stuff."

"You didn't tell me there was a shack out there. Who built it?"

"To tell you the truth I don't have any idea. It's always been there as long as I can remember. It's pretty damn old."

That really aroused Bennie's interest. Whenever he saw an old deserted farm, or just a house, he always wondered who had lived there and if any of them were still alive, and what they'd done for a living, and even speculated about what kind of people they were, or had been. He always hoped they'd been happy and that some terrible tragedy hadn't driven them away.

Because of his fascination with old houses, he vowed to learn who had built the shack on Kid's island—and their fate.

He had his stuff all packed the night before, including canned grub he'd been snitching all week on the sly so Ma wouldn't notice and give him a hard time. Kid brought most of the grub, taking the Model A to town shopping for it, with Newt's blessing. Bennie stashed his full knapsack, blanket, and .22 in the barn and slipped out long before sunup. Hank followed dutifully, staying close for a while till he found out which direction they were headed, then succumbed to a dog's duty to range afield. He was only seven or eight months old but he already knew his business in that respect *for sure*, from the sense dogs are born with.

Bennie half expected to hear Ma's voice yell after him and order him back to do some damn fool chore, but she was sound asleep. When she did wake up she went right to his bedroom, planning to give him his orders for the day whether Pa approved or not, and was irritated to find his bed empty. She rushed downstairs, thinking he might be in the bathroom and when she found he wasn't, grew even more irritated. A little later Pa woke up and heard her loudly banging pans and pots around on the stove. Bennie had confided to him that he was going to sneak out early, so Pa suspected what was bothering Ma. She was being noisy to wake him up so she could jaw at him as a scapegoat. He grinned and rolled over for another snooze.

"*To hell with her!*" he thought. "*But I don't mean that too literally. She might decide to like it just to be ornery.*"

Pa chuckled at his newfound cleverness. He thought of Klondy and said to himself, "*Jesus Christ! I never knew what loving was about all these years.*"

He dimly recognized that his feelings for her were still the same as in Nome with the added bonus of knowing what to do about it. "*What a woman!*" he thought as he dozed off.

Bennie knew the names of a few of the plants and birds he saw while he and Kid hiked. He wanted to know the name of everything and what purpose it served. Kid knew. He'd spent most of his free hours during his whole life in these woods and could read the forest and fields like a familiar book. Now he read that book to Bennie. Their progress was a nature walk, since Kid didn't mind talking as they weren't hunting. Hunting was different since a voice warned animals that someone was coming. It wasn't probable they'd have seen any of the wary forest animals anyhow, unless they made a careful upwind stalk. The whole life of little wild things was one of either hunting or being hunted. Kid knew they'd see enough wild critters when they reached his lake, where he planned to make a special effort to teach Bennie how to move silently upwind in the woods like a wild creature, with eyes and ears (and in his own case even his nose) always alert to avoid missing anything.

The country they traversed first was largely marsh or big fields that had been created by clear cutting the former pine woods. What they saw most of were red-tailed hawks and sparrow hawks, but only from a distance. Hawks had long ago learned that men carry guns that can kill from a long ways off. They'd also learned that some people used everything that moved in the woods for target practice.

"Lots of hawks," Kid said. "They live off mice and snakes and grasshoppers. The only time sparrow hawks go after sparrows is when there isn't anything easier to catch."

Bennie was glad to learn that hawks cut down the snake population.

"Any rattlers in here I ought to be watching out for?" Bennie asked.

"Too far north," Kid said. "Lots down in the Dells where they have winter shelter. No place to hole up here."

"Thank God for small favors."

One thing this unfamiliar country had in common with the woods he'd known was the wonderful spicy smell. He was never able to define exactly what it consisted of, probably a combination of living bloom and dead mast underfoot. He knew everything was part of a cycle and went back to earth to have a rebirth someday, maybe as something else.

He wondered if he might be part of a tree in some future century. He thought, "*Worse fates than that. They live a long while and don't have to go to school. Besides I'd have lots of company with birds and little animals living in me. Maybe trees have souls and I'd be the whole tree, able to think and everything.*"

He glanced around and wondered if some of the trees they were passing might be watching them. It was a happy thought. But for now he satisfied himself with just inhaling great breaths of woods smell. He noticed Kid doing the same thing and wondered if it was unconscious.

Kid said, "Lots of mink out here in the marshes. We'll trap them next winter when they're prime. They bring good money. Muskrats sell too, but they don't bring as much."

Bennie could identify the calls of redwing blackbirds, the predominant bird sound as they progressed. They must be common over a large range of country, he reasoned. They'd been around Wahbonsee, even down along the noisy railroad tracks by the creeks, and around Blackhawk, especially out by Three-Mile Creek. He knew they preferred to hang around in the reeds near water. He'd loved their cheery whistling call from the first time he'd ever heard it.

Kid stopped and pointed. "Can you make out a bird over there on the ground?"

Bennie focused his eyes and searched where Kid was pointing. "Look for what looks like a reed. It's a bittern. We must have sneaked up on him. When they think you might see 'em they turn toward you and scrooch all up and point their head up so they look like the reeds around them. They even sway in the breeze."

"I don't see a thing," Bennie said.

"We'll make him scoot," Kid said, and headed that direction. When they got closer the bird took off.

"I'll be damned!" Bennie said. "How did you ever see him to begin with?"

Kid shrugged. "You'll get so you see everything if you spend enough time out here."

Bennie sure aimed to do that. He loved every step of their progress. He'd never seen so many bluebirds, and other birds he'd never seen before were all around, flying or hidden and calling.

Kid pointed out into an open pool and said, "That's a coot. Watch him. Pretty soon you won't see him."

Sure enough, his butt came up and head went in the water and it was so fast it almost looked like he disappeared right before their eyes. "On the bottom by now," Kid said.

"Jesus," Bennie sighed, "I'll never learn all this stuff."

"Sure you will. It just takes a few years."

That suited Bennie just fine. He never wanted to leave this place. He'd been born here, jerked away by economics (and Ma), and had found his home again.

After a few hours of sweaty progress, Kid said, "Gettin' pretty near."

Bennie heard a call that he'd learned on their progress this far and thought he'd show Kid he remembered the sound: "oong-Ke-chunk." He said, "A bittern, right?"

Before Kid could answer, the sound turned to what sounded like someone pounding something into the muddy ground.

"Is someone out here?" Bennie asked. "Is that your secret?"

Kid grinned. "No and yes. That wasn't a bittern you heard, and someone may be out here imitating a bittern."

He cupped his hands to his mouth and exactly imitated both sounds Bennie had just heard. "Best to give the secret password," Kid said, conspiratorially. "Might get a load of buckshot up our kazoo if we don't."

"*Holy Christ!*" Bennie thought. "*He didn't tell me this was going to be like Robin Hood and his Merry Men.*"

Bennie got his first glimpses of open water through the aspen and birch trees. Then a human figure emerged from a clump of little trees, and sure enough it was holding a double-barrel shotgun. He was still several yards away, a man wearing the standard woods uniform of bib overalls and blue workshirt. Lank grey hair protruded in spikes from the sides of an old felt hat.

"Who the hell is that?" Bennie asked in a low voice.

"You'll find out. Don't ask too many questions around here at first. I told 'em we were coming."

Bennie wondered how. "*Maybe telepathy*." He didn't know Kid meant he'd told them several weeks before in order to get a stamp of approval. It had finally come, which was why Kid had taken so long about taking Bennie out here, aside from the matter of time off.

"How," Kid said, raising his hand to the shotgun wielder like a Hollywood Indian.

"How," the other said, but didn't release his two-hand grip on the shotgun.

"This is Bennie," Kid said.

The man looked him over from dark blue eyes, set deeply under overhanging brows. He needed a shave pretty bad, but wasn't actually wearing a beard.

Bennie asked himself, "*Where have I seen this guy before, or someone that looks a lot like him?*" But he couldn't place him. "*Maybe the movies. He sure has the looks to be a character actor in a Western.*"

Finally, as though seeing something he liked, or at least could tolerate, the other shifted his shotgun into the crook of his left arm and offered Bennie a hand to shake.

He said just about the last thing Bennie expected to hear. "I'm your *nutty* Uncle Bob."

Bennie's mouth dropped open. His nutty uncle laughed.

Finally Bennie joined him since he couldn't see much else to do.

Bob's handshake was like a vice. "*Damn good thing I've been milking cows or I wouldn't survive this.*" Bennie was sure Bob didn't even know he was bearing down though—he just didn't know how strong he was.

Bob knelt down and scratched Hank's ears. The pup took to him at once and sat down wagging his tail, looking up at Bob with soulful eyes. Bennie recalled he'd heard somewhere that the simple-minded got along with all animals. Only Bob didn't act simple-minded. He got up in a swift fluid motion without pushing his hands on his knees to help as most people his age had to. He said, "C'mon," and set off down a path. "Annette will have something in the pot for us." Bennie and Kid had to trot to keep up with Bob's long strides.

"*So that's Kid's secret. It's a hell of a neat secret if you ask me.*"

Bob led the way to the lakeshore and pushed aside some bushes that concealed a canoe.

"Hop in," Bob said, "and sit down in the middle. I'll hold her steady. Yer dog can swim after us."

Hank didn't hesitate to take to the water and swim beside them.

Bennie could see they were headed for an island that was heavily overgrown with brush and trees.

His *nutty* uncle paddled skillfully and after a short haul of maybe a hundred yards grounded the canoe in the shallows and hopped out, steadying it for them to debark. After they were out he pulled it up out of sight into the brush, then set off over a small knoll and into a depression where a teepee was pitched next to a small board shack.

"Home," Bob announced. "It beats the nuthouse."

Hank followed, still soaking wet, and performed his doggy duty by shaking himself off on them. Bob laughed.

Bennie had a pretty strong idea by now that Bob didn't belong in the nuthouse. He belonged here. He recalled how the whole family had always referred to his Aunt Mary as crazy like a fox. She'd married that Greek restaurant owner hadn't she (?)—and was weathering the Depression on her own secure island back in Waubonsee.

"Annette!" Bob yelled. "Where the hell are you?"

He pointed to a pot hanging over the fire and added, "She can't be far or she'd maybe let the stew burn. That ain't her style. Too hard to haul grub out here. And we don't waste anything, either."

Annette came out of the teepee. "Taking a snooze," she said. "I guess this is Bennie." She was obviously at least part Indian, Bennie judged from the black eyes from which he got a direct look, eyes just like Kid's. She offered her hand and her grip was almost as firm as Bob's.

Bennie thought, "*They don't make 'em like this in towns, that's for sure.*"

Kid said, "This is my Aunt Annette, Ma's sister."

Another shocker for Bennie. And she was a looker. If Kid's ma looked like her sister, he could see why the bucks were sniffing around all the time while her husband was in the pen.

"Squat," she invited. "I'll get some bowls and we can dig into that stew."

That reminded Bennie that he hadn't eaten anything but a few berries they'd picked on bushes they passed on the way out and that his backbone was getting pretty familiar with his belly button.

Bob and Kid sat on the grass cross-legged and Bennie imitated them. Annette served them and then dished up a bowl for herself. She'd set out a plate of bread, obviously homemade. Bennie dug in like the others, eating the bread in big bites as he downed the stew. It was all delicious. He thought, "*I don't know much about Annette yet, but if she can't do anything but cook she sure passes the test.*"

Hank moved from one to the other to find out whether he'd be able to bum some food. Annette dished him up a bowl of the stew to which Bob made no comment despite mentioning earlier that they didn't waste anything. He just grinned. Obviously feeding a pup didn't register as wasting something in his mind. Annette broke up a couple of pieces of bread and put them into the bowl too. Hank dived into that, front feet spread as though to keep away anything that might crowd in to swipe his chow, but wagged his tail all the while.

Finished, Bennie reached for the makin's and wondered if he'd get coffee, or whether they rationed it as a scarce luxury out there. The graniteware coffee pot sitting in the coals was so big he hadn't been sure that's what it was, until he smelled the coffee cooking inside.

Annette answered his question by producing tin cups from inside the shack. She even poured for them. A funny thought ran through his mind, "*That business about Indian women waiting on their men hand and foot was no hay, I guess. Not only that, but she's a real looker. I sure wouldn't kick her out of bed. She can't be any older'n Kate. I'll bet I could give her jollies with the best of 'em.*" He wondered if lusting at your uncle's private stock was coming close to some kind of sin.

"*Up sin,*" he told himself, "*I'm already in Heaven.*"

He rolled a cigarette that would have done credit to one of Kid's big Bull

Durham *turds* and thought to offer Annette the makin's. She gratefully accepted them. Bennie noticed Bob smoked a pipe. He wondered what Bob would do with one of Newt's private stock of quality cigars. Maybe what Nelson did. He also wondered if he was going to be allowed to let Newt in on the secret of Uncle Bob. Time would tell.

After they finished their smokes, Bob said, "I'm going to take a leetle nap."

He first rolled up the sides of the teepee then slipped inside. Annette cleared up the dirty dishes to take down to the water and wash them. Bennie said, "I'll help," and went along. That got a surprised, then a grateful look from her. He followed behind and watched the sway of her ample hips in her housedress and ogled her sturdy brown well-formed legs and felt the beginning of a hard-on. It didn't bother him. By now he knew enough about women that he didn't give a damn if she noticed a big rail sticking out in his pants. Most of 'em were flattered if they noticed—at least the ones that recognized what it was, and it sure gave the honest ones hot pants to know they'd excited a man that much. The ones like that were the only ones worth spending time with. He knew that Kate had been aroused by a bulge in his pants because she told him, and after that he got a rail around her every time after the first time he'd had her. He sure as hell wished she were here now.

"Let me show you around," Kid said, when they came back from washing dishes.

He led the way into the shack. It had two double bunks along opposite walls. "We'll sleep in here if it rains." Hank thoroughly inspected the inside, sniffing around all the walls and memorizing the place. Bennie knew dogs and cats needed just one circuit of a place to indelibly map it in their heads.

The rest of the furnishings consisted of a small pot-bellied stove with a cooking space on top, a table, four chairs, a cupboard, and a place to hang clothes on an iron pipe. One wall had shelves that obviously served as a pantry. It was well stocked, and a couple of bulging sacks on the floor probably held potatoes and onions.

Outside was a chicken yard and small coops on the ground. It was closely fenced with chicken wire all around, including on top. Noticing Bennie's questioning look at this, Kid said, "Keeps out varmints. Foxes and skunks mostly. But hawks too. The skunks go for the eggs, and the foxes go for both. We got a few coyotes, too, and even have a wolf snooping around sometimes. They're pretty scarce anymore. A twenty-buck bounty on them has pretty well wiped them out."

"Waddya think?" Kid asked.

Bennie grinned. "I think I'll do like Uncle Bob and catch some shut-eye. Wake me up for supper."

"If I'm awake," Kid said. "If I'm awake."

Bennie had said to himself, "*Paradise for sure*," over a number of things since coming back *Up North*, but this was the best yet, the thought passing dreamily through his mind just before he dropped into a sound sleep.

He planned to spend as much time here as he could manage. Maybe if Ma finally ran him out he'd come out here and live like a true Woodsie.

After supper that evening Bob made a separate fire and tossed green grass on it occasionally to make a smudge to keep off mosquitos. It worked too.

He explained, "I like to sit around and look at a campfire, but I don't care much about swatting mosquitoes while I do it."

Bennie loved staring into the flames of an open fire. It was good for daydreaming. He wondered what a *nut* dreamed about looking into a fire, assuming Bob was one. He had to admit Bob wasn't like any other person he'd met. Newt came closest. His Uncle Johnny down at Country Grandma's was patterned out of the same kind of cloth, too. But Bob led the pack.

After a while an almost full moon rose across the water, forecasting its arrival for ten or fifteen minutes before with a growing luminosity in the eastern sky. Then one bright eye peeked over the horizon and turned the trees on the far shore into lace for a few minutes until it sailed above them.

The air cooled rapidly here on the lake as soon as the sun set. Bennie savored that and the mysterious smell of it, a blending of everything that grew there whether alive or dead. He would learn that past seasons leavings were sometimes more fragrant than new blooms. He rolled another weed, passed around the makings, then lit his and savored that first drag like a true addict. Then he put his hand on Hank's head where the pup was sprawled next to him snoozing. Hank sighed.

"Yeah," Bennie said. "I know what you mean, Hank."

A whippoorwill called in the distance. Somewhere an owl hooted. After a few minutes of silence he was startled by a deep throated baying that brought Hank to his feet, hair standing up on his back. He growled and conned the woods across the lake. It was the wildest sound Bennie had ever heard and raised the hair on the back of his neck. At first he'd thought some big dog was ranging the woods, then he knew what it had to be. *A wolf.*

The woods grew instantly quiet. Little animals froze in place or quickly scooted for their burrows. Night birds cruising the area changed course to definitely locate the source of the sound so they could do their symbiotic duty to potential prey, and cry alarm directly above the big predator, like a crow lookout.

"Wolf," Bob said. "Keep the pup here or he might get et."

It didn't look to Bennie like that was going to be a problem. Hank may have had a wolf foster mama, but he had sense enough to read trouble with the best of them. He actually leaned against Bennie—probably, Bennie figured, to absorb a little courage—and trembled slightly. Maybe someday he'd be big enough to challenge a wolf, but that day wasn't here yet. Hank was only about half-grown at best.

The wolf moved away, and they heard him bay one more time from the top of a far knoll.

"Howling at the moon. Maybe telling his old lady where he is," Bob guessed.

Bennie wanted to ask how he knew it was a male, but thought he hadn't better. He'd bet Bob knew, though, and Kid, too.

When he finally lay down and pulled a blanket over him, Hank snuggled with his back next to him, sighed softly, and was soon in a deep sleep. The last thing Bennie heard before he corked off was the whippoorwill. If Hank barked alarm at some time during the night, he was too dead to the world to hear him. The next thing he knew was opening his eyes to see first light in the east across the lake. He looked around for the pup and saw him in the lake having a morning dip. His splashing was probably what had awakened him.

Everyone else was still sawing wood. At least he knew Kid was, because he wasn't over a few feet away. Bob and Annette had gone into the tent to sleep and neither was in sight yet.

"*Hank's got the right idea,*" he thought. "*I'll slip around the island out of sight and take a dip myself.*"

The water was cold and woke him up thoroughly. He treaded water, sunk up to his chin, which obviously worried Hank, who swam around him and explored to see where the rest of him had gone. Bennie swam to shallow water, waded out, and Hank checked him over when he got on the bank to make sure his best buddy was all there.

Bennie stood straight, inhaling deeply of the woods smell and listening to the early birds singing out their territorial songs. Then another wonderful smell mingled with the woods odors. The mouth-watering odor of fresh coffee. Also bacon frying. That reminded him he was hungry as that wolf had probably been.

He was dry enough to slip back into his clothes, which he did quickly, then headed back to camp.

Hank, beside him, obviously felt the same way he did about the wilds. It showed in his springy trot, head up, eyes shining, tail whipping, looking occasionally at the boss to see that he approved or if he wanted something—that is, when he didn't have to investigate some more interesting thing on the ground or off somewhere in the surrounding woods.

That much exposure to his family seemed to fortify Kid for taking Bennie over to see his mother. He's said it was a crummy place that almost caused a truant officer to faint, but from Kid's clean appearance all the time and what he'd said about his mother, Bennie doubted it. Poor maybe, but not crummy.

They drove over in the Model A. The cabin was set back in the woods, just like their old place, and reached by a rutted dirt road through a birch grove.

"Toot the horn," Kid said, so Ma knows nobody is trying to sneak in and steal something. "Otherwise you might get a load of birdshot out of old Faithful."

He did as he was told, and a woman who looked a lot like her sister came out onto the porch that ran the full length of a cluttered front porch.

"No dog?" Bennie asked.

"Injuns eat them, haven't you heard?" He snorted. "Can't afford to feed one right all the time, so Ma says we can't keep one. I told her now that I got a job we should get one, but she makes me put the money in a bank account."

Bennie was shocked to hear that. He hadn't thought they were so poor.

"This is Bennie," Kid said.

Kid's mother looked Bennie over from head to foot. "I heard a lot about you," she said.

He liked her honest, direct look and the house dress she wore was sparkling clean. Her raven black hair was fixed in two long braids down her back.

"Good, I hope," Bennie said, because it was the thing to say. He was actually embarrassed and searching for words.

She took his hand and shook it. "Mostly," she said and let it hang. "Come on in and I'll fix you two something to eat. If you're like Sylvester you're always hungry."

She led the way. Kid nudged Bennie and said in a low voice, "Don't you start calling me Sylvester."

The cabin was fragrant with the smell of herbs used for cooking, and wild flowers, which were set in fruit jars wherever there was room for them. A huge hook rug in progress was thrown across a chair. They had entered by a long front room that ran across the entire front of the cabin. One end was open into the kitchen that extended to the back of the cabin, with a row of windows above the sink. A hand pump was at one side of the sink.

"You two flop out here and I'll warm up the stew. I've got fresh bread, too."

This didn't sound like starvation to Bennie, and he wondered how it had been before Newt hired Kid. Probably slim pickings a lot of the time.

The furniture was all old wood stuff, nothing overstuffed, but it was solid and had what he figured were homemade cushions on the chairs, covered in cretonne, and probably with cheap cotton batting inside. They were stitched, he noticed, just like the ones Ma made, to keep the cotton from balling up.

After they put down a couple of bowls of her stew, which was delicious, Kid's Ma said, "You're welcome over here anytime. I don't see many people with Circling Hawk gone. He'll be home soon. He'll be glad to see you, too. We'll have a little home-coming party when he gets back and I want you to be sure to come."

Bennie wondered who else would be coming. Some of the men who'd been trying to get her into bed with the Chief gone? Their wives? Pretty little Indian girls? His Nutty Uncle Bob. He'd have to ask Kid.

"I'll be here with bells on," Bennie said. "And you've got to come over and meet Ma and Pa."

She frowned slightly, and he wondered if Kid had told her yet that Ma was half Sioux. She probably wasn't welcome in the homes of many whites.

He said, "Did Kid tell you Ma is Sioux? Her mother is Sitting Bull's niece."

She brightened at that, and looked at Kid reprovingly. "He didn't tell me." Her look clearly inquired why he hadn't.

Kid said, "It slipped my mind."

She said, "Don't let too much like that slip your mind. It could be important." And to Bennie, "I'll be glad to drop by and bring your Ma over here, if you think you should."

"I'll do that," Bennie said. "Probably pretty soon. And she'll want to come to the homecoming, too. So will Uncle Newt, if you don't mind an old paleface reprobate."

"Kid told me about him. I'd like to meet him."

CHAPTER FORTY-FOUR

Why Didn't You Do That to Me Before?

– Ma –

Eben and Ma often worked together in Ma's precious garden. They both had green thumbs. Neither seemed to be bothered by the sun while they hoed or planted or watered, working side by side like troopers, sweating and grunting. As a result the table always had fresh vegetables, and Bennie loved his vegetables, especially tomatoes. But even green beans, which he'd hated all his life were delicious when they came right out of the garden, and there was nothing like fresh peas shucked out of the pod just before Ma started supper. Shelling the peas was often his job. He'd never exactly liked cucumbers, but now Ma soaked them in vinegar as a salad and he even got a taste for them.

After his trip with Kid, Bennie returned to the farm routine, but always in the back of his mind was the thought of slipping away to that hideout again. He didn't tell Pa that his Nutty Brother Bob was living out there although Bob hadn't said whether he should or not.

In fact Bennie didn't say much at all except that he liked camping in the woods. Ma didn't even get on his back for sneaking off early and evading her killjoy effort to rob him of pleasure. Bennie considered that a little odd. He'd been a Ma watcher all his life, since he'd been condemned to spend so many years living alone with her, and was the first to notice a change in her. She often whistled as she worked, something she hadn't done since they lived alone in Wahbonsee and Pa was gone so much.

Now Bennie would watch Ma and make sure she didn't know he was doing it, which wasn't easy since her Indian blood seemed to warn her when someone might be observing her closely, or staring at her from behind. Bennie also noticed she smiled sometimes, seemingly over nothing.

Bennie thought, "I wonder what the hell bit her all of a sudden."

If he'd known, he'd have laughed. *Pa had bit her*. Literally, too.

When Ma kept pestering him to jump her, he'd decided to oblige, not that she had any sexual attraction for him after years of abusing him about sex and everything else. But when she snuggled up to him in bed as she'd started doing every night after he'd first been out with Klondy, he turned over and gave her the business. And he'd learned how to do it from Kate and Grace and Klondy. He wasn't the clumsy oaf that had turned Ma into a sexual dud in the first place. He'd become a pretty fair lover without realizing it.

So he took his time. He now knew exactly what keys to touch and how to caress them to get music out of the old piano. Ma didn't know what was happening. He got her off the first time by working her clitoris. At first it was flat as a pancake and she didn't respond. But biology overcame a lifetime of improper conditioning.

Pa was less reluctant to take his time than he might have been, since he had doubts he'd be able to get a hard-on with a sexless woman after knowing what a truly responsive one should be like. He wanted to give himself plenty of time. The gals who'd taught him in the past couple of years had been responsive if nothing else. Good-looking too. Ma was still good-looking as far as that went. She almost looked like the gal Pa had first taken into the bushes years before in Riverview.

Ma began to respond and feel a sensation she hadn't felt since Prince Charming had knocked her up with Lillian years before. She asked a question that actually startled Pa.

"What are you doing to me?"

Pa was also startled to realize that she was lubricating. She'd always been dry as a bone and he'd had to force his way in. (Not the least of the reasons that she always described sex like "sawing wood." Or why women of Ma's generation called sex "a woman's painful duty.")

She was spasmodically lunging to his ministrations and breathing in hard, short breaths. By then she didn't give a damn what was happening to her.

In a few minutes she had her first real orgasm, and it was a dilly. Pa got excited when he realized what he'd done and jumped her bones, taking it easy and waiting till he felt her respond. He had also learned to kiss as something more than the usual dead mackerel that American women were used to in their clumsy lovers. That didn't hurt a thing.

What Ma did as he entered her came naturally to all women, Pa supposed, although he wasn't great at introspection. She came to meet him with lunging hips and he knew he was going to get her off that way too.

When they separated and lay getting back their breath, Ma asked a stupid question, or at least he thought it was a stupid question. "Why didn't you do that to me before?"

That was a stumper. If he'd known how, it was probable that the lives of a lot of people would have been happier, certainly his and Bennie's and undoubtedly Roy's and Lillian's, to say nothing of Ma's.

But that wasn't why Ma smiled often and whistled as she worked. The war between her and Pa had gone on too many years to end in an embrace. Pa had discovered a perverse streak in himself, and it pleased him. He'd taken to disappearing in the woods on long Sunday walks. Uncle Newt knew where he went. Over to Klondy's farm. And he always came back fairly fagged out from something besides walking. As a result he wasn't a damned bit interested in Ma and in fact wished he'd never shown her what the hell it was all about. She'd got downright demanding.

Perversely he'd worm out of his "painful duty" by saying, "*You always said I was too old for that. Well, I am. Besides I think we both are*."

That got a sullen silence. But a transformation was taking place that explained why Bennie had caught Ma again whistling and smiling to herself. Pa had started it. She was horny a lot of the time and for the first time in her life. It was a pleasant sensation, but frustrating, and Ma wasn't one to be frustrated for long without doing something about it.

One day when she thought everyone was out of the house Eben came in quietly, planning to catch a little nap and when he didn't find Ma in the kitchen, assumed she was also taking a nap, which she sometimes did in the afternoon. He was extra quiet as he slipped up the stairs to his room so as not to disturb her. A strange noise was coming from Ma and Pa's bedroom, and he wondered if Hank had got locked in there. He was about to open the door and noticed it was already open just a crack and couldn't help but peek in.

Eben wasn't the kind to get startled, but what he saw startled him. Ma was naked on the bed, playing with herself. She'd finally figured out what most girls learned young. In her case she reasoned that if a man's finger could do it, so could hers.

Now, as Eben watched, he realized that she didn't know that anyone else was alive, her eyes fixed, staring at the ceiling, hips lunging to meet an imaginary lover, lips parted, breathing heavily, her hand moving faster and faster, the other hand caressing her nipples, until finally with one last great lunge and a little cry, she crossed her legs, spasmodically ducked her head down on her breasts, and finally subsided, breathing heavily.

Eben had watched without guilt, fascinated, aroused by his identification with her passion and the sight of her body, with its ample breasts, curving hips and slim, well-formed legs that met where her hand had been buried in lush black hair. He slipped away as quietly as he'd come, but his dong had come up hard as iron at the sight and even started lubricating. He hadn't seen Ma as a woman to love before then, but he'd had a sudden awakening. It shook him so deeply he had to go out into a stall in the barn and jack off, feverishly remembering the scene he'd just watched.

The next time they worked together in the garden he kept wondering what it would be like to touch her. And to touch her with no clothes on, better yet.

Ma had got a different feeling about him as well. She'd liked him a lot since he was considerate and not like other men had been around her. He wasn't exactly good-looking, and he wasn't a big strapping man, but he wasn't homely either. Now he came into her sights since she had learned what a man could do for her. Gradually she formed an idea about him and it went back to the days when she'd accidentally attracted Prince Charming when she worked for the Browns. She hadn't intended then to expose herself naked in a hall to the good Prince, but it had happened and he'd done what comes naturally for men. She knew it was what had attracted him to her.

Ma tried to figure out how she could manage to attract Eben that way without being too obvious. She thought, "*If I can't get one man, I'll get another. I don't need Russ and don't really like him anymore.*"

She'd suffered from her years long war with Pa, just as he had with her. She wanted a man, but not *that* man. Having an orgasm had changed her completely. Now she knew what her sisters had been talking about—not Mary, of course, but certainly *Lizzy* and the younger ones. She'd always thought they were simply immoral. Now she told herself, "*Boy did I ever have something to learn.*"

She supposed she could go through life masturbating, since nothing came more naturally after Pa had shown her where the little man in the rowboat was located, and it relieved her tension for a while, but she wanted more than that.

She laid her plans carefully. First she made damn sure that Bennie drove the Lincoln when the men went over to the tavern on Saturday night.

She told him, "Your Pa has been getting tanked up and I'm afraid he'll kill himself driving home."

It made sense to Bennie. Besides, Newt had described a new young gal over there. "A blond. A real looker. And nice, too. You should see her cans."

Bennie had been unsuccessfully looking around for a woman to fill in where Kate and Grace had fitted into his life just before he'd left Blackhawk. He was damn hard up for the real thing.

Ma's next move was to get Eben to stay home, which wasn't too hard, since she needed help with canning. When she heard the Lincoln pull out, she thought, "*I've got at least six hours. They won't be back until midnight.*"

Ma didn't know how Eben felt about her. She might have suspected if she knew he'd peeped in and discovered the new Ma. It would have made her more confident of the outcome of her plan.

After they finished with the canning, she said, "I'm going to take a bath."

That brought a picture to Eben's mind of watching her.

He settled down in the parlor with a magazine and tried not to think about it. That didn't work. Especially when Ma came downstairs and down the hall of which he had a plain view and let her robe flap open, seemingly by accident, which gave him a full view of her body.

His jaw must have dropped.

Ma said, "Oops," and added, "I'm sure you've seen a woman before."

She actually laughed at the look on Eben's face. An elf she hadn't suspected in her spoke next for her. "Wanna wash my back?" she asked.

Eben didn't need an elf to reply to that one. "Hell yes!" he said and came down the hall into the bathroom with her.

They had hours in bed before anyone came home, and Eben didn't go to his own room until they heard the Lincoln pull into the yard.

That was why Ma was smiling and whistling those days.

It was also why she didn't give a damn when Pa asked one day out of a clear blue sky:

"How would you like to get a divorce, Em? You can have the damned farm. Eben and Bennie can run this place."

Ma had her suspicions why Pa was so willing to let go of the first security he'd ever had, and was on the verge of mouthing off about it, then thought better of it.

All she said was, "You file and pay for it."

It came as a shock to Bennie, but after thinking it over it made sense.

The night Ma had put the make on Eben the first time, Bennie had watched Pa and Klondy down at her tavern and was smart enough to realize what was going on there.

He wasn't too interested in that though, being busy "'scoping" out the new blond with the big cans. Her name was Annie.

In bed she'd said, "You really know what you're doing. How old are you? Not over eighteen, I'd guess."

He didn't want her to treat him like a kid, and let it go at that. He said, "You're a pretty good guesser. How old are you?"

"Gentlemen never ask a woman that."

"I'm not a gentleman. In fact my Ma thinks I'm a degenerate."

She laughed. "So—I'm nineteen. And don't ask me how a nice girl like me got in a business like this."

"I wasn't aiming to. I was going to ask if you'd like to come out to the farm for dinner some Sunday."

She looked startled. "Whores don't visit around the neighborhood. Your ma would have a fit."

"What she don't know won't hurt her. I'll tell her you're the new first-grade schoolteacher from town. She almost never goes to town, and if she did she wouldn't check up on that."

Annie guffawed and said, "You're a scream. Besides you're nice. You got me hot as quick as any man I've ever been with. In fact most of them don't move me at all—it's just a job."

She looked at him seriously.

"So?" he asked.

"I'm game if you are. What about your pa?"

"He's probably getting it off with Klondy right now. They're old friends from Nome."

He told Kid about it and Kid warned him, "You'll get the clap." Then added, "But in her case it might be worth it. Mind if I try her out?"

Bennie laughed. "You're on your own. I'm not in love with her."

But he wondered if he wasn't at least a little bit. He wondered if a man wasn't in love with every woman he got it off with—a little bit.

CHAPTER FORTY-FIVE

Poor, Motherless Waif

– *Rose* –

Rose was fourteen and felt like she'd lived forever. Until Bennie and his family entered her life, she'd thought of simply ending it all, but was afraid to. She often wondered how she'd do it, and concluded the best way might be to put a hay rope around her neck and jump from the loft in the barn.

Her family had broken up after her mother died in agony, of cancer, and her father, unable to bear it, committed suicide. She'd eventually become a ward of the County. Some of the homes she was sent to were good and some bad. After a while they got jumbled in her head and she no longer tried to separate them. She hated being poor, hated being alone and passed around with no one to love.

Her life with Prune Face and Elephant Ears was just another sad episode in an endless tragedy. It was the worst of them all. There was Felice always standing over her, a prune with her mouth constantly pursed like she'd been sucking on a lemon, and Elephant Ears, who looked at her out of his little eyes in a way that made her afraid. That was worst of all. She'd never minded hard work, but there were times when she understood exactly how her pa had felt, as if inside she was irrevocably broken, a vital piece cut out and lost.

In school she sometimes fell asleep at recess or during lunch hour, when the rest of the kids were playing in the yard, and it was always Ella Mae, who was in her class, who shook her awake when the bell sounded.

"Don't they let you sleep at home?" Ella Mae asked one day.

Rose swallowed hard, remembering how she'd been up before dawn to start the wash, and how she'd have to finish what was left before she could have any supper.

She said, "I don't have a home. It's more like a jail."

It all came out—little cruelties, the loneliness, and how she'd thought more than once about stringing a rope from a beam in the barn and going to join Ma and Pa.

Ella Mae was shocked. "Don't ever think like that. Everything passes."

Rose couldn't hold back the tears. "When?"

"When God says."

"I don't believe in God anymore."

Ella Mae put her arms around her unhappy little friend. "Sure you do. You just forgot. Why'n't you walk home with me and Rufus when school's out?"

At that small gesture, Rose sobbed again, but she bobbed her head. "I'd like to."

Ella's brother, Rufus, was the best athlete in the school and a good student like his sister. In time Rose learned why he wasn't allowed to play in regular football games with other schools, but only in practice. Rufus was black. If it hurt—and it must have—he never showed it. *He knew his place.*

Winnebago wasn't the problem, the whole team liked and respected him; it was the other towns' teams that refused to play against a "nigger." Privately, Rose always thought the real problem wasn't his color but the fact that Rufus was so good that if he played the other teams would lose.

The Browns had lived in Chicago until the Depression began. They had managed to save something out of their little income, and had enough to move to Winnebago when things got hard. Mr. Brown's name was Morris, and everybody called him Morrie, and the sign on his shop said, "Morrie's Shoe and Boot Repair."

Everyone liked him and said, "Morrie knows his place; the whole bunch do," which meant that he lived cheerfully with the fact that local businessmen never invited him to their business meetings over lunch, and that Mrs. Brown, whose name was Rachel, but whom everybody called Ma, lived with the fact that she hadn't a single friend in town.

Ma Brown took one look at the pale, thin little girl with the hungry eyes and decided then and there that some white people didn't deserve to have kids. She mothered Rose with all the warmth of her nature, and was pleased when she saw the first, tentative smile appear on her face.

"Poor, motherless waif," she muttered to herself. "Like a bird that got shoved out of the nest too soon." She stifled anger building inside her. No sense losing her temper over what she couldn't change. She was good at controlling that kind of anger. She'd been doing it since she was old enough to understand the injustice of the world.

Rose wasn't aware of Ma Brown's thoughts, or of the fact that Ella and Rufus knew all that anyone needed to know, and more, about injustice from living in Chicago where they'd got "street smart" very young. The Browns' wisdom was to change Rose's life forever.

The other thing that had changed Rose's life was meeting Bennie, whom she loved from the first moment she saw him. He'd gotten out of the car that first time and looked at her with interest, and, she thought, pity. But there was kindness in his hazel eyes. She saw that, too, in the instant before she looked away, looked down at her feet, dirty and bare though the weather had turned cold, at the patched skirt that was all Felice gave her to wear at home. (She was always careful about how she sent Rose to school, though, because the teachers might notice, and the County would get down on her and maybe take away her slave.)

Rose had wanted in that instant to be beautiful. For Bennie. Her want turned to shame and then helpless rage—at Felice and Elephant Ears, even, unreasonably, at her ma and pa for leaving her, and especially at herself, poor, sad most of the time, and unloved. That's when she'd turned and ran and hid, refusing to come out, even when Felice screamed her name over and over.

More than ever then, she wanted something she might be able to actually get and keep. Something to love with complete devotion. She recognized from the first time she saw Bennie that he filled that bill, and that was when she started to love him with a ferocity that frightened her.

Ella Mae had told her what love was like between a man and woman, and after that, every day, and especially at night before she fell into exhausted sleep, she pictured herself in Bennie's arms. That gave her the first encouragement to live as long as she could, live until she could make him love her as she did him. Hope had entered her life for the first time in years, and she even smiled to herself when she was sure no one would see her.

In her daydreams she was beautiful, with her hair piled up on her head like a movie star and breasts like her ma had, full and womanly. She felt for her own breasts, still small but filling out, partly due to Ma Brown's feeding her after school, often with wonderful cake that had pink frosting, served with big glasses of milk. Felice never cared when Rose didn't eat as much at their place afterward, being grateful for saving more, even pennies, to swell their bulging bank account. If she'd known why Rose was eating less at home, she'd have been torn between stinginess and an aversion to having her ward associate with "niggers."

Rose was happiest when she was invited to the Todd farm some weekends, and Felice didn't object, provided all the chores were done to her persnickety standards. Rose being gone saved another few meals. Still, Rose always ran as fast as she could to the big Lincoln before Felice changed her mind and called her back. That had happened twice so far, and with Felice she never knew. Bennie knew that too, and always gunned the big car away as soon as Rose jumped in and slammed the door.

But with Bennie and his ma and pa, and Newt and Eben, she could forget for a while, pretend they were her own family. She especially loved Uncle Newt and even old Nelson. They all teased her and made a fuss over her. She didn't know what to make of Kid at first but decided he was like a brother when she got to know him, even if a lot of people would have said he was *only* an Indian.

She knew Kid liked her the day he pinched her arm and said, "Uh, pretty good muscles. How you like come to my teepee—cook, wash my socks? Stumbling Bear trade plenty ponies for white squaw."

She giggled, then blushed, wishing it was Bennie who was teasing her. At least, though, Bennie always asked her along when the boys went to the woods, and talked to her like she was a real person and not just his kid sister in a ragged skirt and too-tight blouse. She hoped he'd notice her budding breasts, but if he did, he didn't show it, and she had no idea how to bring her unfolding womanhood to his attention.

Still, just being with him was almost enough. He shared his growing knowledge of the woods, the plants and birds, and she was happy to simply be with him. Kid sometimes grinned when Bennie got his new woodsmanship tangled up a little, but he never said anything.

The creek was running full after a heavy rain, and she hesitated at the edge, wondering if it was deep since the water was roiled and muddy, frightened that maybe she'd get soaked and have to swim out.

"Come on. It's okay," Bennie said, but still she stood, frowning, as she watched the swift, muddy flow.

Bennie didn't rush her. He thought, "She's just a little thing, and scared."

That bothered him when he thought about it. Hell, she was only a girl, and she'd had a hard time of it. He'd seen her face when Felice let out with a string of accusations, and wondered if she'd been whipped. The idea made his stomach tighten up. Whipping Rose would be like beating Hank, who never did anything to deserve it and the thrashings Ma gave him before he was old enough to fight back.

"C'mon, I'll carry you," he said and scooped her up before she could protest.

Automatically she put her arms around his neck to steady herself. Then she realized what she was doing. It was how she'd imagined it would be to be held by Bennie—warm, safe, happy. And something more. She wanted to hold onto him forever, to kiss him the way Ella said grown-ups did and the urge was so powerful that she closed her eyes so he wouldn't read in them what she was feeling.

When she did open them, to sneak a look at him, he seemed grim, his jaw set, his hazel eyes on the far bank.

Kiss me! She wanted to cry. *Love me!* But she stayed quiet, nestled against him.

Bennie was having his own struggle. She was giving him a hard-on and it was coming up fast—Rose, this little girl whom he'd always treated like a sister. Except she wasn't, and he wasn't thinking of her as one now. She was a woman suddenly, and smelled sweet and clean, and he could feel her small breasts through his shirt, the warmth of her breath on his cheek.

Distracted, he slipped on a rock and almost fell. "Hold on," he muttered, more to himself than her.

She clung to him tightly. He could feel her heart beating like a tiny drum, feel the swell in his pants, and in the moment before he reached the other side, he looked at her and was startled by the intensity of her eyes on his for an instant.

Abruptly he set her down. She was trembling and hoped he didn't see. He hoped she didn't glance down at his pants.

"Thanks," she said. It came out a whisper.

He turned quickly to set out on their walk again, following Kid who was already out of sight. He rushed away mostly so he wouldn't be embarrassed, though he suspected she wouldn't notice the tent in his pants or know what caused it if she did.

"Let's go," he said. "Kid'll think we got lost and come back lookin' for us."

She'd forgotten Kid, forgotten everything but Bennie and the urging of her body. In a daze she followed him along the narrow, shaded path.

That night in bed she went over the whole, magical happening. "Bennie," she whispered. "Bennie," and her hands moved over herself, relearning her breasts that tingled as she touched them, the curve of her hips, the secret place that was now wet and demanding. It was Bennie holding her, touching her, inside her, like Ella Mae had said. She whimpered and arched her body to meet herself. Then she lay still, breathing hard.

She couldn't wait to ask Ella Mae what that had been all about.

Ella Mae laughed. "You're just growin' up," she said. "You came for the first time."

"Came?"

"Got yourself off. You'll do it with a man someday and it's even better."

"Have you ever done it with a man?"

Ella Mae grinned. She wasn't about to tell that some of the men in town were taking her into barns and even their houses when their wives were away, and doing it to her for money. Even Elephant Ears wanted to, until he found out her price. She figured he probably went home to the barn and jacked off instead.

"Sure, honey. Back in Chicago when I wasn't nearly as old as you. We ain't like white folks always holding it in, and bragging about how good we are, and the men always hard up and playing with themselves."

"What do you mean playing with themselves?" Rose asked, fascinated by the whole subject.

"Doin' what you did, only like they do."

She described the whole affair and what men's things looked like and how they got big and hard and shot "jizzum," as she called it.

Later, one day when Rose had sneaked away and taken a nap up in the hayloft she heard a noise downstairs and peeked down through the hay window and saw Elephant Ears playing with himself. He milked himself slowly at first, and she marveled at how big a man's thing got as he worked faster and began to moan and breath hard, then started thrusting like a dog doing it, and with a final sharp cry, thrust his hips forward and almost jumped in the air and shot jizzum all over. He ended up, bent over, face down, panting.

Rose felt her own passion rise from sensing how a fellow human must feel in the throes of passion, even an ugly one like him, but was also repelled by him. Even at that she was sorry for him because she knew why he was taking care of himself. She didn't see how any man could do it with Felice. She was also careful that Elephant Ears didn't see or hear her up above him. Ella Mae had warned her what a grown man like him might do to her if he was "horny," as she called it. He'd rape her.

She wished Bennie would rape her. She knew she'd love it and made up her mind to try to interest him in her body.

She'd have been very unhappy, and wouldn't have understood it, if she knew he was generally too played out from meeting Annie on the sly to pay attention to any other woman, and she thought of herself as a woman—especially now since she could better imagine how she'd really feel in Bennie's arms.

CHAPTER FORTY-SIX

The Coach

Bennie loved to play football. For the rest of his life, football and Coach Redballs, as they all called him were inseparable in his mind. His name was Radbaltze, but they all called him Redballs because he seemed to have something that kept him mad all the time. He wasn't big, but he was mean. He'd been quarterback for State and made quite a reputation back when the Big Ten was a power in football, and Redballs had quarterbacked State to a victory over most of the teams in the Big Ten at least once. He was an icon in Wisconsin. Bennie had heard about Redballs before he'd come out for the team's first practice session, and Kid had pointed him out the first day of school.

Teachers would send for "the Coach" when they had problem boys on their hands and he'd come and jerk them out of their seats and take them into the hall. Soon the kids in class would hear the fuss when "the Coach" banged the kid's head somewhere down the lines of metal lockers in the halls.

Afterward even some of the bigger boys would come back into the room, shame-faced, with tears streaking their faces and uncomfortably slink back to their desks. Sometimes kids would snicker, but Bennie never did after he'd been around long enough to have seen one of Redballs's displays. By then he'd been exposed to him on the practice field. He thought, "The son of a bitch will never do that to me."

Then the incident took place that made him and Kid and Bobo Zentz into school heroes.

Bennie was in the line in practice scrimmage, crouched to spring at his opposite number as soon as the ball was snapped from center. Redballs came up behind him and yelled, "Lower or you'll get shoved on your ass!" He kicked him in the butt to make his point and Bennie saw red at once, and sprang up and rushed him, tackling him and setting him on his can. When they both leaped up, Redballs took a swing at him and Bennie ducked and swung right back and chopped him alongside the head, staggering him.

He thought, "Shit! I should have put everything I had in it and I'd have knocked him on his ass."

He threw down his helmet, turned and said, "You can have your fuckin' football team, Coach!"

Redballs, in a rage, hit him from behind and knocked him down, yelling, "No fuckin' snot-nosed kid gets away with hitting me!"

That's when another snot-nosed kid, Kid, hit Redballs with a roundhouse punch from behind and knocked him on his ass.

The coach got up, shook his head and went after Kid, who dodged away. Then Bobo Zentz, who weighed 220 even at age fifteen tackled Redballs and took him down. As though they'd planned it ahead of time, Bobo, Bennie, and Kid roughed Redballs, grinding his nose in the dirt, while Bobo sat on him. They finally let him up.

Bobo shook his finger at him. "Don't try any more of that on us!" he warned. "We ain't kids anymore! And my pa raised me to hate bullies! If he has to come down here, he'll break every bone in your body!"

The coach eyed him balefully, but made no move. Then he ran his gaze over the other two. Following that he let out a stream of the foulest language Bennie had ever heard, including from Cees's brother Jim, who'd been in the Navy.

After that, Redballs did the last thing anyone would ever have expected from him. He laughed. Not only that, it was a real laugh.

He said, "You three sonsabitches are the kind of football players I've been looking for. We'll kick ass on every team in the state."

He offered his hand and they all shook it.

Everyone in town knew it happened, but the school didn't try to expel them, which was just as well. The community might have burned down the place and hung Redballs and old principal Brick. The local mind cottoned to that sort of roughhousing. (The principal was known, of course, as Brick the Prick, and also as "the principal prick" even though he was a pretty good guy.)

Bennie played his heart out for old Redballs after that, and so did the rest of them. And they did kick ass. Never lost a game.

But a lot of learning about football went into the affair before then. And Assistant Coach Lance, who'd been no slouch of a football player himself, taught Bennie as much as Redballs did. Bennie liked him a lot better than Redballs, but respected the latter, too, after that introduction.

Harry Lance laughed a lot, and all the girls in the school were in love with him and found they ought to take accounting, which he taught in addition to being assistant coach. Being girls they probably loved him for the wrong reasons, such as his curly hair, baby blue eyes, and dimpled face. He looked soft but was far from it, as the boys who scrimmaged with him soon learned. They hadn't called him The Rock for nothing during his football career and he still was rock hard and damn fast yet, ten years after he'd left college. He'd been a lumberjack during the summers when he was in college.

The woods around Winnebago, with its premier hunting and fishing, was why a little burg had attracted the caliber of coaches like Redballs and Lance. They were outdoorsmen and had no ambitions to be big names, even though they were both competitive as racehorses. When football season was over they took to the woods and streams as soon as the final school bell of the day rang. Neither was married, probably due to lack of a suitable field to find the right kind of gal for a football coach, though plenty of milkmaids had their eyes on them. The Depression wasn't a time when people married young anyway, and that was usually because they couldn't afford it. These two could both afford it, but Bennie later observed that both coaches wouldn't have been above screwing the pretty older high school girls. Everyone in the community suspected the two coaches were willing to oblige dissatisfied wives, and they were sure that included Principal Brick's pretty young wife. Bennie, along with the whole community except Brick, and Coach Lance, who had inside information, was sure Redballs was banging her regularly, but that didn't make it a fact.

In any case, the saying was, "Why buy a cow when milk's so cheap?"

Milk was not only cheap but plentiful for football heroes, as Bennie would learn before long. He sampled all the good-looking girls that hit on him. There was a song popular in the twenties and still sung then that went:

> *You've got to be a football hero,*
> *To get along with a beautiful gal.*

Bennie loved the smell of crisp fall evenings when they hit the field for practice after school. Even better was the bracing air on nights when they played home games. Maples, oaks, elms, willows, and birches lined the nearby river bank, their fallen leaves imparting the mellow, fruity smell of plants making tribute to the earth that nurtured them. That, and the smell of leaves being burned by homeowners who'd raked up their lawns. This to him would always be the smell of football, rather than sweat and piss. (*Ever wonder why you never saw a football player duck out to take off a bunch of cumbersome padding to take a leak?*) Sometimes, before practice was over, the moon rose and laid its silvery swatch of light across the river, lending total enchantment to this American ritual of fall.

To him the yelling and cheering of spectators was secondary. He played as the *ideological fiction* prescribed: for the sheer hell of it. If he got set on his ass he never got mad as long as it was done fair and square. With him it really wasn't a matter of "whether you won or lost, but how you played the game." Kid was a good deal the same. Nonetheless, they both had the fire that wouldn't let them give up, a reservoir where they found another ounce of energy, even when it felt like their lungs would burst, or their legs turn to rubber. When they were tackled hard, or on the bottom of a pileup, with wind knocked out of them, hurt so bad a normal person would cry like a baby, they simply got up as soon as they could get some air in their lungs and forced themselves to wade back in.

Watching them, Redballs said to Lance, "Goddam, Harry. Those are real fuckin' football players. We got ourselves some winners at last. It's a pity they won't let us put Rufus in with them."

Lance nodded. "Killers," he said.

"Damn well told!"

Love-sick girls always came out to watch practice scrimmages. Rose came every night, but had to go home earlier than she would have liked to, of course. Bennie would sometimes single her out to talk to briefly if he wasn't on the field, but had no idea why she came other than to put a little excitement in her drab home life. He was completely oblivious to the way she looked at him—in fact, didn't even notice.

The snake was ready to crawl into that Garden, too. Two years established Winnebago High's football team as Bennie's and Kid's show—it was *their* team. The whole state knew who Kid and Ben were; they were the sensations from that little jerkwater up north. They were *Kid the Arm* and *Ben the Streak*, star passing back and fleet right end, even reported every week in the Milwaukee and Madison papers. And why not? They shut out the former state champs, undefeated up till then. The score was 28 to 0. Nine other guys helped, but in the public mind the flashy stars battled for that zero in the record book, man! And zero was a big goose egg with no way around it for the former champs. No one noticed that Bobo Zentz blocked like a whole line himself. Winnebago went wild for its two flashy heroes. They were about to go even wilder over what the two stars did the next season.

It came about because Rose was Ella Mae's best friend. Bennie saw nothing wrong with having the black girl and her brother Rufus out to the farm, and neither did anyone out there. Bennie's family had always been as near to color-blind as whites get. Also as irreligious. Bennie never saw the inside of a church, not that the two things had any connection. Newt, of course, had had a black buddy, Leland, when he was a kid, and went through the Civil War with him, almost to the end. In addition, Leland's pa, Magawn, had been like an extra father to Newt when he was little, and taught him how to do good work with as little effort as possible by using his head as the first tool needed on any job. It was pretty clear where Newt would stand on black equality.

Whenever Rufus came out to the farm, the three boys always passed and kicked a football around, and sometimes got into real scrimmages. Rufus was the only one Bennie knew who could run him down in a straight-away race.

Newt watched him and later took Bennie aside and asked, "How come I never see Rufus on the field?"

Until then Bennie had never questioned the community standards prevailing at that time. He felt the dawning of moral indignation when he searched his mind for how to describe the situation to Newt.

When he did, Newt snorted, "That's a bunch of bullshit. Naturally he feels bad about it. Does he ever say anything about it to you guys?

"He must feel bad, but he's never said anything. I'd guess he's been raised to realize that's just the way it is."

"We'll see about that," Newt said.

"What're you gonna do?" Bennie asked. He knew Newt. When something was wrong Newt almost always felt he should change it for the better if he could.

Newt said, "I don't know for sure just yet. I'll have to think about it. But there isn't that much time—is he in your grade?"

"One year ahead of me."

"Hell, he's only got this year to make a name for himself and get the credit he deserves."

That was all Newt said at the time, and several days passed during which Bennie almost forgot it. Then Newt got him and Kid aside after one Sunday dinner and made a suggestion about what they had to do.

"*Yuh* know," he started, "right or wrong are sometimes hard to figure. Wrong is a two-sided coin. One side is actually doing wrong, and the other is standing around with yer finger up yer ass and not doin' anything about it when you see wrong bein' done."

He let that sink in while he got a cigar prepared just right, lit it, and blew a smoke ring. Watching, Bennie sensed that something out of the ordinary would soon be expected of him and Kid if they wanted to live and do well around Newt, which they surely did. Bennie hardly expected to hear what that was going to be, and when he did he got an awful sinking feeling in his stomach.

"You two," Newt said, "have to quit the team when school starts if they won't let Rufus play in regular games. You got no choice."

Both boys were struck dumb. Kid was the first to say something. He looked at Bennie and said, "He's right. They treat Rufus worse than they treat us Injuns about most things. It's a wonder they let me and you play. Hell, Bennie, you're a "breed" when it comes right down to it. But we look nearly white. If we were black on top of Injun, can you imagine how that'd work out?"

"They'll probably try to hang us if we quit," Bennie said.

Newt grinned. "Remember Nathan Hale, the guy who said he only regretted that he had one life to give for his country. Of course, some son of a bitch most likely put those words in his mouth after he got jerked to Jesus. But there comes a time when you've got to stand up and be counted. The black people are *still* slaves when you come right down to it. And it's a cryin' shame."

"O.K.," Kid said. "I'm game. I don't care to sit in a damned classroom for nine months just so I can play football for three. I'll quit school. I'll probably catch hell from Ma, but she'll see it's right. Look what happened to Pa for being right."

"That's a fact," Bennie said. "Ma will have a fit, too."

"Let her," Newt said. "If she gets too mean about it, go over and live with your Pa. Klondy might assign you your own whore."

Kid said, "Knowin' Klondy, she might sneak down to yer room when yer old man is sawing wood. I wonder how that stuff is." He looked inquiringly at Newt, who suddenly blew smoke at the sky and ignored him.

Bennie laughed. It sounded so good he thought maybe he'd move over there anyhow. Something would change his mind about that, too, in a few months and it was just as well he didn't know it yet.

The first day of school, Bennie and Kid went into Coach Redballs's office together. The coach looked up and judged that their faces concealed something they didn't really want to talk to him about.

"Well?" he prompted them.

Kid blurted out, "We've decided we can't rightly play football unless Rufus is allowed to play in regular games."

The coach's look plainly said, "*Are you two tetched?*"

What he said was to Coach Lance who was in his office next door, "Hey, Harry, come in here."

Lance came in looking inquiringly around at the three. "Who died?" he asked, reading their looks.

"Nobody, yet," Redballs said. "But it's a toss up about who or what's apt to. Tell him," he said, nodding at Kid.

"We ain't playin' unless Rufus can play in regular games. It's not right."

Lance couldn't have agreed more, and had thought it himself, but had the discretion not to make an issue of it. He liked Winnebago and his job.

"Say something," Redballs said to Lance.

"I think they're dead right," Lance said.

Redballs shook his head and looked more morose than he had.

"So do I," he admitted reluctantly. "Let's go see Brick."

Principal Brick looked up from behind his desk at the cavalcade that entered his office, his face carefully masking both surprise and expectation. He couldn't think of anything else to say, so said, "To what do I owe this honor? Have you decided to let me play left end? Somehow from your looks I think I'd rather play *left out*." He laughed weakly at his own joke.

He'd brought his Ph.D. to a jerkwater high school, rather than to a university, so he could live the contemplative life without having to publish or perish. The contemplative life was just about to be derailed.

Redballs took the bull by the horns. He said, "It turns out that something has been bothering all four of us for quite a while."

He hesitated so long about saying the rest that even Brick, normally a man who didn't prod anyone, finally said, "Well, spit it out. It must not be good news."

"We've decided it's time to face up to the fact that not letting Rufus Brown play in regular games is morally wrong."

Brick looked stunned. He blurted out the last thing anyone would have expected from him. "*Morally wrong, my ass! If it comes down to it football is probably morally wrong. It's a disguised form of the same damned thing the Romans did when they threw the Christians to the lions!*"

Harry Lance laughed. He did it because he knew something none of the rest did. He was the man actually getting the warm welcome out at Brick's house that the community suspected Redballs of getting. He laughed at the thought that this wasn't exactly the mouse-like Brick that his little dove portrayed him to be.

"What the hell's so funny?" Brick asked. "If I go along with this they'll probably ride all of us out of town on a rail."

Redballs surprised Bennie by saying something he'd read himself in a book: "As Lincoln said about the guy in that shape: 'If it wasn't for the honor' the poor sap would rather have walked. *Think of the honor*."

"Honor, my ass!" Brick snorted. "I want you four to sleep on this and if you don't change your minds come back and tell me. Then we can all traipse over and tell it to the school board at their meeting next week. See if you can hold our two damn fool football stars off that long." He paused, looking into their faces. "By the way, hand me that Milwaukee *Journal* on the table by the door on your way out."

Lance handed it to him, the look on his face showing his puzzlement over such a request after the interview they'd just had. Seeing the question on his face, Brick said, "I want to look over the help wanted section. I agree entirely with you four, and I *know* what the board will say."

Brick was right. The board said a lot of things but it boiled down to what the board's pesident, Dan Wade, the local bank president, said in a nutshell for the rest of the board.

"What the hell do you think this is? No goddam community in the state will let our football team get off the bus if we have a nigger on the team!"

Brick had already lived through this scene while he tossed and turned in bed the night before. He'd also looked over that Milwaukee *Journal* and found a job by a long distance call to a Miami girls' school. His only condition was that they had no organized sports. They didn't. And they couldn't pass up an applicant with a Ph.D. who'd work for peanuts. Brick consoled himself with the thought, "*What the hell, I'm tired of long winters that freeze your balls off.* Maybe with lower fuel bills we can still make ends meet."

"What the hell do you have to say for yourself?" Wade roared at Brick in his best *fake-angry* voice that always made subordinates shrink.

Brick handed him his resignation and walked out. It should have made the local paper.

It should have made *Life* magazine!

Especially since both coaches quit with him. It didn't even make the Madison or Milwaukee papers after the inquiring reporters learned the issue and reported it to their editors.

The consensus was, "We can't run this. We'd all look like bastards. Especially since we've been sitting still for this for years without getting on it. No telling what Eleanor Roosevelt might do. We might get the shitty end of the pork barrel stick. Old FDR listens to her and whatever you say for him, he does run the goddam party."

So Bennie and Kid went to Vocational School, still eligible to play two more years on the football team. Rufus didn't. When Wade got his cronies organized, a small group kicked hell out of Rufus's pa, and trashed his shop. The Browns moved back to Chicago. *Like they all had said, "Morrie knew his place."*

Wade thought he'd got off scot-free and was congratulating himself when Newt walked in and closed his account with the bank—a quarter of a million great big bucks.

"What the hell is this about?" Wade wanted to know.

"Letting that '*nigger*' play on the team was my idea to begin with," Newt said. "Is that clear enough?"

"What the hell business was that of yours?"

"I went through the Civil War," Newt said. "Remember what it was all about when we got down to it? My best friend was black. I was raised with him. He took a minie ball for me and died in my arms. I even kissed him for his mother just before he died, you son of a bitch! "

Newt was yelling and had tears in his eyes before he spun and stalked out.

Wade was genuinely shocked for the first time in many years.

And if that hadn't been bad enough, Klondy came in the next morning and withdrew a hundred grand more. If Wade learned anything no one ever noticed, since he died of a heart attack shortly afterward and his bank closed its doors. Thanks to the New Deal no depositor lost a nickel. The only two who would have lost anything had already taken out their money.

Newt issued the final pronouncement on the episode: "*Now ain't that a cryin' shame about Wade*."

Winnebago had another goose egg football season like those that had previously been its norm. Even Bobo had enrolled in the Vocational School, but no lynch mob tried to kick the shit out of his 280-pound gorilla of a father, or of Bobo either.

Bennie and Kid got the cold shoulder from most of the people who'd regularly come out to cheer them. It was an early lesson in human nature for both of them. They realized that there was not a one of the crowd who now shunned them that didn't know the grounds on which the two stars had nobly turned their backs on glory.

The fearless local *Tomahawk* never reported in its columns the fates of Redballs and Lance.

Brick had acted on his wife's suggestion that he help Redballs and Lance find jobs at a small local college in Florida that had just fired its coaches due to a sagging football team. (She had some idea about continuing to make ends meet due to a warm climate, but not the same warm ends her husband did.)

In the next few years that sagging football team was turned around and went into orbit with a three-season undefeated-streak, a national record at the time. That wasn't reported in the *Tomahawk* either.

CHAPTER FORTY-SEVEN

Rose Comes Home

After his first full year on their farm, Bennie knew he'd be satisfied with a lifetime as what Ma called a "dirt farmer." He was confident he'd make a good farmer, too, regardless of what anyone called him. No matter how hard and long he had to work, he was always happy now.

Cowboying was O.K., and so was running a trap line, but the income from both of those was pretty uncertain; for that matter so was dirt farming out in the West where people cowboyed. But on a farm in Wisconsin where it usually rained enough every year, even if the income, especially the cash part of it, sometimes was pretty skimpy, there was always enough to eat. And taxes were modest, so they could be paid by raising eggs and producing milk and butter to sell to creameries. And there was always a way to wring out a little surplus to buy what seed you couldn't raise yourself, and buy sturdy workclothes at *Monkey Wards* (as all the farmers called Montgomery Ward's). Bennie wasn't a show horse and didn't care if he ever owned a suit. Cheap, sturdy clodhopper shoes, bib overalls, and durable Rockford Sox at ten cents a pair satisfied him.

Ma still made most of his shirts on her old Brunswick foot-pedal sewing machine and liked to do it. He'd be set for life, he figured, if he could find a wife as practical as Ma. (He hoped they'd get electricity before she died so he could get her an electric sewing machine.)

Since Pa was now living over at Klondy's, Eben had moved into the bedroom with Ma, which suited Bennie. He wasn't a moralist, and was glad to see Ma truly happy. He didn't know enough of her past to realize that it was the first time she'd been happy since she'd played hooky in the cornfields of Illinois and communed with *Chaubenee*.

Newt and Nelson now alternated Sunday dinners at Ma's and Klondy's, and sometimes Bennie and Kid went over to Klondy's and joined them. When they did they fibbed and said they were taking off into the woods. This didn't really fool Ma since she was well acquainted with their teenage appetites and knew they were getting fed somewhere.

On some of these excursions to Klondy's, Kid and Bennie would drive in and pick up Rose. If Felice had known that her chattel was being exposed to a madam, she'd have had convulsions. In Rose's case, it was good for the girl. Since she'd lost her friend, Ella Mae, she had no one to lean on for frank advice. For example, Klondy told her how to avoid an unwanted pregnancy, which she thought every girl should know. Klondy had read the rapt looks that Rose shot at Bennie, even if he was too unsuspecting to notice; and Klondy knew better than most where that was apt to lead.

Bennie became the regular chauffeur for the bachelor visits to Klondy's on Saturday nights. If Pa went down there anymore, it was as chauffeur for Klondy in her Chrysler sedan. Eben still went sometimes, but didn't sample the wares anymore, and was satisfied sipping his Squirt and people-watching.

Annie had reluctantly moved on, as such girls were required to do, but Bennie latched onto an amiable blond named Pat, whose boobs were bigger than Annie's. He was making enough money to buy condoms (universally known as rubbers) so he wasn't afraid of catching something. He even bought some rubbers for Kid and talked him into getting his ashes hauled. "You don't want to risk growing hair in your palms," he told Kid.

Kid said, "A bad back is more like what you really get from flogging off."

They were headed home one Sunday morning very early, and about to run into a situation that would change Bennie's whole life.

Nelson and Eben were snoring, propped against each other in the back seat. Newt was next to them smoking a cigar, still wide awake and savoring the night air blowing in the open windows. Kid rolled a couple of cigarettes and lit one, handing it to Bennie, then sat back and lit his own, inhaling a deep drag.

He said, "Ah . . . the sacrifices youth makes to keep our elders out of trouble."

If he expected Newt to rise to the bait, he was disappointed.

Kid suddenly sat up straight and pointed through the windshield. "What the hell is that?" he exclaimed.

"Where?" Bennie asked.

"Up there," Kid pointed, "right side of the road."

Bennie saw a white something, bobbing like it was trotting. "Maybe a deer," he said.

"Naw, a person. Naked." Kid said.

Bennie didn't question Kid's woods-wise eyes. The figure broke into a run and dodged off the road into the woods out of the headlight glow as though it thought someone in a car would be hunting it.

"Holy shit!" Bennie said.

"What?" Newt asked.

"Someone up the road just dodged into the woods," Bennie said.

He'd slowed the car to almost a crawl and dropped into low.

"Naked, too," Kid said.

"Naked? Someone must be nuts or in trouble. Pull up when you get to where they are."

Bennie stopped a few yards short of where they'd seen the thing dart off the road.

"Mosquitoes'll eat the poor son of a bitch," Kid said.

"Get the flashlight," Newt ordered. By then he was getting out, Kid right with him, beaming the flashlight around where the thing had disappeared. "You stay here," Newt told Bennie, "and back up a little so the lights cover more ground."

Eben and Nelson were awakened by the racket.

"What's goin' on?" Eben asked.

"We ain't sure," Bennie said. "Someone was runnin' up the road naked, and jumped in the woods when we came along. Newt and Kid are out looking to see who it is."

"Jesus Christ!" Eben exploded.

Just then the white figure jumped up from behind a bush and headed for the deeper woods. Kid darted after and tackled it, the flashlight flying out of his hand. Bennie pulled closer and said, "Maybe Kid needs help."

Newt, who was out there with him, thought the same thing and quickly retrieved the flashlight and followed after the two figures thrashing in the brush. Eben jumped out to join the fray.

A high-pitched scream of terror, followed by an animal cry, startled Bennie. All the tales of supernatural beings he'd ever heard came to mind. Maybe Kid was being killed by a vampire or something. Nelson must have thought the same thing; he shot out of the car and headed up to the fray faster than Bennie'd ever seen him move.

Shortly the men came out of the brush, dragging a thrashing form that was obviously a person, now moaning like something in mortal pain. Bennie eased the Lincoln up and heard Newt say, "Keep her here a minute."

He motioned Bennie to pull abreast of them.

Newt ducked into the back seat and came out with the lap robe. He passed it to Nelson. "Put this around her," he said.

"What is it?" Bennie asked.

Newt didn't answer, if he heard. He was guiding the figure under the robe into the back seat. Eben got in front to make more room in the back seat.

"Who is it?" Bennie asked this time.

"It's Rose."

"Rose? Should we turn around and take her home?"

Newt snapped, "Not by a jug full, you damn fool! Whatever scared her out of her wits happened back there—she ain't got no home. You must be blind."

Bennie was astonished by Newt's abrupt words, but they started him thinking how, even at the very first, Newt must have suspected something when he asked Rose if she was mistreated.

Rose, trembling and weeping hysterically, didn't even recognize them, or where she was, and Bennie wondered if she were dying. The idea scared him. For the first time he realized how much he'd grown to like her.

Newt put an arm around her. "You're all right now, honey. We won't hurt you. We're taking you where you'll be safe." He crooned the words over and over in a hypnotic, pattern, sensing that in her terror she didn't realize that she was with friends.

Bennie was amazed to realize that Newt could be so tender.

He said, "Ma'll know what to do," and speeded up, hoping a deer didn't jump in their path—or, worse yet, a cow.

By the time they pulled into the yard, Rose was asleep.

"Git yore ma out here," Newt ordered Bennie. "We want another gal around when she wakes up, so she won't have the whips and jingles again."

Ma came out barefoot. Bennie threw the flashlight beam on Rose. She looked awful small, huddled next to Newt's huge form.

"How'd we best get her outa here?" Newt asked Ma.

"Has she got anything broken?"

"I don't think so."

Their voices disturbed Rose; she wriggled, moaned softly, and let out a huge sigh, then settled back against Newt.

"Just hand her out to me then," Ma said. "If she wakes up, she can walk."

Newt handed her out feet first, holding his end up with his big hands under her arms, sliding after awkwardly as best he could.

He said, "She had one hell of a scare of some kind—probably don't want to wake up and think about it."

"I'll take her now," Ma said. "There's not much to her."

Ma was as strong as a lot of men. She took Rose in her arms and headed for the house. Bennie ran ahead, lighting the way.

"We'll put her on the kitchen couch for now. Get a lamp."

Ma gently lowered Rose to the long window seat. The robe slipped off and Bennie was startled to see a lush growth of pubic hair. He'd thought she was too young for that, deceived by her slight build. Ma quickly covered her again and glared around at the gawking males. "Everybody go somewhere else," she ordered, then as an afterthought said, "one of you stay here and tell me what happened." She indicated Newt with a nod. "You, Bennie, go get a comforter and pillow. You other louts bring me the horsehair rocker from the front room."

To Newt she said, "I aim to sit up with her in case she wakes up and doesn't know where she is. Nothing is worse than that. Now, tell me what happened."

"I don't rightly know. We run across her trottin' up the road with just that shred of her shimmy around her neck. She didn't know which end was up, I reckon."

"Close to Felice's?"

"No. Almost five miles outa town, I'd guess."

Ma turned that over in her mind, correctly assuming something at Felice's had terrified the girl and she'd tried to run as far away as she could get. She could imagine what. Being Ma, she simply knew a "morone" had to be at the root of Rose's fright. Some dirty-minded man had done something to her, and God only knew how far he'd got. She made a note to examine Rose carefully after she got rid of the men.

"What did she do when you came along?"

Newt described how she'd jumped off the road and the hassle they'd had catching her, not leaving out her terror and hysteria.

He was startled to hear Ma say, "Some son of a bitch is going to pay for this! That homely bastard Bertram's probably been molesting her for years. Did you notice how haunted she acts all the time—as though she's afraid something's going to happen to her?"

"Yeah," Newt said. "Like something is sneaking up behind her."

"That's it, exactly."

Eben and Nelson trundled in the rocker, and Bennie arrived right behind them with the comforter and pillow.

"Now, everybody out. If I need anything, I'll let you know."

"You want us to stay over here?" Newt asked. "We can bed down in the hay loft."

"No. You come back over in the morning and maybe by then I'll know what happened to her." As Newt was going out the door she said, "Doesn't Bertram look like a morphadite to you?"

Newt grinned. He knew she didn't expect an answer. It was a pronouncement, not a question. Newt divined from her "morphadite" remark exactly what she was thinking and figured she was right.

Eben and Bennie lit a lamp and headed upstairs. Ma could hear them moving around, getting their individual lamps lit, undressing, and rolling into bed. She heard Kid start the Model A, slip it into gear and pull out down their lane without his usual gravel-tossing start, undoubtedly out of a considerate desire not to wake up Rose. She turned the lamp low and settled into the rocker, her eyes on Rose with a tender expression she made sure no one ever saw.

Ma shut her eyes and turned over the possibilities in her mind. She was lulled by the soothing, musical cricket chorus floating through the open window. Frogs croaked down at the pond. One of their cows called to its calf. Far off a whippoorwill cried. It all sounded safe and normal, but Ma, who'd lived through such terrible experiences as running for help when her pa chased her ma with a knife, knew what helpless terror could do to a person, especially a kid.

She'd already decided that Bertram was the guilty party without even knowing what the crime was, if there was one, and thought of Jim Tynan's rope cure. That was the kind of medicine that ruled out repeat performances. Too bad old Jim hadn't actually hung her pa—or beat his brains out while he had him down in the chicken shit. She thought that would be the medicine for Bertram too, and ought to be administered on general principles whether he'd done anything or not. She'd always hated the pink-eyed, tight-fisted cretin anyhow, though she couldn't say why, other than his repulsive looks. He reminded her of Andy Gump in the newspaper cartoon strips.

Rose stirred and moaned and Ma quickly opened her eyes. Rose whimpered, "No! No, please don't!"

Ma put a gentle hand on her forehead. It wasn't feverish, but slightly moist and cool. She kept the comforter up around Rose's neck anyhow. After a person suffered a shock, their resistance was low and they could easily catch pneumonia. She thought of closing the window above Rose's head, but decided the fresh air would do her good. An occasional gust of moist night air sighed through the screen, making a pleasant sound, cooling the kitchen as it eddied through the house and out the other windows and the open doors.

When Ma awoke, the horizon above the distant woods was faintly luminous. She turned her head. Rose was studying her intently, with a puzzled look. Ma wondered if the girl had lost her memory, as people sometime did to avoid thinking of painful or terrifying events.

Rose, still dazed, said, "You're Bennie's ma. Where am I?"

"At our place. You'll be safe here."

"How did I get here? I started to come, but I don't remember getting here. You were the only people I could think of who'd *maybe* help me."

"We'll help you. The men found you running down the road."

"Yes. I remember now. I saw the car lights. I thought *they* were coming to bring me back. I ran into the woods."

"You thought *who* was coming to take you back?"

"Felice. Bertram. Or maybe just him."

Ma didn't miss the fear, hatred, and loathing Rose put into that one word, *him*.

"What did he do to you?"

Rose looked away, then back at Ma as she debated what to say—and how.

"He was always after me. I told Felice, and she said it was my imagination because he was just like a father to me."

Ma thought, "*Father, my foot!*" Bertram couldn't have made a father for a troll in her opinion.

"What did Bertram do to you last night?"

Rose hesitated, wondering if Ma would believe her. She reviewed what had happened in her mind, trying to think how to politely tell it.

Rose wouldn't have had the words to explain what happened, except what Ella Mae had told her and they were hardly polite, but she didn't have any other words for it and decided to plunge ahead and tell the whole story.

"I thought I was home alone since they went to town visiting. Bertram must have walked back from town and sneaked in without my hearing him. I finished my bath and went to my room. I just got my nightie on when he slipped in, shut the door and bolted it."

"What did he do then?"

"He came after me. He didn't have any pants on and had a big hard-on."

Ma wondered how Rose knew what a hard-on was, but didn't interrupt.

Remembering, Rose wrapped her arms around herself. "I jumped on the bed and off the other side. He laughed and . . ." (here she paused, almost afraid to say the words she'd learned, but forced herself to continue)"he started *jacking off* and said, 'Maybe watching this'll make you hot?' Then he came after me again and threw me on the bed. I should have jumped out the window before then and ran, but I was too scared to think of it."

"What did he do then?"

"He ripped off my nightie and got on top of me, and pushed his leg between mine. His breath smelled like a backhouse."

Ma's mouth was open, breathing rapidly, taking this all in, her eyes almost glassy. This was better than her "rape" magazines. Indignation almost made Ma sick to her stomach. "Men!" she thought. "*Dirty bastards*!"

"He was too strong and forced my legs apart and was trying to push his thing in. I said, 'You'll go to jail for rape.' And he laughed and said, 'Who the hell'd believe a *tramp* like you?'"

"I said, 'Wait till Felice gets home, you're supposed to do this with her.' He was breathing real hard, but he laughed at that and said, 'Who could do it with that scrawny chicken? I like young meat.'"

She recalled that calling her a *tramp* was the thing that had given her the sudden burst of strength to fight him off. She recognized that she was a *nothing* in his eyes, probably in Felice's too.

Ella Mae's words came back to her, "If they do try to get you, kick them in the nuts," followed by her description of exactly how to do that.

Rose continued, "I bit his big, fat nose as hard as I could and hung on, and he tried to get away and fell out on the floor. I jumped out the other side of the bed and he said, 'I'll kill you for that!' He came for me, and I kicked him in the nuts." This time she didn't hesitate to use vulgar language. "That doubled him over, and he started to vomit and I had time to push out the screen and jump out. Then I started running. The only place I could think of to come was here."

Ma was stunned by Rose's language and wondered where she picked it up, but shortly came to her senses. She said, "I'm glad you did. You can stay with us."

Rose said, "They'll have the County come and bring me back. I ran away once before and they did that."

"They won't this time."

Ma sounded so sure of herself that Rose almost believed her. She felt a lot better. "Can I have a drink of water now?" she asked.

Ma brought her a glass full and she drained it all.

"More?" Ma asked, but Rose had actually fallen asleep with the glass still at her lips; it rolled onto the comforter. Ma took the empty glass and put a gentle hand on Rose's forehead. She still wasn't feverish, a good sign.

"Take you back my foot!" she mumbled. "I'll cut someone's throat first."

Newt, Nelson, and Kid, full of curiosity, were back by breakfast time, and Ma herded everyone out of the kitchen into the dining room.

"Eben," she directed, "you help me carry in dishes to set the table. You're the only one I trust not to fall over your feet and maybe wake up Rose. I'm going to cook on that kerosene stove in the shed."

Eben warned her as he always did, "Watch that sucker so you don't blow yourself up tryin' to light it. How about you set the table while I get the stove goin'?"

He knew better than to suggest that he do the whole cooking job, even though she'd been up all night.

Ma got in her little joke, deliberately deflecting questions from the curious men about what Rose'd told her. She said, "After breakfast we'll talk. It'll keep till then."

When they'd finished eating, Ma kept them waiting still longer while she went to see how Rose was and stayed a long time just looking at her peaked little face, now peaceful in sleep. Ma wanted to touch her but was afraid she'd wake her up.

She came back and announced, "Still dead to the world, the poor thing. Let's sit on the front porch so there's less chance of disturbing her."

She took her place in the swing, Eben next to her, the rest in the old rockers or on the homemade benches. Ma watched Newt's ritual for getting his cigar going to suit him and smiled a rare sort of smile for her—mischievous.

"Bennie," she said. "If you think I don't know you smoke you must think I'm pretty dense. Go ahead. You too Kid."

Bennie almost choked. Kid laughed. Then everyone laughed.

Bennie felt funny rolling a weed in front of Ma, but somehow managed and got it lit. He passed the makin's to Kid, and as usual Kid rolled his fat *turd* that the cigarette paper barely fit around. Despite her distracted mind, Ma noticed that, knew why as Bennie had, and grinned inwardly.

Newt passed a cigar to Nelson and offered Ma one in fun.

"There's a limit," Ma said.

Nelson pretended to be getting out his pipe to crumple up his cigar in, then hastily shoved it back in his pocket.

"Go ahead, I don't care if you eat it," Newt told him.

Finally Ma told everything that Rose had said regarding her horrible experience the night before.

When she finally finished she half-expected somebody to say something dumb. She knew if Pa was still around he might say, "Nonetheless, Felice is my sister and we'll have to take the girl back."

He might say it anyhow when he heard about this, and she intended to phone him and lay him out before he did.

Eben said in a hard voice, "We should have that bastard Bertram put away where he belongs."

"Easier said than done," Newt chipped in.

Eben said, "I don't see why the hell it should be."

Newt explained, "It's what the little son of a bitch told Rose, "Who the hell'd believe you?' The State treats her kind like dirt."

"Why tell anyone she's out here?" Bennie asked.

"They'd find out sooner or later," Newt said. "They always do, and it would be all the worse for her then."

"We're going to adopt her," Ma said. "I don't care what we have to do. That kid needs a home. If that pasty-faced sister of Pa's and the idiot she married put up a squawk I'll put a hatchet in both their heads."

"Whoa," Newt said. "Slow down. There's ways to get around them."

"Tell me one," Ma said.

Newt said, "I got a hunch I know how to handle the situation. Money talks. Meanwhile it won't hurt to do what Bennie said—for a few days—just keep her here on the sly."

Eben said, "What if they figure out where she must have gone and send the sheriff out?"

Kid said, "In that case I'll hide her where no one'll find her."

Bennie figured he knew where that would be. A good place. Uncle Bob would pump buckshot up the ass of anyone who tried to take her off the island.

Before they could question Newt on his plan, Rose herself broke up the talk, poking her head out the door, wrapped in her comforter. She said, "I smelled food."

Ma jumped up. "I'll get you something."

She fed her at the kitchen table. Rose dug into a man-sized breakfast, not saying anything.

When she was finished eating Ma took her upstairs and rooted out some of Lillian's old dresses from a trunk. They were too big for her, but better than nothing. Ma draped one of them on her, first shooing the men out. "I knew those would come in handy some day," Ma said. "I'll cut them down for you; and we'll have to get your things somehow."

"I don't have many things," Rose said.

"Don't worry," Ma said. "We'll straighten this all out."

Rose wasn't so sure. Fear still nagged at her. She'd almost got away before and was dragged back. She remembered the unsympathetic faces of the sheriff and County case worker when they lectured her on where she'd go if she tried that again. To reform school "where your ungrateful kind belong," were the words she never forgot. They'd even held her in a jail cell for a couple of hours during which she'd wept and looked around for a way to kill herself.

"I'm never going back to that place," Rose said. "I'll run away again . . . or kill myself if I have to."

Eben had come to the door and heard that. "You'll do no such thing," he said. "You got a family now."

To Ma Eben said, "Did you tell her we aim to adopt her?"

Ma smiled one of her rare smiles of genuine pleasure. She hadn't known how "adopt" would sit with Eben. She was uncertain, knowing Eben hadn't been the type to have a steady woman, much less a family. Nothing in Ma's past prepared her to realize that she might be making him as happy as he made her.

Newt said, "I reckon you two will have to get spliced if you're goin' to adopt a kid."

Eben looked startled. To Ma he said, "Do I have to get down on my knees to propose?"

Ma looked as startled as Eben had. Then she grinned. "Why not?"

"These're my best overalls and I don't want to wear out the knees too soon."

That got a laugh out of everyone. Nelson said, "By Yimminy, aye gits to be a best man, maybe."

Newt said, "I'll flip you for it."

Ma said, "I ain't said yes yet."

Rose watched all this as though she didn't believe any of it. She reckoned maybe her own family might have been this crazy if it had hung together. For her part she loved it. She'd almost forgotten her terrible experience for a moment, then it crashed back in on her and she suddenly felt awful.

"I think I've got to throw up," she said, and ran for the bathroom. Ma went right after her in case she choked and needed help.

When they came out Rose was pale and weak, Ma said, "Let me take you up to your new bedroom."

It used to be Nelson's, but by then Ma had scrubbed it a half dozen times, just to make sure it was clean, disinfected it with ammonia solution, and papered it in a bright flower design with a white background.

Before Newt left that morning he said, "Give me a couple of days to check into what we can maybe do. Like I said money talks." He had a hunch Klondy knew right where money talked loudest or she wouldn't be openly running a whorehouse.

Ma got Rose into bed and stayed in the room until she was sure the girl was sound asleep. If she was any judge Rose would sleep the sleep of the dead for many hours, blotting out the whole sad, frightening experience.

When she was sure she could leave, Ma went downstairs to the phone and got hold of Pa. He didn't put in a word all the while she told him what had happened, then after a long silence, stunned Ma by saying almost what Eben had.

"We've got to put that degenerate Bertram where he belongs. You keep that girl there no matter what, and don't let anyone lay a hand on her."

"We're workin' on Bertram's case. Newt's got an idea how to fix them good."

"What's that?"

"I don't know for sure, but he said money talks."

Pa had been around Newt long enough to know how that worked. Newt always learned where the political wind was blowing from. Nonetheless he was still angry. He said, "If you need me to go over and see those bastards, ring me."

A few days passed while Newt was busy as a bee on the telephone, and making a couple of trips somewhere.

When he was ready he assembled the family group to pay a visit to Felice and Elephant Ears.

Bertram had almost come to think it would all blow over, that Rose had run away, but Felice was suspicious when he urged her not to look for the girl because it was good riddance.

"Why not?" Felice demanded. "She's the best worker we ever had, doesn't eat much, and hardly ever gets sick."

"She's been after me like a little whore," he said, thinking he was being very clever. He knew that although Felice had no use for him as a man, she thought every woman might be after her prize catch. But even Felice found his story hard to believe. She'd observed how Bertram had been looking at the girl, and how he looked at all good-looking women when he thought she wasn't watching him. She wondered if he was really the harmless ogler that she'd always considered him to be, like most men were. She remembered he'd slipped away from her in town the night Rose had disappeared.

Bertram felt like puking when he heard the Lincoln pull up in front of the house and saw Pa, Ma, Newt, Bennie, and Rose get out, followed by Eben, who'd said, "You can always use another witness. Besides I'm family now."

Bertram had prepared Felice for this possible confrontation with the best lies he could think up, but he wasn't sure she bought it.

He knew he had to explain his lacerated nose where Rose had bit him, at least to Felice, and told her he'd stumbled into their pile of old barbed wire taking a shortcut home across fields in the dark and cut himself trying to get out of the mess. He wasn't sure she believed that, though. His nose looked too much like it had been bitten.

Regardless of other uncertainties, he wasn't in doubt about the purpose of the contingent that got out of the Lincoln. They grimly headed for the house, Pa first, Ma close behind, then that giant grand-uncle with the icy blue eyes that gave Bertram the heebie-jeebies. But it was the sight of Rose that disclosed beyond a doubt why they were there. He thought of sneaking out the back door, heading into the woods and running away. Then he thought of all that money in the bank. It was his, and he wasn't leaving it, and besides, if he ran away they'd know for sure Rose was telling the truth.

"Answer the door," Felice yelled from the kitchen when she heard the loud knocking.

Nauseated, he steeled himself to brazen it out, but couldn't stifle a chill down his spine.

"Hi, Russ," he said to Pa, trying to sound natural.

Pa pushed him aside.

"Is Felice here?" Pa asked curtly, giving Bertram a cold eye that suggested he'd like to knock him down. This wasn't soft old Russ, but a man he'd never seen before, the veteran of a violent frontier.

"Yeah," Bertram said weakly. "C'mon in everybody."

Rose had come last, hanging onto Bennie's arm, and looked at Bertram like she'd just kicked up a poisonous snake. Bertram wasn't able to look her in the eye. He felt his pecker almost retract into his belly at the sight of her, but didn't have the mother wit to wish it had a few nights before at the sight of her. His bung hole also puckered to keep from fouling his pants. He'd had both reactions before for the same reason, but it had been a long time ago and he'd tried to put it out of his mind.

Felice came in looking surprised, wiping her hands on a dish towel, saw Rose and looked even more surprised.

She said, "*So she ran away to your place? I might have known. Why didn't you bring her back sooner? Rose, go to your room! I'll see to you later.*"

Pa said, "*Rose doesn't have a room here anymore.*"

Felice's sudden anger showed in her reddening face. She sneered at Pa. "Who do you think you are all of a sudden, ordering me around in my own home?" The "all of a sudden" didn't escape Pa, who knew Felice once had called him Honorable Patches behind his back, even while she sponged off of his labor. And maybe she still did call him that, for all he knew. Her attitude now meant she thought he'd got a big head as Newt's charity case, driving a Lincoln he could never have afforded, buying a farm, even eating better than they had for years. Now he was even better off with Klondy, as Felice knew.

Stung, Pa retorted, "Maybe you'd rather have us come back with the sheriff. Or how would you like to see us in court?"

That set Felice to thinking hard.

"What do you mean?"

Newt interrupted, "This sonofabitch," he pointed a finger at Bertram, "tried to rape this little girl. This is damn serious business, so don't give us any of your snotty lip—I pegged you in the cradle, kiddo."

Then he poked his finger hard into Bertram's chest, then again, and again, and emphasized the last poke with "We aim to put this degenerate where he belongs and nail you for neglecting this girl." He pinned Felice with an icy glare.

Felice paled. She'd never been sure that this forbidding-looking giant wasn't at least half cracked. She came back in a shaken voice and said, "I think I'll call the sheriff."

Newt snapped, "You do that. After what I told him, he'll be expecting your call. We'll most likely call him out here to pick up Bertie before we're done anyhow."

Felice said, "Not on my phone, you won't!"

But that threw a scare into her and it showed in her face. Bertram had turned white and his jaw trembled. Watching him, Newt said, "Look at his face! And he's shakin' like a *'hydrophoby' skunk.'* He's guilty as they come."

"Guilty?" Felice tried to argue. "You can't prove a thing. Guilty of what?" she asked as though Newt hadn't got the "rape" charge across to her. She was stalling, trying to get some idea to counter them. She needed her Bertie, a useful cretin, just as she found Rose useful, and didn't want to lose either of them.

Ma spoke for the first time. She pointed her finger at Bertram and, with pure poison in her voice, said, "We told you what he's guilty of. Attempted rape! If you'd have protected this kid," she pointed to Rose, "like any *decent* person would, nothing would have happened. Our menfolks were comin' home from town and rescued her. She was running down the road, hysterical, and had nothing on but this!"

With a calculated dramatic touch, Ma jerked the collar and tattered shards of the top of Rose's nightie from her purse and shook it under Felice's nose. "That ugly elephant-eared bastard ripped the rest of it off her in her bedroom when he tried to rape her! He probably burned the rest of it so you wouldn't find it."

"I don't believe it!" Felice said, but anyone could tell from her face that she did. She looked like someone who'd just seen a rattlesnake crawl under her bed and was wondering how to get it out.

"That figures," Ma said. "I always said you were a simpleton and that proves it!" She pointed a finger at Bertram, eyes flashing, "The girl was scared out of her wits and you're going to pay for it!"

Ma looked the way she had when she'd been ready to smack Bennie as a kid, as he recalled, and he hoped she'd pop Felice one side the head hard enough to knock her down. He knew Ma was strong enough to do it, or even knock her cold.

"Maybe that's so and maybe it isn't," Felice came to Bertram's defense, but she didn't ask Elephant Ears to deny it.

Newt read her mind and got in the final blow. "I thought it would be a good idea to see if he had a record for this sort of thing. I had an investigator look into him and he found some records down in Dane County where Bertie here went to high school. The girls in school were all scared of him for some reason. One of 'em named Olga in particular. She's still alive and sung like a canary when she found out what we wanted to know. That's why he disappeared from Dane County just before he came up here." He let that hang. "The only reason Olga didn't have him put away was that her family didn't want the scandal to come out."

That Newt knew the name Olga really shook Bertram. He turned red, then pale and looked as though he'd like to become invisible.

Even before Newt added the final touch, Felice was wondering if Bertram could be a threat to her own precious being. Suppose he wanted to resume their hateful, very brief, sex life? She had to admit the truth to herself. All her adult life, she'd assumed that all men were after her jewel beyond price.

No one could have convinced her that no man with good eyesight would want her, not even on a million-dollar bet. It was a mystery to everyone why Bertram had married her. It had been a two-way street. She wondered if Rose would come back if she kicked Bertram out. After all Rose had been the best worker she'd ever had (free or otherwise). She wondered if offering to pay her fifty cents a week would help.

Pa interrupted her unhappy thoughts, "We came here because you folks are family, Felice, and I thought you deserved a chance to do the right thing."

Ma laughed loudly. "Her?" she asked.

Pa looked pained.

Felice asked no one in particular, "And what did you think was the right thing? To turn my hired girl over to you?"

Bennie wondered how anyone sane could think that was the main issue by this time. (She sounded like Hitler's propaganda.) *It came to him for the first time in his life that a lot of people around him were nuts and he'd never noticed.*

"Well," Pa said, "Em and Eben plan on adopting Rose. She's never been happy here. We just wanted to convince you it didn't make sense to put up a fuss over it. Maybe get it in the papers, since you have to live here and try to hold your head up in the community."

Felice ignored the important part of that and snapped, "The only reason she didn't like it here is I made her work."

Rose retorted in a voice so harsh for her that Ma took a good look at her and wondered if she really knew her. "*You* never *made* me do anything. I'd have worked even harder if you'd treated me decent."

"Will you come back if I make Bertram leave?" Felice asked.

Rose began to realize, as Bennie had, that this woman was cracked. She spit out the words, "*I'd rather die!*"

Felice looked sulky, still squirming on the hook as she said, "You may have to come back whether you like it or not. I'm going to go to the County if you don't stay here right now. These people can't adopt you. They aren't even married. My own dear brother here is living with a whore."

Pa looked like he'd like to slap her hard. Bennie wished he would.

That did it for Newt. He said, "Let's cut the bull, Felice. We gave you a chance to do the right thing because you're family like Ed said, much as we hate to face it."

Felice detested Newt, always had, ever since she'd realized he saw right through her. Something in her snapped and she said, "You can go to hell. You're not family. Where were you all those years?"

"Makin' enough money to put you in jail for neglecting your duty toward this kid, for one thing," Newt said. "The County already knows all it needs to know about this case. I spent the last couple of days makin' sure of that. If you want to buck them, maybe you'd like to go to court. Rose's got a new home, and that's all there is to it. As for being married, we thought of that. Eben and Emma got married yesterday. We forgot to invite you to the wedding, I guess. If you want a hearing it'll be after we send Berty here up the river. If I can swing it, we'll send you along to look after him, on a rap for neglecting and mistreating this girl. Money talks!"

She knew he had plenty of money.

Bertram spoke for the first time and said, "Keep your trap shut, Felice. And you ain't about to run me out, kiddo." He only thought the rest of the sentence, which would have been, "*and spend my hard-earned money*."

To the others he said, "Suppose we just forget any *unproven* charges about me, and you can have the girl."

Newt snorted, "Unproven my ass!" But he faced the facts and looked over the crowd and asked, "Do we make a deal with this bastard and avoid a big hassle?"

The notion of Bertram getting off in such a case didn't bother him since he'd decided to kill the son of a bitch as soon as the affair blew over.

Ma startled everyone by saying, "I'm not making any deal on letting this degenerate go scot-free. We can adopt Rose whether these shitasses like it or not. I want this *degenerate* behind bars!" She spit out the word so it had exactly the right inflection to cover the case and jabbing her finger in Berty's chest, she finished, "You'd better get yourself a lawyer!"

Pa wasn't the only one stunned by Ma's choice of words. They all were—even Newt who'd thought he fully understood how tough she was.

Rose interrupted. She could hardly believe what she heard herself saying, and saying most positively at that. "Why don't we just forget it? I'll have to testify won't I? I don't want to! I'll forgive and forget if they just let me come live with you without any trouble."

She knew what an ordeal it would be for her to testify, even if it was the truth.

Ma wasn't too happy with that, but she reflected about how Rose must feel. What Bert had said was true, about how the world, and that included a typical jury, would regard Rose. She'd read enough of her "rape" magazines to know what a shifty lawyer could do to a witness.

"O.K.," she said. "But I know there are laws called Statutes of Limitations and I doubt there is one on rape. We can probably prosecute Bertie here for attempted rape if we decided to till the day he dies."

Bertie squirmed and wished he was anywhere but there. He asked himself, "How the hell can this be happening to a guy with a lot of money in the bank?" He'd always thought money was the deciding factor about the right or wrong of anything that counted. It didn't occur to him that he should have jacked off in the barn as usual, instead of in front of a minor girl, and then tried to rape her to boot, especially one who detested him.

They were all pretty sure they'd have no more trouble with Bert and Felice. As much couldn't be said for Bert having trouble with Prune Face, however. As they left, Newt savored that probability and said, "I'd like to get an earful of what those two have to say to each other after we leave."

He thought, but neglected to mention, "*Wouldn't it be a howl if Berty tried to rape Felice?*" He knew if he got *any* from her, that's the way he'd have to do it. The thought made his stomach turn. He considered the idea of killing them both, instead of just Elephant Ears.

As they got in the car Ma said, "I should have slapped Felice's face. I always itched to do it from the first time I laid eyes on her homely phiz."

Bennie rode beside Rose in the back seat on the way home, holding her hand all the way. He rationalized his tenderness as human kindness, a matter of just consoling a fellow human who'd had a hell of a hard time of it most of her life. Besides, she was *almost* his little sister, even if she had given him a hard-on. Then he noticed that her leg pressing against his felt good, and started to get a hard-on again.

Rose didn't know that, but would have been happy if she had. She was growing up and knew her mind exactly. She was going on sixteen now. She wasn't sure what "sweet sixteen" meant, but if it meant the way she felt, she understood why it was sweet. She pushed against Benny a little closer, making it seem like she was just getting into a more comfortable position. She wasn't the least bit ashamed of what it did to her. She just wondered when Bennie would wake up.

Uncle Newt, sitting by the window next to Bennie, appeared preoccupied with smoking a cigar and, Rose hoped, wasn't paying attention to them. Finally, she got control of her feelings, and sat quietly, happier than she'd ever been before and glad that no one felt like talking. She didn't think she could make sense if someone expected her to say something and wondered if anyone else had ever felt this way.

She was going to have a home. A home with Bennie there in the next room every night, and where she could see him and talk to him every day. Maybe some night he'd sneak next door. If he didn't, maybe some night she'd sneak next door. She blushed at the thought.

Adopting Rose was almost a formality because Uncle Newt had the way greased. The judge even reached down from the bench and shook hands with all of them, and didn't act as though he thought Rose was a *tramp*. Money had talked, indeed.

When the family got home after the court hearing, Ma and Rose went off together to Rose's room like a couple of conspiring kids. Bennie could hear Ma and Rose laughing. The sound drifted down plainly from upstairs and Bennie gave Eben and Newt a look that said, "Don't that beat a hog flying?"

The house was going to be a different place and it didn't take long for that to make itself known. Ma set up her sewing machine and started making Rose a new outfit, several dresses, skirts, blouses, and even aprons. Most of the house dresses could be made from the material Ma had been squirreling away for years. For a few extra things, Bennie drove them in to Marshfield in the Lincoln and shot a few racks of pool while he waited. Afterward Ma bought them all lunch in a first-class restaurant.

When Rose had come out of the store in a new dress, and wearing high-heel shoes, he did a double take on her. Ma had shot the works on the kid and the saleswoman had helped them. Rose looked like a woman. She even had rouge and lipstick on. He saw her for the first time through different eyes. She was the prettiest woman he'd seen in town.

He asked himself, "How come I never noticed her before now?"

CHAPTER FORTY-EIGHT

Bennie's Indian Season, Part One

— SPRING 1941

War had been raging all over the world for almost two years, especially in Europe. America was tearing itself apart, trying to decide if it should get into the war on the side of the Allies—which was obviously the side of civilization—before it was too late.

As usual America was going to do the right thing, but wait far too long while do-gooders and cowards dragged their feet or lay down kicking and screaming like kids having tantrums. Among the do-gooders were *Hoobert Heever* and Charles Lindberg (our boy Lindy). *Heever* simply enhanced his bad reputation, but Lindy managed to undo all the favorable publicity his career had merited him up until then and would never quite recover it.

> "*Lindy turned out to be a shithead.*"
> —*Buck Doaks*
> (Speaking from semi-retirement)

While he was plowing that spring, Bennie's eyes often were attracted to the sky by the ominous drone of dozens of roaring airplane engines. Formations of bombers in training for war swept across America. FDR had managed to shove through Congress a rearmament program that included supplying arms to our allies in Europe and Asia. These were Britain, the Netherlands, and France, who were trying to hang onto empires that were doomed, and Australia and China, the latter hanging on against the Japs by the skin of its teeth. China was feebly assisted by military aid carried slowly and laboriously across the mountains on the Burma Road. The aid consisted of war supplies from both Britain and America. Other help came directly to China from an outfit called the Flying Tigers, which was an only slightly-disguised *American* Air Force commanded by a former American Army Air Corps officer, Claire Lee *Chennault*. His Tigers flew American P-40s and raised hell with the Jap Air Force, putting up a fight in which they scored respectably against the overpowering numbers of the Rising Sun.

All of this made headlines almost every day.

Bennie and Kid were sure they'd be going to war sooner or later, that it was only a matter of time. Meanwhile they intended to make the most of the free days that would be left. Newt aimed to help them. He thought it was time to educate them about some of the brutal realities of war.

As General Sherman had said, "War is cruelty, and you cannot refine it."

He also said it more pithily with his better known pronouncement:

"War is hell!"

Sherman was one of the foremost to prove his own definitions. After all, he'd burned Atlanta on purpose, and Columbia, South Carolina, sort of by accident. There were still a few around like Newt, who could remember when news of Sherman's war was in the newspapers. Even out on the plains, where Newt had spent a lot of the Civil War, the news from the more conventional war back east was avidly followed in the newspapers and magazines such as *Harper's* when Newt's outfit could lay its hands any of them. Seeing how hot Colonel Smith's boys were for war news and home news, which they practically inhaled from the newspapers, passing them around until they were worn out, had impressed Newt. Even as a stripling, he was already a book addict. He took up following the war in the newspapers.

More and more Newt's mind wandered back to his days with the regiment, especially the time after they were sent out onto the Plains.

Since he and Nelson had finished their bachelors' nests, he had a lot of time to occupy and spent much of it reliving the past in his mind. He caught up on his reading and reread a lot of his old favorites such as Grant's and Sherman's memoirs. These were a lot more interesting to him than to most readers because he'd seen both of these generals in the flesh at Shiloh, the one big battle in which Smith's regiment was engaged before being ordered west to fight Indians.

By contrast Nelson didn't mind idle time because he'd had so little of it in his life, and spent a lot of days taking long naps or listening to his battery-powered radio while browsing through magazines. Bennie had exposed him to *Western Story Magazine*, and he never missed an issue. At other times he was off fishing, in the woods gathering berries in season, or just wandering. He never carried a gun, and Newt kidded him, "Someday a bear might get you."

"Naw," Nelson scoffed. "Bears and me understands each other."

"How's that?" Newt asked, probing for an opening to needle him.

Nelson grinned since he knew Newt well enough to recognize what he was after, and said, "They get one whiff of me and say, 'By golly, this damned old Swede smells as bad as we do,' for one thing."

"By Christ, I'll buy that! Did you ever have an old he bear try to hump you?"

Nelson ignored him, and Newt got off the subject since it wasn't panning out as he hoped. Newt enjoyed that kind of life, but he'd always felt a responsibility to pass on his thinking and experience. In Bennie he recognized a fellow spirit. He intended to do his best to prepare him for life—and he hoped it would be a long one, such as he himself had been granted.

"*And,*" he thought, "*maybe more useful than mine. I hope he marries Rose and they raise some nice kids and have a good life right here on the farm. There ain't no freer kind of living to be had today anywhere in the world.*"

Of course the government was sticking its nose into farmers' affairs more and more every day, but it was a price of prosperity. Farmers had been going broke by the millions when FDR saved their bacon, almost over their dead bodies, with programs of price supports, controlled production, soil conservation, and now rural electrification, which would bring farm women conveniences known only to city folks.

Newt thought, "*Life's gonna be a hell of a lot better, and I hope I'm still around to see at least the start of it. Hell, as far as that goes, it's been getting a whole lot better ever since the Civil War. I can remember that the world was already changing fast when I brought Pa home from the War on a stretcher. As one example, women weren't cooking in pots hung in the fireplace, or chained to spinning wheels anymore and could buy ready-made clothes, or get cloth already made up and sew it into clothes on one o' them new-fangled sewin' machines.*"

Bringing his Pa home reminded him of their soldiering days in the West, starting when their regiment had been sent to fight Indians under General Sully.

He thought, "*I'd like to take one more look at 'er and see how much it's changed out there across the Missouri,*" and considered how he would go about that. "*I'll need someone to drive the Lincoln. Want to see it on the ground, not out of a train window. Besides trains don't go where we went—at least not entirely. I'll take Bennie. And Kid, too. He'll want to see where his heathen ancestors made their last stand.*

"*Hell, talk about Custer's Last Stand—it was Sitting Bull that made a last stand.*"

He laughed at a sudden thought. "*Or maybe it was really old Bull's First Stand, come to think about it. He never bothered anybody until they poked a stick in his hole and tried to run him out. He came out all right. Well, I was there, too. But that was ten years after the War was over. I'd better look the Little Big Horn over one last time too. Maybe tell Bennie what really happened instead of how it came out in books.*"

He was sitting in front of his cabin smoking a cigar in a big camp chair he'd built for himself out of two by fours and canvas, a pillow behind his head, blowing smoke rings and staring off into the distance and not really seeing his surroundings but observing the past as it was reborn in his head.

Kid came outside rolling a cigarette. He was living with Newt most of the time now. His Pa was out of the pen and taking care of things at home. Newt glanced at Kid and indicated a chair just like the one he was in, and said, "Set. I been figuring. As that cuss on the *Lone Ranger* program says: 'I got a plee-an.' A good one, too."

Kid laughed. They all listened to the *Lone Ranger* regular as clockwork on Nelson's radio. "Who's gonna git in trouble this time?" Kid asked. "I mean besides me?"

Newt never changed expression. He puffed awhile to get his cigar going good again and said, "You and Bennie, only it's the kind of trouble you young farts will like, if I know kids your age, and I think I do. I need a vacation. I want you two along to drive me where I can do what the magazines call 'reliving my youth.' How does that grab you? I want you to bring Bennie over here if he's not busy, and we'll plan it out."

Kid's heart took an elated jump at that prospect. He'd never been west, or even out of Wisconsin. Bennie felt the same way when Kid came over to tell him about it.

They spent a week planning their trip and getting together equipment and supplies.

Newt went over their final list and said, "If we ain't got it, we'll buy it."

The night before they set out, Bennie had trouble going to sleep, excited at the prospect of what had been, to his mind, a utopian excursion that he'd only dreamed about up till then.

He was dozing off when something aroused him. He thought Hank was trying to climb on the bed, at which he tried his luck every once in a while. "Get down, Hank!" He swept his hand out to push the dog away and was startled to find something soft and warm and yielding that was definitely not Hank.

"I'm not Hank," Rose said.

"Are you all right?" he asked, concerned that she might have suddenly taken ill.

"Yes," she said, softly. "Move over. I want to talk to you."

He wondered for a moment if she was losing her mind. "You can talk from out there," he said.

"Just move over and let me in."

She sounded determined.

"I'm getting cold out here."

Then she pulled back the covers and slipped in beside him.

"That's better," she said.

"*This isn't right.*" Bennie thought. "*She's almost my sister.*"

Then a little voice in his head that reminded him of Buck Doaks said, "You must be some kind of dodo. Grab the kid and help her warm up."

The voice was followed by a snicker.

"You can really warm her up if you try."

By now Rose had snuggled close to him.

"You're nice and warm."

Bennie knew enough about women by then to realize that she wasn't having some sort of seizure, as he might have thought if he hadn't outlived Ma's advice.

But Ma's conditioning of him had been superseded by advanced training (by whores).

He knew that Rose was simply growing up.

The snide voice in his head said, "She's horny, just like most girls her age, only most won't admit it."

Bennie put his arm under Rose and pulled her close. He was getting one hell of a hard-on and didn't give a damn if she was almost like a sister or not. Very gently he kissed her. Her inexperienced lips didn't quite know what to do, but her body did. She pressed against him hard, and he was surprised at how strong she was.

After several kisses he expertly slipped his tongue into her mouth and moved it around. He was tremendously aroused by the sound and feel of her heavy breathing and the soft little murmurs she was making. He hoped to hell she wouldn't get any louder and wake up Ma down the hall. He wasn't worried about Eben; he knew he wouldn't care and would understand. Fortunately, as he well knew, once Ma corked off it usually took a tornado to wake her up.

He helped Rose out of her nightie. He always slept naked so didn't have anything to take off. Gently he slipped his hand down and stroked her silky pubic hair and wondered if she'd ever come before. He doubted it. Remembering what Kate had said, he decided to get her off that way first so she'd know what to expect. He didn't want to hurt her. He pulled his arm from under her neck and got up on his elbow so he could lean over and kiss her breasts while he massaged her clitoris. He hadn't really noticed how her boobs had grown in the time she'd been with them. He hadn't noticed a lot he should have and made a vow to make up for lost time. He pressed his body against her leg while he stroked her and felt himself start to come. The novelty of having an inexperienced, yet passionate woman in his arms aroused him tremendously.

He thought, "*Jesus Christ I don't want to ruin it by coming all over her!*"

He pulled away and tried to get control of himself, barely succeeding. Her passion had aroused him to a peak that made self-control all the more difficult.

"Oh, Bennie! Oh, Bennie! Oh, oh, oh!" She came hard and long and gripped his hand tightly between her legs, and continued holding him even after her peak had passed. After she caught her breath he kissed her tenderly, loving the feel of her mouth.

Finally, in a very little voice she said, "I love you, Bennie. I've loved you since the first time I saw you. I had to come here tonight because you're leaving tomorrow and something might happen and you'd never know."

Then, after a pause she said, "Why don't you take me with you? I can sneak over and get in bed with you every night."

Bennie thought, "*Sneak hell! Uncle Newt and Kid wouldn't give a damn if we shacked up the whole trip. But this is a man thing. They really wouldn't want a girl along, not even Rose.*"

Bennie didn't say anything, but got up on his knees between her legs and let himself down gently. He rubbed his erection gently up and down on her entrance where he knew it would contact her clitoris, and made sure she was lubricating heavily before he started into her. She was making little contented noises again. He was surprised how naturally she lifted her legs without him showing her, as though she'd done it a hundred times. She had in her imagination.

None of the experienced women he'd been with had made him feel so wonderful, and he wondered why. She was only a girl, and a terribly inexperienced one at that. It would take a while for him to realize that the reason was that he was falling deeply in love for the first time, and with a woman he could respect completely.

Gradually he eased into her and only by a tremendous effort of will kept from coming at the first stroke. "I've got to hold out, no matter what," he told himself. "I want her to come right with me the first time."

He felt himself losing it regardless, and was elated to feel her letting go with him. Most girls couldn't the first time unless you stuck with them a long while, but most girls weren't deeply in love already with the man doing it with them. She gripped him hard and pulled him in deep as he streamed off his tremendous load in her. It left him gasping for breath, hardly able to hold himself up.

She was breathless too, and it seemed to her she had gone far away for a little while, to a place she'd never been, a wonderful dream world, or maybe Heaven. She drifted back gradually, but with her eyes closed she was still in a wonderful warm place with pink light all around, floating on a cloud where Bennie kissed her again and again, on her lips, her eyelids, her neck and hairline.

He astounded himself by hearing what he was whispering between kisses, repeating it over and over. "You little darling. You little darling doll. I love you, Rose. I love you. I'll always love you, forever and ever."

"I love you, too, Bennie," she said. "With all my heart. I'm going to live for you and nobody else ever—the rest of my life belongs to you."

"Me too," he whispered close to her ear. "Me too, darling." He playfully nipped her ear lobe, then kissed her again, a long, gentle kiss that he wished would last forever. Finally she turned her head and said, "Let me up for air," and the words came out with a small gusty laugh. Then she giggled.

Bennie loved the whole thing, but suddenly a sobering thought jolted him, "*Christ, I should have pulled it out and came on her tummy! Maybe I just got her pregnant!*" But it had felt sweeter and sweeter and he couldn't have stopped if he knew he'd have to die for shooting off *in* her. Besides, he thought, "*I love her. She loves me. We can get married if she's pregnant. What if we are young? Romeo and Juliet were a hell of a lot younger.*"

He didn't even ask himself, "What will Ma say?" The thought didn't occur to him as it might have a few months back. Now, if he'd thought about it at all, he'd have concluded that Ma might approve. She'd been only seventeen when she had Lillian.

Rose was asleep beside him in a few minutes, but woke up later and crawled on top of him. "It's me, again," she whispered when she knew he was fully awake.

"I know it's you," he said. "Did you think I'd expect two *wild women* to sneak in all in one night?"

She laughed. "I wouldn't let one. You're mine now and you'd better get used to it."

"Who's fighting it?" Bennie asked.

They repeated the whole thing, and it was even better than the first time, both of them taking their time and learning one another.

Afterward they talked in low voices for a long while, planning their life together. Bennie had his arm under her neck and kissed her cheek or hairline every once in awhile as they talked. Naturally they would get married as soon as they could convince Ma they weren't too young. And they'd have a family. Maybe a big one.

"I want a boy and a girl at least," Rose said. "Maybe two of each." She was thinking of her own family and how much fun they'd had together before the trouble shattered and dispersed them.

"I want at least a girl if we never have another kid," Bennie said. "One just like you. And I'll spoil her all to pieces just like I'm gonna spoil you from now on."

She jumped on that. "You can start by taking me with you on your trip."

He didn't see a single damn way to get out of it after that and talked Newt and Kid into it the next day, which wasn't hard to do. Both loved Rose.

That was how the Lincoln got packed full of a camping outfit, with Newt and Rose in the back seat with their feet crowded by a pile of tents and other camping stuff and canned goods. The only thing that marred Bennie's total pleasure was that they had to leave Hank behind.

"We'll be stopping' at hotels and tourist courts and most of 'em don't take in dogs," Newt had vetoed the idea. "I hate it as bad as you do, but a lot of the time he wouldn't like it, tied up outside or shut up in the Lincoln. Besides he might get loose and get lost, or someone might steal him if we left him tied out at night."

Even Bennie couldn't think of an argument against that.

When they alternated drivers, Newt up front with Kid doing the driving, if anyone in the front knew the new lovers in back were glued together, kissing a lot, they pretended not to notice.

Bennie had a lewd thought and could hardly stifle a laugh. "*I never knew how much better the scenery looks with at least a half a hard-on all the time.*"

Newt was his usual history lesson, and told them, "The covered wagons used to start by our place in LaSalle every spring as soon as the grass was up. You couldn't travel west till the grass was good enough to keep the livestock fed. Folks traveled only as fast as a hoss could go, and if a man didn't have sense enough to keep his hosses or mules, or maybe oxen alive, he died out in the sticks, or at least walked back to civilization. It made for folks with a lot more sense on the average than today. Of course we had our share of damn fools. Some city folks should never have left home. It was hard on the whole outfit if a man was a damn fool—on his woman and kids, the livestock, and everybody that had to travel with them, but especially on the womenfolks."

They headed southeast at first, instead of west.

"Want to show you where Fort Winnebago was, down at Portage. That's where the frontier was then," Newt said. "My gramp was down there during the Blackhawk War in 1832. You don't hear much about that war. You know why? It wasn't much to be proud of. Most of our wars with the Indians weren't. We'll follow old Blackhawk's trail through Wisconsin then jump the Mississippi and head west—out where I spent most of the Civil War chasing Indians until they rushed us back to Missouri when the Rebs decided to shoot their bolt there; they come under old Pap Price. He was Governor of Missouri once. Politics made him a general, and like a lot of them he wasn't much shucks at it. He was a rare son of a bitch though. Must have weighed three hundred pounds; too fat to get on a horse, and rode in a buggy or wagon. The dumb son of a bitch never won a battle I ever heard of, yet he was popular as hell. It's hard to figure."

When Newt got wound up, Bennie never got tired of listening. There was more history in some of his ramblings than you'd find in a library full of history books by professors who never ventured off a campus in their lives, except maybe to Europe to look at old castles, museums, and Roman aqueducts.

Bennie knew about such things too, from reading, but he thought, "*The Romans and Greeks had their day. We owe 'em just like we owe all our ancestors. But I don't give a shit whether I ever see the Acropolis or the Colosseum. This is my day and this is my kind of country.*"

He surveyed the woods and fields they drove past, the window down and the spring air flowing in bearing a tang that you could kill for. The world was coming back to life after lying dead all winter, dead like it could only get in places as icy cold as Wisconsin. Hibernating life burrowed deeper, stayed dormant longer, and the ground froze at least a foot deep, as he knew from trying to put in a fence post that January. He thought, "*Hell, even people hibernate up here as much as they can, if you think about it. Who the hell goes outside unless they absolutely have to? Not me, that's for sure.*"

They stayed at tourist courts, rather than camped out, at first. Bennie asked at a couple of places if they'd have taken a dog and found out Newt had been right. Most places didn't allow dogs even if they were well housebroken. Some of them didn't look like they'd care to put up a young man and a mere girl in the same room. He and Rose got a couple of funny looks, but Newt was good window dressing. Whose grandpa would let a boy shack up with a young gal? So they registered as man and wife and got away with it.

Their first camp outdoors was at the scene of the battle of Wisconsin Heights, which Bennie had passed once before on his way *up north*. That seemed like a lifetime before but was only four years. Thinking back, he wondered if he'd ever lived before then.

"*Was I ever in Waubonsee? In Blackhawk?*" he asked himself.

The memory of those sorry days was sour, but life had finally got better.

He wondered how much better his life could be. He felt sure it would get even better since his eyes had been opened by Rose and he realized he was in love. Life was like a dream when you were in love.

He thought, "*I do love Rose, and it ain't puppy love. I've been with a lot of grown women. I never felt like this with anyone. And we're gonna live happily ever after, just like in those fairy tales.*"

With war hanging over them he knew that was whistling in the dark. He also had a suspicion that it didn't do to dictate to God and tried to be as humble as possible with his hopes. That was the Indian in him asserting itself. He often prayed and didn't mention his way of praying because he knew that most people wouldn't understand. When he thought of the life he wanted with Rose he asked, "*Please, God, I've never asked for much, but I want this one for sure if you can see your way to it.*"

She was asleep on the back seat beside him, breathing gently with her lips parted a little. He wanted to kiss her but didn't want to wake her up. A feeling so deep and tender he couldn't describe it flooded his whole being and he knew it was true love, just like in the books. He gently took her hand and she stirred a little but didn't wake up. He willed all of his strength into her and hoped she felt his love enveloping her. He wondered what he'd do now if something happened to this wonderful, incredibly innocent and sweet person. The thought didn't occur to him what she might have to live through if something happened to him. And it might with a war that could engulf Uncle Sam any day.

Near the Wisconsin Heights battle site, they saw a farmer working on a fence alongside the road and stopped to get directions.

A weathered old fellow who reminded Bennie of Nelson looked up when they stopped and got out of the car. He looked the big Lincoln over then looked at them, puzzled. Bennie knew what he was thinking. The car looked like city slickers, but their clothes looked like Woodsies.

"Howdy," Newt said. "Hate to bother you, but I told the kids we'd look over the place where my gramp fought old Blackhawk in 1832."

The old boy regarded them from weathered blue eyes that had seen a lot of years.

"Is that so?" he asked. "Well, I reckon you came to the right party. Happens my family's owned the place just about since the fighting was over. My own granddad was a lumberman and squatted on a section right here and proved up on it. You don't look like the kind that would be shootin' my cows or horses or leaving gates open, I reckon."

Newt said, "You got that right. After I finally seen my first gate, I always left 'em the way I found 'em. We're all farm folks from *up north* in Wood County."

The farmer nodded. "I figured you wasn't from too far off. Us folks get the look I guess. I'd show you where to go myself but I want to finish up here. You just go down the road to the next lane on the right and turn in. It's a ways up to the house. Tell Ma I said it was O.K. She'll show you the lane out back of the barn. Just keep on 'er and you can't miss. Goes right down to the river. The big hill is where most of the fightin' was."

Newt remembered his dad showing him that hill three-quarters of a century before, and wondered if his memory was accurate. He'd soon find out.

"Well, thankee kindly," Newt said. "We're mighty obliged. I reckon not everyone would be so helpful."

The farmer said, "I wouldn't be that helpful for just everybody. Like I said, you folks got woods wrote all over you." He looked at Rose, and added, "Even this pretty young gal." He grinned, and Rose smiled.

Then like a gun with one more pop in it, he added, "If many people knew where it was, I'd post it. But it's a funny thing. None of them fancy pants government dudes ever come up here to put up a marker about that fight. Come to think of it, we don't need no marker. I'd get overrun with tourists, especially when they found out you can still find junk from the battle all over back there around the big hill and all the way down to the river. Arrowheads, pieces of guns. My pa said when he was little you could even see the places where the Indians had their campfires. Anyhow, yer welcome as can be. I'd appreciate it if you don't advertise the place. Maybe I'm the only one around that even thinks about that fight these days. The neighbors—none of 'em—ever talk about it and they don't teach it in the schools; not even over to Sauk City, and its named for old Blackhawk's tribe. Funny thing, ain't it?" he said again to no one in particular.

"It is." Newt said. "Maybe nobody's proud of it. Anyway we ain't gonna blab about what we see. Besides no one but a few freaks like us are interested anymore anyhow."

That got a laugh out of the farmer. "If you see any spooks back there, they're harmless. Some get out this far sometimes and I've had 'em watch me milking and doin' chores. I'd like to hire a few for their board." He laughed again, and they joined him.

"Fat chance," Kid said. "Us Injuns are all too lazy to work."

The farmer gave him a careful look. "I guess you're an Indian all right."

Kid said, "Sioux." He pointed a finger at Bennie. "He's a quarter-blood himself."

"The hell you say? Well, I ain't got any beef ag'in' your kind. I reckon you got a royal screwing like Blackhawk."

"Still gettin' it," Kid said.

That got another laugh all around, including Kid who'd learned young there wasn't a hell of a lot he could do about race prejudice except live with it.

The farmer watched the Lincoln grow smaller in the distance and then turned back to his fencing. "Appear like nice folks," he said to himself.

They followed the farmer's instructions and found a neat white two-story house set in a grove of oaks. The farmer's wife heard them coming and came out and looked them over with a reserved expression, then thawed when she learned that her husband had sent them.

"Just up through the barnyard and over the hill," she said. "If you'll excuse me I got to get back to churnin'."

They wound their way back through the hills on a deeply rutted wagon road, Bennie driving cautiously in low. The Lincoln made it right to the big hill where most of the fighting took place.

The farmer had been giving them the straight story about stuff from the battle still to be found, especially arrowheads, and Kid found a ramrod for an old muzzle loader.

Bennie could feel ghosts hovering near the camp that night, knowing they were out there beyond the light of the fire. He bet if Hank was with them he'd have growled occasionally at something none of them could see or hear. Rose snuggled closer to Bennie and pulled her jacket closer around her.

"Spirits," Kid said.

No one questioned him.

When she and Bennie got into his pup tent and snuggled close, she thought about those lost ones out there in the night, souls hovering where they died with no monument to rally around. The place where they'd died was their only monument, this lonely land where their mortal remains had lain to be eaten by wolves without a single person to mourn for them—not a one, for any man, woman or kid. She didn't know about things like that as Bennie did, but she was learning.

He'd told her that he read that one brave had stayed behind, sitting on a rock next to the body of his wife who'd died of exhaustion, waiting to be killed so he could join her in the spirit world. She was still holding their dead baby that had starved to death since she didn't have any milk. The scouts who reached the brave obliged him and scalped them all.

Earlier Newt had stared into the fire, his thoughts far away, then finally said what he was thinking, "I read about the fight in books when I was a kid. Heard it from some who'd been there. They made it sound like the battle of Gettysburg if you believed what the old timers said about that. But Blackhawk had his own story wrote before he died. Said he had only fifty men here to fight off the hundreds of whites while the rest of his braves helped the women and kids over the river. I believe him. At that the soldiers were mostly scared out of their wits, ready to run. A couple of months before, back in Illinois a couple of hundred of them run like hell from Blackhawk and only half a dozen braves. When a few more Indians came up they got really chased and slaughtered like scared puppies waiting for the club. That footrace got the name *Stillman's Run* after the officer in command of the sorry business."

The sad part of that, as Newt's gramp had told him, was that the first bunch of Blackhawk's Indians to confront Stillman's rabble had been sent by the old chief to offer the surrender of his tribe. They were taken into the camp of the whites and some were killed; others escaped. After that, Blackhawk saw no alternative but a running fight to escape, and it lasted all summer. Wisconsin Heights was the prelude to the end that occurred at Bad Axe.

Rose thought of all this before she dropped off to sleep. She could see stars through the front of the tent and a lone cloud blotted them out for a minute. The wind sighed in the bare trees like spirits talking to one another. She snuggled closer to Bennie under their blankets.

They aimed to see Bad Axe before heading for the far west and got there a couple of days later, after stopping in some pleasant little towns just to "mosey around," as Newt said. One had the interesting name Viroqua, and Rose wondered how it got its name. Another was Soldiers Grove, and she could figure how that got the name.

Their route was through rugged hills and valleys known in geography books as the Western Hill and Valley Region of Wisconsin.

Bennie recalled he'd once dreamed of being at Bad Axe—and of how he tried to save the women and children of the Sauk tribe from Wabasha's Sioux. This was the place where Wabasha's braves laughed at him, then sent a shower of arrows after him as he swam away in the Mississippi. Wabasha, Kid had said, was his great-grandfather, or was it his great-great, or was he kidding? Bennie wasn't going to ask. It might have spoiled something.

Bad Axe wasn't marked either. There was a Victory Ridge, a Bad Axe River, a Battle Hollow, and Battle Creek, and a little town named Victory, but not so much as a sign said what battle, or *whose* victory.

Newt said, "Let's ask around and see if anybody knows anything. Or even knows where the actual fight was."

They stopped in a little café for lunch. A slack-lipped fellow with graying hair and weak gray eyes came to take their orders. He was obviously cook and waiter in one package. He brought water and gave them menus, then was about to leave when Newt said, "I wonder if you could tell us where the battle of Bad Axe took place."

That got a vacant look.

"I heard the name," he said, "but I never heard where it was."

Newt thought, "*If I lived in a place where there was a big fight with Indians I'll be damned if I wouldn't find out where it was.*"

When the fellow was out of hearing, Bennie said to Kid, "What a gem he is. I wonder if we'll get poisoned." But the food was remarkably good. The doltish proprietor wasn't much of a historian, but a pretty damned good cook.

As they were leaving, Newt asked, "You know anyone who might be able to tell us where the battle of Bad Axe was fought?"

The man shook his head. "Can't say as I do."

They couldn't find a soul who knew a thing and never were able to find the battle site. They camped high above the river for one night and a random hike the next day turned up little or nothing for sure. Bennie wondered why this battle wasn't marked either. He thought, "*Because we're ashamed of it! That's why they never put it in our school history books. This one was even shittier than some of the other ones we pulled on the poor bastards.*" He remembered his grandmother saying, "I was afraid to go to a parade when the soldiers still wore blue uniforms. I thought they'd get me even then. Isn't that funny?"

He wondered as they drove beside the Mississippi after camping one night, what place along the bank he might have dived in under a shower of arrows as his own reward for sticking up for the desperate fugitives in that dream. He thought, "*Hell, why should I bleed for the bastards? I might have Indian blood, but maybe I ought to be ashamed of it. Their own kind was always killing them, too.*" Somehow that didn't seem like an excuse that ought to satisfy somebody with a sense of fair play. He'd heard too many cop-outs that amounted to shrugging and saying "everyone else does it." He'd also heard that a lot of folks went to hell. It didn't appeal to him. Not copping out, not roasting in the bad place if there really was one. He thought, "*If there ain't, we sure need one, especially for Hitler and his kind. And the Indians deserved it for killing their own when they were being chased by their common enemy after Bad Axe, the palefaces that were stealing their land.*"

The thought of war hanging over them was always in the back of every mind in America in those years, especially in the young men like Bennie and Kid, who knew they'd go as soon as the shooting started. Bennie had thought of going before it started. There was a draft now, which wasn't popular, but so far 900,000 boys had been drafted. (When the draft law came up for renewal a few months later, it would pass in Congress by one vote.)

Bennie knew he'd get caught by the draft sooner or later if the war went on, sooner if America got into it. But since he'd discovered Rose, the idea of volunteering appealed to him less. He thought of her all the time, day and night, and how sweet it was to hold her and feel her heart beating against him. He often told himself, "*I'm sure glad I met a few like Kate and Grace and Klondy's gals so I knew what to do. I could have hurt Rose, and she'd have ended up hating sex like Ma.*" (He didn't know the full story about the new Ma.) The thought of Rose ending up unhappy and unloved was just about the most awful thought he could imagine. And sex with love was a wonderful thing. He thought, "*I hope I live to be a hundred and we can do it till we die, and if I can't still get it up like Newt when I'm old, at least I can hang around and take care of Rose.*"

He couldn't believe how tender and protective she had made him. Just looking at her caused butterflies inside him, like when he was a kid and got a silver dollar in a letter from Grandpa Todd, only this was better.

He thought, "*Why was I so dumb about her? I even saw her naked, taking a bath, out at Kid's lake and never thought she'd want to do anything with me. She was already beautiful then and I had to jack off that night thinking about her, but I was still an innocent dunce.*"

His snide inner voice said, "*Dunce? Very true! A real retard. She was probably beginning to wonder what the hell was the matter with you.*"

Sometimes she caught him looking at her and smiled, her eyes locking with his and growing dark and mysterious. At those times her breath stopped for a moment and she felt the same thrill he did. She always said a little prayer that was prompted by her unhappy past, "*Please God, don't take him away from me now that we've found each other. I couldn't bear it.*"

They crossed the Mississippi River at LaCrosse and headed west into Minnesota. It looked about like the country that Bennie was used to. Newt had them go through Northfield, where the James and Younger Gang had stuck up the bank and got shot out of existence by a bunch of Yankee farmers with grim faces and jut jaws. The James brothers got away, many gang members were killed, and the Younger brothers went to the pen.

Newt's comment about that was, "I'll bet the bastards wished they'd stayed down in Missouri." The bank building was still there and in the window was a picture of that posse, some of the toughest-looking birds Bennie'd ever laid eyes on. He thought, "*I can see why the James Gang got their asses shot off.*"

Newt next took them through New Ulm. He told them, "This is where the Sioux War of 1862 started. The usual reason. A bunch of whites were screwing the Indians until they took about all they could stand. Before it was over they'd killed a few hundred whites and got blamed for the whole affair. But that was the reason Colonel Smith's regiment was sent west after Shiloh. The next couple of years we campaigned against the Sioux, the poor devils. There was two columns, the one up here under General Sibley and the one we were with, under General Sully, that operated in Dakota and Montana. We had quite a time of it and I loved every minute of it. By then I was twelve and a seasoned campaigner, and seasoned chicken and pig thief too. I was taught by experts. We'll swing over that way and start at Sioux City where we headed out from. Might as well go by Spirit Lake on the way. There was a massacre there before the Civil War, started again by the whites. Old Inkpaduta's Santee got all the blame for that, too. They were damn well drove out on the plains and never came back, and Inkpaduta was at the Little Big Horn with his tribe when Custer got his."

That was the campaign that really interested Bennie. He'd been interested in Custer since the year he discovered him in the library in Waubonsee in a book titled *On the Plains with Custer*, by Edwin L. Sabin. That's when he met Pro Bono Publico and learned that her name was the motto of West Point, the national military academy that Custer had attended and where he'd graduated last in his class (and first in a class all by himself).

Bennie knew that the Little Big Horn was on their itinerary later and that Newt and his grandpa, *Johnny Todd*, had both been there the day Custer was wiped out with five companies of his cavalry. Bennie even knew what companies they were—C, E, F, I, and L—and who commanded them. These company commanders were Custer's favorites, and that favoritism had created the factions that split the regiment. That may not have been the least of the reasons why Custer's orders were ignored and he was abandoned to fight it out by himself. The main reason, Bennie always thought, aside from bad luck, was the cowardice of Custer's second-in-command, Major Marcus Reno. Newt had hinted at a full story that had never been told before. Bennie knew Newt was bound to tell it when they got there. Maybe he'd saved the story because he planned all along to go there someday with Bennie and tell what he'd learned right on the spot where it took place.

Before they jumped off to the Plains proper, Newt had to show them Yankton, where he and Johnny Todd had holed up in a hotel room overlooking the court house, intending to ambush Jack McCall if he was acquitted of the killing of their pal, Wild Bill. Newt had Bennie drive around looking for the place, but it was no longer there.

"If it was still here, I'd stay overnight," Newt said.

They asked at the Chamber of Commerce and got no help. They were shown where Custer camped on the way west with the Seventh Cavalry, however. They drove out of town past the place.

CHAPTER FORTY-NINE

Bennie's Indian Season, Part Two

Bennie was stunned by his first view of the Plains. He'd seen pictures of the vast flat landscape, but photographs couldn't capture the feeling of an endless expanse of earth. They had stopped in Pierre for the night, then headed out up the Missouri River early in the morning.

"This is the way we went with General Sully," Newt had said. "By steamboat as much as we could. And all our supplies came the same way."

Bennie stopped the car and got out to savor the air and look around. He climbed a low rise beside the road, Rose trailing behind him. Atop the rise, he stood and turned around slowly, scanning the distant horizon. Bennie realized he'd never really seen the land before. Always there had been trees or hills surrounding him, a canopy of green or, in winter, bare branches pressing in on him. He mused aloud, "I never knew how high the sky was."

Rose who knew he was experiencing a private moment and who had tried to become invisible, whispered, "What?"

Bennie, aware of her once again, said, "I just realized how high the sky is."

She looked up, leaning her head back and stayed like that for a few seconds. "It isn't high," she finally said. "High isn't there. It just goes on forever."

Her words prompted him to look up just as she had, then down and turn completely around, his eyes circling the whole horizon, then look up again. He shivered, feeling that his eyes had attached invisible moorings to this endless space, that it was now an extension of his body and that he might fly around in himself and out there at the same time.

He stared at the sun, still low in the east, and squinted. He remembered the Indian Sun Dance, and decided to fix his gaze on the sun and see if he felt anything unusual. The red orb grew smaller and appeared to recede. His heart raced. He'd seen this phenomenon once before back in Waubonsee, as sick as he'd ever been, expecting to die and terribly frightened. He'd wanted to call out to Ma for help, but knew she'd scoff at his fears, tell him he was merely delirious again and it would go away. He remembered that he had prayed that it would and that God would let him live a while longer.

Now, though, he wasn't frightened, but exhilarated. He was flying toward the sun while it diminished, attempting to catch it. When it grew somewhat larger, he almost laughed at what crossed his mind: "*What will I do with it if I catch it?*"

This wasn't like his terrifying challenge as a child when he was sick and delirious. Alone in bed he'd been overwhelmed by the thought, "Suppose I have to eat the sun? Suppose that's my destiny? How can I do that?" It had been too overwhelming to even consider.

He felt as if he were growing more and more weightless, and he was startled but not frightened. It was as if he might be able to take off and leave the earth and follow the sun. It was so real it startled him, but he wasn't frightened. The thought was so compelling that he grabbed Rose's hand and held onto her hard; in case he really did take off flying he wanted her with him.

"*It's my Indian blood*," he thought. "*I'm coming home. Country Grandma was from out here. She must have missed it terribly all her life and never told anyone.*"

"I've got to remember to ask her," he told himself. "I can do it when we stop by her place on our way home."

They had to go to Country Grandma's in Illinois and pick up Ma, who would be visiting her mother. And Newt wanted to visit his old home at LaSalle, and "see Cannonball's grave," he'd said, "and put flowers on Ma and Pa's graves."

These thoughts brought Bennie back to earth. He walked back down the hill still holding Rose's hand tightly.

"I felt funny up there," Rose said, "Did you?"

He squeezed her hand. "Naw, but it's sure pretty out here." He was out of breath, and the land still seemed to be floating around him.

What had happened was too confusing to admit, even to her. "*As though I've just been born*," he thought, and knew he had to think a long while before he tried to tell anyone, and perhaps he might not ever be able to do it. A voice spoke to him and said, "*Tell God!*" and he experienced a profound shiver such as he'd never felt before.

Rose sensed something from his grip, and said, "You're having a chill. It's pretty cool up here in the morning. You should have brought a jacket."

"You didn't," he said, trying to shake off his mood with banter.

"I'm a hot mama," she said, laughing. "And it's your fault."

That broke his mood, and they returned to the Lincoln, laughing. Newt and Kid noticed the two coming back, hand in hand, and acting like a couple of three-year-olds, and figured they knew why.

As they drove north, Newt said, "Gotta stop at Fort Lincoln. That's where me and old Johnny Todd rode out with Custer on his last campaign."

The town of Bismark didn't impress Bennie, but the ruins of the old fort across the Missouri River did. The village of Mandan had grown there since Custer's time at Fort Abraham Lincoln, and south of it lay the ruins of the fort, haunted by echoes of the past—mingled voices, the sound of hoofs, jingling trace chains, bugle calls, hoarse shouted commands, and above all the howling force of the blizzards that scourged this notoriously frigid place.

Bennie left Rose snoozing in the Lincoln and sneaked off from Newt and Kid, who were inspecting the foundations of what had been Custer's quarters, and walked at least a half mile to a rise where he could see a long way.

The wind had picked up, bending the tall grass and was distinctly chilly under a clouding sky, yet welcoming. Taking Rose's advice, he'd learned to carry a jacket in this country at every hour of the day and now put his on. He savored the wind and was sure it carried voices from the past—laughter of long-departed army people—especially the coarse voices and joking of men after warm weather had liberated everyone from confinement around fireplaces in the family quarters, or the stoves in smelly barracks. He wondered if any of the soldiers had been rugged enough to go for a spring swim in the Missouri, as the Indians did. It would be a challenge in waters from melted ice and snow flooding down from the Rockies hundreds of miles upstream.

Most of all, this hallowed place turned his imagination to happy times, the laughter, and heedless gabble of men and women going on the first picnics of the warmer weather. He knew there must have been young lovers such as he and Rose among the many people living at the fort.

"Hell," he told himself. "Custer and his wife, Libbie, were young lovers when it came right down to it. He wasn't thirty-seven yet when he died, and she was a few years younger than him."

Custer commanded here. Had left this place on his final, fateful campaign, with Newt and his own grandpa along as packers. Bennie knew that Uncle Newt was planning to take them to the place where Custer died with all the men in five of his cavalry companies, and he planned to drag out of Newt every bit of information he could. His grandmother never talked of those days, and he'd been too young to press her, but it would be different when he saw her again. She had been there, too, just like Newt.

He slowly swept his gaze around the horizon, trying to ignore civilization across the river. It was 1876 again, and Custer was about to leave on his last campaign.

Tell me wind, can you recall
Those magic days before the fall
Of the dashing warrior with yellow hair,
his lovely wife all thought so fair?

Did they stroll here and sometimes stand
Beside each other hand in hand
And savor together as lovers do
The magic of being one, though two?

This was the historic ground from which Custer had ridden away on a fateful day in May 1876. Many swore that as he departed, with the band playing "Garry Owen" and "The Girl I Left Behind Me," they saw the long column of horsemen marching up into the clouds.

"*Like me*," Bennie thought. "*Flying to the sun*."

Libbie had stayed the night with her beloved Autie in the first camp out of Fort. Lincoln. What did they say at the last? Why did she ride rapidly away the next morning, head down, weeping? Had she, too, seen the ghostly horsemen? Did she have a premonition that this was their final parting on earth? Poets like to think so. Bennie liked to think so.

Custer had taken hundreds of men with him to Valhalla, where one hoped they hurt no more. Taken them, so to say, "To Garry Owen in Glory," as Custer's favorite band piece had it. The Irish drinking song "Garry Owen" was made immortal by Custer (and Hollywood), and Garry Owen had done no less for Custer. It was a name that would always be associated with him and his famous Seventh Cavalry.

A passing thought caused Bennie to grin. "*I wonder if women are allowed in Valhalla, if maybe Libbie finally joined him there? If she did, Custer probably had the band play 'The Girl I Left behind Me' when he went to meet her*."

A new thought saddened him.

"*Maybe they never met again.*"

A deep love such as the Custers', such as his and Rose's, dying forever, was the saddest thing he could imagine. He refused to accept it.

Where he stood was where the tragically fallen had all lived. This was where a great heart-rending event in American history had been set afoot. But God surely would make it all right in the end.

For him it had started in a book in a library far away, but here was the reality—in this land that held voices of the past. He felt the magic in his whole being. He knew that the earth possesses many fey places where people have striven mightily and won or lost. *And the land remembers, even if not a single soul does.*

He remembered how he had felt as a little boy along the Fox River where the G.A.R. vets congregated in the sun outside their hall, nostalgically recalling their youth. He remembered how they had known men who had actually seen George Washington on his big horse, and heard his thunderous voice rallying retreating troops. He had vowed then to remember and carry on the tradition. Time demands that we never forget the great deeds of out past. Right or wrong, they are our heritage and have to be lived with.

"*Those who cannot remember history . . .* "

"*Custer still might have been alive, a G.A.R. vet. I wish I could have met him, too.*"

"*Maybe I will, in Valhalla,*" he thought. The idea pleased him.

"But not yet," he told himself. "I'm having too much fun living."

CHAPTER FIFTY

Bennie's Indian Season, Part Three

"Right down there is where Custer got shot," Uncle Newt said, pointing. "He fell off Vic into the water."

Bennie felt a sharp pain near his heart as though he'd taken a mortal wound. Up till then he'd always thought Custer had heroically led the remnant of his men to the end, being the last to die, like in the pictures you always saw of Custer's Last Stand. Now he believed that Custer had died here, or maybe was mortally wounded here and carried up on the hill to die. *He might have lived if the rest of the regiment reached them and a doctor could have tended him!* Bennie had never grasped the Last Stand as real until just then. *Heroes, especially towering heroes like Custer didn't really die.*

He looked down at the fabled Little Big Horn roiling along but could form no words for what he was thinking.

Did Custer know it was the end when the bullet tore into him? Was he still conscious for a second as he toppled into the water? What would it be like to know for a split second that "Custer's Luck" had run out?

Did he think, "Goodbye, Libby, love! I'm sorry to leave you like this!"

Hell, he hadn't even had to be there. General Grant had ordered him to be left home. He'd pissed off old Grant and the old boy knew how to hold a grudge, as Newt had said.

Bennie was sure Custer never could have believed that death was destined to come for the Boy General on such a scruffy battlefield. Not God's chosen. Bennie knew that because he was sure nothing like that would ever happen to him, the *Boy Farmer*. But a war was coming. He knew now for the first time for sure that anyone could die. Even fabled Autie Custer, the Boy General.

Newt's voice shattered his reverie.

"By the time we got here, Custer had put me and Johnny Todd on as scouts. We'd been up here with Herendeen, who was another scout with Custer, that was the year before, and we helped set up Fort Pease, on the Yellowstone. We knew the country.

"The campaign ended right down there. Instead of leaving his dead ass float away in the river like they would a common soldier, everyone jumped down to pull the sacred idol out of the drink. Maybe it was just as well. None of the other officers had the force to carry out his plan. They wouldn't have had a snowball in hell chance across the river in old Sitting Bull's bailiwick without Custer to direct the foray *in and out*, any more than they pulled together over there on the hill where they carried Custer."

He swept his arm upward toward Custer Hill, where the Last Stand took place. "Between the Sioux and Cheyenne I'd bet they had five thousand fighting men. But the Army was like the Rebs, who thought one Reb could whip ten Yankees. Some of them, officers especially, thought one cavalryman was good for ten Injuns. It was more like the other way around."

Newt's voice went on, "The damned fool asked for it. Nobody else I ever heard of would have tried what he did but him. Well, maybe Chinese Gordon would have.

"Custer sent me and Johnny Todd up here and told us, 'Keep an eye on how it's going and if we don't pull it off, get the hell out of here and go back and join one of the other battalions. *Reno should have got my order to pull back by now*—and Benteen should be coming up. Join up with them and tell 'em where I am. In any case I aim to concentrate over there where I left Keough,'" Newt swept his arm to the northeast like Custer must have, "'and wait for Terry. He ought to be up there tomorrow at the latest.'"

Bennie knew from their map that Terry was due up Tullock's Creek just over the divide and could have got there the same afternoon that Custer fought alone. Well they hadn't pulled it off, and old woman Terry hadn't struggled up till two days later, because he ran off like a tenderfoot scout trying to blaze a new trail.

Newt said, "When we found out how many Injuns was down there, Custer knew he had to hit them so they didn't get away and run into Terry. Terry and Gibbon had even less men than us. Custer had the major force in the field. Of course he should have circled the wagons like old Granny Crook did, but it wasn't in his blood."

Bennie asked, "Why do you think he attacked? He knew by then how many fighting men were down there. His scouts told him that morning, but he didn't believe them till he got a good look on Weir Point, I guess."

Newt almost said, "He attacked because he didn't know how to do anything else." But he knew that wasn't true. He knew, from listening to Custer leave orders for the two companies he left behind on the hill under Keogh's command, that he figured he might be able to capture enough women and kids to get the Injuns to palaver with him. By then Terry might come up, and they could fight it out with better odds if it came down to it. He was delaying.

"Custer wasn't the heedless fool that people like to say he was," Newt said, "Custer was in a hell of a tough fix and he knew it, but he'd been in a lot of tough fixes before then. He was doing the best he could. I'll bet he wished he had his old Michigan Cavalry Brigade. Even they'd have had a tough time whippin' that many Injuns, especially with them fightin' to protect their women and kids right down there."

Newt fell silent, looking over where the Indian camp had been, and Bennie was glad. He heard the birdsong of redwing blackbirds floating up from the river. He wondered if they'd been singing in that long ago year of 1876, even as the battle came on.

That night, when all of the men who had come to this fatal place where Custer lay dead, the birds had been silent, he was sure. Everything had been silent on the field of the dead except the feasting of coyotes and maybe the rumble of distant thunder. Lightning had flickered around the horizon—a lonely sight on an otherwise dark night. A few scattered drops of rain fell. From the Indian camps came the sounds of mourning for lost loved ones.

Some of Reno's beleaguered troops up on the hill thought they heard the "hideous shrieks" of Indians celebrating with scalp dances. Bennie doubted it. Mourning women, more likely, shrieking out their anguish. The Indians would respect the mourning of those who had lost husbands, brothers, sons, lovers; children too young to realize they'd lost father's they'd never know. He thought, "*They loved each other just like we do.*"

And it finally came home to him what a tragic place this was. Bodies die. They survive only in the memory of those who knew them. Country Grandma remembered her father, who'd received his mortal wound here. He'd lived a few days, carried away on a travois, later buried in a cave in the Big Horn Mountains. Bennie wondered if his bones were still there. Maybe scavengers had scattered them long ago. At least Sitting Bull was buried in the ground where the wolves and coyotes wouldn't eat his dead carcass and drag his bones away.

An odd idea struck him then. "I wonder what Libbie Custer would have thought if they wanted to bury old Sitting Bull up at West Point next to Autie after Bull was murdered."

"What the hell," he told himself, "he was a great American general, too. Maybe someday we'll do it."

He looked up the hill at the monument to Custer and his warriors and asked himself, "Where is your monument, Gramp, where is yours, Uncle Sitting Bull?"

The answer was simple. Only in memories such as Country Grandma's and Newt's and nowhere else.

Where the Heart Was

Redwing blackbirds sing eulogies here today
Just as they did then
To those forever gone away—
Red and white.
Tears for them all.
Winter winds blow here,
Drifting cold white snow
Across the honored graves on the hill
In the neat paleface cemetery.

The Indian scaffolds are gone.
The year has yet to come
When Indians will become Americans.

CHAPTER FIFTY-ONE

Bennie's Indian Season, Part Four

Bennie, lost in his own thoughts, hadn't realized that the rest had scrambled down the hill to the river where what was known as Medicine Tail Coulee ran into it. They had joined another group of people who must have walked down the Coulee. Reluctantly he abandoned his lookout on the hill, prompted by curiosity and went to join them.

Rose came to meet him.

"Who are they?" he asked her.

She said, "Doctor Somebody-or-other and some Indians that were here like Uncle Newt at the time Custer was killed. The doctor is writing a book about it."

Bennie wondered what a doctor was doing writing about Indians instead of germs or something, not realizing that this was a different kind of doctor.

Newt had been talking to them. He winked at Bennie and said, "This here is the *world's foremost authority* on Custer's Last Stand, so you'd better listen to what he has to say."

The doctor gave Bennie a dismissive look and turned to his own group. He had an interpreter to communicate with the very old Indians with him, a woman and two men. It sounded like jabbering to Bennie, and the doctor was obviously hard of hearing, which complicated his job.

"Can you understand what they're saying?" Bennie whispered to Kid.

Kid nodded. "It's little different than at home, but I can follow it. Sioux is Sioux, I guess. I learned it in the cradle, only I didn't have a cradle."

The three youngsters backed away a little.

"Did Newt tell him he saw Custer killed?"

"I don't think he wants them to know he was here," Kid said.

There seemed to be a heated discussion in the doctor's group.

Bennie heard him complaining, "How can he say that? Everyone knows no cavalry got down this far."

The interpreter passed that on to the Indian the doctor had referred to.

The Sioux waved his arms and swung them up the Coulee, then pointed across the river, talking earnestly.

"What is he saying?" Bennie asked.

Kid was trying to keep a straight face. He said in a low voice, "He says what amounts to 'Bullshit!' Says he was right over there and there was a heap of soldiers over here. They charged into the water and their chief got shot and they fished him out of the drink and skedaddled, just like Newt said."

The old woman put in a few words and pointed across the water where the other had pointed. Bennie could see tears in her eyes, and figured she had lost a loved one there. She said something and at her words, Kid's face assumed such a surprised expression that Bennie couldn't help but notice. Kid looked at Bennie with that strange expression still on his face, and asked, "What did you say your great-granddad's name was that got his here?"

"*Four Ponies*, was what Grandma told us. Why?"

Kid said breathlessly, "Unless there was two Four Ponies, that woman has to be your great-grandma. She says her man, Four Ponies, was shot over there. What did they tell you *her* name was?"

For a minute he couldn't recall her name—hadn't thought of it since he'd been in Waubonsee. He felt like his legs might buckle.

Rose took his arm. "My, God!" she exclaimed. "This only happens in movies."

Bennie was rooted to the ground. He groped for the name on the letters from the Indian agent that used to answer Country Grandma's letters to her mother. So here she was still alive. Her name was on the tip of his tongue. He'd always thought of bringing Country Grandma out here to see her mother before she died. But he never expected to meet the old woman like this.

He said to Kid, "Ask her if her name is *She Sees Them First*?"

Kid moved close to her, took her hand to get her attention, and asked the question.

She looked at him mildly surprised, and asked, "Are you from Standing Rock, too?"

"No," Kid said. "I am with him," and he decided to play his role to the hilt whether Bennie was ready or not, and pointing at Bennie said, "He is your great-grandson from the land where the sun rises."

She looked as though a spirit had suddenly leaped up in front of her. Her old mouth opened wide, showing her few remaining teeth, and fear captured her wrinkled face. She thought Kid had second sight and might be a Spirit.

The interpreter said to the doctor, "This kid speaks Sioux."

"What's going on?" Newt asked.

She Sees Him First suddenly swayed. Her hands went to her head and she clutched at her face, breathing rapidly. Kid and Bennie, being closest, grabbed her and gently helped her sit down.

"Here! What's going on?" the Doctor cried. "What did this young hoodlum say to upset her"

"Watch your tongue," Newt said. "This boy is as respectable as you'll ever be. He's with me."

The doctor eyed him with an expression that left little doubt that was no recommendation in his mind, then said, "And this old lady is with me and deserves to be treated with respect regardless." He left unspoken, after "regardless," his implication "even if she is *only* an Indian."

Newt said, "So does the boy. So do I. I listened to your academic palaver, and I savvy a little Sioux myself. This man," he pointed to the old Indian who'd been telling the doctor how it really was, "told it to you like it was. I was right up there on the hill when Custer was shot out there in the water."

"I doubt it."

Bennie and Kid had been fanning She Sees Them First with their hats, and the old Indian men watched impassively, having understood everything that had been said in their tongue, and waiting for the outcome while the palefaces wrangled.

Newt looked like he was thinking of decking the starchy dude. Instead he got a grip on himself and grinned.

"Doubt which?" Newt asked. "That Custer was shot out there, or that I saw it from up there?"

"Both."

"Before you go off the deep end, what that *hoodlum* told the old woman was that my *grandson* is her great-grandson." Bennie would later remember that slip of Newt's tongue—*grandson*—but he was too confused just then to take everything in. He wasn't sure he'd been ready to let anyone know who he was until he'd had a chance to think it over. And he was sure Newt really hadn't wanted to put himself in line to appear as a windy old-timer in the newspapers after the good doctor told his story, if he did.

The interpreter who was in charge of She Sees Them First was a civil service employee from the Indian Bureau and responsible for bringing her and the two men with her from Standing Rock to cooperate with the doctor on his book. He had also leaned down to help the old woman, but was listening as well to what Newt and the doctor said.

He decided it was time that someone took charge.

"Keep your shirts on. I'm Amos Donaldson from the Standing Rock Agency," he said for Newt's benefit. "We'll get all this straight after we're sure you haven't shocked this old lady into a heart attack. It seems to me you may know what you're talking about, since you knew her name just from what she said."

Bennie said, "My grandma was adopted by a white family when she was young. She always told me her mother's name was She Sees Them First and her father was Four Ponies, who was mortally wounded here. I remember Grandma writing letters to her mother, and we tried to get her to visit her mother before she died. She never had the money to do it. Besides, I don't think you could get her off the farm even to do that. Somebody must have read those letters to her Ma and wrote her answers for her."

The interpreter's attitude definitely changed from uncertainty to dawning conviction when Bennie told him that. Donaldson said, "I read those letters to her, and answered them if your grandmother's name is . . ." He paused, trying to remember.

"Feltman," Bennie said. "Mary Feltman. In Illinois."

"That's it. Feltman. She wrote again just lately."

To the doctor he said, "These people are undoubtedly who they say they are, or at least the boy is." Experience had led him to reserve judgment on claims such as Newt's.

Newt said, "If you got doubts about me, I'd just as soon you stick to 'em. I should have kept my trap shut. I got riled there for a minute. In fact I don't want the story to go any further, if it's all the same to you."

She Sees Them First interrupted them by saying, "Help me up. I'm all right."

Everybody tried to help her at once.

She dusted herself off and looked at Bennie, then at Kid. She grinned and asked Kid, "Is this boy really my great-grandson as you say?"

Kid assured her he must be, judging from what she'd said of herself and her husband, Four Ponies.

Her eyes glowed and she placed a hand on Bennie's arm and squeezed it. Bennie felt like it was his turn to sit down. Then he did exactly the right thing. He put his arms around her gently and held her. He was surprised that she didn't smell like he'd been led to believe Indians must smell. Instead she smelled like fresh grass. He realized she was crying. Tears were in his eyes, and he looked at Rose, who was pretty teary, too.

The doctor simply looked nonplussed. He finally managed to say, "I guess maybe I talked out of turn. I'd like to talk to you people if I may. We have a wagon over there with a lunch in it. Would you like something to eat?"

Newt thought, "*I can see that this son of a bitch is a survivor. If blustering won't do it, ass kissing will.*"

The doctor wanted them to come with him to Hardin, where he had billeted his Indians. It turned out that they were staying in Hardin at the same tourist court where Newt had got them rooms. They agreed to get together there and talk more that evening. Newt's party retraced their steps to the Battlefield Headquarters, where they'd left their car. Kid noted with satisfaction the nonplussed look the good doctor gave him when the "hoodlum" got into the driver's seat of a big Lincoln limousine.

That evening they carried chairs out from their rooms and all gathered in the cooling evening air under a huge cottonwood. It was dusk, that lonesome time of day that Bennie loved best. He thought, "What a great place and time for storytelling."

She Sees Them First was obviously directing most of her talk to him, interpreted by Amos Donaldson. Bennie choked up over this strange honor he hadn't expected. Looking at her great-grandson with loving eyes, the old woman told him, "Your grandmother was such a good little girl. She and the other children were playing in the river when the soldiers came." She told the rest of that fateful day's events as they happened, and it was just as Country Grandma's stories had come down to him through Ma. Ma had seldom got her mother to talk and there wasn't much that Bennie recalled, but it had been enough to bring about this amazing reunion.

She Sees Them First told how the next year, while Sitting Bull's band was trying to evade the troops under General Miles, her little girl *Red Moon Rising* had been captured by the white soldiers. She cried as she told how it had been almost more than she could bear to lose first her husband, Country Grandma's father, then her little girl.

It had been the time that ruined life for her ever after. She was silent awhile, then said, "She writes to me you know, and this man reads her letters to me and answers them." She didn't mention that the letters from her daughter were always tear-stained. "And now you are here," she said, reaching over and touching him as though to assure herself he really was there. He took her hand in his and squeezed it gently and got a remarkably hard squeeze in return. She held onto him.

"*Red Moon Rising*," Bennie said to himself. "*Grandma never told anyone that. How nice it sounds*."

Once, when he and Ma were visiting *out home*, Grandma had told him while he watched her bake that she'd like to take a moonlight ride in a buggy one last time. He'd talked his Uncle Johnny into taking down the buggy that hung in a shed, and oiling its wheels so they could take Grandma for a buggy ride for "old times' sake." A red moon had been rising then. He wondered what Country Grandma had thought of that, if she even related it to her Indian name.

Old Martha, one of their mares who'd been put out to pasture, seemed as happy to be in harness again as Grandma was over the treat. Bennie was sure the time of year had been early September, since Ma soon had to take him back to Waubonsee for the start of the hated school year. The night air was already taking on a chill, and Grandma wore her old sweater that buttoned down the front and a shawl on her head.

While still holding his great-grandmother's hand, Bennie blurted out to no one in particular, "Why can't we take her with us to see Country Grandma?"

Donaldson didn't think so, because of her age and the strain on her, and also because regulations forbade it. He said, "If you have the money, and the regulations don't stand in the way, we may be able to arrange to bring her by train, though."

Newt said, "If all it takes is money, it's on. Just let me know how much, and what we have to do." He turned to Bennie, "If we can't do that, how about bringin' yer Grandma out here?"

"She'd never come," Bennie said positively. "She's married to the farm 'out home.' She'd be sure it was going to stop running if she left it even a day. She wouldn't go to Germany with Grandpa to visit his family for the same reason."

Donaldson said, "I'll see what we can do, and let you know what you have to do."

It was pretty obvious that he was as enthralled as any of them by the dramatic coincidence of Bennie's bumping into She Sees Them First, who was truly his great grandmother.

The good doctor wasn't moved by that, but something else bothered him severely. He complained, "My book is written. I've sent all but the final draft to the publisher. I'll have to rewrite it if the troops actually got to the river. This is very embarrassing. It could hurt my reputation if word gets out."

Bennie surmised from his look that Donaldson could barely disguise his distaste for the nearly deaf, opinionated academic. He said, "Didn't other Indians tell you of this before now?" He was sure they had and refrained from adding, "Why didn't you believe them?"

He already knew the answer. "They were Indians and not to be believed; besides *their stories made no sense*." True, if you had already swallowed the white survivors' tales of universal heroism and bravery. Or their scapegoating lies.

Before the doctor could say anything, Newt put in, "I don't think you need to change your story, Doc, and I'll tell you why it's just as well not. Same reason I never said anything, because by the time I got back where I could have talked, America already had invented the heroic version of Custer's Last Stand. I got run off into the hills and me and my pal just slipped off downriver in our own buffalo boat, completely disgusted with the Army's bungling. We didn't stop till we hit Yankton. By then there were already drawings in the newspapers and magazines of Custer firing his pistol or waving his saber (that he never brought with him by the way, none of the troops did), the last man to die, fighting against overwhelming odds. The country needed that illusion then, and still needs it, especially now.

"Maybe Custer really did die up on the hill where they found him. He may have only been wounded at the river; *might have recovered as far as that goes, if they'd fought off the Indians and he could have got doctored in time*. Someone shot him in the head, but not the Injuns, I'd guess—maybe one of his own men at the last who knew he was still alive, so's to spare him being captured and tortured while he was helpless. I can see his brother Tom doing that. If anyone asks me to repeat my story, I'm gonna say I never said it."

He turned to the doctor and said, "How about that?"

The doctor was silent awhile then said, "It makes good sense." He had the grace to laugh, since he knew that the interpreter and Newt, and even the kids, must recognize it as a selfish course that obviously took him off the hook.

Bennie asked She Sees Them First a question that had been bothering him ever since he had read of Sitting Bull and the Army's campaigns to subdue the Sioux. "Was Sitting Bull a chief or only a medicine man as some of the books say?"

She looked indignant for a moment, then, since she knew the Army had tried to demote him to a scheming medicine man, she suspected why he had asked and said, "Sitting Bull was the grandson of Four Horns, the great chief of the Sioux. I am the grandniece of Four Horns. Our fathers were brothers, so I am his cousin. Sitting Bull was the hereditary chief of the Uncpapa. Before he was a chief he was a great warrior with many coups. Many were jealous of him, such as Gall and John Grass. The Agent McLaughlin at Standing Rock was jealous of him after we were forced to go live there. He had him killed because he was a chief and had more influence over the Indians than McLaughlin, who was a mean schemer. He claimed to be the friend of the Sioux, but he was really our greatest enemy.

"That was a very bad time that year that Sitting Bull was killed. We had heard that Wakan Tanka was going to drive the white men away and we could live like we had before, in the time when we were happy. We danced the Ghost Shirt dance while we waited. But after all it turned out to be just another dream.

"It was a sad time for all of us again. Many soldiers came and killed Big Foot and a lot of his people at Wounded Knee Creek—even women, and the old ones, and children, but that was far to the South. Even at that, we heard of it and we were afraid they would come to Standing Rock and kill us all because we were Uncpapa—Sitting Bull's band. We thought they would try to get even for our victory over the Long-Haired Chief at the Greasy Grass where we were this morning." (Bennie knew that Greasy Grass was what the Sioux called the Little Big Horn.)

Bennie told Donaldson he'd like to know if the Indians knew that Custer (the Long-Haired Chief) was who they were fighting, and Donaldson asked She Sees Them First.

"We knew none of the white chiefs then," she said.

Donaldson said, "That all came out of books later. But about Sitting Bull, even today the Sioux will tell you that Sitting Bull was their greatest chief."

Seeming to want to confirm all she had said about her famous cousin, She Sees Them First added, "At the Greasy Grass, Sitting Bull was the Old Man Chief."

Donaldson related that and explained, "That meant he was the head cheese over all the other tribes for that one meeting. Only he had the prestige to get and hold that many Indians together at once."

"Ask her how many Indians she thinks there were."

"As many as the ants if you kick over their hill," she said, not having words to describe exact numbers. Then, remembering, she added, "And that's the way our warriors looked over on the hills where all the soldiers were killed. I looked over there and watched them and went with the other women afterward, because I didn't yet know that Four Ponies had been shot."

Bennie had a sudden funny notion, but thought he'd better not mention it, which was, "I wonder if she cut anyone's balls off." He bet she'd have been capable of it, especially if someone had told her that Four Ponies had been mortally wounded.

Looking directly at Bennie with her black gleaming eyes, she said, "We carried your great-grandfather, Four Ponies, two days on a travois while he still clung to life. Then he died. We buried him in a cave in the Big Horn Mountains. If we hadn't had to run he may have lived."

Bennie thought, "Another score to hold against the palefaces."

After they talked a while longer about small things, it was obvious that She Sees Them First was tuckered out, dozing off and nodding in her chair. Donaldson took her to her room.

The doctor had a short talk with Newt that Bennie couldn't overhear, then left without saying goodnight.

Bennie and the rest all went to Newt and Kid's room for a final reprise of their day.

"Jesus!" Bennie said, letting out a huge sigh. "I feel like I've been born again."

"*Maybe you have*," Newt said.

Rose had been quiet during the whole evening and finally said, "That poor old woman. She looked so happy. I hope she lives to finally see her daughter."

"And her daughter lives to see her." Bennie added. "And I can hardly wait to see how Ma takes it all."

Rose said, "She'll probably want to adopt her grandma."

"What the hell did that old prune of a doctor want?" Kid asked.

Newt laughed. "He said it seemed like a good idea to leave the old story intact. Maybe even patriotic. I suspect he thought I'd buy that to avoid being exposed as a big windbag myself, if for no other reason."

"Did you buy that?"

"Hell, yes. It was my idea in the first place, wasn't it?"

Bennie slept restlessly, and Rose beside him wondered what terrible nightmares he might be having. She thought of awakening him, but decided to let him thrash out whatever was bothering him.

Before he was able to fall asleep Bennie wrestled with a jumble of ideas that overwhelmed his consciousness, the main one being, "Holy Christ, we are all a big mixture of races, everyone related to everyone else. It figures we all have black blood, too, though no white man wants to admit it, and maybe most of blacks wish they were white so they'd get treated better, not that they have to be ashamed of their color. Look at Rufus, our real star of the football team. I could do worse than have Rufus for a brother and Ella Mae as a sister. And their ma sure made a mother for Rose when she needed one bad.

"Come to think of it, I could do a lot worse than have a *scheming medicine man* for a . . . let's see, how am I related to Sitting Bull? Grandma called him Uncle, but I know that's a term of respect for elders, though she was sure his blood relative." He had looked up family lines once and was able to figure out at last that he was Sitting Bull's first cousin three times removed, which meant the third generation after his. "And I'm related to the great chief of the Sioux, Four Horns. I could do a lot worse than that, too. Something like related to George Washington. He remembered the term "Old Man Chief," and almost snorted at the thought that Mark Twain would have had Huck Finn exclaim, 'Ain't that grand and gaudy?' Well, I guess I'll just have to sleep on it. Maybe I'll make Rose address me as Young Man Chief. That's grand and gaudy enough for anybody." He grinned up at the dim ceiling, "I can hear her saying, 'Chief, my foot!' But that's what I aim to be from now on, at least in my own mind. Maybe hereditary, too. Give me something to shoot for. At least I'm a hereditary something-or-other. Maybe just a member of the human race. I could do a lot worse than have a great-grandma like She Sees Them First, and a grandma named Red Moon Rising and I know that for sure, since I've known both of them personally."

Earlier, he'd said he felt as though he'd been born again, but now concluded maybe he hadn't been born at all until that very day. To be born maybe you had to know who you were for sure. A funny thought struck him, which was, "*If that's true, a lot of big shots haven't been born yet and may never be. It's the guys like my nutty uncle Bob who know for sure who they are and love it. And Kid. Uncle Newt sure as hell knew who he was when he crawled out of the womb. But, how about me*?" It left him vaguely disturbed. Finally he told himself, "*I'll think about that tomorrow, like Scarlett O'Hara in the book*," and with that thought was able to fall into a deep sleep.

Sitting Bull materialized just as Chief Waubonsee had. Bennie had seen a lot of pictures of the chief and had no doubt who he was.

"I waited a long while for you, boy," Sitting Bull reproved him sternly.

He looked just like his most familiar photo, calm and dignified, wearing a single feather with his long hair in braids bound in leather falling in front of his shoulders.

Bennie was not unduly surprised to see him, but was puzzled by one thing. "How come you speak English?" he asked.

"I don't," Sitting Bull said. Bennie understood and didn't inquire of himself where he'd learned Sioux.

He asked his first cousin three times removed, "Did you want to tell me anything special?"

"No. But we have the same blood in us. I often have relatives drop by just to visit. It's one of the few pleasures old ones have. Do you happen to have any tobacco, speaking of pleasures?"

Bennie handed over his makings and watched the chief roll a big *turd* of a cigarette that reminded him of Kid's. He held a match for him and watched the same beatific expression of satisfaction capture the chief's face that he himself got when he inhaled that first big, heavenly drag into his lungs.

"I always wanted to meet you," Bennie confessed.

The chief, a realist, said, "I'm not surprised." He might have added truthfully, "Everyone does."

"I had some questions I wanted to ask you."

The chief was silent for a while, not surprised by that either, and said, "Shoot, kid."

"What did you think of Custer?"

"We didn't know Custer. Later we learned who he was. He was a fighter."

Bennie recognized that to this old warrior that meant everything that needed to be said.

Recalling Newt's surmise that the Sioux would have tortured Custer if he had been captured, Bennie asked about that. "Would you have?"

"Why not? His men shot our women and children like they were animals to be hunted. It was our home. Of course we did that to enemies. We hoped it would keep others from coming ever again."

"But you did it to other Indian tribes, too."

"Same reason. They came stealing our horses and women. They should have stayed home."

"You raided them."

Sitting Bull grinned. "And we got tortured if we were dumb enough to get caught."

"Name of the game, huh?" Bennie was astonished to hear himself say that in such an offhand manner. He was beginning to feel more comfortable with the chief, maybe like he felt with his Uncle Johnny, who certainly looked like an Indian. In fact he looked a lot like Sitting Bull, and why not?

"You bet." Sitting Bull answered his question. "Only we played the game better than almost anyone. The Cheyennes did right smart at it, too. Any more foolish questions?"

"Have you forgiven the white men, as so many of them have forgiven you?"

"Forgiven us? For what? We didn't start the trouble. They came to steal our hunting grounds and killed us if we tried to keep them away." He ignored the rest of the dumb question.

"I'm part white. Mostly white. How about me?"

"You're kin. That's different. Most whites really *suck*!"

It was then that Bennie suspected he was dreaming. He laughed. He asked Sitting Bull the same question he'd asked Ralph Esselborn about how he'd come to use the modern word "*suck*."

"I get around these days."

"The U.S. is about to get into another big war. Do you think the Sioux should fight alongside the whites?"

"Fighting is what men are born for. It's their chance to be *warriors*, to count coups."

Here was that word *warrior* again. Waubonsee had said, "You will be one of us," meaning a warrior.

With that Bennie could see the chief was fading away like the Chessy Cat and tried to keep him there, but failed.

"Goodbye," he called, "Goodbye, *Tatanka Io Taka*," and waved. The chief's arm and hand waving back were the last part of him to disappear.

Bennie woke up then and the chief's waving arm melted into the spot where Rose stood looking down at him and for a moment he didn't recognize her or where he was.

"Who were you saying goodbye to?" she asked.

"Sitting Bull."

Over breakfast she repeated, "Sitting Bull, eh?"

"Yeah, none other."

Kid asked, "What was that all about?"

"I had a long talk with Sitting Bull last night."

Kid said, "I'm not surprised. I had a long talk with Crazy Horse. Mostly about pretty women."

Newt said, "I slept like a log." Then added, "I wonder how the learned doctor/professor slept?"

CHAPTER FIFTY-TWO

Where Pa Got Shot

The return trip was a replay of the trip out, with one poor road after another in most rural areas of the West. The usual crummy tourist courts were all that were available, unless you had the money to stay in hotels. Newt did, and they lived in style when they hit a town that had one. Some of these had pretty good restaurants.

They were tourists, wandering at will. Newt took them through Deadwood to see where his old pal Wild Bill had been killed, shot in the back by Jack McCall. Bennie talked them into going through Abilene, where Wild Bill had augmented his fame as a frontier marshal. He found the place a great disappointment, a little burg that had become a fusty farm town with no sign it had ever been the first famous hell-roarin' cowtown.

Then they headed down the Missouri River toward Kansas City, near which the battle of Westport took place. Bennie now knew that Westport was the battle where Newt's Pa had received a crippling wound from a shot in the back by a bushwhacker. Bennie had once thought he'd been killed and that Newt had killed the man who did it. He did indeed kill the man who shot his Pa in the back, but his Pa had come home and lived and practiced law again for a good many years, until Newt's Ma died.

Newt asked around for directions with about as much luck as they'd had at Bad Axe. Finally they went to the library and discovered the problem by looking over a detailed map. The trouble was that the Westport battleground was now inside Kansas City. Westport had become a part of the bigger city, with cars running where horses had pulled cannon one fateful day long ago.

"The hell with it," Newt said. "Let's drive out east a ways. We fought out there on the Big Blue River the first day. Maybe I can spot where we fought."

Finally after a day of fruitless wandering, during which Newt couldn't find anything to suit him, they drove to Independence and put up for the night at a hotel.

After dinner Newt shoved back his chair, lit a cigar, and ordered another cup of coffee. He said, "The place where Pa got shot has to be back over in Kansas City somewhere. I always hated the name of the place, and especially Westport. Always figured it's where my family was ruined. Nothing was ever the same after that. I guess you'll have to settle for me announcing this ball game, rather than seeing it out at the ballpark.

"Anyhow it all started when old Pap Price made a last-ditch try to take back Missouri. He was a half-ass Rebel general, but like I told you before had been governor of Missouri before the war—did a good job in the Mexican War, and was a big stick in politics. He came all the way up from Arkansas and through Missouri with a wagon train even though he needed to move quick if he was gonna pull it off, and he rode in a carriage himself. But his men loved him. He probably drove lightnin' generals like Jo Shelby and Fagan and Marmaduke nuts though. Haw—get that name Marmaduke—isn't that a great name? No wonder he was a fighter. I'll bet he had to fight every day in school because it sounds like some kind of English sissy, but he was a long ways from that. Before the fight here was over, he ended up afoot and was captured by a plain soldier. He busted his arm when his horse fell with him, and get this—was wearin' overalls like a farmer, not that he was trying to disguise himself, it was all he had and probably glad to have 'em.

"Anyhow, Old Pap Price came west along the Missouri River, taking his damn time about it. Nobody ever said he was much of a general. They tell me when they camped he used to lay on a Turkish carpet and guzzle his toddies.

"Two Union columns were comin' along behind him under General Pleasanton and General Smith. Funny thing, but Custer served under both of them at one time or another. Pleasanton made him a brigadier general just before Gettysburg.

"We were in position waitin' for Price over on the left near the Missouri when it started. But outfits got scattered all around, horses runnin' and every man for himself for a while. We got run out of there that day when Shelby flanked us, and we fell back to Westport and set up another line. It was a different story the next day and we got 'em on the run after Pleasanton came in on their flank."

Newt had drawn a rough map on the white tablecloth, which got him a dirty look from the waitress until she got interested in what he was telling the kids. The tip he left later would have bought two tablecloths.

He went on, "I stuck with Pa, and my sidekick Leland stuck with me. Little Cannonball took it all like the trooper he was. By then I was carryin' Pa's double-barrel English rifle. He always used two Colts and had a repeating Henry rifle, too. Pa believed in fighting right alongside the troops, not hangin' back an' just tellin' 'em what to do after the shootin' started. Hell, nobody listened to orders after the fuss started. Couldn't hear 'em anyhow unless somebody yelled right in their ear.

"We fairly well had them whipped, and we got off our hosses and was just standin' around lettin' the hosses take a little blow and taking a drink from our canteens when a little bunch of guerrillas sneaked up behind us. The first I knew was when I saw Pa sort of flinch—I heard the shot and saw him topple over, real slow, trying to keep on his feet. Some son of a bitch shot him in the back from where he was skulking in the brush, and I could see his ugly mug grinnin' through a big bushy beard. I jumped over and grabbed one of Pa's six-shooters, his old Walker he'd carried in Mexico, since my rifle was hung on the ring on my saddle on the other side of Cannonball. I was comin' up and aiming with it, but I saw I'd be too late. The bastard was taking a dead bead on me. That's when Leland jumped in and took the round for me."

"Who was Leland?" Rose asked. Bennie had wondered the same thing. He'd never heard Newt mention him before.

Newt didn't answer right away, looking away in the distance through his after-dinner cigar's smoke. He was quiet for a long while. Finally he said, "He was the best friend I ever had. And he saved my life."

Bennie hadn't heard of Leland since Newt had never told the full story of his boyhood in LaSalle. Bennie had realized there must be something too painful to even talk about that he didn't want to remember. Now it was all coming out.

"Did Leland die?" Bennie asked.

Newt surprised them by snorting, remembering something. He then sobered and Bennie was shocked to see tears in Newt's eyes. He'd always thought the old man was hard as nails, incapable of tears. Newt said, "I didn't mean to laugh, but when we were young together I told Leland I didn't aim to die, ever. And he thought I could manage affairs so he wouldn't either and he sure didn't want to since we both had so much fun living. I promised him I'd never let him die.

"Anyhow, he took the shot for me and gave me time to plug that ugly bushwhacking son of a bitch right between the eyes. They told me later he was a famous guerrilla by the name of Todd that had rode with Quantrill. I never found out if that was true or not.

"Anyhow, there I was with Pa down and Leland down. Pa was unconscious and I went over thinking he was dead. About then old Doc Bedel rushed up and shoved me away and felt for Pa's pulse.

"That's when I noticed Leland lookin' up at me, and I bent over him. He said, 'Newt, you ain't gonna let me die, are you?' But I knew he was dying. I got down and took his head in my lap and held him and saw the blood runnin' out of a big hole in his chest, and watched Doc Bedel with Pa out of the corner of my eye. You can't imagine how I felt. Leland's blood was soakin' through my pants and I remember how it was still warm and made me feel like puking. I hate to think of it and almost never do, except sometimes I dream of it. I wanted to be God so I could undo it all, and I remember my throat was dry and I was seeing stars and dizzy and having trouble breathing too.

"But I managed to say to Leland, 'Naw, I ain't gonna let you die. Before you know it we'll all be back in LaSalle gettin' well.'

He looked relieved and smiled and shut his eyes. 'Thanks, Newt,' he said, and breathed a great big sigh and died. I kissed him then for his mother and held him for a long while.

"We was back in LaSalle all right, but nobody but me got well, if you could call it that. We buried Leland in the white folks' cemetery, too. Pa saw to that. But Pa never walked again. And he was in pain all the time. He hung on till Ma died, though. At the end he must not have weighed more than a hundred twenty pounds, and had weighed almost a hundred pounds more most of his life."

Newt was quiet for a long while and Bennie wondered what he was thinking, looking off into space as though no one else was there. Finally he said, "I always wonder if Ma didn't will herself to die before her time since she knew Pa hurt so bad and was tryin' to stay alive just for her and no other reason."

The idea of someone doing that had never occurred to Bennie. But a bigger shock was to learn that Newt's best friend had been black—and had died for him to boot.

He thought, "*No wonder Newt put up a fight over the football thing in Winnebago, when they wouldn't let our best player in regular games because he was black.*"

It explained a lot else, such as the way he stuck up for blacks as fighters in the rag-chewing sessions with Eben about the World War, after Eben mentioned they kept the blacks behind the lines mostly doing dirty or unimportant jobs, despite their records as Indian fighters.

The last thing Newt said was, "The day after we laid Ma away, Pa killed himself. Sat on a keg of black powder smokin' a cigar. Everyone was afraid to try to stop him because they was scared he'd blow them up, too. I wasn't there or I'd've tried. I didn't want to live myself for a long while after Ma and Pa went. Pa finished his cigar and touched it to the fuse and was smiling when it blew him to smithereens. In those days people knew they were going to join their loved ones in Heaven and that's all there was to it. It was why you could get an army to run into a storm of minie balls and grape shot out of cannons. Try that today."

CHAPTER FIFTY-THREE

Abe Lincoln Country

They drove east through beautiful farming country and crossed over into Illinois.

"This is all Abe Lincoln country," Newt said as they angled north toward the Illinois River. "My Pa and Abe practiced law in all the little towns here on their circuit. Lincoln and Douglas had some of their debates up here, too. Like I said I was at the one at Ottawa with Pa. It's just up the Illinois River from LaSalle.

"I reckon we got time to visit Spring Brook before we go up to LaSalle, though."

Groves of timber clung to the the Illinois River banks. Farms separated them, and Bennie could see the broad silvery sheet of water. He'd bet that farming here, as along any major river, was a hazardous business when the river left its banks, as he was sure it sometimes did, flooding for miles on either side of its normal channel. He deduced this since in some places the entangled brush and dead trees could still be seen, especially when they drove past a creek valley. The detritus of floods had obviously eddied up into these convenient avenues, and was abandoned there by the receding waters.

A road turned to the river and crossed a bridge, and Newt wanted to stop on the other side, since the bridge was too narrow to park without blocking any traffic that might come along. Newt got out and walked back to the middle of the bridge, not having spoken a word.

Kid recognized the signs and cautioned, "He wants to be alone. Let him. I have those spells."

"Everyone does," Rose said. "Even us downtrodden women."

"Downtrodden my foot!" Bennie snorted. "You've run this trip the whole way."

That only got a small smile from Rose. "If you say so," was all she said.

Newt looked upstream a long while, remembering those squat steamers of the Civil War days with their strange names like *Die Vernon* and *Carondelet*. It came back like a travelogue:

He said to himself, "*The Illinois was runnin' full when we set out. I can still see it, a mile wide some places, and water flooded into the low spots along the banks, six or eight feet up on some of the trees.*

"*The river was prettiest in the early morning with haze hanging over it.*

"*I remember thinking since I couldn't see anything but fog: 'Suppose I'm dead and this is Heaven. Where are all the angels? Where is God? I guess the pilot will have to do up there in his private domain.*'"

Newt crossed to the other side of the bridge and looked downstream.

He said to himself, "*We went right past here, of course. It took us a couple of days to make it to St. Louis, even goin' downstream like we did. Fog held us down to a crawl for a while.*"

After Newt got back in he seemed to be back in the present. He said, "That took me back a long time. We went right past there on our way to war." Then he quickly changed the subject to deflect questions about something that he didn't want to talk about just then. He said, "Spring Brook is just a few mile down the pike now."

Newt directed Bennie to the right spot, which was still at the edge of the small town. They parked and got out, Newt turning to survey where the old place had been. He could see it again in his mind.

He said, "I never figured out what made Johnny Todd come back here and go to school, then get hitched and have a family. I never figured it was his style—like me."

Bennie, carried back to a world he'd really never been in, but really had in another enchanted way in Pa's stories in Waubonsee, walked into the large lot and headed for the brook. On the way he noticed where the house foundation had been, the ground still mounded up the way he'd seen old trenches in photos of battlefields.

He said to no one in particular: "I'll come back and try to figure this out. I want to go over where Pa threw rocks into the water."

The others left him to his thoughts and wandered around themselves.

Kid said to Rose, "This is the way I'd feel around an old village. People are all the same, I expect."

She nodded agreement. "Bennie's in seventh heaven. He's heard so much about this place. It must have been the happiest time for his pa because it's about all of his past that he cares to talk about."

It had been a rainy year, and the brook ran fast and high, making its musical noise as it headed out for its long journey to the sea. Redwing blackbirds filled the air with their whistles. "*Just like the Little Big Horn*," Bennie recalled. "*They must be America's historical bird. At least they are for me.*"

He tried to recall all that Pa had told him about living here. "*Right about here Pa was probably chucking rocks and watching them skip when his pesky sisters tried to get him to come play house and he'd gone to hide, with his dog, Fritz, tagging along. I guess I'll skip a few rocks here myself. There's a lot of dandy flat ones that are made for it.*"

He turned to go look for the foundations of the buildings and was surprised, but not too surprised, to find the buildings themselves, the big white house, the barn where Gramp's rangy black horse, Ned, and the cow, Gertrude, were kept. He'd been feeling a sense of anticipation all day, as though some delicious revelation awaited him, and told himself, "*I'm not sure what's happening but I'm going to make the most of it.*"

He walked over to the barn and went inside. A very big and well-fed white cat was sprawled on the seat of a buggy that was parked out of the weather. The cat opened one eye and went back to sleep. "You must be Travelin' Man," Bennie said to him. "Here, let me pet you, Fathead." As though understanding his words, the cat again opened one eye and to anyone who could understand cat, obviously said, "Go right ahead. I thought you'd never ask."

Travelin' Man turned over on his back after Bennie had scratched his ears for a while and he *scritched* his tummy, while the big tom began to purr loudly. Bennie realized that something had come up behind him and turned to find a big collie looking at him as much to say, "Why are you petting Fathead, when I'm around?"

He kneeled and gently offered his hand to be sniffed before he offered to touch the dog, though he knew it had to be Fritz and that he himself might actually be his pa, magically returned to his youth. After he'd scratched the dog's ears thoroughly he grabbed it, inviting a tussle and got one, after which Fritz took off running in circles, coming just close enough to invite him to try to grab him. When the tussle was over Bennie's bent down to Fritz's level, and the dog licked his ears thoroughly and then sat and looked at him as though to say, "You must have something to eat on you. You used to sneak stuff out from breakfast." The best Bennie could do was with a few potato chips wrapped in a wax bag in his pocket for emergency rations on the road.

"Try these," he said.

Fritz liked them so well he closed his eyes while he chewed. The chewing attracted Travelin' Man's attention and he jumped down and worked on the crumbs that dropped from Fritz's mouth.

Bennie left them at their work and approached the house with its wide porch. Immediately inside the front door was a big room with the fireplace.

He spent a long time wandering, upstairs and down, feeling the long-gone people around him, perhaps even the old Frenchman, Bouyer, silently but approvingly watching *history's chosen one magically returned to the ancient fold he'd never actually lived in.*

He thought, "Pity I didn't know how to tune in on this station when I was at the Little Big Horn. Maybe I can go back and do it next year, and Shiloh and Chickamauga, too." It gave him a very queasy feeling in his gut.

"I guess I'll go back out and look for Ned and Gertrude before they take this away from me." He cut past the fenced orchard and took a couple of apples for Ned. Horse and cow were grazing amiably in the corner of the picket fence at the back of the lot.

Ned saw him coming first and started to meet him. It was pretty obvious that he was used to someone bringing him a goodie. Gertrude looked up lazily and went back to eating grass.

"You're a big one all right," Bennie told the black horse that delicately took the apple he offered. "Must be almost seventeen hands."

While Ned chewed Bennie rubbed his ears and cheeks, then put his arms around his neck and pulled his head close to him, as he did to their big horses at home. Ned pulled away as soon as he finished his apple, looking for more. Bennie gave him the second apple and stood back surveying the whole area, engraving the picture on his memory. "*Pa won't believe this when I tell him*," he said to himself. "*If I tell him*."

"I've seen enough," he told the others as he rejoined them. "Let's head for LaSalle."

The enduring wind whispered messages from the past—a wolf's lonely diphthong, Fritz barking in reply, Travelin' Man scratching on the door to be let in on a cold night, the splash of a rock thrown into the brook by a small, happy boy . . . long ago.

CHAPTER FIFTY-FOUR

Cheek Mansion Memorial

It was close to sundown when they finally crossed the river into LaSalle.

Kid was driving with Newt beside him nursing the last of a good cigar.

Newt said, "I don't see any bands out to meet me, or red carpets rolled out."

Kid asked, "Did you expect them? Did you wire ahead?"

"Come to think of it that completely slipped my mind. Old age I guess."

Kid snorted. "Good thing you didn't. They might've met you with a rope."

"Possible," Newt agreed. "If they didn't cut the last of it up and put bands on it to sell for cigars. As I recall you can't get a good cigar in the place."

"If we had Nelson along, he'd have brought some."

"Pig's eye," Newt said. "Union Workman maybe. Turn right at the next corner, I think. The old burg hasn't changed that much in all these years. Only difference I see is the trees are a lot taller."

"You got the turn right," Kid said. "The sign says *Cheek Road*."

They passed another sign that read *CHEEK MANSION MEMORIAL MUSEUM AHEAD*.

The road was wide and curved, sweeping around the top of a rise. Bennie was "rubbering" from the back seat, wanting to see the old Cheek Home as soon as it came into sight. He was glad they'd arrived before dark.

"Slow down," Newt said, "so we don't miss her. This is all grown up since I was here last."

As they drew closer another sign in the shape of an arrow proclaimed: *CHEEK HOME MUSEUM, NEXT RIGHT*.

"Here she is," Newt said. "The driveway must be hid in the bushes."

Kid swung right into a drive framed by two stone pillars with a sign hung between them reading *HISTORIC CHEEK HOME*. A little further along another sign proclaimed:

CHEEK MEMORIAL MUSEUM.
ANCESTRAL HOME OF COLONEL ROBERT CHEEK,
FRIEND AND ASSOCIATE OF ABRAHAM LINCOLN,
WHO OFTEN STAYED HERE.

Kid said, "Pretty impressive. I get the idea the Cheeks lived around here. You ever thought of changing that last sign though?"

Newt almost missed Kid's question, lost in taking in his old home.

"First time I've seen the sign . . . and change it to what?" he finally asked and soon wished he hadn't.

"To home of Colonel Robert Cheek's notorious son, Newt Cheek, who won the Civil War single-handed, despoiled maidens, and generally raised a lot of hell."

Newt laughed. "Damn few around anymore to say I didn't win the war all by myself. I may start claiming I did."

"Suppose someone asks for proof?"

"Why I'll say, 'That son of a bitch, Jeff Davis ain't around anymore. But I am. I rest my case.' Who could argue with that?"

"Where the hell *is* the house?" Kid asked, seeing nothing but trees and shrubs.

"It's set back a way from the street. Yard's grown up some."

"I can tell that."

Kid followed the driveway into a portico. On their left was a limestone landing before a paneled door framed by leaded glass windows. On each side were brass fixtures holding porch lights.

"You sure we got the right place?" Kid asked. "I always figured you for the log cabin type."

Newt said, "It's the right place all right. Just grown up bushes since the War."

A forbidding, white-haired matron came out on the porch, attracted by the auto noise.

For a proper old lady she surprised them with a voice like a hog caller. "We're closed. I'm sorry. You can come back in the morning."

Newt got out of the car and came around to her side. "That's a real disappointment. They told me this was the only place in town I could get a big water glass of whiskey free."

She looked startled for a minute, then exclaimed, "Newt! Newt Cheek, you old reprobate! I'd recognize you if you were two hundred."

He grabbed her and hugged her. "You ain't no spring chicken yerself, Maud," Newt said. "How old are you?"

"None of yer derned business."

"I see yer still a Todd all right. Shifty. How long has it been?"

She figured for a few seconds and then said, "Thirty-two years. When you were back trying to talk some sense into my nephew Eddie. He just had to marry that damned little German that somebody knocked up fer him, didn't he?"

Bennie was almost bowled over by the language coming out of this proper-looking old lady, so much so that it didn't dawn on him for a moment that Ma was "that damned little German."

Newt turned to the car and said, "Bennie, I want you to come out here and meet Johnny Todd's youngest sister. She's yer great-aunt, Maud."

"*Jesus Christ!*" Bennie exclaimed to himself. "*She has to be a minister's daughter if she's Johnny Todd's sister.*" He got out hesitantly, not knowing quite what to do or say. He'd never known he had a great aunt Maud, and if he had wouldn't have expected her to be like this old girl.

Maud looked him over, and thought, "*I sure put my foot in it lettin' the cat out of the bag that his Ma got knocked up, didn't I, Maud, you old fool? I wonder if he knew. How the hell did I know who he was?*"

She recovered and said to Benny, "Yer a big one. But you don't look like a Todd. Got my pa's long nose though."

Maud reminded Bennie of Klondy, judging from what he'd heard coming out of her. This wasn't a Victorian lady. He wondered if maybe they had a madam in the family and he hadn't heard about her.

Maud grabbed him, gave him a hug and a big kiss. She was strong as an ox, even though she had to be eighty if she was a day.

"Who're these?" Maud asked when Kid and Rose got out.

Bennie said, "This is Rose. She's my *adopted sister*. And this is Kid, my best friend."

Maud looked Rose over closely. She said, "I reckon *adopted* don't make you blood kin, does it?"

Rose blushed and didn't know what to say and wasn't sure she was expected to say anything.

Bennie read Maud's mind. "*The old gal sure as hell figured the two of us out quick enough. I guess it was something in my voice. This one is sure nobody's fool.*"

Maud turned to Kid and said, "You and my nephew both look like Indians. You more'n him. His Ma is half Sioux, you know."

Kid, who took an instant liking to Maud, said, "Happens I did know. I'm a Sioux. Bennie's *only* a breed."

Maud laughed. "A breed, eh? Like in the movies. I go to all the Westerns that come to town. I always wanted a 'breed' in the family. Those movie breeds got more piss and vinegar than those sissy white heroes. Give me a nice, sinister knife wielder anytime instead of one of them dudes with pearl-handled six-shooters, a 'geetar,' and fancy tight pants."

Here was one to Bennie's liking. "*Holy shit!*" he exclaimed to himself. "*Leave it to Newt to find a caretaker like her. She's probably got her own six-shooter under her pillow. And maybe a resident lover, come to think of it.*" He forgot to throw in a pint bottle of whiskey stashed under the undies in her dresser drawer.

Maud broke up the greetings with, "Well, come on in. Have you et? And where were you plannin' to put up? I got room here. Kept yer ma and pa's bedroom made up and have it cleaned once a week regular. Yer old bedroom too, Newt. I always knew you'd blow in like a bad penny before you croaked. We may have to stretch the bed a little though. We don't have *Procrustes* on the premises."

"*Procrustes*, eh?" Bennie thought. "*You never can tell what'll come out of a little old lady. But then even I got Greek mythology in the dumb schools I went to.*"

Another more intriguing thought grabbed him and he asked himself, "*From the way they act I wonder what went on with these two when they were young? I know what went on, if Newt had anything to say about it.*"

They entered the mansion through a high-ceilinged front hall. The setting sun filtered through a beveled-glass window, making kaleidoscopic patterns on the wall. Newt looked around silently. He had always been enchanted by the light here at this time of day.

Maud threw a switch and brightened the entry further with mellow light from a wall sconce designed to simulate candles. Under the west window was a shiny dark walnut hall seat with customary coat rack on the back and umbrella stand beside it, holding several umbrellas. A paneled door of matching wood concealed a cloak closet on the other side.

Maud led the way into the hall that ran to the rear of the house and turned right into a cavernous room where arrows of sunlight filtered through partly opened shutter slats highlighting floating dust particles in the long fingers of light.

She quickly threw another light switch to conceal the floating dust. Three overhead chandeliers transformed the room.

Newt looked up at them and said, "New since my time. At least the electric part is."

Bennie looked up and admired fancy cut-glass globes with ornate teardrop pendants that sparkled like diamonds. The ceiling was a startling sky blue, which complemented the flowered wallpaper. Framed photographs covered the walls. He had to restrain an impulse to look them over, since he was sure they were ancestors of whom he'd heard.

Newt took a deep breath. "It even smells the same."

Maud said, "I have fresh flowers brought in every day. In remembrance of your ma. She always did that, as you probably recall."

It brought back the fragrance of roses and sweet-scented stock, and always lilacs.

The spring he'd set out for the war with his pa swam into his memory, a rainy spring, air so heavy with the perfume of lilacs it felt like you could grab a rain-sprinkled hand full of the scent. At dawn it filled the yard—and the house as well, eddying in on cool breezes that always followed a rain.

He heard his mother's voice again telling him, "Newt, come with me and bring that basket. I want to cut some lilacs."

His pa and ma both loved flowers, especially lilacs. The shaded yard was sprinkled with flowering plants beneath oaks and elms that were already mature when his pa had the place built. He'd laid it out to preserve as many trees as possible so they'd have shade right from the time they moved in. Lilacs also partially hedged the porches, interspersed with bridal wreath, forsythia, and snowballs. On the south and west, honeysuckle and clematis climbed on trellises, shading the porches there in the heat of midday.

Newt lowered himself carefully into one of the antique upholstered chairs, lest it was fragile, leaned back just as carefully, then let out a gusty sigh. Bennie imagined a little balloon over his head, like in comic strips, that read, "Home."

Maud said, "Flop right in, cousin. They're replicas of antiques, and pretty sturdy."

"Just like home anyhow," he allowed. To himself he said, "*I'll have to tell Maud the kind of dump I live in nowadays before we leave. Maybe I'd better not, on second thought. She may want to come home with me. She's too old and fat for me. But there was a day . . .* "

"Why don't you all sit." Maud said. "I'll get Newt that water glass of whiskey, then set Minerva at starting supper. She's some cook. Anybody particular about what they eat?"

All shook their heads. Bennie thought, "*I could eat dog with my Injun ancestors about now.*"

She left with a swish, her rapid footsteps echoed down the long hall, but she was soon back with Newt's hooker of booze. "I don't reckon you young ones drink this stuff yet." She didn't wait to find out, since she'd decided they weren't going to get it from her if they did. "How about a cold Coca-Cola or something?"

"I'd love one," Rose said. "Can I come help you?"

"Just sit awhile. I'll bet you're all tired. Have you been driving long?"

"When you come and sit with us," Newt said, "I'll tell you what we've been doing and where we've been the past few weeks."

Maud came back with a tray of cokes, one for herself as well. She'd rather have had what Newt was drinking but thought it would set a bad example for youth.

"Minerva has started supper," she said as she dragged over a straight chair and settled next to Newt.

"We stopped at Spring Brook on the way in. Not much left of Johnny's place," he told her.

She said, "I know. I told Johnny they were tearin' the place down and asked him if he wanted to buy back his old home and keep it for old times' sake. He died before he could answer the letter. It sold for a song."

"You should have bought it yourself."

"I didn't have the money. Schoolteachers still don't make much."

"You should have told *me*."

"I didn't know where you were."

Newt looked a little sheepish. "Yeah," he said. "I ain't the world's best letter writer, I guess."

"World's worst would come closer," Maud said. "But I'm not complaining. A letter every ten years or so beats none at all. By now I figured you were dead, as long as it's been and as old as you are."

Newt ignored that, realizing she was trying to get his goat.

Bennie listened to this interplay and thought, "*Well, at least I found out she wasn't a madam. I'll bet she was one helluva school marm. More like a frontier marshal. I'll bet no one gave her any shit in class.*"

Minerva rang a bell for supper, and Maud led the way down the long hall. "We're eating in the kitchen tonight," Maud said. "Too short a notice to set out the fancy dishes and silverware and keep the butler on duty."

She introduced them all to Minerva, who reminded Bennie of Rufus's mother back in Winnebago.

That butler business caused Newt to give Maud an inquiring look, to see if maybe she really had one.

"Butler?"

"Yeah. Minerva's husband, as a matter of fact. He's Magawn Washington's grandnephew."

"The hell you say. Will he be here tomorrow?"

"I'll make sure he is. Anyhow, I reckon you folks will be able to get along without a butler for one night."

"We'll get by," Newt said. "It may not measure up to some of the hotels we stayed at out west, but we'll make do. What do you need a butler for anyhow?"

Maud laughed. "You may not believe it, but a lot of political bigwigs use the place for private parties. The governor was even here last year."

Newt said, "I ain't sure that's in the charter I gave the city."

"Tell the mayor. He'll want to meet you. Besides it makes enough money to pay for the upkeep on the place."

"The mayor won't meet me if he doesn't know I'm here, will he?"

Minerva was quietly taking this all in as she went about supervising the table, seeing that everyone had enough of everything. Bennie wondered if she had eaten, and if she was allowed to sit at the table when only Maud was there. He was sure that was the case.

After supper Bennie said, "If you don't mind, Aunt Maud, I'd like to look at some of the pictures I saw hung in the hallway.

"Hop to it."

"Me, too," Rose said, "unless you need me to help clean up."

Newt said, "I'll look them over with you in the morning and tell you who the ones I knew are. Right now I want another cup of coffee and a seegar here at the table. You two don't mind cigar smoke, do you?" he asked Maud and Minerva.

"Love it," Maud said, "and Minerva smokes 'em herself."

"I don't either!" Mineva protested, but grinned broadly. "Leland does, though. Cheap ones."

Kid said, "I'm going to sit out here too."

He knew that Bennie wanted to be alone with Rose to savor the essences of his family's past. Kid was attuned to communing with his surroundings and could strongly feel memories emanating from the walls themselves everywhere he'd been in this big house.

The voices in the kitchen faded as Bennie and Rose went down the hallway, but the happy murmur following him was pleasant to hear. This had been a happy place until it all ended in great tragedy. The happiness lingered though; he could feel it everywhere.

"What a wonderful old place," Rose whispered in his ear, taking his arm as they walked down the long hall.

"Yes," Bennie said. "I aim to look it over from top to bottom if Newt lets us stay long enough."

"Unless I miss my guess, he isn't gonna be in a big hurry to leave the old home place. Did you see how he looked?"

"Like a kid come home," he said,. "And what a home!"

Newt's stories hadn't told the half of it. The charming personality of the building itself was strongly enfolding him, not only the nostalgic essence of old historic houses, an aroma that words could never describe, and also some other ineffable thing that could only be felt. Such places talked to special people, and he'd learned young that he was one of a blessed few who sensed the past, imbibing "long ago times" by rubbing elbows, not only with ghosts but with inanimate surroundings, as he had in the library museum in Waubonsee. Some would say objects have no memory. Bennie knew better. He had realized early that ancient places remember. Not only remember, but speak of what they recall, as well. And long-gone people whisper secrets. But only to those who will listen to precious revelations that emanate from every nook and cranny. He was certain there were many spirits here, straining to pass him messages, precious spirits who'd lived during an older time, the era that had given them birth and life and the will finally to inhabit the hallowed grounds of history.

"*Come. I give wisdom. Listen by the waters . . .* "

He remembered how, years before when he was a wide-eyed boy, the ancient willows along the Fox River had told him how a drummer had whittled from one of their youthful branches the drumstick in the nearby G.A.R. Museum beside the river. He never doubted their message. A home-grown stick had beat the drum displayed beside it, pounding its taut head where crossed flags were painted in red, white, and blue. It was as much a veteran as any, had called the troops to battle with the "long roll" at places with magical, hallowed names—Shiloh, Chickamauga, Missionary Ridge—where thousands who believed in "the Last Best Hope of Earth," had given their "last full measure of devotion."

Bennie thought, "*And this is certainly a hallowed house if ever there was one. Abraham Lincoln walked this hall, slept under this roof, not only once, but many times. And Lieutenant Colonel Robert Cheek, my great whatsis, maybe even grandfather, courageously went off to our most glorious war from here and came back a physical wreck. I can feel him and Abe both here for sure.*"

Eventually they all congregated again in the sitting room. Newt gave the kids a tour of the paintings and photographs on the walls, starting with his mother and father, whose portraits were side by side above the mantle. A shiver rippled down Bennie's spine at seeing what they looked like for the first time in living colors. His pa had had no photos of them. They were strikingly good-looking people, the spirit of happiness that had pervaded their personalities had been expertly captured by the artist.

"Did they really look like this?" he asked Newt, since he knew artists sometimes idealized, and sometimes really couldn't catch accurate likenesses.

"Perfect." It was all Newt managed to get out, lost in memory.

"How old were they then?"

"It was before the War. Pa was probably thirty and Ma a few years younger."

Later, after they sat down again and gabbed awhile, Newt said, "I imagine you young ones are about beat. Maud and I will want to set up till the wee hours gabbing."

The others all read that as, "Maud and I want to talk alone."

Maud said, "I'll get you all settled. Bring your bags in."

Newt whispered something to Maud, and she nodded. Bennie could figure what he'd told her since she led him and Rose into Newt's parents' bedroom with only one comment: "I reckon you two are headed for wedding bells."

She ducked her head back in for a moment and said, "If you want a bundling board, I think there's one in the closet there. Your Uncle Newt had a religious upbringing and always carried one courting." She laughed and blew them a goodnight kiss.

"In a hog's whatsis," Bennie yelled after her.

"Should I set up the bundling board?" Bennie asked Rose.

"If you want a divorce before you get married," she said. "I like to snuggle."

"No kidding? Tell me about it."

That night Bennie had another of his vivid dreams. The bedroom was quiet and mysteriously dark except for faint light from the bathroom, where he'd left the light on and the door slightly ajar in case Rose got confused in a strange place.

Music woke him—a faraway piano and a woman's sweet voice.

He listened awhile, then got up and carefully slipped out into the hall and to the head of the stairs. Light was reflected from the sitting room, and the sound floated up from there. He sneaked down the stairs and peeked into the room.

Night had faded away, and the sitting room was aglow from a setting sun just as he had seen it first that afternoon.

Seated in a chair was Newt's Pa, listening raptly to the singer. Next to come into view as Bennie sneaked further down the stairs, was Newt's Ma, playing the piano, with a boy who had to be Newt turning the pages of music for her.

"*So that was what Newt looked like as a kid. He sure was a long, skinny drink of water, but handsome like his Pa.*"

The singing voice carried clear and true.

"*Beautiful dreamer, wake unto me . . .*"

Her husband joined her in the next line,

"*Starlight and dew drops . . .* " And here his voice broke, but he went on valiantly through, "*are waiting for thee*," then couldn't hold back laughing at himself when he saw the woman smiling and the music turner grinning.

They all laughed heartily together, but the woman kept playing and finally recovered enough to resume singing, this time without any help.

Bennie looked the boy over very carefully. "*Newt*," he reassured himself. "*Up till now I've never been able to believe he was a kid once.*"

He carefully assessed the long, gangly figure, the face dominated by glowing, bright blue eyes, with a tow head sporting the same golden hair as his pa.

He believed that he was seeing them as they really had been, whether he was dreaming or not.

Until then *Colonel Bob Cheek* had been nothing but a revered family name, no more real to him than a Greek statue. Bennie had tried to visualize him, but no image had ever jelled. He imprinted this face in his mind, tried to become a camera so as never again to forget this living face. He'd seen it first the night before, in the portrait in the sitting room, but that wasn't the same. The painter had been skillful and brought his subjects to life, but what Bennie saw now was much more vivid. Besides, pictures were inanimate and didn't talk or sing, or laugh. These figures were alive in every sense, even down to making funny croaking attempts at singing.

"Am I dreaming?" he asked himself. "If I am, I don't want to wake up yet."

But he'd always found that you woke up just when you wanted most to stay asleep. And, sure enough, he felt himself waking up and tried not to. He opened his eyes, not sure where he was.

Rose was quietly sleeping beside him, but where were they? Some tourist court?

No—this was Newt's old home, and Leland's, and Bob Cheek's, where his beautiful blond wife played the piano every evening. He knew. He'd seen living people there in the sun-dappled room.

The faces, the piano, and singing, hadn't yet faded. He hoped they never would.

CHAPTER FIFTY-FIVE

Where Are You, Cannonball?

First light was tinting the eastern sky when Bennie woke up again and got out of bed. He peeked around the blinds and down into the backyard. Objects were just beginning to assume shapes as night faded.

"That's where Cannonball is buried," he thought. "I'll slip down and say hello to him before anyone is up, and smoke a weed while I'm out there."

He quietly sneaked his pants and shoes into the bathroom and put them on there so he wouldn't disturb Rose, then slipped out the door and down the dark stairs, feeling his way. He half-expected the sitting room to light up and the music recital to resume where it left off.

Outside the air was deliciously damp and weighted with the mingled perfume of flowers and greenery. Not a breath stirred, but early birds had already started calling. He descended the back steps and looked around to decide which way he should go. An ancient carriage house stood in a corner of the yard, and he thought it was likely the animal burial ground would be behind it. He threaded his way through the bushes and almost stumbled across a stone bench, beyond which he could dimly discern a bronze statue of a horse mounted on a cut granite base.

The bench had undoubtedly been placed there for visitors to sit and think whatever thoughts the sacred spot brought to mind. He sat down and took out the makings. The sky brightened and he could make out the proud head, the pricked ears of an alert war horse—and in his mind plainly saw the prancing animal carrying his young rider off to war. A bronze plaque was mounted on the stone base of the monument, unreadable from where he sat. He got up and moved close where he could make out one word in large, raised letters:

CANNONBALL

He struck a match and held it to the plaque so he could see the smaller letters below:

Where is Cannonball?
I think I know.
In the Great, Green Pasture
Where horses go!

This sentimental remembrance written by one who had loved his doughty miniature war horse—undoubtedly Newt—brought tears to Bennie's eyes.

From Newt's stories of a time now gone forever, Bennie could almost hear the most vivid imagined thing that had imprinted in his mind. The marching drums:

Boom,
Boom,
Boom, boom, boom!

The mortal remains of an animal eternally at rest under this stone had been through "the resounding clash of arms" and seen its own Civil War, had seen it through the smoke—heard it, smelled and felt it. Even tasted it in the sometimes brackish or bloody waters it had to drink or go dry in the heat of battle. Newt had said Cannonball was fearless and tireless. Whenever he spoke of his departed horse his voice was soft, tender, and always sad.

"Well, Cannonball," Bennie said. "I love you, too. I wish I could have given you a pat . . . or better yet, an apple."

He knew himself well enough to realize the emotion that was rising in him demanded that he make some gesture to express respect. He said aloud, "I guess I'll have to roll a weed—a big one like Kid's *turds*—so it lasts long enough for a ceremonial Injun smoke in your honor, Cannonball, while we're here alone."

It was getting lighter by the time he fired his cigarette. Looking upward to blow the first ceremonial puff of smoke, he was startled to detect from the corner of his eye something moving beyond the monument, which he made out as an arm moving there; another human was beyond the monument. Who? Why? He focused his eyes and saw that someone was seated on a bench similar to his on the far side of the memorial. He realized who it had to be and why he had come there before sunup.

"*I might have known*," he thought.

He remembered how, years ago right after they first moved back *up north*, he had been about to go upstairs and get Newt out of bed for breakfast, right after he'd downed his first of Eben's classical farm breakfasts himself, and had earned Eben's snort of derision as he told him, "Kiddo, Newt's been up for hours. He's over in the woods helping Nelson get out some firewood."

Newt had come out here before sunrise, just as he had, to commune with his faithful old pal. Bennie felt like he was intruding on a sacred reunion. He rose and started to slip away.

Newt said, "You don't have to run off. My *good old boy* and I have had our talk. He's just fine."

"Can you really hear him?" Bennie asked.

"Plain as day. We always understood each other without actually saying a word out loud," Newt said. "Ain't that so, Cannonball? This is Bennie. He's good with horses. He'd have babied you just like I did."

Bennie thought, "*Damn well told I would have!*" He realized he was listening hard, expecting a reply from Cannonball, but didn't feel foolish doing it after the dreams he'd been having; he wasn't about to believe that anything was impossible. He could, indeed, feel the living presence of Newt's vital little horse. He wondered if the critter came up from the ground, as he'd seen Johnny Todd do, and sometimes grazed around there at night when he wasn't apt to be seen. *Up north* there was a famous phantom horse that many people had sworn they saw. They knew it wasn't a real horse because it dematerialized when it knew it had been sighted.

"Cannonball's statue looks just like he did," Newt said. "I paid a bundle for it. I'll show you some pictures of him later on when we tour the *gallery* over there." He aimed his thumb at the house. The gesture and remark suggested to Bennie that Newt wasn't entirely happy that he'd turned over the family home to the public.

The sun, just below the horizon, lit the scene in progressively greater detail, showing Cannonball's bronze outlines in clear relief. The sculptor had succeeded in bringing his subject to life.

Bennie and Newt sat and silently enjoyed a magical interlude together.

Kid quietly joined them after a while. Bennie handed him the makin's for his first morning smoke.

The three smoked companionably, all feeling the pull of historic surroundings. After a while Newt said, "C'mon, I'll give you a tour." He led the way to the carriage house. He was happy to discover it hadn't been altered since its horse days.

"This was where I kept Cannonball in bad weather," he said, pointing out a stall.

The old brick building smelled of moldy hay, stale air, and antiquity. Bennie could imagine a team of carriage horses, and Colonel Cheek's riding horse too, snugly in here with Cannonball during cold, blustery weather, all contentedly chewing on fresh hay. Or maybe crunching an ear or two of corn fed in very cold weather.

Newt led the way outside and, walking under a canopy of ancient oaks and elms, came to the brow of the hill at the back of the lot. From this lookout the river was in plain sight, luminous and misty, painting a broad bright path on the face of the land.

Bennie thought, "*Once that was the principal highway. In fact, once it was the only one. Even for Indians and explorers in canoes. After whites came, the first roads were boggy trails, churned to either dust or mud, depending on the weather, threading between trees in the woods and around swampy spots on the prairies. How different from today. First the railroads came, and after them, cars that needed good hard roads all over the country. What a hell of a shame. I'd have preferred the steamboat days.*"

As though to please him a stern-wheeler rounded into sight like a ghost emerging from the mists, pushing a flat of barges before it. "*Not run by steam anymore,*" Bennie told himself, "*but picturesque as hell anyhow.*"

They silently watched the boat push the barges until it was out of sight.

"I don't know about you galoots," Newt said, "but I'm starving. Let's go see if anything is going on in the kitchen. If it isn't we can look around and find the stuff to make breakfast ourselves. Or drive downtown and find a restaurant if one's open this early."

"Bound to be a trucker's café," Kid said.

On the way to the house they met a sleepy-eyed Rose coming their way.

"Why didn't you wake me up?" she complained to Bennie. "I'll bet you men have been out visiting Cannonball."

Bennie felt guilty. "I'll take you over to his grave then we can go in and see about breakfast."

"It's started. Can't you smell it?"

Bennie wrinkled his nose and inhaling, caught the faint aroma of frying bacon and brewing coffee.

It caused his stomach to churn, but he ignored it and said, "C'mon. Breakfast can wait."

Rose made a perfect picture of a reverent horse lover as she stood and looked up at Cannonball. Then, like a typical woman, she said, "He was cute."

Bennie laughed. "So are you." He took her in his arms and kissed her long and tenderly, then harder as her warm body pressed tightly against him aroused him. He noted Cannonball eyeing them over Rose's shoulder and said to himself, "*I'll bet you know just how this makes me feel, old boy. It runs in the family.*"

It was undoubtedly his imagination that Cannonball winked.

He said to Rose, "I'll show you the old carriage house later. I sort of feel like showing you now, but they'd notice the straw on the back of your clothes when we come up to breakfast."

"Just like a man," she said. Then added, "And I love it."

Over her shoulder she said, "Goodbye, Cannonball. And I still think you're cute."

Glancing back, Bennie agreed. *Cute, but tough.*

CHAPTER FIFTY-SIX

Mike Mullins Returns

The phone rang just after breakfast and Maud picked it up, answered with a "hello," then stood listening. "I'll ask him," she said.

"Somebody wants to know if a kid named Newt is here. Says a little bird told him you 'was.'"

"Who the hell is it? And how did he find out I'm here?"

Maud shrugged.

She spoke into the phone and said, "He wants to know who you are."

She pulled the phone from her ear and said, "He says Mike Mullins."

Newt grinned. "Give me that phone."

He grabbed it and said, "How are you, you old chicken-stealing son of a bitch? Or are you some other Mike Mullins?"

He listened awhile and said, "You must be a hundred. You sound pretty good for an old fart . . . Yeah. I'm ninety-one, myself, not exactly a kid anymore. Any of the others still alive?

"We'll have to get together. I can send our car around for you. I don't reckon I'll have to put in any likker since I suppose you're all too damned old to drink anymore."

Loud squawking from the phone that Bennie could make out from across the room, sounded to him like, "In a rat's ass!"

"Where the hell do you live? I'll come over with the car myself. You get ahold of the other boys. What time should I be there?"

He scribbled something on the pad by the phone and hung up grinning, tore off the sheet of notepaper and slipped it into his pocket.

"Don't that beat a hog flyin'?"

"What?" Maud asked.

"Old Mike Mullins is still alive, and a couple of the other boys from Smith's regiment."

"I coulda told you that. They get their ugly phizzes in the paper every Memorial Day and whenever they get picked up by the cops for trying to fondle young women."

"You made that up," Newt said. "But if it happened as often as they thought about doing it they'd be on the front page every day, I'll bet." He went on,

"We gotta go over and round up a bunch of them at ten. You mind if I bring them here? If you'd rather not have a bunch of old degenerates around, I can take them to a restaurant that maybe has a private back room to keep virgin-fondling degenerates out of sight of the regular customers."

Maud said, "Bring them here. I know the whole bunch of senile damn fools. Some of 'em bring visiting relatives out here and brag they knew yer paw like a brother. And I didn't say those were *virgins* they tried to fondle."

"Most of 'em did know Pa like a brother."

Bennie said, "We got a lot of time for you to show us around here before ten."

Long before ten Bennie, Rose, and Kid had become acquainted with the faces of all the officers and most of the enlisted men, especially Nicodemus Cochrane, who stood head and shoulders above those in pictures with him, and a number of horses of Smith's old regiment.

When he came to Cochrane's picture Newt said, "Did I ever tell you what happened to him up at Athens, Iowa, in our first battle. Got his cock shot off in his hand, and two fingers with it, while he was takin' a piss. Pardon my French, Rose, but that's exactly what happened. I met him years later around the turn of the century, in Chicago. He was a big stick in politics. Never run for office, but pulled strings. Also supported a lot of charities. The Catholic Sisters all loved him. But he was so crooked they probably had to screw him in the ground when he died, and the cardinal probably said his service anyhow. But cardinals know that being crooked is how most get rich and have money for charity. Nick had a helluva good heart. I asked him why he didn't run for office himself and he said, 'Can you imagine how I'd make out when my opponent started calling me Cockless Cochrane, or Dickless Nick?' I got his point. But they all kowtowed to him and he never got in the papers like Bathhouse and Hinkeydink and the boys. Or in jail either, like a lot of 'em did.

"Here's a picture of me on Cannonball," Newt said. "I had a bunch taken. This one was up in Dakota. You can tell by the *mountains* in the background."

Bennie looked fondly at the little pinto horse, and behind him the endless prairie, flat as a pool table all the way to the horizon. "I believe I saw those same *mountains* not too long ago, myself," Bennie said. "They call 'em the Phantom Hills as I recall."

Newt came to another photo and said, "Here's the cannons old Grant tried to get back from Colonel Smith and got his knuckles rapped by Lincoln. This was taken just before Shiloh. Grant never forgive poor Smith. He finally resigned in 1864 and ran for Congress. Got elected, too. And that's how Pa got to be colonel of the regiment. They both should have been major generals by then, but Grant was a petty little son of a bitch when he wanted to be and kept them from it, and Lincoln stood for it. You might say old Abe was selectively idealistic. He dodged a lot of fights where he didn't see any percentage in it. He recognized Grant as the coming man almost from the first, and didn't do too much to peeve him—in fact I can't think of a thing besides those cannons."

Bennie thought, "Here's a view of Grant we never hear about. *Petty little son of a bitch.*"

Kid chimed in and asked Newt, "You think Grant was crooked like some books say?"

Newt said, "I don't think so. Not an out-and-out crook himself. His family was though—on both sides *and he knew it*—he was just a little too simple and trusting for his own good. He was a damn good general though. As Lincoln said when his enemies tried to sidetrack Grant's promotion, 'I can't spare him. He fights.' That says a lot. So many of them wanted to do anything but, and sat on their asses waiting for more supplies or horses or something. You can read about 'em, especially McClellan, but another pair were Buell and Rosecrans."

Bennie thought, "*If Colonel Smith was in Congress by then, I'll bet he never missed a chance to gore Grant's ox, for all the good it did him.*"

Minerva's husband, Leland, showed up about nine, and Newt went into the Sitting Room with him for a confab. He motioned the kids to follow.

"I want you to meet my gaggle of kids," Newt told him. "This is Bennie, my grand-nephew, and Rose and Kid. I reckon you pretty nearly qualify as a member of the family, Leland. Your grandpa was just like a father to me. Taught me how to do a lot of things without wearing myself out in the bargain."

He offered Leland a cigar, and not a cheap one like Minerva said he usually smoked. Leland looked at it, recognized its quality, then sniffed it. "Do you mind if I put it away for after dinner tonight. I almost never get one like this."

Newt got out another pair of them, one for each of them, and said, "Why don't we light up now and you can save that one for later."

He'd already made up his mind to send Leland a box of them for Christmas.

Leland said, "Magawn lived till I was about ten, I guess. I can remember him talking about you and his own son Leland, who I'm named after, and your pa. He thought a heap of your pa."

"And Pa thought a heap of him." Newt's voice changed and dropped lower,

"I guess you must be named for Leland. Did you know he saved my life and lost his in the bargain?"

"I heard the story."

Newt's eyes grew misty and Leland looked away, trying to keep from crying himself.

Newt was not really there for a minute or two, seeming not to know anyone was in the room with him. He could hear again in his mind the joyous racket that two boys once made in this house until they would be banished to outdoors in nice weather, or to the attic on rainy days. Finally he drifted back to the present and brokenly said in a low voice, "He was the best friend I ever had. And the bravest, though he didn't even know it himself. I'd have got him a medal if I could."

Bennie, who was present through this tableau and almost crying himself, thought, "Speaking of *Last Full Measure of Devotion*." He looked at Rose. She didn't even try to conceal the tears in her eyes. She wanted to touch Newt, to hold him like he was her little boy, and console him. Bennie felt the same way, at a loss what to do or say, so kept his emotions to himself and let Newt play out his tragedy alone. Finally, the old man recovered and shook his head.

"It was all so long ago," he said to no one in particular. "And so unnecessary, except that a lot of people are no damn good. Politicians especially."

Leland nodded in agreement. "FDR is the first one we've had since Teddy Roosevelt that gave a damn about us blacks."

Bennie had heard that one discussed enough around the supper table *Up North* and knew it was true. The Republicans like Colonel McCormick even called FDR's wife the "Niggers' Mammy" and they said even worse about FDR himself.

Bennie thought, "Talk is cheap. FDR knows, like Lincoln did, that 'all men are created equal.' And, like Lincoln, he puts his money where his mouth is."

Finally Newt and Leland turned to small talk that didn't interest him, and Bennie motioned to Rose to slip out of the room with him. Kid followed them.

Bennie said to Kid, with a wink, "How about doin' the driving when Newt goes over to pick up his old pals. Rose didn't get to visit Cannonball or see the grounds."

Kid grinned, knowing that two young lovers wanted to be alone on this sacred turf. "Glad to," he said. "I'd like to look over the town a little. Looks like an interesting old burg. I'll bet it was a hell-roarer in the canal boat days, from what Newt told us. Probably as bad as Deadwood."

Bennie and Rose went out through the kitchen to the backyard. He figured that Maud and Minerva had disappeared on their domestic rounds somewhere in the cavernous house. In fact, Maud had sent Minerva out on a couple of errands that would have made Bennie and Rose laugh if they'd known of them, or at least the way Maud had sent her would have.

She'd told Minerva, "Go down and put the 'Closed Today' sign up at the entrance, then drive downtown and stock up on booze. I don't want those old farts to drink me dry. Me and Newt have got some personal reminiscing to do this evening, and I know him well enough to know he won't want to do it with a dry whistle."

Kid had drifted back and joined Newt and Leland to be on hand when it was time to go pick up Mike Mullins and his old friends. He'd heard Bennie talk about the old G.A.R. vets in Waubonsee and looked forward eagerly to seeing a crop of his own. There hadn't been a one around Winnebago when he was old enough to appreciate them, although a lot of the Indians had gone to the war, including Kid's grandpa. Kid didn't remember him, but his pa had retold stories his gramp had told him. Kid had never got around to telling Bennie or anyone else about that. He was glad he hadn't. He thought, "*Maybe I'll spring it on Newt and the other G.A.R. boys if they fly too high.*"

His gramp had had a good experience or two and told stories about dumb palefaces and the lumps they got while they were getting used to the woods and the bushwhacking Rebs down South.

Bennie hadn't yet connected the name Mike Mullins with the hobo Pa had met at the cave when he was a boy, although he'd mentioned him in the evening stories that Ma called *windjamming* back in Wahbonsee. Right now he had something else on his mind.

It was early enough that the tantalizing summer woods smell still enveloped Bennie and Rose as they wandered across the yard. The dense green shrubbery and ancient trees were heavily populated with song birds, and robins hopped on the lawn, reluctant to surrender the right of way to people interrupting their wrestling matches with the night-crawlers they were trying to pull out of the ground.

Cannonball's monument was completely screened from the house by bushes and trees. They walked there first and sat on the same bench that Bennie had occupied before sunup.

"I'm sorry I didn't bring you with me this morning. It was beautiful out here with the sun just coming up. But I didn't really know where I was going."

She squeezed his hand. "It's all right. It's beautiful now, too, and I'm here."

She looked it all over silently and finally said. "This is a wonderful place. I always tried to picture it from Newt's stories, but I never could."

"Neither could I."

They sat quietly side by side, each deep in private thoughts for a few minutes.

"C'mon, let me show you the river. There was a stern-wheeler on it this morning pushing a bunch of barges. I hope there's one now. I love to watch them and wonder where they've been and where they're going."

His words set off an uncomfortable train of thought in Rose. "*I wonder where we came from and where we're going. And why?*" She was vaguely aware that this question came to her now because she loved Bennie so much, and felt it here more than she ever had,

"*I wonder where he's going.*"

She silently prayed again, as she did whenever she thought of that, and tried not to remember how little good prayer had done when her mother had died screaming in pain. She blotted out the thought of even the possibility of losing him and having their idyll come to an end. "*I know we all die,*" she reasoned. "*And in the first place I think that's unfair as can be if we're happy.*" It brought to her mind Stephen Foster's sentimental song "Ah, May the Red Rose Live Always," and its haunting words:

"*Why must the beautiful ever weep, why must the beautiful die?*"

She knew that people thought you shouldn't call men "beautiful" because that might reflect on them as "sissies," but she didn't care; she thought Bennie was beautiful, and the strange thoughts he'd revealed to her about life were all beautiful, too. She knew he would be a historian someday, even if he stayed a farmer as well. But she could also see him as a professor on a small college campus imparting his wisdom and philosophy to young people. She'd thought she'd like to live in a snug little house in a small college town and be known as the wife of a beloved professor.

Standing on the rise above the river, hand in hand, a wave of love engulfed her and left her trembling. Bennie felt her shaking and turned to her, concerned. "What's the matter?" She fell into his arms sobbing. "I love you so. I don't want to lose you, ever. I hope we live together a hundred years."

He said nothing for a while, simply squeezing her and feeling her warmth and the clean smell of her hair. He thought he knew exactly how she felt. He wanted to hold her, and fend for her, forever and ever. "You won't lose me," he said. "And I want to live with you for a hundred years. I wish we could live forever just like we have been and have a raft of kids to love."

He kissed her then and held the kiss for a long, long time, feeling passion rising strongly in him. He looked around for a place they could lie down concealed and led the way into the shrubbery looking for exactly what he wanted, going to a dell with tall grass and soft ground as though he knew it would be there. He held her hand and helped her lower herself to the ground, then quickly came down beside her, pulling her close and kissing her hard, over and over.

The novelty of making love with clothes on only heightened his passion and he couldn't restrain himself long, especially with Rose coming to meet him as wildly driven by love as he was.

Rose was absolutely sure that Bennie had planted their first baby in her at the moment they finally thrust together that last eager time. They lay side by side awhile, both completely spent.

She was even more certain that she was going to conceive when he recovered and kissed her long and gently as he always did, helping her stop trembling and relax. A small hot spark of life seemed to burn inside her, and it was very real to her.

When their lips separated finally, she said, "I love you so much, darling."

"I love you, too."

"I love you three."

It started an old fun ritual. Sometimes she loved him "ten" before they stopped the game, laughing.

When they walked back toward the carriage house, which Bennie intended to show her, she said, "You know what happened back there?"

"Yeah," he said. "I believe I do, and I liked the hell out of it."

"That's not what I mean."

"I was too busy to notice anything else. Did you see Maud peeking out of the bushes or something?"

"No silly."

"What then?"

They were standing beside Cannonball when she told him.

"You just became a father."

He wasn't ready for a remark like that, but knew that she might very well be right.

"If I did, I hope it's twins. A girl and a boy."

Rose squeezed his hand. "I'll do my best."

"Maybe it'll be triplets."

"Let's go easy here. I'm new at this. And it hurts. If it's triplets you can have the third one."

"I'd have them all if I could keep you from hurting."

She believed him. She had never known a man so gentle and considerate, unless it was her father. She thought, "Some men are as maternal as women, but they never get credit for it. Most of them hate to admit it themselves. And people, like the ninnies that most of them are, say, 'Men are all alike.' I know better."

CHAPTER FIFTY-SEVEN

All Out of Jail

Minerva got back with a load of booze just ahead of Kid in the Lincoln loaded with history. She found Bennie and Rose in the kitchen with Maud.

"Trouble's here," she announced, laughing.

As they hurried down the hall to greet the visitors, Bennie could hear jabbering of mingled voices outside.

He wasn't prepared to see a young man with the veterans, especially one wearing bright blue trousers with a red stripe down the leg and a khaki shirt. He recognized a Marine uniform from pictures he'd seen. Who was he and why was he here? He judged this fellow was about thirty or so and took in the pilot's wings pinned over the left pocket of his shirt. That increased his interest because he'd been thinking more and more that if he had to go to war he'd like to get into the Air Force. He hadn't realized that the Marines and Navy also had what amounted to air forces. Being a pilot was beyond his ambition, since he hadn't finished high school. He and Kid had talked it over and figured they'd make good gunners or mechanics.

Newt led the way to the door and held it open for the four very old men with him, all walking with canes and wearing glasses. They hobbled behind him at their best pace, which was slow at best. The Marine steadied each of them up the single limestone step onto the landing. Kid, who kept back out of the way, watched with interest and gave Bennie a "you're going to appreciate this crew" look.

Maud met them inside and almost yelled, since she knew most of them were hard of hearing, "Well, I'm glad to see you're all out of jail at the same time." That got the chuckles she expected.

One said, "Yeah, Maud, and my parole officer knows I'm here."

She shot back, "I know that, Mike. He just phoned to check up."

Bennie looked Mike over and the realization dawned for the first time that this could be the Mike of Pa's story about the cave, since he knew that his name was Mullins and he was from around there. Somehow he'd always thought that Mike Mullins must be dead when Pa told of those old days. If this was *the* Mike of the story, Pa would be happy to hear he was still kicking.

Mike's hair was completely white, but he still stood erect, helped by his cane, and obviously had been broad-shouldered, although his coat hung on him, like clothes bought years before did when people shrunk as they got older.

All of the vets wore their G.A.R. uniforms, Bennie was happy to see, dark blue pants and coats and broad-brimmed hats, with the sacred G.A.R. wreath on them.

Maud said, "I got lots of chairs set out for us in the sitting room." She led the way. "In a while I'm going to feed lunch to all of you galoots that have teeth." Bennie didn't catch which one of them said sotto voce, "I don't need teeth for what I'd like most."

Newt took over after they were in the sitting room and said, "I want you fellows to meet my grandnephew, Bennie. He's Johnny Todd's grandson. I guess you all know who Johnny was. His pa was Ike Todd, our regimental chaplain. Johnny was my cousin."

"And a hell raiser like you," one of the vets said.

The recollection of Ike Todd got a couple of laughs. Bennie wondered if they remembered that old Ike had damn near fallen off his horse when the parade started as they headed for war. Or had he done everything in the same clumsy manner? Bennie recalled that he'd wondered if Newt had been telling him the truth about how old Ike had bailed out Johnny Todd, Newt, and Wild Bill after they cleaned out a pool hall in a brawl. Bennie got his confirmation now. The same man said:

"I remember how you two made the papers when you cleaned out Malone's pool hall with pool cues, along with Wild Bill. Comes to me that old Ike bailed you out."

"How can I forget?" Newt asked. "Jim said Old Ike was a hard case, but his heart was in the right place. We thought that would be a good time to head west again."

Bennie knew that all the local people always had called Wild Bill simply Jim, as they'd known him before he left home and got famous on the frontier.

Bennie shook hands with them as Newt introduced him, "My grandnephew, Bennie. Meet Mike Mullins and Denny McMillen, and Pete Dawson. They was all in Smith's regiment when I was mascot. Left town with it and stuck all the way."

Mike said, "A helluva mascot. He taught us religious boys to drink."

Their hands were dry and scaly to his touch when he shook hands with them, as he'd learned to expect of old people, but all had surprisingly strong grips, as a generation that knew little besides hard physical work. Every one of them looked well-scrubbed and had on a clean white shirt. But they smelled musty, nonetheless, like old people, and old buildings, and history.

When Newt got to the fourth one of them, he said, "This last old sot here used to be a schoolteacher, then he got smart and joined the Marines. Tom Curry."

Bennie figured that might account for the Marine with them. Probably a relative who joined because "ole grandpa whatsis" had been a Marine and bragged about the Corps.

Newt said to Rose and Kid, "Come up here, you two."

And to the visitors, "This is Bennie's sister, Rose, and sidekick, Kid."

Bennie almost laughed at that simplification of "sister," and remembered one of Newt's sayings: "*Incest is O.K. as long as you keep it in the family.*"

"*They'd die if they knew what we've been up to a little while ago. Or maybe not. Pardon me, God, for thinking like that about a sacred subject.*"

He wasn't too worried about God, since by then he'd figured out that God was pretty understanding about human tendencies and didn't set much store in overly pious cases like his great-granddad Ike.

Newt turned to the young Marine and gestured to Bennie and Rose, saying, "This is Tom's grandson, Flint Curry. At least Tom says he's his grandson."

The Marine grinned, catching Newt's implication he said, "I came along a little late in Pa's life, I guess. And Pa was sort of late in Gramp's. Of course, as the saying goes, we might have had *good* neighbors."

All eyes turned to Tom to see how that struck him. He held a cupped hand to his ear and said, imitating Fibber McGee on the popular radio show: "What's that you say, Johnny?"

That got the laugh he expected.

Maud said, "Set down everybody and get settled."

They didn't need a second invitation since old legs didn't take kindly to standing too long. After everyone was settled, she asked, "Would any of you sacred relics possibly want a little chemical libation?"

Mike said, "If you don't tell my parole officer, I might take a leetle touch of the critter."

She got a unanimous vote on that.

Newt said, "Bennie's interested in *our* war. Read all my books on it and a lot I don't have."

That focused these old-timers on Bennie, as Newt had expected. Mike Mullins said, "Maybe you two experts would tell us old farts what it was all about, then."

Newt said, "I'm not sure about us, but I read where someone asked a Reb why he was fighting, and he figured about that awhile and the best he could come up with was, "Because y'all 'r' down chere."

"That about fits it, I guess. I jined up to see the world and git out of a small burg fer a while." He snorted and, while he had the floor, got in his opinion before anyone could make a jibe about that: "It was one helluva war any way you look at 'er. And we might just have another one if I'm any judge from readin' the morning papers."

He looked around to see how that sat. Heads nodded agreement.

Newt said, "The sooner the better. *The longer you wait, the harder it is to kill off sons of bitches like Hitler*." As an afterthought he added, "*And Jeff Davis*."

"Hell fire," Mike Mullins said, "Hitler makes ole Jeff Davis look like a schoolboy."

Newt said, "That's a fact, come to think of it. I never thought I'd hear of anyone that made old Jeff look good, but Hitler sure as hell does." He looked at Flint Curry to see what an active-duty Marine he might have to say and got his money's worth in a few words.

"Hitler is a first-class madman. He has to be stopped. We all know it's coming. We've been trying to get prepared, but it hasn't been easy with dummies like Lindberg and his America First jugheads and a bunch of pacifists. We're going to have to whip the Japs, too. *And maybe hang Lindy*."

Then he remembered that Rose was in the room and said, "Pardon my French, miss, but those are facts. We'll all go down the drain if we don't wake up."

There wasn't much to say to that, and he was glad to see that Rose didn't blush. She simply nodded, although she didn't want to see the country get into a war and her reasons were purely selfish. She didn't know how she could possibly live if she lost someone else she loved, and losing Bennie would be ten times as bad as any of the others had been.

Denny spoke for the first time, "It looks to me like we're wakin' up—finally. And FDR may turn out to be our Lincoln. He's tough if I'm any judge, although you might miss it under that slippery front he puts up."

"What do you mean, *slippery*?" Mike asked, bristling. "He's the best damn president we've had since his cousin Teddy."

"I know that. But even Lincoln was slippery the way I meant it. A politician has to be. That's all I meant. A leader has to slick out a bunch of dummies in order to lead. It looks to me like FDR is doing it."

"Amen," Newt said.

The old-timers' talk soon turned exclusively to small recollections such as how, in *their war*.

Newt and Mike got the most fun out of the chicken-stealing story that had almost got Mike into deep trouble with Newt's pa.

Flint caught Bennie staring at his wings and in a low voice said, "You'll get drafted pretty soon," and looking at Kid added, "so you two might as well get in the *premium* service."

Bennie recognized a recruiting pitch for the Marines and said, "Me and Kid would like to be pilots but we both got kicked out of school."

That interested Flint and he motioned them to the other end of the room. None of the old-timers seemed to notice their leaving. Rose stuck with Bennie.

They told Flint why and how they got kicked out of school.

Bennie said, "I guess we could never get pilot's wings like you college guys, but we'd like to be around airplanes, maybe keep 'em flying. We're both good with tools."

That sounded safer than flying to Rose, and she hoped if they went that was the kind of jobs they'd have.

Flint said, "I never finished high school. I ran away and 'jined' the Marines when I was sixteen in 1927. Got in Aviation, and since the commanding officer liked me, I finally got in the enlisted flying program."

"But you're an officer now." He knew what the silver bars were on his shoulders.

"What they call a mustang." He laughed briefly over the phrase and explained, "That's what they call officers that came up through the ranks, rather than from the military academies or reserve officers' programs in college." He shrugged. "It pays the same. And I'd have given an arm to be a pilot if being one-armed didn't keep me from being one in the bargain. I always wanted to fly."

"So did I," Bennie said. He remembered the hawk that said he'd be "one of them." He craned his neck to watch every plane that flew over and always had. There were getting to be a lot more of them now, and sometimes there'd be a formation of big ones. He knew from pictures that the last big formation that had passed over *Up North* were B-24 bombers, and he'd counted thirty of them before the elements all passed in echelon, the smooth heavy engine rumble finally dying into stillness. Bennie noticed that for a while after they passed, the woods were very still, such as after the wild things had heard a wolf howl and laid low lest it come after *them*.

He'd tried to imagine himself piloting one of the "big ones," as the ads put it, but couldn't, knowing he'd never qualify for pilot training. Now he saw another avenue open and for the first time seriously thought he might become a pilot. Maybe if they were so hard up for pilots that the Air Force was putting out posters in store windows that read: "YOU TOO CAN FLY, FLY THE BIG ONES!" they would scoop up kids like him and Kid.

Rose watching him, read his mind, and wasn't happy. Didn't he know he was a father now? Bennie felt her gaze on him, but avoided looking at her. He knew she often read his mind, as people could who were very close. He had no intention of going out and getting himself killed. His hunches were pretty good and he simply knew he'd survive a war, no matter how long it lasted. Women fussed too much and worried too much over their men and probably had since people had lived in caves or trees or wherever they lived back then.

In his mind he already saw himself returning home triumphantly; maybe even a boy general. "In that case," he told himself, "I might stay in." In this fantasy Kid returned with him and they were both pilots with a lot of medals.

Flint said, "If you decide to enlist, get in touch with me first. I may be able to pull some strings. Guys like me know the officers who are getting up there in rank today. We learned to fly together in prehistoric times." He snorted over his own little joke. "I might even be able to get you over to Hawaii with me after you finish boot camp. I'm stationed outside of Honolulu at a place called Barber's Point."

They talked awhile about things in general, especially living on a farm in northern Wisconsin. Flint said, "I came off the farm. Sometimes I wish I'd never left. How's the hunting up there?"

"Good," Kid chipped in. "And I can take anybody right to game every time. It's my Injun blood. Or take 'em where it ain't, either, come to think of it. Me and Pa guide guys from the cities and see that they get lots of exercise. We save the deer for the tribe, though. We need them." He grinned and added, "Bennie here is only a quarter-blood Sioux, but I'm full blood. His aunt Maud here calls him a 'breed' and said she always wanted one in the family. I almost got him trained so he can find his way home out of the woods."

Flint laughed, as Kid had expected. "I wish my leave lasted till hunting season. I'd like to come up and try my hand at it. I have a notion it'll be my last chance before we're hunting different game for a few years."

"Come ahead," Kid said.

"How about game wardens?"

Kid guffawed. "Newt shoots them as soon as we get a new one. Besides seasons don't apply to us pesky redskins."

"You're not kidding?" Flint asked.

"Hell no. You can ride up with us. There's room in the Lincoln."

"I've got my own car. I could follow you up and head back to San Diego from there as well as here."

Rose felt her heart sink. She knew that Flint would have Bennie and Kid thinking that they should join the Marines even before they were drafted. Both boys had patriotism coming out their ears, even though Kid was always complaining about the way palefaces had treated his ancestors. People didn't treat Indians a whole lot better even yet. Rose began to hate Flint even though she knew it wasn't right and certainly not logical. She couldn't help it, despite recognizing that he was a real nice man and one that was on the front line, ready to be first to fight for freedom and all that. Lindberg might not be a great patriot, but she liked Lindy's ideas better than Flint's and Newt's. *Old Hitler wasn't America's business.*

Bennie finally got his chance to talk to Mike Mullins and opened with, "My Pa knew a Mike Mullins when he was a kid. He told me a story about how this Mike had showed him a cave on his old family farm across the river."

Mullins eyes brightened. "That was on our place. They've made a damned park out of it. Even cut down the old apple trees. I remember your paw. He was about twelve and at first he was scared I was gonna take him down in a cave and knife him like Injun Joe in *Tom Sawyer*. That was a long time ago. So you're that kid's son? You sure don't look like him."

"My ma is half Sioux." He told Mike about his Indian side and how they'd just been up to the Little Big Horn.

Mike threw back his head and looked at the ceiling, remembering something and trying to recall it plainly. "I met a lot of Sioux in the War. Killed more of them than they did of me. At least one or two I can remember. When we was campaigning under Sully in Dakota. Not bad people. Who could blame them for fighting for their homes? They had some good ideas about how to live, too."

Kid was taking this all in, and put in, "We still do, but nobody listens to them much."

"Like what?"

Kid hadn't expected an old, old man to be interested, but he had a quick enough answer. "Like hangin' a bunch of those dude book farmers down at Madison that drained the marshes to make room for a lot of new farms, and killed off our wild rice in the bargain. Then they decided it was a mistake to farm up there in the first place, so they raised taxes and stopped maintaining roads so no more farmers would come and the ones there would starve out."

Bennie was listening open-mouthed. He hadn't known any of that or suspected that Kid knew it.

"Sounds about right for the way dude professors operate," Mike said.

He turned to Rose and changed the subject. "You're about a pretty a gal as I ever saw," he told her.

She blushed and smiled.

To Bennie he said, "I hear she's only your adopted sister and you two are sparkin' according to Newt, is that so?"

Bennie nodded.

Mike asked, "Speakin' of old Sioux customs, how many ponies would you take fer this squaw?"

Rose laughed out loud. "No deal," she said.

Mike tried to keep a straight face, but his eyes gave him away.

Later Kid got hold of Mullins alone and said, "If you want to see if you can still get your jollies, you should come up and visit us, and see Bennie's pa again for old times' sake. He'd love it."

"What's that got to do with my jollies?" Mike asked.

"Bennie's pa got divorced from his ma and married the local madam. She always has some good lookers. Hell, you ain't much older'n Newt and he gets it off regular down there at Klondy's."

"Jesus Christ!" Mike said. "I might just be up to see you."

Before the old-timers left for home, Flint's grandpa told how he'd been part of the Marine guard on the *Kearsarge* and witnessed the fight when it sunk the famous Rebel raider *Alabama*, off Brest, France.

This gave Bennie a new slant on the Civil War. He'd hardly thought of the part the Navy played in it, and of course the Marines with them. But reviewing it in his mind he realized that without them it would have been completely impossible to subdue the South.

Kid drove the old-timers home again, and when he returned, Newt said, "I'm ragged out. Talkin' over old times is fun, but it wears an old feller out. I think I'll take a nap."

Maud said, "To say nothing of getting sleepy from a big lunch and several good pulls on a bottle. That crew will probably all fall in bed and won't be up till breakfast."

"Good idea all around," Newt said. "I might not either. What do you say to my stayin' another day to rest up?"

"I wouldn't hear of anything else."

She thought it would be a good idea and had intended to talk him into it to keep her head on. She hadn't told him the local newspaper sharks had wanted to get an exclusive interview with "the son of old Colonel Bob Cheek." The only way she'd been able to hold them off was to tell them to come the next day, even though she wasn't sure Newt would still be there.

That made sense to the newspaper, since they saw the other vets all year, but not Newt. He not only hadn't been home for years, but he was a Cheek, even though he wasn't technically a vet. They knew he'd killed the famous guerrilla chief that *back-shot* his pa, and in any case Colonel Bob Cheek and his family were still big news around the area even though there'd been a couple of wars since his time. Colonel Smith, the first colonel of the regiment, had no relatives living locally. They'd died out or moved away over the years, although the regiment was always known as Smith's.

The Civil War was the last war where soldiers all from one place had been kept together so that their descendants talked about them almost every day. And that war had been America's sacred crusade to save the Union and free the slaves. History classes and books, as well as popular novels kept that idea alive and bright in the public mind. Even *Gone with the Wind* kept alive that nostalgic, sentimental era, despite being oriented to the Southern view. The North could afford to be forgiving and generous—they won.

CHAPTER FIFTY-EIGHT

I Can Stand Almost Anything

Bennie's sleep that night wasn't broken by glowing dreams of the past. Becoming a father takes a lot out of a fellow, even a young virile one. After holding Rose close and kissing her goodnight, tenderly and long, he remembered almost nothing until he awoke with sunrise flooding the room.

Rose had lain awake a long while, thinking. She imagined she could feel their son moving in her already, so sure was she of what had happened between her and Bennie that morning. She smiled up in the darkness and a picture of a little boy still at the creeping stage—definitely a younger issue of Bennie—danced into her mind. She watched him try to get up and walk, urging him to succeed in her mind. Finally he made it from one piece of furniture to another, then took a few steps without holding on, and she realized she had been holding her breath until he succeeded. She smiled over the look that captured his little face as he recognized what he'd done all by himself, an expression that clearly said he thought he'd just accomplished something wonderful. She thought, "*He really did.*" She was sure she could discern from his earnest expression that he dimly realized he had just embarked seriously on a strange journey into the mysterious affair he'd learn to know as life.

To her, most of life had been little more than a bad joke until Bennie had come along. She prayed that their son would never have the terrible times that she and Bennie had had in growing up during the Depression. She especially prayed that he wouldn't suffer the loss of those he loved, as she had. She wondered how she'd ever survived it. Sticking it out had earned her mental toughness. She told herself, "*I can stand almost anything and survive; anything except losing Bennie!*" She had to struggle a long while to put that out of her mind, but finally shook off the unhappy possibility and returned her thoughts to happier things.

Of course their boy wouldn't suffer what his parents had. She wouldn't permit it. She and Bennie would live to see a big family grow and give them grandchildren and maybe great-grandchildren while they lived to a happy old age.

Bennie tried not to waken Rose, but was defeated by her resolve before she went to sleep that she wouldn't miss anything again by being a slug-a-bed. He was tiptoeing to the bathroom and glanced her way and saw her eyes following him. She smiled. "*Caughtcha* this time, didn't I?"

"Oh, hell. I recall you got to be a mother yesterday and was figuring you needed all the rest you could get."

"Get back in here and I'll show you how much rest I need."

Later, he tried the journey to the bathroom a second time and noticed Rose snoozing.

"*I love you, little new Ma,*" he said to himself and sneaked out. On his way downstairs he added with great satisfaction, "*I reckon the Boy-Lover was too much for her.*"

He wasn't surprised to find Newt up and alert, smoking a cigar and sipping coffee at the kitchen table.

Minerva greeted Bennie with, "How about a cup of coffee, and I'll fix you eggs and anything you like with 'em?"

"Ham," he said. "And some of those good fried spuds you made yesterday."

Newt said, "I got a little private investigating to do today before we leave. If you youngsters would like to pass on it, I'll probably be able to handle it alone."

Just then Kid ambled in and said, "Do what alone?"

Minerva looked at Kid and raised her eyebrows to ask what he wanted for breakfast. "Same as yesterday," he said, which meant the same thing Bennie was having.

Newt was silent a while, taking a big puff on his cigar, stringing out the suspense as he often did.

Rose wandered in, looking sleepy, yawned, then said, "You three aren't going to leave me out of anything this time."

Bennie eyed her mock-seriously. "We were just going to take Newt down to the local den of iniquity," he told her. He had no hesitation about talking like this around her, since she knew where either he or Kid chauffeured his older charges almost every Saturday night back home.

"I can snooze in the car while you wait."

Newt told her, "He made that up. I've got religion recently. I thought maybe you people had noticed. But I did have a little trip in mind. I'm planning to unlock the attic and look around up there. Maud said it hasn't been opened up for years. In fact, she didn't even have a key. I had her get a guy out yesterday to make a key."

He pulled it out of his pocket, a big old-fashioned key.

"Leland and I used to play up there on rainy days. Pa's trunk was full of treasures from the Mexican War that we used to look over and play with."

"Like what?" Bennie asked.

"Lots of old truck up there, some from as far back as the Revolution, I'd guess. Of course, in those days that wasn't all that long ago. About as long ago as the Civil War is today. To me that seems like yesterday sometimes."

Bennie thought, "*To me, too, sometimes. Then other times it seems like it never happened.*"

"What else might be in that trunk?" Kid asked.

"I kinda had a notion the old Colt Walker I used to kill the son of a bitch that *back-shot* Pa might be in that trunk. Maybe his sword, too."

In the background Minerva had been listening to every word and would have liked to come up to the attic with them, but was too polite to ask. Besides, she knew her place, the deferential status that even northerners expected her people to accept.

"What're we waiting for?" Bennie asked after Rose had finished her pancakes. "Let's go round up Newt and get with the attic?"

They found Newt wandering along the brow of the rise overlooking the river. "Has Maud showed up, yet?" he asked. "Cain't go without her. She said she'd divorce me if I did. She musta had a hard night if she ain't up yet."

"I didn't know you were the marryin' type," Kid said.

"I ain't. That was the problem with Maud. That and we were cousins, of course, not that it makes much difference. A lot of 'em get married and don't have idiot kids like they say, either. Anyhow, it turned out she *was* the marryin' kind, which was why I left these parts."

Rose, as she listened, started thinking that Newt should have got married. He was a wonderful old character. His outward rejection of emotion struck her as skin deep, and she thought he always looked wistfully lonely when he observed romantic conduct in others.

"She was too young for you," Kid said.

"Not really. The French have a formula. A woman should be half a man's age plus seven years. On that scale she's way too old."

"Now she is," Kid said. "But you musta been thirty when she was born."

"Twenty-one, to be exact. She's just under seventy if I calculate right."

"Who's just under seventy?" Maud materialized from behind them. Not even Kid had heard her approach on the soft grassy turf.

Newt turned and said, "An old flame."

"Which one?"

"I can't remember, but old whatsername was a helluva woman."

Maud inspected his face for some clue regarding his true feelings.

Maud snorted. "You had dozens of 'em breathin' heavy for you around here when you were young. Lord knows why. Maybe poor eyesight. If you'd been handsome like your paw I could understand it."

She didn't fool Rose. Under this light banter some flame still flickered on both sides.

Rose's eyes always misted over when she encountered tragedies, and the worst tragedy in her mind, after lost loved ones, was lost love. Bennie noticed her sudden tears, and since they were standing to one side, whispered, "What's the matter?"

"I'll tell you later," she whispered back.

She thought, "*How could I have lived if Bennie hadn't fallen in love with me? Did Maud once go through that with Newt?*"

"Well," Maud said, "let's go look at the haunted attic."

"Haunted?" Newt asked.

"Didn't you hear footsteps up there at night?"

"Can't say as I did."

"I did," Kid said. "When Newt wasn't snoring too loud to hear 'em." Kid's bedroom was right next to Newt's.

Newt gave him a sharp look. "Footsteps, eh?"

"Yeah, footsteps."

Newt took the lead, moving at a faster walk than usual. "Let's go see about this," he said over his shoulder.

There was an edge of urgency in his voice. Catching that, Bennie wondered if there were some secret here that only Newt knew about, a secret that had to do with ancient memories, and musty relics stored away for decades in a dim attic where a ghost walked at night, perhaps condemned to stay there in lonely exile until some ritual took place that would liberate it. Was Newt bound on an errand of liberation? The old man projected an air that suggested he knew something unusual.

"Why didn't you tell me about those footsteps sooner?" Newt asked Maud, and laterally Kid.

Maud said, "They kept while you were in Alaska all those years, and might have been dead for all we knew. I guess I didn't mention 'em because I'm used to them."

Maud led the way up the squeaky, narrow steps to the third-floor landing and turned for Newt to unlock it.

The big key turned easily in the lock, since the locksmith had oiled and operated the mechanism several times to make sure it worked smoothly. Bennie felt like Alice in Wonderland, who had used a magic key, not knowing where the door that it unlocked would lead. He was sure it would be a Wonderland experience, especially if they found the Colt Walker. Bennie had been holding his breath while Newt turned the key in the lock and swung the door open. The interior was dim, but lit by large, round windows at each end, although he could see only one of them when Newt opened the door.

They all moved inside. Rose took his hand, and he knew why. Despite Newt's happy memories of this boyhood playground, another pervasive sense of sadness hung over the dim, musty room. Perhaps even some remotely threatening spirit pervaded this locked-away, barn-like space and had invaded it after its happy earlier days. His eyes began to adjust to the gloom and he made out old rough-cut rafters that sloped steeply to the peak of the roof. A sudden noise, the scuttling feet of some creature, startled everyone.

"Probably a squirrel lives up here," Newt said. "They used to get in under the eaves no matter how hard we tried to keep them out. Pa could never understand why they kept coming back. Good thing he never found out me and Leland was feedin' 'em. The squirrel mamas liked a snug nest inside instead of out in the rain in the oak trees. Can't say as I blame them. Maybe the ones we fed are the great-great-greats of this one."

"If it's a squirrel," Kid said. "It didn't sound like a squirrel to me."

"What did it sound like?" Bennie asked.

"I'm not sure," Kid said in an unaccustomed voice that made Bennie look at him sharply. Kid wasn't looking at him, but had his head cocked to one side, eyes slightly unfocused, looking down. Was his Indian sense alerting him to what others couldn't feel? Bennie's own usually sensitive antennae didn't tell him a thing. He concentrated on communicating with that side of himself, focusing his Indian side and indeed started to feel there was something lurking here besides squirrels, or other rodents, but he wondered as he always did—for example, about such things as his conversation with Waubonsee—if he brought the ghosts with him, or if they were already there. Were ghosts merely memories that some attuned people materialized in the right place, or vice versa?

His hand must have tightened on Rose's, since she looked at him questioningly. He said nothing, looking around silently at the clutter. Wires to hang clothes on had been strung years before and unused clothes hung on them, covered with yellowing old bed sheets, which themselves were coated with years of accumulated dust. Sealed boxes, and some open ones were stacked or scattered, and they were not the familiar cartons of the modern world, but sturdy wooden boxes, the only kind known in Newt's youth.

Newt thought, "*If we want to look in those we'll have to get a hammer.*"

"Here's Pa's trunk," he announced.

He stood looking at it for a long while without making an effort to open it.

Decades fell away and he could hear rain pattering on the roof. Leland's always happy face swam into view. "What'll we play today, Newt?" he asked. "Pirates," he heard another issue of Newt reply. "Today, I'll be Blackbeard and you can be Lieutenant Maynard, and kill me with Pa's sword."

He plainly recalled Leland's eyes looking at him and his voice: "I'll be Blackbeard. I'm black and you ain't. Besides it wouldn't be right if I killed you. Ma says I'm supposed to look after you like she did her folks down South."

Newt's thoughts returned to the present. "*He sure as hell looked after me.*"

Newt said, referring to Leland's modern day namesake, "I wonder why I didn't remember to bring Leland up here. Is he downstairs?"

Maud said, "I'll go get him."

"Bring Minerva, too."

"Well, here goes," Newt said. "A Treasure Chest like Captain Flint's. We always called Pa Captain till after the Civil War."

The lid lifted quietly and rested open on leather hinges.

"No Colt Walker here," Newt said, looking at the collection in the top tray.

He picked up a rich russet leather wallet that had seen a lot of use and opened its compartments. "Lookee here," he said. "Some old greenbacks. The kind they made when I was young. Big ones that you could almost fan yourself with." He waved the handful around. "Worth more, too."

"Let's see one," Kid said.

Newt handed him the wallet and all, then turned back to the tray and picked up a handkerchief made of expensive linen. "Pa always used these," he said. "And here's his G.A.R. wreath and gilt buttons." He next withdrew a medal and silently held it in his hand, turning it and examining it with reverence. "Pa's Congressional Medal of Honor. It's a wonder Grant didn't prevent him from getting one. Probably didn't know about it. Lucky for old Useless S. that Colonel Smith didn't get into the Senate. Grant would have died a major general because Smith would have filibustered his promotion until the last horn blew."

Bennie, who had a good deal higher opinion of Grant than Newt, said, "Maybe we'd have lost the Civil War."

"We did anyhow," Newt said. "Most useless war ever fought. Slavery would have died of its own weight."

He took up another wallet-size leather case up from the tray, opened it on its little brass hinges, looked at the inside quickly, and snapped it shut without showing it to anyone. Bennie knew it was an old photo holder from those days, having seen them in the G.A.R. Museum. They were designed to hold two opposing photos that could be displayed when the holder was hinged open and set on end. Newt shoved this in his side pocket without comment, and the others recognized that something about it prevented him from showing it to them—at least for the time being. Bennie scanned Newt's face for a clue and detected a mistiness in his eyes that hinted he was having a hard time to keep from crying. "*Maybe his ma and pa again*," he reasoned.

They heard Maud and the two servants coming up the steps and dropped the subject of slavery, waiting for them to come see what treasures Newt found next.

Bennie scanned the attic further and almost jumped at an apparition that materialized, staring directly into his eyes from the shadow just under the peak of the roof over a round window. It was the perfect face of Newt's father, an optical illusion, formed perhaps by some slant of light and conjunction of the rafters and cobwebs. He stared at it but called no one's attention to it. He'd seen such things before and no one else seemed to. The Moodore Ghost's apparitional appearances for example. He expected this one to dematerialize as such phenomena always had, but it didn't. A chill rippled up and down his spine as he realized, "*Maybe it's really him this time. If it really is, then he must be the ghost that walks here! Has he come to tell me something like all the rest did.*"

Another haunting thought intrigued him: "*Suppose Old Abe comes here sometimes to keep him company. They both died tragic deaths. And Newt's pa was one of the best friends Abe ever had. Never asked him for a single favor. Abe must have appreciated that.*" He moved his head to scan the attic, but could see no other faces. When he looked back, Colonel Bob's face was gone.

"*What did he want to tell me?*" Bennie asked himself. He was sure that this ghost, like all the others had a message for him.

Voices echoed in his mind, all saying: "*You will be one of us!*"

Ralph Esselborn's voice, especially, saying: "*Never run!*"

"*I don't aim to!*" he promised. And then, whether it was his imagination or not, Abe Lincoln seemed very near, and he told himself, "*You can't save the Last Best Hope of Earth by running, even if you have to give Your Last Full Measure of Devotion.*"

"*Is this really happening?*" he asked himself as he always had when these interludes took place.

Rose, still holding his hand, asked, "Where are you?"

That broke the spell and Colonel Bob reappeared briefly, smiled, and disappeared.

"I'm not sure," he said. "Are you?"

She said, "It's almost unreal isn't it? I can feel the past all around us."

Kid, overhearing, said, "Amen!"

This had all happened in the span of seconds but seemed like a long while to Bennie.

When the newly arrived three had gathered around, Newt said, "Well, let's pull out the tray and see what's down below."

Bennie heard Newt's sharp intake of breath as he held the tray aside.

"There she is! Pa's Colt Walker. And his uniforms and sword too."

He handed the tray to Leland to set down somewhere and took up the pistol and immediately aimed it at an imaginary target. "Bang!" he said, and performed an imitation of the heavy pistol's recoil. Talking then only to himself and perhaps to the ghost of his pa, he said, "This is the baby I got the dirty son of a bitch with." He examined it more closely and said, "It's empty."

He handed the pistol to Leland to hold and told him, "If your namesake hadn't died for me, I'd have been killed instead of him and never evened the score for Pa. Or maybe Leland would have evened the score for both of us. He was a dead shot himself, and cool under fire. He never *ran away* like some did. It wasn't in him."

"You evened the score for him, too, Mr. Newt," Leland reminded him. He looked straight into Newt eyes and saw something he'd never see in his life—the lingering spark called up by the memory of killing. He looked into the frightening, pale blue eyes of a cold-blooded killer who relished the memory of revenge.

A strong chill rippled up Leland's spine. To quickly get off the subject, he said, "I always wanted to know what that other long ago Leland looked like, but there ain't a picture of him downstairs."

Newt knew why and felt ashamed—in those days the blacks had no spare cash for frills like picture taking, and no whites wasted money having pictures taken of their servants. He knew that Leland was asking him if he had such a picture. And by the wildest chance he had the only one he could remember, outside of shots taken in the field during the war, of which he'd never had copies.

He reached into his pocket and handed Leland the little leather picture case and took back the pistol so he could use both hands to open it.

Newt said, "That's Leland with his ma when he was a little boy. On the other side is Magawn, his pa."

Leland looked inside, his face a rapt study in respect or perhaps a sort of magical nostalgia for what he'd never really known. He handed the case to Minerva, who looked at it the pictures a long while, then held it so everyone could see. On one side was an older black man, on the other a proud-looking mama with her boy, who had been trying not to grin since he'd been told that would spoil the picture. It didn't suppress the mischievous light in his big luminous eyes, however.

Minerva burst into tears. "The poor little thing," she said. Leland took the picture case from her and handed it back to Newt, then took his wife into his arms. He was crying, too, and didn't care who knew it. To console Minerva he said what was true in a very broken voice: "He wasn't little anymore when he saved Mr. Newt's life."

Rose held out her hand to Newt for the picture case, took it, and looked carefully at all the faces and burst out with, "He was cute as a bug." Then she burst into tears and impulsively held her arm around Minerva's heaving shoulders as best she could manage, since she had to hug Leland's arms to do it.

Bennie felt like he was in church. He had reaffirmed by this scene one of the most important things he'd ever learned, and he'd learned it long before. It was that what mattered was inside people, not outside. And that all humans were one race in fact. "*We've got to learn that,*" he told himself, "*and it doesn't look like it's going to be very soon, or easy either.*"

When everyone regained a degree of composure, Newt was still standing with the Colt Walker dangling at his side in his right hand.

He offered the pistol to Bennie. "Heft this baby," he said.

Bennie had often been told the Walker weighed almost five pounds and scarcely credited that, but now knew it was true. This was a monster weapon, developed by Sam Colt and Captain Walker of the Texas Ranger Battalion in the Mexican War.

Bennie was lost for a while, aiming the gun at a phantom target.

"It's yours," Newt said.

At this, the spectral vision of Colonel Bob returned to him, this time over the sights of the pistol, only now it was the face in the picture over the mantle in the sitting room. Colonel Bob, smiled, waved, and was gone. "*Did Newt and I just liberate a ghost?*" Bennie asked himself. He was ready to believe he was losing his mind and quickly dropped the pistol to his side and stood trembling.

"What's the matter?" Newt asked him. But the old man knew what was the matter with him. Bennie was sure that Newt was by some occult means fully aware of what they had just done together.

The rest of their investigation was a complete blank to him later, except for the packet of letters Newt had taken from the trunk. "I'll have to read these later," he'd said. He didn't say who had written them.

Bennie wondered if the letters might contain a message for him that Newt would convey when the time came. In any case it reaffirmed what he'd felt strongly: it was his destiny to be a warrior like Colonel Bob, and his son Newt, and Newt's best friend Leland, and all the rest, especially Custer. He absolutely knew this momentous truth, just as Rose had known she became a mother the day before.

It had been his destiny since he'd first stirred in Ma's womb.

Remembered voices spoke to him:

Waubonsee (at Devil's Cave): "One day you will be one of us."

Ralph Esselborn (up north): "I was in the war. We're going to get into another one. You'll be in it."

The Smart-ass Hawk (up north, the same day as Ralph, when he'd asked it what he'd be one of): "A warrior, you dumb shit! Couldn't you figure that out for yourself?"

LISTEN BY THE WATERS!

"Well, I'm going to be a warrior. I was born for it. And the Hawk was a symbol that told me I'd fly unless I miss my guess. It was no accident, either, that Flint showed up and told me how to be a pilot.

"And I'm going to be the goddamdest warrior anyone ever saw. I'll be an Ace like Eddie Rickenbacker. I'll come home from the war with medals down to my knees. Maybe make boy general."

After lunch, to which they invited the local editor for his interview with Newt, they went to the cemetery to decorate the graves. The florist had delivered several large bouquets that morning. They fitted them all into Maud's stationwagon, which Minerva drove, Leland in the right seat like a copilot should be. They followed the Lincoln. Maud rode in front as navigator, with Bennie driving.

She directed him to a place just opposite a tall monument, and pointed. "There it is. Biggest one in the place."

It certainly exceeded his expectations. From fifty feet away he could see the carving on the stone, but not make it out clearly. They all got out and approached the huge monument, which stood at least thirty feet high on a polished marble base. The base supported a fluted column on top of which an angel held in its arms a female figure in the style of Michelangelo's *Pietà*.

Newt knew the significance of that. His father had always promised to care for his wife throughout eternity. Here was that promise in stone.

The marble base was inscribed:

COLONEL ROBERT CHEEK
FIRST ILLINOIS MOUNTED VOLUNTEERS
1821–1879
HIS BELOVED WIFE, AMELIA ELLEN TODD CHEEK
1825–1879

Bennie was astounded to discover they had died so young. He thought, "Why, life cheated them both!"

A smaller stone nearby in the same plot was inscribed:

LELAND WASHINGTON
1850–1864
A SOLDIER OF THE REPUBLIC IN SPIRIT.
IN LOVING REMEMBRANCE OF A
FAITHFUL FRIEND OF
THE CHEEK FAMILY

They buried both memorials in flowers.

Rose, speaking through tears, said it for them all: "It's all we can do for the people we loved when they're gone, isn't it? Except remember them in our hearts. Then we die too and take even the memory with us. It's all too sad."

Kid drove them as they left LaSalle late that afternoon. Bennie in the back seat occasionally fondled the Colt Walker. Or reread the inscription on it

The personal arm of Captain Robert Cheek.

He thought, "*It's sort of odd that Newt's pa didn't call it a 'weapon' or a 'pistol' . . . or even 'firearm,' since a sword could be called an arm.*"

Newt had also taken with him his father's uniform and his sword in its scabbard, with belt and shoulder straps still attached, to which was also slung the holster for this pistol. They lay, carefully wrapped in a bed sheet, in a place of honor on top of the baggage in the rear seat.

Next to Bennie, Rose dozed, a faint smile on her face. He watched her indulgently, her breath gently flowing in and out of slightly parted lips, and said to himself, "Well, little mom. It'll be a long while before either of us die so we, at least, can keep them all alive that much longer in our hearts."

He thought that over, and added, "After that it will be up to all those kids you want to have to keep memories bright. If we raise 'em right, they'll know it's their responsibility."

CHAPTER FIFTY-NINE

A Boy Could Imagine Anything

Creeks and rivers whisper to knowing ears:
"I have been to the sea and back a million times."

Bennie had long known that rivers nurtured, had distinct personalities, could speak, had souls. He already knew this when he wandered along the Fox River when he was eight. An intensely educational decade had passed for him since then, but he could still recall vividly the sight of willows that dipped graceful branches into the Fox's water creating bubbly designs that changed every instant. A boy could stare at them and imagine anything.

As they sped eastward from LaSalle, Bennie had time to watch the scenery. He occasionally caught glimpses of the Illinois River, which they paralleled. He wondered what he would learn from it if he lived where he could visit it often.

He had first learned an important lesson from the Fox River at Waubonsee where an earlier Bennie—that dirt-poor, lonely boy who had been too often sick—had wistfully watched the motorboats of the rich knifing through the water, pushing V-shaped waves ashore behind them. These miniature tidal waves hypnotized him. He couldn't help but stare at them until the last one ebbed and the river became calm once again.

The most useful message he received from the river was, "Toss your clothes off, kid. No one will see you way out here. Wade in and learn to swim in me. You don't need a boat."

So he learned to swim all by himself—aside from a few snide suggestions from Buck Doaks—such as, "Stick to shallow water at first, where you can walk on the bottom if you start sinking," then, after he could swim a long ways in shallow water, Buck tossed him a reasonable question, "Did it ever occur to you that you can swim just as far in deep water now as you can in this puddle?"

He got the point and ventured to swim across the river and back. Midway across he thought how deep the water must be under him and almost sank from fear. Buck urged him on with encouraging words: "Who the hell will I have to talk to if you sink like a rock, you ninny? Get going!" With some trepidation, he turned and swam back. The experience gave him a lot of the self-confidence that he had needed. A few years later he was swimming across Lake Koshkonong and back, which must have been at least a couple of miles, and when he finished he was sure he could have done it again without resting. He never tried, though. There was always too much attraction for a red-blooded American boy instead to practice outdoor social graces, such as stealing a picnic lunch from some careless rich dummies, or at least richer than he was, and filling up.

Still he couldn't help but be envious of those with fast boats. Even a rowboat would have pleased him if he had one of his own.

He had been introduced to the Illinois River when he was six and Uncle Johnny came to meet him and Ma in Riverview to take them *out home*, and had obligingly stopped his Dort touring car on the iron bridge when Bennie begged time to watch a passing stern-wheeler pushing its barges. In those days he hadn't known that the Illinois was one of the most historic American rivers, avenue of French explorers, highway of the fur trade, the first tentacle of a transportation octopus whose nucleus was Chicago. He learned all that later from books.

The Illinois's banks had also been the familiar stamping ground of legendary Chief Tecumseh, who was killed in the War of 1812, and of his faithful fighting friend, Chief Chaubenee. After Tecumseh's death a rudderless, aging Chaubenee became a fat, peace-loving beggar who was famous for warning many whites that Blackhawk's Sauks were coming to scourge them. This earned Chaubenee a monument that ended up in back of a saloon in Riverview as civilization advanced. In addition to bestowing a monument, grateful whites rewarded him by stealing his homeland and pauperized him and his people.

Rose, who had been dozing beside him, awakened slowly, looked around to orient herself, then grinned at Bennie, who was watching her. He leaned over and kissed her and she closed her eyes, wishing to sleep a little longer. Before, dozing off again, she remembered that they were headed to Country Grandma's. Rose had heard much about her from both Bennie and Ma, especially about her Indian background and mysterious loss of a fabulous inheritance. By now Ma should be *out home* with her mother. Rose looked forward to seeing Ma again, since they were more like two girls together than adopted daughter and mother.

She had wished Ma could come with them on this trip. In any case, Rose was thrilled, thinking of the discoveries to be expected *out home*, especially if Ma's Sioux grandmother She Sees Them First could join them. But at the same time she was homesick for her familiar north woods and scenes from it swam in her mind as she fell asleep.

Newt, with whom Amos Donaldson of the Indian Bureau had promised to keep in touch by wire, hadn't yet heard if Country Grandma's mother would be allowed to leave the reservation. If Newt had known how those arrangements were miscarrying due to careful bureaucratic planning, the air would have been blue around him from more than cigar smoke.

Rose certainly hoped She Sees Them First would obtain permission to come visit her daughter, especially for Bennie's sake. She knew that Bennie planned to get Newt embroiled in discussions with Country Grandma and her mother about the battle of the Little Big Horn, since they had all been there, whether any of them enjoyed reliving it or not. He had a true historian's nose for digging out information and determination to preserve facts for posterity.

Bennie perked up like a dog coming into familiar territory as they approached Riverview, passed over the Illinois and Michigan Canal at the "widewater" and ascended the approach to the new span that had replaced the old iron truss bridge. The new bridge was necessary to accommodate a manyfold increase in auto and especially truck traffic, since the old one had been a one- and-a-half-lane affair, especially for trucks, which were wider than buggies and most farm wagons. Because of that, the first car or truck to reach the bridge had had the right of way over others coming from the other direction. One hoped the others would stop and wait their turn to cross and that no one would rudely get out of line. (Some inevitably did and caused fistfights and one shooting on the bridge during the years after motor vehicles came into use.)

The new bridge rose steeply to at least twice the height of the old one to allow passage of new, taller river traffic. Stern-wheelers were rapidly being replaced by tugs with high stacks and rigging, and the channel had been deepened for occasional seagoing vessels with tall masts from which loading booms swung.

Just beyond the bridge they were motioned by a uniformed state trooper into a line of cars at a roadblock. Several other uniformed officers were up ahead looking into cars. Recognizing what they were, Newt said, "Somebody must have stuck up a bank or something."

Kid pulled over and stopped, then moved ahead in his turn until opposite a trooper who bent down and looked them over through the open windows.

"What's going on?" Kid asked.

"Lost person. We want everyone to be on the lookout for this one especially. She doesn't speak English and won't understand how to get by in this neck of the woods, so we want everyone to try to help her or at least notify us right away if they see her. Besides, she's an old lady."

"How will we recognize her?"

The trooper grinned, "You'll know her all right. You may not believe this, but she's a Sioux Indian off a reservation out west someplace and we were told she's dressed just like the Indians we see in movies, with high buckskin leggings and all."

"Jesus Christ!" Newt exploded. "That's got to be *She Sees Them First.* That dumb son of a bitch Amos Donaldson brought her back here without asking us first, and let her get lost!"

Newt's outburst instantly got the trooper's full attention. "That's her name! How come you know it? And about Donaldson? He's the guy who phoned in the alarm. He's back there in town chasing his tail."

The trooper looked like he was about to search their trunk for the lost woman.

Newt said, "We were supposed to meet her, but she wasn't supposed to come until we told them it was O.K. to bring her. Some damned dumb bureaucrat screwed up."

That was hitting a little close to home, and the trooper didn't look happy. Since he didn't know what else to do he fell back on being officious. "Pull out on the shoulder. The sergeant will want to talk to you."

Rose said to Bennie, "The poor old lady. She'll be terrified."

Bennie thought, "*Don't count on it.*"

This old girl was related to Sitting Bull, and old Bull managed to navigate unfamiliar terrain first rate. Bennie wouldn't have been surprised *from what he'd read of Sioux tactics traveling in strange country* to hear that *some farmer* had recently lost a horse. It was the preferred Sioux transportation even now. Neither would Newt, who had ample experience with Plains Indians and, unlike Bennie, *he hadn't gotten most of it out of a book.*

She Sees Them First had enjoyed her first time riding on a train. In fact her trip to the Little Big Horn had been the first time she'd been very far off the Standing Rock Reservation since the *hostiles* had been confined there. She had come back from Canada with Sitting Bull in 1881 and had no reason to leave until she'd been taken to the Little Big Horn by Amos Donaldson and that had been by auto.

She'd found the train a little scary when it first moved, since it accelerated to a speed at which she'd never traveled, and swayed, thumped, and squealed while it did, but she soon forgot that in the enjoyment of watching the ground whip past and disappear behind them. She expertly appraised every horse and cow they passed, and marveled at the numbers of whites she saw as the train moved eastward through many towns. But best of all was the dining car, where she could eat as much of everything as she wanted. A black man would just bring more if Donaldson asked him to. For his part Donaldson was enjoying this part of the trip as much as she, since the Bureau was footing the bill, intending to pass it on to Newt as he'd agreed (in writing, with five carbon copies).

When passengers heard who she was, she became an object of great attention, and a pet of some, who asked to be introduced to a relative of Sitting Bull. She accumulated pockets full of candy and someone even gave her a red rose. She understood that she must be an important person now and liked it, although she couldn't even imagine the reason for her new status.

Her first night in a berth had been something else to get used to. After a while she settled down, lying on her side with two pillows to prop up her head, and watched the passing lights of ranches and towns through the slit of window where the porter hadn't quite pulled the curtain down all the way. At last, after hours of half-dreaming about how it had become possible that this was happening to an old woman, she started to wonder what those she'd known, who were now gone, would think of it. Gradually she felt herself dropping off to sleep, with clear visions of some of them in her head, especially Four Ponies, who had been a good, brave man.

Her last drowsy thoughts were about going to see their daughter, Red Moon Rising—she wondered what the person she remembered only as an obedient and helpful young girl would look like, and most of all if she would still truly love her mother? After all, she was probably more like a white person now. Her letters always said that she loved her mother—every one of them. They all ended with a scrawl that Donaldson had told her was the word "Love," and her signature followed, "Mary," not Red Moon Rising. She had memorized what those words looked like. But letters were only pieces of paper that she couldn't even read for herself. Pieces of paper, like smoke signals, conveyed messages, but you couldn't look the senders in the eyes or hear their voices, which was the only way you knew the truth. Mr. Donaldson had given her the letters, even though she couldn't read them. She remembered what they said almost word for word. And she had no trouble reading the tear-stained pages.

Well, time would tell, and she would soon know. There was no doubt in her mind that she still loved the daughter she'd lost and mourned over so many years before. The memory had never dimmed of how bereft she'd been, and how worried for a little girl in the hands of the *Wasuchus*, assuming she was still alive. She had prayed that her daughter *was* alive, because even as a captive she might escape and make her way back to her people. Whenever she thought of how sad it had been, tears came to her eyes—even yet. She remembered her almost overwhelming happiness when her lost daughter had tracked down her whereabouts and sent her first letter. She had been so glad then, but it wasn't like having her little girl back. Her wrinkled face was wet with tears which she wiped away with the back of her hand just before she dropped off to sleep.

It took two days to reach Riverview, and Mr. Donaldson was right beside her almost all the time, but he had to take care of personal needs, too. She understood that and obeyed his instructions to stay where he left her until he returned. Just before they got to Riverview they had been sitting on the observation platform of the last car, which she enjoyed immensely.

The conductor came out to notify them they'd almost arrived at their destination and to be certain they didn't miss their stop.

Donaldson had said to her, "You stay here for a minute," and left with the conductor.

He knew that newsmen's snoopy noses had ferreted out the fact that they were coming because some had already waylaid them at earlier stops. She Sees Them First, put off by their insistent voices, exaggerated gestures, and intense faces, instinctively mistrusted newsmen and became agitated if they stayed around long. They reminded her of Indian agents.

This time Donaldson wanted to make final arrangements with the conductor to get her off the train secretly, after all the other passengers had debarked. But he was taking no chances that an engineer, anxious to keep on schedule, would leave while they were still on the train, or, equally as bad, depart with them deposited in Riverview and their baggage still on the train. He had been irritated enough when the Bureau had insisted that they travel on the schedule prescribed by the tickets they had arranged for them, whether Newt approved or not. He had agreed to this only because he knew how disappointed her relatives would be if She Sees Them First were denied permission to leave at all by some aggravated official. He assumed he could put them up at a hotel in Riverview if it came down to it—even at his own expense, since he was sure Newt would repay him. He hoped Newt had got at least one of the telegrams he'd sent to alert him to the change of plans.

A constant worry for him was that he'd been cautioned by the Agency doctor that the old woman had a weak heart, and he didn't think it would help his record if she died on his hands. In any case, he had plenty of time for a final conference with the conductor, since the train had come to a full stop on a siding, waiting for another to pull out of the station.

It was then, while she was alone, that the old Indian woman saw the puppy crawling beside the tracks on three legs, the other dangling and bloody. She wondered if it had been run over by the train, as wagons sometimes ran over puppies on the Reservation. The thought of leaving it to die, as it surely would without help, was too much for her. She carefully climbed over the railing, her arthritic body protesting every move, and tried to let herself down to the track bed, losing her grip and dropping the final foot. The jar to her backbone almost paralyzed her for a moment, even though she was strong and agile for her age, as well as determined in the way that only an Indian woman could be. (After all, some had been known to drop out of a column fleeing the soldiers, have a baby, possibly unattended by even a friend, and rejoin the column within a few hours.)

The puppy saw her coming and sensing that she would help it, tried to drag itself to her. She saw the fear drain from its eyes, supplanted by hope. When she picked it up and cuddled it to her breast she realized that it was almost skin and bones. It weakly tried to lick her.

She crooned a Sioux song to it, a minor key repetition of encouraging words such as she would have to a frightened child that had been hurt. She realized then that somehow she had to get herself and it safely back onto the train. However, if she laid it on the rear platform it might become frightened and scramble back off as she slowly clambered back up, assuming she could even manage that. As she worried about that, the train moved slowly away toward the depot a half mile down the tracks.

She watched it grow smaller, knowing she couldn't possibly catch it. That didn't worry her so much as knowing that Mr. Donaldson would be angry with her. Well, it would all work out and she would explain it to him. He was a good man and would understand. Patience and hope were strong in her kind who had fruitlessly waited for centuries for someone to help them. She carried the puppy in her arms and started down the tracks after the train. A trestle interfered with following directly because she wasn't sure her uncertain balance could keep her upright on the spaced ties.

There was a gully below the trestle with a small meandering creek running through it. Very carefully she maneuvered down the bank, puppy still in her arms, occasionally whining a little, and made it to water. She allowed it to drink its fill before she attempted to tend to its injuries. She knew how to use water to clean wounds. It was all her people had had when she was young. After cleaning the rip in the little animal's broken leg, she made a bandage from a piece of her shawl, and a splint from a willow branch, using the knife she had never told Mr. Donaldson she had brought along. No discreet Sioux woman went among whites without a knife concealed under her skirts in a sheath fastened to her leg. Donaldson, as familiar as he was with her people, didn't know that and wouldn't understand. No Sioux, *man or woman*, going among whites would have done it without at least a knife.

After bandaging the puppy, she surveyed the area for an easy enough route for her old body to work up out of the creek bed and decided she would have to walk upstream a ways to find a low enough spot to make it out.

When, panting heavily, she finally managed that, she was in an orchard at the back of a deep yard, through which she could make out a distant house. It was shady there and she was tired. She picked an apple and took a bite, found it delicious and ate the whole thing. The pup watched her eat with its hunger showing plainly on its face. She looked around and saw that there were plenty of grasshoppers in the tall grass and caught a couple. There were dozens of them hopping in sight. *At least she and the pup wouldn't starve right away with plenty of apples, wild game (even if only grasshoppers) and water on hand.*

Pretty soon she would find some white person and ask them for help, maybe up at the house she saw. The people there wouldn't understand her need, but would call help when they were sure she meant no harm. In time she figured that Mr. Donaldson would issue an alarm and she would be found by searchers, regardless. That's what happened when children strayed away from the Reservation. Just now she needed to rest for a while.

It was then that she was gripped by a familiar sharp jab of pain around her heart and had to sit down. An old tree with a wide trunk provided her a spot to sit down and rest her head. After a short nap, her breathing became easier and the pain subsided. But she was still very tired. She roused, then lay down, curled up in the grass with her arms for a pillow and sank into a deep sleep, the puppy curled in the curve of her lap. When she awakened, stars were out, and at first she couldn't remember where she was. The puppy's whine reminded her. It was faithfully there, although she knew it was hungry and hurting. A few grasshoppers were poor fare to recuperate from a wound on, although her people had done it during famines.

She decided she would just have to wait until morning to move around. At her age she couldn't see so well and might stumble over something and fall, or fall into a hole and break something. The puppy whined again. She hugged it gently and said to it, "*Poor thing, you're hungry. But you will have to be patient and wait.*" She was sympathetic, but not overly concerned, since she was used to being hungry. She'd been hungry most of her life, so that finally she hadn't even realized she was hungry sometimes. "*It will live*," she told herself, "*And*

I must live, too, to save its life and find it a home. Maybe Mr. Donaldson will let me keep it."

The chilling night air suggested building a fire, but she had no way to do it. For the rest of the night she would sit with her back to the big tree again, holding the puppy close to keep it warm and trying to make her shawl cover them both. She dozed fitfully, awakened occasionally by the little animal's whimpering or the distant sound of a dog barking. She knew the little dog must hurt badly at the times when he whined and knew too well how that felt, too. She stroked him then and willed her strength into him as medicine men did. She was a "healer" herself, and knew it worked like an anesthetic, since the dog settled down again each time.

At first light she took up her orphan charge and slowly made her way further into town. She saw no one up yet, but a few autos moved in the distance. She could see taller buildings a few blocks away and headed there because she knew it was in places like that where restaurants were located, and they threw out edible garbage. She instinctively chose an alley that ran behind some stores. She had been in white man villages near the Reservation enough to know that these narrow streets were where the backs of restaurants abutted. With good luck she would find a feast for both her and the puppy in a garbage can. She could never understand why whites threw out so much food, especially when they allowed her people, and even other whites, to starve.

She found what she sought and the two of them had a feast together, the pup eagerly biting the food and nipping her fingers sometimes as he did. She was unaware that the cook who had come in early to start breakfast, had heard her out back and called the police to report a prowler.

The sun rose shortly after that and attracted her attention to a tall monument, golden in the sun's rays, a short distance up the alley. It had some sort of figure on top. Lost though she was, the figure interested her. As she walked nearer, the odor of the place repelled her, a rank smell she knew from the breath of the disgusting men who got drunk on the reservation.

She looked up at the large statue and saw that it was an Indian.

"*He looks like Sitting Bull,*" she told herself in amazement.

She knew that the whites made such statues to honor each other, but had never seen one of an Indian.

"*Do they know him here?*" she asked herself.

It didn't make sense. She knew they must hate him since he had killed so many of them who came asking for it.

There was a plaque on the base of the statue, but of course she couldn't read it.

The words there read:

CHAUBENEE

FRIEND OF THE WHITES

It was there that the police cruiser found her.

In a few moments she was reunited with Mr. Donaldson at the police station and was amazed to see with him her great-grandson, Bennie, and those others she had met at the Little Bighorn. She certainly hadn't expected to meet them like this and wondered how they knew she would be here. Tears welled in her eyes. She was still holding the puppy and held it out to Bennie, saying to Donaldson, "Tell him I want to keep it, and if I can't I want him to have it."

Bennie very carefully handed the puppy to Rose and drew his great-grandmother into his arms, patting her shoulders as though he were consoling a little lost kid. In a way he was. He felt her sobbing against his shoulder. "*Who says Indians don't cry?*" he asked himself and felt uncontrollable tears coming to his own eyes.

CHAPTER SIXTY

The Lost Sioux

After Donaldson found out what had happened from She Sees Them First, and explained that and their unannounced schedule to Newt, everyone calmed down. The sergeant in charge was obviously irritated to recognize that he couldn't think of any way to detain them with paperwork. He looked for assistance to the sheriff, who'd come over as soon as alerted to the finding of the lost Indian woman. The sheriff shook his head to the sergeant to indicate he had no help to offer.

The sergeant concluded, reluctantly, to let Newt and his party simply walk out. He couldn't even think of some kind of form to have them sign in quintuplicate. He hoped the chief wouldn't chew his ass later for forgetting some procedure he could have dredged up, or for not inventing some red tape on the spot.

Newt stuck his head back in and asked the sergeant, "Is there a vet in this burg?"

"A what?" The question surprised him.

"A veterinarian."

"Oh, yeah. For the pup. Straight down the street about four blocks on the left." He motioned with his thumb. "You'll see the sign, but he won't be open yet."

Outside on the walk they milled around and Newt said, "Let's get our stomachs taken care of, then get the pup down to a vet. I'll bet *Shesees* here could use some decent chuck. So could the pup. We gotta go back and check out at the hotel, and they got a pretty fair restaurant, so that ought to fill the bill."

Newt was surprised to see the same waitress who'd been on at supper the night before, and when she brought menus, said, "Jeezus, do they work you all the time?"

She grinned. "Morning girl is off sick,"

The grin was because she had spotted Newt as one of the last of the big-time spenders. She would have been convulsed to hear that he called himself "the last of the spent big-timers." He was, in any case, eternally sympathetic to anyone who had to work in a restaurant and never tipped less than a buck, which was a lot of money. Cigarettes were only a dime a pack, so a buck bought a carton of them.

The waitress also realized who Shesees was and was thrilled to be serving her breakfast. Such an unusual disappearance had made the *Herald* the night before, with a follow-up special that morning, although there were no pictures. The story of the lost Sioux was all over town. Newt expected a newsman to show up and try to get some pictures and ask stupid questions (such as what Sheesees thought about Custer's Last Stand) and hadn't decided whether to pity a fool born incapable of holding an *honest* job, or threaten to kill him. He liked the latter idea better, but unfortunately it could lead to delaying their journey.

After they were settled at a big table, Donaldson supervised Shesees's selections, which boiled down to "a lot."

She smiled at the prospect of another flood of food just as she'd got on the train, then looked over at Kid and peppered him with a barrage of Sioux. He nodded and told her something.

"What was that about?" Bennie asked.

"She said the pup is still asleep in the back seat of the car, probably, but she knows it's hungry, so she wants me to take it some of her breakfast as soon as it gets here."

Newt said, "Tell her we'll get it some breakfast of its own. They probably have some scraps from last night we can carry out right quick."

He motioned to the waitress and got that show on the road.

Shesees turned loose another barrage on Kid and included Donaldson in her arc of fire.

Kid said, "She wants to know what we think she should call the pup. She says maybe she'll call it *Broken Leg*, or maybe *Little Brave*."

Rose, who had been toting the pup ever since Bennie had handed it to her said, "Ask her what she thinks about *Little Warm One*, or *Licks a Heap*?"

Kid passed that on and *Sheseez* laughed and said something back.

"She likes *Licks a Heap*," Kid said, "and says that the little squaw is very bright.

Rose said, "It's a good thing I didn't say *Peeing Bull*, or I might have got in trouble and been very dull."

"Did he leak on you?" Bennie asked.

"A heap," Rose said. "Before we check out, I'm going to change my skirt and wash off."

Newt said to Bennie, "We ought to let the folks out at your grandma's know we're on the way at last. They got a phone?"

"I don't think so. They don't even have indoor plumbing or water as far as

I know. But the guy down the road is a *progressive* farmer, and I'll bet he does. Let me check the phone book."

"If he does, ring him up," Newt said.

He did, and Bennie got Claud Willis's wife, Clarissa. She said, "I'll go over and tell 'em you'll be on the way. And if you're coming out here I wouldn't hear of your not dropping over to say hello, for old times' sake. I told your grandmother that we could take a couple of people over here at night if she doesn't have enough beds."

At the veterinarian's, Shesees carried Licks a Heap in personally. When she learned that they'd decided to keep him a few days for "cage rest," she asked Kid, "Do you think the vet looks like a good man?"

Kid made a show of looking him over carefully and assured her he did. Actually he thought he looked like an illustration of Captain Hook he'd seen in a book, but realized they'd pull his license—as the vet also must realize—if he mistreated an animal, so figured it would be safe to leave *Licks* there.

"He'll be O.K.," Kid said. "I'll come in and check on her tomorrow." The vet's assistant, an attractive corn-fed type girl, gave Kid the idea that coming in to check would be a pleasure. The way she looked at him, as though she suspected he'd mentally hustled her into a bed at least twice, suggested that would be O.K. with her, too. Newt hadn't let him go to a single whorehouse on the whole trip, and he was so horny he was surprised that no one noticed him tooting.

After those necessary tasks were out of the way, Bennie drove them out of town and back across the bridge where they'd been stopped the day before. Memories of past trips across the Illinois here caused a constriction in his chest such as a kid gets on Christmas morning. All of his memories of Country Grandma's were happy except the constant apprehension at meals from knowing that Ma was looking for any excuse to send him away from the table and make him cry.

He thought, "*She sure sings a different tune since I've got big enough so she can't beat me up anymore.*" He didn't stop to reflect that Country Grandpa, or as Jim Tynan had called him, "That mean little *Cherman* rat, Grandpa Feltman," had given Ma the blood line that planted both traits into her: being mean in the first place, and reforming only when he was afraid not to.

He got a surprise when he turned onto the narrow country road that led two miles out into the waving cornfields down to the old home place. It had been graveled and recently graded as well. When Pa had driven it in the old Buick, or Uncle Johnny in the Dort, or Clermont, or whatever his latest car had been, it had been rutted and dusty or else muddy. After a rain it was always almost impossible to negotiate, causing cars to skid around from side to side in deep, black mud. Only low gear would do. The bad road also led to prayers that one wouldn't sink to the running boards and get stuck fast. The prayers had been answered about one out of two, so that half the time someone waded through the mud, up to the farm and had Country Grandpa hitch up a team of horses to pull them out. The worst part of the road had been the quarter mile just before the home place, so the towing wasn't as much a chore as it might have been. A year or two before they'd moved back *up north*, Uncle Johnny had talked the old man into buying a Fordson tractor that made the towing job a lot easier.

Ma was down at the front gate waiting for them. It was always kept shut since the farmers along there let their cows out on the road to graze the free grass along the edges and naturally any cow finding an open gate would have to come through it. Country Grandma didn't need cows trying to push down the fence around her garden or accidentally tramping on the inevitable chickens' nests scattered around in the weeds by wily hens trying to hide them, since such bootleg nests were where a good number of the eggs Grandma sold were laid.

Bennie spotted Ma waiting by the gate and knew she wanted to be the important one to lead in the precious cavalcade. An imp reminded him of her mean record when he was a wide-eyed, hungry kid at the table and she'd enjoyed making him cry. He pretended not to see her, and merely waved as he speeded by, gunning it up a little just as he passed. He hoped she'd think he'd forgotten where the place was and assume he hadn't recognized her. He could hear a protesting bellow through the open window.

Rose said, "That was Ma. Isn't that your grandma's place?"

Bennie grinned. "So it is. I must have forgot what it looked like after all these years."

Only Kid realized that Bennie went past on purpose to get Ma's goat.

Bennie said, "I'll have to go up to Willis's driveway to turn around." It was a quarter-mile up the road.

Kid said, "Are you sure you really forgot?"

"To tell you the truth I thought I'd pay her back for a few licks she got in on me when she used to bring me out here as a little kid."

Rose said, "That's mean."

"Not if you knew the debt I was paying off."

As he swung around the Willis's barnyard, Clarissa came out of the house to see who they were. He pulled up next to her on the way out and was glad to see she hadn't worn out. She'd always been a feast for male eyes in the neighborhood and still was.

"Well, *hello*," Clarissa greeted him. "You *are* little Bennie, aren't you?"

Bennie said, "Yep. Hi, Clarissa."

"Why are you down this far?"

"I forgot where the old place was," he fibbed. "I'm headed back. See you later."

She probably didn't believe him, judging from her look, but stood back and waved as they departed. When he got back down to Ma, he was pleased to see she was in the middle of the road, looking steamed. He ignored her scowl as he pulled abreast of her and said, "I forgot where the place was."

Her look plainly said, "Bullshit!" But she was too curious to see what her grandmother looked like to complain. She looked into the back seat, then motioned him into the driveway, rather than have a reunion out on the road. He stopped between the house and the cob-shed, as they called it, in front of the old familiar screened porch.

Country Grandma emerged in her customary garb, a cheap house dress and her inevitable apron. She had been practicing Sioux in her mind and speaking it to herself out of anyone's hearing, which meant mostly in the back house, She had discovered that over the years, even though she never spoke Sioux, or tried to teach the language to her kids, she had constantly memorized the old words by speaking Sioux in her mind. She had relived remembered conversations, and could still form the old sounds with her mouth and tongue. She could even remember the words of Four Ponies and hear his voice as she was sure it had sounded. But she was still terribly afraid that she was wrong in her recollections, that She Sees Them First would wonder what strange language Red Moon Rising was jabbering at her in. Her heart was in her mouth and her breath very short.

She waited by the back door of the Lincoln while Donaldson helped her arthritic mother back out of the Lincoln and carefully search for the ground with one foot. Then the old woman turned and looked at her daughter.

Country Grandma had the strangest feeling that she was suddenly young again. In Sioux she said, "*Mama.*" Even her voice sounded like a child's.

Then the two women were embracing, crying like children.

She Sees Them First said over and over, "Little one. Lost one. I cried and cried." Then she said, "Now you are back."

Ma came puffing up the drive and surveyed the scene with a poker face. She was the only one dry-eyed. Even Newt had to pretend he was getting a cigar ready to light.

Bennie eyed Ma and thought, "*Go ahead. Figure out some way to spoil it.*"

But she failed for once. Instead she simply watched with shifting emotions flickering across her face, none of which he could read to his satisfaction. She seemed perplexed for the most part.

Shesees finally stepped back and wiped her eyes with the back of her hand and looked around, her gaze coming to rest on Ma. "You are a Sioux," she said. "You must be my granddaughter."

Donaldson quickly interpreted that.

Ma made no move, and was silent. Shesees was uncertain whether she should hug Ma. Finally Country Grandma said, "Hug her, Emma. Don't just stand there like a ninny. She's my mother!"

That seemed to unleash something in Ma and she took the old woman in her arms and actually hugged her. "Does she understand English?" she asked no one in particular.

Bennie said, "Not a word."

Ma said, "She doesn't even smell bad."

That was too much for Bennie. He exploded, "For Christ's sake, Ma, get human for once or I'll dunk you in the horse trough!"

Rose was the only one who looked even slightly shocked at Bennie's explosion. She knew Ma could be human and realized that something more complex than meanness was motivating her now, and also that something she didn't know about was behind Bennie's exasperation that make him explode in such an uncharacteristic manner.

Rose finally decided to laugh and broke the tension by saying, "Ma is just being Ma. At least she's honest. That's what I thought the first time I hugged her, but I didn't blurt it out."

Ma shot her a grateful look. She said indignantly, "That's right. I've heard about her all my life and I'm going to love her *if it kills me*."

At that everyone but Shesees laughed, even Country Grandma, who knew her solemn little daughter like a book and loved her for the side that had unselfishly helped her survive overwork, from the time Emma was about three and had understood instinctively that her mother desperately needed help.

Shesees looked around for someone to explain to her why everyone was laughing, but got no direct answer. She looked at Emma to see if something in her look suggested she had been making fun of her and that everyone was laughing at a dumb old Sioux squaw. She would not have been surprised. It was what life had led her to expect from whites, and she viewed even her daughter as mostly white by now. A lot of poisonous memories needed erasure from her mind before she would believe she was truly accepted here. Yet she had desperately wanted to come. Now she wondered if it had been a mistake. Would she have been happier just to live out her allotted days on Standing Rock with others like her, getting by on a skimpy diet in poor living quarters, too hot in summer, too cold in the winter.

Newt put in, "Tell her, Kid, that Em said she's strong like she expected a Sioux to be, even an old one."

Kid did as he was told, which caused Shesees to smile. She said to Kid, "Tell her I was strong enough to carry a hurt puppy a long way yesterday."

Bennie told the story to Ma.

That broke the ice. Anyone who loved a dog was all right in Ma's book. Ma was "dog simple" for sure.

Just then Uncle Johnny came up from the barn, where he'd actually hidden out on the pretext of doing some job that needed doing. He had a taste for making appearances that even Teddy Roosevelt would have envied. He made one now, carrying one of their cats. Shesees looked at him a long while with an undefinable expression. Finally she said, "You look like Uncle Sitting Bull."

"What did she say?"

Kid told him.

"Well, what the hell do you know about that? A handsome guy, I guess."

He grabbed Shesees and said, "Hi, Grandma. We're sure glad you got here at last." He gave her a big squeeze.

Bennie thought, "*Uh-oh. Here's a big love match in the making.*"

After he turned his grandmother loose, Johnny looked around and asked Bennie, "How about introducing me to all of these other people." He looked over Newt and said, "I reckon you're Uncle Newt."

Newt had been studying Johnny and decided he was going to like him. Naturally he also decided he'd pretend he didn't.

"Goddam if that ain't a fact," Newt said. "Mostly they call me that old S.O.B. Cheek, though." He didn't offer to shake hands.

Johnny laughed and ignored the slight.

"And this is Kid," Bennie said.

Kid shook Johnny's hand and said, "How."

Johnny laughed again. "I reckon you're another breed like me."

Kid said, "Full-blood, not that it makes a rat's ass."

Johnny finally got to Rose last, because he'd like to have got to her first. He did like the ladies, and vice versa.

Country Grandma had been trying to follow all this and broke in to get control, "I've got a bunch of chairs set around the dining room table and coffee is on. I made some kuchen too. I'm fixing chicken and dumplings for dinner." ("Dinner," of course, meaning what later became "lunch," during the same decades that the evening meal, that had been "supper," was gradually replaced by "dinner.")

Bennie had already appreciatively sniffed the familiar and distinctive smell of Country Grandma's chicken stewing slowly on the old woodstove, a tantalizing odor like no other. He figured she put some secret ingredient in it that no one else knew about.

Country Grandma led the way inside, saying, "We can decide where everyone can sleep later. We'll have to double up, but we're used to that. I asked the Willises if we could put someone down there if we don't have enough room."

Inside, Country Grandpa sat in his rocker reading the Bible and pretending to be oblivious to everything going on, and furthermore not interested. Bennie had been looking forward to watching him and Newt together.

Country Grandpa liked to pretend he was already old and feeble, which usually got him a lot of respect he didn't deserve; also borrowed respect that he couldn't get any other way. Actually he was fifteen years younger than Newt—which made him seventy-six. He didn't get out of his chair when they came in, and Country Grandma ignored him, making no effort at introductions. It was a snub well earned by him for years of being a gold-plated prick. She savored having the upper hand after a lifetime of suffering his bullying.

Newt took this in and figured it out immediately. He'd heard enough from Ma about her pa to read him like a book. Also to figure out Ma got her mean streak from him. He went over and stood where Country Grandpa could hardly ignore him. When the other looked up, he said, "Readin' the Bible, eh? I wonder if I can borrow yours every once in a while, while I'm here. I lost mine on our trip somewhere. A man needs his Bible."

Country Grandpa didn't have the mother wit to know he was being ribbed, but he also had no idea how to take the remark, or how to take the forbidding-looking giant towering over him. Newt's face revealed absolutely no guile. If Newt had really thought a favorable reference to the need for reading a Bible would impress the other, he would have missed the mark by a mile. Bennie had told him long before, when mentioning his grandfather, that the horses out in their stalls had more reverence for God than Country Grandpa. Bennie suspected the old man of having no illusions about himself, or where he would be going either, if he really believed the Bible.

Bennie and Kid, who had both noticed Newt's needling, were trying to keep from splitting and barely succeeded. Kid had had a thorough briefing many times from Bennie about "that old *Cherman* S.O.B. Feltman."

Bennie saw his grandfather silently extend the Bible to Newt. He said,

"Take it now." He grinned in the sneaky, obsequious manner that he reserved for his betters.

Country Grandma seated her mother in a chair at the head of the table with a home-made cretonne-covered pillow in it to ease the weary seats of honored guests. She said to her mother, "You rest while I get you coffee and something you'll like that I baked myself."

She recalled how to make the coffee Sioux style: one-quarter sugar, one-quarter cream, and the rest strong coffee. When she brought that and a big slab of kuchen, she sat down beside her mother and said to her daughter, "Em, you serve the others."

While her mother ate, she sipped her own coffee and took special notice of Rose for the first time, eyeing her over the brim of her cup.

She thought, "*So you're Bennie's? If I'm any judge he's lucky.*"

She Sees Them First was like a little kid that needed to pinch itself to make sure happiness wasn't a dream. She munched her delicious kuchen and washed it down with mouthfuls of coffee, filling up because the next meal might be a long time coming, but she also surveyed everything around her and filed the memories away. In a few days she would be back at Standing Rock and might never again see her daughter and her family.

She sat at the end of a long table in the dining room extended across the whole small house. Before an addition had been tacked on, it had been a community room where Country Grandma and Grandpa slept behind a curtained partition. The many kids had slept up in the loft, which was reached by a ladder. It was an oven in summer and icebox in winter, which the kids had toughed out the best they could. One of them was always sick, but they all survived.

Behind Shesees was a window that looked out across a tiny yard with the barnyard beyond. Outside that window a short distance was the rock wellhouse in which her daughter had locked herself when her husband insanely chased her with a butcher knife. He was lucky Shesees hadn't been there, or she'd have brained him with one of the rocks left around after the wellhouse was built, and beat him to death with it.

Few looking at her now, serene and outwardly happy, would have suspected that side of her, except those like Newt who had fought the Sioux and knew that a soldier's training was like kindergarten compared to that of any Indian, whether man, woman, or child, and that their warfare continued for a lifetime. At any moment, enemies on horse-stealing forays or raiding parties seeking revenge might attack, the soldiers might come. Other hazards were always to be guarded against: a grizzly bear might loom out of a creek bottom, a herd of buffalo stampede toward a village. And worst of all, everyone could come down with some white man sickness, and dozens would die. Those almost too weak to stand tried to care for the sick and dying and carry away the dead.

This was the background of the calm veteran seated at the head of Country Grandma's table. No one would place flags on her grave on Memorial Day, if she had a marked grave, but she was a soldier of the Republic's wars as much as any of those who had been at places of great suffering like Valley Forge, or slaughters like Antietam; a soldier of the Republic as much as Newt's father, or her husband, Four Ponies, Bennie's great-grandfather, whom she'd nursed after the Custer fight and lost her battle to save. Only she among the living knew where the cave was in which his remains could be found, lying at honored rest with his weapons and the bones of his favorite war horse surrounding him. But, because she was here, he would soon be here, too. Memories would resurrect him.

Country Grandpa got up and without saying a word, hobbled away through the passageway known as the "entry," into the new house. It was time for his long daily nap, which would last until he smelled supper cooking.

Country Grandma noted her mother yawning and asked, "Are you worn out from your trip and all the excitement?"

Her mother thought about that—she *was* bone-weary, not from her trip, necessarily, but from a long life filled with much living and a lot of trouble.

Shesees assayed her options: she could sit here and talk, but they could do that later, for days as far as she knew, or she could rest somewhere. She supposed they'd put her on a bed and shush everyone into being quiet so she could sleep, but she might not sleep. She might watch rapidly scrolling scenes from the past in her mind, and she'd rather not; they made her impatient and although she usually *did* go to sleep as a refuge.

"I think I'll take a walk. Maybe you will come with me."

No one made an effort to join Shesees and her daughter as they went out together. Everyone had been listening, and recognized that the old woman wanted to be alone with her daughter. Bennie suspected more than that. He knew that he had always heard messages from the "old ones" who had lived the same tough frontier life that Shesees had and died here. He would have bet his life she'd sensed the same thing and expected it. She wanted to go out to feel the land and listen, to see if her daughter could hear the voices, or if she had become so white that she was hopeless.

Bennie slipped to the door and watched them slowly moving away together, wading through chickens pecking at tidbits on the ground, going out the barnyard gate, and walking into the field behind the barn. He wondered how far they might go. Shesees had proven that she could make a half-mile on her old legs, carrying a puppy to boot. He knew his grandmother was almost tireless and probably walked five miles a day just doing the chores and keeping house.

He turned, hearing Ma come up behind him, taking a place beside him at the fence, silently watching. He wondered if she felt slighted because they hadn't asked her to come with them. Her face revealed nothing.

Ma was remembering how, when she was Little Emma, she used to go out there to hide from Mary.

She thought, "*Maybe they'll go all the way down to the creek. Maybe Grandma will hear Chaubenee's wife calling. I wish I could have.*"

Maybe . . .

If she "Listens by the Waters."

If anyone were apt to do that, and actually hear voices it was Shesees. Bennie had never told anyone, especially Ma, about hearing Waubonsee.

CHAPTER SIXTY-ONE

Babes in the Woods Together

Bennie had looked forward to seeing his older brother, Roy. He had last seen him when Pa drove the Buick away from the dismal flat that had been their home in Wahbonsee, if such a place could have been described as a home. Roy had pedaled his bike in from the farm mainly to see Bennie off. After all they'd been "babes in the woods" together for almost a decade. That had been in the summer of 1936.

Roy had never come to see them *up north*, and Bennie knew why from the occasional letters he'd got from him—would have known in any case. Roy had revealed without actually writing it that he had no desire to see Ma and renew old hurts, but he did write that he sympathized with Bennie who was condemned to live with her for a few more years. Like Bennie, Roy had wanted a mother to love, and love him, and perhaps needed one more than Bennie did. Roy was the soft-hearted one. The big brother who had always come running to help Bennie, or anyone else that needed it.

As for Roy's feelings for Pa, it would have been hard to figure. Bennie doubted if Roy missed a shadow father who hadn't exerted much influence on his boys except with his stories of the past. A desire to visit Pa wouldn't have attracted Roy to come *up north*. They hadn't exchanged a single letter in five years.

Roy might have come if they needed a hand on the farm—he loved farm life—but knew from Bennie's letters that they had too many hands on the plow already.

Bennie was deeply disappointed to learn that it wasn't in the cards to see Roy on this trip, since he'd just been drafted into the Army and was in Basic Training down at Fort Robinson, Arkansas. He wasn't disturbed to learn that he wasn't going to meet Sister either, since she was off gallivanting with her mentally lightweight husband on a vacation trip to visit distant relatives in Minnesota. Sister had known that her Sioux great-grandmother was probably coming for a visit, but hadn't cared and in fact would have preferred that no one knew she had Indian blood.

Bennie had been observing Ma wistfully watching her mother and Shesees as they walked out of sight without her, and thought he knew how she felt. For all of her snide remarks and outward indifference, Ma wanted to be a part of that old Sioux family that was being magically reknit in this unlikely place.

Bennie suspected that Ma would have liked to go along and be a little mouse listening to what the two Sioux women talked about, even if she couldn't understand a word they said. He'd have liked to do the same thing, and figured he'd know from the tone of their voices if they were transported back to the old time when they'd been a little girl and her mama. From what he'd seen so far that seemed to be the case. Sensing what they must feel made him happy, like finding a long lost treasure.

Kid came over, stood beside him and guessed what he was thinking. He said, "Wonderful, isn't it?"

"Yeah. But look at poor Ma. She wants to stick her nose in there in the worst way."

"If I know your ma, that's the way she'll do it."

Bennie laughed. "I guess so. Let's go over and cheer her up."

They walked over to the fence where Ma stood, staring at the place where the two had disappeared among the rows of tall corn. Ma glanced at Bennie and Kid without warmth. She'd knew why they were there and didn't want sympathy.

"I hope they don't get lost," she said.

"Fat chance," Kid said. "I'd bet your grandma could walk back to the reservation in a straight line.

"Maybe even in a snowstorm," Bennie put in.

Ma gave them both dirty looks. She said, "I think we should go after them to see that they don't fall in the creek and drown."

Bennie said, "It's not over a foot deep for a mile either direction except when it floods. Besides you can't swim."

Ma glowered at him, spun on one foot and left, marching toward the house in her best indignant stalk.

The family history that Bennie longed to learn of, hidden for years in unhappy memories, came out after supper that night. He had set the stage for it himself. He sensed that this would be the best time, when it was so new to them all that they hadn't erected barriers to mask emotions or conceal sad memories. They were still sitting around the long dining-room table over coffee, the men smoking. Bennie had prompted Kid who he managed to seat next to Shesees, to subtly start the discussion in the right direction by pointing at

Newt and saying to the old woman, "You know he was at the Little Big Horn with Custer?"

She said, "Yes, he said that the first day. They didn't believe him. I could tell from what you told me he said that he was there."

Country Grandma was following this exchange closely, and looked at Newt as though she'd seen him truly for the first time.

Because she had never talked of that time, and had always been diffident around strangers, Bennie was astonished when she looked at Newt and asked, "You were there when my father was killed?"

Newt nodded, thinking, "*I could have been the one that fired the bullet that killed him.*" He wondered if this woman was thinking the same thing.

She said, "That was a terrible day. I was a little girl, playing in the river with the other children and we were all happy and splashing like kids do, making a lot of noise. We didn't hear the soldiers coming."

Newt wanted to ask, "Couldn't you hear the shooting down where Reno was?" but he didn't want to interrupt her. He couldn't remember if he had heard it either. Sound often traveled in strange ways.

Kid told Shesees what they were saying. She turned her head to each as they spoke, watching her daughter and Newt as they exchanged words, trying to understand them from the tone of voice.

Country Grandma said to Newt, "The first I knew you were coming, the little girl next to me—I can't remember her name—screamed, and I looked at her and she was holding her arm, and it was dangling by a thread of flesh and spurting blood. I thought an evil spirit had attacked us. She ran out of the water screaming for her mother. Then the bullets started hitting the water around us and we could hear the guns going off and we were all afraid and ran like chickens with their heads cut off. I can remember screaming and I couldn't stop."

Newt's face wore an expression Bennie had never seen on it; of terrible sadness. Newt realized that he, or Johnny Todd also, might have fired the shot that almost cut an innocent little girl's arm off. He recalled the "nits breed lice" remark someone had made at the time they started shooting. And here was the grandson of one of them, listening to how one side of his family had deliberately killed the loved ones of the other.

Kid told Shesees in a low voice what was being said.

She broke in, "I remember that. We heard the shooting and I rushed out to find Red Moon Rising. At first I thought the little girl with her arm shot was her, than I tried to stop the blood with a ball of dry grass and cloth I tore off my sleeve. Her mother came then, and I went back looking for Red Moon and found her. The village was ready to run until we heard that our men at the other end drove away the soldiers that had come from the south."

She suddenly wailed in an unearthly voice. "I lost my man. I lost my man. He lived two days and we talked and he said, 'I am going to Wakan Tanka now and I want you always to take care of Red Moon Rising.' *And then the next fall I lost her too*!"

To Bennie's amazement, the most sympathetic one of them all was Country Grandpa, that old *Cherman* son of a bitch. He had prompted Kid with the words, "What did she say?"

Kid told them, while Shesees, unaware of anyone else, swayed from side to side with her eyes closed, tears streaming from them, continuing with a sing-song wail, a Sioux song of grief.

Bennie thought, "She still loves Four Ponies like it was yesterday."

Country Grandpa said, "That was terrible. Like Germany. Always at war. That damn Kaiser and Bismark. It's why I ran away."

Everyone looked startled.

Country Grandma, who'd been trying to console her mother, heard her husband and looked at him as though she were seeing him for the first time, as though she'd never suspected he might be human. "*Well, what reason had he ever given anyone to suspect that*?"

She thought, "*I'll think that over later*," and turned her attention back to Shesees. "I'm going to put her to bed now."

Bennie watched, thinking, "*Just like the little girl is now the mother. Maybe she is. Time plays funny tricks on us.*"

He recalled reading that time was called "the old annihilator." He asked himself, "*Annihilator, of what?*"

He had just seen a prior time not only recreate itself, but create a new present. Here was something to puzzle over.

He looked at Rose and was not surprised to see her eyes filled with tears. She said, "How tragic. And wonderful. I love that old woman."

"So do I. We've got to figure out how she can live here the rest of her days."

CHAPTER SIXTY-TWO

The Old Reprobates

Bennie was not surprised that Uncle Johnny and Newt hit it off like the old reprobates they were. It didn't take them long to hatch an escapade.

"They're going to do what? Come again." Kid said, when Bennie told him.

"Newt and Johnny are going to get laid, but they plan to take my grandpop along and get his ashes hauled, too. Johnny figures it's been about twenty years since Gramp has had it in anything."

"Maybe one of the calves," Kid said, and laughed.

Bennie said, "I doubt it. That's out West with sheep. Wouldn't you love to see a scene like that in a Western movie? I can see some fancy-pants phoney settin' his guitar down real careful and chasing a sheep."

"I don't think Hopalong Cassidy would go for it."

"Hell no, but he don't strum a geetar either," Kid said.

They were outside the barn smoking a morning weed. It was early and still dewy, with the sun barely up above the trees to the east by the creek. They were sleeping in the old lean-to on the barn, just as Bennie had when he was little and there were more kids and grandkids there at the same time than could be laid out around the house on the floor. Johnny and Newt were also sleeping up in the lean-to. Hay made a nice fragrant mattress, but Bennie missed cuddling up to Rose, who shared a bed with Ma in the front room in the new addition. Country Grandma and her mother had the bed in Grandma's bedroom, and the old *Cherman* had his own bed and bedroom as befit the patriarch, fallen though he may have been.

Rose had her suspicions that the men might be going out for more than a beer and game of pool, but wisely held her tongue. She was sure Bennie wouldn't do anything that would hurt her if she found out about it. She watched them disappear down the road in the Lincoln, waiting till the taillights disappeared before she strolled back up the lane, where she found Ma sitting alone under the box elder; Rose sat down beside her on the auto seat that Johnny had installed out there to lounge in. Neither spoke, nor had to. It was cooling down, and a breeze carried the smell of green, growing corn to them. Fireflies winked wherever Rose looked. Unfortunately a few mosquitos were winking too, if it could be called that, but country people got used to them and hardly noticed.

Ma finally said, "It's like I never left home."

Rose knew she intended to explain that and waited.

"I used to go down to the creek where Ma and Shesees went together and listen for Chaubenee's wife to say something to me."

"Who was that?"

"Chaubenee was a famous Indian chief and a friend of Tecumseh. They have a statue of him in Riverview."

"When Chaubenee was old he was called the 'friend of the whites' because he warned them of Blackhawk coming to get them so they could all run to town and protect themselves better."

"Why was his wife down by the creek?"

"She was hurrying home to their camp before dark, and it had been raining hard. The water was high and she drowned."

"The poor old woman."

"People say they see her ghost there sometimes, but I never did." Ma's voice was wistful as she said it. "I thought she might talk to me since I'm half-Indian."

"Maybe she will yet. We can walk down there together tomorrow if you want to."

"Let's. I'd like to do that. And maybe Ma and Grandma will come along."

Rose thought, "It's the first time she's called Shesees Grandma. That's a good sign."

The next morning Rose invited Sheesees to walk again down to the creek, but she sadly declined. "*Tell her,*" she said to Kid, "*that I will go in a few days. I am old and tired. But very happy now.*"

Shesees understated her weakness, too worn out from the excitement and didn't want to tell anyone that her heart hurt every so often so that she had trouble breathing.

Rose told Ma that Sheesees was worn out, and said, "Why don't just the two of us go, and you can tell me if it's changed since you were little."

"Poor old woman," Ma said. "I can see how she'd be worn out." Ma saw where she got her own toughness and was finally coming to love her grandmother, though she would never have admitted it, even to herself.

Ma led the way, circled behind the barn where the milk cows in the pasture looked them over as they passed, then went back to grazing. Ma continued, walking down a corn row from habit, because she used to go that way so no one saw her, especially Mary. It would have been easier to go on the other side of the fence in the edge of the soy bean field, but that wouldn't do. Besides, she didn't like the looks of soy beans and didn't even like the name. When she was little they hadn't even heard of soy beans; hay was redtop and timothy and clover. And how sweet the clover had smelled on a dewy morning. Soy beans didn't smell nearly so good, even cut and drying in windrows.

At the far end of the long rows of corn they emerged into a grassy strip along the edge of the woods. A fox had been raiding the corn and fled at the sight of them, scooting into the woods.

"See the blackberries," Ma said, recognizing them from a distance. They're still here. There ought to be gooseberries and raspberries, too."

The strip of woods wasn't wide, and they saw the bright water of the creek sparkling through open vistas in the woods, and Ma could hear its familiar murmur over the rocky bottom there.

She stopped at its edge and looked up and down. Here the trees formed an umbrella almost all the way over the water, making it dim and cool.

"Let's take off our shoes and wade," Ma suggested, in a voice Rose had never heard, like a happy kid. "But be careful where you wade. Shitepokes pick up the clams and fly high and drop them on the rocks to break them open so they can get into them and eat the meat. There are lost of sharp shells on the bottom."

"Shitepokes?"

"Yeah," Ma said. "Actually sea gulls that fly over from Lake Michigan, but we always called them shitepokes since that's what they did best. Look around and you can see all this white stuff. They're full of it, I guess. You had to hope that none of them flew over you or you might get crowned." She laughed. "I did just once and washed it off as quick as I could."

After wading and splashing around for awhile, they climbed out and sat on a grassy knoll.

"Suppose soldiers had sneaked up and shot at us," Ma said, "like at poor Grandma. She must have had a terrible life. God knows, Ma didn't have a picnic either."

Rose thought, "*How about you? Until just the past few years your life was as hard as theirs*." Then it occurred to her that Ma didn't even know her life had been *too hard*.

"Where do you think Chaubenee's wife drowned?" she asked Ma.

"I don't know. They found her body on a sand bar just below here a little ways. Jim Tynan showed us the spot one day."

"Who was Jim Tynan?"

Ma grinned. "He tried to hang Pa for chasing Ma with a butcher knife. Ma locked herself in the pump house—the same one that's still there—and I ran for help and brought Jim Tynan. A bunch more neighbors showed up, and Jim wanted to hang Pa to that big limb on the box elder that we were sitting under last night."

"Why didn't they?"

"Ma begged them not to, like a ninny."

"What did they do then?"

"Made Pa promise never to lay a finger on Ma again, and Jim told him if he did he'd be back and blow his head off with a shotgun. He would have, too. Mary told me that Jim had Pa down and was trying to beat his brains out on the ground even before they strung him up on a rope and pulled him up a time or two so he could feel what choking was like."

"*My God*," Rose thought. "*I didn't know the half of the life this woman has had. No wonder she doesn't laugh much.*"

"Did he leave her alone after that?" Rose asked.

"Yes, and after Jim Tynan died, Johnny was old enough to beat the tar out of him, so he kept him in line." She was silent a long while and Rose wondered what she was thinking. Finally she said, "Before he chased her with a knife, Pa kicked her in the stomach where she was carrying my sister, Lizzie, and she was born two months early that night over at the Tynans."

The night before Bennie had tooled the Lincoln down the familiar road he'd traveled so often as a kid, when Pa drove the Buick and got stuck as often as not. It seemed to him as though they were always getting to Country Grandma's just after a heavy rain. The newly graveled road was a big improvement. He was headed for a place that locals had dubbed *Ungodly on the Amazon*. No one seemed to remember why. Actually it was the small wide spot on a paved road. The wide spot may have been little, but it had a mayor, Franco DiTulio, whose brother had a saloon in Coal City. Franco was also fire chief and police chief, ran the profitable filling station, and owned an even more profitable and popular place, known in those days as a road house, that catered like Klondy's place *up north* to the fundamental needs of the lusty local lads. It also had gambling. The local wags said of that and the other main attraction: "Likker in the front and poker in the rear."

As they debarked from the Lincoln under the neon sign that read simply "DiTulio's," Bennie inhaled the familiar smell of all saloons, stale alcohol. The usual flashing neon beer signs radiated their message through the front windows.

Country Grandpa went on point as soon as he smelled the booze. He was notorious for keeping bottles stashed all over in the farm buildings for his occasional nip on which to keep going.

Kid said, "Ah, it smells like home."

Inside almost everyone greeted Uncle Johnny. The standing joke was that he paid the utility bill there. Franco, from behind the bar, greeted him, "Yanoh," his pet name for him. "Long time no see. It's been almost a week."

Uncle Johnny waved idly his direction and led the way to a big round table.

A well-constructed bar waitress came over, smiling. Bennie had a notion she might do more than bring drinks if it were the right customer.

"Hello, Yanoh," she said and looking over the whole table, "What'll it be, boys?'

Johnny said, "Hi, Caroline. Make mine the usual."

Kid said under his breath to Bennie, regarding Newt and Country Grandpa, "Some boys."

Kid's and Bennie's orders of orange pop stopped Caroline, and she gave them a surprised look. Johnny had beer, the two old rips had straight whiskey.

Johnny said, "Pity that Indian Bureau guy went to bed early. He don't know what he's missing."

"Neither do I," Kid said. "Yet."

Johnny laughed. "They'll all be out and parade by in time. Take your pick. And come to think of it, that Indian Bureau guy might not be missing out on much either up where he's staying."

Bennie recalled Clarissa's warm greeting to him when he'd pulled through there the day they arrived.

The old *Cherman* hadn't yet clued in to what was in store for him. He was happy with whiskey and looked it. Bennie, watching him, thought, "*I hope I never get so whiskey is all I need to get that gleam in my eye. I wanna be like Newt with Billy Goat Balls till I drop over*."

It took a couple of whiskeys to prepare Country Grandpa to take the plunge. By then Kid had picked a tall, willowy girl with sleepy black eyes and disappeared with her.

Grandpa noticing asked Newt, "Where are they going?"

A shocking thought went through Johnny's head, "Maybe the old man has never been in a whorehouse!" This was true.

Newt said, "Look over these young gals when they parade through. A man can have any one of them for a few bucks."

Grandpa had heard of such places. He also had considered them sinful and never expected to be in one. After his third shot he didn't particularly give a damn.

He looked over the crop with approval whenever one showed up after that. He now understood why they showed up with a man who'd gone back somewhere with them, down a dimly lit hall. The men always looked happy, and if they were at a table with others, usually had a laugh with the boys upon their return. Once Grandpa heard the inquiry, "How was that stuff" and the reply, "The worst I ever had was outstanding."

The old *Cherman*'s mind started working on that, and he could feel something active in his jeans that he knew could still come up. In fact he still jacked off every once in a while and could come with the best of them, maybe because he'd had so much practice at it when he was younger, out of necessity.

It took one more shot of booze to get him really primed. By then Johnny had put Franco up to having one of the girls come over and sit on Grandpa's lap. "I'll pay her extra," Johnny said. "It may take her a while to get him up to it, if he can still do it."

With that sort of preparation, Mary, the girl who sat on Gramp's lap, was surprised to feel it coming up under her and gave the old boy a good look. He looked to be all of sixty, but she knew that wasn't too old. She'd have been shocked to learn how old he really was. When she got him organized to go back with her, she had to steer him a little until he got his whiskey legs under control, then he went spryly.

Newt said, "I reckon I'll try one myself."

Bennie and Johnny were all that was left at the big table. Johnny said, "How about you?"

"Not anymore. I got what I want, and I'm not going to give her a dose or something."

"You can use a rubber."

Bennie shook his head. "It just doesn't appeal to me anymore. Maybe someday I'll need some variety, but not yet."

Johnny nodded. "Rose is a real nice girl. And as pretty as they come. I don't blame you. Are you two planning to get hitched?"

"As soon as we get home."

"Good. I ain't the marryin' kind, but I think most men need a wife. I reckon I'll go back with *one of my wives*. I like the one Kid took back."

Those who wanted to sample the wares were all back long before Country Grandpa came out. When he finally got back he looked happier than Bennie had ever seen him.

Bennie commented on that to Uncle Johnny when he came back. "Maybe we can get an inside report from the house on how he made out. I doubt that he'd say much about it."

He was surprised to hear his grandpa say in reply to Newt's "How was that stuff?"

"Pretty *tem* good!"

The report from his young benefactress was even more illuminating and was passed along by Johnny after they got home and were up in the lean-to getting undressed for bed by lantern light.

"She said, 'The old fart kept it up for an hour and finally got it off. He wore me out. He's strong as a bull, too. I'll bet he could pitch hay with the best of them.'"

Johnny said, "I told her he did pitch hay."

She said, "Bring him back anytime. He's hung, too."

That naturally got a laugh out of everyone.

Bennie thought, "I guess I inherited it from both sides."

At the breakfast table he observed the old man closely, and saw no evidence of fatigue. His appetite was better than average, though.

Grandpa stopped them all with the remark, "Mary, I think you ought to get your mother to stay with us from now on."

Country Grandma looked at him as though he'd just broken out with the tenor part of an opera.

"What?" she asked.

"I think you should have your mother stay with us until she dies. She needs a home."

Bennie thought, "I heard getting it off kept bulls from being ornery, but it's the first time I saw it work on people."

Newt said, "Maybe we can arrange that."

Donaldson said, "I doubt it. The Bureau won't stand for it."

Newt asked, "Did the Bureau ever hear of a famous law case called *Standing Bear vs. Crook*?"

Donaldson sighed. "I see you've had someone looking into it already. My boss won't like it."

Newt laughed. "The South didn't like freeing its slaves either. Money talks."

Newt explained *Standing Bear vs. Crook* to them later. He said, "Seems like a Ponca Indian named Standing Bear wanted to leave the tribe that was put on a reservation in Oklahoma where he didn't like the weather and come back to Nebraska where the Poncas always lived. The government wanted to send him back to Oklahoma, but he sued them—in fact old General Crook put him up to it. His case finally went to the Supreme Court, and it turned out they thought Indians were citizens just like anybody else if they wanted to be. After all, it was what the U.S. government had been preaching to them for a century or so. General Crook went along with the thing as defendant since he had Standing Bear in irons, more or less, and was glad he lost the case. Whatever else you say for old Rosebud George, he was always for the Injun."

And that was how Shesees came home, or home came to her. It wasn't decided in a day, although they knew before they headed back up north that the deal was greased.

Country Grandpa got in the last word, pointing to Kid, "He told me about Wakan Tanka. I'm gonna learn Sioux from Mary and her Ma now, and I can pray to him, too. I ain't getting' any younger and can use all the help I can get when my time comes."

"*Damn well told! Me too!*" Bennie thought.

Actually he didn't think that Grandpa believed any of what he read in the Bible and spouted off about. He'd heard him say too many times, "It'll all come to nothing in the end."

Bennie thought, "*For his kind anyhow.*"

Uncle Johnny privately told Bennie, "The Old Man told me that when he dies I should just bury him in the manure pile, so we get some good out of him, at least."

It didn't surprise Bennie to hear that, either.

The parting of Ma, Grandma, and Great-Grandma was as tearful as Bennie had expected, except that he didn't think he'd break down and cry himself when he hugged Shesees goodbye. She hugged him back hard and said something.

Kid said, "She said, *God Bless You*!"

Rose and Shesees had a similar hugging match.

Bennie was looking forward to seeing how Ma would handle it. She hugged her grandmother, but gingerly, as though she thought she might break an old woman. Her stoic nature forbade tears, too. She'd rather have died than show maudlin emotion *like others*.

Shesees seemed to understand, and stepped back and smiled at her. Red Moon Rising had explained to Shesees about the little girl Emma who had worked so hard to help her, and about her life afterward, too. The old woman thought, "*There has been little happiness in her life. Like the Sioux after the white man took our land and we stopped roaming free.*"

Country Grandma wasn't afraid to cry watching them all. And *Shesees* had tears in her eyes all the while. She gave Kid a big hug just as she had Bennie. To him she said, "Tell them all that Shesees loves them and wishes them a long, happy life."

She and Country Grandma stood in the road and waved after the Lincoln as long as it was in sight.

Concealed by a grape vine behind the new house, where he could see the road without being seen himself, Country Grandpa, the old *Cherman*, watched too and waved goodbye to them. He knew that he'd just had the happiest week of his life since he'd been a little boy in Germany, and now he was ready to be buried in the manure pile. "*But*," he thought, "*while I'm waiting I'm going to go out to shoot pool a lot with Johnny.*"

CHAPTER SIXTY-THREE

This Man Could Get Bennie Killed!

Ma had heard from Rose about Flint Curry, the Marine pilot who most likely would induce Bennie to join the Marines if he got a chance.

They were back *up north* and almost settled in again, when Flint phoned and Ma took the call. She really didn't want to put Bennie on to talk to him, but didn't see how she could avoid it.

"Flint," she heard Bennie say, and she hated the tone of elation. Ma had a nose for threats to her family, and thought, "*This man could get Bennie killed!*" Of course the tractor might do as much any day, or a horse kicking him in the head by accident, but at least he'd be home when it happened.

After talking for a couple of minutes, during which Ma tried to decipher Bennie's thoughts, he hung up.

She looked at him for a report. He said, "He's over at the airport at the Falls. He flew up in a rented plane from Milwaukee. I told him we had room to put him up here."

"I heard you say that. Why did you tell him that?"

"Because we do."

Ma looked sour. Rose had heard Bennie talking on the phone and came into the kitchen and asked, "What's going on?"

Bennie told her and her heart sunk. She'd hoped Flint would forget all about them.

Ma said, "I don't think we have any room for him here."

Bennie said, "That's O.K. Pa and Klondy can put him up."

Ma's expression was worth at least a hundred dollars. She hadn't anticipated such a horrible possibility. Bennie would be over there with that bad influence of a madam in addition to getting recruited by a wild Marine to go off and get himself killed.

She sighed. "We might as well put him in the room next to yours."

Rose said, "If he starts trying to talk you into joining the Marines, I'll sneak over and cut his throat some night."

Bennie said, "I've already decided to join the Marines if they're going to draft me. They're talking about lowering the draft age to eighteen, you know."

"You can get a deferment. You'll be a married man with a *son* by then. And an essential farmer besides."

They'd got Ma's blessing on the marriage *as young as they were*, and the date was already set. Besides, Ma was no fool and had noticed that Rose had that special look of women carrying a baby, although she didn't show even a little yet. It was too soon.

Bennie decided to drop the explosive subject of joining the Marines and said, "I've already ordered a special pair of overalls with a crease sewed in them to get married in."

"My foot," Rose said. "We're going somewhere and buy you a suit."

Ma said, "Sears and Wards both have good ready-made ones cheap; you can even order them from the catalog."

Bennie said, "I don't care where we get it. I'll probably never wear it again until my funeral."

He was sorry he'd said "funeral" as soon as he looked at Rose. She paled and the happy smile faded from her face. "Please don't talk about funerals," she said.

Ma felt exactly the same way. She may have thought once that Bennie was a degenerate, but she was beginning to appreciate him and thought maybe he'd amount to something, since he seemed to be listening more to her advice. Or Rose's advice, which amounted to the same thing. Rose had a lot of good sense, which Ma had concluded as soon as she recognized that Rose always listened to her and took her advice—which usually amounted to orders—and did it without argument.

"Anyhow," Bennie said, "I'm going to drive over to the Falls and pick up Flint, now that it's settled he's going to stay here. I think I'll go get Kid and take him along."

"How about me?" Rose complained.

"You're welcome as can be. He might take you up for a plane ride."

"Not on a bet. If God intended people to fly he'd have given them wings."

"You'd better stay here then, because he didn't give you wheels either."

That got him a dirty look.

"Let's go," he said, "ignoring the look. "We don't want to keep Uncle Sam's boys waiting."

Flint was in the little shack that served as the airport's office and headquarters. It was tacked onto a tiny hangar. In front of the hangar was a biwing plane that looked like all the fighters from the war in France that Bennie had seen in photos. The only difference was that this one had two cockpits.

Flint came out to the car as they pulled up and looked in the window at Bennie, then stuck in his hand and shook.

"Didn't think I'd come up, did you?" he said.

Rose thought, "*I wish you hadn't, damn you!*"

He looked exactly like what would get the boys off the farm, glamorous in a set of aviators coveralls, with wings sewed over the left pocket and captain's bars on the shoulders, and he was wearing the traditional "go to hell" long silk scarf. She thought, "It's a wonder he isn't wearing a helmet and goggles."

He'd thought of leaving them on, but had left them in the plane, although he knew they made great recruiting aids and he'd already made up his mind that since Bennie and Kid would be going to war soon anyhow, they might as well get in the *premier* service.

He stuck his head into the back window and grabbed Kid's hand, too, then looked across at Rose and came around the car to open the door for her. She was impressed with this little courtesy and the way he took her hand and helped her out and held onto it a second longer than he had to and squeezed a little.

"Hi, beautiful," he said.

She blushed, but smiled in spite of herself and said, "I'll bet you say that to all the girls."

"Whenever I get a chance, and only if they're really beautiful."

She felt herself beginning to like this man, and despised herself for it.

When Bennie and Kid were out of the car, he said, "Come on over and I'll show you the crate I flew over here in."

It was indeed a crate, which was why they were called that. A flimsy collection of aluminum tube framework over which doped fabric was stretched. It also had a fabric wing that wouldn't have survived a hailstorm. Under the wing fabric, the spars and ribs were wood, held together by glue and silk cord, but Bennie didn't know that, or that they were remarkably strong nevertheless. It was the type of plane the Wright brothers appreciated in a world that was turning to all-metal aircraft. You couldn't build an all-metal aircraft in your garage.

"How about taking a hop?" Flint asked. "Who's first? How about you, Rose?"

She backed away as though she thought he might throw her into one of the cockpits. "No way," she said. But this time she left out "the God would have given me wings bit." Bennie had cured her of that chestnut.

"I'm your man," Bennie said.

"I'll flip you for it," Kid said.

"O.K."

Kid won the flip.

"I brought parachutes," Flint said. "Never can tell when one of these crates might fall apart." He said that for effect to see if it would bother Kid, or Bennie.

It bothered Rose and confirmed her worst fears. You read about aircraft having wings fall off every so often. She didn't realize that it seldom happened, and when it did some idiot had done something he shouldn't have.

Flint fitted Kid into a chute and gave him rudimentary instructions in its use, then got him into a helmet with goggles. He climbed up onto the left wing and pulled Kid up after him and settled him into the front cockpit, which was partially under the top wing. Once Kid was properly seated, Flint leaned in and showed him how to fasten the seat belt. Then he hopped down and climbed into the rear cockpit.

"It's got an electric starter," he said to Bennie, who was standing beside the rear cockpit watching him get tied down. "Otherwise I'd have to show you how to 'prop' it to get it started."

"To what it?"

"Prop it. Spin the prop by hand. You've seen it in movies."

"Oh, yeah."

"Now get out of the way, and don't get near the prop and especially not when I come back, until it stops turning."

By then the man who ran the airport, a combination mechanic and pilot, had come out.

He stood back as Flint yelled, "Switch off," then in a little while, "Contact," as he started the prop turning.

The engine snorted into life and settled down to a smooth pattern. Flint gunned it a couple of times, then pulled it back to a steady idle.

The airport manager pulled the chocks from under the wheels, being careful to stay well clear of the spinning prop.

Bennie watched as Flint gunned the power to pull the plane into motion, and was fascinated by the little tornadoes of dust the prop raised on the ground as the plane trundled away toward the end of the field. He heard the engine running up, but didn't know enough about flying yet to know that Flint was reading the engine instruments at takeoff power to see that everything appeared normal before taking the runway. Then the plane rolled forward again and swung around, aligned with the runway, and surged into motion, engine roaring, gradually reaching a crescendo as it steadily gained speed, the tail rose, and soon the machine smoothly left the ground. A professional would have appreciated what they saw, but Bennie was too new at it to realize he'd just seen one of the smoothest takeoffs that had ever been made there.

The airport manager knew, however, and his mouth was open slightly, eyes glued on the plane, following its progress. Like all pilots, he watched every takeoff and landing if he was in view of it, and often the climb until a plane was out of sight. Flint never got out of sight.

He climbed to a thousand feet and made a sharp turn, coming back in a dive and skimmed down the runway, pulled up, and rolled one complete revolution and then did a chandelle to the left, coming out of it and climbing normally until he reached a safe altitude, then gracefully turning back to come over the runway at a higher altitude. Bennie watched the plane diving to pick up speed, and stood with his mouth open while Flint looped it directly over the runway, went up again just to the top of another loop, half-rolled the plane to right side up, and flew away, climbing.

The airport manager next to Bennie said, "That son of a bitch really knows how to fly." He was so interested in watching he didn't even make the customary apology to Rose about pardoning his French.

This time Flint dove at the airport, pulled up and climbed gracefully, half-rolled the ship upside down, let the nose drop and pulled into level flight just above the ground, continued across the field and pulled up again, half-rolled and repeated his performance, then pulled up into a chandelle and winged over into a turn onto the final approach to the runway, power pulled back and made a perfect three-point landing.

When the plane was parked, recalling that he had to wait till the prop stopped, Bennie slowly walked over to it. He noticed that Kid wasn't getting out too spryly. In fact he wasn't getting out at all yet. Bennie had heard that people got air sick and when he was close enough yelled in at Kid, "Did you puke?"

Flint hopped out, leaving his chute in the seat and climbed up on the wing to help Kid out if he needed it. He said, "If he puked you could smell it."

Kid, looking a little pale yet, crawled out. "If you'd kept that up a little while longer it wouldn't be puke you could smell."

Flint laughed. "I'm an expert. I know exactly what dose of medicine a patient can stand."

He turned to Bennie. "It's your turn next, if you want to try a dose of the same. Of course I can always fly straight and level like I do for girls. That's what I'll do when it's Rose's turn."

She said, "Rose isn't going to have a turn, and that's final."

Bennie said, "I'm game. If I puke, I puke."

Flint got him fitted into the parachute and then into the front cockpit, gave him the helmet and goggles and helped him fasten the seat belt and tighten it. Bennie looked over his surrounding. The plane had a distinct smell, of both the material it was made of and of gas and oil residues that clung to it. He didn't mind the smell. He looked over the dials in front of him on what he would have called a dashboard, not yet knowing that in the aviation world it was an instrument panel. Some of the gauges moved a little and one spun up rapidly as Flint goosed the power to start moving.

Bennie couldn't have described exactly how he felt as the plane wobbled across the rough ground, cushioned by the slightly springy landing gear. He surveyed the surrounding woods as they spun around with the rapid turns a plane made on the ground, compared to a car. He decided he was a little bit scared and thought he must be a sissy, even though he had been up before in Waubonsee and Blackhawk. Well, he'd be damned if he let on, even if it killed him.

After checking the engine, Flint pulled it back to idle and yelled, "You all set?"

"I guess," he yelled back.

No conscious thoughts occupied his mind while he watched the plane aligned exactly with the middle of the runway and felt the power smoothly applied, which pushed him back in the seat. He watched while the tail came up, and when they stopped rumbling along over the rough runway knew they must have left the ground and were flying.

He asked himself, "What the hell am I doing up here?"

He recalled what Rose had said about God and wings. But then he felt another strange sensation as he watched objects below get smaller and their sense of speed diminished with height. He was just about to decide he really was going to like flying, when Flint reduced power, and he wondered if the engine had quit, which set his stomach crawling in anticipation of something frightening. The plane's nose rise slightly, then all hell broke loose as the horizon abruptly turned over a complete revolution and returned to level. The unexpected violent thrashing through the air and unaccustomed whistling racket that went with it caused his heart to jump painfully. He unhappily recalled what Kid had said about shitting his pants. His bung hole was puckering, and he wanted to yell, "Get me to hell back on the ground, goddammit!"

Flint pulled the power completely off and yelled, "That was a snap roll."

Bennie thought, "*I don't care what it was, I want back on the ground!*"

But he wasn't going to have his wish right away. He knew he was absolutely powerless to control the plane himself, and thought he'd have about as much luck controlling Flint, who seemed determined to scare the daylights out of him. He watched the horizon rapidly moving past in a smooth steep turn. At least it *was* smooth, rather than abrupt. He tried to lean away from the low side for fear of falling out, his hands gripping the sides of his seat, though he knew the safety belt would undoubtedly hold him in. He was too new at it to realize that the plane's G forces were holding him in his seat as well. He told himself, "*If I get killed, I get killed!*"

Flint turned back toward the runway and Bennie was sure the Marine madman at the controls planned to do at least everything he'd done with Kid, and maybe more. He already had with the snap roll. He spontaneously gripped the edges of his seat again, while hearing the increasing rush of air as they accelerated toward the field, then fought off shutting his eyes as he felt his weight increasing with G forces when Flint pulled up into a loop. They came over the top and dived, and Bennie was sure they were going to crash straight into the ground. His heart was in his mouth and his stomach tied in a knot, and they stayed that way while Flint pulled up well before they hit the ground and whipped into a steep turn and chandelled up until the plane hung on the prop just short of a stall, then gracefully settled to the attitude for a normal climb.

He thought, "The crazy son of a bitch is going to do something else I'd just as soon pass on," but he lost some of his fear wondering what it was going to be, and also through relief that he wasn't getting sick to his stomach. He almost enjoyed looking around at the scenery as Flint maneuvered for his next stunt.

This time Flint did a repeat of the graceful half loops he'd performed with Kid, back and forth over the runway. Bennie actually enjoying them after the first one, since they were perfectly smooth. After the second one he thought, "Ah, now we'll land," and felt relief already. He was a little premature, since Flint climbed the plane out again, this time higher than he had before.

At the top of their climb he reduced power and yelled, "You've heard of tail spins. They look pretty scary, but there's nothing to them."

He then pulled up the nose, the plane shuddered as it stalled and Bennie felt the stick slam back between his legs, while the right rudder pedal shot fully forward. The left wing whipped violently up past the horizon, then the nose fell sharply to the right and the ground below was spinning crazily. A road went past then came around again, and they repeated the pattern, the ground rushing closer. He started to get dizzy and this time nauseated as well. At the peak of his discomfort, Flint slammed the stick forward simultaneously with kicking in full left rudder, the spinning motion slowed, then stopped abruptly, and the plane whipped into a straight dive, aligned with the road that had been spinning, and Flint smoothly brought it level, adding power as he did.

Bennie was wrung out and hoped to hell it was over. He thought, "*Jesus Christ, what ever gave me the dumb notion I wanted to fly*?"

Flint pulled off the power and yelled, "Put your feet on the rudders and take hold of the stick and follow through with me on the landing so you can feel what I'm doing."

He did as he was told, but there was almost no strength in his arm. He thought, "It's a good thing I don't have to get this thing on the ground. Suppose he had a heart attack. I'd have to bail out." That, too, was a thought that didn't please him.

He was only half-conscious of what he was doing as they landed and taxied in to their parking spot.

He hoped he didn't look as drained as Kid had, but was sure he must.

He got out with no help and removed his helmet, tossing it back on top of the parachute.

Flint asked, "Waddaya think?"

Bennie grinned weakly. "It takes a little getting used to, I guess"

Flint said, "I gave you a real hard dose of it. I wanted to kill you or cure you right up front. That was mild compared to dog fighting. We'll fly some more and I'll let you fly. I've got some Gosports coming in the mail in a few days and I'll be able to talk to you without pulling off the power and yelling."

"*I can hardly wait*," Bennie thought, not knowing or caring what Gosports might be.

Kid had been listening and said, "I have a feeling I'm going to make a great infantryman, or something."

Flint laughed. "Don't cash out till I let you fly straight and level and just look over the scenery."

He turned to Rose and said, "Now it's your turn. I won't do any of that stuff I did with them. Just take you for a scenic tour."

Rose said, "Not if I live to be a million."

He didn't push her or see any reason to. The Marines didn't recruit women, especially not as pilots. He thought, "*And that's the way we'd better keep it. Woman are too inflexible to fly. Christ, if a truck pulled into their lane on the highway, they'd let it hit 'em head on before they dodged into the lane the truck swerved out of, because they've been told you shouldn't drive on the wrong side of the road.*"

When they got home, Ma came out to meet them and said, "Where have you been? You were gone so long I thought you must have had an accident."

This was pure Ma. She always thought someone was going to have an accident. And if a plane went overhead, she always thought it sounded like it was in trouble, without the slightest idea how one would sound if it really was.

Flint read the ill-concealed disapproval on her face when Bennie introduced them.

Her displeasure over Flint didn't extend to cooking a lousy meal for him, however. Ma's stomach came first, and besides Eben wouldn't have been happy. Eben might even toss out a bad meal and cook a good one himself. You couldn't tell about him, and she'd never been able to train him as she had Pa. He simply walked out when she nattered at him and didn't come back for hours, and once he was gone all night, never telling her he'd slept in the hay loft.

Ma hated to admit to herself that she liked Flint's looks, his pugnacious jaw and killer blue eyes, like Jim Tynan's. She normally didn't like blonds, but his almost white hair went with the rest of him, and on him was attractive. Besides he had an air about him of fearlessness and authority that she could feel. The feeling that you got from the unfathomable eyes of the deadly jungle cats she'd seen in zoos.

Bennie got Flint settled in Rose's old room. It was available since there was no secret anymore how it was between them, and Ma never quivered when Rose said she was moving in with Bennie.

Flint said, "I'm dog tired. I must be getting old. All I did today was drive to Milwaukee from LaSalle, then fly up here and take you guys for a little spin."

"Yeah," Bennie said, dryly. "I suppose we all get old in time. I'll see you in the morning. Sleep as late as you want to."

He got his first chance to privately compare notes with Kid on flying as he drove him over to Newt's in the Lincoln.

"Waddya think?" he asked.

"Like I said, I think I'll make a great infantryman."

"Are you serious?"

"Serious as hell. How about you?"

"I think I'll give it a little more of a try. I sure as hell didn't like the spin. I thought I'd heave my cookies for sure."

"I thought I'd heave mine even taking off, but somehow I kept it down. Anyhow, you couldn't pay me enough to do it anymore. You hop to it. I will take him hunting though."

"He'll like that. And I want to take him over so Pa can meet him."

Hunting got on the agenda first thing in the morning. Kid drove over in the Model A and brought his old single-barrel and a .32 Special Winchester deer rifle. Bennie had a Model 94 .30-30 and a .12 gauge pump shotgun. Flint had brought only a .30-30, which was the most popular deer hunting caliber in the country then. Bennie had seen him retrieve it and his suitcase from the shack at the airport, where he'd deposited them before he took up his victims.

They packed to camp a few days in the woods, just as Bennie and Kid always did. Evenings were beginning to get chilly in late August and the campfire felt good.

After supper their first night, while they were lying around the fire smoking, Flint said, "This is the life. After the war when I retire, I aim to buy a little place up in this neck of the woods, find a good woman who likes the outdoors, and live out my days."

"You sound awful sure about that war," Kid said.

"It's coming. The longer we put it off, the more trouble we're going to have. The Corps's been getting ready for it for years, but Congress is just waking up, the stupid bastards! FDR has known it for a couple of years and has been trying to hold their feet to the fire. Churchill over in England has known it ever since the son of a bitch Hitler came to power. We can't live in the same world with people like the Germans and Japs without having them sitting on our doorstep sooner or later, *if we don't hit them at home and keep them there!*"

Bennie had heard the same argument at the supper table for a number of years. Pa, Newt, Eben, and Nelson all felt the same way. But there were plenty who didn't. Rose came to mind. He told himself, "*I've got to convince her. We've got to go for the sake of women and kids as much as anything. It's a pity she hasn't read as much history as I have.*"

"Those who cannot remember history . . ."

Flint left after an idyllic week. He'd had Bennie up for a few hours of instruction and given him a real feel for flying, even letting him make several landings without touching the controls himself.

"You're a natural," he pronounced. "All you need is a little more instruction and you can solo. Barnes here, who runs the airport, is an instructor—he can solo you. I paid him for ten hours in advance."

"You didn't have to do that. I got some dough."

"You can pay for some more. *That ten hours is my investment in national security*. And be sure and stay in touch."

"I'll do that. I really like to fly now that I'm gettin' the hang of it."

Flint grinned. "You'll never really get the hang of it—*just come close, maybe*."

"Whatever," Bennie said, "but I feel like a bird up there sometimes."

Flint said, "Tell me about it," shook hands, and got into the plane. He waved as he taxied out to take off. Bennie was surprised Flint didn't swoop back and roll over the runway, but his suitcase and rifle and extra chute would probably have fallen out. He simply rocked the wings after taking off and bored off into the blue.

Bennie watched the plane until it turned into a speck then disappeared from sight.

The day before Flint left, Klondy had had them all over to Sunday dinner. Bennie wanted to expose Rose to the war talk he knew would develop around the dinner table with Pa and Flint both there, to say nothing of Newt. He got the surprise of his life when Klondy gave war its best pep talk.

She said, "My gramp was in the Civil War and always said, just like Newt, that if we'd faced up to the grim facts sooner we'd have saved a lot of lives, maybe not even had a war. It took Lincoln to put some stiffening in the national backbone. FDR is trying to do it now. My pa was in the Spanish American War, and maybe I shouldn't say it, since I've never told anyone, but I had a son when I was only seventeen and he got killed in the World War."

That was a shocker for Bennie, and he looked at Pa's face to see how he was taking it. It didn't seem to bother him a bit.

To Pa she said, "I never told you, but I don't think it makes any difference. He's gone, and even if I wasn't married to his pa, that doesn't cut any ice either. I loved them both, and the kid died for his country. He was only twenty-one. He never even got to vote, but we believed in patriotism then. I remember reading in history class in grade school how Stephen Decatur made a toast: '*My country, may she always be in the right, but my country right or wrong.*' If the English fighting by themselves over there right now aren't in the right, I don't know what right is. *It's time we wake up and start acting like we know what right is again and help them. They're fighting our war.*"

Bennie hadn't expected that Klondy had that kind of speech in her and took his first real good look at her.

Rose didn't appear convinced by Klondy's unexpected eloquence, but Bennie was glad she heard it. He realized that Rose was a special case since she'd lost her ma and pa and seen her family, once so idyllically happy together, scattered to the winds.

But his mind was made up, and he'd have to bring her around to realizing why. All the more reason if, as she kept saying, they were going to have a kid. He wanted his country, "the last best hope of earth," kept that way for the sake of all the generations coming, not only American, but in the whole world. Humans everywhere had a right to own themselves, their hearts, their consciences, and souls. They might lose sight of it for a while to fill their stomachs, but it came back to wanting to be free in the long run.

He had gradually realized that *not only his* kid would be born free because so many who had gone before had been willing to give "their last full measure of devotion," but every baby in the world was born wanting to be free, looking for someone to set them free if they weren't, and to keep them that way.

He wondered, "*Why do I know this? It must be from reading so much history—and biography.*"

Biography was his favorite way of learning history. He turned that over in his mind and saw that history boiled down to people doing things they wanted to do, that human nature had dictated the course of history since the dawn of mankind and, "*Every baby in a dictatorship is born an enemy of the state, because God built them to be free.*"

It was a comforting thought. The "last best hope of earth" gained a lot of allies *in the long run* wherever it set a people free, or showed them the way to be free on their own.

CHAPTER SIXTY-FOUR

Flying Gets in Your Blood

Bennie decided Uncle Newt was his best bet for advice regarding how to go about telling everyone he was going to join the Marines whether they liked it or not.

Newt's first caution was, "Best get hitched before you get stubborn about it. The gal may not marry you if you get on your high horse. She may give you the choice between her and your pride. What will you do then?"

"I think she's pregnant, and so does she. I don't think she's apt to tell me to get out of her life now."

"This isn't your usual gal," Newt said. "No tellin' what she might do and stick to it, too. Let some time go by. Maybe you'll get drafted and you can blame Uncle Sam. Maybe we'll get into it ourselves. We'd damn well better before it's too late!"

"Hell, Congress just repassed the draft law by one vote. They aren't apt to lower the draft age unless a war actually starts. I could be out here as a plow jockey for years."

"I reckon that flying business lit a shuck under yore tail."

"I guess. It gets in your blood. I can hardly wait till the next time I get in the air."

"Man, you got it bad. I've flown with a lot of bush pilots in Alaska, and I don't know a one that isn't that way. You wouldn't believe the places they fly in all kinds of weather."

"Yeah, I would. I read an article about it. Like Flint. He said he always wanted to fly, and boy is he good at it."

"Well, I guess you'll be good at it, too."

"If working at it will do it, I'll be the best. Maybe if I'm a pilot in the war I'll go to Alaska and be a bush pilot when it's over."

"You'd take to Alaska," Newt said.

His talk with Newt gave him little encouragement to make any move as soon as he'd like to. He started thinking about the wedding. It was only a week away, and Ma and Rose were scheming like a couple of kids about how to make it gaudy and memorable. It was only going to be a small family affair, but by now the family was considerable (and didn't include Felice and the Cretin). Ma even decided to let Klondy come if "she had the nerve," which stunned Bennie. He had a notion Klondy would have the nerve. He thought, "*Wouldn't it be funny if she and Ma got to be good friends.*" He'd heard of odder things. After all in some ways they were a lot alike, strong-willed and self-sufficient *survivors*, above all.

It was turning into a glorious, flaming red-and-gold Wisconsin fall, still warm and sunny during the day, with crispness capturing the air immediately after the sun set. In the morning, hoar frost clung to the grass and bushes and sometimes even the lower leaves of the trees. Bennie knew it was caused by warm, moist air flowing over the cooler earth, which caused condensation, but knowing why it was there didn't diminish its beauty and wonder.

He took Rose down to his rock for a picnic one nice morning and when the sun was high, they peeled off their clothes and gingerly tiptoed out into the cold water, gradually moving into deeper water and submerging. He was fascinated as always by her graceful body, breasts swaying as she moved, the lovely triangle of brown luxuriant hair where her thighs joined.

Consumed by an overpowering surge of passion, he grabbed her and crushed her against him as they faced each other chest-deep in the water. Desire flamed up in them both and she came strongly to him, eyes deep black pools of mystery, shining now with love and also humor, as she said, "You may '*skwush*' your son."

"*Skwush*" was a pure Ma-ism, one of Ma's invented words that came right to the point regardless of not being in any dictionary.

Bennie kissed Rose gently at first, then harder, then fiercely, and she was equally animal in her sudden arousal, pressing her whole body against him eagerly, thrusting against his rising erection. When he unglued his mouth from hers, they both came up for air, and she said, breathlessly, "I think we ought to get out and lie down on the grass. I'm suddenly really tired." Then she giggled.

"Me too," he said. "I hope you won't mind me using you as a mattress."

He was already leading the way out, holding her hand. She said, "Like I said, you might *skwush* me and our son."

"I'll risk it if you're game."

"I'm game," she said as she lay back and looked up at him coming down to her, reading the depth of passion in his eyes and happy to realize she was causing it.

Too shortly, he pushed up on his arms above her and said, "Boy, that didn't take long."

She smiled, trying without success to look enigmatic, but only managing to look impish, and said, "Maybe you'd like an encore."

He carefully lowered his body against her again and rubbed his lips gently over hers, wetting them with his tongue, then plunged his tongue deeply into her mouth to meet and entangle with hers.

"Fancy that," he said, pulling away his lips briefly, but thrusting his hips at her. "That's the quickest I ever got in shape to pitch another inning after a draining like I just had. I believe you're going to seduce this *innercent* youth again." He knew that was in the cards because his erection had hardly gone down before he felt it swelling again.

"Tough," she said, "you'll just have to live with it. It's been a hard year all over."

He laughed. "Hard, like just now, or in bed last night, you mean?"

It was *that* kind of fall for them. Young, deep, passionate love dominated their lives, and he never once mentioned joining the Marines again. She was as happy as she could get, thinking, "*Maybe he's come to his senses. He doesn't have to go at all, much less go first, since he'll be a father, who is also a farmer and farmers are always deferred.*"

The day was perfect for a wedding, as Rose had prayed it would be, since she wanted to get married outdoors under the ceremonial maple tree, as she thought of it, where Uncle Newt used to gather them all for his stories. To her it was a cherished place, since that was where they had all sat when she first came to visit Ma and Pa Todd, long before she lived there, a place where she could secretly watch Bennie before he had awakened to the fact that she was growing into a woman who was in love with him.

The only problem regarding the marriage, since she wanted a regular ceremony with some trimmings to remember it by, was getting a minister. She didn't want a Justice of the Peace affair. They cast around for a minister but none were willing to come out to perform a ceremony, not only because it was "way out in the sticks" but (though none openly said so) because none of the family belonged to a church—and besides, Bennie was the son of a reprobate who was not only divorced, but remarried to the madam of the county's leading whorehouse.

Newt could have rounded up almost any minister, using his usual persuasiveness—a big donation for the minister's exclusive use. But Kid had a better idea.

"Why don't we get our Injun preacher, Thundering Water?"

"Is he a real minister?" Ma asked.

"Yep," Kid said. "Went to one o' them regular Bible schools, got a piece of paper to prove it, and wears dark blue shiny pants on top of it. He can rant with the best of 'em, too, and make his voice quaver just right, like God's going to pop in any minute."

"Sounds proper to me," Newt said.

"He falls short a little on being a hypocrite, though," Kid put in.

"Oh, well," Newt said, "In that case maybe we'd better look around a little more."

Rose, who'd been listening to her fate being weighed by the usual unqualified males, said, "Never mind. He'll do."

Bennie liked the idea of an Indian minister.

The ceremony was set for eleven in the morning so there would be plenty of time for a big lunch afterward, and essential naps later.

They weren't planning on a honeymoon. Few in the farm country ever considered such things because they couldn't afford either time or money for frills. The only possible time to get away from heavy farm work was winter, and few could afford a trip to a warm climate for a honeymoon, which was the only kind of place that made sense. (If you had to stay cooped up in a house to stay warm, anywhere would do for a honeymoon.) Bennie and Rose could have afforded a honeymoon almost anywhere since Newt offered to finance one, but the deciding reason that kept them home was that Rose wanted to help Ma with the last of the season's canning.

It made sense to Bennie, who had no desire to go anywhere after their summer trip. Besides he wanted to sneak off to fly as often as possible. He now had thirty hours flying time, and Marty Barnes had soloed him after only seven hours. He was about to get his private license so he could carry passengers, and he dreamed almost every night of flying.

Flying carried him up there with that smart-talking sparrow and wise-ass hawk, who'd told him he'd be a warrior on his first day out in the woods after they came back *up north*.

He imagined now that he knew how birds loved the freedom high above the earth like the hawk, or even darting around low, wary, and quick in the case of the sparrow.

Bennie loved to circle and swoop lazily, taking in the scenery and sometimes doing a loop or barrel roll, which kept only positive G forces on the plane, which, Marty cautioned him, were all the old bird was designed to stand. Marty said, "Screw up and you'll pull the wings off and be seriously dead. I can't spare that old bird. It's the only one I've got." Bennie didn't miss the implication that he could spare anyone dumb enough to do such a thing, but not the plane he did it in.

But mostly he practiced takeoffs and landings, which Flint said was where you really learned and used all of your skill, aside from dog fighting.

Bennie could hear Flint's voice saying, "Flying like the airlines do isn't real flying. You don't learn anything, just boring holes. Sure, the airline guys get a lot of hours and instrument flying too, and they get good on instruments, but occasionally that gets them in over their heads because airlines are always trying to make an extra buck, flying when they shouldn't do it, and kill people. Experience can't repeal the law of gravity while you're carrying too big a load of ice."

"We're good at instrument flying too because we have to be, and good at navigation out in the middle of nowhere over water, finding our way home to an aircraft carrier before we run out of juice. And *when* we get into the war, carriers won't have any lights at night so they stand out like a Christmas tree, or have a radio homer for us to fly to. It'll be seat-of-pants stuff. We'll get lights just long enough to aim at the deck when we're almost overhead and have the right identification and not before."

It sounded to Bennie like every mission was a suicide mission if that's the way it would be. He wasn't far wrong. And he never forgot that Flint had said, "*when*" not "*if*" we get into the war.

That's where things stood when they all gathered for the wedding ceremony. Kid and his ma and pa were the first to show up, bringing the minister with them. Kid's pa (who preferred to be called Circling Hawk, his own name for himself) was wearing a jacket over his freshly washed bib overalls out of consideration for the solemn occasion.

"Come to kiss the bride," he announced.

Kid's mother nudged him and said, "I come to crown you if you don't behave. And don't overdo it at the punch bowl!"

"Who me?"

"Yeah, you."

That got things off to a good start for a fun day. Circling Hawk wandered off to join Newt, who'd just walked over through the woods with Nelson. The chief knew that Newt was always good for an expensive cigar.

Bennie had had butterflies in his stomach since the day before, even though he and Rose had been married for months for all practical purposes. He thought, "That's dumb. People shouldn't let ceremonies get to them."

He was also holding his breath to see if Klondy would be with Pa. When

Klondy not only showed up with Pa but was driving the car as well, Bennie thought, "*This is going to be worth watching.*"

It wasn't, though. Both Ma and Klondy were true steel, and met as though they'd been seeing each other at church for years. They even shook hands, which women didn't usually do. Bennie didn't miss the long appraisals that they gave each other, however. Finally Klondy smiled and said, "I hope we get to be friends."

For once Ma had the grace to smile back, even though enigmatically, and not say something like, "That'll be the day."

"*I wonder where this will end up?*" Bennie asked himself.

Like Bennie, Rose had butterflies in her tummy. Ma was keeping her out of sight, which she said was the thing to do with the bride to avoid bad luck. Besides she wanted to keep anyone from seeing the wedding dress she'd made for Rose. It was made from some white satin Ma had had since the Lord only knew when, with puffed sleeves, a high neck with a collar of pink roses Ma had spent hours sewing by hand to look like real ones, and a long, tight-fitting skirt section, reaching almost to Rose's shoe tops. Ma insisted you had to wear a hat at your wedding and they got a white hat to match the dress, that clung close to Rose's head. Ma had wanted her to buy a wide-brimmed hat with a fashionable curved brim, but Rose had turned it down as too fancy (and expensive). Any hat she wore would have been put in the shade by her long chestnut hair flowing almost to her waist in back, restrained by one pink ribbon with a small brooch holding the knot in it. The color exactly matched the rose collar.

Bennie thought she looked as regal as a queen when she finally came out and took Newt's arm to figuratively "walk down the aisle."

Thundering Water played his part to the hilt, especially after a couple of fortifying, early visits to the punch bowl with Circling Hawk.

The little group that stood behind the bride and groom were Ma and Pa, Newt, Nelson, Eben, Kid's parents, Klondy, with Kid as best man. One of the neighboring Anderson girls had been invited over as bridesmaid and brought her two sisters, which more or less made it mandatory to invite their parents, Fred and Alma Anderson, the only outsiders. It hadn't occurred to Bennie before what an insular existence they led, a little family almost entirely different than their neighbors in most respects, especially the money behind them.

Two last-minute additions to the family came after Thundering Water started the "We are gathered here's, etc." Nutty Bob and Kid's aunt walked in from the woods. Pa turned to see who'd arrived and did a double take on Bob, not entirely ready to credit his eyes. Bennie had never breathed a word about him to any of the family.

Rose, oblivious to everything but the fact that her girlish dream of someday marrying Bennie was coming true, hardly knew what was going on. She did take in the unorthodox cathedral of hazy woods in the distance and the flaming red canopy of leaves above them. It reminded her of the title of a book she'd read, *Heaven Can Wait*.

It was all over too soon, with Thundering Water saying: "I now pronounce you man and wife."

She turned to Bennie, her eyes shining with happy tears and lifted her mouth to him. He did a proper job of it, so much so that Kid tapped him on the shoulder and said, "Can I cut in?"

Bennie released Rose, and Kid did next honors, with Thundering Water right behind him, followed by Circling Hawk. Pa gave her a fatherly peck on the cheek, then Eben gave her a real smackeroo. Rose thought, "Lucky Ma."

Last came Nelson and Newt, both smelling of booze, as all the rest had, only a little more so, she thought.

Nutty Bob stayed in the background, then drifted away when everyone was busy with the kissing and congratulating. By arrangement with Kid and Bennie, he was going to stay in the barn and wait for one of them to bring out Pa later to talk awhile. Bob wasn't sure that Ma wouldn't call the sheriff and try to have him put back in the loony bin. He realized that she'd disliked him from the first time she'd laid eyes on him.

Rose and Bennie broke away after lunch and went up for a "*nap.*" She was physically and emotionally drained.

By sundown all of the guests had left, and Ma was cleaning up, when Rose came down to help. Ma looked her over for wear and tear and couldn't see any signs of it, since the nap had refreshed Rose wonderfully.

Ma thought, "*If I'd searched the globe I couldn't have found a woman for Bennie that I thought would be as good for him.*"

"How does it feel to be a Todd now?" she asked.

"Wonderful. I have to pinch myself to realize Bennie is actually mine. I loved him from the day I first laid eyes on him."

Ma smiled, but was thinking, "*I hope you have better luck as a Todd that I did. The only good thing to come out of it was my kids, especially Bennie.*" Of them all she'd always thought Bennie would be the one to amount to something.

CHAPTER SIXTY-FIVE

I Remember Pearl Harbor

"Some came running."

[FLASHBACKS]

— 1932

Was I coming down to Pearl Harbor all that time? "I remember Pearl Harbor."

— 1937

Voices were speaking across the world but Bennie, at age fifteen, was scarcely aware of them, even though they were reported on the "air waves" and in newspapers and news magazines—two most popular of the latter were *Time* and *Life* . . .

* * * * *

Sports were a national craze that salved troubled minds. The Depression was alleviated but was far from whipped.

* * * * *

The Four Horsemen of Notre Dame, sports heroes, would remain in the public eye and consciousness for years, since three became famous football coaches. But they were not the Four Horsemen that shaped the next decades—*the bloody Horseman would do that.*

. . . The rider on the Red Horse was about to take the stage front and center, and Bennie's life would take an Apocalyptic path, along with tens of millions of others worldwide.

Fifty million people would die in what Winston Churchill called the "unnecessary war"—that is, unnecessary if one believes the world should have stood up to injustice soon enough—it didn't. It seldom does.

— September 1941

Bennie tried to hide his head in the sand. But it was uphill work trying to strangle the unmistakable conviction that he was a shirker. Here he was with his sleeves rolled up, not ready to fight, but standing at a sink helping two women can berries.

He argued with himself, "I've got to stay here as the Boy Farmer. *I'm married, about to be a father one of these days, God willing, so I've got to recognize that all those romantic ideals are just that—romantic baloney. I'm not the Boy General and never will be. Custer went to West Point and I dropped out of high school. A big difference. Let them draft me and then Rose and Ma can't squawk!*"

Such thoughts were damned small consolation to him, but obviously a great consolation to a lot of others he'd heard down at Klondy's place:

"They're gonna have to drag me over to get my ass shot off!"

"Volunteer, my ass! The British and French got themselves into it. Let them get themselves out of it."

"Lindy's got it right. America first."

"I'll go when my time comes, and not before."

"Hell, if the Japs start any trouble, the Pacific Fleet'll sink them so fast their heads will swim!"

"It's not our fight. Let them come over here first."

Bennie's usual inner circle was sitting around a table, Newt listening to that kind of talk and looking like he'd like to take the shirking sonsabitches outside and kick some sense into them, or bore a hole in them with the .45 that by then everyone knew he carried like it was grown to him. They'd seen him shoot it, too.

"Why, the son of a bitch could hit a man with that cannon every time at a hundred yards. Even if he was running. I wonder where the hell he learned to shoot like that."

No one gave Newt any trouble, and his reputation was the reason, that and the fact that his eyes told the story as well—he'd as soon shoot you as look at you, and everyone suspected you wouldn't be the first by a long shot.

So when Newt grabbed the fellow by his sleeve that had just said, "*It's not our fight. Let them come over here first*," and pulled him over to their table and said, "Sit down, sonny," it seemed to the guy like a good idea to do as he was told.

Newt speared him with a cold eye and said, "You don't know what the fuck you're talking about, and I'm tired of hearing that kind of crap!"

Conversation died. Everyone there realized what might happen any second if the big bruiser decided to give Newt any guff.

Newt turned up the volume, aware that he was getting an audience, "Coming over here is the problem, kid. That's exactly what they'll do if we don't stop them over there. Would have after the World War, if they'd won. It'd been only a matter of time. It's only a matter of time now. If we'd lived up to our responsibilities and joined the League of Nations and put some backbone into it, none of this would have happened. If Chamberlain had some backbone and stood up to Hitler when he still had a chance, this wouldn't have happened. Instead he came home to England and bragged about how he got 'Peace in our Time.' Peace my ass! You can see what kind of peace he got.

"I don't expect to change anybody's mind, but I don't want to have to sit around here and listen to any more empty-headed horseshit. Now get the hell out of my sight!"

The big kid looked like a rabbit confronted suddenly by a snake, and not only got up, feeling lucky to be alive, but quickly got his hat and mackinaw and left the place without so much as glancing back.

Newt swiveled his head around like Wild Bill with a look that said, "Anyone else?"

There wasn't.

Bennie was afraid to ask Newt what he thought of his own grandnephew being a "shirker," but he didn't think it was a good time. Newt had never yet bit his head off, but there was always a first time, and he looked like he was in a mood where he might do it.

Kid broke the heavy silence. "I'm going to go down and sign up. Newt just made up my mind. Ma and Pa feel just like Newt does. Indians may not be first-class citizens yet, but we will be. If Hitler came over here nobody would be."

He looked apologetically at Bennie and added, "*It's different with you. If I was married with a kid on the way, I wouldn't go 'til I had to.*"

"That makes sense," Nelson said. "But good for you, Kid."

Bennie wasn't sure, however that "making sense" didn't include dodging a bigger responsibility than you owed your family.

Eben said, "If I was young enough, I'd go again. I wrote a letter and asked, and got turned down just like I expected."

Pa, who had "escaped the draft" in the world war because of a wife, kids, a dependent mother, and his minor sister, Felice, in addition to being a farmer, came as close to disagreeing with Newt as anyone there dared.

He said, "If your first allegiance isn't to your family, then whatever you put ahead of your family won't be worth a shit anyhow."

He wasn't eloquent enough to explain that what he meant was that patriotism stemmed from loyalty to your family. He was afraid to look Newt directly in the face when he said it, but he knew he had to say it. He didn't want to lose Bennie any more than Ma and Rose did. He quickly added, "But Newt is dead right. If we don't stop them over there, we'll have to fight them here."

Lucky for Pa, Newt got his meaning right off, and recognized they were really saying the same thing.

Bennie took all this in silently.

Almost every day he looked up and watched military formations of bombers pass overhead on training missions. At such times, he always got a picture of himself in a fighter plane, escorting them, or shooting down enemy bombers like the Royal Air Force in England, which many Americans had volunteered to join. He wanted to "stop them over there," and had made up his mind he was going to go. He'd break the news "as tactfully as possible," but would go under any circumstances.

He needed someone to sign his papers because he was too young yet. He thought, "*I'll have to talk this over with Newt. He'll sign for me. We'll be in deep shit with Ma and Rose when they find out, but they'll get over it.*"

[FLASHBACK—1936 AND 1937]

Riverside Park
(On the way back up north)

"He'd miss Riverside Park. It might even miss him . . . sometimes land does."
(Walk beside the Little Big Horn.)

"Where are you, George Armstrong Custer?"
"Where are you Sitting Bull—Crazy Horse?"
"Where are you, Blackhawk?"
"Where are you, Ben Edwin Todd? (Bennie.)
"Yes, where are you, Bennie, our own, he who pissed in Uncle Bart's lemonade jug?

Rare are they with the guts to prescribe poison, or 'bid the guns to shoot!'" (Or even piss in a jug of lemonade.)

"Where are they all?"

BEYOND THE HILLS OF HISTORY.

Some like Bennie,—oops, old whatsisname! Faceless,
while insipid runners-up from the proper side of the tracks are pictured in Daily Gazettes.
Nameless—except as afterthoughts.
Some, gone forever—Like Ralph Esselborn.
Others waiting—like Bennie—

Until the DRUMS OF THE REPUBLIC

Sound the long roll—the call to fight worldwide injustice for the Republic of Man.

The call to eternal Glory, should they give their "last full measure of devotion."

CHAPTER SIXTY-SIX

The Army Air Corps

Bennie got his first letter from Kid from Camp McCoy, the nearest Army post to Winnebago. Bennie was surprised to learn that Kid hadn't got into the Marine Corps.

Kid wrote, "I don't care to fly, so there's no special point to getting in the Marines. I can stay around home at least while I'm in Basic Training.

"You're never going to guess who's over here and has me under his wing. Old Coach Redballs. He had a reserve officers' commission and is a captain now. He's the athletic director and aims to put me on the football team. He said, 'You're too valuable as a *morale builder* to let you get your ass shot off if we get into it.' Get that 'morale builder' shit! He's 'just like that' with the commanding general who was a jock at West Point, played football against Red Grange and the Four Horsemen. *Fancy that.*

"Bennie, if you want to fly you ought to join the Army Air Corps. They're advertising all over the Post here on bulletin boards. You won't need *pull* to get into their pilot training program. If you can pass a written test you're a natural to get your wings and be an officer. You're bound to pass the physical. They're looking for warm bodies. I can tell you from what I've seen so far that being an officer is a hell of a lot better than being an enlisted man.

"I took just about the same written test for O.C.S. (Officers Candidate School) that you will for flying school, and even scored high on it. You'd pass the aviation cadet written test in a minute. Anyhow, if I'm lucky, I'll be a second lieutenant one of these days. I can hardly believe it. They call them 'ninety-day wonders' since the course is ninety days long.

"Of course, if you get in, Redballs might not let you go to flying training. You might fall out of a plane and not be a 'morale booster' anymore.

"I told him about you and he said, 'Talk him into enlisting and I'll get him over here and we'll have the champion football team of the whole army. The General can get you back here after you finish O.C.S. or I wouldn't let you go in the first place. You guys could turn pro after you get out and make a lot better money than you can farming.'

"Think that over."

—

This didn't make being Boy Farmer any more attractive to Bennie, but he still hesitated. By now Rose was beginning to show in front and he loved her all the more for knowing she was going to have their kid. It was a hell of a predicament for a natural-born "warrior." What would he do if she left him, which she might do if she thought he was *turning his back on what really mattered*? The thought of living without her was absolutely unbearable.

That was where affairs stood when Bennie chauffeured Newt, Nelson, and Eben down to Klondy's to hoist a few the night before Pearl Harbor.

Ma never batted an eye over Eben's resumption of his visits to his old haunts, but might have if she knew the full story of what went on.

There was some discussion at their table regarding the negotiations in progress with the "Japs."

Newt was in a talkative frame of mind. He led out, "I recall when our troubles with Japan started. 1905. They shellacked the Russians good a couple of times. Teddy Roosevelt got a Nobel Prize for negotiating an end to the fighting. I reckon both sides were just as glad. Japan couldn't have kept up the war, and the Russians had enough trouble at home.

"Teddy Roosevelt got it right, though. We had to watch the Japs from then on. They were out to take over the Pacific. Maybe we ought to let 'em. FDR is sticking his nose in and asking for it. We've shut off Japan's oil, their scrap metal, and now he's closed the Panama Canal to them. It looks to me like they don't have much choice but to fight. Can you blame 'em? They've got a couple of envoys down wrangling in Washington right now. Probably their last-ditch proposition. We think we have to protect China because they're our friends. Countries don't have friends. Only folks that happen to have their eggs in your basket just then. Read your history books. But Orientals aren't predictable in any case, whether they're Chinese or Japanese or any other kind. You simply can't trust the bastards. You can look for a war to start any day, but you can't say FDR isn't asking for it. Maybe he wants one so we can jump in and help England before it's too late."

"A good idea," Nelson put in.

Bennie usually paid full attention whenever Newt gave one of his lectures, but he was feeling listless. He missed Kid at the gathering, and wished he himself hadn't come. He was glad to get home and slip into bed with Rose.

Rose tired easily those days, and often went to bed early. He slipped under the covers with her, and as usual she roused and snuggled against him. He kissed her, heard her sleepy, contented sigh as she went right back to sleep, and was asleep himself almost when his head hit the pillow. Asleep, he didn't have to think of his dilemma.

Besides, the U.S. might not get into the war after all. Maybe FDR would play Japan's game after all. But he agreed with Newt that this would be too bad, since we were only postponing the inevitable. Everyone with a lick of sense knew that if Germany and Italy won, we'd be isolated and have to fight them sooner or later in order to continue indispensable trade with the rest of the world. Successful negotiations between the Japanese and U.S., however, could put off Bennie's decision for a while. He'd probably be drafted and could serve his country without getting in Dutch with his family. Most likely he could stay near home on Coach Redballs's football team. At least he'd be in the Army and not feel like a slacker. Besides, he'd missed playing football. Deep inside he realized that line of reasoning was actually a cop-out. He wanted to be in a position to go in harm's way if a war came.

The next afternoon Ma hurried out to where Eben and Bennie were milking. She almost never came into the barn, and Bennie knew that something serious must be wrong.

He said, "What's the matter?"

She said, "The Japs attacked Pearl Harbor this morning."

Bennie stood up so fast he kicked over the stool.

"Are you sure?"

"I'm sure. It's on the radio. Come listen for yourself. They sunk most of the Pacific Fleet, it sounds like."

"The milkin'll keep, I guess," Eben said. "Let's go listen for a while." Ma was walking rapidly back toward the house.

"I thought the house might be on fire," Eben added.

There was a house afire, all right, but not the small one they were snugly living in. It was the big one that everyone lived in!

Rose's practical mind went immediately to the possible consequences of the news. Bennie's swift entry to the house was a signal of what she might expect. When there was danger, many stood back and watched;

"Some came running!"

She knew which kind she'd married.

How could she keep such a man from answering his country's call in its gravest hour of need? And would it be right if she did?

She sat glued to the radio with the rest. Newt and Nelson came over, having picked up the news on Nelson's battery radio, and they listened glumly as each humiliating new bulletin came in. Each worse than the last. It appeared that thousands of sailors had been killed on the sunken battleships, and a lot of soldiers in other places around the island of Oahu where the Japs had strafed our air fields.

Bennie was stunned, and the look on the faces of the rest told him they felt the same. Ma looked grim. She didn't want Bennie to go to war, and possibly get killed, but she, too, was a fighter. She'd been raised since her days at Johnny Run School, as everyone was, on a diet of patriotism. She had come to see, during the World War, that wars were sometime unavoidable, considering human nature. In spite of that she could never quite overcome the holdover from her childish wondering why we had wars if they hurt people like their neighbor, George Spiller. She especially didn't want them to hurt her sons. In that she had the company of every mother in the world.

She thought, "*They're bound to take him now,*" and clenched her hands in her lap, but then relaxed again as an idea for a last-ditch weapon to slow down the process struck her. "*Well, maybe he has to go, but I'll be damned if I'll sign any papers and let him enlist a day before he has to go anyhow.*"

Ma read the occasional letters she got in the mail at the kitchen table—they were usually only from her sisters or mother. Eben had brought the mail and gone into the front room as he always did to look at the new seed catalogs. He'd noticed the official letter, but its significance hadn't registered on him. The government was always sending out notices about something.

She opened the official letter from the government, thinking it must be about one of the new farm programs, not noticing that it was from the Army, not the Department of Agriculture.

Her eyes read the words, but they meant little at first.

"*The War Department regrets to inform you that your son, Roy Todd, was among those soldiers killed in the attack on Pearl Harbor.*"

She thought, "*How can that be? His last letter said he just got out of Basic Training?*"

Then she remembered he'd said he was being sent somewhere as a replacement.

A follow-up letter from his commanding officer in Hawaii would tell her rest of the story in time. He'd been sent to Hawaii to help fill out an infantry unit and had only been there a day when the Jap attack had swept the islands.

She sat at the kitchen table, the letter in her weak grasp, where she'd let her hands fall into her apron. She was alone and wanted to cry and realized she'd almost forgotten how.

She hadn't thought much about Roy, since he hadn't written or visited after they left Illinois. She knew why but would never admit that it was her fault.

Like Bennie, Roy had been born at home, with only the help of Pa's mother. She remembered when he'd first been placed in her arms and she put him on a breast and felt his little mouth sucking in her life-giving milk. She had loved him then, and knew now that she always had, despite her inability to show it, or treat him better.

She was suddenly overwhelmed, regretting every time she'd hit him, which had been often before he was old enough to protect himself. She'd even thought "good riddance" when he'd left home to work for her sister on the farm. She regretted that too. Most of all. He'd have loved to come back *up north* just as Bennie had, and she'd denied him that pleasure. Now he was gone and would never have pleasure of any kind again.

That realization broke the dam and started her crying and her reluctant surrender made it come out with a strange, agonized noise like a wounded animal. Eben heard her and came running.

"What's the matter?" he asked, rapidly crossing to her side.

She handed him the letter.

"My, God," he said.

He'd never known Roy, except from what Bennie and Pa had told him, but what he'd heard told him that Roy had been a kid with an intensely loving nature. Eben's own life had been that way, too, so he was sure how Roy must have felt, abandoned through no fault of his own. Yet Eben couldn't bring himself to blame Ma. Of all the people on earth, he'd probably been the first one to fully understand her, and he did love her in spite of everything.

He lifted her up from her chair, pulled her into his arms and held her, anguished because he realized he could do nothing to stop the big sobs that shook her body. She'd just have to get it out in her own way and own good time.

Finally she quieted down and said softly, "I loved him,"

"I know you did."

"But I never told him," she said, and started to sob again.

Rose came into the kitchen, attracted by the strange noises. "What's the matter?" she asked. "What's happened now?"

Eben shook his head to warn her away to prevent Ma from being embarrassed over her loss of her usual composure, but Ma said to Rose, "Roy is dead."

Rose thought, "*How terrible for poor Ma!*"

She'd never known Roy, but from Bennie's remarks about how Roy had looked out for him as a younger brother, she'd come to love the *good* boy who'd had an even harder time with Ma than Bennie, but couldn't bring herself to blame Ma any more than Eben could. Ma was what she was, and had her good side that she always tried to conceal. Rose also understood, due to similar experiences in her life, that Ma believed if you were overly demonstrative about what you loved, it would be taken from you.

Ma's undoing had been her inborn conviction that only *Ma always* knew best. "*Why couldn't people understand that she had to control them for their own good, especially Pa and 'her' kids?*"

In the case of "her" children, she had been especially protective, striking out at them when they failed to obey her. "*They had to recognize that her orders were for their own good!*" It had been maddening to see creatures that owed their life to her unable to grasp her purpose.

Rose put her arms around Ma and Eben and the three stood together, both unified and struck dumb by grief.

"*It might be me next time*," Rose thought, "*and who will comfort me if Bennie is killed?*"

She had read signs in him that disturbed her, since she knew him well. With his Indian blood, there was no way to keep from trying to avenge his brother's death. She recognized his deep inner malaise. Several times he'd been unable to respond to her need for their passionate love making and apologized as being overly tired. Young as she was, she understood that he was blaming her, undoubtedly only subconsciously, of robbing him of his manhood.

She left Ma and Eben and went back upstairs and lay on the bed, pulling a comforter over her, since the house was always cold upstairs in the winter. She lay on her side and drew her knees up to keep warmer, overwhelmed by thoughts she would rather not have had. Her final conclusion didn't please her, and she fell asleep to avoid thinking of it, but even in sleep she felt the truth.

It had been, "*I've got to let him go now, even if he gets killed. It's better than having him walk around dying inside from the thought that he's shirking.* Besides we can't let cruel people and cowards run the world, *no matter what.*"

CHAPTER SIXTY-SEVEN

Yankee Doodle Dandy

— January 5, 1942

It was Bennie's birthday, and Ma and Rose had baked a cake, which they brought out after supper with candles lit. He blew out all twenty in one breath, as he was expected to.

Newt and Nelson were there for the event and Newt said, "I wonder how I'd do on ninety-two of 'em."

"When's your birthday?" Ma asked. "I forgot if you ever said. Anyhow, we'll give you your chance."

"First of April," Newt said.

"April Fool's Day? Are you kidding."

"Actually, I made that up. It's the Fourth of July."

"Are you sure you didn't make that up?"

"Nope. Honest Injun. The Fourth of July."

The words of George M. Cohan's song "Yankee Doodle Dandy" came to Bennie's mind:

> *A real live nephew of my Uncle Sam,*
> *Born on the Fourth of July.*

Well, Newt was a Yankee Doodle Dandy if there ever was one.

The phone rang and Eben picked it up, then looked quizzically at Bennie as he held it out and said, "It's a Captain somebody or other. I didn't quite catch the name."

Bennie immediately thought that Flint Curry must be calling him.

"Hello," he said, questioningly.

"This is Coach Redballs," the voice on the phone snorted, followed by a real laugh.

"Coach!" Bennie's heart beat picked up. "I never thought I'd hear your voice after you left here."

"Neither did Kid. When the hell are you going to get in and come over and join us?"

Bennie looked around at the curious faces turned toward him, listening, and took the phone around the corner into the front room as far as the cord would let him and spoke in a low voice.

"I got problems with that," he said. "I'm married. Besides my brother got killed at Pearl Harbor, and Ma doesn't want me sticking my neck out until I have to."

"How do *you* feel about it?"

"I'd have been in the day after Pearl Harbor if it was up to me."

Rose heard that much from the kitchen and her heart sank. She knew who "Coach" had to be because Bennie had let her read Kid's letters.

"Put your wife on. Kid told me who she is. I remember the pretty little girl who used to come to football practice every night."

Bennie called Rose in and handed her the phone.

"It's Coach Radbaltze. He wants to talk to you."

Rose heard the familiar voice say, "Hello, honey," and wanted to snap back, "Don't honey me!"

The coach made his pitch, and it was a good one. "Bennie will be drafted pretty soon, and when he is there won't be any way I can control where he goes. If he enlists now I can keep him here until the war is over. It won't last long. He can come home on weekends and you can visit him over here."

"Are you sure?" She wanted to believe him, but it sounded too good to be true.

"Sure I'm sure. At least if he enlists down at Madison. I've got it greased down there. He'll come over here for Basic Training, and then I can get him permanently assigned to the Post here. Think about it. And put Bennie back on."

She handed the phone back to him silently. He tried to read the look on her face but failed.

The coach said, "I told her I could get you over here permanently provided you enlist down at Madison. I have the recruiters down there in my hip pocket. You'll come here for Basic, then I can get you assigned to the Headquarters and keep you till hell freezes over. The commanding general is a football nut. He knows all about you and Kid. If he leaves, the next one will be the same. Generals all want to shine because good publicity helps them get promoted and there's nothing like having a winning football team on post for that. It makes the *Army and Navy Journal* and everyone reads it, even old General Marshall in Washington, and he's the head cheese."

Bennie told everyone in the kitchen what the coach had said. Ma didn't look convinced. "They all lie," she said, without specifying who "all" were. It was the old Ma talking. All "men" lied "to get their way."

"Sounds good to me," Newt said. "Especially the idea of having some control over where you're going. There's no glory in getting your ass shot off. Look what happened to Pa."

War had long before lost its glamour for Newt, although he wasn't blinded to the necessity for war if you couldn't avoid "killing" trouble. Newt was a born killer, but he wasn't stupid. When a groundhog case came up you didn't run. But until then, it paid to go first class and make life as convenient as possible.

When Bennie and Rose were in bed, he wisely kept quiet, waiting to see if she had anything to say about the coach's call.

They lay side by side, as always before they went to sleep, with his arm under her neck, snuggled close. After a while she said, "I've been thinking."

"Oh. Oh." he said. "Now I'm in for it."

"Don't be silly. I've been watching you. You aren't happy, and we both know why. You feel like a shirker after having your brother killed and Kid in the Army. I can understand how a man would feel about that. If it were up to me, I'd never let you off the farm, regardless of what anyone thought, but as it is you might as well be off the farm. You're not here half the time, anyhow."

He knew it was true and held his tongue.

"Your brother got drafted and sent right to where the shooting was going to start and look what happened to him."

Bennie hated to think of Roy being gone forever and never seeing his face or hearing his voice again. In his mind Roy was a hero, though he'd probably never fired a shot at Pearl Harbor.

After Rose was quiet for a very long while, Bennie said, "So?"

"So, if you really believe the coach, I'm not going to stand in the way of your signing up, so long as you do it down at Madison like he said."

"That leaves Ma to convince."

"I'll talk to her."

"And say what?"

"That our best chance of not losing you forever is to make sure you aren't drafted like Roy was and sent off somewhere, God knows where, to get killed first thing."

"You think she'll buy it?"

"If I buy it, and I do, I think she will. I've got more to lose than she does in your case."

The next morning Rose found a minute alone with Ma in the kitchen. She sat down at the table while Ma fussed around the sink as she always did, unable to rest for long. Rose watched her, trying to get up her nerve as well as figuring how to start.

Finally she said, "I've decided to let Bennie join the Army if he wants to."

Ma stopped without turning from the sink. "I knew you would. So have I."

Stunned on both counts, Rose was quiet for a long minute, waiting for Ma to turn and look at her.

"How did you know?"

"I wasn't born yesterday. Besides I have Indian blood. I woke up last night and just knew." Her face as she said it resembled her grandmother *Shesees* in her prophetic moments, then changed to the familiar mulish Ma-look that wished to hear no contradiction of what she'd said.

"Will he be back?"

Ma avoided Rose's gaze, came over and sat down at the table. Her knees felt weak, and she had trouble navigating the short distance to the chair. She felt lost and empty. Her spiritual sources had been elusive, though she had always been able to tap them if she concentrated; had ever since she was a little girl out in the cornfield trying to hear the departed spirits of Chaubenee or his poor drowned wife.

"I think I'll have some coffee," she said in a subdued voice. "Would you like some?"

Rose said, "Why not." She sensed Ma's sudden weakness and said, "I'll fix it for us," and got up to do it. As she turned to the stove, she said, "You didn't answer my question."

Ma was silent a long while and Rose thought she might not have heard her, or simply wasn't going to answer, but finally Ma said, in that same subdued voice, "I don't know."

She sounded so strange that Rose turned to look at her.

She saw tears welling in Ma's eyes for the second time ever. Before she'd seen Ma crying over Roy, she'd often wondered if she had any tears left.

Rose put down the coffee pot and went to Ma, stooping and putting her arms around the older woman, for a moment in the role of consoling mother.

Finally getting back to her earlier question, "Will he be back?" she answered it herself. "Only God knows if Bennie will come back," Rose said. "I hope so and pray all the time that he will. I love him so."

"So do I," Ma confessed. That admission didn't come easily. Maybe until then Ma hadn't really known that, just as she hadn't realized she loved Roy, either.

Newt and Pa were going down to Madison with Bennie, Pa to sign the papers, and Newt for moral support, and also because he wanted to "get out for a while and look at some new scenery."

Bennie started to pack a suitcase the night before. He put it on the bed and said to Rose, who was watching him, "We'll need enough for a couple of days. I'll have to take a physical examination according to Kid, then we come back here and will have a few weeks before they call me. There's room in here for your things, too."

Rose said, "I'm going to stay here with Ma."

Bennie wasn't ready for that.

"Why?" he asked her. "We should spend as much time together now as we can." He felt lost as it struck him fully for the first time that he would be leaving this familiar place that he loved and the people he loved, and might never return.

Rose bit her lip to keep it from quivering. "You know I want to be with you, I don't want to be away from you for a minute I don't have to, but . . . but I don't want to watch you sign what could be your death warrant."

She broke down then and he held her tenderly and kissed the top of her head. He had never felt such a need to be protective, to make his own strength enter her body, nor had he actually known the true depth of his love for her. He almost lost his resolve. "*What am I doing to her?*" he asked himself. "*And why? Did Custer ever ask himself how Libbie felt whenever he went off to be a hero?*"

He hugged her so tight she gasped, "I can't breathe." But she knew why he was doing it and realized she'd been hugging back as hard as she could.

"You can wait outside in the Lincoln," he said, trying to lighten the moment and make them both feel better.

She made a weak try at laughing. "It's not funny. And please don't try to make me come with you."

"Let's go to bed," he said. "I can finish packing in the morning."

He had never felt so tenderly toward her, and as soon as they were under the covers cuddled as close as possible, Rose clinging tightly to him, seeking the kisses he rained on her, then, both aroused to an unaccustomed pitch Bennie entered her, trying to remember to be gentle so he wouldn't hurt the baby growing in her.

She gasped in his ear, "I won't break. Cut loose."

The next morning Bennie, standing in the yard waiting to drive away, stood aside for a last look at his beloved land.

Snow still buried the fields and stood deep in the woods. The black trunks of trees were starkly clear in their bareness—patiently awaiting another spring.

The woods weren't sheathed in their usual winter morning haze, and he could see deeply into them. Something moved. A doe moving cautiously from the brush, looking around shyly, probably gauging her chances of slipping out to snatch a wisp or two of the hay Bennie had spread early that morning to give the cows something to browse on until evening milking time.

Pa, Newt, Ma, Eben, and Rose all were quietly watching, knowing he was making a last survey of this place they all loved, perhaps him most of all.

Rose knew how he felt best of any of them because she felt exactly the same way. "*Our hearts are here*," she said to herself. "*This is the earth where we both gave our birth yell.*"

Bennie, no longer aware of anyone else being near, thought, "*Christ, how I love this land!*"

A lump gripped his throat, and sudden tears dimmed his eyes.

As he planted a goodbye kiss on Rose's lips, he drew back and said, "You haven't changed your mind, have you?"

"About coming to Madison? Or about you going to war? In the second case it's 'No, I haven't changed my mind," since I never made it up. Everybody else did it for me."

"What does that mean?"

"It means I love you. Now get going before I bawl and spoil it all. Get back soon. I intend to make the most of our last few weeks together." Then she whispered, "Just like last night."

He grinned and whispered back, "Christ. I may not survive to make it to the war. Help me into the car, will you?"

Bennie kept his eyes on Rose in the rearview mirror as long as she was in sight, then turned to watch the passing land, as beautiful in winter as in the fullness of summer.

He remembered something he'd read about Wisconsin when it was a pristine Indian paradise:

— 1660

> *"The country was so pleasant, so beautiful and fruitful that it grieved me to see that the world could not discover such enticing country to live in."*
> *—Pierre Radisson*

Epilogue

Newt and Pa left Bennie with the recruiter and came outside for a smoke, seating themselves side by side on a bench facing the door.

"Warm for this time of year," Newt said. "Not exactly spring, but not exactly winter either. Remember how we'd come out in our shirtsleeves in Nome when it finally warmed up to zero?"

"I hate to think about it."

Newt noticed that the State capitol building was reflected in the recruiting office door behind their own images. The Wisconsin state capitol building reminded him of the Capitol in Washington D.C., the symbol of the nation and all it stood for.

The words from the Pledge of Allegiance to the Flag passed through his mind: "And to the Republic for which it stands . . ."

He'd learned very young to be loyal, not so much then to the "flag," about which people didn't yet make a big fuss, but to the Republic for which it stands.

Then he had answered the call of the *Drums of the Republic*.

"*I would yet if the bastards would let me!*" he thought.

He saw Bennie coming from the other side of the door to get Pa to come in and sign the papers. As the door swung shut behind Bennie, the big flag on the capitol and the building itself merged into a single cameo framing Bennie like a Norman Rockwell painting.

Newt thought his ears were deceiving him when, at that instant, he heard drums and bugles burst into sound behind him:

Ta-de-da, de-da-dee, da-da!

Ta-da-dee-da, da-da-da-da!

Boom!

Boom!

Boom!

Some eager-beaver high school marching band director had his band out practicing early while the weather was good.

Newt felt the beginning of tears.
It was May 1861 again.

Hear the drums,
The Drums,
The Drums of the Republic marching.
Where are the drums of the Republic?"

The Drums of the Republic were returning from *Behind the Hills of History* as they always had when the need truly arose. So that:

"Government
Of the People,
By the People,
For the People,
Shall Not Perish from This Earth."

* * * * *

BID THE GUNS TO SHOOT!